Paley Demosthenes

Select private orations

Paley Demosthenes

Select private orations

ISBN/EAN: 9783337278779

Printed in Europe, USA, Canada, Australia, Japan

Cover: Foto ©Andreas Hilbeck / pixelio.de

More available books at **www.hansebooks.com**

DEMOSTHENES

PART II

CONTAINING

PRO PHORMIONE, CONTRA STEPHANUM I. II.;
CONTRA NICOSTRATUM, CONONEM, CALLICLEM;

WITH

INTRODUCTION AND ENGLISH COMMENTARY

BY

J. E. SANDYS, Litt. D.

FELLOW AND TUTOR OF ST JOHN'S COLLEGE, AND PUBLIC ORATOR
IN THE UNIVERSITY OF CAMBRIDGE.

WITH SUPPLEMENTARY NOTES BY

F. A. PALEY, M.A., LL.D.

EDITOR OF HESIOD, THE GREEK TRAGIC POETS, ETC.; LATE EXAMINER
IN CLASSICS TO THE UNIVERSITY OF LONDON.

EDITED FOR THE SYNDICS OF THE UNIVERSITY PRESS.

SECOND EDITION, REVISED.

CAMBRIDGE:
AT THE UNIVERSITY PRESS.
1886

PREFACE TO THE FIRST EDITION.

MY earliest interest in the Private Orations may be said to date from the time when it was my privilege as an undergraduate to attend, in the year 1865, a course of lectures by my friend Mr Moss, then Fellow and Lecturer of St John's College, and now Head-Master of Shrewsbury School. His selections included two of the six speeches edited in the present volume, the *Nicostratus* and the *Conon*; but, as the notes taken down from his lectures were too scanty to form even the basis of any attempt at constructing a complete edition, my commentary on those speeches has been mainly the result of independent reading and research, though I gladly acknowledge the help that is due to his soundness of judgment on several points on which I have consulted him while revising my notes on the *Conon*. In the case of the *Nicostratus*, when my own commentary was nearly ready for the press, I had the further advantage of attending in the spring of 1874 some of Dr Kennedy's professorial lectures on the Private Orations. From the excellent translation of his brother Mr Charles Rann Kennedy I have here and there quoted a few extracts; and if I have now and then drawn attention to an apparently erroneous interpretation, I have done so with the consciousness that in each case it is only a trifling blemish in what is nearly perfect of its kind. Similarly, several questionable explanations, retained even in the sixth edition of Liddell and Scott's *Lexicon*, have been duly pointed out in the course of my commentary, as it is only thus that a labourer in a limited field can offer any acknowledgement of his large indebtedness to their labours[1]. The lexicography of Demosthenes cannot indeed be said to be at present in a completely satisfactory condition, as general lexicons have still to rely in a great measure on Reiske's *Index Graecitatis*, which, with the portion of his *opus magnum* including his notes on the speeches in this volume, was posthumously published exactly a century ago.

The volume opens with a speech on behalf of Phormion, in bar of a claim on the part of Apollodorus for the recovery of capital alleged to have been transferred to Phormion by Pasion, the father of Apollodorus. This is followed by two on behalf of Phormion's opponent Apollodorus, charging with false witness one of

---

[1] Some of these have since been corrected in the seventh edition.

the deponents called on Phormion's side in the previous trial. These three speeches, though not actually delivered in the same lawsuit, virtually represent the arguments of the two opposite sides, and a comparison of their conflicting statements has an interest similar in kind, though different in degree, to that derived from reading the longer and more important orations of Demosthenes, *On the Embassy* and *On the Crown*, in constrast with those of his great rival Aeschines. The orations of Antiphon, the earliest of the Attic Orators, include indeed four sets of ingenious speeches written for the prosecution and the defence in cases of homicide, but his cases are merely imaginary, and the orations are intended as rhetorical exercises alone. The first three selections in this volume supply us with the only instance in all the remains of Attic oratory, where the legal issues ´ raised on both sides in a suit of purely private interest, lie before us as they were actually presented to an Athenian tribunal. Whether Demosthenes actually wrote for both sides is a vexed question, briefly discussed in the course of the Introduction; it is a question that has provoked a large number of dissertations, the titles of which I have recorded on a page devoted to a conspectus of the literature of the subject up to the present date. But the volume now published, while it happens to be the first English commentary on any of the

selections included in it, is also the first attempt
either in England or elsewhere to put together an
edition of all these three speeches in their connexion
with one another[1]. As compared with the work
demanded by the second half of this volume, where
I have been conscious of moving more freely over
ground familiarised by more frequent reading of that
portion with private pupils between 1867 and 1870,
and for public lectures at a later date, the task of
writing the first half has proved a somewhat tedious
one, owing partly to the necessity of constantly keeping
in view all the nine speeches in which Phormion's opponent, Apollodorus, is more or less directly concerned,
and of forming an opinion on the numerous points of
literary criticism and chronological detail involved in
the controversy on the authorship of those orations.

Those who, after finishing the *pro Phormione*, do
not care to study minutely the whole of the two
speeches against Stephanus, ought, at the very least, to
examine the vigorous attack on Phormion which extends
from § 71 to § 82 of the first of those two speeches.
They should also endeavour to obtain a connected view

---

[1] Mr Penrose's handy volume (now out of print) contained the
Speeches against *Aphobus*, *Onetor*, *Zenothemis*, *Apaturius*, *Phormio*
(Or. 34, πρὸς Φορμίωνα), and *Lacritus*. The *Eubulides*, *Theocrines* and
in Neaeram are the only private orations included in the learned
edition of Demosthenes by Dr John Taylor (fellow of St John's Coll.
from 1726 to 1752), printed at the Cambridge University Press in
1748, 1757 and 1769.

of the argument by reading consecutively the italicised abstracts inserted at suitable intervals in the course of the commentary. With the help of these abstracts the general reader, the barrister, for instance, who has not remembered all the Greek of his younger days, may perhaps, if tempted to dip into these pages, form some opinion of his own on the forensic oratory of Athens; but my more immediate object in this part of my work has been to obviate any occasion for unduly burdening the notes with those literal renderings which are always welcome to students of the less industrious sort, by supplying instead either a free paraphrase or a condensed summary, as the occasion requires.

The latter half of the volume includes the *Nicostratus*, which was delivered by the same speaker as the two orations against Stephanus, namely by Apollodorus, and also the *Conon*, which is certainly one of the most celebrated of the minor speeches of Demosthenes. To these selections, both of which throw much light on the social life of Athens, I have added the *Callicles*, which, though less well known than the others, will be found one of the pleasantest, while it happens to be the shortest, of all the Private Orations.

The first volume of the Select Private Orations includes the speeches *contra Phormionem* (Or. 34), *Lacritum* (35), *Pantaenetum* (37), *Boeotum de nomine* (39), *Boeotum de dote* (40), and *Dionysodorum* (56). In the preface to that volume it has been already explained that the two volumes are a joint edition on the part of

Mr Paley and myself, and I may here repeat that while Mr Paley is mainly responsible for the first volume, I am similarly responsible for the whole of the Introduction and for nearly all the notes of the second, though I have had the advantage of receiving from him a careful revision of all the proof-sheets of my commentary, and a large number of supplementary annotations, many of which have been incorporated with my own, and duly acknowledged by being placed in square brackets and followed by his initial.

J. E. S.

October, 1875.

IN preparing the second edition of this volume, the work has been thoroughly revised, and the suggestions with which I have been favoured by scholars who have had occasion to use it, have been carefully considered and in many cases adopted. Some redundant passages have been removed, and room has been found for many additional notes and references. Account has also been taken of the recent literature of the subject, and particularly of the volume on Demosthenes in the important work of Professor F. Blass, entitled *die Attische Beredsamkeit.* Lastly, the manuscripts of Demosthenes in the Paris Library have been specially examined by me during the early part of the present year, and the readings ascribed to them in the former edition have been verified and corrected accordingly.

J. E. S.

October, 1886.

CONTENTS.

PAGE

SELECT LIST OF EDITIONS, DISSERTATIONS AND BOOKS
OF REFERENCE xiii

SYMBOLS USED IN RECORDING VARIOUS READINGS . . xvi

TABLE OF ATTIC MONEY xviii

INTRODUCTION TO OR. XXXVI. xix

   ,,   ,,   OR. XLV. xxxii

   ,,   ,,   OR. XLVI. xxxvi

ON THE AUTHORSHIP OF OR. XLV, XLVI. . . . xxxix

INTRODUCTION TO OR. LIII. li

   ,,   ,,   OR. LIV. lx

   ,,   ,,   OR. LV. lxviii

TEXT AND NOTES.

ORATION

XXXVI. ΠΑΡΑΓΡΑΦΗ ΥΠΕΡ ΦΟΡΜΙΩΝΟΣ . . 1

XLV. ΚΑΤΑ ΣΤΕΦΑΝΟΥ ΨΕΥΔΟΜΑΡΤΥΡΙΩΝ Α. . 55

XLVI. ΚΑΤΑ ΣΤΕΦΑΝΟΥ ΨΕΥΔΟΜΑΡΤΥΡΙΩΝ Β. . 121

LIII. ΠΡΟΣ ΝΙΚΟΣΤΡΑΤΟΝ ΠΕΡΙ ΑΝΔΡΑΠΟΔΩΝ
ΑΠΟΓΡΑΦΗΣ ΑΡΕΘΟΥΣΙΟΥ . . 142

LIV. ΚΑΤΑ ΚΟΝΩΝΟΣ ΑΙΚΙΑΣ . . . 174

  EXCURSUS (A). On the defective verb τύπτω . . 221

    ,, (B). On the quantity of ἔμπυος . 226

    ,, (C). On the meaning of αὐτολήκυθος . 227

    ,, (D). On the club called the Τριβαλλοί . 229

LV. ΠΡΟΣ ΚΑΛΛΙΚΛΕΑ ΠΕΡΙ ΧΩΡΙΟΥ . . 231

  INDEX 260

SELECT LIST OF EDITIONS, DISSERTATIONS AND BOOKS OF REFERENCE

ON THE SELECTIONS INCLUDED IN THIS VOLUME.

TEXT.

(1) J. G. BAITER *and* H. SAUPPE. *Oratores Attici*, in one volume 4to, Zürich, 1850. (2) IMM. BEKKER. *Demosthenis Orationes;* stereotyped edition, 8vo. Leipzig, 1854-5 [earlier editions, Oxford 1822, and Berlin 1824]. (3) W. DINDORF. *Demosthenis Orationes* [Leipzig, 1825, Oxford, 1846], *editio tertia correctior*, (Teubner) Leipzig, 1855, reprinted in subsequent years; of vol. ɪ Or. 1—19 there is an *editio quarta correctior*, revised by F. BLASS. 1885. (Vol. ɪɪ Part 2 includes Or. 36; and Vol. ɪɪɪ Part 1, all the remaining selections of the present volume.)

COMMENTARIES.

I. GENERAL.

(1) G. H. SCHAEFER. *Apparatus Criticus ad Demosthenem Vinc. Obsopoei, Hier. Wolfii* [1572]. *Jo. Taylori* [1748, 1757] *et Jo. Jac. Reiskii* [1770—1775] *annotationes tenens. Commodum in ordinem digestum aliorumque et suis annotationibus auctum edidit Godofredus Henricus Schaefer.* London, 1824-7, Vol. ɪᴠ pp. 590—618 (on Or. 36); Vol. ᴠ pp. 167—214 (on Or. 45 and 46); pp. 346—407 (on Or. 53, 54 and 55). (2) G. S. DOBSON, *Oratores Attici, Graece cum notis variorum*, xᴠɪ vols. London, 1828. Vol. ᴠɪɪ, Dem. Or. 21—38; vol. ᴠɪɪ, Or. 39—59; Vol. ɪx *Reiskii Annotationes*, etc. Vol. xɪ *Reiskii indices Graecitatis.* (3) W. DINDORF. *Demosthenes ex recensione Gulielmi Dindorfii*, Oxford, Vol. ᴠɪɪ [1849] *Annotationes interpretum ad* Or. xxᴠɪɪ—ʟxɪɪ.

II. SPECIAL.

(1) A. WESTERMANN. *Ausgewählte Reden des Dem.*, part 3, pp. 111—131, *Rede gegen Konon* (Or. 54). Also contains *adv. Aristocratem* and *in Eubulidem.* Berlin (2nd ed. 1865). (2) G. HUETTNER. *Dem. pro Phormione oratio adnotatione critica instructa et commentario explanata*, pp. 104 [without text], (Jung) Erlangen, 1885.

LEXICOGRAPHY AND TEXTUAL CRITICISM.

(1) HARPOCRATION. λέξεις τῶν δέκα ῥητόρων, ed. W. Dindorf; Oxford, 1853: (also Pollux, and Anecdota Graeca, ed. Bekker;

and Hesychius, ed. Schmidt). (2) T. MITCHELL (after Reiske 1775). *Indices Graecitatis in Oratores Atticos*, 2 vols. and *Index Graecitatis Isocraticae* Oxford, 1828 [uniform with the Oxford edition of Bekker's *Oratores Attici*]. (3) P. P. DOBREE, *Adversaria;* cura Scholefield; Cambridge, 1833 (ed. Wagner, Leipzig, 1875).

DEMOSTHENIC LITERATURE.

I. GENERAL.

(1) ARNOLD SCHAEFER. *Demosthenes und seine Zeit.* 3 vols., esp. vol. III part 2, *Beilagen: die Reden in Sachen Apollodors* (Or. 36, 45, 46, 53 etc.) pp. 130—199. Rede wider Konon (Or. 54) pp. 247—252; gegen Kallikles (Or. 55) pp. 252-7. Leipzig, 1856-8; new ed. of vol. I, II and part 1 only of vol. III, 1886- ; part 2 will not be reprinted.

(2) F. BLASS. *Die Attische Beredsamkeit*, esp. vol. III *Demosthenes;* Leipzig, 1877.

II. SPECIAL.

On Or. 36, 45, 46 and 53.

(1) **C. D. Beels.** *Diatribe in Dem. orationes* I *et* II *in Stephanum* (Or. 45 and 46), pp. 122, Leyden, 1823. (2) **Im. Hermann.** *De tempore, quo orationes quae feruntur Demosthenis pro Apollodoro et Phormione scriptae sint, disputatio* (on Or. 36, 45, 46, 53 etc.) pp. 22. Erfurt, 1842. (3) **A. Westermann.** *Untersuchungen über die in die Attischen Redner eingelegten Urkunden*, pp. 136 (esp. pp. 105—113 on the depositions in Or. 45 and 46). Leipzig, 1850. (4) **W. Hornbostel.** *Ueber die rom Dem. in Sachen des Apollodor verfassten Gerichtsreden*, pp. 42. Ratzeburg, 1851. In the *Neue Jahrbücher für Philologie* 1854, 2, pp. 504-5 there is a suggestive review of this dissertation by **C. Rehdantz**, who also gives a short account of Apollodorus in his *ritae Iphicratis Chabriae Timothei*, 1845, pp. 191-3, (where he promised a special dissertation of his own, which unhappily never appeared). (5) **Im. Hermann.** *Einleitende Bemerkungen zu Dem. paragraphischen Reden*, (Or. 36 etc.) pp. 23. Erfurt, 1853. (6) **F. Lortzing.** *De orationibus quas Dem. pro Apollodoro scripsisse fertur*, pp. 94. Berlin, 1863. (7) **J. Sigg.** *Der Verfasser neun angeblich von Dem. für Apollodor geschriebener Reden. Besonderer Abdruck aus dem sechsten Supplementbande der Jahrbücher für classische Philologie*, pp. 396—434. Leipzig (Teubner), 1873. (8) **I. E. Kirchner.** *De litis instrumentis quae exstant in Demosthenis quae fertur in Lacritum et priore adv. Stephanum orationibus*, pp. 40. Halle (Hendel), 1883. (9) **R. Lallier.** *Le procès du Phormion; études sur les moeurs judiciaires d'Athènes.* Annuaire de l'Association pour l'encouragement des études grecques en France; année xii p. 48—62. (10) **G. Perrot.** *Démosthène et ses contemporains*, in the *Revue des deux mondes*, 1873, 6, pp. 407-39 (on Or. 36, pp. 428-39); reprinted in *Mémoires d'archéologie, d'épigraphie et d'histoire*, pp. 337—444, Paris (Didier), 1875.

(11) **R. Duncker.**   *Inter privatarum causarum orationes Demos-thenicas quae pro genuinis habendae sint quaeque pro falsis breviter exponitur.*   Greiffenberg, pars i, 1877.   (12) **P. Uhle.**   *Quaestiones de orationum Demostheni falso addictarum scriptoribus,* i (Or. 35, 43, 46; 50, 52, 53, 59), Leipzig (Fock) 1883: ii pp. 32 (Or. 33, 34, 56), ib. 1886.

On Or. 54.

(1) **G. Perrot,** *Revue des deux mondes,* 1873, 3, pp. 927–53 (esp. 946–53).   (2) **C. Zink.**   *Adnotationes ad Dem. orationem in Cononem,* pp. 30.   Erlangen (Jung), 1883.

GREEK ANTIQUITIES.

(1) **A. Boeckh.**   *Die Staatshaushaltung der Athener,* ed. 2, 1851; ed. 3, 1886.   *Public Economy of Athens :*—1st German ed. translated by Sir George Cornewall Lewis, 1828, 1842; 2nd German ed. translated by Lamb, Boston. u. s., 1857.   (2) **K. F. Hermann,** *Lehrbuch der Griechischen Antiquitäten,* (a) *Staatsalterthümer* ed. 5, Baehr and Stark, 1874: new ed. by A. Hug.   (b) *Privatalterthümer,* (including Law), ed. 2, Stark, 1870; ed. 3 (excluding Law, see below), Blümner, 1882.   (3) **W. A. Becker,** *Charikles,* ed. K. F. Hermann, 1854, ed. Göll 1877; abridged English transl. by F. Metcalfe, 1845, ed. 3, 1866.   (4) **B. Büchsenschütz,** *Besitz und Erwerb im griechischen Alterthume.*   Halle, 1869.

Greek Law.

(1) **J. B. Télfy.**   *Corpus Iuris Attici;* Pesth, 1868.   (2) **Meier und Schömann.**   *Der Attische Process;* Halle, 1824: new edition revised by **J. H. Lipsius**; Berlin, 1881–6.   (3) **K. F. Hermann.** *Griechischen Antiquitäten,* new ed. vol. ii part 1, *Rechtsalter-thümer,* ed. Thalheim, 1884.   (4) **C. R. Kennedy.**   (a) *Articles* in Dr W. Smith's *Dict. of Greek and Roman Antiquities,* 2nd. ed. London 1848, reprinted in subsequent years, [a new edition preparing.   Joint Editor, W. Wayte].   (b) *The Orations of Dem.* translated with notes and dissertations, 5 vols. London, reissued 1880.   (5) **E. Caillemer.**   (a) *Articles* in Daremberg and Saglio, *Dictionnaire des Antiquités Grecques et Romaines,* parts 1—10, A—cup, pp. 1—1600, Paris (Hachette) 1873–86.   (b) *études sur les antiquités juridiques d'Athènes* 1865–80, [scattered essays, some of them very difficult to procure; a collected edition would be welcome].   (6) **R. Dareste.**   *Les plaidoyers civils de Démosthène,* traduits en Francais, avec arguments et notes, vol. i pp. 385 ; ii pp. 364 Paris (Plon) 1875.

EXPLANATION OF THE SYMBOLS USED IN THIS EDITION IN RECORDING VARIOUS READINGS.

As a general rule, wherever our text (that of W. Dindorf's third Edition) agrees with that of the Zürich editors, we have not thought it necessary to notice any variations in the mss. Where Dindorf differs from the Zürich editors, the difference is in most cases due to the greater weight given by the latter to the readings of the Paris ms Σ.

Z stands for the *Zürich* text of Demosthenes as printed by J. G. Baiter and H. Sauppe in their excellent edition of the *Oratores Attici*, in one volume (1850).

Bekker st. is Bekker's stereotyped edition published at Leipzig in 1854. The readings adopted in his Berlin ed. 1824 have been occasionally recorded. When Dindorf differs from the Zürich editors, he generally agrees with Bekker. When a note begins with Bekk., it is meant that Dindorf's text is supported by Bekker's Berlin and Leipzig editions; then, after a slight space, follows the reading of the Zürich editors (Z) with the mss supporting it, introduced by the word *cum*.

The mss thus quoted by the Zürich editors are as follows :

Σ or S in the *Bibliothèque Nationale*, Paris (No. 2934), on parchment; of century X. "Primae quidem classis unus superest Parisinus S" Dindorf, praef. ed. Oxon. p. vi. This is admitted on all hands to be the best ms, and its readings are very often accepted by Bekker and still more frequently by the Zürich editors. A careful description of it was published by Voemel (Σ *codicis Demosthenici conditio describitur*) in 1853. For a protest against *excessive* reference to its authority, see the Preface of Shilleto's fourth edition of the *De falsa legatione*, pp. vii, viii, xiv. By examining the ms I have ascertained that the readings assigned to it in the former edition, on the authority of the *apparatus criticus* of the Zürich editors, are wrong in the following instances, in Or. 45 § 87, the ms has καὶ παράδειγμα, not παράδειγμα; in 46 § 6 ἐν (not ἐν τῷ) γραμματείῳ; in 46 § 12 ἐξεῖναι ἐπ' ἀνδρί (not ἐπ ἀνδρὶ ἐξεῖναι) θεῖναι; and in 55 § 5 it has ὑμῖν, not ἡμῖν. In the last instance, the same mistake has found its way into the critical notes of Dindorf's Oxford ed.

F.   *Codex Marcianus* (No. 416), in the Library of St Mark's at Venice, on parchment; of century XI.   The best MS of the second group or family (Dindorf), but closely followed by the *Codex Bavaricus* (B).

Φ.   In the same Library (No. 418), on parchment; of century XI.

k.   In the *Bibliothèque Nationale* Paris (No. 2998), on cotton paper (bombycinus), *forma quadrata;* of century XIV.   Contains Or. 54 (κὰτα Κόνωνος).

r.   In the same Library (No. 2936), on parchment *forma maxima;* of century XIII.

A¹.   *Augustanus primus*, formerly at Augsburg (*Augusta Vindelicorum*), now at Munich (No. 485), on parchment, *paene quadratus;* of century XI (according to Dindorf), or XII (according to the Zürich edition).

B.   *Bavaricus*, now at Munich (No. 85), on cotton-paper (bombycinus) *forma maxima;* of century XIII.

γρ.   A contraction for γράφεται, used in the MSS themselves to introduce the marginal citation of a various reading.

TABLE OF ATTIC MONEY.

	Values in English money.	
8 χαλκοῖ = 1 ὀβολός	1·62*d*	1·3̇*d*
6 ὀβολοί = 1 δραχμή	9·72*d**	8*d*†
100 δραχμαί = 1 μνᾶ	£4 1*s*	£3 6*s* 8*d*
60 μναῖ = 1 τάλαντον	£243	£200

Like the τάλαντον of 6000 δραχμαί, the μνᾶ was not an actual coin but only a term used in keeping accounts to denote a sum of 100 δραχμαί.

* This is the equivalent given in Hussey's *Ancient Weights and Money*, pp. 47, 48, followed in Smith's *Dictionary of Greek and Roman Antiquities*, s. v. DRACHMA. It assumes that an Attic drachma contains only 65·4 grains Troy of pure silver. As a shilling contains 80·7 grains of pure silver; a drachma is reckoned as $\frac{65 \cdot 4}{80 \cdot 7}$ of a shilling, or 9·72 pence.

† This is the equivalent proposed in Professor W. W. Goodwin's article on *the Value of the Attic Talent in Modern Money* in the *Transactions of the American Philological Association* 1885, xvi, p. 117—9. It has been ascertained that the Athenians coined their silver pure, and the best specimens of Attic coinage prove the weight of the drachma to be 67·38+ grains Troy of pure silver. The average price of *pure* silver for the last quarter of a century having been 57 pence per ounce of 480 grains, it follows that the amount of silver in a drachma is worth $\frac{67 \cdot 38}{480}$ of 57 pence = 8·001375 pence.

N.B. Neither of the above estimates takes account of the different *purchasing powers* of silver in ancient and modern times.

INTRODUCTION TO

OR. XXXVI.

ΥΠΕΡ ΦΟΡΜΙΩΝΟΣ.

In the early part of the fourth century B. C. there was a noted man of business at Athens, named Pasion. He was originally a slave in the employment of a firm of bankers, but by his industry and integrity he won the confidence of his employers, Antisthenes and Archestratus, and was rewarded by receiving his liberty from the latter and by succeeding both of them in their business[1]. In the *Trapeziticus* of Isocrates, he appears as defendant in a suit brought by the son of a trusted minister of Satyrus, prince of Pontus, and is charged, whether rightly or wrongly, with appropriating a sum of money deposited with him by the plaintiff, with destroying documents detrimental to his own interests, and with other sharp practice of a somewhat unscrupulous character. To examine the justice of these charges is no part of our present duty, nor indeed have we the data for arriving at any decisive result; suffice it to say that, in the language of his very opponent in that action, he

---

[1] Or. 36 § 43 sq.—On the *Trapezitae*, see Becker's *Charicles* scene IV; K. F. Hermann, *Privatalterthümer* § 48; Büchsenschütz, *Besitz und Erwerb* pp. 500—510; Perrot in *Revue des deux mondes* 1873, 6 p. 408, reprinted in *Mémoires d'archéologie, d'épigraphie et d'histoire*, 1875, p. 337—444; also Göll's *Kulturbilder* I 189—197, and Huettner's *Dissertation* on this speech, 1885, p. 98—104.

is described as one of those bankers who enjoyed a wide
connexion and had the management of large sums of
money, and whose position as men of business had won
them a general confidence[1]. The speech composed by
Isocrates probably belongs to the year B.C. 394, when
Pasion, though no longer a slave, was only a resident
alien (μέτοικος)[2]; at a subsequent date, on rising to the
privileged position of enjoying as a denizen (ἰσοτελὴς)
such civic rights as were not of an expressly political
nature, he acquired some property in land, and distinguished himself by his public spirit, on one occasion in
particular presenting the State with a thousand shields
from his own manufactory, and five triremes equipped
at his own expense[3]. In recognition of these services,
Athens rewarded him with the rights of her citizenship[4].

Among those who had business relations with him
we find Athenians of high position like Timotheus, the
celebrated general[5], and Demosthenes, the father of the
orator[6]; his bank in the Peiraeus enjoyed, in the Euxine
and elsewhere, a credit co-extensive with the commerce
of Attica : even eight years after his death, Apollodorus,
of whom we shall hear more anon, had only to declare
himself as Pasion's son to be at once enabled to raise
a loan in a foreign land[7]; and in later ages, in the
imaginary letters of Alciphron, the Atticist who in the
latter part of the second century of our era attempted
to revive the memories of the times of Menander, we find
the vulgar money-lender contrasted with a banker of

[1] Isocr. *Trapez.* § 2.
[2] Isocr. *Trapez.* § 41.
[3] Or. 45 § 85.
[4] Or. 36 § 47, Or. 46 § 15, Or. 53 § 18, Or. 59 § 2 ψηφισα-μένου τοῦ δήμου τοῦ Ἀθηναίων Ἀθηναῖον εἶναι Πασίωνα καὶ ἐκ-γόνους τοὺς ἐκείνου διὰ τὰς εὐερ-γεσίας τὰς εἰς τὴν πόλιν.

[5] Or. 49 πρὸς Τιμόθεον ὑπὲρ χρέως. Cf. note on Or. 36 § 53, p. 48.
[6] Or. 27 § 11.
[7] Or. 50 § 56 διὰ τὸ Πασίωνος εἶναι καὶ ἐκεῖνον ἐπεξενῶσθαι πολ-λοῖς καὶ πιστευθῆναι ἐν τῇ Ἑλ-λάδι οὐκ ἠπόρουν, ὅπου δεηθείην δανείσασθαι.

blameless reputation, who bears the appropriate name of Pasion[1].

Pasion, in his old age, finding his eyesight failing him, and being only able to walk with difficulty up to Athens from his bank in the Peiraeus[2], four or five miles distant, transferred his business, including not only his bank but also his shield-manufactory, on lease to his managing clerk Phormion[3], who, like his employer, was himself originally a slave[4], and obtained his freedom as the reward of honest service[5]. We read of him as a generous and energetic man of business, and his skilful management is said to have been the very saving of the property of his former master[6]. From the nature of the case, as well as from certain chronological considerations, it may be concluded that the lease to Phormion belongs to a date before, but not long before, Pasion's death in B.C. 370[7]. In B.C. 372, we find the latter still managing his business on his own account[8], and we may therefore fix on B.C. 371 as the probable date of the lease. Pasion left behind him a widow, Archippe by name[9], and two sons by her, the elder, Apollodorus, who was four-and-twenty years old at his father's death[10], and the younger, Pasicles, who came of age eight years after (namely, in B.C. 362)[11]. In his will he provided that his widow should be married to Phormion, with a dowry of two

---

[1] Alciphron III 3. See note on Or. 45 § 70.—Mr Mahaffy in his *Social Greece* gives a slight sketch of Pasion, to illustrate the business habits of the Greeks, pp. 382—6; cf. Perrot, quoted on p. xix.

[2] Or. 52 § 13 quoted in note on Or. 36 § 7.

[3] Or. 36 § 4, Or. 45 § 33.

[4] Or. 45 §§ 71—76.

[5] Or. 36 § 30.

[6] Or. 36 §§ 49—53.

[7] Or. 46 § 13 ἐπὶ Δυσνικήτου ἄρχοντος, Ol. 102, 3 = July 370—July 369 B.C.

[8] Or. 49 §§ 29, 59. In the archonship of Alcisthenes, Ol. 102, 1 (Arnold Schaefer, *Dem. u. s. Zeit*, III 2 p. 132).

[9] Or. 45 § 74.

[10] Or. 36 § 22.

[11] Or. 36 §§ 10 and 37 compared together (A. Schaefer, u. s.).

talents, a dwelling-house valued at one hundred minae, maid-servants, gold ornaments and all that formerly belonged to his wife[1]. By this will, Phormion also became one of the guardians to Pasion's younger son, Pasicles. He was to continue lessee of the bank and shield-manufactory until Pasicles came of age, and it was the father's wish that until that time the property should remain undivided. Owing, however, to the extravagance of the elder son, the guardians, acting in the interests of their ward, determined on a partition of all the property, with the exception of the bank and shield-manufactory leased to Phormion, half the rent of which was for the present paid to Apollodorus, and half reserved for Pasicles, the minor[2].

Apollodorus was at Athens in B. c. 370 and appears to have been present at his father's death-bed[3], and some time after this, he was abroad in the public service as trierarch, probably in the year B. c. 368[4]. It was during his absence that, in accordance with his father's will, his mother was married to Phormion ; the son, on his return home, resented this arrangement, and as the courts were not open at that time for private lawsuits, he took steps to bring a public indictment against Phormion, for criminal outrage on his mother ($\gamma\rho\alpha\phi\grave{\eta}$ $\ddot{v}\beta\rho\epsilon\omega\varsigma$). However, a reconciliation was brought about and the charge was not pressed[5].

In B. c. 362, when Pasicles came of age, his guardians gave an account of their trust, which was acknowledged as correct, and Phormion's lease of the bank and manufactory terminated with a discharge given him on the part of Apollodorus from all liabilities under the lease. The elder brother then, having the prior choice, took the

---

[1] Or. 45 § 28 *ad fin.*
[2] Or. 36 §§ 8—10, § 34.
[3] Or. 49 § 42.
[4] Or. 45 § 3; 46 § 21. See note on p. lvii *infra.*
[5] Or. 45 §§ 3, 4.

manufactory, leaving the banking business to his younger brother[1]. For a short time the brothers appear to have superintended their property in person; but not long after, possibly a year subsequent[2] to the partition, a new lease of the bank and the manufactory was granted to certain persons, at a rent which was the same as that which had been paid by Phormion[3], namely, 2 talents and 40 minae[4], out of which one talent[5] was due to Apollodorus for the manufactory, and the remainder to Pasicles for the bank. This second lease was granted not by Pasicles alone, but by Apollodorus acting in conjunction with his younger brother.

Phormion, meanwhile, being quit of his trust as guardian, and of his lease of the bank and manufactory, established a banking business on his own account, and, like his former master, Pasion, obtained a recognition of the general esteem in which he was held, by being presented with the citizenship. The date of this event was B.C. 361[6]. In the year B.C. 360, after a protracted service as trierarch in the Northern Aegean and the neigh-

---

[1] Or. 36 §§ 10, 11.

[2] The Rev. A. Wright, Fellow and Lecturer of Queens' College, has favoured me with some criticisms questioning the probability of any interval having elapsed between the two leases. 'Apollodorus,' he observes, 'was not a man of business habits: Pasicles was a mere lad, not likely to undertake the management of a bank, even with the most confidential clerk. I can find nothing to indicate that they did thus hold the property except ὕστερον in § 12 which is hardly decisive, and can scarcely be maintained in face of the direct evidence the other way in § 37. It is more probable (and this will solve the further diffi-culty started in the note on § 12 μισθῶν ἑτέροις), that Apollodorus, knowing Phormion's lease to be expiring, looked out for some other lessees, and entered into an engagement for a lease with Xenon &c. some months before the lease expired. Xenon would enter on the property as soon as Phormion quitted it, whereas some days might pass before the νομή was completed. And so Phormion may actually have acted as lessor.'

[3] Or. 36 § 12 τοῦ ἴσου ἀργυρίου.

[4] Or. 36 § 51, cf. § 11.

[5] Or. 36 § 37 *ad fin.*

[6] Or. 46 § 13, ἐπὶ Νικοφήμου ἄρχοντος, Ol. 104, 4 = B.C. 361—360.

bouring waters, Apollodorus returned to Athens to find his mother at death's door. She died six days after; but not before she had seen and recognised her son, though according to his own account she was unable to make such provision for him as she had intended[1].

The mother's death was the signal for a fresh outbreak of the differences between Apollodorus and his step-father Phormion. The step-son put in a claim for 3000 drachmae, which was submitted to arbitrators, who established the claim and induced Phormion for quietness' sake to pay it to Apollodorus. The latter then gave Phormion a second release from all claims[2].

Phormion, however, had not yet seen the last of his litigious step-son; the latter, after numerous lawsuits with his father's debtors, in which he succeeded in recovering no less than 20 talents[3], was at last prompted, by pecuniary exigencies due to his extravagance, and by feelings of envy at Phormion's prosperity, to put in a claim about twenty years after the father's death for another sum of 20 talents, alleged to have been transferred to Phormion by the father as part of the working capital ($\dot{a}\phi o\rho\mu\dot{\eta}$) of the business[4].

The defendant, as we learn from the speech *pro Phormione*, expected that Apollodorus' contention, that Phormion must have received such capital, would be supported by presumptive proofs alone. He would argue that, without such a fund, it was incredible that Phor-

---

[1] Or. 50 § 60 quoted in note on Or. 36 § 14.

[2] Or. 36 §§ 15—17.

[3] Or. 36 § 36.

[4] Why *twenty* talents were claimed does not appear, but we may conjecture that that amount arose out of the eleven talents mentioned in Or. 36 § 11, with the addition of interest. Phormion's lease lasted for 8 years; 11 talents, at say 10 per cent. simple interest (not an uncommon rate at Athens), would with the interest amount to exactly 20 talents in 8 years (and a fraction of a year over, $\frac{2}{11}$).

mion, who was merely a liberated slave, should have managed the business and risen to opulence, while he himself, a rich man's son, had been reduced to penury (§ 43). To give stronger proof than these *a priori* probabilities had been made impossible, he would assert, by Phormion's having induced his wife to destroy Pasion's papers (§ 18); he would also denounce the lease and the will as forgeries, and would make out that it was only while Phormion promised him a high rent, that he kept silence on his claim, but as he had not fulfilled these promises, he was compelled to bring the case before the court (§ 33).

The arguments here anticipated by the defendant appear again in the first speech against Stephanus (Or. 45), a speech arising out of the present lawsuit. The case came in the first instance before an arbitrator, Tisias[1] by name, but was left undecided by him, and was accordingly brought before a public tribunal. The writer of the Greek argument, generally supposed to be Libanius, calls the suit a δίκη ἀφορμῆς, though it has been doubted whether there is any ancient authority for the existence of such a suit under that designation[2]. However, the phrase ἀφορμὴν ἐγκαλεῖν occurs in the speech itself (§ 12), in reference to the plaintiff's claim to the capital of the bank.

To meet this claim, Phormion, instead of waiting for the plaintiff to bring his case before the court and then confronting his opponent with a' direct denial and joining issue on the merits, preferred putting in a special

---

[1] Or. 45 § 10.

[2] Dareste, *les plaidoyers civils de Dém.* II 145: ' *Est-il vrai que les Athéniens eussent créé une action spéciale pour les affaires de ce genre?* ' But cf. Caillemer, *le contrat de prêt à Athènes,* p. 28—31, where δίκη ἀφορμῆς is distinguished from δίκη ἀργυρίου, δίκη χρέους and other terms, and accepted without suspicion as a term of Attic law. Similarly in Meier und Schömann, *Att. Process,* p. 510.

plea in bar of action, a plea technically known in Greek law as a παραγραφὴ, shewing cause on the part of the defendant why the case should not be allowed to come on for trial at all. The two pleas urged on the defendant's behalf are (1) that the plaintiff had given him a discharge from the original lease of the bank and manufactory, and also a second discharge from a subsequent claim settled by arbitration (§§ 23—25); (2) that the plaintiff's suit contravened the statute of limitations, in which the term of five years was fixed as a sufficient time for injured parties to recover their dues, whereas the plaintiff was putting in a claim after the lapse of more than twenty years from the date of the lease (§ 26). To maintain these pleas is the object of the speech *pro Phormione*, though it is only a small portion of it that is directly concerned with them, such technical pleadings being naturally unpopular with juries, who regarded them as mere makeshifts, to gain time and evade the ends of justice[1]. Hence a large part of the speech is devoted to arguing on the case itself, thus proving that the defendant's resort to special pleading was not due to any fear of meeting the plaintiff on the main issue. All this was of course irrelevant to the real question before the court, and counsel would hardly be permitted by any judge now-a-days to travel so widely out of the 'record.' In such a case, the defendant spoke first[2]; thus, while he

---

[1] Cf. Isaeus Or. 7 § 3 εἰ μὲν ἑώρων ὑμᾶς μᾶλλον ἀποδεχομένους τὰς διαμαρτυρίας ἢ τὰς εὐθυδικίας κ.τ.λ.

[2] See note on Or. 36 Arg. line 25 *ad fin.* The writer of the life of Demosthenes in the *Orations on the Crown* published by the Clarendon Press appears to have overlooked this in stating: 'it is clear that in the speech to which Demosthenes, in behalf of Phormion, composed a reply, Apollodorus had dwelt much on the fact of Phormion having been his father's slave' (p. xxxiii). Apollodorus did not address the court at all; he could not speak *before* the case, for the special plea had been opened on the side of the defendant, and the jury would not listen to him after.

was under the slight disadvantage of the *onus probandi*, he had on the other hand the benefit of the first hearing, and might at once produce a favourable impression of the strength of his case, which would put a stop to further litigation.

Phormion, being of foreign extraction and unpractised in public speaking, does not address the court in person (§ 1); his friends speak in his stead, and the case is opened on his behalf in an oration composed but almost certainly not spoken by Demosthenes[1], which forms the first of the selections included in the present volume[2].

The speech contains several notes of time which approximately determine the date of its delivery. In § 26 we are told that 'more than twenty years' have elapsed since the lease granted by Pasion; in § 19 we find that 'eighteen years' have passed since the partition of the property effected by the guardians in consequence of the extravagance of Apollodorus; and in § 38 the same period is described in general terms as 'about twenty years.' Pasion died in B.C. 370 and the above indications point to the year B.C. 350 as the probable date of the speech. As we have already observed, the lease would be granted to Phormion before B.C. 370, and

---

[1] The contrary might be inferred from the language of Deinarchus *contra Dem.* § 111, (Δημοσθένους) λογογράφου καὶ μισθοῦ τὰς δίκας λέγοντος ὑπὲρ Κτησίππου καὶ Φορμίωνος (Compare p. xli). But the authority of Aeschines, in a speech delivered only seven years after the *pro Phormione*, supports the opinion expressed in the text, *de fals. leg.* § 185, ἔγραψας λόγον Φορμίωνι (cf. Or. 46 § 1 οἱ γράφοντες καὶ οἱ συμβουλεύοντες ὑπὲρ Φορμίωνος). Lortzing, *Apoll.* p. 14, who agrees with A. Schaefer, *Dem. u. s. Zeit*, p. 169.

[2] It is unnecessary in this place to give a detailed account of the speech itself, as its contents are analysed in the italicised abstracts printed at convenient intervals in the course of the commentary. The reader who desires a general view of the drift of the argument may do well to read all the abstracts consecutively before settling down to the perusal of the Greek.

probably after B.C. 372, i.e. in B.C. 371. Thus 21 years would have passed since the grant of the lease. At first sight the term of eighteen years above mentioned might seem to point to B.C. 352[1], but it appears certain that the partition of property was not effected *immediately* after the death of Pasion. Some allowance must be made for the time during which the extravagance of Apollodorus was running its course (§ 8), before the guardians came to the conclusion that a partition of the property was inevitable; and the term of eighteen years is reckoned, it will be observed, not from the death of Pasion but from the division of his estate.

Again, the speech of Apollodorus against Nicostratus, § 13, shews that after his return from his Sicilian trierarchy which on independent grounds may be placed in B.C. 368, he was not yet in possession of his share of the estate. We find that he was compelled to raise money on the security of his house and to pledge some of his plate; we may therefore conclude that the partition was not earlier than B.C. 368, and the 'eighteen years' bring us once more to B.C. 350 as the date of the speech.

Further, the lease of Phormion lasted eight, that of the subsequent lessees, ten years; but it would be far from correct to assume that this points to the lapse of only eighteen years from the death of Pasion to the delivery of the speech, and consequently to B.C. 352 for the date of the latter; for (1) the previous lease began *before* the death of Pasion, (2) the subsequent lease does not appear to have followed immediately on the expiration of the first lease[2], and (3) the second lease had ter-

---

[1] This date is accepted by Droysen (*Zeitschrift für d. Alterthumswissenschaft* 1839 p. 930), Hornbostel (*Apoll.* p. 20), and A. Schaefer (u. s., p. 168 —9).

[2] § 11 εὐθὺς ὡς ἀφεῖσαν τουτονὶ τῆς μισθώσεως νέμονται τὴν τράπεζαν κ.τ.λ., § 13 ἐμίσθωσεν ὕστερον Ξένωνι κ.τ.λ.

minated before the date of the speech[1]. The date B.C.
352, besides being open to the objection that the phrase
'more than twenty years' has to be explained away as
a round number, in other words as equivalent to *less*
than twenty years, only just allows time for the two
leases, with no margin over, either for the interval between the first and second, or for the further interval
after the second; while B.C. 350 is consistent with both
these data[2].

The only difficulty in our accepting this date arises
from the reference to Callippus in § 53, as then alive in
Sicily. Now Callippus left that island for Rhegium in
the spring of B.C. 350 at the latest, and was killed in the
same year. This would reduce us to the alternative of
either supposing that the news of these events had not
yet reached Athens, or resorting to the heroic remedy of
striking out the words as spurious[3]. Otherwise, it may
be worth while to suggest as the date the latter part of
B.C. 351; this would involve our reckoning the term of
'more than twenty years' from the beginning of B.C. 371
to the end of B.C. 351 *inclusive*, and similarly the
eighteen years from the partition would be counted
inclusively from B.C. 368 to B.C. 351.

---

[1] § 14 ἐλευθέρους ἀφεῖσαν...καὶ
οὐκ ἐδικάζοντο οὔτ' ἐκείνοις τότ'
οὔτε τούτῳ.

[2] Ol. 107, 3 = B.C. 350—349.
This date is supported by Fynes
Clinton; Böhnecke (*Forschun-
gen auf dem Gebiete der Atti-
schen Redner*, I 43, 67); Imm.
Hermann (*de tempore*, &c. p.
11 and *einleitende Bemerkungen
zu Dem. paragraph. Reden* p.
16); Rehdantz (*Jahns neue
Jahrb.* LXX p. 505); Lortzing
(*Apoll.* p. 15—18); Sigg (*Apoll.*
ap. *Jahrb. f. class. Philol. Suppl.
Bd.* VI Hft. 2 p. 406—8); Blass,
Att. Ber. III 405; and Huettner,
Disputatio p. 18.

[3] This has been proposed by
Sigg u. s., p. 408, who objects
to them as breaking the sym-
metry of the sentence οὐχὶ Τιμομάχου κατηγόρεις; οὐχὶ Καλλίππου; οὐ πάλιν Μένωνος; οὐκ Αὐτοκλέους; οὐ Τιμοθέου; οὐκ ἄλλων
πολλῶν; But we here have six
rhetorical questions divided into a set of two beginning with
οὐχὶ, and a set of four beginning with οὐ. The transition
from the former to the latter is
marked by πάλιν.

The speech is undoubtedly the genuine work of Demosthenes; this is proved not only by the testimony of Aeschines[1] but by the frequent quotations of ancient lexicographers and grammarians, and the internal evidence is equally conclusive. It holds a high place in his Private Orations; among the merits of its earlier portions may be noticed the closeness of its reasoning and the lucid arrangement of its argument, while its later portions are rendered interesting by the strong invective of the personal attack on the plaintiff and the dignified tone of the appeal to the court in favour of the defendant. All the points are supported by evidence, and except where the public services of the defendant are apparently unduly depreciated[2], there is every evidence of fairness on the part of the speaker. It is a forcible oration, in which we clearly recognise the characteristic feature that gives Demosthenes the superiority over Lysias, the great master of clear narration, and over his own instructor Isaeus, the best lawyer of all the Attic orators, namely, the ethical warmth of colouring, by which the dullest details are lit up with a fresh life and interest[3]. In the words of an able French critic, 'de tous les plaidoyers civils de Démosthène, le plus beau peut-être, celui où l'orateur a mis le plus d'art et de véhémence, c'est le discours qu'il a composé pour le banquier Phormion.' He calls it elsewhere, *un chef-d'œuvre dans son genre*[4]. Professor Jebb has with equal truth touched upon 'the moral dignity of the defence for Phormio[5].'

The result was decisive; the court, according to the statement of Apollodorus himself, upheld the plea of the

---

[1] *de fals. leg.* § 165, quoted in full on p. xl.

[2] See §§ 39—42 with notes, and esp. A. Schaefer, u. s., p. 168.

[3] *die ethische Wärme welche selbst einem nüchternen Stoffe Leben verleiht.* A. Schaefer, u. s., p. 168.

[4] Perrot, *Revue des deux mondes*, 1873, 6 pp. 407, 436.

[5] *Attic Orators* i 309.

defendant, and refused to listen to any reply on the part
of the plaintiff.   More than four-fifths of the jury must
have voted for the defendant, as we learn that the
plaintiff was condemned to pay the ἐπωβελία, i.e. a sixth
part of the twenty talents claimed, a fine amounting in
this case to as much as three talents and twenty minae.
We are not surprised to learn that the plaintiff left the
court in high dudgeon (Or. 45 § 6).

INTRODUCTION TO

OR. XLV.

ΚΑΤΑ ΣΤΕΦΑΝΟΥ
ΨΕΥΔΟΜΑΡΤΥΡΙΩΝ Α.

THE effect of the verdict given in support of Phormion's special plea in bar of the action brought by Apollodorus, was to prevent the latter from raising the same issue again, except in an indirect manner. It was still open to him to bring an action for false evidence against the witnesses on whose testimony Phormion had relied; such an action was known as a δίκη ψευδομαρτυριῶν, and if the plaintiff made good his case against the accessories, he could next proceed against the principal who produced them, by an action for subornation of false witness (δίκη κακοτεχνιῶν[1]); and in the event of his succeeding in the latter, he might then bring forward afresh his original suit (in the present instance a δίκη ἀφορμῆς).

Apollodorus accordingly brought an action for false testimony against one Stephanus, who was called on Phormion's side in the previous trial. This witness deposed to neither of the points on which the special plea was raised; he was neither produced to prove the date of the original lease, shewing the lapse of the term fixed by the Athenian statute of limitations, nor did he give evidence to the release and quittance effected between

---

[1] Or. 49 § 56, Or. 47 § 1.

Apollodorus and Phormion; he simply attested a point
which was, strictly speaking, irrelevant to the special plea
and really belonged to the main issue.   He was called,
with others, to prove a legal challenge[1] given by Phormion
to Apollodorus, demanding that, if the latter declined to
admit that a document put in evidence by Phormion was
a copy of Pasion's will, Apollodorus should himself open
the original; he deposed that Apollodorus declined to
open it, and further that the said copy was a counterpart
of the original[2].

The plaintiff denies that any such challenge had been
made and declares that his father left no will.   He contends that (1) had the challenge been given, there could
have been no reason for his refusing to open the document
(§§ 9—14); (2) it was unnecessary to demand his acknowledgment of the correctness of a copy, when according to
his opponents the original might have been readily produced (§§ 15—19); (3) the terms of the deposition were
false because it assumed that Pasion made the will alleged,
whereas he made no will at all; its terms ought to have
run, *not* 'the will of Pasion,' but 'the will Phormion
asserts to have been left by Pasion' (§§ 24—26).   His
argument on these points is a singular combination of
shallowness and subtlety[3], as may be seen in further
detail by referring to the italicised abstract of the somewhat difficult sections here referred to.

He next argues that the terms of the 'will' prove it
was forged by Phormion in his own interests (§§ 27—28),
that the 'will' was inconsistent with the 'lease,' that the
latter was also a fabrication (§§ 29—36), and that the
discharge pleaded by Phormion was false (§§ 40—42).   In
anticipation of the defendant's probable reply, that his

[1] Or. 36 § 7.
[2] Or. 45 § 10.
[3] *nur einige schwache, ja ganz* *nichtige* τεκμήρια...; *gegenzeu-* *gen...hat er nicht.* Sigg, *Apoll.* p. 412.

responsibility is limited to two points only, (1) Phormion's giving the challenge, and (2) the plaintiff's refusal of it, the plaintiff insists on binding the defendant to the exact terms of his testimony (§§ 43—46). He further submits that, if in the reply any attempt is made to denounce his original action as fraudulent, all such reference to the past must be suppressed by the court as irrelevant to the issue before it (§§ 47—50). If the defendant urged it was not his own evidence, bearing as it did on the main issue, but the evidence of those who gave witness to the special plea, that was fatal to the plaintiff in the former trial; the answer was, that the evidence on the main issue crippled his case on the special plea (§§ 51—52).

At this point the speaker passes off into petty personalities of a curious description, denouncing the defendant for giving false evidence against him, regardless of the family tie of Apollodorus' marriage with a first cousin of Stephanus, and thus transgressing what he calls by a rhetorical flourish the unwritten laws of natural affection (§§ 53—56); he declares and very inadequately proves, that a legal document on which he had relied in the former trial had been stolen by Stephanus (§§ 57—62); denounces him for truckling to prosperity, for selfishly disregarding the rights of the poor and the claims of the public on his ample resources (§§ 63—67), for his sour and sullen unsociability, and for his merciless extortion as a miserable money-lender (§§ 68—70).

Turning then from the nominal defendant Stephanus to his principal, Phormion, who is the real opponent in the present as in the previous lawsuit, he launches out into a vigorous invective against him, for his gross ingratitude towards the speaker's family who were the very founders of his fortunes (§§ 71—76), contrasts his own orderly life and public services with his opponent's immorality (§§ 77—80), charges him with appropriating money that belonged to Pasion, from whom all his wealth had originally come. Born a barbarian and sold as a slave, he had yet had the audacity to criticize the antecedents of the plaintiff's family (§§ 80—82).

After an ungenerous and gratuitous insinuation, to account for his younger brother Pasicles taking Phormion's part (§§ 83—84), he turns to the jury, reminds them of his father's benefactions to the state, implores them to protect him from one who was once a slave to his family, and from that slave's creature Stephanus; and, while reminding them incidentally of some of the points on which he relied, concludes by claiming a verdict against the man who, by his false evidence for Phormion, had robbed him of his revenge in the previous trial (§§ 85—88).

The defendant Stephanus replied at considerable length[1]. The purport of his defence appears to have been very much what the plaintiff had anticipated in §§ 43—46. In particular, he contended that he was responsible for attesting to the challenge alone and not for any further details incidentally included in his evidence. The existence of the will had been attested by other witnesses than himself, and the court's acceptance of Phormion's special plea was due to *their* evidence on the main issue, and also to the evidence given by *others* on the plea itself, proving the original lease and the subsequent discharge.

---

[1] Or. 46 § 1.

INTRODUCTION TO

Or. XLVI

ΚΑΤΑ ΣΤΕΦΑΝΟΥ
ΨΕΥΔΟΜΑΡΤΥΡΙΩΝ Β.

THE reply of Stephanus is followed by a second speech on
the part of the plaintiff, Apollodorus. In contrast to the
presumptive proofs and the passionate declamation of
his former effort, we here find, in a far less lengthy and
less ambitious form, little more than a series of technical
arguments supported by quotations from such parts of
the Athenian code as appeared to bear, however remotely,
on the case in question.

He charges the defendant with having given 'hearsay evidence' and cites the law against it (§§ 6—8);
declares that Phormion, under the mask of the defendant's
deposition, has given evidence in his own cause, which is
illegal (9—10); he even deduces the falsehood of the deposition from the material on which it was inscribed;
instead of being written hurriedly on an ordinary wax-
tablet to attest on the spot a *bona fide* challenge, it was
drawn up in a more permanent form implying a deliberately fraudulent design (11). He attempts to prove
that his father made no will at all, and quotes a law
forbidding a man's making a will if he had male issue
lawfully begotten (14). He further urges that his father
was disabled from disposing of his property by his 'adoption' as an Athenian citizen—a legal quibble arising from
the ambiguity of the term relating to adoption, which
really refers to the family and not to the state, as the

plaintiff disingenuously implies.   He also insinuates that his father was debarred from making a will by being under undue influence and of unsound mind (15—17).   He further. contends that his mother was technically an 'heiress,' and by law held in ward by her nearest relative, namely himself; that her marriage was therefore invalid, being made in his absence, without his consent and without any legal adjudication, and that Pasion's disposal of his wife by will was thus illegal (18—23); that the father's 'will,' if ever made, was vitiated by the fact that there were sons of full age now surviving (24); and that the defendant and Phormion had conspired to defeat the ends of justice (25—26).   After a parting sally on Phormion for his disregard of the laws, and a final thrust at the defendant, defying him to shew how he could possibly have known that the document attached to his challenge was a copy of Pasion's will, which he had never seen, and after also asserting that no one ever had a copy made of his own will[1], but kept it by him till his death, he concludes by asking the court to grant him the redress demanded by the claims of justice and the laws of Athens (27—29).

Thus the plaintiff assigns four legal reasons in support of the plea that Pasion's will was a forgery: (1) Pasion was a citizen by 'adoption'; (2) his widow was an 'heiress' legally at the disposal of her son and not her deceased husband; (3) he had legitimate sons, both of whom were now grown up and their coming of age would invalidate any will on the part of the father; (4) he was of unsound mind.   On these four points we have only to remark that the first rests on a verbal quibble[2].   (2) There is no indication elsewhere in other

---

[1] See Becker's *Charicles*, Scene xi, note 37.
[2] See note on § 14, and M.

Dareste *les plaidoyers civils de Dém.* II p. 307—8, where the law is briefly discussed.

speeches of Apollodorus that his mother was technically an 'heiress,' indeed there is reason to suspect that she was not even a native of Athens at all (§ 23); besides, as regards the alleged invalidity of his mother's second marriage, the plaintiff had already in his former speech expressed his acquiescence (Or. 45 § 4). (3) The intention of the law was that if a father, having legitimate male issue, made a will independent of their interests, the terms of the will as affecting other persons were to become valid in the event of the male children dying before they came of age. Thus a father could not disinherit his lawful heir, but he was not prevented from making a will in which the rights of the heir were duly regarded[1]; and indeed, we find that Apollodorus and his younger brother had divided their father's estate between them, and that the former in particular had succeeded to a dwelling-house which was once his father's property. (4) The suggestion of lunacy is inconsistent with Apollodorus' own description of his father's last illness in another speech, by which it appears that he was then clear-headed enough to give his son a particular account of all the sums due to him from his numerous creditors[2].

On the whole it is obvious that the plaintiff must have been conscious of having a very bad case indeed, and that to maintain it he was compelled to resort to the most contemptible subterfuges[3].

The date of the two speeches must be placed shortly after that of the speech in the suit between Apollodorus and Phormion, i.e. very soon after B.C. 351 or 350.

---

[1] Lortzing, *Apoll.* p. 82—3; Dareste, u. s., II p. 293.

[2] Or. 49 (Timoth.) § 42.

[3] *Beide reden, ganz besonders aber die zweite, sind voll bloszer sophismen und spiegelfechtereien so handgreiflicher und oft fast lächerlicher art, dasz u. s. w.* Sigg, *Apoll.* p. 412 and A. Schaefer, u. s., p. 177.

On the authorship of the Two Speeches against Stephanus.

We have seen that the authorship of the speech *pro Phormione* is undisputed; it is doubtless the genuine work of the great orator himself. Whether he is also the writer of both, or at any rate the first, of the two speeches against Stephanus, and of the others delivered by Apollodorus, which have come down to us among the works of Demosthenes[1], is a vexed question, an exhaustive treatment of which would demand an elaborate treatise beyond the compass of the present introduction. All that can here be offered is a brief discussion keeping in view, and where necessary correcting and supplementing, the arguments suggested by previous writers on the subject, and tested by the results of an independent investigation.

In the speech *pro Phormione* the case is supported by two important documents; (1) the lease granted to Phormion, (2) the will left by Pasion. In both the speeches against Stephanus (a witness, it will be remembered, in the former trial), the lease and the will are denounced as a fabrication and a fraud; more than this, while in the previous oration a warm eulogy is passed on the career of Phormion as a blameless man of business and as a generous citizen of irreproachable character, in the two latter the speaker avails himself of all the artifices of subtle insinuation, all the vehemence of unscrupulous invective, to paint his opponent's character in the darkest colours. The question arises whether the two latter speeches, or either of them, could have been written by the same person as the former.

Narrowing the enquiry for our present purpose to those speeches alone which Apollodorus delivered against Stephanus, we may in the first instance examine the *external evidence* (whether contemporary with Demosthenes or not) which may be adduced in support of the genuineness of the two speeches in question.   In

---

[1] The speeches by Apollodorus (with the dates assigned to them by A. Schaefer) are Or. 52 πρὸς Κάλλιππον, B.C. 369—8; Or. 53 πρὸς Νικόστρατον, after B.C. 368; Or. 49 πρὸς Τιμόθεον ὑπὲρ χρέους, B.C. 362; Or. 50, πρὸς Πολυκλέα περὶ τοῦ ἐπιτριηραρχήματος, about B.C. 357; Or. 45 and 46, κατὰ Στεφάνου ψευδομαρτυριῶν α΄ and β΄, about B.C. 351; Or. 59 κατὰ Νεαίρας, after B.C. 343;—Or. 47, κατ᾽ Εὐέργου καὶ Μνησιβούλου was delivered after B.C. 356, but not by Apollodorus, though it was probably *written* by the same orator as most, if not all of the above-mentioned speeches, and possibly by Apollodorus himself.

the first place we must set a passage in Aeschines in which he
denounces the orator as a traitor, charges him with writing for
a pecuniary consideration a speech for Phormion the banker and
with shewing this speech to Apollodorus, who was then prosecuting
Phormion on a charge imperilling his status as a free man[1]. Here
it will be remarked that the description of the trial is vague, and
the penalty, to which Phormion would have been liable, much ex-
aggerated; but it is more important to notice that Aeschines says
nothing of Demosthenes *writing* a speech for Apollodorus either
in the lawsuit with Phormion, or in his subsequent suit against
Stephanus. If Aeschines is speaking the truth, then at the worst
all that he says is, that, in his opinion, Demosthenes acted in
bad faith by betraying his client's interests and allowing his
opponent to become informed of the arguments which would be
brought against him. But it may be noticed that this course
is not necessarily inconsistent with good faith on the part of
Phormion's friend, as the orator may have seen no reason for
concealing his client's case from his opponent,—especially as the
speech on that client's behalf would be the opening speech, and
the case would be in no danger of being damaged by any previous
attack on the part of the plaintiff. Demosthenes may have been
anxious to reconcile the parties and, if possible, to put an end
to a quarrel which was threatening the disruption of Pasion's
family; and so strong was his client's position, that to inform
Apollodorus of the case against him and even to shew him the
very manuscript itself with the friendly advice to drop the lawsuit, would have been no detriment to Phormion's interests[2].

Considering all the calumnies raked up by Aeschines against
his great rival in the two orations *de falsa legatione* and *contra*

---

[1] Aeschines, *de falsa legatione*
§ 165, τὸν δ' ἀγαθὸν σύμβουλον
τί χρὴ ποιεῖν; οὐ τῇ πόλει πρὸς
τὸ παρὸν τὰ βέλτιστα συμβουλεύειν; τὸν δὲ πονηρὸν κατήγορον
τί χρὴ λέγειν; οὐ τοὺς καιροὺς
ἀποκρυπτόμενον τῆς πράξεως κατηγορεῖν; τὸν δὲ ἐκ φύσεως προδότην
πῶς χρὴ θεωρεῖν; ἀρά γε ὡς σὺ
τοῖς ἐντυγχάνουσι καὶ πιστεύσασι
κέχρησαι, λόγους εἰς δικαστήρια
γράφοντα μισθοῦ τούτους ἐκφέρειν
τοῖς ἀντιδίκοις; ἔγραψας λόγον
Φορμίωνι τῷ τραπεζίτῃ χρήματα
λαβών· τοῦτον ἐξήνεγκας Ἀπολλοδώρῳ τῷ περὶ τοῦ σώματος
κρίναντι Φορμίωνα. Id. *contra
Ctesiphontem* § 173, περὶ δὲ τὴν
καθ' ἡμέραν δίαιταν τίς ἐστιν; ἐκ
τριηράρχου λογογράφος ἀνεφάνη,
τὰ πατρῷα καταγελάστως προ-
έμενος· ἄπιστος δὲ καὶ περὶ ταῦτα
δόξας εἶναι καὶ τοὺς λόγους ἐκφέρων
τοῖς ἀντιδίκοις ἀνεπήδησεν ἐπὶ τὸ
βῆμα.

[2] A. Schaefer, u. s., III 2, p.
178, and Rehdantz there referred to.

Ctesiphontem, we venture to think that, if he had had any ground
whatever for asserting that Demosthenes actually *wrote* a speech
for Apollodorus, a speech virtually directed against Phormion,
though nominally against one of his witnesses only, he would
certainly have seized his opportunity and made the very most of
so damaging a fact. But he says no such thing; and even
Deinarchus, another strong opponent of Demosthenes, makes no
such charge against him, though he has an opening for so doing
in a passage in which he refers to the orator's 'delivering' a speech
for Phormion[1].

Later writers, however, though less likely to be familiar with
the facts, are bolder in their denunciations; in Plutarch's life of
Demosthenes, we read that the orator 'is said to have written for
Apollodorus his speeches against Phormion and Stephanus, for
which he justly fell into disrepute, as he also wrote a speech
for Phormion in his lawsuit against Apollodorus.' He adds,
with a reminiscence perhaps of the trade of the orator's father,
'it was as bad as selling swords to both sides from the same
manufactory'[2].

The insertion of the speeches against Stephanus among the
works of Demosthenes may perhaps be accounted for by the

[1] Deinarchus *contra Demosth.*
§ 111 p. 108, εὑρήσετε...τοῦτον
ἀντὶ λογογράφου καὶ μισθοῦ τὰς
δίκας λέγοντος ὑπὲρ Κτησίππου
καὶ Φορμίωνος καὶ ἑτέρων πολλῶν πλουσιώτατον ὄντα τῶν ἐν τῇ
πόλει. A recent editor of Deinarchus, Dr F. Blass, writes to
me suggesting that the passage
is interpolated,—a suggestion
which he has recorded on p. vii
of his edition. Deinarchus, he
conjectures, wrote only καὶ μισθοῦ τὰς δίκας λέγοντος; had he
wanted to enter into detail, he
must have added 'Phormion
the banker' and 'Ctesippus the
son of Chabrias', because these
cases were by that time probably forgotten. The bare addition ὑπὲρ Κτησίππου καὶ Φορμίωνος καὶ ἑτέρων πολλῶν is, he
says, exactly what a grammarian would insert to remind
his pupils of the speeches they
had read in the course of their
studies.

[2] Plutarch, *Dem.* chap. 15,
λέγεται δὲ καὶ τὸν κατὰ Τιμοθέου
τοῦ στρατηγοῦ λόγον, ᾧ χρησάμε-
νος Ἀπολλόδωρος εἷλε τὸν ἄνδρα
τοῦ ὀφλήματος, Δημοσθένης γράψαι
τῷ Ἀπολλοδώρῳ, καθάπερ καὶ
τοὺς πρὸς Φορμίωνα καὶ Στέφανον,
ἐφ᾽ οἷς εἰκότως ἠδόξησε. καὶ γὰρ
ὁ Φορμίων ἠγωνίζετο λόγῳ Δημοσθένους πρὸς τὸν Ἀπολλόδωρον,
ἀτεχνῶς καθάπερ ἐξ ἑνὸς μαχαι-
ροπωλίου τὰ κατ᾽ ἀλλήλων ἐγχει-
ρίδια πωλοῦντος αὐτοῦ τοῖς ἀντιδίκοις. (Cf. chap. 4, Δημοσθένης
ὁ πατὴρ... ἐπεκαλεῖτο μαχαιρο-
ποιός.) Comp. *Dem. et Cic.* c. 3,
χρηματίσασθαι ἀπὸ τοῦ λόγου
Δημοσθένης ἐπιψόγως λέγεται, λο-
γογραφῶν κρύφα τοῖς περὶ Φορμίωνα καὶ Ἀπολλόδωρον ἀντιδίκοις.

conjecture that Callimachus, who, as head of the Alexandrine library, undertook the prodigious task of settling the canon of the Attic Orators[1], may have been misled either by the passage of Aeschines above quoted, or by the partial resemblance of the first speech to the style of the orator, into supposing that Demosthenes himself was the writer; or again may have included them among his orations as incidentally illustrative of his genuine works. That there was once a time when Apollodorus himself was regarded as the writer of the orations spoken by him which have been handed down to us among the works of Demosthenes, may perhaps be fairly concluded from a *scholium* on the passage of Aeschines above referred to, noting 'from this it is clear that the speeches referring to the estate of Apollodorus are *not* written by him, but by Demosthenes'[2]. Thus, Plutarch's story of the duplicity of Demosthenes, which with slight variations is repeated by still later writers[3], may have originated in a misunderstanding of the language of his enemy's accusation[4]. The phraseology used by one of them in particular (Zosimus by name, a grammarian who, if we credit the conjecture attributing to him part of the *scholia* on Aeschines, may have actually written the *scholium* in question,) shews how easily, even

[1] Rehdantz ap. A. Schaefer, u. s., p. 317—322. The earliest reference to the Ten as a distinct group is to be found in the title of a lost work by Caecilius of Calacte,— χαρακτῆρες τῶν ί ῥητόρων. But the form of the title implies that it was a group already recognised (Introd. to Cicero's *Orator* p. xii).

[2] Aesch. ed. Schultz, p. 311, ἐκ τούτου δῆλον ὅτι καὶ οἱ περὶ τὴν οἰκίαν (οὐσίαν coniecit A. Schaefer)᾽Απολλοδώρου λόγοι οὐκ ᾽Απολλοδώρου ἀλλὰ Δημοσθένους. The rhetorician Tiberius, περὶ σχημάτων c. 14 (referred to by A. Schaefer), quotes from Or. 45 § 83, and introduces his citation with the name not of Demosthenes but of Apollodorus, καὶ πάλιν ᾽Απολλόδωρος ʻἐγὼ γάρ—οὐκ οἶδα,' though he professes in c. 1 to confine himself to ὅσα παρὰ Δημοσθένει κατενοήσαμεν. In c. 31 he begins an extract from Or. 36 § 52 with the words, ἐν τῷ ὑπὲρ Φορμίωνος πρὸς τὸν ᾽Απολλόδωρον. Weil, *les Harangues de Dém.* p. xi, demurs to any weight being assigned to the quotation from Tiberius.

[3] Anonym. p. 155, Suidas *Dem.* c. 3, referred to by Lortzing, *Apoll.* p. 23.

[4] The taunt about 'selling swords to both sides' is not borrowed from the passage in Aeschines. L. Schmidt, *Paed. Archiv* xxv (1) 58, in a review of this volume, points out, however, that it may have been due in the first instance to some other personal opponent of Demosthenes (Weil, u. s.).

before his time, Callimachus and Plutarch may have been misled
by a careless expansion of the language of the orator's rival—
language which we have little hesitation in regarding as the
original source of the subsequent tradition[1].

The argument from *internal evidence* is more intricate, and
the style of all the orations delivered by Apollodorus has been discussed with much minuteness by several modern critics. Without entering, however, into undue detail on those speeches which
are not included in the present volume, we may briefly state certain
peculiarities of diction to which Arnold Schaefer, who, in his admir-
able work on the *Life and Times of Demosthenes*, was the first to
treat the subject systematically, has specially drawn attention,
as running through all the speeches delivered by Apollodorus,
and distinguishing them from the genuine writings of Demosthenes[2].

We find, then, a feebleness of expression shewing itself in
repetitions of the same word within short intervals from one
another[3]; this clumsiness is most noticeable in the case of
the pronouns οὗτος and αὐτός[4]. Again, clause after clause begins
with the same relative pronoun, or the same hypothetical par-
ticle[5]. Such carelessness of expression is naturally attended
by looseness of rhythm; thus, tested by the frequency of *hiatus*,
the speeches delivered by Apollodorus are inferior in composition

---

[1] Zosimus *vit. Dem.* p. 119
R., λογογραφεῖν ἀρξάμενος καὶ
εἰς τὰ ἰδιωτικὰ καὶ εἰς τὰ δημόσια
καὶ πολλοὺς ἐκδοὺς λόγους πρὸς
ἑαυτοὺς ἤλω ἀμφοτέροις λόγους
ἐκδοὺς κατ᾽ ἀλλήλων. He lived
in the time of the Emperor
Anastasius, A.D. 491—518.

[2] A. Schaefer *Dem. u. s. Zeit*,
III 2, 184—199, *Der Verfasser
der von Apollodor gehaltenen
Reden*, 1858. Since then, the
subject has been elaborately
discussed by F. Lortzing (1863)
and J. Sigg (1873). For the
full titles of their treatises, see
p. xiv.

[3] Or. 45 § 4, γιγνομένου...
γίγνονται...ἐγίγνοντο, *ib.* § 63,
συνέβαινεν ... βαίνων. — Or. 46
§ 28, διαθηκῶν... διαθηκῶν...δια-
τιθέμενοι ... διατίθενται. Simi-

larly in § 2, διατιθεμένῳ τῷ
πατρί is thrice repeated and ὁ
πατὴρ διέθετο twice. For other
repetitions see §§ 3, 5, 8, 25.

[4] Or. 45 § 64, τούτῳ...τοῦτον
τούτου...τούτου, § 86, ἑαυτόν...
τούτου ... ἑαυτόν...ταῦθ᾽... τούτου,
and similarly § 34, § 83.—Or.
46 § 21, οὗτος...αὐτόν...αὐτοῦ
τούτου...αὐτάς...ταῦτ᾽, and § 6.
But cf. Or. 36 §§ 12, 20 and 42.

[5] Or. 45 § 49 οὕς...οὕς § 81,
εἰ...εἰ...εἶτα...εἰ. Or. 46 § 23,
εἴπερ...εἴτε...εἴτε...εἰ μὲν...εἰδὲ
...εἴπερ. τοίνυν though common in the genuine orations
occurs 14 times at least in the
29 sections of Or. 46. '*Non
negari potest vividioribus trans-
grediendi figuris, quibus D. ex-
cellit, carere nostras orationes*'
Lortzing p. 33.

to the certainly genuine speeches of Demosthenes, though an exception must be made in favour of the first speech against Stephanus[1]. Even this speech supplies instances of unrhythmical construction[2], and examples of anacoluthon or bad writing; and in particular an awkward combination of participles may be noticed in the first as well as in the second oration[3].

On passing to the question of the degree of mastery over the subject-matter and the general argument which is displayed in the various speeches, a distinction may be drawn between the earlier speeches on the one hand (e.g. those against Polycles and Timotheus) where the narrative is monotonous and tedious, and the conclusion somewhat lame and feeble; and the two speeches against Stephanus. The latter shew signs of an improvement which Schaefer ascribes to the prolonged experience in litigation which the speaker had enjoyed since his earlier efforts. The general style of all these orations, differing as it does from that of Demosthenes, and bearing marks of a kind of consistency of its own, points (so Schaefer suggests) to one person as the writer of them all, and that person in all probability Apollodorus himself. He often appeared before the law-courts not only in private suits on his own account, but also in public causes; and, when he was a member of the Council, he made important proposals, and brought them before the general assembly of the people. Even assuming that he resorted to others for assistance in his private lawsuits, yet, as soon as he appeared in a more public character, he would find it necessary to speak for himself, and without some oratorical ability he could hardly have undertaken so many public causes. In the second speech against Stephanus we find him pluming himself on his cleverness[4]; and in that against Neaera he is called upon to address the court on behalf of a younger and less experienced speaker[5]. Apollodorus obviously laid himself out

---

[1] Benseler *de hiatu* p. 147, *auctor alterius orationis* (Or. 45) *sermonem ita conformare solebat, ut vocalium concursus evitaretur et auctor alterius* (Or. 46) *ita ut hiatus non evitaretur.*

[2] The passage referred to is in § 68, ἐγὼ γὰρ — προσελθεῖν πρῶτον, but the objection is perhaps hypercritical. For anacoluthon, cf. Or. 45 § 3; for bad writing, Or. 46 § 17.

[3] Or. 45 § 83, Or. 46 § 13 (Lortzing p. 88, 89).

[4] § 17 οὐδὲ ἐδόκουν ἐμὲ οὕτω δεινὸν ἔσεσθαι ὥστε ταῦτα ἀκριβῶς ἐξετάσαι.

[5] Or. 59 § 14, νέον ὄντα καὶ ἀπείρως ἔχοντα τοῦ λέγειν, while Apollodorus πρεσβύτερός ἐστι... καὶ ἐμπειροτέρως ἔχει τῶν νόμων.

for attempting to play a prominent part at Athens; in the *pro
Phormione* the jury are specially warned against his loud and
impudent self-assertion[1], and elsewhere we even find him apolo-
gising for his loudness of voice (as well as his hurried gait
and ill-favoured countenance), as his misfortune and not his
fault[2].

Such then is the general drift of the arguments, to which a
brief sketch can only do imperfect justice, which lead Schaefer to
the conclusion that the speeches against Callippus, Nicostratus,
Timotheus, Polycles, Euergus and Mnesibulus; both of those
in prosecution of Stephanus; and lastly, that in accusation
of Neaera,—speeches delivered in the above chronological order
between the years B.C. 369 and 343,—were all composed by
one person, who had a distinctive style of his own, and that
person probably Apollodorus himself, with whose transactions
no less than seven of these speeches are concerned.

The above conclusion is however open to criticism on the
ground that it gives no adequate account of the incomparable
superiority of the first speech against Stephanus, not only to
the others delivered by Apollodorus, but in particular to the
second speech in the very same trial. It is marked by a closeness
of argument, and a forcibleness of invective, worthy of a far abler
writer than the composer of the other speeches. It seems futile
to explain this superiority by ascribing it to a gradual improvement in the speaker's rhetorical ability brought about by time
and experience[3], when the second speech is so meagre and lifeless,
and when the last of the series, namely that *in Neaeram*, instead

---

[1] Or. 36 § 61, κραυγή καὶ ἀναίδεια.

[2] Or. 45 § 77. A. Schaefer
understands the passage differ-
ently; after referring to the
loudness of voice attributed to
Apoll. in Or. 36, he continues:
'Wenn dagegen Apollodor er-
klärt: *Ich rechne mich selber,
was Gesichtsbildung, raschen
Gang und laute Rede betrifft,
nicht unter die von der Natur
glücklich begabten...,* so will er
damit nur ein selbstgefälliges
prunken und stolzieren von
sich ablehnen, ohne andeuten
zu wollen, er sei missgestalt

träges Schrittes und schwach-
stimmig.' This misses the
sense; the words when taken
correctly as in the text, confirm
the quotation from Or. 36, and
do not appear even remotely to
contradict it. Cf. Lysias Or.
16 §§ 18, 19.

[3] A. Schaefer, u. s., p. 191.
Prof. Schaefer, in a kind communication received since I
wrote the above, endeavours to
account for the greater polish
of style shewn in Or. 45 by the
fact that Apollodorus had the
strongest motives for doing his
very best in his opening speech.

of shewing any advance as compared with the first speech against
Stephanus is certainly inferior to it, and is characterized by a
diffuseness and laxity of style, and by other faults besides. And
again, the explanation that the second speech is only a δευτερο-
λογία, and therefore inferior to the first, is hardly adequate.
Hence, while we would ascribe the second to Apollodorus himself, and find in its constant quotations from the Athenian code
of law a characteristic touch, reminding us of his legal learning
as attested in the oration *in Neaeram*[1], we are driven to the
conclusion that in the first he had recourse to the assistance
of an abler rhetorician than himself. There is scarcely sufficient
proof that that rhetorician was Demosthenes. It must however
be candidly admitted that of all the speeches delivered by Apollodorus, the one that on personal grounds is least likely to have
been written by the composer of the oration for Apollodorus'
opponent Phormion, is less far removed from the style of Demosthenes than any of the remainder, though again and again we
have words never used by the orator himself in his undisputed
writings[2]. In one passage indeed (§ 77) we have a close parallel
with the *Pantaenetus* (§ 55)[3], which seems to point to a common
authorship, and if the latter speech is rightly assigned to the
year 346 or thereabout, in other words, is placed *after* the speeches
now under consideration, we can hardly explain the parallel
except by the hypothesis of a common source, or else by the
less probable assumption that Demosthenes, who was almost
certainly the writer of the *Pantaenetus*, having heard or read
the first speech against Stephanus, a speech directed virtually
against his own client Phormion, borrowed from the phraseology
of the latter oration, with which he was thus familiar. The Attic
Orator, Hyperides, is known to have written one speech at
least against Pasicles[4], who, though a brother of Apollodorus,
took the side of his opponent Phormion, and a conjecture has

---

[1] § 14, ἐμπειροτέρως ἔχει τῶν
νόμων, and § 15 ὑπὲρ τῶν θεῶν
καὶ τῶν νόμων καὶ τοῦ δικαίου
καὶ ὑμῶν αὐτῶν, compared with
Or. 46 § 20 ὑπὲρ τῶν αὐτῶν καὶ
ἐμοῦ καὶ τοῦ δικαίου καὶ τῶν
νόμων.

[2] § 14 παροξυσμός, § 19 παραπέτασμα, § 70 ἀοίκητος (in sense
'houseless'), § 85 ἐπίχαρτος,
§ 63 and § 65 ὑποπίπτειν τινί
(also in Or. 59 Neaer. § 43).

[3] Or. 37 §§ 52, 55 quoted in
note on Or. 45 § 77. The *Pantaenetus* was probably the later
speech of the two.

[4] κατὰ Πασικλέους and πρὸς
Πασικλέα περὶ ἀντιδόσεως, Fragm.
137—140, p. 88—9 ed. Blass.

been half hazarded that it was for Apollodorus that those speeches were composed[1]; but there is no adequate reason for assigning the first speech against Stephanus to that orator, and a comparison with his four extant orations has led me to notice only one important coincidence of expression[2].

On the whole, then, we may conclude (1) that the second speech was not only delivered by Apollodorus, but probably composed by him; (2) that the first was written for him, possibly not by Demosthenes, but by some rhetorician unknown to us, whose assistance he was led to secure either by the pressure of his other engagements, or by a consciousness of the difficulty of the task that was before him, and a mistrust of his own unaided ability to compose more than the legal rejoinder to the defendant's reply.

Those who attribute the speeches against Stephanus, or at least the first of them, to the authorship of Demosthenes, are bound to supply some reasonable motive for his changing sides after taking the part of Phormion against Apollodorus. If such a desertion to the enemy's camp was due to his discovery that the documents relied on in the first trial were forgeries, and that the deponents called to prove them were guilty of false witness, we cannot but think that Demosthenes, if he had been the writer of a speech immediately arising out of the former trial, would have been prompted to stronger expressions of indignation against the fraud practised on the jury on the previous occasion.

While we dismiss as irrelevant any attempt to try the alleged duplicity of Demosthenes by the standard of the professional etiquette of the English bar, and refrain from entangling our discussion with parallels suggested by questions of modern forensic casuistry, we may at any rate remark that, though we have no sufficient warrant for assuming that the orator was above pecuniary considerations, a certain sense of honour would probably have kept him from accepting a fee to write down the very side which he had but lately written up; and we may fairly conclude that such conduct was held dishonourable from the fact that even for divulging Phormion's case to his opponent, Demosthenes is, whether truly   falsely, charged by Aeschines with playing a traitor's part.

---

[1] Hornbostel, *Apoll.* p. 35.

[2] Or. 45 § 74 ἀνεκδότους ἔνδον γηράσκειν, compared with Hy-perides III 28, 4, ἀνέκδοτον ἔνδον καταγηράσκειν and III 27, 22, ἄγαμον ἔνδον καταγηράσκειν.

Again, it is urged that the first speech against Stephanus was written for a different trial to that on behalf of Phormion. This can hardly be regarded as an extenuating fact in favour of Demosthenes as the writer of the leading speech in both trials, since the second cause arose immediately out of the first, and there can be no question about the irreconcileable difference between the facts of the case as stated in the two orations, and the terms used in the one and the other in describing the character of Phormion. Even apart from motives of honour, the lower ground of expediency would presumably have sufficed to prevent Demosthenes from writing to defame the character of one who, by his opponent himself, was admitted to be a wealthy and prosperous man of business, and from supporting by preference the failing fortunes of an impoverished pettifogger.

Such, then, at the very strongest, are the principal arguments that may be adduced against the genuineness of the two speeches against Stephanus. In conclusion, it is only fair to submit the only hypothesis on which it is not impossible that Demosthenes may after all be the real author of, at any rate, the first oration.

We have already seen that it is highly probable that the speech against Phormion belongs to the latter part of the year B. c. 351 (p. xxix) and that the speeches against Stephanus may fairly be placed in the year B.c. 350[1]. It was a year in which the efforts of Athens to recover Euboea and to protect Olynthus placed her in a position of grave financial embarrassment. To meet this, Apollodorus, as a member of the senate, moved a decree that it should be submitted to the vote of the public assembly whether the surplus of the revenue should be paid to the Theoric fund for religious festivals, or applied to the expenses of the war. The proposal was approved by the senate and accepted by the public assembly; and the latter passed a decree appropriating the surplus to military purposes. Hereupon one Stephanus, who is not to be identified with the defendant in the speeches before us, impeached Apollodorus on the ground of his having brought forward an illegal decree; and he obtained a verdict, which led to the fine of one talent being inflicted on Apollodorus[2]. In this impeach-

---

[1] The *archon eponymus* of that year [Ol. 107, 3] was one Apollodorus, probably *not* the son of Pasion.

[2] Or. 59 §§ 3—8, esp. § 4, διαχειροτονῆσαι τὸν δῆμον εἴτε δοκεῖ τὰ περιόντα χρήματα τῆς διοικήσεως στρατιωτικὰ εἶναι ἢ Θεωρικά; Grote, *H. G.*, chap. 88; Curtius, *H. G.*, vol. v, p. 269 (Eng. Transl.); Hornbostel, *Apoll.* p. 39, 40; A. Schaefer,

ment, Stephanus was probably the tool of Eubulus and the peace-party, and although there is no proof that Apollodorus acted at the suggestion of Demosthenes and the opposite party, the proposal of Apollodorus would doubtless meet with the orator's approval, as is clear from the financial policy cautiously propounded by the latter in the Olynthiac orations[1], and, when it was too late, carried to a successful issue twelve years afterwards in the autumn of 339, only one year before the catastrophe of Chaeroneia.

It may therefore be questioned whether political motives may not have induced Demosthenes to throw Phormion overboard and to support Apollodorus by writing the first speech against Stephanus. On this hypothesis it may be presumed that Apollodorus, having lost his lawsuit against Phormion owing to the powerful advocacy of Demosthenes, and being almost crushed by the consequences of his defeat, resorted to. Demosthenes in the hope of recovering part at least of his resources, and proposed to run the risk of bringing forward his motion on the Theoric fund, on condition that the orator wrote him a speech against the obnoxious witness Stephanus.

My friend Dr F. Blass (the author of several important works on Greek Oratory) has favoured me with a suggestive letter[2], supporting this hypothesis and also shewing that the style of the first speech against Stephanus, apart from its general resemblance to that of Demosthenes[3], coincides with it in a hitherto unnoticed peculiarity, that under certain limitations the orator generally avoids the juxtaposition of more than two short syllables, the exceptions being for the most part cases where the three syllables fall within the compass of a single word[4]. To examine the minute criterion here proposed is beyond my present purpose. It is sufficient to state (as my learned correspondent would obviously acknowledge), that while its absence may suggest the spuriousness of any given oration, its presence does not prove its genuineness. It may also be admitted

---

u. s., III 2, p. 180 and (for the chronology here followed) *ib.* p. 330. Some (*e.g.* Weil, *Harangues de Dém.* p. 163) would place the Euboean expedition in B.C. 348, and Dr Blass would therefore place in that year the motion of Apollodorus and the delivery of Or. 45.

[1] Olynth. III §§ 10—13.
[2] 12 Sept. 1875 ; see also his *Att. Ber.* III 32, 412—4 (published in 1877).
[3] Sigg, *Apoll.* p. 415—432.
[4] See p. 7 of his dissertation on the Letters ascribed to Demosthenes, (Oct. 1875); also *Att. Ber.* III 99—101.

that the testimony of Harpocration is in favour of the Demosthenic authorship of the first speech[1] (though the value of that testimony is impaired by his attributing the second speech[2] to the same author); and that the parallelism of § 77 to a passage in the *Pantaenetus* already noticed is on the whole more easily explained by ascribing the first speech to Demosthenes than by any other hypothesis[3].

[1] See quotations in notes on Or. 45 §§ 1, 15, 63, 66, 74, 80, 84.

[2] Cf. Or. 46 §§ 7, 11, 20.

[3] Since the above discussion was first published, it has been justly observed that the genuineness of the first speech against Stephanus 'could hardly have been doubted but for the desire to vindicate the orator's morality....The morality of Demosthenes' conduct may in this case perhaps be dubious, but it is not so palpably bad as has been supposed....But...he attacks his late client's character with a coarse violence and a wantonness which goes beyond the conventional invective of the law-courts. He writes for Apollodorus as Apollodorus would have written himself, not sparing even the speaker's own mother. And it is precisely here rather than in the change of sides that we feel the real discredit lies' (S. H. Butcher, *Demosthenes*, 1881, p. 136).

INTRODUCTION TO

Or. LIII

ΠΡΟΣ ΝΙΚΟΣΤΡΑΤΟΝ
ΠΕΡΙ ΑΝΔΡΑΠΟΔΩΝ ΑΠΟΓΡΑΦΗΣ
ΑΡΕΘΟΥΣΙΟΥ.

In this speech Apollodorus, the litigious son of Pasion,
appears in support of a lawsuit arising out of an information laid against one Arethusius, for refusing to pay a fine
due to the public chest. According to Athenian law, if
a state-debtor concealed his effects, any citizen who discovered the fact was at liberty to draw up, and lay before
the proper magistrate, a written statement containing an
inventory or specification of the goods in question. The
schedule thus drawn up was called an ἀπογραφή, and this
name was also given to the legal process in support of it[1].
The informant, in the event of his making good his case,
was entitled to the reward of three-fourths of the valuation (§ 2); if he failed, he was fined a thousand drachmae,
and suffered a partial disfranchisement which prevented
his appearing again as a prosecutor in a public cause
(§ 1).

In the present instance, Apollodorus has handed in a
specification in which two slaves are stated to be the
property of Arethusius, and therefore liable to confiscation
as a partial payment of his debt to the public treasury.

---

[1] Meier and Schömann, p. 253; Hermann, *Public Antiquities*,
§ 136, 13.

Hereupon, a brother of Arethusius, named Nicostratus, puts in a claim to the slaves, and in the speech before us Apollodorus has to shew that the claim is false and that the slaves are really the property of Arethusius. To prove this he calls evidence in §§ 19—21, and this is the only portion of the speech which is really relevant to the issue before the court, while the greater part of it, up to this point, is devoted to a narrative of the relations between Apollodorus and the two brothers. The object of this is to shew that the former had been most ungratefully treated by the latter, especially by Nicostratus, and that he was therefore, according to the Athenian notion, fully justified in revenging himself for his private wrongs by supporting a public information against his opponent. To prove the purity of his motives and to ingratiate himself with the court, he waives at the very outset his claim to the reward to which the informant in such cases is legally entitled.

Among the speeches of Lysias we have three concerned with causes relating to claims of money withheld from the state (ἀπογραφαί): the speech 'for the soldier' (Or. 9), that 'on the property of Aristophanes' (19), and that 'against Philocrates' (29). The first two are for the defence; the third, for the prosecution. But in all three, the promoter of the ἀπογραφή is represented as the prosecutor; in the present case, although the promoter of the ἀπογραφή is Apollodorus, we should probably consider him as the defendant and Nicostratus as the plaintiff. Apollodorus was apparently in possession of the effects disputed; his opponent Nicostratus puts in a claim against him, and the speech before us is therefore a speech for the defence[1]. Owing to the general character of its contents, it is usually classed among the

---

[1] Caillemer, s.v. *Apographē*, in Daremberg and Saglio's *Dict.*

Private Orations, and it may be conveniently studied in conjunction with them. But it cannot be too clearly stated, that, in so far as it arises directly out of a refusal to pay a fine to the public chest, it is essentially a speech delivered in a public cause.

Apollodorus states that Nicostratus was his neighbour in the country and formerly his trusted friend, that they had done kindly services for one another, and that in particular he had lent to Nicostratus, free of interest, a sum which he was himself compelled to raise on the security of part of his property. So far from being grateful, the borrower at once laid a plot to escape payment of his debt, made common cause with the opponents of Apollodorus, and induced a third party (one Lycidas) to bring against him a suit demanding that certain property should be produced in court. Among those who were entered as witnesses to the delivery of the summons requiring him to produce the property, was Arethusius, a brother of Nicostratus, as above mentioned. The summons, it is alleged, was never served, consequently Apollodorus did not appear, and judgment went against him by default. Subsequently, Apollodorus prosecuted Arethusius for fraudulent citation ($\psi\epsilon\upsilon\delta o\kappa\lambda\eta\tau\epsilon i\alpha\varsigma$ $\gamma\rho\alpha\phi\acute{\eta}$), which was regarded by Athenian law as a *criminal* offence, while on the contrary a witness in the cause itself as distinguished from one who attested a summons, was, if he gave false evidence, only liable to a *civil* action[1]. Before the case came on, Arethusius committed several acts of outrage against Apollodorus, laid waste his orchard and violently assaulted him, and when the case for fraudulent citation, and apparently for the other criminal acts, was

---

[1] Harpocration, quoted on § 17 *ad fin.*, inaccurately uses the (possibly generic) term $\delta i\kappa\eta$, instead of $\gamma\rho\alpha\phi\acute{\eta}$, with reference to $\psi\epsilon\upsilon\delta o\kappa\lambda\eta\tau\epsilon i\alpha$.

brought before the jury, Apollodorus, under these aggravating circumstances, obtained a verdict against Arethusius with the greatest ease. Indeed, it was only owing to the entreaties of his brothers, with the acquiescence of the prosecutor, who was unwilling to face the odium which would ensue, that Arethusius escaped the penalty of death[1], and had inflicted on him a fine of one talent, for the payment of which his brothers became jointly responsible. Arethusius pleaded poverty and refused to pay: thereupon Apollodorus took the legal steps required (as above described) for the confiscation of his property, and in his specification claimed for the state, among other effects, two slaves as a partial security for the payment of the fine. Nicostratus resists this claim as regards the slaves in question and claims them as his own property, though even in that case, as the speaker points out, they should be confiscated, since Nicostratus had guaranteed the payment of the fine and had failed to make good his guarantee. In §§ 22—25 Apollodorus describes the unsuccessful attempt of his opponents to entrap him into accepting a legal challenge, which would have committed him to a virtual admission that the slaves were private property; and in §§ 19—21 calls evidence to prove, that the person recognised as the responsible owner of the slaves was Arethusius, and not the present claimant Nicostratus.

Passing from the general contents of the speech as above sketched, we may turn to a brief consideration of its literary style and special peculiarities. We are at once struck by the disproportionate space of twenty sections

---

[1] Boeckh, *Public Economy*, trans. Lamb, p. 496 note 2, while noticing that other criminal acts are involved, considers that the present passage proves that the punishment of death might be inflicted in a case of ψευδοκλητεία, but this seems scarcely probable.

devoted to purely preliminary details, as contrasted with the short compass within which lies the real gist of the case. The long account of the reasons prompting the speaker to seek for revenge, is unlike the manner of Demosthenes, and a certain feebleness and diffuseness may be noted in the narrative immediately following the exordium. Among minor details may be observed a tendency to add unnecessary and superfluous clauses, defining more clearly what has just gone before[1]. Again, we find needless repetitions within the limits of a single sentence[2]; further, we have a certain clumsiness in the repetition of pronouns such as οὗτος and αὐτός[3]; we observe a disproportionate number of harsh constructions[4], and it is curious to notice that a phrase occurring in this speech, which is unexampled in the undisputed writings of Demosthenes, finds its nearest parallels in speeches delivered like the present by Apollodorus[5]. We may also trace a general resemblance to the style of that against Neaera, the greater part of which was delivered by the same person, a speech which it is impossible to attribute to the authorship of Demosthenes[6]; and, lastly, there is a

[1] e.g. not content with Ἀρεθουσίου, οὗπερ ἐγέγραπτο εἶναι in § 2, the writer in § 10 has the words, Ἀρεθούσιος οὗ τἀνδράποδ' ἐστὶ ταῦτα ἃ νῦν ἀπογέγραπται, again in § 14 Ἀρεθούσιος οὗπέρ ἐστι τἀνδράποδα ταῦτα, and similarly in § 19. The words in § 7 ἐδεῖτό μου βοηθῆσαι αὐτῷ ὥσπερ καὶ ἐν τῷ ἔμπροσθεν χρόνῳ ἦν περὶ αὐτὸν ἀληθινὸς φίλος, are partially repeated in § 8 and § 12. Again in § 24, τὰς βασάνους is unnecessarily followed by the closer definition, ὅτι εἴποιεν οἱ ἄνθρωποι. (Cf. A. Schaefer, u. s., p. 187—190; Lortzing, *Apoll.* p. 30 etc.; and see especially Blass, *Att. Ber.* III 462.)

[2] e.g. § 4, οἰκείως διεκείμεθα... οἰκείως διεκείμην.

[3] § 6 *ad init.* αὐτὸν...τούτου... αὐτῷ...αὐτός. Also, *ad fin.* τούτου ...τούτου...αὐτὸς...τοῦτον τούτου ...αὐτῷ...αὐτόν. Cf. §§ 4 and 8.

[4] See §§ 11, 12, 24, 29.

[5] § 15, ἐβάδιζον ἐπὶ τὸν κλητῆρα τὸν ὁμολογοῦντα κεκλητευκέναι ...τῆς ψευδοκλητείας compared with Or. 49 § 56, μὴ... ἐπὶ τόνδε κακοτεχνιῶν ἔλθοιμι; and esp. Or. 52 § 32, ἐπὶ τὸν Κηφισιάδην βαδίζειν τὸν ὁμολογοῦντα κεκομίσθαι καὶ ἔχειν τὸ ἀργύριον.

[6] Or. 59 (κατὰ Νεαίρας) is condemned by ancient critics

certain want of warmth in the peroration, unlike the vigorous style of the great orator himself.

On the whole, without entering into minuter detail, we may consider the internal evidence is such as to throw grave doubts on this speech being the genuine work of Demosthenes, and we are not surprised to find its genuineness called in question by the lexicographer of the Attic Orators, Harpocration[1], though Plutarch refers it without suspicion to the authorship of Demosthenes, and fancifully contrasts the literary fame of the orator with the military reputation of the general of that name in the Peloponnesian War[2].

We have now to consider the data for arriving at the time when the speech was delivered. In § 9, Apollodorus describes himself as short of money, owing to differences between himself and Phormion, who was keeping him out of the property left him by his father Pasion, who, it will be remembered, died in B. c. 370. Again, in § 14 we are told, that at the time of the events there related, Apollodorus had not yet brought to a preliminary hearing the suits he had instituted against his relatives (Phormion and others). The suit against Phormion respecting the banking capital (Or. 36) was delayed until about B.c. 350. But a much more direct indication is given by a reference

(ὕπτιον ὄντα καὶ πολλαχῆ τῆς τοῦ ῥήτορος δυνάμεως ἐνδεέστερον *Arg.*). Among modern critics, Reiske is its sole supporter. Among the minor points of resemblance, apart from the general style, may be quoted Or. 59 § 16 ἃ μὲν ἠδικημένος, ὦ ἄνδρες Ἀθηναῖοι, ὑπὸ Στεφάνου... ὡς δ' ἐστὶ...τοῦτο ὑμῖν βούλομαι σαφῶς ἐπιδεῖξαι compared with Or. 53 (Nicostr.) § 19 ἃ μὲν τοίνυν ἀδικούμενος, ὦ ἄνδρες δικασταί, ὑπ' αὐτῶν...ὡς δ' ἔστιν... ἐπιδείξω ὑμῖν (noticed by Rehdantz, *vit. Iphicr.* p. 194). Add Or. 59 § 14. Also the tedious references to the plea of revenge, Or. 59 § 1 ὥστ' οὐχ ὑπάρχων ἀλλὰ τιμωρούμενος κ.τ.λ. and cf. § 18 ἐκ μικρῶν παιδίων with Or. 53 § 19, ἐκ μικροῦ παιδαρίου, while παιδάριον μικρόν, though common enough in itself, also happens to occur in Or. 59 § 50.

[1] εἰ γνήσιος s.v. ἀπογραφή, quoted in note on § 1, p. 134.

[2] Plut. *de gloria Atheniensium* chap. 8.

in § 5, to a trierarchy involving the speaker's absence from Athens; and it was shortly after his return that the events described in the context occurred. He had to sail round the south of the Peloponnesus, and after touching there to take certain ambassadors to Sicily. It seems probable that we should identify this trierarchy with that mentioned in Or. 45 § 3, which belongs either to B.C. 369 or B.C. 368[1]. The latter date is more probable, not only for the reason given in the note on that

---

[1] On a ψήφισμα respecting the alliance with Dionysius I see Kirchhoff in *Philologus* xii 571, where the writer holds that there were embassies sent to Sicily in 369 and also in 368. Cf. Lortzing, *Apoll.* pp. 3 f., 10; Sigg, *Apoll.* p. 403 f. (Blass, *Att. Ber.* iii 460).

Droysen (*Zeitschrift für d. Alterthumswissenschaft* 1839 p. 929) places the speech in Ol. 107, 1 = B.C. 352—1, and Böhnecke (*Forschungen* p. 675) in Ol. 107, 2 = B.C. 351—350. They connect the Sicilian trierarchy of Apollodorus (1) with the despatch sent to Athens in Ol. 106, 3 = B.C. 354—3 by a leading man in Syracuse, Callippus by name; and (2) with a request for assistance on the part of the Messenians, recorded by Pausanias (iv 28 § 2). Arnold Schaefer, however, points out that we have no authority for stating that the Athenians sent any reply to the overtures of Callippus by sending a special embassy to Sicily, and Apollodorus would have been the last man in the world to have anything to do with Callippus, who was his personal enemy (see note on Or. 36 § 53). Besides, Apollodorus would then be in the 40th year of his age, and would have had considerable experience of business, whereas when he undertook this trierarchy, and when he shortly after assisted Nicostratus, he was quite a young man and inexperienced in the ways of the world (§§ 12—13). As was seen by Rehdantz, who places the speech in B.C. 368 (*Jahn's Neue Jahrbücher* lxx 505), we must not refer the allusions in §§ 9 and 14 to the lawsuit of Apollodorus against Phormion which was met by the latter's special plea (Or. 36), but to the threatened litigation of the first few years after his father's death. Now, after the summer of 369 the Athenians, in consequence of help sent by Dionysius I. to his allies the Spartans, were engaged in negociations with that tyrant which led to the conclusion of a peace and alliance. With these negociations we may connect the Sicilian trierarchy of Apollodorus. The ambassadors whom he had on board could not confer with the Spartans without landing at Gytheion, as the Peloponnesus was for the most part in arms on the side of the Thebans. (Abridged from A. Schaefer, u. s., p. 145—6.)

passage, but also because at this period no one was
required to be trierarch oftener than once in three years,
and we know that Apollodorus was so employed in
B.C. 362; hence he may have been trierarch in B.C. 365
and B.C. 368, but probably not in B.C. 369[1]. Thus
if we allow a fair interval of time for the events mentioned in the speech subsequent to the trierarchy, we may
fix on B.C. 366 as the probable date of its delivery. Now,
if Demosthenes was born in B.C. 381, he was still a minor
in B.C. 366 and too young to have been the writer of the
speech ; if, as is most probable, his birth was in B.C. 384,
he was only just of age when the speech was delivered,
and had enough to do in looking after his own affairs, and
preparing, under the guidance of Isaeus, to join issue with
his guardians, without writing speeches for other people.
Consequently, the probable date of the speech, coinciding
as it does with the internal evidence and with the doubts
of Harpocration, makes it almost impossible to ascribe it
to the authorship of Demosthenes.

But whether written by Demosthenes, or, as is much
more probable, by another, most likely by Apollodorus
himself, there can be no reasonable doubt that the speech
was actually delivered before an Athenian tribunal. As a
study of character, the narrative of the relations between
the speaker and his opponents is not without an interest
of its own ; and the moralist may there find a fresh
exemplification of the wise saw of Polonius,

---

[1] Cf. Sigg, *Apoll.* p. 404, who
(with Lortzing) also draws attention to the indication of
time in § 4 ἐπειδὴ ἐτελεύτησεν
ὁ πατήρ...χρόνου δὲ προβαίνοντος.
But it is fair to remark that the
subsequent expression 'whenever I was abroad, either on
public service as trierarch, or
on my own account on some
other business,' while it is not
necessarily inconsistent with
a *single* voyage as trierarch,
which is all we can assume if
we place the period in B.C. 366,
is better suited to a date which
would allow of more than one
absence on public service.

> Never a borrower or a lender be,
> For loan oft loses both itself and friend.

The speech includes several passages of peculiar intricacy, in which the language of Athenian lawcourts and the vocabulary of Attic horticulture will demand special illustration in the course of the commentary[1]. The knotty points of legal terminology, which may embarrass the beginner, may prove attractive to experts,

> *qui iuris nodos et legum aenigmata solvunt;*

though others perhaps will be better pleased to dwell on the details of the speaker's country-home, and will not be sorry to leave for a while the lawcourts of Athens, for the vineyards and orchards, the olives and roses of Attica.

[1] notes on §§ 14—16.

INTRODUCTION TO

OR. LIV

ΚΑΤΑ ΚΟΝΩΝΟΣ ΑΙΚΙΑΣ.

THIS is a speech for the plaintiff in an action for assault and battery, which arose as follows. One evening the plaintiff, a young Athenian named Ariston, accompanied by a friend, was taking his usual stroll in the market-place of Athens, when he was attacked by the defendant Conon, and his son Ctesias and four others. One of these last fell upon Ariston's friend and held him fast, while Conon and the rest made an onslaught on Ariston, stripped him of his cloak which they carried off with them, threw him violently into the mud, and assaulted him with such brutality that he was for some time confined to his bed and his life despaired of (§§ 7—12).

Ariston, on his recovery, had more than one legal course open to him (§§ 1 and 24). Conon had, in the first instance, rendered himself liable to summary arrest for stripping off his cloak, and he was still amenable either to a public indictment for criminal outrage ($ὕβρεως$ $γραφή$) or to a private suit for assault and battery ($αἰκίας$ $δίκη$). To take the former of these last two courses would have proved a task too arduous for so youthful a prosecutor as Ariston, and he accordingly followed the advice of his friends and adopted the safer and less ambitious plan of bringing an action for

assault. The case was submitted in this form to a
public arbitrator, and as his award, whatever it may
have been, was not final, the plaintiff brought his suit
before one of the legal tribunals, possibly that known as
the Forty, state-officers chosen by lot who went on
circuit through the demes of Attica, and under whose
cognisance, besides some minor matters, all private
lawsuits for assault were placed[1]. Two points were
essential to the proof of the case, (1) that the defendant struck the plaintiff who was a free-man, with intent
to insult him; and (2) that the defendant struck the
first blow and was not acting in self-defence under the
provocation of a previous assault.

The plaintiff, after a brief statement of the reasons
which led him to prefer bringing a private suit instead
of a public indictment against his assailant, and after
the usual request for a favourable hearing, gives a
graphic account of the origin of the feud between
Conon's sons and himself (§§ 3—6); he then passes on
to a vivid description of the scene in the market-place
and the brutal assault there committed by Conon and
one of his sons (§§ 7—9), and calls medical and other
evidence to prove the serious nature of that assault and
its nearly fatal result (§§ 10—12).

He next anticipates the defence which is likely to
be set up by Conon, who, he understands, will make
light of his son's misconduct and try to pass it off as
a mere freak of youthful pleasantry; he contrasts the
flippancy of the proposed defence with the more serious
spirit of the laws of Athens, which provide penalties
for even minor offences to preclude the perpetration of

---

[1] Or. 37 (Pant.) § 33, ἡ μὲν
αἰκία καὶ τὰ τῶν βιαίων πρὸς τοὺς
τετταράκοντα, αἱ δὲ τῆς ὕβρεως
(δίκαι) πρὸς τοὺς θεσμοθέτας. See
esp. Caillemer in *Dict. des Antiquités* (Daremberg et Saglio)
s.v. *Aikias dikè*; or Meier and
Schömann, *Att. Process* p. 80.

graver crimes (§§ 13—20); and he submits that the plea of youth can only be urged in mitigation of punishment and is at any rate inapplicable to Conon himself, a man of more than fifty years of age, who, so far from restraining his sons and the other assailants, was actually the ringleader of them all (§§ 21—23). The defendant was amenable to the laws against highway robbery and brutal outrage and, had death ensued, would have been chargeable with murder (§§ 24, 25).

He further describes the evasive conduct of the defendant during the preliminary arbitration (§§ 25—29); denounces the falsehood of the evidence put in by persons who were boon-companions of the defendant, deposing that they found the plaintiff fighting with the defendant's son, and that the defendant did not strike the plaintiff; contrasts it with the evidence of impartial persons on his own side attesting to his having been assaulted by the defendant (§§ 30—33); and comments severely on the bad character of the witnesses for the defence (§§ 34—37).

He then warns the court not to allow themselves to be imposed upon by the hard swearing and the sensational imprecations which, he is informed, will be resorted to by the defendant, whose antecedents prove his reckless disregard of things sacred; while he himself, averse though he was to taking even a lawful oath, had for the truth's sake offered to take such a pledge; and, as that offer had been declined by the defendant, he would now for the satisfaction of the court swear solemnly that in very truth he had been brutally assaulted by his opponents (§§ 38—41).

After pointing out that even in this private suit public interests were at stake, he very briefly refers to the way in which his family and himself had done their duty towards their country, while his opponents had done nothing of the kind. 'Even supposing,' he says in conclusion, 'we are of less service to the state than our opponents, *that* is no reason why we should be assaulted and brutally outraged.'

The only clue to the date of the speech is to be found in a passage in § 3, whence we conclude that it was delivered two years after orders were given at Athens for a military force to go out on garrison duty to Panactum, a fort on the Boeotian frontier. We read of such an expedition in B.C. 343[1]; and this would bring us to B.C. 341 as the year of the trial. It has been suggested, however, though no reason is assigned, that this is too late a year, and that there is warrant for believing there was regular military service, as opposed to a special expedition, on the Boeotian frontier in B.C. 357, to protect Attica from a diversion on the part of the Boeotians shortly before the Phocian war, during which there was no occasion for such precautions, as the Phocians kept the Boeotians occupied in another direction[2]. Thus, the military movements referred to in § 3 belong to the time either shortly before or shortly after the Phocian war, in other words, either to B.C. 357 or 343, the speech being thus placed in B.C. 355 or 341 respectively. In the course of an *Excursus* on p. 229, I have pointed out that the reference to the Triballi in the days of Conon's youth supplies us with a hitherto unnoticed coincidence in favour of the later date.

The speech has deservedly won the admiration of

---

[1] Dem. *de fals. leg.* (B.C. 313) § 326, περὶ...τῆς πρὸς Πανάκτῳ χώρας μεθ᾽ ὅπλων ἐξερχόμεθα, ὃ ἕως ἦσαν Φωκεῖς σῷοι οὐδεπώποτ᾽ ἐποιήσαμεν.

[2] A. Schaefer, *Dem. u. s. Zeit*, III 2, p. 251, who notices that on Dem. Mid. § 193, ὅσοι τὰ φρούρια ἦσαν ἔρημα λελοιπότες the Scholiast remarks φρούρια δὲ λέγει μεταξὺ τῆς Ἀττικῆς καὶ Βοιωτίας. πολέμου γὰρ τότε πρὸς Θηβαίους ὄντος διὰ τὴν Εὔβοιαν ἀναγκαῖον ἦν τὰς ἐκ τῆς Βοιωτίας εἰσβολὰς παρὰ τῶν Ἀθηναίων φυλάττεσθαι.

ancient and modern critics alike. It is one of the few private orations whose genuineness has never been doubted[1]. The orator Deinarchus is reported to have plagiarized from it[2], the old grammarians often refer to it, and the Greek writers on Rhetoric quote it more frequently than any of the other private orations[3]. In particular Dionysius of Halicarnassus, in his treatise on the eloquence of Demosthenes, after quoting a vivid description from the orator Lysias, one of the highest merits of whose style was the power of clear and graphic narration, selects for comparison the equally vivid passage in the present speech where the plaintiff describes the disorderly doings of his opponents in the camp at Panactum and in the market-place of Athens (§§ 3—9). His criticism is to the effect that the extract from Demosthenes is fully equal to that from Lysias in clearness, correctness, and perspicuity of style, in conciseness and terseness, in unadorned simplicity and in truthfulness of detail. He also commends the skill with which the language of the speaker is kept true to character, and appropriate to the subject, and finds in the narrative much of the winning persuasiveness, the charming grace, and the other merits of style that mark his quotation from Lysias[4]. A modern writer on the literature of the speeches of

---

[1] Blass, *Att. Ber.* III 399.

[2] Eusebius, *Praepar. Evang.* quoting from Porphyry (περὶ τοῦ κλέπτας εἶναι τοὺς Ἕλληνας), x 3 p. 775 Migne, Δείναρχος ἐν τῷ πρώτῳ κατὰ Κλεομέδοντα αἰκίας πολλὰ μετενήνοχεν αὐτοῖς ὀνόμα- σιν ἐκ τοῦ Δημοσθένους Μετὰ (*sic*) Κόνωνος αἰκίας.

[3] e.g. Hermogenes quoted on §§ 1, 4.

[4] Dionysius, *de admir. vi dicendi Dem.* 13, ταῦτα οὐ καθαρὰ καὶ ἀκριβῆ καὶ σαφῆ καὶ διὰ τῶν κυρίων καὶ κοινῶν ὀνομάτων κατε- σκευασμένα, ὥσπερ τὰ Λυσίου;... τί δ' οὐχὶ σύντομα καὶ στρογγύλα καὶ ἀληθείας μεστὰ καὶ τὴν ἀφελῆ καὶ ἀκατάσκευον ἐπιφαίνοντα φύ- σιν, καθάπερ ἐκεῖνα;...οὐχὶ δὲ καὶ πιθανὰ καὶ ἐν ἤθει λεγόμενά τινι καὶ τὸ πρέπον τοῖς ὑποκειμένοις προσώποις τε καὶ πράγμασι φυλ- άττοντα; ἡδονῆς δ' ἄρα καὶ πει- θοῦς καὶ χαρίτων, καιροῦ τε καὶ τῶν ἄλλων ἁπάντων, ἃ τοῖς Λυ- σιακοῖς ἐπανθοῦσιν, ἆρα οὐχὶ πολλὴ μοῖρα;

Demosthenes has well remarked that no selection from the Private Orations can be considered complete which does not include the *Conon*[1]; and many years after that remark was made, it was excellently edited for school-reading with a brief German commentary by Westermann. It has also been the subject of an appreciative criticism by Perrot who writes as follows:

'Dans le discours contre Conon...Démosthène réunit aux qualités qui firent le succès de Lysias celles qui distinguent Isée. De Lysias, il tient l'art d'entrer dans le caractère et dans le rôle du personnage qu'il fait parler, de se transformer en lui, si l'on peut ainsi parler, de produire l'illusion la plus complète. Par la vraisemblance et la vivacité du récit, par l'art d'y semer des détails sensibles et pittoresques, de faire voir la chose telle que l'on a intérêt à la présenter, il est bien près d'égaler son modéle...Où Démosthène est tout à fait superieur à Lysias, c'est dans ce qu'il a appris d'Isée : il tire des témoignages un bien autre parti, il les place, les encadre, les développe et les discute avec une bien autre habileté ; il connaît bien mieux les lois, il remonte à leurs principes, il en expose les sens et la portée avec une autorité dont rien chez Lysias ne peut donner l'idée. Enfin, pour n'insister que sur les différences les plus notables, les figures de pensée dont Lysias ignore encore l'usage animent et colorent son style : c'est le dilemme, c'est l'apostrophe, ce sont des interrogations brusques et passionnées, ce sont des mouvemens oratoires dont l'élan et la variété nous avertissent que l'éloquence attique n'a plus de progrès à faire, qu'elle touche à sa perfection[2].'

One of our own scholars, in the course of a short chapter devoted mainly to the Private Speeches contained in the present volume, has well observed :—

[1] *In einer Sammlung aus den Privatreden des Demosthenes dürfte...diese nicht fehlen.* A. G. Becker's *Literatur des Dem.* p. 122, 1830.

[2] G. Perrot, *Revue des deux mondes*, 1873, 3 p. 952—3.

The whole story is told and commented on with exquisite grace. The tone is that of a middle-aged[1] man of precise habits, who knows little law, and would have known less had it not been for the defendant; anxious to seem calm, but not quite able to smother his indignation; a little wanting in a sense of the ludicrous, and so keenly alive to his own respectability—which is a recurring topic—that he must apologise for being aware that such rowdyism even exists[2].

To the modern reader the main interest of the speech is to be found perhaps in the lifelike pictures of Athenian manners incidentally sketched in its pages; and several scenes have accordingly been borrowed from it and interwoven with the narrative of Becker's *Charicles* in illustration of the private life of the ancient Greeks[3]. In particular, we here read of the disorderly clubs formed by young men about town, who, after holding a carouse, would sally forth into the streets to assault quiet people and play practical jokes at the expense of inoffensive citizens. To these indecorous societies the defendant's sons belonged, and the defendant himself in his youth was a member of a club called after a lawless tribe of Thrace, an association that finds its modern parallel in the fraternity, which in the days of Addison took its name from the wild Mohocks of North America, and was for some time the terror of the streets of London. The practical jokes of young Athens in the days of Demosthenes re-appear, some seven centuries later, in a less objectionable, not to say harmless form, in the pleasantries practised by students at the University of Athens at the expense of the 'freshmen' ($o\dot{i}$ $\nu\epsilon\acute{\eta}\lambda\nu\delta\epsilon s$), who, at the first moment of their arrival, were struggled for by the young allies of the rival lecturers, good-humouredly

[1] Youth, rather than middle age, is suggested by § 1 $\dot{v}\pi\grave{\epsilon}\rho$ $\tau\grave{\eta}\nu$ $\dot{\eta}\lambda\iota\kappa\acute{\iota}a\nu$ (and the context).

[2] S. H. Butcher, *Demosthenes*, 1881, p. 134.

[3] p. 136—139 (with notes) of the 2nd Germ. ed. by K. F. Hermann = p. 80—83 of abridged English ed. of 1866.

chaffed by them, and escorted with mock gravity through the market-place to the public bath, where, after a feint of frightening them, their tormentors considered the act of initiation completed, and were very good friends to the freshmen ever after[1].

The pages of the Greek orators abound in references to house-breaking and highway robbery, to street-brawls and other disorderly acts imperilling the public security[2]; and in the present speech we find that the plaintiff could not take a quiet walk along the market-place of Athens, beneath the rock of the Acropolis, past the temple erected as a memorial of the patriotic self-sacrifice of the daughters of an ancient king of Attica, and by the very scene where the tyrant Hipparchus was slain, without finding himself the victim of a brutal and outrageous assault. In times such as these at Athens, one who was tempted to take an evening stroll with a friend, if invited in language like that of Sebastian in *Twelfth Night*,

> I pray you, let us satisfy our eyes
> With the memorials and the things of fame
> That do renown this city,

might have replied, with Antonio,

> Would you'd pardon me,
> I do not without danger walk these streets.

---

[1] Gregor. Nazianzen, Or. 43 *in laudem Basilii magni* c. 16, who describes the initiation as τοῖς ἀγνοοῦσι λίαν φοβερὸν καὶ ἀνήμερον τοῖς δὲ προειδόσι καὶ μάλα ἡδὺ καὶ φιλάνθρωπον. Gregory's young friend Basil was one of the few who were spared the ordeal on coming into residence (in A. D. 351).

[2] e. g. (Dem.) Or. 47, κατ' Εὐέργου καὶ Μνησιβούλου, Lysias Or. 3, πρὸς Σίμωνα and fragm. 75 (ed. Scheibe), a long passage quoted by Dionysius as a parallel to the *Conon* (as already stated, p. lxiv). Cf. Becker's *Charicles*, Sc. v, note 9, and Mahaffy's *Social Life in Greece*, p. 319.

INTRODUCTION TO

Or. LV

ΠΡΟΣ ΚΑΛΛΙΚΛΕΑ ΠΕΡΙ ΧΩΡΙΟΥ[1].

Tiis is a speech on the side of the defence in an action
for damages alleged to have been incurred by the plaintiff, Callicles, by reason of a wall having been built on
the defendant's property to the obstruction of a water-
course carrying off the drainage of the surrounding hills.
The farms of the plaintiff and defendant lay in a hilly
district of Attica, separated from one another by a public road; and the defendant's father, Tisias, on coming
into possession of his farm and finding that the water
which flowed from the high ground had made an inroad
into his property and was cutting itself a regular channel, built a stone-wall round it to prevent the water from
making any further encroachment. No protest was
raised on the part of the plaintiff's family either at the
time or for many years subsequently; Tisias lived fifteen
years after building the enclosure, and, after his death, a
mountain-torrent caused by a heavy shower of rain
overthrew an old wall on the plaintiff's land, flooded his
property and damaged some of his stores. Thereupon
the plaintiff brought an action for damages, alleging that
the flood was due to the stream being diverted to his
own side of the road by the proper water-course having

---

[1] περὶ χωρίου βλάβης is the title given by Harpocration, in *one*
of his articles (s.v. χλῆδος Or. 55 § 22).   But cf. § 15.

been blocked up by the building of the wall on the defendant's property.

The speech for the defence opens by casting on the plaintiff the imputation of bringing the action with a view to getting possession of the defendant's property (§ 1). The speaker, a son of Tisias, whose name is not given, pleads that the wall was built by his father fifteen years before his death, without any objection on the part of the plaintiff's family, and challenges the other side to prove the existence of the water-course alleged to be obstructed by the wall (§§ 3—7); he had offered to refer the dispute to the arbitration of impartial persons familiar with the neighbourhood, but the plaintiff had refused the offer (§§ 8, 9); he then describes carefully the position of the two properties on the opposite sides of the public way, and accounts for the building of the wall (§§ 10, 11). He next calls evidence to prove that the alleged water-course was part of his private ground, as it contained an old burial-place, and an orchard besides (§§ 12—15); he further shews that, as the water would naturally flow down the public way, there was no occasion for such a water-course (§§ 16—18), and that there was no such channel immediately above or below his own property (§ 19). The plaintiff's loss was due to his own carelessness and he was most inconsistent in bringing this action (§ 20); the other neighbours who had suffered severely made no complaint, whereas the plaintiff had lost nothing worth mentioning (§§ 21, 23—25). Again, his opponents had themselves advanced their wall (and thus encroached on public property); they had also raised the level of the road (and thus led to the water being liable to be diverted from the road itself to the lands adjacent). After once more referring to the plaintiff's interested motive in bringing the action, he states

in conclusion that, though the plaintiff had refused his
offer, he had been ready to take the legally recognised
oath and to swear that he had not caused the damage
alleged, feeling that that would be the strongest argument
with a jury who were themselves on their solemn oath.

The general style of the *Callicles*, as indeed that of
the *Conon*, is not unlike that of Lysias, and speeches
on similar subjects, one on a water-conduit and another
on a disputed boundary, are known to have been composed by the orator Hyperides[1], but the genuineness of
the speech before us can hardly be seriously contested[2],
though it has been suggested that it was written by
Demosthenes in his younger days[3]. It is quoted without
hesitation by Harpocration and the rhetoricians alike, as
the work of Demosthenes himself. The narrow limits
of the speech and the somewhat trivial nature of the
subject will account for the exordium not being succeeded, as elsewhere, by any formal narrative or statement of the case; instead of this, the narrative of the
facts is only incidentally included in the course of the
speech, and is blended and interwoven with the thread
of the argument. Here and there the argument is
brightened by a touch of quiet humour, as in the
passage where the speaker, arguing on the supposition
of his allowing the rain-water to make an inroad into
his property, after exhausting several alternatives of
dealing with the stream when once it was there, ex-
claims in conclusion, 'What *am* I to do with it? for I
presume the plaintiff won't compel me to drink it up!'

[1] περὶ ὀχετοῦ and περὶ τῶν
ὁρίων p. 88 (ed. Blass) fragm.
134 ὅπως τὸ ἀνώμαλον τοῦ χωρίου
τῇ τῶν ἀνδήρων καὶ ὀχετῶν
ἀφαιροῖτο κατασκεύη. fragm. 158,
οχετόκρανα (= αἱ τῶν ὀχετῶν
αρχαί).

[2] Bekker however in the
Leipzig ed. vol. III, 1855 considers it doubtful; and it is
rejected by Sigg, *Apoll.* p. 401
note.

[3] A. Schaefer, u. s., III 2,
256.

In the course of the speech we have also several indications of the provisions of Athenian law respecting those rights of water, with the Roman law of which we are far better acquainted. We gather that the inferior tenant held his land subject to the limiting obligation, or *servitus* as Roman lawyers would have called it, of giving free passage into his own land for the water, in particular the rain-water, flowing from the superior tenement; and in a passage of Plato's *Laws* we find provisions suggested for regulating the relations between neighbours in rights of this description and requiring the superior proprietor to do everything in his power to relieve the inferior proprietor from unnecessary inconvenience[1]. Again, the law did not allow the diversion of the natural and regular channel of the water by the building of a wall or by any similar construction. Callicles appears to have had no case, as his property did not immediately adjoin that of the defendant but was separated from it by a public way which provided sufficiently for carrying off the water. In some instances, but (as the defendant contends) not in the present, a regularly recognised water-course, or ditch, traversed several successive properties, and it is clear that no individual proprietor could intercept this. It also appears that the proprietor of any land bordering on a public way generally turned his drainage on to the road (§ 26)[2].

The legal issue in the *Callicles* appears to turn in a great measure on the nature of the water-course, the existence of which is maintained by the plaintiff and denied by the defendant. The encroachment made by the floods, before the defendant's father became the pro-

[1] p. 844, quoted in note on § 19.

[2] Cf. M. Caillemer's article on *Aqua* in Daremberg et Saglio, *Dict. des Antiquités.*

prietor, led to a stream of intermittent rain-water gradually forming a channel for itself (μᾶλλον ὡδοποίει § 11) through a burial-ground[1] planted with fruit-trees. The plaintiff appears to have contended that the channel thus formed was a water-course within the terms of the law; the defendant relies on the existence of the trees and the tombs to prove that it was *not* a recognised channel, but part of his private ground, accidentally inundated, and repeatedly traversed by water, more than fifteen years before. It was this damage, he contends, that led to his father building the wall for the protection of his property.

Lastly, we have several points that are curiously suggestive on the state of the country-roads in the hilly districts of Attica; the road itself is assumed to be the natural channel for the drainage of the neighbouring hills, and a proper water-course beside the road is declared to be a thing unheard of. In fact, like some of the present roads of Attica, as described in a modern writer's amusing sketches of Greek brigandage, the road and the stream were one and the same thing, and, except in dry weather, the former hardly existed[2].

---

[1] For purposes of *irrigation*, Plato would allow the tenant to divert water from streams that were common property by cutting himself a channel anywhere except through a private house or through temples or tombs. Legg. p. 844 A, τῶν ὑδάτων πέρι γεωργοῖσι παλαιοὶ καὶ καλοὶ νόμοι κείμενοι οὐκ ἄξιο παροχετεύειν λόγοις, ἀλλ᾽ ὁ βουληθεὶς ἐπὶ τὸν αὑτοῦ τόπον ἄγειν ὕδωρ ἀγέτω μὲν ἀρχόμενος ἐκ τῶν κοινῶν ναμάτων...ᾗ δ᾽ ἂν βούληται ἄγειν, πλὴν δι᾽ οἰκίας ἢ ἱερῶν τι νῶν ἢ καὶ μνημάτων, ἀγέτω.

[2] Edmond About, quoted on p. 231.

ΠΑΡΑΓΡΑΦΗ ΥΠΕΡ ΦΟΡΜΙΩΝΟΣ.

ΥΠΟΘΕΣΙΣ.

Πασίων ὁ τραπεζίτης τελευτῶν ἐπὶ δύο παισὶν ἐξ
᾿Αρχίππης, ᾿Απολλοδώρῳ καὶ Πασικλεῖ, Φορμίωνα
οἰκέτην ἑαυτοῦ γενόμενον, τετυχηκότα δὲ ἔτι πρότερον ἐλευθερίας, ἐπίτροπον τοῦ νεωτέρου τῶν παίδων
Πασικλέους κατέλιπε, καὶ τὴν μητέρα αὐτῶν, παλ- 5
λακὴν ἑαυτοῦ γενομένην, ἔδωκεν ἐπὶ προικὶ γυναῖκα.
᾿Απολλόδωρος οὖν νέμεται πρὸς τὸν ἀδελφὸν τὴν
πατρῴαν οὐσίαν πλὴν τῆς τραπέζης καὶ τοῦ ἀσπι-
δοπηγείου· ταῦτα γὰρ Φορμίων ἐμεμίσθωτο παρὰ
Πασίωνος εἰς ὡρισμένον χρόνον τινά. καὶ τέως μὲν 10
ἐλάμβανε τὸ ἥμισυ τῆς μισθώσεως ἑκάτερος, ὕστερον
δὲ καὶ αὐτὰ νέμονται, καὶ γίγνεται τὸ μὲν ἀσπιδο-

1. τελευτῶν ἐπὶ δύο παισὶν]
'Dying with (*in possession of*)
two children,' i.e. 'leaving two
children behind him at his
death'; an idiom not unfre-
quent in late Greek, e. g. He-
rodian (fl. A.D. 238) iv 2 § 1,
ἔθος ἐστὶ ῾Ρωμαίοις ἐκθειάζειν
βασιλέων τοὺς ἐπὶ παισὶ διαδό-
χοις τελευτήσαντας. Or. 27 Arg.
5. παλλακὴν] 'Quo iure Libanius Archippam, quae et in
testimonio Pasionis (Or. 45 § 28)
et alibi (36 §§ 30, 31; 46 § 13)
uxor (γυνὴ) eius dicitur, hoc
loco παλλακὴν vocaverit, non
apparet' (Huettner).

6. ἐπὶ προικὶ] For the construction cf. Or. 28, Aphob. B, § 16,
τούτῳ τὴν ἐμὴν μητέρα ἐγγυῶν
ἐπὶ ταῖς ὀγδοήκοντα μναῖς, ib. §
19; 41 § 6. The marriage portion of Archippe amounted to
five talents, as we learn from the
First Speech against Stephanus,
Or. 45 § 74, cf. ib. § 28, ἠκούσατε τὸ πλῆθος τῆς προικὸς, τάλαντον ἐκ Πεπαρήθου, τάλαντον
αὐτόθεν, συνοικίαν ἑκατὸν μνῶν,
θεραπαίνας καὶ χρυσία κ.τ.λ.
12. αὐτὰ] They share between
them the properties themselves,
viz. when Phormion's lease of
them had expired.

πηγεῖον Ἀπολλοδώρου Πασικλέους, δὲ ἡ τράπεζα.
ἀποθανούσης δὲ καὶ τῆς μητρὸς ὕστερον, νειμάμενος
15 καὶ τὴν ἐκείνης οὐσίαν, ἐνεκάλει τῷ Φορμίωνι ὡς
πολλὰ ἔχοντι ἑαυτοῦ χρήματα. καθίσαντες οὖν ἑαυτοὺς διαιτητὰς, ὥς φησι Φορμίων, Ἀπολλοδώρῳ προσ-
ήκοντες, Νικίας καὶ Δεινίας καὶ Ἀνδρομένης, ἔπεισαν
Ἀπολλόδωρον διαλύσασθαι πρὸς Φορμίωνα τὰ ἐγ-
20 κλήματα λαβόντα πεντακισχιλίας. ὁ μὲν οὖν Ἀπολλόδωρος μετὰ ταῦτα πάλιν εἴληχε δίκην Φορμίωνι
ἀφορμῆς· ἀφορμὴν δὲ οἱ Ἀττικοὶ καλοῦσιν ὅπερ ἡμεῖς 944
ἐνθήκην. ὁ δὲ Φορμίων παραγράφεται, νόμον παρεχόμενος τὸν κελεύοντα περὶ ὧν ἂν ἅπαξ ἀφῇ τις καὶ
25 διαλύσηται μηκέτι ἐξεῖναι δικάζεσθαι. ἅπτεται μέντοι

21. εἴληχε] In Grammarian's Greek, this stands either for λαγχάνει or ἔλαχε. So πέπομφε is used in the Argument to Or. 34, line 31, and so πεποίηκεν below. P.]

δίκην ἀφορμῆς] 'A suit referring to capital,' 'a suit for the recovery of banking stock.' § 12 ἐγκαλοῦντ' ἀφορμήν.

22. οἱ Ἀττικοί] Harpocration s. v. ἐπιψηφίζειν : παρὰ τοῖς Ἀττικοῖς: s. v. πρυτανεία : παρὰ τοῖς ἄλλοις Ἀττικοῖς (after naming Isocrates).

23. ἐνθήκην] Harpocration s.v. ἀφορμή· ὅταν τις ἀργύριον δῷ ἐνθήκην, ἀφορμὴ καλεῖται ἰδίως παρὰ τοῖς Ἀττικοῖς. And similarly Hesychius, and Phrynichus, ed. Rutherford p. 304. For this late Greek equivalent to ἀφορμὴ references are given in Sophocles' Lex. of Rom. and Byzantine Greek to Phrynichus 223 (fl. A.D. 180) and Basilius of Caesarea III 320 (fl. c. A.D. 379).

παραγράφεται κ.τ.λ.] 'Phormion raises a special plea in bar of action, by appealing to a sta-

tute enacting that, on matters on which a release and quittance has once been granted, no subsequent litigation shall be lawful.' See note on § 25 ἀφεὶς καὶ ἀπαλλάξας. Pollux: παραγραφή· ὅταν τις μὴ εἰσαγώγιμον λέγῃ εἶναι τὴν δίκην, ἢ ὡς κεκριμένος, ἢ διαίτης γεγενημένης, ἢ ὡς ἀφειμένος, ἢ ὡς τῶν χρόνων ἐξηκόντων (§ 26) ἐν οἷς ἔδει κρίνεσθαι· where are enumerated the four principal circumstances under which an ordinary action is not maintainable. (Cf. C. R. Kennedy, Dem. Lept. &c. Vol. III Appendix, IX p. 378; Meier and Schömann, Att. Process, p. 644—9.)

παρεχόμενος] ' adducing,'= προϊσχόμενος. A use of the participle analogous to παρέχεσθαι μάρτυρας (Or. 27 § 8), said of one who is pleading his own cause, and so, inf. § 54, and often elsewhere. P.]

25. ἅπτεται τῆς εὐθείας] Sc. δίκης. 'Touches on, handles, grapples with, the general issue,' εὐθυδικία being the direct course

καὶ τῆς εὐθείας ὁ ῥήτωρ, δεικνὺς ὡς οὐκ εἶχεν ἡ τράπεζα χρήματα ἴδια τοῦ Πασίωνος. τοῦτο δὲ πεποίηκεν, ἵνα ἡ παραγραφὴ μᾶλλον ἰσχύῃ, τῆς εὐθείας δεικνυμένης[a] τῷ Ἀπολλοδώρῳ σαθρᾶς.

———

Τὴν μὲν ἀπειρίαν τοῦ λέγειν, καὶ ὡς ἀδυνάτως

[a] δεικνυομένης Z.

of an action argued on the merits of the case, as opposed to παραγραφή. Or. 34 ὑπόθ. 1. 32, and ib. § 4, εὐθυδικίαν εἰσιόντα. Or. 45 § 6 (where Apollodorus is speaking of the defendant in the present case) προλαβών μου ὥστε πρότερον λέγειν διὰ τὸ παραγραφὴν εἶναι καὶ μὴ εὐθυδικίᾳ (fortasse -αν) εἰσιέναι.

27. τοῦτο δὲ πεποίηκεν κ.τ.λ.] 'He has done (or 'does') this to give greater force to the special plea, by proving that, even on its own merits, the case of the plaintiff is quite untenable.' (σαθρᾶς, thoroughly rotten, unsound, Or. 18 § 227.) Cf. ὑπόθεσις of Or. 32 (Zenoth.) δεικνυσιν ὡς θαρρεῖ μὲν τῇ εὐθείᾳ, ἐκ περιουσίας δὲ αὐτῷ καὶ παραγραφὴν ὁ νόμος δίδωσιν.

§§ 1—3. *The defendant Phormion's obvious inexperience and incapacity for public speaking make it necessary for his friends to state his case on his behalf. They confront the plaintiff Apollodorus with a special plea in bar of action, not to waste time and evade the main issue, but to secure a final settlement of the case. Their friend, the defendant, has conferred many kindnesses on the plaintiff; and has further been released from all the legal claims of the latter, only to find himself at last the victim of a vexatious lawsuit. However, a brief recital of the transactions of the litigants will prove that the plaintiff's case is utterly untenable.*

1. τὴν ἀπειρίαν τοῦ λέγειν] Like all slaves at Athens, Phormion (once the slave of the banker Pasion) was of barbarian birth; and though subsequently rewarded with the rights of freedom and citizenship, remained unable to speak good Greek. In a later speech arising out of the present action, Apollodorus, himself the son of one who was once a slave, taunts him with his foreign extraction and his indifferent pronunciation. Or. 45 § 81 βάρβαρος ἐωνήθης, and § 30, ἴσως αὐτὸν ὑπειλήφατε, ὅτι σολοικίζει τῇ φωνῇ, βάρβαρον καὶ εὐκαταφρόνητον εἶναι, ἔστι δὲ βάρβαρος οὗτος τῷ μισεῖν οὓς αὐτῷ προσῆκε τιμᾶν, τῷ δὲ κακουργῆσαι καὶ διορύξαι πράγματα οὐδενὸς λείπεται. In § 77, Apollodorus himself apologizes for his broad brogue or loud voice (λαλεῖν μέγα); the speaker of πρὸς Πανταίνετον makes similar excuses for his διάλεκτος (Or. 37 §§ 52, 55); and a like tribute to the sensitiveness of an Attic audience is paid by the Mytilenaean in Antiphon's de Caede Herodis (Or. v § 5) δέομαι ὑμῶν ...ἐάν τι τῇ γλώσσῃ ἁμάρτω, συγγνώμην ἔχειν μοι καὶ ἡγεῖσθαι ἀπειρίᾳ αὐτὸ μᾶλλον ἢ ἀδικίᾳ ἡμαρτῆσθαι. Cf. Cicero Or. §§ 24—27.

ἀδυνάτως ἔχει] 'Is quite in-

ἔχει Φορμίων, αὐτοὶ πάντες ὁρᾶτε, ὦ ἄνδρες Ἀθηναῖοι· ἀνάγκη δ᾽ ἐστὶ τοῖς ἐπιτηδείοις ἡμῖν, ἃ σύνισμεν
πολλάκις τούτου διεξιόντος ἀκηκοότες, λέγειν καὶ διδάσκειν ὑμᾶς, ἵν᾽ εἰδότες καὶ μεμαθηκότες ὀρθῶς τὰ
δίκαια παρ᾽ ἡμῶν, ἃ ἂν ᾖ δίκαια καὶ εὔορκα, ταῦτα
2 ψηφίσησθε. τὴν μὲν οὖν παραγραφὴν ἐποιησάμεθα
τῆς δίκης οὐχ ἵν᾽ ἐκκρούοντες χρόνους ἐμποιῶμεν,
ἀλλ᾽ ἵνα τῶν πραγμάτων, ἐὰν ἐπιδείξῃ μηδ᾽ ὁτιοῦν

capable,' referring mainly to his inexperience and want of facility in speaking. Thus in Antiphon *u. s.* v § 2 ἡ τοῦ λέγειν ἀδυναμία is contrasted with ἡ ἐμπειρία τῶν πραγμάτων. It is suggested by Blass, *Att. Ber.* III 405, that ἀδυνάτως refers to feebleness of health, but this appears improbable.

ὁρᾶτε] In a general sense, 'you all of yourselves observe.' Or. 3 Olynth. § 1 τοὺς λόγους... ὁρῶ γιγνομένους.

τοῖς ἐπιτηδείοις] as his συνήγοροι. Hyperid. Euxen. 25 τί τούτου τῶν ἐν τῇ πόλει βέλτιον ἢ δημοτικώτερόν ἐστι...ἢ ὁπόταν τις ἰδιώτης εἰς ἀγῶνα καὶ κίνδυνον καταστὰς μὴ δύνηται ὑπὲρ ἑαυτοῦ ἀπολογεῖσθαι, τούτῳ τὸν βουλόμενον τῶν πολιτῶν ἀναβάντα βοηθῆσαι κ.τ.λ.

λέγειν καὶ διδάσκειν] Dem. is particularly fond of coupling together words that are nearly synonymous with one another, e.g. in the next line, εἰδότες καὶ μεμαθηκότες, and in the next, δίκαια καὶ εὔορκα, § 4 ἀκοῦσαι καὶ μαθεῖν, § 12 λέγειν καὶ ἐπιδεικνύναι, § 18 πεπραγμένα καὶ γεγενημένα, § 29 ὄντι καὶ ζῶντι, § 32 δόντος καὶ ἐπισκήψαντος, § 47 κοσμεῖν καὶ περιστέλλειν, § 61 φυλάττετε καὶ μέμνησθε. Also § 16 αἰτίας καὶ ἐγκλήματα (cf. § 61), § 2 ἰσχυρὰ καὶ βέβαια.

Similarly in Or. 20 § 163 λέγειν καὶ διεξιέναι, 21 § 17 εἰπεῖν καὶ διηγήσασθαι (Huettner). This characteristic of his style is noticed by Dionysius Hal. περὶ τῆς Δημ. δεινότητος 58, and is illustrated by Blass, *Att. Ber.* III 94.

ἃ ἂν ᾖ δίκαια κ.τ.λ.] The relative clause to ταῦτα ψηφίσησθε is placed before it partly for increased emphasis, partly to bring δίκαια closer to τὰ δίκαια in the previous context.

2. ἵν᾽ ἐκκρούοντες χρόνους ἐμποιῶμεν] 'With the evasive object of wasting time,' or (with Kennedy) 'for the sake of evasion and delay.' The phrase χρόνους ἐμποιεῖν occurs in Or. 9 § 71, 23 § 93. Cf. Or. 47 § 63, διατριβὰς ἐμποιῶν......τεχνάζων τοῦ χρόνον ἐγγενέσθαι. For ἐκκροῦοντες, cf. Or. 54 § 30; 40 § 45 τὴν δίκην ὅτι πλεῖστον χρόνον ἐκκρούειν, ib. 43; and for the general sense, Thuc. III 38, χρόνου διατριβὴν ἐμποιεῖν and κατὰ Στεφ. Λ, § 4, p. 1102, χρόνου γιγνομένου καὶ τῆς γραφῆς ἐκκρουομένης. Liddell and Scott (ed. 6) give a phrase ἐκκρούειν χρόνον, 'to waste time,' and, to prove it, inadvertently refer to the last passage and to the words of the text, where χρόνους clearly comes after ἐμποιῶμεν (corrected in ed. 7, 1883).

ἀδικοῦνθ᾽ ἑαυτὸν οὑτοσὶ, ἀπαλλαγή τις αὐτῷ γένηται
παρ᾽ ὑμῖν κυρία. ὅσα γὰρ παρὰ τοῖς ἄλλοις ἐστὶν ἀνθρώποις ἰσχυρὰ καὶ βέβαια ἄνευ τοῦ παρ᾽ ὑμῖν ἀγωνί-
945 σασθαι, ταῦτα πάντα πεποιηκὼς Φορμίων οὑτοσὶ, καὶ
πολλὰ μὲν εὖ πεποιηκὼς Ἀπολλόδωρον τουτονὶ, πάντα 3
δ᾽, ὅσων κύριος τῶν τούτου κατελείφθη, διαλύσας καὶ
παραδοὺς δικαίως, καὶ πάντων ἀφεθεὶς μετὰ ταῦτα
τῶν ἐγκλημάτων, ὅμως, ὡς ὁρᾶτε, ἐπειδὴ φέρειν τοῦτον οὐχ οἷός τ᾽ ἐστὶ, δίκην ταλάντων εἴκοσι λαχὼν
αὐτῷ ταύτην συκοφαντεῖ. ἐξ ἀρχῆς οὖν ἅπαντα τὰ

ἀπαλλαγὴ κυρία] A legal and valid (or final) acquittal from all future actions, πραγμάτων. Cf. Harpocr. quoted on § 25.

ἄνευ τοῦ παρ᾽ ὑμῖν ἀγωνίσασθαι] 'Without standing a trial in your court.'

πεποιηκὼς...εὖ πεποιηκὼς...... διαλύσας ... παραδοὺς ... ἀφεθεὶς] Although all these participles refer to Phormion, who is the subject of the first part of the sentence, the principal verb συκοφαντεῖ refers to Apollodorus. To obviate the harshness of this anacoluthon it has been proposed (by G. H. Schaefer) to follow one of the mss, the *Augustanus primus*, in reading πεποίηκε for πεποιηκὼς, and also to strike out καὶ before πολλὰ, and place a full stop at ἐγκλημάτων. [But we should still expect ὅμως δ᾽, or ἀλλ᾽ ὅμως. Perhaps it is better to regard this as an instance of the '*nominativus pendens*.' P.] The Zürich editors refer to Funkhaenel, quaest. Dem. p. 75 sq.

3. τούτου] Apollodorus.

διαλύσας κ. παραδοὺς κ.τ.λ.] 'Having duly paid and delivered up everything——and having thereafter received a discharge from all further claims.'

For διαλύειν τι, cf. 20 § 12 κοινῇ διαλῦσαι τὰ χρήματα, 28 § 2; 29 § 7; 41 § 8. For another construction διαλύειν τινά, cf. § 50.

ἀφεθεὶς—ἐγκλημάτων] Or. 45 §§ 5, 40; Lys. 3 § 25 ἐφειμένους τῶν ἐγκλημάτων, Isaeus 5 § 1 ἀφήκαμεν ἀλλήλους τῶν ἐγκλημάτων.

ἐπειδὴ φέρειν τοῦτον οὐχ οἷός τ᾽ ἐστὶ] i.e. since (or, at a time when) Phormion cannot submit any longer to the unconscionable claims of Apollodorus (and therefore declines to make any further concessions), the latter has vexatiously instituted the present action. The subject of the subordinate clause appears to be Phormion. For the sense, compare the language ascribed to Apollodorus in § 33, μίσθωσιν ἤθελεν αὐτῷ φέρειν Φορμίων πολλήν...ἐπεὶ δ᾽ οὐ ποιεῖ ταῦτα, τηνικαῦτα, φησὶ, δικάζομαι, and especially κατὰ Στεφ. Α, § 5, ἐπειδὴ ποιεῖν τε οὐδὲν ᾤετο δεῖν ὧν τότε ὡμολόγησε, καὶ τὰ χρήματα ἀποστερεῖν ἐνεχείρησεν ἃ τῆς τραπέζης εἶχεν ἀφορμὴν, δίκην ἠναγκάσθην λαχεῖν. For φέρειν cf. 21 § 197 ὃν...οὐ φίλοι δύνανται φέρειν.—For δίκην λαχὼν, cf. Or. 54 § 1, ἔλαχον δίκην n.

συκοφαντεῖ] Cf. Or. 55 § 1 n.

πραχθέντα τούτῳ πρὸς Πασίωνα καὶ Ἀπολλόδωρον ὡς ἂν δύνωμαι διὰ βραχυτάτων εἰπεῖν πειράσομαι, ἐξ ὧν εὖ οἶδ᾽ ὅτι ἥ τε τούτου συκοφαντία φανερὰ γενήσεται, καὶ ὡς οὐκ εἰσαγώγιμος ἡ δίκη γνώσεσθε ἅμα ταῦτ᾽ ἀκούσαντες.

4   Πρῶτον μὲν οὖν ὑμῖν ἀναγνώσεται τὰς συνθήκας,

——πραχθέντα τούτῳ, Or. 34 § 36 n.

Πασίωνα] Pasion, originally the slave of Archestratus (§ 48), and accountant to the banking-firm of Archestratus and Antisthenes, was set free by his masters and succeeded them in their business (§§ 43—48). The *Trapeziticus* of Isocrates, which belongs to B.C. 394, while Pasion was probably still a μέτοικος, and not yet rewarded with the citizenship of Athens, purports to be a speech written in prosecution of Pasion for defrauding a subject of Satyrus, king of Bosporus. The father of Demosthenes had some money in Pasion's bank (Or. 27 § 11). Pasion, according to his son, Apollodorus, had conferred many benefits on the state, e.g. by presenting five triremes and a thousand shields (Or. 45 § 85), and his credit was good throughout all Greece (Or. 50 § 56). He died in B.C. 370 (Or. 46 § 13). *Introd.* pp. xix—xxi.

οὐκ εἰσαγώγιμος] Or. 45 § 5 (of this very trial), παρεγράψατο τὴν δίκην ἣν ἔφευγε Φορμίων οὐκ εἰσαγώγιμον εἶναι. See ὑπόθεσις l. 23, παραγράφεται, n.

§§ 4—11. *Statement of the transactions of Phormion with Pasion and Apollodorus. After Phormion had become his own master, but before he had received the rights of Athenian citizenship, Pasion gave him a lease of the Bank and the Shield - Manufactory. Subsequently Pasion became ill and died, leaving a will whereby Phormion married his former master's widow (Archippe), and became guardian to his younger son (Pasicles). The elder son (Apollodorus) proceeded to appropriate large sums out of the common estate, and the guardians accordingly deemed it prudent on behalf of their ward to determine on a partition of all the effects except the Bank and Shield-Manufactory, leased to the defendant, who was one of the guardians. The defendant paid a moiety of the rent of that property to the elder son, Apollodorus, who when Pasicles came of age discharged the defendant from his liability under the lease and from all further claims. The said property was thereupon divided between the two brothers, the elder exercising his option in favour of the Shield-Manufactory, as the safer though less remunerative business, and leaving the Bank, with its higher but more hazardous revenue, to his younger brother.*

4. ἀναγνώσεται] sc. ὁ γραμματεύς, the clerk of the court, as in §§ 21, 24, 40.—συνθήκας: The terms are given in Or. 45 § 32, μίσθωσιν φέρειν τοῦτον ἄνευ τῆς καθ᾽ ἡμέραν διοικήσεως δύο τάλαντα καὶ τετταράκοντα μνᾶς τοῦ

καθ' ἃς ἐμίσθωσε Πασίων τὴν τράπεζαν τούτῳ καὶ
τὸ ἀσπιδοπηγεῖον. καί μοι λαβὲ τὰς συνθήκας καὶ
τὴν πρόκλησιν καὶ τὰς μαρτυρίας ταυτασί.

ΣΥΝΘΗΚΑΙ. ΠΡΟΚΛΗΣΙΣ. ΜΑΡΤΥΡΙΑΙ.

Αἱ μὲν οὖν συνθῆκαι, καθ' ἃς ἐμίσθωσεν ὁ Πασίων
τούτῳ τὴν τράπεζαν καὶ τὸ ἀσπιδοπηγεῖον ἤδη καθ'
ἑαυτὸν ὄντι, αὗταί εἰσιν, ὦ ἄνδρες Ἀθηναῖοι· δεῖ δ'
ὑμᾶς ἀκοῦσαι καὶ μαθεῖν ἐκ τίνος τρόπου προσώφειλε
τὰ ἕνδεκα τάλαντα ὁ Πασίων ἐπὶ τὴν τράπεζαν. οὐ 5
γὰρ δι' ἀπορίαν ταῦτ' ὤφειλεν, ἀλλὰ διὰ φιλεργίαν. ἡ

ἐνιαυτοῦ ἑκάστου...προσγέγραπται
δὲ τελευταῖον ' ὀφείλει δὲ Πασίων
ἕνδεκα τάλαντα εἰς τὰς παρακαταθήκας.'

ἀσπιδοπηγεῖον] Or. 45 § 85,
ὁ ἐμὸς ὑμῖν πατὴρ (Pasion)
χιλίας ἔδωκεν ἀσπίδας.

τὴν πρόκλησιν] Probably a
challenge to Apollodorus for the
production of the articles of
agreement between Pasion and
Phormion. On the term in
general, see Or. 54 § 27, προκαλοῦνται, n. and infr. § 7 n.

ἤδη καθ' ἑαυτὸν ὄντι] 'Doing
business on his own account, as
his own master,' no longer subject, as a slave, to the control of
another, though still a μέτοικος.
This rendering is supported
by C. R. Kennedy and M. Dareste. Similarly in Reiske's index: 'when he had left his
master's service, and gone into
business for himself, in his own
name, at his own risk.' καθ'
ἑαυτὸν is often used of being
'by oneself,' separate from
others; 21 § 140 καθ' ἑαυτὸν
ζῶντι, 10 § 52 γεγόνασι καθ'
αὑτοὺς ἕκαστοι.

προσώφειλε κ.τ.λ.] The defendant has to explain how it
comes to pass that Pasion is

entered in the articles of agreement as owing eleven talents
to the bank. He shows that
this sum had been lent by
Pasion on the security of certain
lands and houses on which
Pasion as the creditor, being an
Athenian citizen, would have
a claim, in the event of the
loan not being refunded or the
interest regularly paid. As
Phormion the lessee of the banking business had not yet acquired the rights of citizenship, it was therefore arranged
that Pasion should not transfer
these securities to Phormion
but keep them in his own
hands, and credit Phormion with
their value: in other words,
enter himself in the articles of
agreement as debtor to the bank
to the amount of eleven talents.

For προσώφειλε, the compound
verb followed by the simple
ὤφειλε where the repetition of
the preposition is not necessary, cf. Cic. Catil. IV 1, per-
ferrem...feram. Cf. Or. 53 § 4.

5. ἀπορίαν ... φιλεργίαν] 'Not
want but thrift,' or (with Kennedy) 'Not on account of poverty, but on account of his
industry in business.' In Or.

μὲν γὰρ ἔγγειος ἦν οὐσία Πασίωνι μάλιστα ταλάντων
εἴκοσιν, ἀργύριον δὲ πρὸς ταύτῃ δεδανεισμένον ἴδιον
πλέον[b] ἢ πεντήκοντα τάλαντα. ἐν οὖν τοῖς πεντήκοντα
ταλάντοις τούτοις ἀπὸ τῶν παρακαταθηκῶν τῶν τῆς 946
6 τραπέζης ἕνδεκα τάλαντα ἐνεργὰ ἦν. μισθούμενος οὖν

[b] μᾶλλον r a me collatus.

45 § 33 Apollodorus insinuates that the debt arose from Phormion's mismanagement.

ἔγγειος οὐσία] 'Property in land,' 'real property,' also called φανερὰ οὐσία. Harpocr. ἀφανὴς οὐσία καὶ φανερά· ἀφανὴς μὲν ἡ ἐν χρήμασι καὶ σώμασι καὶ σκεύεσι, φανερὰ δὲ ἡ ἔγγειος. Lysias, fragm. 91, τοῦ νόμου κελεύοντος τοὺς ἐπιτρόπους τοῖς ὀρφανοῖς ἔγγειον τὴν οὐσίαν καθιστάναι (Suidas s. v. ἔγγειον).

ἀργύριον πρὸς ταύτῃ] In addition to this he had money of his own (personal property) lent out on interest to the amount of more than fifty talents. The larger amount so employed shows that he was a usurer by practice or profession. P.]

ἐν οὖν τοῖς πεντήκοντα...ἕνδεκα] We have just been told that Pasion had more than 50 talents of his own money (ἀργύριον ἴδιον) lent out at interest, and we now find that ἐν τοῖς πεντήκοντα ταλάντοις there were 11 talents from the bank-deposits, profitably invested. The latter could hardly be called ἴδιον ἀργύριον, unless the words are used loosely in the general sense of 'personal property' as opposed to ἔγγειος οὐσία or 'real property.' But we should perhaps strike out ἴδιον and attribute its insertion to an accidental repetition of πλέον, as ΙΔΙΟΝ and ΠΛΕΟΝ are not very unlike one another. Blass accepts this,

pointing out that ἴδιον is also open to objection on rhythmical grounds. Or again, keeping ἴδιον we might alter ἐν οὖν into ἐπ' οὖν 'in addition to,' 'over and above' the 50 talents. Heraldus proposed σὺν οὖν, and G. H. Schaefer unsuccessfully attempts to show that ἐν may mean 'besides,' by quoting the quasi-adverbial use of ἐν δὲ in Soph. Ai. 675, O. C. 55, and O. T. 27.

[In the sense of 'in addition to' he should rather have said πρὸς than ἐπί. Perhaps ἐν means 'mixed up with,' i.e. out at loan to the same borrowers as his own money was (Boeckh *P. E.* p. 480 Lewis[2] = 622 Lamb). A man may borrow of me, as a banker, privately £500, and I may let him have £500 more belonging to the bank. On the large profits thus made by bankers, see Boeckh, *P. E.* p. 127 Lewis[2]. P.]

'Pasion a prêté en tout 50 talents, à savoir 39 de ses fonds personnels, et onze des fonds provenant des dépôts faits à la banque...Tous ces fonds sont indistinctement prêtés au nom de Pasion (ἴδιον), qui est seul créancier des emprunteurs, tout en restant débiteur des déposants.' Dareste, who agrees with A. Schaefer, *Dem. u. s. Zeit* III 2, 132.

ἐνεργὰ] 'Out on interest,' 'profitably invested,' as opposed to ἀργὰ 'lying idle.' Or. 27 § 7

ὅδε τὴν ἐργασίαν ταύτην τὴν[c] τῆς τραπέζης καὶ τὰς
παρακαταθήκας λαμβάνων, ὁρῶν ὅτι μήπω τῆς πολιτείας αὐτῷ[d] παρ᾽ ὑμῖν οὔσης οὐχ οἷός τε ἔσοιτο εἰσ-
πράττειν ὅσα Πασίων ἐπὶ γῇ καὶ συνοικίαις δεδανεικὼς ἦν, εἵλετο μᾶλλον αὐτὸν τὸν Πασίωνα χρήστην
ἔχειν τούτων τῶν χρημάτων ἢ τοὺς ἄλλους χρήστας,
οἷς προειμένος ἦν.   καὶ οὕτω διὰ ταῦτ᾽[e] ἐγράφη εἰς

[c] ταύτην τὴν Bekk. αὐτὴν Bekk. st. et Z cum Σ (coll. § 13). αὐτὴν
τὴν Voemel cum A[1]r.   [d] αὐτῷ Bekk. Z et Voemel (cf. tamen
Buttmann. in Mid. exc. x).   [e] ταῦτα Z.

τά τ᾽ ἐνεργὰ αὐτῶν καὶ ὅσα ἦν ἀργὰ,
§ 10 ταῦτα μὲν ἐνεργὰ κατέλειπεν
...τὸ δ᾽ ἔργον αὐτῶν πεντήκοντα
μναῖ, 56 § 29 τὸ δάνειον...ἐνεργὸν
ποιεῖν.

παρακαταθήκη] Plato defin.
p. 415 δόμα μετὰ πίστεως. Claims
for the repayment of such banking deposits form the subject of
two of the forensic orations of
Isocrates, the *Trapeziticus* and
the ἀμάρτυρος πρὸς Εὐθύνουν.

6. μήπω τῆς πολιτείας κ.τ.λ.]
No one could lend money on
the security of land unless in
default of payment (Or. 35 § 12)
the lender had the right to take
possession of such land, and
this right of possession was
confined to citizens to the ex-
clusion of μέτοικοι (or resident
aliens) like Phormion. In a similar case a special exception
was once made by the Byzan-
tines: Aristot. Oeconom. II 4
μετοίκων τινῶν ἐπιδεδανεικότων
ἐπὶ κτήμασιν οὐκ οὔσης αὐτοῖς
ἐγκτήσεως, ἐψηφίσαντο τὸ τρίτον
μέρος εἰσφέροντα τοῦ δανείου τὸν
βουλόμενον κυρίως ἔχειν τὸ κτῆμα
(Büchsenschütz, *Besitz und Erwerb im Griechischen Alterthume*,
pp. 492—3, K. F. Hermann,
Rechtsalt. p. 89 ed. Thalheim).

[On the insecurity of lending
money on houses or lands, except for citizens, see Boeckh,
P. E. pp. 140 and 654 Lewis[2],
who observes on this passage
that 'no resident alien could
safely lend money upon houses
or other landed property, a
privilege which was confined to
the citizens.' Of course μήπω
οὔσης, 'si nondum esset,' is very
different from οὔπω οὔσης, 'cum
nondum esset.' P.]

ἐπὶ γῇ...δεδανεικὼς] Cf. ἔγ-
γυον, or ἔγγειον, δάνεισμα and
Or. 34 § 23 ἔγγειοι τόκοι. (K.
F. Hermann, *Privatalterthümer*
§ 49, 9 and Büchsenschütz *u. s.*
p. 490.)

συνοικίαις] See n. on Or. 53
§ 13 τίθημι τὴν συνοικίαν ἑκκαί-
δεκα μνῶν. Houses built in
blocks and let out to families
were commonly so called. [This
is οἰκεῖν μετ᾽ ἄλλων opposed to
μονόρρυθμοι δόμοι in Aesch. Suppl.
960. The συνοικίαι were chiefly
let as lodgings for the μέτοικοι.
(See C. R. Kennedy, Dem. I p.
252.) Boeckh, *P. E.* p. 140. P.]

ἢ τοὺς ἄλλους χρήστας] 'Than
the others, to whom Pasion had
lent it, debtors to the bank.'
Perhaps the word χρήστας is
interpolated. P.]

οἷς προειμένος ἦν] In the me-

τὴν μίσθωσιν προσοφείλων ὁ Πασίων ἔνδεκα τάλαντα, ὥσπερ καὶ μεμαρτύρηται ὑμῖν.

7   Ὃν μὲν τοίνυν τρόπον ἡ μίσθωσις ἐγένετο, μεμαρτύρηται ὑμῖν ὑπ’ αὐτοῦ τοῦ ἐπικαθημένου· ἐπι-
γενομένης δὲ ἀρρωστίας τῷ Πασίωνι μετὰ ταῦτα,
σκέψασθ’ ἃ διέθετο. λαβὲ τῆς διαθήκης τὸ ἀντίγραφον καὶ τὴν πρόκλησιν ταυτηνὶ[f] καὶ τὰς μαρτυρίας
ταυτασὶ, παρ’ οἷς αἱ διαθῆκαι κεῖνται[g].

[f] Bekk. ταύτην Z cum ΣΑ¹r.
[g] παρ’ οἷς—κεῖνται interpolata esse censet Huettner.

dial sense. Liddell and Scott s. v. προΐημι B iii refer to this passage for the sense ‘to give away,’ ‘ to give freely.’ But it here means ‘to lend’ as in Plato Demod. 384. Cf. Or. 56 §§ 2, 48, 50.

ἐγράφη ... προσοφείλων ἔνδεκα τάλ.] Or. 45 § 29 προσγέγραπται ἔνδεκα τάλαντα ὁ πατὴρ (Pasion) ὀφείλων εἰς τὰς παρακαταθήκας τούτῳ, and § 34 ἐῶ τἄλλ’ ὅσ’ ἂν περὶ τῶν ἔνδεκα ταλ. ἔχοιμι εἰπεῖν, ὡς οὐκ ὤφειλεν ὁ πατὴρ, ἀλλ’ οὗτος ὑφῄρηται.

‘Ces onze talents provenant de dépôts constituaient une dette exigible de la part des déposants, et par suite un danger pour la banque du moment que le contre-valeur n’était pas facilement et promptement réalisable. C’est pourquoi Pasion donne à Phormion sa garantie pour les onze talents. Il reste créancier de ses emprunteurs, mais il devient débiteur, envers la banque, d’une somme égale de sa créance sur ces derniers.’ Dareste.

7. τοῦ ἐπικαθημένου] ‘The manager, the clerk, of the bank.’ Elsewhere Phormion himself is described by Apoll. as τὸν ἐπικαθήμενον ἐπὶ τῆς τραπέζης (Or. 49 § 17) and καθήμενον καὶ διοικοῦντα ἐπὶ τῇ τραπέζῃ (Or. 45 § 33), Isocr. Or. 17 (Trapez.) § 12, Pollux iii 84 ἐπικαθήμενος τραπέζῃ, S. Matt. ix 9 καθήμενον ἐπὶ (in charge over) τὸ τελώνιον.

ἀρρωστίας] Pasion’s failing health is touched upon in Or. 52 § 13 ἀδυνάτως ἤδη ἔχοντα καὶ μόγις εἰς ἄστυ ἀναβαίνοντα καὶ τὸν ὀφθαλμὸν αὐτὸν προδιδόντα and in Or. 49 § 42 ἔλεγεν ἀρρωστῶν ὅ τι ὀφείλοιτο αὐτῷ ἕκαστον.

μαρτυρίας..παρ’ οἷς] = μ. τούτων τῶν μαρτύρων παρ’ οἷς, ‘the depositions of the persons to whose keeping the will has been entrusted’ (cf. Isaeus 6 § 7; 9 §§ 5, 6, 18). In times when there were no probate-courts, it is obvious that the greatest precautions had to be taken to prevent forgeries by interested parties. In Or. 45 § 19 one Cephisophon deposes that his father had left behind him at his death, a document endorsed ‘ Pasion’s Will,’ which Apollodorus (ib. §§ 5, 22) denounces as a forgery (οὐδεπώποτε γενομένη...κατεσκευασμένη). The alleged terms are given ib. § 28, quoted in part in ὑπόθεσις 1. 6 n. The plural παρ’ οἷς is inaccurate, as the will appears to have

ΔΙΑΘΗΚΗ[h]. ΠΡΟΚΛΗΣΙΣ. ΜΑΡΤΥΡΙΑΙ. 8

Ἐπειδὴ τοίνυν ὁ Πασίων ἐτετελευτήκει ταῦτα δια-
θέμενος, Φορμίων οὑτοσὶ τὴν μὲν γυναῖκα λαμβάνει
κατὰ τὴν διαθήκην, τὸν δὲ παῖδα ἐπετρόπευεν. ἁρ-
πάζοντος δὲ τούτου καὶ πολλὰ ἀπὸ κοινῶν ὄντων τῶν
χρημάτων ἀναλίσκειν οἰομένου δεῖν, λογιζόμενοι πρὸς
ἑαυτοὺς οἱ ἐπίτροποι ὅτι, εἰ δεήσει κατὰ τὰς διαθήκας,

[h] Bekk. ἀντίγραφον Z cum ΣrA[1].

been in the custody of a single person only.

Probably the only instances we have of a will being in *official* custody are (1) Isaeus 1 §§ 14, 15, where it is in the hands of one of the ἀστύνομοι, and (2) an inscription from Amorgos (*C. I. G.* 2264 n), κατὰ τὰς δια-θήκας τὰς κειμένας ἐν ἱερῷ τῆς Ἀφροδίτης καὶ παρ' Εὐνομίδῃ τῷ ἄρχοντι καὶ παρὰ τῷ θεσμοθέτῃ Κτησιφῶντι (Meier and Schö-mann, p. 37, note 31 ed. Lipsius).

8. πρόκλησις] To establish Pa-sion's will, Stephanus and two others deposed that they were present when Phormion chal-lenged Apollodorus to open the will, and that the latter refused. In Or. 45 Apollodorus sues Ste-phanus for having given false evidence in the present case and discusses this challenge in §§ 8 —19, denying that any such challenge ever took place or that his father left such a will.

Πασίων ἐτετελευτήκει] Or. 46 § 13 ἐτελεύτησεν ἐπὶ Δυσνικήτου ἄρχοντος (B.C. 370).

τὴν γυναῖκα λαμβάνει κ.τ.λ.] Similarly the father of Dem. left Aphobus guardian of his children, and gave him his widow with a marriage-portion and the use of his house and furniture (Or. 27 § 5). The ob-ject of such legacies was to se-cure a faithful performance of the guardian's trust by connect-ing him more closely with the family of his ward (cf. 58 § 31). Diogenes Laertius, i 56, quotes a law, perhaps wrongly ascribed to Solon, τὸν ἐπίτροπον τῇ ὀρ-φανῶν μητρὶ μὴ συνοικεῖν. (K. F. Hermann, *Privatalt.* § 57, 16 = p. 13 of *Rechtsalt.* Thalheim.)

τὸν παῖδα] i. e. Pasicles, who was a minor for 8 years (B.C. 370—362), as appears by com-paring § 10 with § 37. He was probably 8 or 10 years old when his father died ; his elder bro-ther was 24 (inf. § 22).

τούτου] The claimant Apol-lodorus, whom the orator pur-posely represents as thriftless and unscrupulous at the very first.

λογιζόμενοι] 'The guardians, calculating among themselves, that if, by the terms of the will, it proved necessary to subtract from the *common* fund all that the plaintiff should have spent, and then divide the remainder equally, there would be no sur-plus whatever, decided in behalf of their ward on an immediate division of the property.'

κατὰ τὰς διαθήκας] goes with ἐξελόντας alone, and not with τὰ λοιπὰ νέμειν. The partition of the property was sufficiently provided for by the *law*, ἅπαντας

ὅσ' ἂν οὗτος ἐκ κοινῶν τῶν χρημάτων ἀναλώσῃ, τούτους[1] ἐξελόντας ἀντιμοιρεὶ[j] τὰ λοιπὰ νέμειν, οὐδ' ὁτιοῦν
ἔσται περιὸν, νείμασθαι τὰ ὄντα ὑπὲρ τοῦ παιδὸς 947
9 ἔγνωσαν. καὶ νέμονται τὴν ἄλλην οὐσίαν πλὴν ὧν
ἐμεμίσθωτο οὑτοσί· τούτων δὲ τῆς προσόδου τὴν ἡμί-

---

[1] τούτους Z et Bekk. st. cum Σ. τούτοις Reiske, Bekk.

[j] Bekk. st. et Voemel. ἀντιμοιρει (sine accentu) Σ, ἀντιμοιρεῖ (sic)
FΦ. τὰς ἀντιμοιρίας Reiske et Bekk. 1824 cum Λ[1]r.

τοὺς γνησίους ἰσομοίρους εἶναι τῶν
πατρῴων (Isaeus 6 § 25), and did
not require to be directed by the
will. It may be presumed that
the will provided for making
payments out of the estate previous to the legal partition of
the property.

κοινῶν τῶν χρημάτων] κοινῶν,
predicative; while yet undivided
and belonging to both alike.

τούτους] can only refer to τοὺς
ἐπιτρόπους, a construction that
is so harsh that the text is almost certainly wrong.

ἀντιμοιρεὶ] ' Share for share,'
cf. § 32 τὰ μητρῷα πρὸς μέρος
ἠξίους νέμεσθαι. The adverb
does not appear to occur elsewhere, and its form is sus-
piciously like the late Greek
words ἀνωνυμεί, αὐτολεξεί, αὐτο-
ψεί, παμπληθεί, πανεθνεί. In
earlier Greek almost the only
instances found are αὐτοβοεί
(Thuc.) and πανδημεί (Thuc.
Andoc. Lys. Isocr.).

[A more probable reading
would be τούτοις ἐξελόντας ἀντιμοιρίας, 'taking out (and laying
aside for the minor) equal sums
to those taken on each occasion
out of the general property by
Apollodorus.' The syntax ἀντιμοιρεὶ νέμειν seems unnatural, to
say nothing of the form of the
adverb; and ἐξελόντας seems to
require a definite accusative. P.]
Blass prefers τούτοις (neut. re-

ferring to ὅσα) and takes ἀντιμοιρεὶ with ἐξελόντας.

νέμειν...νέμονται] Donaldson,
Gk. Gr. p. 450, observes that
νέμειν is here used ' of a distri-
bution of property by executors;
though we have immediately
afterwards, νέμονται τὴν ἄλλην
οὐσίαν, because the obligation to
divide, under the will, stands in
a certain opposition to the act
of division, which the executors
performed with the same amount
of care and interest as if they
had divided the property among
themselves...Afterwards we have
(§ 10) ἐνείματο οὗτος πρὸς τὸν
ἀδελφόν, of one of the parties
immediately interested.' For
νέμεσθαι used in the middle voice
generally (but not always) of the
heirs, cf. §§ 11, 32, 38, Or. 39 § 6
τὸ τρίτον νείμασθαι μέρος, 47 § 35
νενεμημένος εἴη (τὴν οὐσίαν πρὸς
τὸν ἀδελφόν), Lysias 16 § 10;
19 § 46; 32 § 4; Isaeus 1 § 16
οἱ τούτων φίλοι...ἠξίουν νείμασθαι
τὴν οὐσίαν; 7 §§ 5, 25. The active διένειμεν is applied to the
father dividing his property
among his sons in Or. 43, Macart. § 49 (followed by νειμάμε-
νοι, of the sons) and in Lysias
19 § 46.

νείμασθαι] The subject is not
the ' brothers,' but the ' guardians,' as is clear from the subsequent verbs νέμονται and ἀπεδίδοσαν.

σειαν τούτῳ ἀπεδίδοσαν. ἄχρι μὲν οὖν τούτου τοῦ
χρόνου πῶς ἔνεστ᾽ ἐγκαλεῖν αὐτῷ μισθώσεως; οὐ γὰρ
νῦν, ἀλλὰ τότ᾽ εὐθὺς ἔδει χαλεπαίνοντα φαίνεσθαι.
καὶ μὴν οὐδὲ τὰς ἐπιγενομένας[k] μισθώσεις ὡς οὐκ
ἀπείληφεν ἔστ᾽ εἰπεῖν αὐτῷ. οὐ γὰρ ἄν ποτε, ἐπειδὴ 10
δοκιμασθέντος Πασικλέους ἀπηλλάττετο τῆς μισθώσεως ὅδε, ἀφῆκατ᾽ ἂν αὐτὸν ἁπάντων τῶν ἐγκλημάτων
ἀλλὰ τότ᾽ ἂν παραχρῆμα ἀπῃτεῖτε, εἴ τι προσώφει-
λεν ὑμῖν. ὡς τοίνυν ταῦτ᾽ ἀληθῆ λέγω, καὶ ἐνείματο
οὗτος πρὸς τὸν ἀδελφὸν παῖδ᾽ ὄντα, καὶ ἀφῆκαν τῆς
μισθώσεως καὶ τῶν ἄλλων ἁπάντων ἐγκλημάτων,
λαβὲ ταυτηνὶ τὴν μαρτυρίαν.

ΜΑΡΤΥΡΙΑ.

Εὐθὺς τοίνυν, ὦ ἄνδρες Ἀθηναῖοι, ὡς ἀφεῖσαν 11
τουτονὶ τῆς μισθώσεως, νέμονται τὴν τράπεζαν καὶ

[k] ἐπιγιγνομένας Z et Voemel *cum* ΣΦΦ. ἐπιγεν- Bekk.

9. ἀπεδίδοσαν] The guardians paid Apollodorus the share
due to him, viz. half the rent of
the bank and shield-manufactory. ἀποδιδόναι is 'to pay a man
his due,' as in Isaeus 5 § 21 οἷς
ἔδει αὐτὸν ἀποδόντα τὴν τιμὴν,
ἡμῖν τὰ μέρη ἀποδοῦναι, and frag.
29 ἀποδεδωκότι τὰς μισθώσεις. Cf.
Or. 41 § 9 τὴν τιμήν; 34 § 13
δάνειον; 15 § 17 χάριν; 16 § 2
εὔνοιαν. See note on 53 § 10.

ἄχρι μὲν οὖν κ.τ.λ.] 'Down
to this date, then, there is not
the slightest claim against Phormion in respect of the lease.'
For the rather rare construction
of ἐγκαλεῖν c. gen. cf. Or. 54 § 2
and Plut. Arist. 10, 9 τῆς βραδυτῆ-
τος αὐτοῖς ἐνεκάλει. In § 12 we
have ἐγκαλοῦντ᾽ ἀφορμήν.

10. δοκιμασθέντος] The δοκιμασία (see *Dict. Antiq.*) took
place on 'coming of age,' usually at 18, but in the case of

orphans it might be accelerated
a year or two. (A. Schaefer,
Dem. u. s. Zeit, III 2, 19—38
*Der Eintritt der Mündigkeit
nach Attischem Rechte.*)

ἀφῆκαν τῆς μισθώσεως κ.τ.λ.]
Or. 45 § 5 μάρτυρας ὡς ἀφῆκα αὐτὸν
τῶν ἐγκλημάτων παρέσχετο ψευδεῖς, καὶ μισθώσεώς τινος ἐσκευωρημένης καὶ διαθήκης οὐδεπώποτε
γενομένης.

[The forms ἀφήκατε and ἀφῆκαν and παρέδωκαν §§ 14, 44 are
rather unusual. The Attics prefer in the plural the inflexion of
the second aorist, ἀφεῖμεν, ἀφεῖτε,
ἀφεῖσαν. Cf. §§ 11, 14, and
see Veitch's *Greek Verbs.*—The
two brothers Apollodorus and
Pasicles are directly addressed
in ἀφήκατε, not the jury, as is
shown by ἀπῃτεῖτε following.—
For this sense of προσοφείλειν
cf. Ar. Ran. 1134. P.]

τὸ ἀσπιδοπηγεῖον, καὶ λαβὼν αἵρεσιν Ἀπολλόδωρος
αἱρεῖται τὸ ἀσπιδοπηγεῖον ἀντὶ τῆς τραπέζης. καίτοι
εἰ ἦν ἰδία[1] τις ἀφορμὴ τούτῳ πρὸς τῇ τραπέζῃ, τί
δή ποτ’ ἂν εἵλετο τοῦτο μᾶλλον ἢ ἐκείνην; οὔτε
γὰρ ἡ πρόσοδος ἦν πλείων, ἀλλ’ ἐλάττων (τὸ μὲν
γὰρ τάλαντον, ἡ δ’ ἑκατὸν μνᾶς ἔφερεν), οὔτε τὸ
κτῆμα ἥδιον[m], εἰ προσῆν χρήματα τῇ τραπέζῃ ἴδια.
ἀλλ’ οὐ προσῆν. διόπερ σωφρονῶν εἵλετο τὸ ἀσπιδοπηγεῖον οὑτοσί[n]· τὸ μὲν γὰρ κτῆμ’ ἀκίνδυνόν ἐστιν, 948
ἡ δ’ ἐργασία προσόδους ἔχουσα ἐπικινδύνους ἀπὸ
χρημάτων ἀλλοτρίων.

[1] καὶ Voemel *cum* Σ.   [m] Wolf. ἡδεῶν A[1]r, ἴδιον FΣΦ.
[n] οὗτος Bekk. Z et Voemel *cum* Σ.   *om.* rA[1].

11. αἵρεσιν] The choice lay
with him by virtue of being the
elder brother (§ 34).

καίτοι κ.τ.λ.] Phormion argues
that if the plaintiff had had any
private capital of his own in
the bank, he would have chosen
the banking-business in preference to the manufactory. He
did not, and therefore he contends there was no such fund.—
ἰδία ἀφορμὴ is private banking-
stock, as opposed to deposits,
παρακαταθῆκαι (cf. § 11).—τάλαντον = 60 minae.

τὸ μὲν γὰρ—ἀλλοτρίων] ‘For
the manufactory is a property
free from risk, whereas the bank
is a business yielding a hazardous (speculative, precarious) revenue from other people’s
money.’ The bank was not a
κτῆμα, but only an ἐργασία, not a
secure property, but a precarious trading with other people’s
money.

ἥδιον] The labour and trouble
and other disagreeable incidents
of manufacturing shields made
such a property less desirable

in itself than a banking business.
But the bank business was speculative, and involved the risk
of losing the deposits, and therefore the manufactory, with all
its drawbacks, was preferred by
Apollodorus, as being at least
safe. P.]

§§ 12—17. *The plaintiff’s
claim to a sum of banking-stock
alleged to have been held by the
defendant may be proved groundless by many arguments:* (1)
*Plaintiff’s father is entered in
the lease, not as creditor on account of banking-stock assigned
to defendant, but actually as
debtor to the bank.* (2) *On the
partition of the property, plaintiff put in no claim to such stock.*
(3) *After the termination of defendant’s lease of the bank,
plaintiff let it to others for the
same sum and no less; and did
not specially transfer to them
any banking-stock besides.* (4)
*The plaintiff during the life of
his mother, who was perfectly
familiar with all these details,
made no demand on the defend-*

Πολλὰ δ' ἄν τις ἔχοι λέγειν καὶ ἐπιδεικνύναι σημεῖα τοῦ τοῦτον συκοφαντεῖν ἐγκαλοῦντ'[o] ἀφορμήν. ἀλλ', οἶμαι, μέγιστον μέν ἐστιν ἁπάντων τεκμήριον τοῦ μηδεμίαν λαβεῖν ἀφορμὴν εἰς ταῦτα τουτονὶ τὸ ἐν τῇ μισθώσει γεγράφθαι προσοφείλοντα τὸν Πασίων' ἐπὶ τὴν τράπεζαν, οὐ δεδωκότα ἀφορμὴν τούτῳ, δεύτερον δὲ τὸ[p] τοῦτον ἐν τῇ νομῇ μηδὲν[q] ἐγκαλοῦντα φαίνεσθαι, τρίτον δ', ὅτι μισθῶν ἑτέροις ὕστερον ταὐτὰ 12

[o] ἐγκαλοῦντα Z.

[p] om. Z cum ΣΦ. τὸ τοῦτον Bekk. cum marg. Σ.

[q] μηδὲ Σ, μηδ' Voemel. '*quidni* μηδὲ *ante verba* ἐν τῇ νομῇ *positum esse malis? at* μηδὲν *intellegendum est* μηδεμίαν ἀφορμήν' Huettner.

ant; it was only when she died that he set up a fraudulent claim, not for any banking-stock as now, but for a sum of 3000 dr. The claim was submitted to the arbitration of some relatives of the plaintiff, and upon their award the defendant for peace and quietness' sake paid the money and a second time received from the plaintiff a release from all his claims.

12. πολλὰ—ἐπιδεικνύναι] Or. 20 § 163 πολλὰ δ' ἄν τις ἔχοι λέγειν ἔτι καὶ διεξιέναι.

σημεῖα...τεκμήριον] Or. 54 § 9.

συκοφαντεῖν κ.τ.λ.] Kennedy: 'This claim of the plaintiff's to a sum of banking-stock is false and fraudulent.'—ἐγκαλοῦντ' ἀφορμήν, the first distinct reference in the speech to the nature of the plaintiff's case. He alleges that the defendant had a grant of capital from Pasion and had appropriated it.

τουτονὶ...τούτῳ...τοῦτον] The first two refer to the defendant, the third to the plaintiff, Apollodorus. The ambiguity arising from the same pronoun being applied to two different persons, would be readily dispelled by the orator's delivery. Cf. § 42 n.

προσοφείλοντα] sc. 11 talents, §§ 4—6.—τῇ νομῇ, § 8 fin.

μισθῶν ἑτέροις κ.τ.λ.] i.e. to Xenon and the others in § 13. The argument is: assume the defendant defrauded the plaintiff of bank-stock amounting to 20 talents. Then the stock in question could not have formed part of the business when the plaintiff let it to the later lessees. The plaintiff then should either have let it to them at *lower* terms than to the defendant, or have handed over to the bank an equivalent to the stock alleged to be missing. He did neither; he made no fresh transfer and he charged them the same rent. Therefore the property must have been in the same condition as when the defendant originally leased it from the plaintiff's father.—The context compels us to make Apollodorus the subject of the sentence μισθῶν—φανήσεται,

ταῦτα τοῦ ἴσου ἀργυρίου οὐ φανήσεται προσμεμισθω-
13 κὼς ἰδίαν ἀφορμήν. καίτοι εἰ, ἣν ὁ πατὴρ παρέσχεν,
ὑπὸ τοῦδε ἀπεστέρητο[r], αὐτὸν νῦν προσῆκεν ἐκείνοις
ἄλλοθεν πορίσαντα δεδωκέναι. ὡς τοίνυν ταῦτ᾽ ἀληθῆ
λέγω, καὶ ἐμίσθωσεν ὕστερον Ξένωνι καὶ Εὐφραίῳ
καὶ Εὔφρονι καὶ Καλλιστράτῳ, καὶ οὐδὲ τούτοις παρέδωκεν ἰδίαν ἀφορμὴν, ἀλλὰ τὰς παρακαταθήκας καὶ
τὴν ἀπὸ τούτων ἐργασίαν αὐτὴν ἐμισθώσαντο, λαβέ
μοι τὴν τούτων μαρτυρίαν, καὶ ὡς τὸ ἀσπιδοπηγεῖον
εἵλετο[8].

ΜΑΡΤΥΡΙΑ.

14   Μεμαρτύρηται μὲν τοίνυν ὑμῖν, ὦ ἄνδρες Ἀθηναῖοι, ὅτι καὶ τούτοις ἐμίσθωσαν καὶ οὐ παρέδωκαν
ἰδίαν ἀφορμὴν οὐδεμίαν, καὶ ἐλευθέρους ἀφεῖσαν ὡς

[r] Coniecit G. H. Schaefer. ἀπεστερειτο Σ. ἀποστεροῖτο FΦ,
ἀπεστεροῖτο Voemel.

[8] καὶ ὡς—εἵλετο delenda esse censuit G. H. Schaefer ab Huett-
nero approbatus.

but the bank, it will be remembered, became the property not
of Apollodorus, but of Pasicles,
when the latter came of age
and Phormion's lease expired;
we must therefore conclude
that the elder brother acted as
agent on behalf of his less experienced younger brother.

τοῦ ἴσου ἀργυρίου] viz. 2[t] 40[m]
for the whole business, 1[t] for
the shield-manufactory, and
1[t] 40[m] (= 100[m]) for the bank
(cf. § 11). It has been suggested
that τοῦ ἴσου ἀργυρίου is a false
statement, but a careful consideration of §§ 11 and 37 shows
that this is not the case.

13. τοῦδε...αὐτὸν] Defendant
and plaintiff respectively.—νῦν
'in that case,' referring to the
hypothesis εἰ — ἀπεστέρητο. —

αὐτὸν, standing first in the
clause, must mean *ipsum*.

The sense is: 'Surely, if
Apollodorus had been defrauded by Phormion of capital supplied by Pasion, he would *himself* (on *that* supposition) have
had to provide capital from
other sources, and deliver it to
those new lessees.' Otherwise,
he could not have got the same
amount of rent.

ἐμίσθωσεν] Granted the lease
(on behalf of Pasicles). Below
we have ἐμισθώσαντο, referring,
as usual, to the lessees.

αὐτὴν] 'Alone'; explained by
οὐ παρέδωκαν ἰδίαν ἀφορμήν.

14. ἐμίσθωσαν ... παρέδωκαν]
The plurals refer to the two
brothers.

ἐλευθέρους ἀφεῖσαν] Or. 29

μεγάλα εὖ πεπονθότες, καὶ οὐκ ἐδικάζοντο οὔτ᾽ ἐκείνοις τότ᾽ οὔτε τούτῳ.　ὃν μὲν τοίνυν χρόνον ἡ μήτηρ
ἔζη ἡ πάντα ταῦτ᾽ ἀκριβῶς εἰδυῖα[t], οὐδὲν ἔγκλημα
πώποτε ἐποιήσατο πρὸς τουτονὶ Φορμίωνα Ἀπολλό-
949 δωρος· ὡς δ᾽ ἐτελεύτησεν ἐκείνη, τρισχιλίας ἐγκαλέσας
ἀργυρίου δραχμὰς πρὸς αἷς ἔδωκεν ἐκείνη δισχιλίαις
τοῖς τούτου παιδίοις, καὶ χιτωνίσκον τινὰ καὶ θερά-
παιναν, ἐσυκοφάντει.　καὶ οὐδ᾽ ἐνταῦθα τούτων οὐδὲν 15
ὧν νῦν ἐγκαλεῖ λέγων φανήσεται.　ἐπιτρέψας δὲ τῷ
τε τῆς ἑαυτοῦ γυναικὸς πατρὶ καὶ τῷ συγκηδεστῇ τῷ

[t] ἀκριβῶς ταῦτ᾽ εἰδυῖα Z et Voemel cum Σ.　ἀκριβῶς εἰδυῖα ταῦτα
FΦ.　ταῦτ᾽ ἀκριβῶς εἰδυῖα Bekk.

§§ 25, 31 τὸν Μιλύαν ἐλεύθερον εἶναι ἀφεθέντα, 47 § 55 ἀφειμένη ἐλευθέρα...ἀφείθη ἐλευθέρα, § 72 ἀφεῖτο...ἐλευθέρα. Xenon, Euphraeus and the other lessees appear (like Phormion) to have been slaves originally. The family show their gratitude for their services by *giving them freedom* (ὡς μεγάλα εὖ πεπονθότες). It is so translated by M. Dareste. G. H. Schaefer and C. R. Kennedy (perhaps less satisfactorily) understand the words : 'set free from all further claims'; 'gave them a complete discharge'; a sense which is at first sight partly supported by καὶ οὐκ ἐδικάζοντο below.

ὡς ἐτελεύτησεν] The speaker insinuates that Apoll. purposely waited till his mother's death, as her familiarity with all the details of her late husband's property would have thwarted his plots against Phormion. Her death is described by Apollodorus in Or. 50 § 60, 'While I was abroad my mother lay ill and was at death's door, and therefore little able to help in retrieving my affairs. It was just six days after my return that, when she had seen me and spoken to me, she breathed her last, when she no longer had such control over her property as to be able to give me all that she desired.' The death took place in Feb. B.C. 360.

πρὸς αἷς] She had left Phormion's children 2000 drachmas, but Apollodorus claims more than that sum also as his own. His avaricious and mean character is shown by his claim to a χιτωνίσκος, a chemise or 'slave's frock,' perhaps. A man who would make such demands was little likely to omit his present claims, if he had then believed in the justice of them. P.]

χιτωνίσκον] Or. 21 § 216 θοἰμάτιον προέσθαι καὶ μικροῦ γυμνὸν ἐν τῷ χιτωνίσκῳ γενέσθαι.

15. ἐπιτρέψας κ.τ.λ.] The plaintiff submitted the claims to the arbitration of Deinias and Nicias (§ 17), his own father-in-law and brother-in-law respectively. Pollux: ἔλεγον δὲ ἐπιτρέψαι δίαιταν, καὶ ἡ δίαιτα ἐκαλεῖτο ἐπιτροπή.

αὐτοῦ[u] καὶ Λυσίνῳ καὶ Ἀνδρομένει, πεισάντων τούτων Φορμίωνα τουτονὶ δοῦναι δωρεὰν τὰς τρισχιλίας
καὶ τὸ προσὸν καὶ φίλον μᾶλλον ἔχειν τοῦτον ἢ διὰ
ταῦτ᾽ ἐχθρὸν αὐτὸν εἶναι, λαβὼν τὸ σύμπαν πεντακισχιλίας, καὶ πάντων ἀφεὶς τῶν ἐγκλημάτων τὸ
16 δεύτερον εἰς τὸ ἱερὸν τῆς Ἀθηνᾶς ἐλθὼν, πάλιν, ὡς
ὁρᾶτε, δικάζεται, πάσας αἰτίας συμπλάσας καὶ ἐγκλήματα ἐκ παντὸς τοῦ χρόνου τοῦ πρὸ τούτου (τοῦτο
γάρ ἐστι μέγιστον ἁπάντων), ἃ οὐδεπώποτ᾽ ᾐτιάσατο.
ὡς τοίνυν ταῦτ᾽ ἀληθῆ λέγω, λαβέ μοι τὴν γνῶσιν
τὴν γενομένην ἐν ἀκροπόλει, καὶ τὴν μαρτυρίαν τῶν
παραγενομένων, ὅτ᾽ ᾐφίει[v] τῶν ἐγκλημάτων ἁπάντων
Ἀπολλόδωρος, λαμβάνων τοῦτο τὸ ἀργύριον.

[u] ἑαυτοῦ Ζ.

[v] ἀφίει Ζ cum Σ.   ᾐφίει F.   'codices modo hoc modo illud exhibent; vid. Dind. ad 21 § 79, 36 § 24; Rehdantz, ad 3 § 5,'
Huettner.

δοῦναι δωρεὰν] By 'making a present' of the 3000 drachmae, Phormion satisfies Apollodorus without admitting his legal claim to the sum. Or. 19 § 170; 42 § 19; Isaeus 2 § 31 διῄτησαν ἡμᾶς ἀποστῆναι ὧν οὗτος ἀμφισβήτησε καὶ δοῦναι δωρεάν· οὐ γὰρ ἔφασαν εἶναι ἄλλην ἀπαλλαγὴν οὐδεμίαν, εἰ μὴ μεταλήψονται οὗτοι τῶν ἐκείνου.

τὸ προσὸν] Not the 2000 drachmae of § 14; for they were already given by the mother (ἔδωκεν ἐκείνη), but the 'additional articles' χιτωνίσκος καὶ θεράπαινα. [τὸ προσὸν may however refer to πρὸς αἷς κ.τ.λ. supra. He got the 3000 and the 2000 also that had been left to Phormion's boys. He got from him 5000 in all, and gave him a full release from all further claims; and yet now again he says Phormion has kept back some of Pasi

on's money! But (he argues) the discharge then given justifies the παραγραφὴ now put in. P.]

ἀφεὶς...τὸ δεύτερον] The former release is mentioned in § 10 fin. This second release is solemnly given in the temple of Athênê on the Acropolis. Isocr. Trapez. § 20, ταῦτα συγγράψαντες καὶ ἀναγαγόντες εἰς ἀκρόπολιν Πύρωνα......δίδομεν αὐτῷ φυλάττειν τὰς συνθήκας, ib. 17 and Andoc. 1 § 42.

16. συμπλάσας] 'Having concocted,' 'fabricated,' 'patched up,' 'put into shape.' Aeschin. 3 § 77 τῶν θεῶν συμπλάσας ἑαυτῷ ἐνύπνιον κατεψεύσατο. The metaphor (as in the words feigning and fiction) is from the moulding of clay in the hands of the potter. Cf. § 33 πλάσμα.

τὴν γνῶσιν] 'The award' of the arbitrators. Or. 27 § 1, τοῖς οἰκείοις ἐπιτρέπειν and τοῖς

ΓΝΩΣΙΣ. ΜΑΡΤΥΡΙΑ.

'Ακούετε τῆς γνώσεως, ὦ ἄνδρες δικασταὶ, ἣν 17
ἔγνω Δεινίας, οὗ τὴν θυγατέρα οὗτος ἔχει, καὶ Νικίας
ὁ τὴν ἀδελφὴν τῆς τούτου γυναικὸς ἔχων. ταῦτα
τοίνυν λαβὼν καὶ ἀφεὶς ἁπάντων τῶν ἐγκλημάτων,
ὥσπερ ἢ πάντων τεθνεώτων τούτων ἢ τῆς ἀληθείας
οὐ γενησομένης φανερᾶς, δίκην τοσούτων ταλάντων
λαχὼν τολμᾷ δικάζεσθαι.

Τὰ μὲν οὖν πεπραγμένα καὶ γεγενημένα Φορμίωνι 18
πρὸς 'Απολλόδωρον ἐξ ἀρχῆς ἅπαντ' ἀκηκόατε, ὦ
950 ἄνδρες 'Αθηναῖοι. οἶμαι[w] δ' 'Απολλόδωρον τουτονὶ
οὐδὲν ἔχοντα δίκαιον εἰπεῖν περὶ ὧν ἐγκαλεῖ, ἅπερ
παρὰ τῷ διαιτητῇ λέγειν ἐτόλμα, ταῦτ' ἐρεῖν, ὡς τὰ

[w] Σ.   οἴομαι Ζ (see Veitch, Gk. Vbs., and Dindf. Praef. p. xiii).

υπ' ἐκείνων γνωσθεῖσιν ἐμμένειν.
Cf. § 17.—ἐν ἀκροπόλει. So supra
τὸ ἱερὸν τῆς 'Αθηνᾶς. Pollux, διή-
των δ' ἐν ἱεροῖς (VIII 126). Or. 59
§ 46 (of two arbitrators) συνελ-
θόντες ἐν τῷ ἱερῷ, and Or. 54
§ 26, τὸν λίθον, n.

λαμβάνων] 'On the receipt
of this money,' viz. the 5000
drachmae.

17. τούτων] τῶν μαρτύρων τῶν
παραγενομένων, § 16.

τοσούτων ταλ.] § 3, ταλάντων
εἴκοσι.

τολμᾷ] It was acting in open
defiance of the law to bring an
action after a full acquittance
had been given.

§§ 18—21. Anticipation of the
arguments likely to be brought
forward by the plaintiff. *He
will repeat what he stated before the arbitrator, that his
mother destroyed his father's
papers at the defendant's insti-
gation. If so (1) how came the
plaintiff to make a partition of
his patrimony, without any*

*papers to determine its amount?
Unless those claims were false
and fraudulent, which the plaintiff will scarcely admit, he
must have gained possession of
his father's papers, and his
mother could not have made
away with them. (2) Why was
no question raised when the
plaintiff's younger brother came
of age and was receiving from
his guardians an account of
their trust? (3) On what papers
did the plaintiff base all his
many law-suits for the recovery
of large sums due to his father?*

18. τὰ μὲν οὖν κ.τ.λ.] Transition
from the διήγησις or πρόθεσις
to the πίστεις or 'proofs' (Ar.
Rhet. III 13), from the brief
recital of the transactions between plaintiff and defendant
(§§ 4—17) to the legal and other
arguments.

τῷ διαιτητῇ] Pollux: πάλαι δ'
οὐδεμία (?) δίκη πρὶν ἐπὶ διαιτητὰς ἐλθεῖν εἰσήγετο (VIII 126). Cf.
54 § 26, ἡ δίαιτα n.

γράμματα ἡ μήτηρ ἠφάνικε πεισθεῖσα ὑπὸ τούτου, καὶ
τούτων ἀπολωλότων οὐκ ἔχει τίνα χρὴ τρόπον ταῦτ'
19 ἐξελέγχειν ἀκριβῶς. περὶ δὴ τούτων καὶ ταύτης τῆς
αἰτίας σκέψασθε ἡλίκ' ἄν τις ἔχοι τεκμήρια εἰπεῖν
ὅτι ψεύδεται. πρῶτον μὲν γὰρ, ὦ ἄνδρες Ἀθηναῖοι,
τίς ἂν ἐνείματο τὰ πατρῷα μὴ λαβὼν γράμματα ἐξ ὧν
ἔμελλεν[x] εἴσεσθαι τὴν καταλειφθεῖσαν οὐσίαν; οὐδὲ
εἷς δήπου. καίτοι δυοῖν δέοντα εἴκοσιν ἔτη ἐστὶν ἐξ
ὅτου ἐνείμω, καὶ οὐκ ἂν ἔχοις ἐπιδεῖξαι ὡς ἐνεκάλεσας
20 πώποτε ὑπὲρ τῶν γραμμάτων. δεύτερον δὲ, τίς οὐκ
ἂν, ἡνίκα ὁ Πασικλῆς ἀνὴρ γεγονὼς ἐκομίζετο τὸν
λόγον τῆς ἐπιτροπῆς, εἰ δι' αὐτοῦ τὰ γράμματ' ὤκνει
τὴν μητέρα αἰτιᾶσθαι διεφθαρκέναι, τούτῳ ταῦτ' ἐδή-

---

[x] ἤμελλεν Z cum Σ (see Isocr. Paneg. § 83 n.).

τὰ γράμματα] Not Pasion's
will, but his private papers and
ledgers or banking-books, τὰ
γράμματα τὰ τραπεζιτικά (Or.
49 §§ 43, 59 quoted below in
note on § 21, ἐκ ποίων γραμμάτων). Cf. Or. 49 § 5, οἱ τραπεζῖται εἰώθασιν ὑπομνήματα
γράφεσθαι ὧν τε διδόασι χρημάτων, κ.τ.λ. and Or. 52 § 4.

19. ἐνείματο] 'Who would have
taken his share of his father's
property, if he had not the
books from which alone he
could know the amount of property left?' He refers to the
division of the patrimony decided on by the guardians in
consequence of the elder brother spending largely out of the
common fund, § 8 fin. This
event took place eighteen years
before the date of the speech;
which, if we could assume that
the partition was in the same
year as the father's death, viz.
370, would belong to B.C. 352.
This however we cannot assume, indeed the language of

§ 8, πολλὰ ἀναλίσκειν, κ.τ.λ.,
implies that the elder brother's
course of extravagance lasted
some time before the partition
was decided on. We may therefore perhaps place the partition
in B.C. 368, and the speech in
B.C. 350. See *Introd.* p. xxvii f.

ὑπὲρ τῶν γραμμάτων] sc. περὶ
τῆς ἀφανίσεως αὐτῶν.

20. ἀνὴρ γεγονὼς] Cf. § 10,
δοκιμασθέντος Πασικλέους.

ἐκομίζετο κ.τ.λ.] 'Was getting
in an account of the guardianship,' i.e. the accounts from his
guardians. Or. 27, κατ' Ἀφόβου
ἐπιτροπῆς, § 50, πότερον ἐπι-
τροπευθεὶς ἀπεδέξατ' ἂν τοῦτον
τὸν λόγον παρὰ τῶν ἐπιτρόπων;

τούτῳ...τούτου] It is best to refer these pronouns to Pasicles
(with Reiske, Kennedy and Dareste); not to Apollodorus (with
G. H. Schaefer). The sense is:
'Assuming Apollodorus hesi-
tated with his own lips to accuse his mother of destroying
the documents; at any rate,
when Pasicles came of age and

λωσεν, ὅπως διὰ τούτου ταῦτα ἠλέγχθη; τρίτον δ᾽, ἐκ
ποίων γραμμάτων τὰς δίκας ἐλάγχανες; οὗτος γὰρ
πολλοῖς τῶν πολιτῶν δίκας λαγχάνων πολλὰ χρήματα εἰσπέπρακται, γράφων εἰς τὰ ἐγκλήματα "ἔ-
"βλαψέ με ὁ δεῖνα οὐκ ἀποδιδοὺς ἐμοὶ τὸ ἀργύριον, ὃ
"κατέλιπεν[y] ὁ πατὴρ ὀφείλοντα αὐτὸν ἐν τοῖς γράμ-
"μασιν." καίτοι εἰ ἠφάνιστο τὰ γράμματα[z], ἐκ ποίων 21
γραμμάτων τὰς δίκας ἐλάγχανεν; ἀλλὰ μὴν ὅτι
ταῦτ᾽ ἀληθῆ λέγω, τὴν μὲν νομὴν ἀκηκόατε, ἣν ἐνείματο, καὶ μεμαρτύρηται ὑμῖν· τῶν δὲ λήξεων τούτων
ἀναγνώσεται ὑμῖν τὰς μαρτυρίας. λαβὲ τὰς μαρτυρίας μοι.

ΜΑΡΤΥΡΙΑΙ.

951   Οὐκοῦν ἐν ταύταις ταῖς λήξεσιν ὡμολόγηκεν ἀπει-
ληφέναι τὰ τοῦ πατρὸς γράμματα· οὐ γὰρ δὴ συκο-

[y] κατέλειπεν Z et Voemel *cum* Σ.   -έλιπεν Bekk.
[z] τὸ γράμμα Voemel *cum* Σ.

was in course of receiving the
report of his guardians' administration, is there any one who,
under the circumstances, would
not have stated the fact to his
younger brother, and by his
instrumentality had the matter
investigated?'

ὅπως ἠλέγχθη] inf. § 47 ἵνα,
'that so they might have been
proved true or false,' &c.

πολλὰ χρήματα εἰσπέπρακται]
'He has succeeded in recovering large sums of money.' The
famous general Timotheus, under pressure of political exigencies, in the years 374 to
372 B.C., borrowed more than
forty-four minae from the
banker Pasion, on whose death
his son Apollodorus sues Timotheus for payment in a speech
still extant, belonging probably
to the year B.C. 362. (Or. 49,
πρὸς Τιμόθεον ὑπὲρ χρέως.) Cf.
infr. §§ 36 and 54.

21.   ἐκ ποίων γραμμάτων] If
there *were* no papers, then the
grounds of your actions were
fraudulent, συκοφαντίαι, inf.
In Or. 49, Pasion's papers are
expressly cited, e.g. § 43, κελεύοντος ἐνεγκεῖν τὰ γράμματα ἀπὸ
τῆς τραπέζης καὶ ἀντίγραφα αἰ-
τοῦντος...ἐξενέγκας ἔδωκα ζητεῖν
τὰ γράμματα καὶ ἐκγράφεσθαι ὅσα
οὗτος ὤφειλεν, and § 59, τοῖς
γράμμασι τοῖς τραπεζιτικοῖς.

λήξεων μαρτυρίας] 'The depositions in support of' (or
'verifying') 'these plaints.'
For λῆξις, cf. supr. δίκας ἐλάγχανεν, also Or. 45 § 50, τῇ τοῦ
διώκοντος λήξει ἣν ἐγὼ τούτῳ
ψευδομαρτυριῶν εἴληχα, and Or.
33 § 35, ἐγκέκληκε καὶ...τὴν λῆξιν
πεποίηται.

φαντεῖν γε, οὐδ᾽ ὧν οὐκ ὤφειλον οὗτοι δικάζεσθαι
φήσειεν ἄν.

22   Νομίζω τοίνυν, ὦ ἄνδρες Ἀθηναῖοι, μεγάλων καὶ
πολλῶν ὄντων ἐξ ὧν ἔστιν ἰδεῖν οὐκ ἀδικοῦντα Φορμίωνα τουτονί, μέγιστον ἁπάντων εἶναι, ὅτι Πασικλῆς,
ἀδελφὸς ὢν Ἀπολλοδώρου τουτουὶ, οὔτε δίκην εἴληχεν
οὔτ᾽ ἄλλ᾽ οὐδὲν ὧν οὗτος ἐγκαλεῖ. καίτοι οὐ δήπου
τὸν μὲν παῖδα ὑπὸ τοῦ πατρὸς καταλειφθέντα, καὶ οὗ
τῶν ὄντων κύριος ἦν, ἐπίτροπος καταλελειμμένος, οὐκ
ἂν ἠδίκει, σὲ δὲ, ὃς ἀνὴρ κατελείφθης τέτταρα καὶ
εἴκοσιν ἔτη γεγονὼς, καὶ ὑπὲρ σαυτοῦ ῥᾳδίως ἂν τὰ
δίκαια ἐλάμβανες εὐθὺς, εἴ τι ἠδικοῦ. οὐκ ἔστι ταῦτα.
ὡς τοίνυν ταῦτ᾽ ἀληθῆ λέγω καὶ ὁ Πασικλῆς οὐδὲν
ἐγκαλεῖ, λαβέ μοι τὴν τούτου μαρτυρίαν.

§ 22. Argument from the silence of plaintiff's younger brother. *Pasicles, as a minor, had been much more liable to be wronged by the defendant, who as testamentary guardian had control over his ward's property. Pasicles makes no complaint. Therefore (it is tacitly assumed) he had no complaint to make. A fortiori defendant is not likely to have wronged the plaintiff, who at his father's death was a man of four and twenty, and fully able to defend himself.*

Φορμίωνα τουτονί] τουτονί need not refer to Apollodorus, but may be taken with Φορμίωνα, cf. infr. Ἀπολλοδώρου τουτονί, and §§ 15, 18, 26, 28, 47, 57.

οὔτ᾽ ἄλλ᾽ κ.τ.λ.] sc. οὔτε ἄλλο οὐδὲν ἐγκαλεῖ ὧν οὗτος (ἐγκαλεῖ).

τὸν] Construe with καταλειφθέντα, παῖδα being a predicate.

κύριος...ἐπίτροπος] Cf. Or. 38 § 6, τῶν ἐπιτρόπων οἳ μετὰ τὸν ἐκείνου θάνατον τῶν ἡμετέρων ἐγένοντο κύριοι. κύριος here refers to the *property*, ἐπίτροπος

to the *person* of the ward (Schömann on Isaeus 1 § 10).

σὲ δὲ] sc. ἂν ἠδίκει. Notice the double force of the negative, οὐ δήπου οὐκ ἂν ἠδίκει, 'Surely he would not have abstained from wronging one who had been left a minor by his father, and over whose property he had a legal power and authority, as having been left guardian of it, and yet have wronged *you*,' &c. So inf. § 46, οὐδὲ τὸν Φορμίωνα ἐκεῖνος οὐχ ὁρᾷ. [Expectabam, οὐ δήπου σὲ μὲν ἂν ἠδίκει, τὸν δὲ παῖδα οὔ. Shilleto, De Fals. Leg. § 390, not. crit. P.]

ὁ Πασ. οὐδὲν ἐγκαλεῖ] 'Brings no claim against Phormion,' i.e. for property of his father's withheld. Cf. Or. 45 §§ 83, 84, where Apollodorus meets the objection arising from the silence of Pasicles by broaching a suspicion that he is his half-brother only and by insinuating he is really a son of Archippe and *Phormion*. 'Say no more, pray, of Pasicles; no! let him

ΜΑΡΤΥΡΙΑ.

Ἃ τοίνυν ἤδη περὶ αὐτοῦ τοῦ μὴ εἰσαγώγιμον 23
εἶναι τὴν δίκην δεῖ σκοπεῖν ὑμᾶς, ταῦτ' ἀναμνήσθητε
ἐκ τῶν εἰρημένων. ἡμεῖς γὰρ, ὦ ἄνδρες Ἀθηναῖοι,
γεγενημένου μὲν διαλογισμοῦ καὶ ἀφέσεως τῆς τραπέζης καὶ τοῦ ἀσπιδοπηγείου τῆς μισθώσεως, γεγενημένης δὲ διαίτης καὶ πάλιν πάντων ἀφέσεως, οὐκ
ἐώντων τῶν νόμων δίκας ὧν ἂν ἀφῇ τις ἅπαξ λαγχάνειν, συκοφαντοῦντος τούτου καὶ παρὰ τοὺς νόμους 24
δικαζομένου παρεγραψάμεθα ἐκ τῶν νόμων μὴ εἶναι
τὴν δίκην εἰσαγώγιμον. ἵν' οὖν εἰδῆθ'[a] ὑπὲρ οὗ τὴν
ψῆφον οἴσετε, τόν τε νόμον ὑμῖν τοῦτον ἀναγνώσεται
952 καὶ τὰς μαρτυρίας ἐφεξῆς τῶν παρόντων, ὅτ' ἠφίει[b]
τῆς μισθώσεως καὶ τῶν ἄλλων ἁπάντων ἐγκλημάτων
Ἀπολλόδωρος Φορμίωνα[c]. λαβέ μοι τὰς μαρτυρίας
ταυτασὶ καὶ τὸν νόμον.

[a] ἴδητε Z cum correcto Σ.   εἰδῆθ' Bckk.   ἴδηθ' Bekk. st.
[b] ἀφίει Z cum Σ.   [c] om. Z cum ΣrA¹.   add. Bekk.

be called your *son*, Phormion, not
your *master*; and my opponent
(he is bent upon it)—not my
brother.'

§§ 23—25. *The speaker now
passes from the arguments in
support of the main issue (or
the case upon its merits) to
those on which the defendant
raises a special plea in bar of
action.*

*The plaintiff's case cannot
come before the court because
he has given the defendant a
discharge from the original
lease of the Bank and Manufactory, and a second discharge
from a subsequent claim which
was settled by arbitration; and
the laws allow no right of action
where a release and discharge*
have been given or received.

23. μὴ εἰσαγώγιμον] Cf. ὑπόθεσις l. 23, n. — διαλογισμοῦ, a
reckoning up, or producing of
accounts as between the two
parties, Phormion and Apoll.
Cf. § 60.

ἀφέσεως — μισθώσεως] The
order is (γεγενημένης) ἀφέσεως
τῆς μισθ. τῆς τραπέζης κ.τ.λ.
Cf. § 24, ἠφίει τῆς μισθώσεως and
supr. § 10. Or. 33 § 3, πάντων
ἀπαλλαγῆς καὶ ἀφέσεως γενομένης. 45 § 11; 38 §§ 5, 9, 14.

διαίτης κ.τ.λ.] § 16.

24. ἐκ τῶν νόμων] Contrasted
with παρὰ τοὺς νόμους. As he
brought his action contrary to the
law, we have put in an objection
to it which is fully allowed by
the law.

ΜΑΡΤΥΡΙΑΙ. ΝΟΜΟΣ.

25   Ἀκούετε τοῦ νόμου λέγοντος, ὦ ἄνδρες Ἀθηναῖοι,
τά τε ἄλλα ὧν μὴ εἶναι δίκας ^dκαὶ ὅσα τις ἀφῆκεν ἢ
ἀπήλλαξεν. εἰκότως· εἰ γάρ ἐστι δίκαιον, ὧν ἂν ἅπαξ
γένηται δίκη, μηκέτ᾽ ἐξεῖναι δικάζεσθαι, πολὺ τῶν
ἀφεθέντων δικαιότερον μὴ εἶναι δίκας^d. ὁ μὲν γὰρ ἐν
ὑμῖν ἡττηθεὶς τάχ᾽ ἂν εἴποι τοῦτο ὡς ἐξηπατήθητε
ὑμεῖς· ὁ δὲ αὐτοῦ φανερῶς καταγνοὺς καὶ ἀφεὶς καὶ
ἀπαλλάξας, τίν᾽ ἂν ἑαυτὸν αἰτίαν αἰτιασάμενος τῶν

^{d-d} καὶ ὅσα—μὴ εἶναι δίκας propter ὁμοιοτέλευτον omisit Σ, sup-
plevit manus multo recentior.

---

25. ἀκούετε κ.τ.λ.] Or. 38, παραγραφὴ πρὸς Ναυσίμαχον, § 5,
ἀκούετε τοῦ νόμου σαφῶς λέγοντος
ἕκαστα ὧν μὴ εἶναι δίκας, ὧν ἕν
ἐστιν, ὁμοίως τοῖς ἄλλοις κύριον,
περὶ ὧν ἄν τις ἀφῇ καὶ
ἀπαλλάξῃ, μὴ δικάζεσθαι.
Cf. 37 §§ 1, 19; 33 § 3.

ὧν μὴ εἶναι δίκας] Infin. in
relative clause influenced by
λέγοντος. 'Among other cases
in which an action cannot be
maintained, those especially in
which a discharge and release
have been given or received.'

εἰ γὰρ κ.τ.λ.] The sense
is, 'If it is just that, when
once a case has been tried, it
should not be tried again, even
although the defeated litigant
might fairly plead that the
court had been imposed upon,
a *fortiori* there is no ground
for re-opening the question
when a man has judged his
own case and has palpably
decided against himself by giving and receiving a discharge.'

μηκέτ᾽ ἐξεῖναι δικάζεσθαι] Or.
38 § 16 ἅπαξ περὶ τῶν αὐτῶν πρὸς
τὸν αὐτὸν εἶναι τὰς δίκας. 20
Lept. § 147 οἱ νόμοι δ᾽ οὐκ ἐῶσι
δὶς πρὸς τὸν αὐτὸν περὶ τῶν αὐτῶν

οὔτε δίκας οὔτ᾽ εὐθύνας οὔτε δια-
δικασίαν οὔτ᾽ ἄλλο τοιοῦτ᾽ οὐδὲν
εἶναι.

ἐξηπατήθητε] Or. 37 § 20
περὶ ὧν ἔγνω τὸ δικαστήριον, ἔστιν
εἰπεῖν ὡς ἐξαπατηθὲν τοῦτ᾽ ἐποίησε
...ἃ δ᾽ αὐτὸς ἐπείσθη καὶ ἀφῆκεν,
οὐκ ἔνι δήπουθεν εἰπεῖν οὐδ᾽ αὐτὸν
αἰτιάσασθαι ὡς οὐ δικαίως ταῦτ᾽
ἐποίησεν.

αὐτοῦ...καταγνοὺς] The two
subsequent participles are subordinate in construction to
καταγνούς. 'He who has clearly
condemned (given a verdict a-
gainst) himself *by* both granting
and getting a release and discharge.' Madvig *Gr. Synt.*
§ 176, d.

ἀφεὶς καὶ ἀπαλλάξας] It is
clear the words do not mean
the same thing, for below we
have γέγονεν ἀμφότερα· καὶ
γὰρ ἀφῆκε καὶ ἀπήλλαξε. Similarly 37 § 1 and 38 § 1 after ἀφεὶς
καὶ ἀπαλλάξας we have γεγενημένων ἀμφοτέρων, and in 37
§ 19 after ὧν ἂν ἀφῇ καὶ ἀπαλλάξῃ τις we have ἀμφότερ᾽ ἐστὶ
πεπραγμένα.

ἀφιέναι is very frequently
used of the lender, or the
landlord, who, on settlement

αὐτῶν πάλιν εἰκότως δικάζοιτο; οὐδεμίαν δήπου.
διόπερ τοῦτο πρῶτον ἔγραψεν ὁ τὸν νόμον θεὶς ὧν μὴ

of his claims, releases the borrower or the tenant from all further liability (§§ 10, 15, 16, 17, 24). Similarly of a ward releasing his guardian from all further claims, in 38 §§ 3, 4, 6, 18, 27; and of a creditor forgiving a debt, 53 §§ 8, 13. Cf. 56 §§ 26, 28, 29.

ἀπαλλάττειν often refers to the debtor or tenant getting quit of his creditor or landlord by discharging or compromising the debt (34 § 22 τοὺς δανείσαντας ἀπήλλαξεν, 49 § 17; 53 § 11; 33 § 9 and Isaeus Or. 5 Dicaeog. § 28 ἀπαλλάσσειν τοὺς χρήστας). Settling a cross account between lessor and lessee (e.g. Apoll. and Phormion) would involve a double release and quittance on either side. Cf. 33 § 12, τῶν συναλλαγμάτων ἀφεῖμεν καὶ ἀπηλλάξαμεν ἀλλήλους ὥστε μήτε τούτῳ πρὸς ἐμὲ μήτ' ἐμοὶ πρὸς τοῦτον πρᾶγμ' εἶναι μηδέν.

The present passage is the subject of the following article in Harpocration. ἀφεὶς καὶ ἀπαλλάξας· τὸ μὲν ἀφεὶς ὅταν ἀπολύσῃ τίς τινα τῶν ἐγκλημάτων ὧν ἐνεκάλει αὐτῷ, τὸ δὲ ἀπαλλάξας, ὅταν πείσῃ τὸν ἐγκαλοῦντα ἀποστῆναι καὶ μηκέτι ἐγκαλεῖν (recte)· Δημοσθένης ἐν τῇ ὑπὲρ Φορμίωνος παραγραφῇ. ἔστι δὲ καὶ οὕτως εἰπεῖν, ὅτι ἀφίησι μέν τις αὐτῶν μόνον ὧν ἂν ἐγκαλῇ, ἀπαλλάττει δὲ, ὅταν μηδὲ ἄλλον τινὰ λόγον ὑπολίπηται ἑαυτῷ πρὸς τὸν ἐγκαλούμενον. Δημοσθένης ἐν τῇ ὑπὲρ Φορμίωνος παραγραφῇ "ἵν' ἀπαλλαγή τις αὐτῷ γένηται παρ' ὑμῶν κυρία" (§ 2). Cf. Or. 37 §§ 1, 16, 19; Or. 38 §§ 1, 5; Or. 33 § 3. In Bekker's Anecdota pp. 202, 469 we find the same explanation as

that which is given. in the first part of Harpocration's article.

[From the frequency of this legal formula, though a shade of difference may be traced, and perhaps originally existed, between these verbs, I agree with Mr Kennedy (Dem. Pant. p. 230) that it had passed into a technical expression, and that practically they became synonyms. P.]

In Shilleto's copy of Mr Kennedy's translation I find a manuscript note in which, after quoting the explanation given in Bekker's *Anecdota*, he adds: "This is a clear statement and exactly in accordance with the meaning of the words: ἀφίημι, 'I let go, one whom I have a hold of'; ἀπαλλάττω, 'I get rid of one who has a hold of me.' So I ἀφίημι a man on whom I have a claim by my condoning the debt, by receiving payment, postponing it, &c.; I ἀπαλλάττω a man who has a claim on me, by his condoning the debt, by my paying it, by my putting off the payment-day. So he who ἀφίησιν, ἀπαλλάττεται [passive]; he who ἀπαλλάττει, ἀφίεται [passive]. I cannot conceive anything plainer." But owing to the two-fold use of ἀπαλλάττειν, both of *setting free* and *getting rid of* another, the question is not really quite as simple as this would make it appear. Thus in Isocr. Trapez. § 26, after ἀφειμένος and ἀφεῖσθαι τῶν ἐγκλημάτων have been used in §§ 23, 25 of one who is 'released from all claims,' the same person is described as ἀπηλλαγμένος τῶν ἐγκλημάτων, which is possibly a middle use, 'having got himself

εἶναι δίκας, ὅσα τις ἀφῆκεν ἢ ἀπήλλαξεν. ἃ τῷδε
γέγονεν ἀμφότερα· καὶ γὰρ ἀφῆκε καὶ ἀπήλλαξεν.
ὡς δ' ἀληθῆ λέγω, μεμαρτύρηται ὑμῖν, ὦ ἄνδρες
Ἀθηναῖοι.

26   Λαβὲ δή μοι καὶ τὸν τῆς προθεσμίας νόμον.

ΝΟΜΟΣ.

Ὁ μὲν τοίνυν νόμος, ὦ ἄνδρες Ἀθηναῖοι, σαφῶς
οὑτωσὶ τὸν χρόνον ὥρισεν· Ἀπολλόδωρος δ' οὑτοσὶ
παρεληλυθότων ἐτῶν πλέον ἢ εἴκοσι τὴν ἑαυτοῦ συκο-
φαντίαν ἀξιοῖ περὶ πλείονος ὑμᾶς ποιήσασθαι τῶν
νόμων, καθ' οὓς ὀμωμοκότες δικάζετε. καίτοι πᾶσι
μὲν τοῖς νόμοις προσέχειν εἰκός ἐσθ' ὑμᾶς, οὐχ ἥκιστα
27 δὲ τούτῳ, ὦ ἄνδρες Ἀθηναῖοι. δοκεῖ γάρ μοι καὶ ὁ
Σόλων οὐδενὸς ἄλλου ἕνεκα θεῖναι αὐτὸν ἢ τοῦ μὴ

quit of all claims.'—The distinction drawn in Platner's *Process* I 146, is that ἀφεῖναι regards
the release from an existing obligation mainly from the point
of view of the person granting
the release, whereas ἀπαλλάττειν
implies a *two-fold* transaction
and an agreement on the part
of *both* the persons concerned.

§ 26. *The plaintiff's suit is
also inadmissible for another
reason; it contravenes the statute
of limitations, in which the term
of five years is fixed as a sufficient time for injured parties to
recover their dues, whereas the
plaintiff puts forward his claim
after a lapse of more than twenty
years.*

προθεσμίας νόμον] (See Dict.
Antiq. s.v.)—Harpocr. Δημοσθένης ὑπὲρ Φορμίωνος· τὴν τῶν ε'
ἐτῶν ἂν λέγοι προθεσμίαν ὁ ῥήτωρ,
ὡς ἐν τῷ λόγῳ ὑποσημαίνει. See
Or. 38 §§ 17, 27, and cf. Isaeus,
3 § 58, and Plato Leg. p. 954ᶜ.

(Caillemer, *la Prescription à
Athènes*, 1869, and K. F. Her-
mann, *Privatalt.* § 71, 5 and 6
= *Rechtsalt.* p. 106 Thalheim.)

πλέον ἢ εἴκοσι] The speaker
apparently goes back to the time
of Pasion's lease of the banking
business to Phormion, which
cannot well have been later than
B.C. 371, when Pasion was so
infirm that he died a year after.
This would bring the date of the
speech to B.C. 351 at the earliest,
and B.C. 350 cannot be far wrong.
See *Introd.* p. xxvii f.

καθ' οὓς ὀμωμοκότες κ.τ.λ.] Pollux: ὁ δ' ὅρκος ἦν τῶν δικαστῶν,
περὶ μὲν ὧν νόμοι εἰσι, ψηφιεῖσθαι
κατὰ τοὺς νόμους, περὶ δὲ ὧν μή
εἰσι, γνώμῃ τῇ δικαιοτάτῃ (VIII
122). See Dr Hager in *Journal
of Philology*, VI 10.

27. δοκεῖ ὁ Σόλων] A favourite
rhetorical device, to remind the
dicasts of the solemnity and
high authority of the law they
administer.

συκοφαντεῖσθαι ὑμᾶς.   τοῖς μὲν γὰρ ἀδικουμένοις τὰ
953 πέντε ἔτη ἱκανὸν ἡγήσατ᾽ εἶναι εἰσπράξασθαι· κατὰ
δὲ τῶν ψευδομένων τὸν χρόνον ἐνόμισε σαφέστατον
ἔλεγχον ἔσεσθαι.   καὶ ἅμα[e] ἐπειδὴ ἀδύνατον ἔγνω ὂν
τούς τε συμβάλλοντας καὶ τοὺς μάρτυρας ἀεὶ ζῆν,
τὸν νόμον ἀντὶ τούτων ἔθηκεν, ὅπως μάρτυς εἴη[f] τοῦ
δικαίου τοῖς ἐρήμοις.

e Bekk.   καὶ ἅμα καὶ Z et Voemel cum Σ.
f μαρτυρησείη Voemel (μαρτυρησει η Σ).

τοῖς ἀδικουμένοις...τῶν ψευδομένων] i.e. the legal term of five years would be quite sufficient for injured parties to 'recover their rights' if their claim were an honest one, whereas those who set up false claims, (a pointed thrust at the present plaintiff,) would be convicted by the fact that they had allowed the statutable period to elapse without taking action. (ἔλεγχον ἔσεσθαι sc. *si per tot annos tacuissent.* G. H. Schaefer.)   τῶν ψευδομένων is sometimes wrongly supposed to imply that as in Roman law there was no statute of limitations against right of recovery of things stolen, (*quod subreptum erit, eius rei aeterna auctoritas esto,*) so in Attic law there was none in case of falsehood, i.e. that even after five years a claim based on a false assertion might be disputed. (Telfy, *Corpus iuris Attici* § 1587, and K. F. Hermann, *Privatalt.* § 71, 6 = *Rechtsalt.* p. 106 Thalheim.)   Here therefore it merely means κατὰ τῶν συκοφαντούντων.

τὰ πέντε ἔτη] The *well-known* legal term of five years.

τὸν χρόνον—ἔλεγχον] Lysias Or. 19 § 61 τῷ χρόνῳ ὃν ὑμεῖς

σαφέστατον ἔλεγχον τοῦ ἀληθοῦς νομίσατε.

τὸν νόμον ἀντὶ τούτων κ.τ.λ.] That is, 'The contracting parties themselves, and the witnesses to that contract, could not live for ever; and therefore the legislator laid down the law, with its limit of time, designing that, in lieu of living witnesses, the destitute should find therein a deathless witness on the side of right.'

§§ 28—32.   Plaintiff's probable reply anticipated. *Surely he will not ask his audience to resent the defendant's marriage with the plaintiff's mother. Among bankers, there are many precedents for such an arrangement, and on grounds of expediency, as the only means of keeping up the business, Pasion acted prudently in directing that Phormion should marry his widow and thereby binding him more closely to his own household.*

As to the point of honour, 'you may turn up your nose at Phormion's marrying into your family, but remember that in high character, he is more like your father than you are.'

That the marriage was directed by Pasion is not only expressly proved by the will, but is in-

28 Θαυμάζω τοίνυν ἔγωγ’, ὦ ἄνδρες δικασταὶ, τί ποτ’ ἐστὶν ἃ πρὸς ταῦτ’ ἐπιχειρήσει λέγειν Ἀπολλόδωρος οὑτοσί. οὐ γὰρ ἐκεῖνό γ’ ὑπείληφεν, ὡς ὑμεῖς, μηδὲν ὁρῶντες εἰς χρήματα τοῦτον ἠδικημένον, ὀργιεῖσθ’ ὅτι τὴν μητέρ’ ἔγημεν αὐτοῦ Φορμίων. οὐ γὰρ ἀγνοεῖ τοῦτο, οὐδ’ αὐτὸν λέληθεν, οὐδ’ ὑμῶν πολλοὺς, ὅτι Σωκράτης ὁ τραπεζίτης ἐκεῖνος, παρὰ τῶν κυρίων ἀπαλλαγεὶς ὥσπερ ὁ τούτου πατὴρ, ἔδωκε Σατύρῳ

29 τὴν ἑαυτοῦ γυναῖκα, ἑαυτοῦ ποτὲ γενομένῳ. ἕτερος Σωκλῆς τραπεζιτεύσας ἔδωκε τὴν ἑαυτοῦ γυναῖκα Τιμοδήμῳ τῷ νῦν ἔτ’ ὄντι καὶ ζῶντι, γενομένῳ ποτὲ αὐτοῦ⁵. καὶ οὐ μόνον ἐνθάδε ταῦτα ποιοῦσιν οἱ περὶ τὰς ἐργασίας ὄντες ταύτας, ὦ ἄνδρες Ἀθηναῖοι, ἀλλ’ ἐν Αἰγίνῃ ἔδωκε Στρυμόδωρος Ἑρμαίῳ τῷ ἑαυτοῦ οἰκέτῃ τὴν γυναῖκα, καὶ τελευτησάσης ἐκείνης ἔδωκε πάλιν

⁵ ἑαυτοῦ Z.

ferentially concluded from the plaintiff's own admission; for on his mother's death he permitted her two children by Phormion to share her property equally with himself and Pasicles, her two children by Pasion, and thus allowed the legality of this second marriage.

28. θαυμάζω κ.τ.λ.] Or. 37 § 44 ἔγωγε, ὅ τι ποτ’ ἐρεῖ πρὸς ὑμᾶς, θαυμάζω.

τί ποτ’ ἐστὶν ἃ] Cf. note on 54 § 13.

μηδὲν ὁρῶντες] i.e. ἦν καὶ μηδὲν ὁρᾶτε. Goodwin, _Moods and Tenses_, § 52, 1.

παρὰ τῶν κυρίων ἀπαλλαγεὶς ὥσπερ ὁ τούτου πατὴρ] A very close parallel. The banker referred to, like the plaintiff's father, had himself been a slave once, had been set free by his masters, and had given his wife in marriage to one who was formerly his slave. Cf. § 43 fin. and § 48 ἐγένετο Πασίων Ἀρχεστράτου. [On ἐκεῖνος see Or. 40 § 28.]

29. ὄντι καὶ ζῶντι] Who is still ‘alive and in being.’ The redundancy is intended to strengthen the emphasis. Cf. De Corona § 72 τὴν Μυσῶν λείαν καλουμένην τὴν Ἑλλάδα οὖσαν ὀφθῆναι ζώντων καὶ ὄντων Ἀθηναίων.

τελευτησάσης...ἔδωκε τὴν θυγατέρα] After the will had been made, the wife apparently died before the husband and the latter then gave his daughter in marriage to his former servant. The first ἔδωκε therefore must mean, ‘directed in his will that, after his own death, his widow should marry Hermaeus.’ M. Dareste, however, supposes that there is no reference to any will. He holds

τὴν θυγατέρα τὴν ἑαυτοῦ.   καὶ πολλοὺς ἂν ἔχοι τις
εἰπεῖν τοιούτους.   εἰκότως· ὑμῖν μὲν γάρ, ὦ ἄνδρες 30
'Αθηναῖοι, τοῖς γένει πολίταις οὐδὲ ἓν πλῆθος χρημάτων ἀντὶ τοῦ γένους καλόν ἐστιν ἑλέσθαι· τοῖς δὲ
τοῦτο μὲν δωρεὰν ἢ παρ' ὑμῶν ἢ παρ' ἄλλων τινῶν
λαβοῦσι, τῇ τύχῃ δ' ἐξ ἀρχῆς ἀπὸ τοῦ χρηματίσασθαι
καὶ ἑτέρων πλείω κτήσασθαι[h] καὶ αὐτῶν τούτων
ἀξιωθεῖσι, ταῦτ' ἐστι φυλακτέα.   διόπερ Πασίων ὁ
954 πατὴρ ὁ σὸς οὐ πρῶτος οὐδὲ μόνος, οὐδ' αὐτὸν ὑβρίζων
οὐδ' ὑμᾶς τοὺς υἱεῖς, ἀλλὰ μόνην ὁρῶν σωτηρίαν τοῖς
ἑαυτοῦ πράγμασιν, εἰ τοῦτον ἀνάγκη ποιήσειεν οἰκεῖον
ὑμῖν, ἔδωκε τὴν ἑαυτοῦ γυναῖκα μητέρα δ' ὑμετέραν
τούτῳ.   πρὸς μὲν οὖν τὰ συμφέροντα ἐὰν ἐξετάζῃς, 31

[h] καὶ ἑτέρων πλείω κτήσασθαι om. Huettner cum A¹r.

that the woman had either
been divorced from her husband, or was not his lawful
wife.

30.   ὑμῖν...τοῖς γένει πολίταις
κ.τ.λ.]   A compliment to the
audience, designed to smooth the
way for what might otherwise
prove an invidious reference to
the money-making of bankers
in general and to the wealth of
Pasion in particular. 'For *you*,
gentlemen of Athens, you who
are citizens by birth, it is dis-
creditable to prize any amount
of money, however large, more
highly than that honourable
birth (lit. 'no amount of wealth
is honourable for you to accept
in place of your free birth');
but those who (like Pasion) have
received the rights of citizenship
as a free gift either from yourselves or from others, and who,
thanks in the first instance to
their good fortune, were deemed
worthy of the selfsame privileges, by reason of having pro-
spered in money-making and

acquired more wealth than their
neighbours, must do their best
to preserve their pecuniary advantages.'

The sense is, 'though it would
be wrong for those who are citizens by birth to prefer wealth
to citizenship, it would also be
unreasonable for those who are
citizens by adoption to be careless of the wealth which has
gained them that very honour
and privilege.'

αὐτὸν ὑβρίζων κ.τ.λ.]   Dis-
gracing, outraging, casting contumely on, himself and his
family. Though you threatened
Phormion with a γραφὴ ὕβρεως
for marrying your mother (Or.
45 § 3—4), your father was
guilty of no ὕβρις to his family
in arranging for that marriage.

ἀνάγκῃ]   *Necessitate*, 'by a
family tie.' Isocr. ad Dem.
10, Lys. 32 § 5.

ὑμῖν...ὑμετέραν]   'You and
yours.' 'Your family.' Cf. Or.
55 § 5, n.

καλῶς βεβουλευμένον αὐτὸν εὑρήσεις· εἰ δὲ πρὸς
γένους δόξαν ἀναίνει¹ Φορμίωνα κηδεστὴν, ὅρα μὴ
γελοῖον ᾖ σὲ ταῦτα λέγειν. εἰ γάρ τις ἔροιτό σε,
ποῖόν τιν' ἡγεῖ ʲ τὸν πατέρα τὸν σεαυτοῦ ᵏ εἶναι, χρηστὸν εὖ οἶδ' ὅτι φήσειας ἄν. πότερον οὖν οἴει μᾶλλον
ἐοικέναι τὸν τρόπον καὶ πάντα τὸν βίον Πασίωνι,
σαυτὸν ἢ τουτονί; ἐγὼ μὲν γὰρ εὖ οἶδ' ὅτι τοῦτον.
32 εἶθ' ὅς ἐστιν ὁμοιότερος σοῦ τῷ σῷ πατρὶ, τοῦτον, εἰ
τὴν μητέρα τὴν σὴν ἔγημεν, ἀναίνει¹; ἀλλὰ μὴν ὅτι
γε δόντος καὶ ἐπισκήψαντος τοῦ σοῦ πατρὸς ταῦτ'
ἐπράχθη, οὐ μόνον ἐκ τῆς διαθήκης ἔστιν ἰδεῖν, ὦ
ἄνδρες Ἀθηναῖοι, ἀλλὰ καὶ σὺ μάρτυς αὐτὸς γέγονας.
ὅτε γὰρ τὰ μητρῷα πρὸς μέρος ἠξίους νέμεσθαι, ὄντων
παίδων ἐκ τῆς γυναικὸς Φορμίωνι τούτῳ, τότε ὡμο-
λόγεις κυρίως δόντος τοῦ πατρὸς τοῦ σοῦ κατὰ τοὺς
νόμους αὐτὴν γεγαμῆσθαι. εἰ γὰρ αὐτὴν εἶχε λαβὼν
ἀδίκως ὅδε μηδενὸς δόντος, οὐκ ἦσαν οἱ παῖδες κληρο-

¹ ἀναίνῃ Z.   ʲ Σ. ἡγῇ Z.   ᵏ Σ. σαυτοῦ Z.

31. πρὸς γένους δόξαν] Sc.
βλέπων.

ἀναίνει] 'Disdain,' 'scorn,'
'disown,' 'turn up your nose
at' in family pride. Harpocr.
ἀναίνεσθαι κοινῶς μὲν τὸ ἀρνεῖσθαι,
ἰδίως δὲ ἐπὶ τῶν κατὰ τοὺς γάμους
…λέγεται. Δημ. ἐν τῇ ὑπὲρ Φορμίωνος παραγραφῇ.—κηδεστὴν in
general a relation by marriage,
here used of the stepfather.

σὲ ταῦτα λέγειν] Notice the
emphatic pronoun.

[ποῖον—πότερον. In Greek
the difference between the direct
and the indirect question (qualem putas, and qualem putes)
cannot be expressed from the
want of 'subjunctivity.' P.] πότερον being probably masculine,
a comma (omitted in Dindorf's
text) has been added after Πασίωνι.

32. δόντος κ. ἐπισκήψαντος]
By your father's special grant
and injunction.

πρὸς μέρος] 'Share and share
alike.' § 8, ἀντιμοιρεὶ νέμειν,
νέμεσθαι. On παίδων…Φορμίωνι
see note on τὸ τέταρτον μέρος infr.

οὐκ ἦσαν κληρονόμοι] The
proposition is categorically, not
conditionally stated, 'then the
children were not heirs; and if
they were not heirs, then they
had no share in the property.'
The right of inheritance was
confined to the children born
ἐξ ἀστῆς καὶ ἐγγυητῆς γυναικὸς
Isae. de Ciron. § 19, pro Eu-
phil. § 9. Dem. Or. 57 § 53
ἐξῆν τούτοις (τοῖς συγγενέσι) εἰ
νόθος ἢ ξένος ἦν ἐγὼ, κληρονόμοις
εἶναι τῶν ἐμῶν πάντων. Arist.

νόμοι, τοῖς δὲ μὴ κληρονόμοις οὐκ ἦν μετουσία τῶν
ὄντων. ἀλλὰ μὴν ὅτι ταῦτ᾽ ἀληθῆ λέγω μεμαρτύρηται τῷ[1] τὸ τέταρτον μέρος λαβεῖν καὶ ἀφεῖναι τῶν
ἐγκλημάτων ἁπάντων.

Κατ᾽ οὐδὲν τοίνυν, ὦ ἄνδρες Ἀθηναῖοι, δίκαιον 33
οὐδὲν ἔχων εἰπεῖν ἀναιδεστάτους λόγους ἐτόλμα λέγειν
955 πρὸς τῷ διαιτητῇ, περὶ ὧν προακηκοέναι βέλτιόν ἐσθ᾽
ὑμᾶς, ἕνα μὲν τὸ παράπαν μὴ γενέσθαι διαθήκην,
ἀλλ᾽ εἶναι τοῦτο πλάσμα καὶ σκευώρημα ὅλον, ἕτερον
δ᾽ ἕνεκα τούτου πάντα ταῦτα συγχωρεῖν τὸν πρὸ τοῦ

---

[1] addidit Reiske.

Aves, 1640—73. (K. F. Hermann
Privatalt. § 29, 5 = p. 253 Blüm-
ner, and § 57, 2 = *Rechtsalt.* p. 7
Thalheim.)

τὸ τέταρτον μέρος] The property is divided into four parts,
one of which is taken by Apollodorus, another by his brother
Pasicles. The other two go to
the children of the second marriage, who must have been two
in number.

ἀφεῖναι τῶν ἐγκλ.] § 3 ἀφεθεὶς, § 25 ἀφεὶς κ. ἀπαλλάξας, n.

§§ 33—35. Anticipation of
plaintiff's arguments, continued.
He will impudently assert (1)
*that his father made no will and
that the document produced was
a forgery; and* (2) *that the reason
why he forbore to press the
charge at the proper time was
that defendant promised to pay
him a high rent.*

In answer to (1), *if there was
no will, how came the plaintiff
to succeed to the lodging-house
which he holds in accordance
with the terms of the will? In
answer to* (2), *it is in evidence
that after the termination of the
defendant's lease, the plaintiff
let the business to others; had*

*the plaintiff any lawful claim
on the defendant, he ought certainly to have brought it forward
at the time of the subsequent
lease.*

33. εἰπεῖν...λέγειν] Almost
identical in meaning and used, as
often, for variety of expression.
Phil. II § 11, ταῦθ᾽ ἃ πάντες μὲν
ἀεὶ γλίχονται λέγειν, ἀξίως δ᾽ οὐδεὶς εἰπεῖν δεδύνηται. Isocr. ad
Dem. § 41 and Paneg. § 11 n.

πλάσμα κ. σκευώρημα ὅλον] 'A
figment and a forgery from beginning to end.' Hesych. σκευώ-
ρημα· πλάσμα, κακουργία, κατασκευή, τὸ γινόμενον κατασκεύασμα
εἰς βλάβην, and id. σκευωρία·
κατασκευή. Pollux x 15 τάχα δ᾽
ἀπὸ τούτων (sc. σκευῶν) καὶ ἡ
σκευοποιία καὶ ἡ σκευωρία καὶ τὸ
ἐσκευοποιημένον πρᾶγμα, ὡς Ἰ-
σαῖος ἐν τῷ περὶ τοῦ Ἀρχεπόλιδος
κλήρου· διαθηκῶν δὲ τεττάρων ὑπ᾽
αὐτῶν ἐσκευοποιημένων.

In Or. 45 § 42 Apollodorus himself, in criticising the διαθήκη,
concludes with the words πάντα
πεπλασμένα καὶ κατεσκευασμένα
ἐλέγχεται. Cf. ib. 29 πλάσμα
ὅλον ἐστὶν ἡ διαθήκη, and 41 § 24
σκευώρημα.

τὸν πρὸ τοῦ χρόνον] 'During

χρόνον καὶ οὐχὶ δικάζεσθαι, ὅτι μίσθωσιν ἤθελεν
αὑτῷ φέρειν Φορμίων πολλὴν καὶ ὑπισχνεῖτο οἴσειν·
ἐπεὶ δ' οὐ ποιεῖ ταῦτα, τηνικαῦτα, φησὶ, δικάζομαι.
34 ὅτι δὲ ταῦτ' ἀμφότερ', ἐὰν λέγῃ, ψεύσεται καὶ τοῖς ὑφ'
ἑαυτοῦ πεπραγμένοις ἐναντία ἐρεῖ, σκοπεῖτε ἐκ τωνδί.
ὅταν μὲν τοίνυν τὴν διαθήκην ἀρνῆται, ἐκ τίνος τρόπου
πρεσβεῖα λαβὼν τὴν συνοικίαν κατὰ τὴν διαθήκην
ἔχει, τοῦτ' ἐρωτᾶτ'[m] αὐτόν. οὐ γὰρ ἐκεῖνό γ' ἐρεῖ,
ὡς ὅσα μὲν[n] πλεονεκτεῖν τόγδ' ἔγραψεν ὁ πατὴρ, κύριά
35 ἐστι τῆς διαθήκης, τὰ δ' ἄλλα ἄκυρα. ὅταν δ' ὑπὸ τῶν
τοῦδε ὑποσχέσεων ὑπάγεσθαι φῇ, μέμνησθ' ὅτι μάρτυρας ὑμῖν παρεσχήμεθα, οἳ χρόνον πολὺν τοῦδ' ἀπηλ-

[m] ἐρωτᾶτε Z.

[n] ὡς ἃ μὲν Huettner (ωσαμὲν Σ prima manu); ὅσα μὲν Voemel.

the former period.' πρὸ τοῦ sometimes spelt as one word προτοῦ.

οὐχὶ δικάζεσθαι] See Shilleto
on Thuc. 1 p. 153.

μίσθωσιν φέρειν] We have
frequently had μίσθωσιν in the
sense of 'lease'; we here find it
used like μίσθωμα for 'rent'
(§§ 36, 51). Or. 28 § 12 ἀποδέ-
δωκε τὴν μίσθωσιν followed by
λαβὼν τὴν πρόσοδον.

34. πρεσβεῖα] By right of
primogeniture (39 § 29). Pollux: πρεσβεῖά ἐστι γέρα τὰ τοῖς
πρεσβυτέροις δεδομένα. The recognition of any such right
seems quite exceptional in Attic
law. See Hermann's *Rechtsalt.*
p. 54 Thalheim.

τὴν συνοικίαν] "It should be
observed that the Attic language
distinguishes between dwelling-
houses (οἰκίαι) and lodging-
houses (συνοικίαι); accidentally
indeed a dwelling-house might
be let out for lodgings, and a
lodging-house have been in-
habited by the proprietor himself" (Boeckh, *Publ. Econ.* 1 90).

Apoll. may have already had a
household of his own and his
father may therefore have assigned him a συνοικία. (A.
Schaefer *Dem. u. s. Zeit*, 111 2,
133.) Cf. § 6 ἐπὶ συνοικίαις, n.

35. ὑποσχέσεων] He will tell
you, perhaps, that Phormion promised to pay a good rent (ὑπισχνεῖτο § 33), and so for a long
time he withheld further action.

χρόνον πολὺν] 'For a long
time' (ten years as appears by
§ 37), acc. of duration of time,
to be taken with μισθωταὶ ἐγίγνοντο. Kennedy seems to be
mistaken in taking it with τοῦδ'
ἀπηλλαγμένου and translating
'who, *long after* the defendant's
retirement, took a lease.' On
the contrary, the new lease must
have been granted *not long
after* the defendant's connexion
with the business ended, as
eighteen years elapsed from the
division of the property to the
date of the speech, and the first
eight belong to Phormion's lease
and the last ten to the later

λαγμένου μισθωταὶ τούτοις ἐγίγνοντο τῆς τραπέζης
καὶ τοῦ ἀσπιδοπηγείου. καίτοι τόθ᾽, ὁπηνίκα ἐμίσθωσεν ἐκείνοις, τῷδ᾽ ἐγκαλεῖν παραχρῆμα ἐχρῆν, εἴπερ
ἀληθῆ ἦν ὑπὲρ ὧν τότ᾽ ἀφεὶς νῦν τούτῳ δικάζεται. ὡς
τοίνυν° ἀληθῆ λέγω, καὶ πρεσβεῖά τέ τὴν συνοικίαν
ἔλαβε κατὰ τὴν διαθήκην καὶ τῷδε οὐχ ὅπως ἐγκαλεῖν ᾤετο δεῖν, ἀλλ᾽ ἐπῄνει, λαβὲ τὴν μαρτυρίαν.

ΜΑΡΤΥΡΙΑ.

"Ινα τοίνυν εἰδῆτε, ὦ ἄνδρες 'Αθηναῖοι, ὅσα χρήματ᾽ 36
ἔχων ἐκ τῶν μισθώσεων καὶ ἐκ τῶν χρεῶν ὡς ἀπορῶν καὶ πάντα ἀπολωλεκὼς ὀδυρεῖται[ᵖ], βραχέα ἡμῶν
956 ἀκούσατε. οὗτος γὰρ ἐκ μὲν τῶν χρεῶν ὁμοῦ τάλαντ᾽
εἴκοσιν εἰσπέπρακται ἐκ τῶν γραμμάτων ὧν ὁ πατὴρ
κατέλιπεν[q], καὶ τούτων ἔχει πλέον[ʳ] ἢ τὰ ἡμίση· πολ-

° Σ. τοίνυν ταῦτ᾽ Ζ.
ᵖ Bekk. ὀδύρεται Ζ et Bekker st. cum ΦΣΦ.
q Bekk. κατελείπεν Ζ cum Σ.
ʳ πλέον Bekk. πλεῖον Ζ cum Σ. πλείω ΦΦ.

lease of Xenon, &c (cf. §§ 37, 19,
12). The general sense is this:
We have proved that, after
Phormion had given up the
bank, others became and long
remained lessees (§ 13) of it.
Apollodorus ought, the moment
they took it, to have looked
after his dues, and seen that all
his money was in the business.
But he made no claim at all, nay
even thanked Phormion for his
good services in the management.

§§ 36—42. *The plaintiff will
complain that he is utterly destitute and ruined. You must know
then that, from the debts due to
his father and the rents due to
himself, he has received more
than forty talents.*

Oh, but he has lavishly spent
*his money in the public service
on trierarchal and choragic
charges! On the contrary, all
that he gave on his own account
after the property was divided,
barely amounted to twenty minae.
Even assuming his boasted liber-
ality to be true, that is no reason
for giving the defendant's property to the plaintiff, and thus
reducing the former to poverty,
while we see the latter squander-
ing his money in his customary
manner.*

36. μισθώσεων] 'Rents.' Cf.
§ 33 μίσθωσιν φέρειν, n.

ὀδυρεῖται] 21 § 186 ὀδυρεῖται
καὶ πολλοὺς λόγους καὶ ταπεινοὺς
ἐρεῖ.

εἰσπέπρακται ἐκ τ. γραμ.] § 21
ἐκ ποίων γραμμάτων, n.

37 λῶν γὰρ τὰ μέρη τὸν ἀδελφὸν ἀπεστέρει[s]. ἐκ δὲ τῶν
μισθώσεων, ὀκτὼ μὲν ἐτῶν ἃ Φορμίων εἶχε τὴν τράπεζαν, ὀγδοήκοντα μνᾶς τοῦ ἐνιαυτοῦ ἑκάστου, τὸ ἥμισυ
τῆς ὅλης μισθώσεως· καὶ ταῦτ'[t] ἐστι δέκα τάλαντα καὶ
τετταράκοντα μναῖ· δέκα δ' ἐτῶν μετὰ ταῦτα, ὧν ἐμίσθωσαν ὕστερον Ξένωνι καὶ Εὐφραίῳ καὶ Εὔφρονι καὶ
38 Καλλιστράτῳ, τάλαντον[u] τοῦ ἐνιαυτοῦ ἑκάστου. χωρὶς δὲ τούτων, ἐτῶν ἴσως εἴκοσι τῆς ἐξ ἀρχῆς νεμηθεί-

[s] Z et Dindf. et Voemel cum Σ.   ἀποστερεῖ Bekk.   ἀποστερῶν
A[1]r omisso γὰρ.   [t] ταῦτα Z.

[u] καὶ δισχιλίας sine causa addidit Voemel.

ἀπεστέρει.] 'Was continually defrauding' his brother of his shares in many of the debts.

37. τὴν τράπεζαν] The bank alone is mentioned, but it must not be forgotten that Phormion had a lease of the shield-manufactory as well.

ὀγδοήκοντα μνᾶς] The share of Apollodorus, eighty minae, is half the annual rent of the whole business, the shield-manufactory and the bank. Consistently with this, the whole rent, as stated in § 51, Or. 45 § 32, is 2 talents and 40^m (i.e. 160^m) per annum. Of this (as appears from § 11) one talent was paid for the shield-manufactory, and one talent and 40^m for the bank.

Εὐφραίῳ] In Or. 49 πρὸς Τιμόθεον § 44, Phormion and Euphraeus are mentioned by Apollodorus, as having paid from Pasion's bank certain sums of money to persons named by Timotheus. Like Phormion, Euphraeus had risen from a subordinate position, to be one of the lessees of the bank. Cf § 14 ἐλευθέρους ἀφεῖσαν, n.

τάλαντον] This is the rent of the shield-manufactory alone,

as appears from § 11 τὸ (ἀσπιδο-πηγεῖον) τάλαντον ἔφερεν. It is this rent alone that is here referred to. Xenon and his partners paid a total sum of 2^t 40^m for the whole business, consisting of the manufactory and the bank. The rent of the manufactory (1^t) belonged to Apollodorus, that of the bank to Pasicles (1^t 40^m). The rent thus paid *for the whole business* was the same as that which had been paid by Phormion (τοῦ ἴσου ἀργυρίου, § 12). It is from not understanding this, that Voemel was led to conjecture τάλαντον καὶ δισχιλίας, i. e. 1^t 20^m = 80^m = the sum paid by Phormion to Apollodorus. But it was only the *total* rent that was the same in both cases; the way in which it was divided between the brothers was different.

38. ἐτῶν ἴσως εἴκοσι] In § 19 the interval is more strictly stated at eighteen years. It has been suggested by Mr A. Wright that it is here put at 'nearly 20' to help the audience to follow the arithmetic. If so, the item ἐνείματο will become 10^t, though it is really less; and the half of the item εἰσεπράξατο may be put

σης οὐσίας, ἧς αὐτὸς ἐπεμελεῖτο, τὰς προσόδους, πλέον
ἢ μνᾶς τριάκοντα.   ἐὰν δ' ἅπαντα συνθῆτε, ὅσα ἐνείματο, ὅσα εἰσεπράξατο, ὅσ' εἴληφε μίσθωσιν, πλέον
ἢ τετταράκοντα τάλαντα εἰληφὼς φανήσεται, χωρὶς
ὧν οὗτος εὖ πεποίηκε, καὶ τῶν μητρῴων, καὶ ὧν ἀπὸ
τῆς τραπέζης ἔχων οὐκ ἀποδίδωσι πένθ' ἡμιταλάντων
καὶ ἑξακοσίων δραχμῶν.   ἀλλὰ νὴ Δία ταῦθ' ἡ πόλις 39
εἴληφε, καὶ δεινὰ πέπονθας πολλὰ καταλελειτουργη-

at 10^t, though it is really more.
But the total would remain the
same.

τῆς ἐξ ἀρχῆς κ.τ.λ.]   See § 11.
Apollodorus had chosen the
shield-manufactory; and the
rents of it, under his own management, are now reckoned as
part of his general income.

πλέον ἢ τετταράκοντα τάλαντα]

ἐνείματο more than 30^m
   for eighteen years =
   more than 540^m =
   more than   9^t
εἰσεπράξατο 20^t; ἔχει
   πλέον ἢ τὰ ἡμίση or
   more than 10^t, say 11
εἴληφε μίσθωσιν from
   Phormion for the
   bank and manufac-
   tory 80^m for eight
   years   = 10   40^m
               from
   Xenon, &c., for the
   manufactory alone,
   1^t for ten years = 10
                ———
   Total more than 40^t 40^m

ὧν οὗτος εὖ πεπ.]   Referring
probably to Phormion's free gift
of 3000 dr. (§ 15).—τῶν μητρῴων, a fourth part of his mother's
property (§ 32).   Otherwise we
must understand it of an occasional *bonus* for the good-will
of the bank: and to this ἐπῄνει
might refer in § 35.

πένθ' ἡμιταλάντων]   Two and
a-half talents, not four and
a-half as Jerome Wolf and Kennedy translate it (which would
require πέμπτου ἡμιταλάντου).
The plaintiff's unpaid debt of
156^m is with a bitter emphasis
mentioned last in the list of his
resources.

39.   ἀλλὰ νὴ Δία]   Introducing a supposed rejoinder on the
opposite side.   'Oh! but he will
say, All this wealth has been
received, in fact, not by him,
but by the city.'   Cf. Or. 54 §
34 n.

καταλελειτουργηκώς] You make
out that you are cruelly wronged,
after having *lavishly spent*, (as
it were) 'liturgised away,' your
money in the public service.
For this use of κατα- cf. Isaeus
Or. 5 § 43 οὔτε γὰρ εἰς τὴν πόλιν
οὔτε εἰς τοὺς φίλους φανερὸς εἶ
δαπανηθεὶς οὐδέν.   ἀλλὰ μὴν οὐδὲ καθιπποτρόφηκας, οὐ γὰρ πώποτε ἐκτήσω ἵππον πλείονος ἄξιον
ἢ τριῶν μνῶν· οὔτε κατεζευγο-
τρόφηκας, ἐπεὶ οὐδὲ ζεῦγος ἐκτήσω ὁρικὸν οὐδεπώποτε ἐπὶ τοσούτοις ἀγροῖς καὶ κτήμασιν.

[So καταχαρίζεσθαι, 'to give
away in presents,' καταχρῆσθαι,
καταπροδοῦναι, καταδωροδοκεῖν,
καταπολιτεύεσθαι, καθυποκρίνεσ-
θαί τινα, De Fals. Leg. §§ 362,
389.   P.]

κώς. ἀλλ᾽ ἃ μὲν ἐκ κοινῶν ἐλειτούργεις τῶν χρημάτων,
σὺ καὶ ὁ ἀδελφὸς ἀνηλώσατε· ἃ δ᾽ ὕστερον, οὐκ ἔστιν
ἄξια μὴ ὅτι δυοῖν ταλάντοιν προσόδου, ἀλλ᾽ οὐδ᾽
εἴκοσι μνῶν. μηδὲν οὖν τὴν πόλιν αἰτιῶ, μηδ᾽ ἃ σὺ
τῶν ὄντων αἰσχρῶς καὶ κακῶς ἀνήλωκας, ὡς ἡ πόλις
40 εἴληφε, λέγε. ἵνα δ᾽ εἰδῆτε, ὦ ἄνδρες Ἀθηναῖοι, τό τε
πλῆθος τῶν χρημάτων ὧν εἴληφε, καὶ τὰς λειτουργίας ἃς λελειτούργηκεν, ἀναγνώσεται ὑμῖν καθ᾽ ἓν
ἕκαστον. λαβέ μοι᾽ τὸ βιβλίον τουτὶ καὶ τὴν 957
πρόκλησιν ταυτηνὶʷ καὶ τὰς μαρτυρίας ταυτασί.

ΒΙΒΛΙΟΝˣ. ΠΡΟΚΛΗΣΙΣ. ΜΑΡΤΥΡΙΑΙ.

41 Τοσαῦτα μὲν τοίνυν χρήματα εἰληφὼς καὶ χρέα
πολλῶν ταλάντων ἔχων, ὧν τὰ μὲν παρ᾽ ἑκόντων, τὰ
δ᾽ ἐκ τῶν δικῶν εἰσπράττει, ἃ τῆς μισθώσεως ἔξω τῆς
τραπέζης καὶ τῆς ἄλλης οὐσίας, ἣν κατέλιπε Πασίων,
ὠφείλετο ἐκείνῳ καὶ νῦν παρειλήφασιν οὗτοι, καὶ το-
σαῦτ᾽ ἀνηλωκὼς ὅσ᾽ ὑμεῖς ἠκούσατε, οὐδὲ πολλοστὸν
μέρος τῶν προσόδων, μὴ ὅτι τῶν ἀρχαίων, εἰς τὰς λει-

ᵛ Bekk. om. Z cum Σ.

ʷ Bekk. ταύτην Z et Voëmel cum Σr.　　　ˣ addidit Reiske.

ἐκ κοινῶν κ.τ.λ.] i.e. You cannot take the sole credit for the
sums spent *before* the property
was divided. Half of that expenditure came out of your
brother's money (§ 8).

ἐλειτούργεις] See *Dict. Antiq.*;
also F. A. Wolf's preface to Dem.
Leptines (Beatson's trans. p. 40
sqq.) and Boeckh's *Public Econ.*,
Book 4 §§ 10—15. Among the
λειτουργίαι were the τριηραρχία
and χορηγία referred to in § 41
fin.

μὴ ὅτι...ἀλλ᾽ οὐδ᾽] See note
on Or. 34 § 14, and cf. 27 § 7;
43 § 9; 56 § 39. (Madvig's

Gk. Syntax, § 212, and Kühner's
*Ausf. Gram. der Griechischen
Sprache*, II § 525, 4.)

δυοῖν] i.e. more than 40 for
about 20 years, § 38.

μηδὲν—αἰτιῶ] 'Don't accuse
the *state* then,' 'don't be charging the state with being the
cause and object of your lavish
expenditure.'

41. ἃ τῆς μισθ. κ.τ.λ.] The
order is ἃ (ἔξω τῆς μισθώσεως τῆς
τραπέζης κ.τ.λ.) ὠφείλετο τῷ Πασίωνι καὶ ἃ οὗτοι (sc. Apoll. and
Pasicles) παρειλήφασιν.

οὐδὲ πολλοστὸν κ.τ.λ.] 'The
smallest fraction of his income,

τουργίας, ὅμως ἀλαζονεύσεται καὶ τριηραρχίας ἐρεῖ
καὶ χορηγίας. ἐγὼ δ', ὡς μὲν οὐκ ἀληθῆ ταῦτ' ἐρεῖ, 42
ἐπέδειξα, οἶμαι^y μέντοι, κἂν εἰ ταῦτα πάντ' ἀληθῆ
λέγοι, κάλλιον εἶναι καὶ δικαιότερον τόνδε ἀπὸ τῶν
αὑτοῦ λειτουργεῖν ὑμῖν ἢ τούτῳ δόντας τὰ τούτου,
μικρὰ τῶν πάντων αὐτοὺς μετασχόντας, τόνδε μὲν ἐν
ταῖς ἐσχάταις ἐνδείαις ὁρᾶν, τοῦτον δ' ὑβρίζοντα καὶ
εἰς ἅπερ εἴωθεν ἀναλίσκοντα. ἀλλὰ μὴν περί γε τῆς 43

^y Σ.　οἴομαι Ζ (cf. § 18).

not to say (I needn't say) of his
capital.' This explains τοσαῦτ',
tantilla.

ἀλαζονεύσεται .... τριηραρχίας
ἐρεῖ] 'Will in bragging terms
talk of his trierarchal (and
choragic) expenses.' Of such
ἀλαζονεία there are instances
again and again in Dem. and
the other orators, e. g. Midias
p. 566 seqq. Or. 38 § 25 τάχα
τοίνυν ἴσως καὶ τριηραρχίας ἐροῦσι
καὶ τὰ ὄντα ὡς ἀνηλώκασιν εἰς
ὑμᾶς, 20 § 151. In Or. 45 § 85,
Apollodorus appeals to his
father's trierarchies, and in
§ 66 taunts one of Phormion's
witnesses, Stephanus, with
having never done the smallest
service to the state by τριηραρχία
or χορηγία or any other λειτουρ-
γία whatever.

The plaintiff had really some
good reason for being proud of
his trierarchal services. Among
the orations of Dem. a speech
has come down to us (Or. 50,
πρὸς Πολυκλέα) in which Apollodorus states that being appointed trierarch (in B.C. 362)
he gave his vessel a splendid
equipment and liberal wages to
the crew; and for more than
seventeen months traversed the
Hellespont and other waters,
often encountering perilous
storms, in the public service.

42. τόνδε ἀπὸ τῶν αὑτοῦ]
'That he should *continue to
serve you* from his own resources,' &c.—pointing to Phormion, who is also referred to in
τόνδε μὲν two lines further on.—
τούτῳ δόντας τὰ τούτου, i.e. hand-
ing over to the plaintiff (Ap.)
the property of the defendant
(Phormion). For a similarly
ambiguous use of demonstrative
pronouns, see above, § 12 n.

τόνδε μὲν...τοῦτον δ'] Defendant and plaintiff respectively.

εἰς ἅπερ εἴωθεν ἀναλ.] A deliberately vague innuendo, which
is partly justified by the details
of a subsequent section (§ 45).
In Or. 45 § 77, Apollodorus says
with some self-complacency: τῷ
μέτριος κατὰ πάσας τὰς εἰς
ἐμαυτὸν δαπάνας εἶναι πολὺ τούτου καὶ τοιούτων ἑτέρων εὐτακτότερον ζῶν ἂν φανείην.

§§ 43—48. *As to the de-
fendant's wealth, and his having
got it from your father's estate,
you should be the last man in
all the world to use such language. The defendant, like
your own father, made his
money by faithful and honest
service, by personal integrity of
character, and by that good
credit and fair fame which in
the commercial world is the best
kind of capital.*

εὐπορίας, ὡς ἐκ τῶν τοῦ πατρὸς τοῦ σοῦ κέκτηται, καὶ
ὧν ἐρωτήσειν ἔφησθα, πόθεν τὰ ὄντα κέκτηται Φορμίων[z], μόνῳ τῶν ὄντων ἀνθρώπων σοὶ τοῦτον οὐκ
ἔνεστ᾽[a] εἰπεῖν τὸν λόγον. οὐδὲ γὰρ Πασίων ὁ σὸς
πατὴρ ἐκτήσαθ᾽ εὑρὼν οὐδὲ τοῦ πατρὸς αὐτῷ[b] παραδόντος, ἀλλὰ παρὰ τοῖς αὐτοῦ κυρίοις Ἀντισθένει καὶ
Ἀρχεστράτῳ τραπεζιτεύουσι πεῖραν δοὺς ὅτι χρη-
44 στός ἐστι καὶ δίκαιος, ἐπιστεύθη. ἔστι δ᾽ ἐν ἐμπορίῳ

---

[z] καὶ ὧν ἐρωτήσειν—Φορμίων secludenda esse censet Huettner.

[a] Σ. ἔνεστιν Z.   [b] αὐτῷ Z.

Again, if you claim the defendant's property on the ground that he was once your father's slave, then Antimachus, a surviving son of your father's former master, might go still further, and claim your own estate and the defendant's too; yet, though now in a humble position, far below his merits and his proper rank, he does not go to law with them, because they have money to spend while he is in destitution.

Instead of making the most of the good fortune by which your father and the defendant alike received the rights of freedom and citizenship, you are heartless enough to cast contumely on yourself and your parents, and on Athens too, for granting her privileges to people like yourself; you are senseless enough to forget that, by insisting that the defendant's former servitude should not be brought up against him, we are really speaking on your side and defending your own position. The rule, that you lay down to the detriment of the defendant, can as easily be advanced against yourself by the house to which your father was once a slave.

43. ὧν = περὶ τούτων ἅ.

πόθεν—κέκτηται Φ.] In Or. 45 § 80, Apollodorus unfairly says of Phormion, εἰ ἦν δίκαιος, πένης ἂν ἦν τὰ τοῦ δεσπότου διοικήσας. ...Had I dragged you off to prison as a thief caught in the act, with your present property clapped upon your back, ...and had I, supposing you denied the theft, demanded the name of the person from whom you received it, to whose name would you have appealed? οὔτε γάρ σοι πατὴρ παρέδωκεν, οὔθ᾽ εὖρες.

ἐκτήσαθ᾽ εὑρὼν] 'Got it *by good luck*' as a 'godsend,' a 'windfall,' a εὕρημα or Ἑρμαῖον. Passages like the present and the parallel from Or. 45 § 81 (given above) should be quoted in Liddell and Scott s. v. εὑρίσκω, 4).

Ἀρχεστράτῳ] Isocr. Trapez. § 43, Πασίων δὲ Ἀρχέστρατόν μοι ἀπὸ τῆς τραπέζης ἑπτὰ ταλάντων ἐγγυητὴν παρέσχεν. (A. Schaefer *Dem. u. s. Zeit* III 2, 131.)

δίκαιος] 'Honest.'

ἐπιστεύθη] 'Won his master's confidence,' 'was trusted.' So in Or. 50 § 56, Apollodorus describes the wide extent of his

καὶ χρήμασιν ἐργαζομένοις ἀνθρώποις φιλεργὸν δόξαι
καὶ χρηστὸν εἶναι τὸν αὐτὸν θαυμαστὸν ἡλίκον. οὔτ᾽
οὖν ἐκείνῳ τοῦθ᾽ οἱ κύριοι παρέδωκαν, ἀλλ᾽ αὐτὸς ἔφυ
958 χρηστός, οὔτε τῷδε ὁ σὸς πατήρ· σὲ γὰρ ἂν πρότερον
τοῦδε χρηστὸν ἐποίησεν, εἰ ἦν ἐπ᾽ ἐκείνῳ. εἰ δὲ τοῦτο
ἀγνοεῖς, ὅτι πίστις ἀφορμὴ πασῶν ἐστι μεγίστη πρὸς
χρηματισμόν, πᾶν ἂν ἀγνοήσειας. χωρὶς δὲ τούτων

father's connexion and good credit (ἐπεξενῶσθαι πολλοῖς καὶ πιστευθῆναι ἐν τῇ Ἑλλάδι).

44. ἐν ἐμπορίῳ καὶ χρήμασιν ἐργαζομένοις] Kennedy: 'In the commercial world and the money-market it is thought a wonderful thing, when the same person shows himself to be both honest and diligent.' The order is: θαυμαστὸν ἡλίκον ἐστὶν ἀνθρώποις ἐργαζομένοις ἐν ἐμπορίῳ καὶ (ἐργαζομένοις) χρήμασι, τὸν αὐτὸν δόξαι φιλεργὸν καὶ εἶναι χρηστὸν, i.e. a reputation for business-like habits and a really honest character, when combined in the same person, have a striking influence in the money-market and the commercial world.

ἐν should be taken with ἐμπορίῳ only, the construction being (as G. H. Schaefer notices) ἐργάζεσθαι ἐν ἐμπορίῳ with the preposition, and ἐργάζεσθαι χρήμασιν without. Cf. Or. 57 § 31 ἐν τῇ ἀγορᾷ ἐργάζεσθαι with Or. 33 § 4, where τῆς ἐργασίας τῆς κατὰ θάλατταν is followed by τούτοις (sc. τοῖς χρήμασι) πειρῶμαι ναυτικοῖς ἐργάζεσθαι. [ἐν ἐμπορίῳ may also be taken by itself, 'the mart it is thought a great matter,' &c. P.]

δόξαι is slightly contrasted with εἶναι, the outward reputation for business habits with the inward and inherent honesty

(cf. ἔφυ χρηστός below). G. H. Schaefer says, 'dativus regitur a verbo δόξαι. Deinde τὸ ἑξῆς est: τὸν αὐτὸν δόξαι εἶναι φιλεργὸν καὶ χρηστόν.' But the position of δόξαι and εἶναι makes against this construction. Cf. Aesch. Theb. 592, οὐ γὰρ δοκεῖν ἄριστος ἀλλ᾽ εἶναι θέλει.

It is the *combination* of δόξαι φιλεργὸν and εἶναι χρηστὸν that is insisted on, because a forger, for instance, might have all the air of a painstaking man of business without being really χρηστός: and *vice versa*, a man of unblemished *morale* might never get a name for financial skill, or even ordinary business-like habits.

οὔτε—οὔτε] 'As then his masters did not bequeath to Pasion this virtue, but his honesty was natural, so neither did Pasion bequeath it to Phormion; for he would have made *you* honest rather than him, had it been in his power.' The philosophic questions, εἰ διδακτὸς ἀρετή, and τὸ φύσει ἄπαν κράτιστον, are perhaps held in view, though it is seldom that Demosthenes enters on the region of philosophy. P.]

πίστις ἀφορμή] 'If you don't know that for money-making the best capital of all is good credit; then, what *do* you know?'

ἀφορμή] Cf. § 12 n.

χωρὶς...πατρί] An accidental

πολλὰ καὶ τῷ σῷ πατρὶ καὶ σοὶ καὶ ὅλως τοῖς ὑμετέροις πράγμασι Φορμίων γέγονε χρήσιμος. ἀλλ᾿, οἶμαι,
τῆς σῆς ἀπληστίας καὶ τοῦ σοῦ τρόπου τίς ἂν δύναιτο
45 ἐφικέσθαι; καὶ δῆτα θαυμάζω πῶς οὐ λογίζει[c] πρὸς
σεαυτὸν[d] ὅτι ἔστιν Ἀρχεστράτῳ τῷ ποτὲ τὸν σὸν
πατέρα κτησαμένῳ υἱὸς ἐνθάδε, Ἀντίμαχος, πράττων
οὐ κατ᾿ ἀξίαν, ὃς οὐ δικάζεταί σοι οὐδὲ δεινά φησι
πάσχειν, εἰ σὺ μὲν χλανίδα φορεῖς, καὶ τὴν μὲν λέλυσαι, τὴν δ᾿ ἐκδέδωκας ἑταίραν, καὶ ταῦτα γυναῖκ᾿ ἔχων
ποιεῖς, καὶ τρεῖς παῖδας ἀκολούθους περιάγεις[e], καὶ ζῇς

[c] λογίζῃ Z cum Σ.
[d] Bekk. ἑαυτὸν Z cum Σ (cf. Isocr. ad Dem. § 14 n.).
[e] περιάγει Cobet, infra.

iambic line. See Isocr. Paneg.
§ 170 n.—On ὑμετέροις, cf. § 30 fin.
  ὅλως] 'Generally.'
  ἀλλ᾿, οἶμαι...τίς ἂν δύναιτο ;]
Questions of this kind are often
best rendered by a negative
sentence. 'But no one, I feel,
can come up to your covetousness and your general character.' 'Your covetousness &c,
no language, I take it, can ade-
quately describe.' ἐφικέσθαι, sc.
τῷ λόγῳ. Or. 14 § 1, ὧν οὐδ᾿ ἂν
εἷς ἀξίως ἐφικέσθαι τῷ λόγῳ δύναιτο. For the genitive, cf.
Isocr. 4 § 187; 9 § 49; 10 § 13.
  45. χλανίδα] 'A mantle,' a light
upper garment of fine wool.
Aeschin. Timarch. § 131, τὰ
κομψὰ ταῦτα χλανίσκια ...... καὶ
τοὺς μαλακοὺς χιτωνίσκους. Dem.
Or. 21 § 133 (of Midias), χλανί-
δας καὶ κυμβία καὶ κάδους ἔχων.
Pollux vii 48: χλανὶς δὲ ἱμάτιον
λεπτόν. K. F. Hermann, Privatalt. § 21 p. 177 ed. Blümner.
  λέλυσαι] 'Redeemed' from her
owner. Herod. ii 135 (of Rho-
dôpis), ἀπικομένη κατ᾿ ἐργασίαν
ἐλύθη χρημάτων μεγάλων ὑπ᾿
ἀνδρὸς Μυτιληναίου. Ar. Vesp.

1353, ἐγώ σε...λυσάμενος ἔξω
παλλακήν. Dem. Or. 48 § 53,
ἑταίραν λυσάμενος ἔνδον ἔχει. [It
may be remarked that Demosthenes is particularly fond of
using perfect passives in the
medial sense. P.]
  ἐκδέδωκας] Given away in
marriage. Or. 59, κατὰ Νεαίρας,
§ 73, (ἡ ἄνθρωπος) ἐξεδόθη τῷ
Διονύσῳ γυνὴ, and Or. 27 § 69,
θυγατέρας παρὰ σφῶν αὐτῶν ἐκ-
δόντας.
  καὶ ταῦτα γυναῖκ᾿ ἔχων......]
'And that too, when you have
a wife.' In his speech πρὸς
Πολυκλέα, Apollodorus, contrary
to what might be expected
from the present passage, speaks
in affectionate terms of his
wife. Or. 50 § 61, ἡ γυνὴ ἣν ἐγὼ
περὶ πλείστου ποιοῦμαι ἀσθενῶς
διέκειτο πολὺν χρόνον.
  παῖδας ἀκολούθους] Or. 21
(Midias) § 158, τρεῖς ἀκολούθους
ἢ τέτταρας αὐτὸς ἄγων διὰ τῆς
ἀγορᾶς σοβεῖ. Xen. Mem. i 7
§ 2, σκεύη τε καλὰ κέκτηνται καὶ
ἀκολούθους πολλοὺς περιάγονται.
(Becker, Charicles iii 21, ed. 2
= p. 362 of Eng. ed.)

ἀσελγῶς[f] ὥστε καὶ τοὺς ἀπαντῶντας αἰσθάνεσθαι,
αὐτὸς δ' ἐκεῖνος πολλῶν ἐνδεής ἐστιν. οὐδὲ τὸν Φορ- 46
μίων' ἐκεῖνος οὐχ ὁρᾷ.   καίτοι εἰ κατὰ τοῦτ' οἴει σοι
προσήκειν τῶν τούτου, ὅτι τοῦ πατρός ποτ' ἐγένετο
τοῦ σοῦ, ἐκείνῳ προσήκει μᾶλλον ἢ σοί· ὁ γὰρ αὖ σὸς
πατὴρ ἐκείνων ἐγένετο. ὥστε καὶ σὺ καὶ οὗτος ἐκείνου
γίγνεσθε ἐκ τούτου τοῦ λόγου.   σὺ δ' εἰς τοῦθ' ἥκεις
ἀγνωμοσύνης ὥσθ' ἃ προσήκει σοι τοὺς λέγοντας
ἐχθροὺς νομίζειν, ταῦτ' αὐτὸς ποιεῖς ἀνάγκην εἶναι
λέγειν, καὶ ὑβρίζεις μὲν σαυτὸν καὶ τοὺς γονέας τεθ- 47
νεῶτας, προπηλακίζεις δὲ τὴν πόλιν, καὶ ἃ διὰ[g] τῆς τούτων φιλανθρωπίας ἀπολαύσας εὕρετο ὁ σὸς πατὴρ καὶ
μετὰ ταῦτα Φορμίων οὑτοσὶ, ταῦτα ἀντὶ τοῦ κοσμεῖν

[f] Σ.   +οὕτως Ζ.

[g] Ζ et Dindf. cum Σ.   διὰ om. Bekk. et Voemel; 'διὰ ab inter-
prete aliquo ad verbi (ἀπολαύσας) vim explanandam adscriptum est,'
Huettner.

περιάγεις] Cobet, after quoting the above passage of Xenophon (to alter σκεύη καλὰ into
σκευὴν καλὴν), takes the hint
suggested by the last word
περιάγονται, to propose the middle for the active in the present
passage. 'Reponendum est ne-
cessario περιάγει. Discrimen
inter περιάγω et περιάγομαι tam
perspicuum est quam perpetu-
um. Si quem *circumductamus*
spectaturum aliquid, aut omnino
si cui damus operam ut circum-
iens inspiciat aliquid aut
agat, cum περιάγειν dicimur;
sin autem quis quaqua incedit
secum trahit aliquem, cuius
opera officioque utatur, eum
περιάγεσθαι dicitur, ut herus
pedissequos, aut tyrannus satel-
lites.' (*Novae lectiones*, p. 652.)
46. οὐδὲ τὸν Φορμίωνα] 'Nor is
Phormio's position unknown
to him.' Kennedy. For the
double negation, see on § 22.
Though Phormion was once the
slave of one who was himself
a slave of the father of Antimachus, the latter, who is well
aware how Phormion has risen,
does not grudge him his suc-
cess and does not hold himself
aggrieved by him. ὁρᾷ, § 50 and
23 § 100 ἤδη δέ τινα εἶδον.
—ἐκείνῳ, to Antimachus.
ἀγνωμοσύνης] 'Heartlessness,'
'want of proper feeling';
'churlishness.' Or. 54 § 14,
ἀγνώμονας καὶ πικρούς. Or. 14
§ 5; 18 §§ 207, 252; 60 § 20.
[The polite Greeks had many
terms of this kind, ἀγροικία,
σκαιότης, ἀμαθία, ἀπαιδευσία, ἀ-
πειροκαλία. P.]
47. ὑβρίζεις ... προπηλακίζεις]
Or. 23 § 120, ὧν ὕβρισε καὶ
προὐπηλάκισεν, 9, § 60; 18 § 12.
κοσμεῖν καὶ περιστέλλειν] 'Adorn-
ing and cherishing' the right

καὶ περιστέλλειν, ἵνα καὶ τοῖς δοῦσιν ὡς εὐσχη- 959
μονέστατα ἐφαίνετο καὶ τοῖς λαβοῦσιν ὑμῖν, ἄγεις εἰς
μέσον, δεικνύεις, ἐλέγχεις, μόνον οὐκ ὀνειδίζεις οἷον
48 ὄντα σε ἐποιήσαντο Ἀθηναῖοι. εἶτ' εἰς τοῦθ' ἥκεις
μανίας (τί γὰρ ἂν ἄλλο τις εἴποι;) ὥστ' οὐκ αἰσθάνει[h]
ὅτι καὶ νῦν ἡμεῖς μὲν ἀξιοῦντες, ἐπειδήπερ ἀπηλλάγη
Φορμίων, μηδέν' ὑπόλογον εἶναι εἴ ποτε τοῦ σοῦ
πατρὸς ἐγένετο, ὑπὲρ σοῦ λέγομεν, σὺ δὲ μηδέποτ'
ἐξ ἴσου σοι γενέσθαι τοῦτον ἀξιῶν κατὰ σαυτοῦ λέ-
γεις· ἃ γὰρ ἂν σὺ δίκαια σαυτῷ κατὰ τούτου τάξῃς,
ταὐτὰ[i] ταῦθ' ἥξει κατὰ σοῦ παρὰ τῶν τὸν σὸν πατέρα
ἐξ ἀρχῆς κτησαμένων.   ἀλλὰ μὴν ὅτι κἀκεῖνος ἦν
τινῶν, εἶτ' ἀπηλλάγη τὸν αὐτὸν τρόπον ὅνπερ οὗτος
ἀφ' ὑμῶν, λαβέ μοι ταυτασὶ τὰς μαρτυρίας, [j]ὡς ἐγένετο Πασίων Ἀρχεστράτου[j].

[h] Σ. αἰσθάνῃ Ζ.   [i] Σ. τὰ αὐτὰ Ζ.
[j-j] 'verba interpolata,' Huettner.

of citizenship. [A metaphor
from putting on and gracefully
adjusting clothes. Whence he
adds εὐσχημονέστατα. P.]

ἵνα—ἐφαίνετο] Cf. ὅπως ἠλέγχθη, § 20. Goodwin's *Moods
and Tenses*, § 44, 3. Kühner,
§ 553, 7.

ἄγεις εἰς μέσον κ.τ.λ.] 45 § 16.
'You drag it into public view,
point (the finger of scorn) at it,
criticize it ; and all but taunt
Athens with naturalizing (admitting to the freedom of the
city) such a character as yourself.'

48. *εἰς τοῦθ' ἥκεις μανίας*] Cf. §
46, εἰς τοῦθ' ἥκεις ἀγνωμοσύνης.
Madvig *Gk. Syntax*, § 50 ad fin.
27 § 24; 33 § 19; 40 §§ 28, 49,
58; 56 § 3.

μηδέν' ὑπόλογον εἶναι] Lit.
'should not be taken into account against him,' 'should not
detract from his credit.' A metaphor from book-keeping, appropriate in a speech on banking-
stock. Lys. 28 § 13, οὐδὲ ἀδίκως
τούτοις φημὶ ἂν εἶναι ὑπόλογον
τὴν ἐκείνου φυγήν, ib. 4 § 18 ;
Plat. Lach. 189 B.

[Cf. ὁ παράλογος, ὁ κατάλογος,
ὁ μετάμελος, words formed from
a primary use of the simple
noun *governed* by the preposition. Translate: 'And now we, in
requiring that, as Phormio has
left Pasion's service, it should
not be remembered against him
that he was once Pasion's property, are in fact speaking in your
behalf ; while you, in demanding that Phormio shall not be
put on the same footing as
yourself, are speaking against
yourself.' P.]

ΜΑΡΤΥΡΙΑΙ.

Εἶτα τὸν σώσαντα μὲν ἐξ ἀρχῆς τὰ πράγματα καὶ 49
πολλὰ χρήσιμον αὐτὸν παρασχόντα τῷ πατρὶ τῷ τούτου, τοσαῦτα δ᾽ αὐτὸν τοῦτον ἀγαθὰ εἰργασμένον ὅσ᾽
ὑμεῖς ἀκηκόατε, τοῦτον οἴεται δεῖν ἑλὼν τηλικαύτην
δίκην ἀδίκως ἐκβαλεῖν[k]. οὐ γὰρ ἄλλο γ᾽ ἔχοις[l] οὐδὲν

[k] ΣτΑ¹. ἐκβάλλειν Z.   [l] Bekk. ἔχοι Z cum Σ.

§§ 49—52. *The defendant's management of the family property was the very saving of the business, and in this and many other respects he has been a great benefactor to the plaintiff's father and to the plaintiff himself; and yet the latter is now demanding a verdict, which, if granted, will turn the defendant out of house and home, a ruined bankrupt, like those whom we remember. The plaintiff's father, esteeming the defendant more highly than his own son, wisely and prudently left him manager of his leases when he died, besides showing his esteem for him during his lifetime. And that esteem was well deserved, for while the other bankers, to whose losses allusion has just been made, did business on their own account, and therefore had to pay no rent to another, and were nevertheless ruined; the defendant not only paid a rent for the bank but kept up the business for the family of the plaintiff, who, so far from being grateful, takes no account of all this, but even persecutes and calumniates him. Our friend, if for a moment we may call him so, little thinks that honesty is the best policy (as is proved by the defendant's prosperity). The plaintiff at any rate is a case in point; he has (if we are to believe him) lost all his money; had he been* a man of sound sense he would not have thrown it away.

49. ἐκβαλεῖν] In Or. 45 κατὰ Στεφάνου Α § 70, Apollodorus taunts Stephanus (one of Phormion's witnesses in the present trial) with turning his own uncle out of his patrimony for arrears of debt : τοκίζων...ἐξέβαλες ἐκ τῆς πατρῴας οὐσίας.

οὐ γὰρ ἄλλο γ᾽] i.e. If heavy damages are granted the plaintiff, the penalty will prove none other than (will not fall short of) turning the defendant out of house and home. 'Examine the nature of his property closely and you will soon see whose it really is, and into whose hands it will fall, if (which heaven forbid) the court is misled into condemning him.' The property consists largely of deposits at the bank, invested in different speculations, and incapable of being realized at a moment's notice. If Phormion has to pay damages, there will at once be a run upon his bank ; his customers, to secure their property before it is paid away in damages, will claim their deposits, and Phormion, like others before him, will be bankrupt.

ἔχοις οὐδὲν ἄν] Notice the strong affinity or attraction that ἄν has to the negative; which is the reason of the common hyperthesis οὐκ ἄν οἶμαί σε ποιεῖν,

ἂν ποιῆσαι. εἰς μὲν γὰρ τὰ ὄντα εἰ βλέπεις ἀκριβῶς,
ταῦθ᾽[m] εὑρήσεις ὧν ἔστιν, ἐὰν[n], ὃ μὴ γένοιτο, ἐξαπατη-
50 θῶσιν οὗτοι. ὁρᾷς τὸν Ἀριστόλοχον[o] τὸν Χαριδήμου;
ποτ᾽ εἶχεν ἀγρόν, εἶτά γε νῦν πολλοί· πολλοῖς γὰρ
ἐκεῖνος ὀφείλων αὐτὸν ἐκτήσατο. καὶ τὸν Σωσίνομον
καὶ τὸν Τιμόδημον καὶ τοὺς ἄλλους τραπεζίτας, οἳ,
ἐπεὶ διαλύειν ἐδέησεν οἷς ὤφειλον, ἐξέστησαν ἁπάν-
ντες τῶν τῶν ὄντων. σὺ δ᾽ οὐδὲν οἴει δεῖν σκοπεῖν οὐδ᾽ 960
ὧν ὁ πατὴρ σοῦ πολλῷ βελτίων ὢν καὶ ἄμεινον σοῦ[p]
51 φρονῶν πρὸς ἅπαντ᾽ ἐβουλεύσατο· ὃς, ὦ Ζεῦ καὶ θεοί,
τοσούτῳ τοῦτον ἡγεῖτο σοῦ πλείονος ἄξιον εἶναι καὶ
σοὶ καὶ ἑαυτῷ[q] καὶ τοῖς ὑμετέροις πράγμασιν, ὥστε
ἀνδρὸς ὄντος σοῦ τοῦτον, οὐ σὲ τῶν μισθώσεων κατέλιπεν ἐπίτροπον καὶ τὴν γυναῖκα ἔδωκε καὶ ζῶν αὐτὸν
ἐτίμα,[r] δικαίως, ὦ ἄνδρες Ἀθηναῖοι· οἱ μὲν γὰρ ἄλλοι
τραπεζῖται μίσθωσιν οὐ φέροντες, ἀλλ᾽ αὐτοὶ ἑαυτοῖς[s]

[m] Bekk. αὐτὰ Z cum ΓΣΦΒ.   [n] ΣrΑ¹. ἂν Z.
[o] Σ. Ἀρχίλοχον Z.   [p] add. ΣΑ¹. om. Z.
[q] Σ. αὐτῷ Z.   [r] ἐτίμα. Z.   [s] Σ. αὐτοῖς Z.

&c. Goodwin's *Moods and
Tenses*, § 42, 2, n., and Short's
*Order of Words in Attic Greek
Prose*, p. xciv (3) (*b*).

50. Ἀριστόλοχον] In 45 § 64
Stephanus is described as cringing to *Aristolochus the banker*
in his prosperity, and deserting
his son when in great distress
after Aristolochus was ruined
and had lost all his property.

ποτ᾽ εἶχεν ἀγρὸν κ.τ.λ.] 'He
had a farm once,'—'he owned
some land in his day; that
land has passed to many owners
now.' ποτὲ (*olim*) is seldom
found in so emphatic a position.
—πολλοί (sc. ἔχουσι τὸν ἀγρόν).

διαλύειν] sc. (τούτους) οἷς
ὤφειλον 'to settle with, to satisfy,
their creditors.' Cf. Or. 37 § 12

note; 30 § 8; 34 § 40; 49 § 29.

ἐξέστησαν] 'Had to give up,'
'were ousted from.' 45 § 64,
ἀπώλετο καὶ τῶν ὄντων ἐξέστη.
Apatur. § 25, Pantaen. 37 § 49,
Antiphon 2 β § 9, τῆς οὐσίας
ἐκστησόμενος, Ar. Acharn. 615
(K. F. Hermann *Privatalt*. § 71,
3 = *Rechtsalt*. p. 106 Thalheim).
ἐκστῆναι (like ἐκπεσεῖν) would
answer as a passive to ἐκβαλεῖν.
The special word for becoming
bankrupt is ἀνασκευάζεσθαι (contrasted with κατασκευάζεσθαι to
establish a bank); Dem. Apatur.
33 § 9, τῆς τραπέζης ἀνασκευα-
σθείσης. Or. 49 § 68, τοῖς ἀνε-
σκευασμένοις τῶν τραπεζιτῶν. Cf.
infra § 57, ἀνατρέψαι, n.

51. ἑαυτοῖς ἐργ. πάντες ἀπώ-
λοντο] This frequent failure of

ἐργαζόμενοι πάντες ἀπώλοντο, οὗτος δὲ μίσθωσιν φέρων δύο τάλαντα καὶ τετταράκοντα μνᾶς ὑμῖν ἔσωσε
τὴν τράπεζαν. ὧν ἐκεῖνος μὲν χάριν εἶχε, σὺ δ' οὐδένα 52
ποιεῖ λόγον, ἀλλ' ἐναντία τῇ διαθήκῃ καὶ ταῖς ἀπ'
ἐκείνης‌ᵗ ἀραῖς γραφείσαις ὑπὸ τοῦ σοῦ‌ᵘ πατρὸς ἐλαύνεις, συκοφαντεῖς, διώκεις‌ᵛ. ὦ βέλτιστε, εἰ οἷόν τε
σὲ τοῦτ' εἰπεῖν, οὐ παύσει‌ʷ, καὶ γνώσει‌ˣ τοῦθ', ὅτι
πολλῶν χρημάτων τὸ χρηστὸν εἶναι λυσιτελέστερόν
ἐστι; σοὶ γοῦν, εἴπερ ἀληθῆ λέγεις, χρήματα μὲν
τοσαῦτ' εἰληφότι πάντ' ἀπόλωλεν, ὡς φῄς‌ʸ· εἰ δ'
ἦσθα ἐπιεικής, οὐκ ἄν ποτε αὐτὰ ἀνήλωσας.

ᵗ ἐπ' ἐκείνης conicit *Huettner, exsecrationes istas extra testamentum inscriptas esse arbitratus.*

ᵘ add. ΣrA¹. om. Z.

ᵛ Z *et Dindf. et Voemel cum* ΣrA¹. διώκεις, συκοφαντεῖς Bekk.

ʷ παύσῃ Z.   ˣ γνώσῃ Z.

ʸ φῄς *rectius scribi docuit Cobet ad Hyper. or. ed. ii p.* 108
(Hüettner).

bankers on their own account, if truly stated, seems remarkable.

δύο τάλ. κ.τ.λ.] As rent for the bank *and the manufactory.* Cf. §§ 11, 37; 45 § 32.

52. ταῖς ἀραῖς] Solemn imprecations on those who violated the conditions of the will.

ἐλαύνεις, συκοφαντεῖς, διώκεις] ' Harass, calumniate, prosecute.' διώκεις comes rather feebly after the stronger word συκοφαντεῖς, and in spite of the authority of the Paris ꜱꜱ there is much to be said for the old order retained by Bekker: ἐλαύνεις, διώκεις, συκοφαντεῖς. The latter is to some extent confirmed by the Rhetorician Tiberius (περὶ σχημά-των, c. 31), who refers to this passage as an instance of a figure of speech described by another Rhetorician (Alexander, περὶ σχημάτων, c. 10) as ἐπὶ πλεῖον ἐπὶ τοῦ αὐτοῦ νοήματος ἐπιμονὴ μετὰ αὐξήσεως. His words are: ἐπιμονὴ δέ ἐστιν ὅταν τις πλείω ῥήματα ὀρθὰ ἀλλήλοις ἐπιβάλλῃ, ὡς ἐν τῷ ὑπὲρ Φορμίω-νος πρὸς τὸν Ἀπολλόδωρον, ἄγεις (sic), ἐλαύνεις, διώκεις, συκο-φαντεῖς. δείνωσιν τὸ σχῆμα ἔχει.

οὐ παύσει κ.τ.λ.] ' *Do* stop, and make up your mind to this truth, that being honourable pays a man better than being very wealthy.'

πολλῶν χρημάτων τὸ χρηστὸν λυσ.] Honesty is the best policy. The collocation of the cognate words χρήματα and χρηστός may be only accidental.

σοὶ γοῦν] ' In *your* case, at any rate.' From this primary sense γοῦν often takes the secondary meaning ' for instance.'

53   Ἀλλ' ἔγωγε μὰ τὸν Δία καὶ θεοὺς πανταχῆ σκο-
πῶν οὐδὲν ὁρῶ, διότι* ἂν σοὶ πεισθέντες τουδὶ κατα-
ψηφίσαιντο. τί γάρ; ὅτι πλησίον ὄντων τῶν ἀδικημάτων ἐγκαλεῖς; ἀλλ' ἔτεσι καὶ χρόνοις ὕστερον αἰτιᾷ.
ἀλλ' ὅτι τοῦτον ἀπράγμων ἦσθα τὸν χρόνον; ἀλλὰ τίς

* Bekk.   διὰ τί Z et Voemel (διατὶ ΣrA¹).

§§ 53—57. *But though (for
sake of argument) the speaker
has pointed out the results which
would ensue, if the defendant
were condemned, he protests that
he can see no ground for such
condemnation. Plaintiff brings
forward his charge ever so many
years after the alleged offence,
and meanwhile has found time
for incessant litigation, especially
in public causes where his personal interests were but partially
affected. While prosecuting so
many others, how came he to let
Phormion alone? The presumption is that the plaintiff was
never really wronged by him, and
that the claim now put in, so
long after the event, is utterly
false and groundless.*

*To meet these charges, it will
be much to the purpose to produce
evidence of the bad character of
the plaintiff, and also of the integrity and kindly feeling, the
generosity and the public services
of the defendant.*

53.   ἀλλ'...ἀλλ'...ἀλλά] For
this use of ἀλλά cf. Dem. 18 § 24,
τί γὰρ καὶ βουλόμενοι μετεπέμπεσθ'
ἂν αὐτοὺς ἐν τοσούτῳ τῷ καιρῷ;
ἐπὶ τὴν εἰρήνην; ἀλλ' ὑπῆρχεν
ἅπασιν. ἀλλ' ἐπὶ τὸν πόλεμον;
ἀλλ' αὐτοὶ περὶ εἰρήνης ἐβουλεύ-
εσθε (Huettner).

ἔτεσι καὶ χρόνοις ὕστερον] i.e.
'years and ages later,' 'ever so
many years after,' 'years and
years later.' The phrase is
curious and is perhaps rightly
suspected by Seager, who suggests the emendation ἔτεσι καὶ
χρόνοις τοσούτοις ὕστερον (*Classical Journal* 1829, Vol. 30, No.
59, p. 109). It is defended by
G. H. Schaefer, who refers to
Pausanias x 17 § 3, ἔτεσι δὲ
ὕστερον μετὰ τοὺς Λιβύας ἀφίκοντο.
We may compare Lysias 3 § 39,
οἱ μὲν ἄλλοι...ὀργιζόμενοι παραχρῆμα τιμωρεῖσθαι ζητοῦσιν, οὗτος
δὲ χρόνοις ὕστερον. But the
two phrases ἔτεσιν ὕστερον and
χρόνοις ὕστερον, however defensible in themselves separately, do
not apparently occur in combination elsewhere; and it may
therefore be worth while to
suggest either ἀλλὰ τοσούτοις
χρόνοις ὕστερον, or simply ἀλλὰ
χρόνοις ὕστερον just as in the
passage of Lysias above quoted.
In the latter case ἔτεσι καὶ may
be a corruption of a marginal
gloss ἔτεσι κ' i.e. 'twenty years,'
a transcriber's note explaining
χρόνοις by referring to § 26,
παρεληλυθότων ἐτῶν πλέον ἢ εἴκοσι, and § 38, ἐτῶν ἴσως εἴκοσι.
(Mr Shilleto suggests as a parallel to ἔτεσι καὶ χρόνοις, Cic.
Verr. II 3 § 21, *tot annis atque
adeo saeculis tot.*)

ἀπράγμων] Often used of
quiet and easy-going people who
shrink from litigation. Or. 40
§ 32, ἀπράγμων καὶ οὐ φιλόδικος,
42 § 12. Cf. ἀπραγμοσύνη and
its opposites, πολυπράγμων, πολυ-
πραγμονεῖν, πολυπραγμοσύνη. So
also, in the next line, πράγματα

οὐκ οἶδεν ὅσα πράγματα πράττων οὐ πέπαυσαι, οὐ
μόνον δίκας ἰδίας διώκων οὐκ ἐλάττους ταυτησὶ, ἀλλὰ
δημοσίᾳ συκοφαντῶν καὶ κρίνων τινάς;[a] οὐχὶ Τιμομάχου κατηγόρεις; οὐχὶ Καλλίππου τοῦ νῦν ὄντος

[a] τίνας οὔ; Dobree.

πράττων, as is clear from the rest of the sentence, refers to the plaintiff's incessant litigation. Or. 27 § 1, οὐδὲν ἂν ἔδει δικῶν οὐδὲ πραγμάτων. 54 § 24.

κατηγόρεις] Young students are apt to confound the imperfect κατηγόρεις with the present κατηγορεῖς.

κρίνων τινάς] The force of the sentence is much improved by Dobree's almost certain emendation κρίνων τίνας οὔ; οὐχὶ Τιμομάχου κατηγόρεις; κ.τ.λ., where the loss of οὔ would be accounted for by οὐχὶ following immediately after. Or. 37 § 14, πολλὰ δεηθέντος καὶ τί οὐ ποιήσαντος; 47 § 43, δεομένων ἀπάντων καὶ ἱκετευόντων καὶ τίνα οὐ προσπεμπόντων; Felicissime restituit, says Shilleto of Dobree (F. L. § 231).

Τιμομάχου κ.τ.λ.] All these prosecutions are almost certainly connected with the naval operations extending over the plaintiff's protracted trierarchy of seventeen months in the Thracian Waters (in B. C. 362–361). In his speech against Polycles (Or. 50) Autocles, Meno, and Timomachus are mentioned as successive commanders of the fleet (§§ 12—14 and Or. 23 § 104—5); and while he there speaks in general terms of the maladministration of all the commanders (§ 15 τὰ τῶν στρατηγῶν ἄπιστα), he uses the strongest language against Timomachus, mainly for his treasonable collusion with an

exiled relative, Callistratus. (See next note.) Timomachus was condemned, and put to death (Schol. on Aeschin. 1 § 56).

Καλλίππου τοῦ νῦν...ἐν Σικελίᾳ] The context shows that this Callippus (who must not be confounded with the plaintiff in the speech of Apollodorus πρὸς Κάλλιππον Or. 52) can be none other than 'the son of Philon, of the deme Aexone,' who, at the request of Timomachus, conveyed Callistratus on board an Athenian trireme to Thasos from his place of exile in Macedonia, after Apollodorus had stoutly refused to allow his own vessel to be used for so unlawful a purpose (Or. 50 § 46—52). He may, with great probability, be identified with Plato's pupil of that name, with whom another of Plato's disciples, the well-known Dion of Syracuse, lived on friendly terms at Athens on his banishment from Sicily in B.C. 366. In August 357, Dion, with a small force, started from the island of Zacynthus, and during the absence of Dionysius the younger, made a triumphal entry into Syracuse, attended by his friend Callippus, who was one of his captains, and is described by Plutarch as λαμπρὸς ἐν τοῖς ἀγῶσι καὶ διάσημος. Ultimately, in the spring or summer of 353, Dion was assassinated by Callippus, who after usurping the government for thirteen months, was defeated

ἐν Σικελίᾳ; οὐ πάλιν Μένωνος; οὐκ Αὐτοκλέους; οὐ 961
54 Τιμοθέου; οὐκ ἄλλων πολλῶν; καίτοι πῶς ἔχει λόγον
σὲ, Ἀπολλόδωρον ὄντα, πρότερον τῶν κοινῶν, ὧν μέρος
ἠδικοῦ, δίκην ἀξιοῦν λαμβάνειν, ἢ τῶν ἰδίων ὧν νῦν
ἐγκαλεῖς, ἄλλως τε καὶ τηλικούτων ὄντων, ὡς σὺ φής;
τί ποτ᾽ οὖν ἐκείνων κατηγορῶν τόνδ᾽ εἴας; οὐκ ἠδικοῦ, ἀλλ᾽, οἶμαι, συκοφαντεῖς νῦν. ἡγοῦμαι τοίνυν,
ὦ ἄνδρες Ἀθηναῖοι, πάντων μάλιστ᾽ εἰς τὸ πρᾶγμα

in battle by a brother of the younger Dionysius, and *after wandering about in Sicily* and establishing himself in Southern Italy, at Rhegium, was shortly after (probably in B.C. 350) himself killed by his friends, with the very sword (as the story runs) with which he murdered Dion. (Plutarch, *Dion*, 17, 28—58; Plato Ep. vii; Diodorus xvi *passim*.)

In the present passage Apollodorus is stated to have prosecuted Callippus τοῦ νῦν ὄντος ἐν Σικελίᾳ. The Athenian fleet (with Callippus) reached Athens from the Thracian coasts in Feb. 360, and Callippus started for Syracuse from Zacynthus in Aug. 357, so that the plaintiff's prosecution of him cannot well be placed later than the spring of 357, though it may have been two years earlier in 359, and in any case about the same time as his prosecutions of Timomachus, Meno and Autocles. (A. Schaefer *Dem. u. s. Zeit*, III 2, 158—161.)

If the present speech is as late as 350 B.C., Callippus was still alive; at any rate, the news of his death cannot have reached Athens. *Introd.* p. xxix.

οὐ Τιμοθέου;] The charge against Timotheus, the celebrated Athenian general, may have been

connected with his defeat at Amphipolis B.C. 360. At first sight the allusion might be explained of the plaintiff's *private* suit (Or. 49) against the general for sums borrowed from Pasion (cf. above § 36 n.); but the context appears to point expressly to public indictments (δημοσίᾳ in the previous sentence and τῶν κοινῶν in the next); though this reason is not conclusive, as the first part of the previous sentence refers to δίκαι ἴδιαι.

54. Ἀπολλόδωρον ὄντα κ.τ.λ.] *aculeatum et amarum dictum.* Reiske. It is not like *Apollodorus*, it is inconsistent with his true character, to be going out of his way to undertake public prosecutions where his own interests were but partially affected, to the neglect of private suits in which, as he says, he has a direct and an important concern. If Apollodorus had been really wronged by Phormion, he would have prosecuted him before. For the emphatic reference to the name, cf. Cicero, ad Atticum v 2, '...cum Hortensius veniret et infirmus et tam longe et *Hortensius.*'

μέρος] 'In part alone,' as only one aggrieved person, out of many. So τὸ μέρος in Herod. I 120, II 173, and μέρος τι in Thuc. IV 30.

εἶναι τούτων μάρτυρας παρασχέσθαι· τὸν γὰρ συκο-
φαντοῦντα ἀεὶ τί χρὴ νομίζειν νῦν ποιεῖν; καὶ νὴ Δί'[b] 55
ἔγωγε, ὦ ἄνδρες Ἀθηναῖοι, νομίζω πάνθ' ὅσα τοῦ
τρόπου τοῦ Φορμίωνός ἐστι σημεῖα καὶ τῆς τούτου
δικαιοσύνης καὶ φιλανθρωπίας, καὶ ταῦτ' εἰς τὸ
πρᾶγμ' εἶναι πρὸς ὑμᾶς εἰπεῖν. ὁ μὲν γὰρ περὶ πάντ'
ἄδικος τάχ' ἂν, εἰ τύχοι, καὶ τοῦτον ἠδίκει· ὁ δὲ μηδένα μηδὲν ἠδικηκώς, πολλοὺς δὲ εὖ πεποιηκὼς ἑκὼν
ἐκ τίνος εἰκότως ἂν[c] τρόπου τοῦτον μόνον ἠδίκει τῶν
πάντων; τούτων τοίνυν τῶν μαρτυριῶν ἀκούσαντες
γνώσεσθε τὸν ἑκατέρου τρόπον.

ΜΑΡΤΥΡΙΑΙ.

Ἴθι δὴ λέγε[d] καὶ τὰς πρὸς Ἀπολλόδωρον τῆς πο- 56
νηρίας.

ΜΑΡΤΥΡΙΑΙ.

Ἆρ' οὖν ὅμοιος οὑτοσί, σκοπεῖτε.   λέγε.

ΜΑΡΤΥΡΙΑΙ.

Ἀνάγνωθι δὴ καὶ ὅσα δημοσίᾳ χρήσιμος τῇ πόλει
γέγονεν οὑτοσί.

[b] Δία Z cum Σ.   [c] ΣrΛ¹.   αν εἰκότως Z.
[d] coniecit G. H. Schaefer.   om. Z cum libris.

πάντων μάλιστ' εἰς τὸ πρᾶγμα] 'Very *much* to the purpose', '*anything* but irrelevant', 57 § 7 εἰς αὐτὸ τὸ πρᾶγμα πάντα λέγειν. The depositions about to be produced on the general character of plaintiff and defendant, are liable to objection on the ground of their being beside the question. The speaker here meets that objection beforehand.

56. τὰς] sc. μαρτυρίας. 'Testimony to the plaintiff's bad character.'

The four sets of depositions may probably be grouped as follows:

(1) General evidence of Phormion's good character.

(2) On his opponent's bad character.

(3) On Phormion's generosity to those in need (§ 58, ἀκούετε ...οἷον ἑαυτὸν τοῖς δεηθεῖσι παρέχει).

(4) On Phormion's public benefactions (§§ 56, 57, χρήσιμος τῇ πόλει, and § 58 ad fin.).

ἆρ' οὖν ὅμοιος οὑτοσί, σκοπεῖτε] *Look here, upon this picture, and on this.*

ΜΑΡΤΥΡΙΑΙ.

57   Τοσαῦτα τοίνυν, ὦ ἄνδρες Ἀθηναῖοι, Φορμίων
χρήσιμος γεγονὼς καὶ τῇ πόλει καὶ πολλοῖς ὑμῶν, καὶ
οὐδένα οὔτ’ ἰδίᾳ οὔτε δημοσίᾳ κακὸν οὐδὲν εἰργασμένος, οὐδ’ ἀδικῶν Ἀπολλόδωρον τουτονί, δεῖται καὶ
ἱκετεύει καὶ ἀξιοῖ σωθῆναι, καὶ ἡμεῖς συνδεόμεθα οἱ 962
ἐπιτήδειοι ταῦθ’ᵉ ὑμῶν. ἐκεῖνο δ’ ὑμᾶς ἀκοῦσαι δεῖ.
τοσαῦτα γάρ, ὦ ἄνδρες Ἀθηναῖοι, χρήμαθ’ ὑμῖν ἀνεγνώσθη προσηυπορηκὼςᶠ ὅσ’ οὔθ’ οὗτος οὔτ’ ἄλλος

ᵉ legendum fortasse ταῦθ’.   ᶠ προσευ- Z cum Σ.

§ 57 to end. The defendant
not only implores your protection, but claims it as his right.
Generous in his benefactions and
apart from his actual resources
enjoying credit for at least as
much besides, he is enabled by
means of that good credit to be
of advantage, not to himself
alone, but to yourselves as well.
Do not suffer so worthy, so
energetic, so generous a man of
business to be ruined by this
abominable blackguard. Most
of the plaintiff's statements you
will simply disregard as baseless calumny, but you must
order him to prove either that
there was no will (cf. § 33), or
that there is some other lease
besides that produced on our
side (cf. § 9), or that he did not
give the defendant a release
from all claims (§§ 15, 16), or
that the laws allow a claim to
be set up when once such a release has been given (§§ 23—5).
Challenge him to prove any one
of these points, or anything like
them. If, for want of such
proof, he resorts to ribaldry,
don't attend to him, don't allow
his loud and shameless asser-
tions to mislead you; but carefully remember what you have

heard on our side. If so, you
will give a verdict which will be
true to your consciences, true to
the cause of justice. (The clerk
shall read you the law and the
remaining depositions.)

That is our case, gentlemen:
I need not detain you any longer.

57. δεῖται καὶ ἱκετεύει καὶ ἀξιοῖ
σωθῆναι] Requests, implores
and claims your protection. Or.
27 § 68, and 57 § 1, δέομαι καὶ
ἱκετεύω καὶ ἀντιβολῶ.

χρήμαθ’ ὑμῖν ἀνεγνώσθη προσ-
ηυπορηκὼς]   C. R. Kennedy
translates: ‘It has been read
out to you, that he has acquired
such a heap of money as neither he nor any one else pos-
sesses.’ This can hardly be
right, particularly as such a
blunt assertion of Phormion's
affluence would be a very invidious statement for his friends
to make, and would not ingratiate him in the eyes of the
court. εὐπορεῖν χρήματα (or
χρημάτων) has two senses, (1)
‘to be well off’; (2) ‘to supply
money.’ ‘εὐπορεῖν,’ says Lo-
beck(Parerga p. 595), ‘non solum
significat abunde habere…sed
etiam suppeditare: ἐπικουρίαν
ταῖς χρείαις ἐξευπορεῖν Plato Legg.
xi 153; χρήμαθ’ ὑμῖν προσ-

οὐδεὶς κέκτηται. πίστις μέντοι Φορμίωνι παρὰ τοῖς
εἰδόσι καὶ τοσούτων καὶ πολλῷ πλειόνων χρημάτων
ἐστὶ, δι' ἧς καὶ αὐτὸς αὐτῷ καὶ ὑμῖν χρήσιμός ἐστιν.
ἃ μὴ προῆσθε[g], μηδ' ἐπιτρέψητε ἀνατρέψαι τῷ μιαρῷ 58

[g] Bekk. cum A¹r. προεισθε prima manu Σ. πρόησθε Z (vulgo et correctus Σ).

εὐπορηκώς Dem. Phorm. 962. Cf. Apat. 894, 14 (= Or. 33 § 7 εὐπορήσειν αὐτῷ δέκα μνᾶς); de reb. Chers. p. 94 (συνευποροῦντας ἐκείνῳ χρημάτων); Boeot. p. 1019 (= Or. 40 § 36 χρήματα εὐπορήσας); Neaer. 1369, 10; Aeschin. Timarch. p. 121; Lycurg. Leocr. p. 233 ; quibus inter se collatis intelligitur, quanta sit utriusque notionis contagio, a Romanis quoque unius verbi *suppetendi* angustiis conclusa.' (See note on Or. 40 § 36, and cf. 33 § 6 τριάκοντα μνᾶς συνευπορῆσαι.)

Having regard to the context, we must here take the secondary sense of εὐπορεῖν, and explain the passage as follows : 'The depositions read aloud to you show that the defendant has (lit. he has been recited to you as having) provided you on emergencies with larger sums of money than his own (οὗτος i.e. our friend, the defendant's) or any one else's private fortune amounts to; but then he has *credit*, &c.' The sentence πίστις μέντοι κ.τ.λ. shows how it came to pass that Phormion was enabled, as a capitalist in the enjoyment of extensive credit in the commercial world, to advance sums of money larger than the private resources of any single individual.

πίστις] 'Credit.' Cf. § 44, πίστις ἀφορμὴ κ.τ.λ.

58. ἃ μὴ προῆσθε] 'Do not throw this away,' i.e. 'do not sacrifice these advantages to the interests of the plaintiff.'

μηδ' ἐπιτρέψητε ἀνατρέψαι] Possibly an unintentional collocation of two compounds of τρέπειν. One word, however, might suggest the other. 'Do not suffer this wretch to over-turn it,' i.e. overthrow the defendant from his high position and good credit.

[The metaphor is perhaps from overthrowing a fabric of wealth, as in Aesch. Pers. 165, μὴ μέγας πλοῦτος κονίσας οὖδας ἀντρέψῃ ποδὶ ὄλβον ὃν Δαρεῖος ἦρεν οὐκ ἄνευ θεῶν τινός, i.e. 'iniurioso pede proruere.' P.] In Theb. 1076 the context shows that the metaphor is not from an earthquake, but from the capsizing of a ship, πόλιν μὴ ἀνατραπῆναι μηδ' ἀλλοδαπῶν κύματι φωτῶν κατακλυσθῆν, and the way in which the word is used by the orators proves that they also regarded it as a nautical metaphor: Dem. 9 § 69 ὅπως μηδεὶς ἀνατρέψει (τὸ σκάφος), 19 § 250 οὐχ ὅπως ὀρθὴ πλεύσεται (ἡ πόλις) προείδετο, ἀλλ' ἀνέτρεψε καὶ κατέδυσε. Aeschin. 3 § 158 πλοῖον ἀνατρέψῃ and τὴν πόλιν ἄρδην ἀνατετροφότα. It is metaphorically applied in Dem. 18 § 296 to the ὅροι τῶν ἀγαθῶν καὶ κανόνες, in 25 Aristog. 1 § 28 to τὰ κοινὰ δίκαια and in § 32 to τὴν πόλιν; in Aeschin. 1 § 187 to τὴν κοινὴν παιδείαν, in § 190 to

τούτῳ ἀνθρώπῳ, μηδὲ ποιήσητε αἰσχρὸν παράδειγμα,
ὡς τὰ τῶν ἐργαζομένων καὶ μετρίως ἐθελόντων ζῆν
τοῖς βδελυροῖς καὶ συκοφάνταις ὑπάρχει παρ' ὑμῶν
λαβεῖν· πολὺ γὰρ χρησιμώτερα ὑμῖν παρὰ τῷδε ὄντα
ὑπάρχει. ὁρᾶτε γὰρ αὐτοὶ καὶ ἀκούετε τῶν μαρτύρων,
59 οἷον ἑαυτὸν τοῖς δεηθεῖσι παρέχει. καὶ τούτων οὐδὲν
ἕνεκα τοῦ λυσιτελοῦντος εἰς χρήματα πεποίηκεν, ἀλλὰ
φιλανθρωπίᾳ καὶ τρόπου ἐπιεικείᾳ. οὔκουν ἄξιον, ὦ
ἄνδρες Ἀθηναῖοι, τὸν τοιοῦτον ἄνδρα προέσθαι τούτῳ,
οὐδὲ τηνικαῦτα ἐλεεῖν ὅτ' οὐδὲν ἔσται τούτῳ πλέον,

πόλεις; in Deinarchus 1 § 30 to
πράγματα ἢ ἴδια ἢ κοινά, in § 88
to τὴν πόλιν (with ἐπιτρέψετε in
the previous clause), and in
3 § 4 to ἄπαντα τὰ ἐν τῇ πόλει.

In Liddell and Scott (ed. 6)
the phrase ἀνατρέπειν τράπεζαν is
explained 'to upset a banker's
table, i.e. to make him bankrupt.' The only passage quoted
is Dem. 403, 7, where however
there is no reference whatever
to a bankruptcy, but only to
the overturning of a table towards the close of a disorderly
banquet. (The reference to Dem.
743, 1 [= Timocr. § 136] in ed. 7
should be to the *Scholium* on
that passage, quoted below.)

In Andocides de Mysteriis,
§ 130, we have a curious passage stating that in Athens
there was a story current among
the old wives and the little
children, that the house of
Hipponicus was haunted by an
unquiet spirit that overturned
his table ('Ἱππόνικος ἐν τῇ οἰκίᾳ
ἀλιτήριον τρέφει, ὃς αὐτοῦ τὴν
τράπεζαν ἀνατρέπει). πῶς οὖν
(the orator continues) ἡ φήμη
ἡ τότε οὖσα δοκεῖ ὑμῖν ἀποβῆναι;
οἰόμενος γὰρ Ἱππόνικος υἱὸν τρέ-
φειν, ἀλιτήριον αὑτῷ ἔτρεφεν, ὃς

ἀνατέτροφεν ἐκείνου τὸν πλοῦτον, τὴν σωφροσύνην, τὸν ἄλλον
βίον ἅπαντα. But the only place,
so far as I can find, in which
the phrase has a distinct reference to bankruptcy is the
Scholium on Dem. Timocr.
§ 136, where δανεῖσαι τοῖς τρα-
πεζίταις is followed by ἔτυχεν
ὕστερον ἀνατραπῆναι τὰς τραπέ-
ζας (Baiter and Sauppe, *Orat.
Att.* ii 119, 6, 35). See § 50
ἐξέστησαν, n.

αἰσχρὸν παράδειγμα κ.τ.λ.] 'A
disgraceful precedent that the
property of men in business,
who live respectable lives, may
be obtained from you by mis-
creants and pettifoggers.' Kennedy. ὑπάρχει, 'that the laws
allow,' 'that it is a condition of
your polity.'

πολὺ γὰρ...ὑπάρχει] Or. 38
§ 28 ἃ καὶ ὑμῖν ἐστιν ἐπ' ὠφελείᾳ
μείζονι παρ' ἡμῖν ὄντα ἢ παρὰ
τούτοις. Lysias Or. 18 §§ 20, 21;
19 § 61; 21 §§ 12—14.

59. τοῦ λυσιτελ. εἰς χρήματα]
Pecuniary advantage; instead
of being placed between the
article and participle, as would
be most natural, εἰς χρήματα is
reserved for a more emphatic
position.

ἀλλὰ νῦν ὅτε κύριοι καθέστατε σῶσαι· οὐ γὰρ ἔγωγ'
ὁρῶ καιρὸν ἐν τίνι ἂν μᾶλλον βοηθήσειέ τις αὐτῷ.
τὰ μὲν οὖν πολλὰ ὧν Ἀπολλόδωρος ἐρεῖ, νομίζετ' 60
εἶναι λόγον[h] καὶ συκοφαντίας, κελεύετε δ' αὐτὸν
ὑμῖν[i] ἐπιδεῖξαι ἢ ὡς οὐ διέθετο ταῦθ' ὁ πατήρ, ἢ ὡς
ἔστι τις ἄλλη μίσθωσις πλὴν ἧς[j] ἡμεῖς δείκνυμεν, ἢ
ὡς οὐκ ἀφῆκεν αὐτὸν διαλογισάμενος τῶν ἐγκλημάτων
ἁπάντων ἃ ἔγνω ὁ κηδεστὴς ὁ τούτου καὶ οὗτος αὐτὸς
συνεχώρησεν, ἢ ὡς διδόασιν οἱ νόμοι δικάζεσθαι τῶν
οὕτω πραχθέντων, ἢ τῶν τοιούτων τι δεικνύναι.   ἐὰν 61
δ' ἀπορῶν αἰτίας καὶ βλασφημίας λέγῃ καὶ κακο-
963 λογῇ[k], μὴ προσέχετε τὸν νοῦν, μηδ' ὑμᾶς ἡ τούτου
κραυγὴ καὶ ἀναίδεια ἐξαπατήσῃ, ἀλλὰ φυλάττετε καὶ

[h] λόγους maluit Reiske.

[i] Bekk. om. Z et Bekker st. cum Σ ubi per imprudentiam (ut
videtur) ὑμῖν in versu extremo praetermissum.

[j] Bekk. ἥν Z cum Σr (etiam ΦΦ).

[k] καὶ κακολογῇ delenda esse existimat Huettner, 'nam κακο-
λογεῖν idem declarat, quod βλασφημίας λέγειν, et verbum satis
rarum est apud antiquos scriptores; cf. Lys. 8 § 5, Pseudodem.
25 § 94'.

καιρὸν ἐν τίνι] Confused between ἐν τίνι καιρῷ, and καιρὸν
ἐν ᾧ, κ.τ.λ.   Cf. Or. 56 § 24 n.,
and Plat. Rep. p. 399 E βίου
ῥυθμοὺς ἰδεῖν κοσμίου τε καὶ
ἀνδρείου τίνες εἰσίν· οὓς ἰδόντα
κ.τ.λ.   Cf. Isocr. ad Dem. § 5
συμβουλεύειν, ὧν χρὴ...ὀρέγεσθαι
καὶ τίνων ἔργων ἀπέχεσθαι, n.

60.   λόγον καὶ συκοφ.] i.e.
empty talk and baseless mis-
representation.   Forλόγος,'mere
talk,' cf. Or. 20 § 101, εἰ δὲ
ταῦτα λόγους καὶ φλυαρίας εἶναι
φήσεις, ἐκεῖνό γ' οὐ λόγος, 8 § 13
λόγοι καὶ προφάσεις, 20 § 101
λόγους καὶ φλυαρίας.   Similarly
λόγοι in 30 § 34 and λόγος in 20
§ 92.

ἐπιδεῖξαι] Plaintiff is chal-

lenged to *prove* his statements,
not to rest content with vague
calumny.

διαλογισάμενος] See § 23.

ἐγκλημάτων ἃ ἔγνω] Claims
which were the subject of the
award (γνῶσις) of Deinias, 'ἃ
ἔγνω, *quae disceptavit.*'   G. H.
Schaefer.   Cf. § 17 init.

δεικνύναι] sc. κελεύετε, 'tell
him to *try if* he can show,' &c.
To be distinguished from ἐπιδεῖξαι just above.

61.   λέγῃ] '*Go on talking.*'

φυλάττετε καὶ μέμνησθε] 'Keep
in mind and remember'.   Or. 20
§§ 163, 167; 23 § 210 ταῦτα φυλάττετε καὶ μεμνημένοι κάθησθε,
45 § 87.

μέμνησθε ὅσ' ἡμῶν ἀκηκόατε. κἂν ταῦτα ποιῆτε,
αὐτοί τ' εὐορκήσετε καὶ τοῦτον δικαίως σώσετε, ἄξιον
ὄντα νὴ τὸν Δία καὶ θεοὺς ἅπαντας.

62   Ἀνάγνωθι λαβὼν αὐτοῖς τὸν νόμον καὶ τὰς μαρτυρίας τασδί.

ΝΟΜΟΣ. ΜΑΡΤΥΡΙΑΙ.

Οὐκ οἶδ' ὅ τι δεῖ πλείω λέγειν· οἶμαι[1] γὰρ ὑμᾶς
οὐδὲν ἀγνοεῖν τῶν εἰρημένων. ἐξέρα τὸ ὕδωρ.

[1] Σ. οἴομαι Z (cf. § 18).

62. τὸν νόμον καὶ τὰς μαρτυρίας]
The context does not show what
law or what depositions are
referred to : possibly another
νόμος of the same general purport as that recited before,
§ 25 (ὧν μὴ εἶναι δίκας), and further evidence to facts or to the
defendant's character (ἄξιον
ὄντα, § 61).

οὐκ οἶδ' ...... εἰρημένων] The
same sentence *verbatim* is found
at the close of Or. 20 (Lept.),
38 (Nausimach.), and 54 (Conon); and also at the end of
the 7th and 8th speeches of
Isaeus.

ὅ τι δεῖ] Not 'what I should
say further,' (which would require πλέον), but '*why I should
say any more*', '*what need there
is* for my saying any more.'
Similarly in 41 § 25 ἡγοῦμαι μὲν
οὐδὲν ἔτι δεῖν πλείω λέγειν, we
must be careful to take οὐδὲν
before δεῖν and not after λέγειν.

ἐξέρα τὸ ὕδωρ] 'Pour out the
water.' See Midias, § 129. (Cf.
ἐξερᾶν τοὺς λίθους in Ar. Ach. 341,

and τὰς ψήφους in Vesp. 993.)
The only other passage where
the phrase is found is at the
end of Or. 38, where the *whole*
of this short epilogue recurs.

The speaker having concluded his speech within the legal
limits of time measured by the
κλεψύδρα, pointedly calls on the
attendant to empty the 'water-
clock' (54 § 36). The rhetorical
effect is that the court is re-
minded that the speaker has
spared them a longer speech,
and the defendant gets the
credit of having so good a cause
that the orator does not find it
necessary to avail himself of
the full time at his disposal.

The result of Phormion's plea
is thus stated by Apollodorus
Or. 45 § 6, οὕτω διέθηκε τοὺς
δικαστὰς ὥστε φωνὴν μηδ' ἡντινοῦν ἐθέλειν ἀκούειν ἡμῶν· προσοφλὼν δὲ τὴν ἐπωβελίαν καὶ οὐδὲ
λόγου τυχεῖν ἀξιωθείς, ὡς οὐκ οἶδ'
εἴ τις πώποτε ἄλλος ἀνθρώπων,
ἀπῄειν βαρέως, ὦ ἄνδρες Ἀθηναῖοι,
καὶ χαλεπῶς φέρων.

XLV

ΚΑΤΑ ΣΤΕΦΑΝΟΥ
ΨΕΥΔΟΜΑΡΤΥΡΙΩΝ Α.

ΥΠΟΘΕΣΙΣ.

῞Οτε ᾿Απολλόδωρος ἔκρινε Φορμίωνα τῆς τραπέζης ἀφορμὴν ἐγκαλῶν, ὁ δὲ τὴν δίκην παρεγράψατο,
ὁ[a] Στέφανος μετ᾿ ἄλλων τινῶν ἐμαρτύρησε Φορμίωνι,
ὡς ἄρα ὁ μὲν Φορμίων προὐκαλεῖτο ᾿Απολλόδωρον, εἰ
1101 μή φησιν ἀντίγραφα εἶναι τῶν διαθηκῶν τῶν τοῦ 5
πατρὸς Πασίωνος, Φορμίωνι[b] παρασχεῖν ἀνοῖξαι τὰς
διαθήκας αὐτάς, ἃς ἔχει καὶ παρέχεται ᾿Αμφίας,
᾿Απολλόδωρος δὲ ἀνοίγειν οὐκ ἠθέλησεν, ἔστι δὲ ἀντίγραφα τάδε τῶν διαθηκῶν τῶν Πασίωνος. ταύτην
ἐμαρτύρησαν τὴν μαρτυρίαν οἱ περὶ Στέφανον, τοῦ 10

[Δημοσθένους] κατὰ Στεφάνου ψευδομαρτυριῶν α. ‘hanc orationem nobis non videri Demosthenis esse significarimus’ Z.
Argumentum in ultima columna antecedentis orationis 36 addidit
manus recentior in Σ.
  [a] om. Z. addidit Dind. ex Σ.
  [b] om. Z. πατρὸς Φορμίωνος παρασχεῖν libri. correxit Dind. ex
Σ in quo scriptum πατρὸς φορμίωνι πασίωνος, παρασχεῖν.

1. τραπέζης ἀφορμὴν ἐγκαλῶν]
See *Argument* to Or. 36, l. 22 n.
On παρεγράψατο see *ib.* l. 23 n.
  3. Στέφανος ἐμαρτύρησε κ.τ.λ.]
See *infra* § 8. The ἄλλοι τινές
are called ῎Ενδιος and Σκύθης in
the document there quoted.
  4. εἰ μή φησιν] ‘P’. made A.
a proposal, that if A. denies that
the copies put in are copies of
the will of his father Pasion, he
shall let Phormion open the will
itself which is in the custody of,
and is produced by, Amphias.’
  8. ἔστι δὲ ἀντίγραφα κ.τ.λ.]
The clause is continued from
ὡς, ‘that the document produced
is a copy of Pasion's will.’

Ἀπολλοδώρου λέγοντος κατὰ τοῦ Φορμίωνος ὡς ἄρα
τὰς διαθήκας πέπλακε καὶ τὸ ὅλον πρᾶγμα σκευώ-
ρημά ἐστιν. ἡττηθεὶς τοίνυν τὴν δίκην Ἀπολλόδωρος
ὑπὲρ τῆς μαρτυρίας ὡς ψευδοῦς οὔσης τῷ Στεφάνῳ
15 δικάζεται.

---

1   Καταψευδομαρτυρηθείς, ὦ ἄνδρες Ἀθηναῖοι, καὶ
παθὼν ὑπὸ Φορμίωνος ὑβριστικὰ καὶ δεινὰ δίκην
παρὰ τῶν αἰτίων ἥκω ληψόμενος παρ' ὑμῖν.   δέομαι
δὲ πάντων ὑμῶν καὶ ἱκετεύω καὶ ἀντιβολῶ πρῶτον

12. πέπλακε...σκευρώρημα] Or.
36 § 33, πλάσμα καὶ σκευώρημα
ὅλον, and infra § 42.

§§ 1—2. Exordium (προοίμιον).
*Having been defeated by false
testimony in my suit against
Phormion, I have come into court
to claim a verdict against those
who compassed that outrageous
and atrocious wrong. I ask the
jury to give me a friendly and
favourable hearing ; and, if I
make good my case, to grant me
the redress which is my due.*

*In the former trial, the defen-
dant Stephanus in particular
gave false evidence against me,
prompted by corrupt motives ;
and I propose to prove this from
his own testimony. A brief recital of the relations between
Phormion and myself will help
the jury to form an opinion on
the villany of Phormion and the
falsehood of his witnesses.*

The Exordium is not unlike
that of Or. 54, κατὰ Κόνωνος,
where, as here, the προαύλιον
(Ar. Rhet. iii 14) or, as we should
say, the key-note of the whole
speech is struck in the opening
words: ὑβρισθεὶς ὦ ἄνδρες
δικασταὶ καὶ παθὼν ὑπὸ Κόνωνος
κ.τ.λ.—The appeal *ad captan-
dam benevolentiam, πρῶτον μὲν*

εὐνοϊκῶς ἀκοῦσαί μου, also occurs
in Or. 54 § 2, and similarly the
formula εἶτ' ἐὰν (ἠδικῆσθαι καὶ
παρανενομῆσθαι) δοκῶ, βοηθῆσαί
μοι τὰ δίκαια, and lastly the
promise of brevity, ὡς ἂν οἷός
τε ὦ διὰ βραχυτάτων.

καταψευδομαρτυρηθείς] 'Crushed by' (or 'having been the
victim of') false testimony.'
Cf. Or. 33 § 37, and Plat.
Gorg. 472 B. Harpocr. κατα-
ψευδομαρτυρησάμενος· ἀντὶ τοῦ
παρασχὼν τὰ ψεύδη (an ψευδῆ?)
μαρτυρήσοντας. Δημοσθένης ἐν τῷ
κατὰ Στεφάνου. The lexicographer intended doubtless to refer
to Or. 29 (ὑπὲρ Φάνου πρὸς Ἄφο-
βον ψευδομαρτυριῶν) § 6, where
the *middle* participle explained
by him is to be found. The
mistake possibly arose out of a
confusion between the titles of
the two speeches, κατὰ Στεφάνου and ὑπὲρ Φάνου (A.
Schaefer in *Neue Jahrb.* 1870,
vol. 101 p. 523).

δέομαι ... ἱκετεύω ... ἀντιβολῶ]
Cf. *infra* §85, Or.27 (Aphobus A)
§ 68, and 57 (Eubul.) § 1; Lysias Or. 18 § 27, and 21 § 21.
Such combinations of two or
three nearly synonymous verbs
are very common in the undisputed speeches of Demosthenes

μὲν εὐνοϊκῶς ἀκοῦσαί μου· μέγα γὰρ τοῖς ἠτυχηκόσιν,
ὥσπερ ἐγώ, δυνηθῆναι περὶ ὧν πεπόνθασιν εἰπεῖν καὶ
εὐμενῶς ἐχόντων ὑμῶν ἀκροατῶν τυχεῖν· εἶτ᾿ ἐὰν ἀδικεῖσθαι δοκῶ, βοηθῆσαί μοι τὰ δίκαια. ἐπιδείξω δ᾿ 2
ὑμῖν τουτονὶ Στέφανον καὶ μεμαρτυρηκότα τὰᶜ ψευδῆ,
1102 καὶ δι᾿ αἰσχροκερδίανᵈ τοῦτο πεποιηκότα, καὶ κατήγορον αὐτὸν αὐτοῦ γιγνόμενον· τοσαύτη περιφάνεια τοῦ
πράγματός ἐστιν. ἐξ ἀρχῆς δ᾿ ὡς ἂν οἷός τε ὦ διὰ
βραχυτάτων εἰπεῖν πειράσομαι τὰ πεπραγμένα μοι

ᶜ om. Z cum libris. addidit Reiskius.
ᵈ Σ, qui sic ubique. Bckk. αἰσχροκέρδειαν Z.

(e.g. Or. 36 § 47, ἄγεις εἰς μέσον, δεικνύεις, ἐλέγχεις ; ib. 52, ἐλαύνεις, συκοφαντεῖς, διώκεις ; ib. 57, δεῖται καὶ ἱκετεύει καὶ ἀξιοῖ ; Or. 54 § 33, δικάζομαι καὶ μισῶ καὶ ἐπεξέρχομαι). The speech ὑπὲρ Φορμίωνος alone contains nearly forty such passages ; of the speeches delivered by Apollodorus, the first oration against Stephanus has more than 30, while in the rest there is hardly anything of the kind, though in the second speech against Stephanus, § 28, we have δέομαι καὶ ἱκετεύω. (J. Sigg in *Jahrb. für class. Philol. Suppl.* vi p. 419.)

εὐμενῶς] Almost equivalent to εὐνοϊκῶς in the last sentence ; εὐμενής, however, is not so trivial a word as εὔνους. The former is frequent in Attic verse, the latter is generally found in prose ; the former is most often used of the gracious condescension of a deity ; the latter of the kindly feelings of ordinary human beings. Or. 4 § 45, τὸ τῶν θεῶν εὐμενές, illustrates the rule, while the exception in the present passage may be paralleled from Herod. vii 237, ξεῖνος δὲ ξείνῳ...εὐμενέστατον πάντων.

[Add Eur. Alc. 319, οὐδὲν μητρὸς εὐμενέστερον, El. 601, ἔστιν τί μοι κατ᾿ Ἄργος εὐμενὲς φίλων ; Aesch. Suppl. 488 and 518 Dind. P.]

2. τὰ ψευδῆ] ‘ *Additum articulum hoc vel illud testimonium peculiariter indicat, contra* μαρτυρεῖν ψευδῆ (cf. § 41) *vel* ἀληθῆ (§ 52) *tantummodo significat* μαρτυρεῖν ψευδῶς *vel* ἀληθῶς’ (Beels, *Diatribe,* p. 79). See Or. 47 §§ 1, 2 τὰ ψευδῆ μαρτυρεῖν ; ib. § 4 ψευδῆ μ. thrice. [inf. § 5, τὰ ψευδῆ μου κατεμαρτύρησεν, ‘ gave *this* false evidence against me.’ Thus often in the Tragic poets τὰ δεινά, where some special atrocity is described. But here we may render, ‘ has given evidence which was false.’ P.]

τοσαύτη περιφάνεια κ. τ. λ.] ‘ So transparent is the case.’ ‘ So plain and clear from every point of view.’ Or. 29 § 1 (also of false witness), ῥᾳδίως ἐξελέγξας διὰ τὴν περιφάνειαν τῶν πραγμάτων. Isaeus, Or. 7 § 28, τοσαύτη περιφάνεια τῆς ἐμῆς ποιήσεως ἐγένετο παρ᾿ αὐτοῖς...ἐπὶ τοσούτων μαρτύρων γέγονεν ἡ ποίησις. Cf. Hom. Od. ι 426, περισκέπτῳ ἐνὶ χώρῳ, and ib. v 476, ἐν περιφαινομένῳ.

πρὸς Φορμίωνα, ἐξ ὧν, ἀκούσαντες, τήν τ᾽ ἐκείνου[e]
πονηρίαν καὶ τούτους, ὅτι τὰ ψευδῆ μεμαρτυρήκασι,
γνώσεσθε.

3   Ἐγὼ γὰρ, ὦ ἄνδρες δικασταὶ, πολλῶν χρημάτων
ὑπὸ τοῦ πατρὸς καταλειφθέντων μοι, καὶ ταῦτα Φορμίωνος ἔχοντος, καὶ ἔτι πρὸς τούτοις τὴν μητέρα γή-
μαντος τὴν ἐμὴν ἀποδημοῦντος ἐμοῦ δημοσίᾳ τριηραρ-

° τήν τε τούτου Z cum libris.   τήν τ᾽ ἐκείνου Bekker cum γρ.
ΓΦΒ.

ἐξ ὧν...γνώσεσθε] This being
the syntax, ἀκούσαντες must be
taken by itself, ' when you have
heard it.'

ἐκείνου] sc. Φορμίωνος.

§§ 3—8. Narrative (διήγησις).
My father Pasion left behind
him at his death a large property
which got into the hands of
Phormion, who also married
Pasion's widow, my mother
Archippe, during my absence
from Athens on public service.
On my return, I threatened
Phormion with legal proceedings
in consequence of this marriage,
but my case did not come on; and
afterwards a reconciliation was
brought about. Subsequently,
however, on Phormion's refusing to fulfil his engagements and
attempting to rob me of the
banking-stock leased him by my
father, I was compelled to prosecute him at the earliest opportunity.

Phormion thereupon put in a
special plea in bar of action,
and brought forward false witnesses to show that I gave him
a discharge from all further
claims, and to attest to a lease
which in fact was a fabrication
and to a will that never existed.

The result of his plea, which
gave him the advantage of the
first hearing, was that the jury
would not listen to me at all; I
was fined for failing to make
good my case and left the court
in high dudgeon at my ill-treat-
ment. On reflection, however, I
feel that the jury, in their igno-
rance of the real facts, could not,
on the evidence, have found any
other verdict; but I have a right
to be indignant with the false
witnesses who brought about that
result,—and with Stephanus in
particular whose evidence shall
be read to the court. (The evidence is read.)

δημοσίᾳ] To be taken with
ἀποδημοῦντος, ' cum publice (in
causa publica) abessem.' The
fondness of the Greeks for
participles is shown by the addition of τριηραρχοῦντος which
is subordinate to, and explanatory of, ἀποδημοῦντος. Or. 36 § 25,
and Madv. Gk. Synt. § 176, d.

This trierarchy of Apollodorus may almost certainly be
connected with the negociations
between Athens and the Elder
Dionysius towards the close of
his career. It appears from a
decree discovered near the Pro-
pylaea in 1837, and restored by
A. Kirchhoff in the Philologus for
1857 (xii p. 571—8), that Athenian ambassadors were sent to
Syracuse in the summer of
B.C. 369 and in B.C. 368. Cf.

χοῦντος ὑμῖν (ὃν τρόπον δὲ, οὐκ ἴσως καλὸν υἱεῖ περὶ
μητρὸς ἀκριβῶς εἰπεῖν), ἐπειδὴ καταπλεύσας ᾐσθό-
μην καὶ τὰ πεπραγμένα εἶδον, πολλὰ ἀγανακτήσας
καὶ χαλεπῶς ἐνεγκὼν δίκην μὲν οὐχ οἷός τ᾽ ἦν ἰδίαν
λαχεῖν (οὐ γὰρ ἦσαν ἐν τῷ τότε καιρῷ δίκαι, ἀλλ᾽ ἀνε- 4
βάλλεσθε ὑμεῖς διὰ τὸν πόλεμον), γραφὴν δὲ ὕβρεως
γράφομαι πρὸς τοὺς θεσμοθέτας αὐτόν. χρόνου δὲ
γιγνομένου, καὶ τῆς μὲν γραφῆς ἐκκρουομένης, δικῶν

esp. τού[των δὲ τοὺς ἐπὶ Δυσνικήτου ἄρχο]ντος πρέσβ[εις διακο-
μίζειν τὴν ὁμολογί]αν. The trierarchy may be identified with
that of Or. 53 § 5, and probably
belongs to the *later* of these two
embassies in B.C. 368, as we
read in Or. 46 § 21, ἐγὼ μὲν
ἀπεδήμουν τριηραρχῶν, τετελευτήκει δ᾽ ὁ πατὴρ πάλαι, ὅτε
οὗτος ἔγημε. πάλαι, though a
vague word, shows at any rate
that a considerable time elapsed
between the death of Pasion in
B.C. 370 (Or. 46 § 13), and his
widow's marriage with Phormion. (Im. Hermann, *de tempore*, etc. p. 9; A. Schaefer, *Dem.
und seine Zeit*, III 2, 146; and
Lortzing, *Apollodorus*, p. 3.)

ὃν τρόπον δὲ (sc. ἔγημε)—ἀκριβῶς εἰπεῖν] Cf. § 27, διεφθάρκει
ἦν ἐμοὶ μὲν οὐ καλὸν λέγειν.
(Similarly in 40 § 8 τῇ τούτων
μητρὶ ἐπλησίασεν ὅντινα δή ποτ᾽
οὖν τρόπον· οὐ γὰρ ἐμὸν τοῦτο
λέγειν ἐστί.) This affectation
of dutiful delicacy of feeling towards his mother in the early
portions of the speech is rather
inconsistent with the apparently
gratuitous insinuation towards
its close, where he broaches the
suspicion that his own brother
Pasicles (who was eight years
old at his father Pasion's death)
was really her son *by Phormion*
(§ 84).

δίκην ἰδίαν...γραφὴν ὕβρεως] Cf.
Or. 54 § 1, ad fin.

4. πόλεμον] This suspension
of lawsuits, which the plaintiff
found in force on returning
from his trierarchy in B.C. 368,
was due to the hostilities between Athens and Thebes in
the period between the battle of
Leuctra in B.C. 371, and the
death of Epaminondas at the
battle of Mantineia in B.C. 362.
The courts were not sitting for
ordinary business, perhaps because there was no pay for the
dicasts (cf. Or. 39 § 17); and
the only process that was available under the circumstances
was a public action. So (just
below) δικῶν οὐκ οὐσῶν means, as
the courts continued closed for
private suits. ὑμεῖς refers to the
citizens generally, who are said,
in the medial sense, 'to have
had the sessions (τὰς δίκας)
postponed.'

θεσμοθέτας] Isocr. Or. 20, κατὰ
Λοχίτου § 2, περὶ τῆς ὕβρεως...
ἔξεστι τῷ βουλομένῳ τῶν πολιτῶν
γραψαμένῳ πρὸς τοὺς θεσμοθέτας
εἰσελθεῖν εἰς ὑμᾶς. (Hermann,
Privatalt. § 61, 9, 19 = *Rechtsalt.*
ed. Thalheim § 6, pp. 35, 37;
Meier and Schömann, p. 323.)

χρόνου γιγνομένου—γραφῆς ἐκ-
κρουομένης] See note on Or. 36 § 2,
ἵν᾽ ἐκκρούοντες χρόνους ἐμποιῶμεν.
For χρόνου δὲ γιγνομένου, Reiske

δὲ οὐκ οὐσῶν, γίγνονται παῖδες ἐκ τούτου τῇ μητρί.
καὶ μετὰ ταῦτα (εἰρήσεται γὰρ ἅπασα πρὸς ὑμᾶς ἡ
ἀλήθεια, ὦ ἄνδρες δικασταὶ) πολλοὶ μὲν καὶ φιλάνθρωποι λόγοι παρὰ τῆς μητρὸς ἐγίγνοντο καὶ δεήσεις
ὑπὲρ Φορμίωνος τουτονί, πολλοὶ δὲ καὶ μέτριοι καὶ
5 ταπεινοὶ παρ' αὐτοῦ τούτου. ἵνα δὲ, ὦ ἄνδρες Ἀθηναῖοι, συντέμω ταῦτα, ἐπειδὴ ποιεῖν τε οὐδὲν ᾤετο δεῖν
ὧν τότε ὡμολόγησε, καὶ τὰ χρήματα ἀποστερεῖν ἐνεχείρησεν ἃ τῆς τραπέζης εἶχεν ἀφορμὴν, δίκην ἠναγκάσθην αὐτῷ λαχεῖν, ἐπειδὴ τάχιστα ἐξουσία ἐγένετο. 1103
γνοὺς δ' οὗτος ὅτι πάντα ἐξελεγχθήσεται καὶ κάκιστος
ἀνθρώπων περὶ ἡμᾶς γεγονὼς ἐπιδειχθήσεται, μηχα-
νᾶται καὶ κατασκευάζει ταῦτα, ἐφ' οἷς Στέφανος οὐ-

ingeniously, but perhaps unnecessarily, proposes χρόνου δ'
ἐγγιγνομένου, which at any rate
modifies the slight inelegance of
the triple repetition γιγνομένου
...γίγνονται...ἐγίγνοντο. Cf. Or.
47 § 63, χρόνον ἐγγενέσθαι.

φιλάνθρωποι λόγοι] 'Kindly
overtures' (blanditiae, G. H.
Schaefer). De Corona, § 298,
οὔτε φιλανθρωπία λόγων οὔτ'
ἐπαγγελιῶν μέγεθος. Midias, § 75,
οὔτε κλαύσαντα οὔτε δεηθέντα...
οὔτε φιλάνθρωπον ... οὐδ' ὁτιοῦν
πρὸς τοὺς δικαστὰς ποιήσαντα,
where perhaps bribery is tacitly
meant. (Cf. Shilleto on Fals. leg.
§ 117.)

μέτριοι...ταπεινοὶ] i.e. 'both
moderate and reasonable in
their terms.' Fals. leg. § 15,
μετρίους λόγους, where Shilleto
quotes Ulpian: ἤγουν ἐπιεικεῖς,
φιλανθρώπους.

5. ἵνα...συντέμω] The reason for
the speaker's hurrying over this
part of his statement is partly
because the overtures of reconciliation on Phormion's side,

which he takes credit to himself for candidly admitting, are
really more to Phormion's credit
than to his own.

δίκην] i.e. the suit κατὰ Φορμίωνος, to meet which a special
plea is put in on Phormion's
behalf in Or. 36. The words
ἐπειδὴ τάχιστα ἐξουσία ἐγένετο
are possibly meant as a partial
reply (they are at any rate the
only reply given in this speech)
to that portion of Phormion's
plea which traversed his opponent's suit on the ground that
it infringed the 'statute of limitations' (Or. 36 § 26). But it
may be noticed on Phormion's
side that at least 18 years had
elapsed since the death of
Apollodorus' father, and eight
since that of his mother, before
the suit was instituted; and
during the interval the plaintiff
found time for ever so many
lawsuits in cases where his
private interests were but partially concerned (Or. 36 § 53).

τοσὶ τὰ ψευδῆ μου κατεμαρτύρησεν. καὶ πρῶτον μὲν
παρεγρά̱ψατο τὴν δίκην, ἣν ἔφευγε Φορμίων, μὴ εἰσαγώγιμον εἶναι· ἔπειτα μάρτυρας, ὡς ἀφῆκα αὐτὸν
τῶν ἐγκλημάτων, παρέσχετο ψευδεῖς, καὶ μισθώσεώς
τινος ἐσκευ̱ωρημένης καὶ διαθήκης οὐδεπώποτε γενομένης. προλαβὼν δέ μου ὥστε πρότερον[f] λέγειν διὰ 6
τὸ παραγραφὴν εἶναι καὶ μὴ εὐθυδικίᾳ εἰσιέναι, καὶ
ταῦτ᾽ ἀναγνοὺς καὶ τἄλλα, ὡς αὐτῷ συμφέρειν ἡγεῖτο,
ψευσάμενος, οὕτω διέθηκε τοὺς δικαστάς, ὥστε φωνὴν
μηδ᾽ ἡντινοῦν ἐθέλειν ἀκούειν ἡμῶν· προσοφλὼν δὲ
τὴν ἐπωβελίαν καὶ οὐδὲ λόγου τυχεῖν ἀξιωθείς, ὡς
οὐκ οἶδ᾽ εἴ τις πώποτε ἄλλος ἀνθρώπων, ἀπῄειν βαρέως, ὦ ἄνδρες Ἀθηναῖοι, καὶ χαλεπῶς φέρων. λόγον 7
δ᾽ ἐμαυτῷ διδοὺς εὑρίσκω τοῖς δικάσασι μὲν τότε πολλὴν συγγνώμην οὖσαν (ἐγὼ γὰρ αὐτὸς οὐκ ἂν οἶδ᾽ ὅ

[f] ‘*Malim* πρότερος,’ Dobree.

παρεγράψατο κ.τ.λ.] See notes
on p. 2. For μάρτυρας ὡς ἀφῆκα,
see Or. 36 §§ 24, 25; and for the
depositions on the 'lease,' *ib.*
§ 4, and on the 'will,' *ib.* § 7.

6. πρότερον λέγειν] Cf. Isocr.
παραγραφὴ πρὸς Καλλίμαχον
§ 1, φεύγων τὴν δίκην πρότερος
λέγω τοῦ διώκοντος. See on Or.
34 § 4, κατηγορεῖν τοῦ διώκοντος,
and *ibid.* § 1, ἐν τῷ μέρει λεγόντων. — προλαβὼν = φθάσας,
'having got the advantage of
me.'

εὐθυδικίᾳ εἰσιέναι] We might
expect the acc. as in Or. 34 § 4,
εὐθυδικίαν εἰσιόντα, οὐ κατηγορεῖν
τοῦ διώκοντος (cf. Or. 36 *Arg.*
l. 25 ἅπτεται τῆς εὐθείας n.); but
the dat. is found in Isaeus, Or.
6 (Philoctem.) § 53, μὴ διαμαρτυ-
ρίᾳ κωλύειν ἀλλ᾽ εὐθυδικίᾳ εἰσιέναι.

τὴν ἐπωβελίαν] The legal
fine of one-sixth of the amount
claimed (lit. one obol in each

drachma, or 6 obols), inflicted
on the plaintiff in private suits
(see on Or. 56 § 4) if he failed
to secure a fifth part of the
votes. In the present case,
Apoll. had to pay, in addition
to costs, a sixth part of 20
talents, 3^t 20^m = £666, if (with
Goodwin) we reckon the talent
at £200. (Boeckh, *Publ. Econ.*
Book iii chap. 10, pp. 473, 482
trans. Lamb.)—For οὐδὲ λόγου
τυχεῖν cf. § 19, ἀπεκλείσθην τοῦ
λόγου τυχεῖν.

7. οὐκ ἂν οἶδ᾽ ὅ τι ἄλλο εἶχον]
ἂν is often attracted to the negative and separated from its
verb (e.g. εἶχον) by the interposition of οἶδα (as here), οἴομαι,
δοκῶ, φημί (as elsewhere). (Cf.
note on Or. 37 (Pant.) § 16, οὐδ᾽
ἂν εἴ τι γένοιτο ᾠήθην δίκην μοι
λαχεῖν, also Goodwin's *Moods
and Tenses* § 42, 2, and Shilleto
on Thuc. i 76 § 4.) It is quite

τι ἄλλο εἶχον ψηφίσασθαι, τῶν πεπραγμένων μὲν
μηδὲν εἰδὼς, τὰ δὲ μαρτυρούμενα ἀκούων), τούτους δὲ
ἀξίους ὄντας ὀργῆς, οἳ τῷ τὰ ψευδῆ μαρτυρεῖν αἴτιοι
τούτων ἐγένοντο. περὶ μὲν δὴ τῶν ἄλλων τῶν μεμαρτυρηκότων, ὅταν πρὸς ἐκείνους εἰσίω, τότε ἐρῶ· περὶ
ὧν δ' οὑτοσὶ Στέφανος μεμαρτύρηκεν, ἤδη πειράσομαι
8 διδάσκειν ὑμᾶς. λαβὲ δ' αὐτὴν τὴν μαρτυρίαν καὶ
ἀνάγνωθί μοι, ἵνα ἐξ αὐτῆς ἐπιδεικνύω. λέγε· σὺ δ'
ἐπίλαβε τὸ ὕδωρ.

ΜΑΡΤΥΡΙΑ. 1104

ᵍ[Στέφανος Μενεκλέους Ἀχαρνεύς, Ἔνδιος Ἐπι-

ᵍ *testimonium omisit* Σ.   *uncos in hac quoque oratione addita-
mentis huius generis addidimus* Ζ.

unnecessary to accept the suggestion of Cobet οὐκ οἶδ' ἂν ὅ
τι (*Nov. Lect.* 581), or that of
Dobree '*distingue* αὐτὸς οὐκ ἂν,
οἶδ' ὅτι, ἄλλο εἶχον.'

πρὸς ἐκείνους εἰσίω] sc. εἰς
δικαστήριον. 'When I proceed
against *them*,' Endius and Scythes, contrasted with οὑτοσί, the
present defendant. Compare § 17,
ἐπὶ τοῦτον ᾖα, infr. § 41 ὅταν εἰσίω
πρὸς... and Or. 54 § 32 ad fin.
εἰσιέναι, or εἰσελθεῖν, is used of
either litigant (e.g. in Or. 40 § 1,
of the plaintiff; and *ib.* § 5 of
the defendant); and also of the
lawsuit itself in Or. 34 § 18. Cf.
Or. 34 § 1, οὐδεμίαν πώποτε δίκην
πρὸς ὑμᾶς εἰσήλθομεν, οὔτ' ἐγκαλοῦντες οὔτ' ἐγκαλούμενοι ὑφ' ἑτέρων.

8. ἐξ αὐτῆς] *ex ipsa*, perhaps,
rather than *ex ea*.—On ἐπίλαβε
τὸ ὕδωρ cf. note on Or. 54 § 36.

Στέφανος Μενεκλέους κ.τ.λ.]
Like many, if not most of the
documents inserted in the
speeches of the Attic Orators,
this deposition has been re

garded as spurious. Its purport
is to be found in §§ 9—26 and
in Or. 46 § 5. The names of
Tisias, Cephisophon and Amphias are given in §§ 10, 17, and
Or. 46 § 5. Stephanus and
Tisias, as well as Pasion and
Apollodorus are assigned to the
deme Acharnae in the documents only (§§ 28, 46), not in
the speech itself. Στέφανος
Ἀχαρνεὺς appears in an inscription as trierarch in B.C. 322, but
this (it has been suggested) is
not likely to be the defendant
in the present action, for at that
date the latter, if (as is not improbable) he was about the same
age as Apollodorus, would be about seventy; and we can hardly suppose that one who was so
poor a patriot as not to have
undertaken any public services
up to the age of 47 or thereabouts (§ 66), would have embarked on a trierarchy at so
advanced an age. But the name
was far from uncommon, and
the *deme* may (it is thought)

γένους Λαμπτρεὺς[h], Σκύθης Ἁρματέως Κυδαθηναιεὺς
μαρτυροῦσι παρεῖναι πρὸς τῷ διαιτητῇ Τισίᾳ Ἀχαρ-
νεῖ, ὅτε προὐκαλεῖτο Φορμίων Ἀπολλόδωρον, εἰ μή
φησιν ἀντίγραφα εἶναι τῶν διαθηκῶν τῶν Πασίωνος
τὸ γραμματεῖον ὃ ἐνεβάλετο Φορμίων εἰς τὸν ἐχῖνον,
ἀνοίγειν τὰς διαθήκας τὰς Πασίωνος, ἃς παρείχετο
πρὸς τὸν διαιτητὴν Ἀμφίας ὁ Κηφισοφῶντος κηδε-
στής· Ἀπολλόδωρον δὲ οὐκ ἐθέλειν ἀνοίγειν· εἶναι
δὲ τὰ[i] ἀντίγραφα τῶν διαθηκῶν τῶν Πασίωνος.][g]

Ἠκούσατε μὲν τῆς μαρτυρίας, ὦ ἄνδρες δικασταὶ, 9
νομίζω δ᾽ ὑμᾶς, εἰ καὶ μηδὲν τῶν ἄλλων αἰσθάνεσθέ

[h] Λαμπρεὺς Bekker 1824. 'immo Λαμπτρεὺς' Z, et Bekker st.

[i] τὰ Bekker. ταῦτα (Dobree). τάδ' (Sauppe, cf. Arg. line 9).
'Sequebatur enim quod hic deest testimonium Pasionis, cf. § 10 ad
fin.' Z.

have been assigned at random
by the writer of the document.

The name Ἔνδιος Ἐπιγένους
Λαμπτρεὺς is given in one MS
only (Φ). An inscription, however, of B.C. 325 gives the name
Κριτόδημος Ἐνδίου Λαμπτρεὺς
whose father may be the Ἔνδιος
of the text, though the name is
not a rare one.

Lastly, Σκύθης is naturally
an uncommon name for an
Athenian, though found as such
in an inscription. The name
of his father, Ἁρματεύς, does
not occur elsewhere, except in
Stephanus of Byzantium, who
makes it mean 'an inhabitant
of Harma' which he wrongly
supposes to be a deme of Attica,
whereas it was really the name
of a part of the range of Parnes.
(Abridged from A. Westermann's
*Untersuchungen über die in die
Attischen Redner eingelegten
Urkunden*, pp. 105—8.)

Blass, however, sees no ground
for rejecting the documents in
this speech; the names of the
witnesses, as Westermann himself admits, are supported by
the evidence of inscriptions
(Blass *Att. Ber.* III 409). Their
genuineness has been recently
maintained in a careful dissertation by Kirchner, 1883.

προὐκαλεῖτο...ἀνοίγειν] 'Challenged him, (in the event of his
denying that the document Phormion put into the box was a copy
of Pasion's will,) to open the
will of Pasion which &c.' On
ἐχῖνον see note on Or. 54 § 27.

εἶναι τὰ ἀντίγραφα κ.τ.λ.] A
loosely expressed sentence. τὰ
ἀντίγραφα τῶν διαθηκῶν cannot
be construed as the subject, and
unless we accept either τάδ' or
ταῦτ' for τὰ we must rather
awkwardly get the predicate
out of τὰ ἀντίγραφα. The
speaker himself expresses the
sense better in §§ 10, 23
(Westermann, u. s. p. 108).

§§ 9—14. *It is deposed that
Phormion challenged me to open*

πω, τοῦτό γε αὐτὸ θαυμάζειν, τὸ τὴν μὲν ἀρχὴν τῆς
μαρτυρίας εἶναι πρόκλησιν, τὴν δὲ τελευτὴν διαθήκην. οὐ μὴν ἀλλ' ἔγωγ' οἶμαι δεῖν, ἐπειδὰν, ὃ τῶν με-

the will, produced (it is alleged) before the arbitrator; that I refused the challenge and would not open the 'will'; that the document to which they depose is a counterpart of the original will; and then follows the copy.

Let us examine this evidence. In the first place, why should one have refused to open the document?

'Oh! to prevent the jury from hearing the terms of the will.'

But, I reply, the witnesses deposed to the will as well as to the challenge, and thus the jury would hear the terms of the 'will' publicly recited from the 'copy' whether I opened it or not. What was I to gain by refusing? Why! even if they had given no challenge, and had made a mere assertion, and if some one had produced a document purporting to be Pasion's will, it would have been my interest to challenge them and to open the will. In this case, (1) had the contents differed from the terms of the deposition, I should have appealed to the bystanders to bear witness to the discrepancy, which would have been a strong proof that the rest of their case was got up for a purpose. (2) Had the contents agreed, I should have required the producer himself to give evidence. Had he consented, I should have had in him a responsible witness; had he declined, here again I should have had sufficient proof that the affair was a fabrication. On this hypothesis, I should have had to deal with one witness only, instead of with many

(as my opponents have made it out); and of course I should have preferred the former, and so would every one else. For where (as here) there is room for cool calculation, no one would be so foolish as to abandon his own interests and do what would damage his case. And yet, by deposing that I refused to open the 'will,' these witnesses represented me as doing what is improbable, unreasonable, and contrary to all experience.

In brief, the first point which the plaintiff attempts to make in proving the evidence to be false, is that assuming he was challenged to open the 'will,' he sees no reason why he should have refused a challenge which it would have been to his interest to accept. On the other side, it may be noticed that the plaintiff had a strong reason for refusing to open the 'will,' and thus give express recognition to an important document, the contents of which as he himself says elsewhere (§ 21) were detrimental to his own interests. (A. Schaefer, *Dem.* III 2, p. 171). So far, the case clearly tends against Apollodorus.

9.   οὐ μὴν ἀλλ'...] 'Nevertheless', 'however', 'not but that.' The ellipse which this combination of particles always involves may be here supplied by some such words as οὐ μὴν (ὑμᾶς τοῦτο χρὴ θαυμάζειν) or (παραλείπειν τοῦτο χρὴ) ἀλλ' ἔγωγε κ.τ.λ. Kühner's *Gk. Gr.* § 535, 7.

τῶν μεμαρτ....κεφάλ.] sc. ἐμὲ οὐκ ἐθέλειν ἀνοίγειν.—τηνικαῦτα sc. in §§ 15—28.

μαρτυρημένων ὡσπερεὶ κεφάλαιόν ἐστιν, ἐπιδείξω ψεῦδος ὄν, τηνικαῦτ' ἤδη καὶ περὶ τῶν τοιούτων ποιεῖσθαι
τοὺς λόγους. ἔστι δὴ μεμαρτυρημένον αὐτοῖς προκα- 10
λεῖσθαι Φορμίωνα ἀνοίγειν τὰς διαθήκας, ἃς παρέχειν
πρὸς τὸν διαιτητὴν Τισίαν Ἀμφίαν τὸν Κηφισοφῶντος κηδεστήν· ἐμὲ δ' οὐκ ἐθέλειν ἀνοίγειν· εἶναι δὲ
ἃς αὐτοὶ μεμαρτυρήκασι διαθήκας, ἀντιγράφους ἐκείνων. εἶθ' ἡ διαθήκη γέγραπται. ἐγὼ τοίνυν περὶ μὲν 11
τοῦ προκαλεῖσθαί με ἢ μὴ ταῦτα Φορμίωνα οὐδέν πω
λέγω, οὐδὲ ὑπὲρ τοῦ τὰς διαθήκας ἀληθεῖς ἢ ψευδεῖς
εἶναι, ἀλλ' αὐτίχ' ὑμᾶς περὶ τούτων διδάξω· ἀλλ' ἃ
μεμαρτυρήκασι, μή μ' ἐθέλειν τὸ γραμματεῖον ἀνοί-
γειν. ὡδὶ δὴ σκοπεῖτε. τοῦ τις ἂν ἕνεκα^j ἔφευγεν ἀνοί-
1105 γειν, τὸ γραμματεῖον; ἵν' ἡ διαθήκη νὴ Δία μὴ φανερὰ
γένοιτο τοῖς δικασταῖς. εἰ μὲν τοίνυν μὴ προσεμαρτύ- 12
ρουν τῇ προκλήσει τὴν διαθήκην οὗτοι, λόγον εἶχέ
τιν' ἂν τὸ φεύγειν ἐμὲ ἀνοίγειν τὸ γραμματεῖον· προσ-
μαρτυρούντων δὲ τούτων καὶ τῶν δικαστῶν ὁμοίως

^j εἵνεκεν Z cum Σ.

10. ἃς παρέχειν] sc. μαρτυροῦσι. For the infinitive in the
relative clause influenced by the
principal verb, cf. Or. 36 § 25.

εἶθ' ἡ διαθήκη γέγραπται]
'Then follows a copy of the will,'
or (with Kennedy) 'and then
the will is set out.' 'Deinde
sequitur (in testimonio corum)
testamentum exscriptum, sequitur exemplum testamenti.' Seager, Classical Journ. lx p. 267.

11. περὶ...ὑπὲρ] These prepo-
sitions are here, as often, practically synonymous. Cf. infra
§ 50, and Fals. Leg. § 94, p. 371,
οὐ περὶ τοῦ εἰ ποιητέον εἰρήνην...
ἀλλ' ὑπὲρ τοῦ ποίαν τινά.

τοῦ τις ἂν ἕνεκα ἔφευγεν κ.τ.λ.]
'What reason would any one
have had for declining, &c.'

'Malim ἕνεκεν καὶ ἔφευγεν...
Latine porro,' says Dobree, who
would similarly read in Or. 37
§ 27, τίνος γὰρ ἕνεκα καὶ ἔπειθον,
'ut in tali re usitatum est dicere'
(Cobet, Nov. Lect. 606).

νὴ Δία] Or. 36 § 39, and Or.
54 § 34 n.

12. εἰ...μὴ προσεμαρτύρουν]
'Had they not deposed to the
will, as well as to the challenge,
I might reasonably have declined to open the document
(purporting to be a copy of the
will): but, as they actually deposed to both, and as the jury
would have to hear the will
whether I opened it or not, what
was the use then of my refusing
to open it?'

ἀκουσομένων, τί ἦν μοι κέρδος τὸ μὴ ἐθέλειν; οὐδὲ ἓν
δήπου. αὐτὸ γὰρ τοὐναντίον, ὦ ἄνδρες Ἀθηναῖοι,
κἂν εἰ μηδὲν προὐκαλοῦντο οὗτοι, λόγῳ δ᾽ ἐχρῶντο
13 μόνον, καὶ παρεῖχέ τις αὐτοῖς γραμματεῖον ὡς διαθήκην, ἐμὸν ἦν τὸ προκαλεῖσθαι καὶ ἀνοίγειν[k] ταύτην,
ἵν᾽ εἰ μὲν ἄλλ᾽ ἄττα τῶν ὑπὸ τούτων μεμαρτυρημένων
ἦν τἀκεῖ γεγραμμένα, μάρτυρας εὐθὺς τῶν περιεστηκότων πολλοὺς ποιησάμενος τεκμηρίῳ τούτῳ καὶ περὶ
τῶν ἄλλων, ὡς κατασκευάζουσιν, ἐχρώμην· εἰ δὲ ταῦτ᾽
ἐνῆν, τὸν παρασχόντ᾽ αὐτὸν ἠξίουν μαρτυρεῖν. ἐθελήσαντος μὲν γὰρ ὑπεύθυνον ἐλάμβανον, εἰ δ᾽ ἔφευγε,

[k] κελεύειν ἀνοίγειν Φ (γρ. in margine). 'recte, opinor; sin,
deleam καὶ ante ἀνοίγειν' G. H. Schaefer.

κἂν εἰ] The ἂν strictly belongs to the apodosis ἐμὸν ἦν,
but is here, as often, put as
early as possible. Cf. Or. 36 §
42, οἶμαι...κἂν εἰ...λέγοι, κάλλιον
εἶναι. Sometimes the construction of the apodosis shows that
κἂν εἰ is regarded as much the
same as καὶ εἰ, e.g. Plato Meno
72 c, κἂν εἰ πολλαὶ καὶ παντοδαπαί
εἰσιν, ἕν γέ τι εἶδος ταὐτὸν ἅπασαι
ἔχουσι. Kühner, *Gk. Gr.* § 398,
p. 210. Buttmann calls this
"ἂν *consopitum*," where its force
is, as it were, dormant. It is
peculiar to the later or middle
Attic.

§ 13. ἵν᾽—ἐχρώμην] Or. 36
§ 47, ἵνα—ἐφαίνετο n.

ἀλλ᾽ ἄττα τῶν κ.τ.λ.] = ἀλλ᾽
ἄττα ἢ τὰ, i.e. 'had the contents of the alleged will been
different from the terms deposed
to by these witnesses.' For this
rather uncommon use of ἄλλος
with gen. (like ἕτερος, ἀλλότριος,
διάφορος) cf. Xen. Mem. IV
4 § 25, πότερον τοὺς θεοὺς ἡγῇ τὰ
δίκαια νομοθετεῖν ἢ ἄλλα τῶν
δικαίων. ἀλλότριος is so used in
Dem. 18 § 182, but I cannot

find any similar use of ἄλλος in
Demosthenes.—Dobree suggests
ἀλλ᾽ ἄττα ἀντὶ τῶν.

τεκμηρίῳ κ.τ.λ.] sc. τούτῳ
ἐχρώμην τεκμηρίῳ ὡς καὶ τἄλλα
κατασκευάζουσι.—In the next
clause αὐτὸν ('to give evidence
himself') is contrasted with the
several witnesses, οἱ περὶ Στέφανον.

ἐθελήσαντος μὲν] i.e. εἰ μὲν
ἠθέλησε, contrasted with εἰ δ᾽
ἔφευγε. We should naturally
expect ἐθελήσαντα, as the use
of gen. absolute, in reference
to the same person as the acc.
ὑπεύθυνον, is somewhat exceptional, the rule being that the
gen. absolute is generally found
only when there is no other
case in the sentence to which
the participle might attach itself. Cf. however, Xen. Cyr.
I 4 § 2, ἀσθενήσαντος αὐτοῦ (sc.
τοῦ πάππου) οὐδέποτε ἀπέλιπε
τὸν πάππον. (Kühner, *Gk. Gr.*
§ 494 b, Madvig, *Gk. Synt.*
§ 181 R 6.)

ὑπεύθυνον] Liable to a prosecution for false witness.

πάλιν αὐτὸ τοῦθ' ἱκανὸν τεκμήριον ἦν μοι τοῦ πεπλά-
σθαι τὸ πρᾶγμα. καὶ δὴ καὶ συνέβαινεν ἐκείνως μὲν
ἕνα εἶναι, πρὸς ὃν τὰ πράγματα ἐγίγνετό μοι, ὡς δ'
οὗτοι μεμαρτυρήκασι, πρὸς πολλούς. ἔστιν οὖν ὅστις
ἂν¹ ὑμῶν ταῦθ' εἵλετο; ἐγὼ μὲν οὐδένα ἡγοῦμαι. οὐ 14
τοίνυν οὐδὲ κατ' ἄλλου πιστεύειν ἐστὲ δίκαιοι. καὶ γάρ,
ὦ ἄνδρες Ἀθηναῖοι, ὅσοις μὲν πρόσεστιν ὀργὴ τῶν
πραττομένων ἢ λῆμμά τι κέρδους ἢ παροξυσμὸς ἢ φι-

¹ Bekker (st. Leipzig ed.). 'ἂν deesse vidit Schaeferus' Z.

συνέβαινεν κ.τ.λ.] Kennedy
translates: 'And the result was,
that in that way, I had one
person to deal with.' The conditional is only implied and not
directly expressed, in other
words συνέβαινεν (like ἠξίουν...
ἐλάμβανον...ἦν above) is put without ἄν.—'Malim καὶ δὴ κἂν συνέβαινεν et mox ἔστιν οὖν ὅστις ἂν
ὑμῶν,' says Dobree, comparing
§ 33 bis, and also proposing in
§ 34 τίς γὰρ ἂν ἀνθρώπων. The
last two emendations are accepted in Dindorf's text.

[All the imperfects in this remarkable sentence, which does
not read altogether like the
style of Demosthenes, depend
on the preceding ἵνα, 'in which
case it would have happened
that, &c.' The addition of ἄν
would be quite out of place here,
though it is necessary in the
clause ἔστιν οὖν ὅστις ἂν ὑμῶν,
which passes into quite a different construction. P.]

ἐκείνως] 'In the former case,'
lit. 'in that other way,' under
the hypothesis just mentioned
(as opposed to the fact ὡς οὗτοι
μεμαρτυρήκασι), sc. εἰ τὸν παρα-
σχόντ' ἠξίουν μαρτυρεῖν, including
the subsequent subdivision of
that supposition into the two
further hypotheses, ἐθελήσαντος
μὲν κ.τ.λ. and εἰ δ' ἔφευγε κ.τ.λ.

πρὸς πολλούς] sc. τὰ πράγματα γενέσθαι μοι.

14. οὐ...οὐδὲ κατ' ἄλλου πισ-
τεύειν] 'Well then, you cannot
fairly believe it of any one else
either.'

ὅσοις...τῶν πραττομένων] The
participle is best taken not as
gen. after ὀργὴ but after ὅσοις,
which is neuter. Cf. § 15, ὅσα...
τῶν πεπραγμένων. 'In every
course of action attended by
anger, or by getting of gain, or
by any exasperation ('keen resentment,' 'strong provocation'),
or by a spirit of jealousy, one
man may act in one way,
another in another, according
to his individual character.'

παροξυσμὸς] This word, found
twice in the New Testament
(Hebr. x 24, Acts xv 39), is
never used by Demosthenes,
nor indeed does it appear to
occur elsewhere in the sense of
'exasperation' in any of the
earlier Greek writers. In the
Aphorisms of Hippocrates, 1243
(Liddell & Scott), it is a medical
term, in the sense perpetuated
in our 'paroxysm.' The verb
however is found in Or. 57
(Eubul.) § 49, ἡ πόλις πᾶσα...
ὀργιζομένη παρώξυντο, ib. § 2,
Or. 47 (Energ.) § 19; also the
adj. in Or. 20 (Lept.) § 105, λόγοι
παροξυντικοὶ πρὸς τὸ...πεῖσαι.

λονεικία, ταῦτα μὲν ἄλλος ἂν ἄλλως πράξειε πρὸς τὸν
αὐτοῦ τρόπον· ὅσοις δὲ τούτων μὲν μηδὲν, λογισμὸς
δ᾽ ἐφ᾽ ἡσυχίας τοῦ συμφέροντος, τίς οὕτως ἄφρων
ὅστις ἂν τὰ συνοίσοντ᾽[m] ἀφεὶς, ἐξ ὧν κάκιον ἔμελλεν
ἀγωνιεῖσθαι, ταῦτ᾽ ἔπραξεν; ἃ γὰρ οὔτ᾽ εἰκότα οὔτ᾽ 1106
εὔλογα οὔτ᾽ ἂν ἔπραξεν οὐδεὶς, ταῦθ᾽ οὗτοι μεμαρτυρήκασι περὶ ἡμῶν.

15   Οὐ τοίνυν μόνον ἐξ ὧν ἐμὲ μὴ ἐθέλειν[n] τὸ γραμματεῖον ἀνοίγειν μεμαρτυρήκασι, γνοίη τις ἂν αὐτοὺς ὅτι
ψεύδονται, ἀλλὰ καὶ ἐκ τοῦ πρόκλησιν ὁμοῦ διαθήκῃ

[m] συνοίσοντα Z.   [n] θέλειν Σ.

λογισμὸς κ.τ.λ. 'A calm calculation of one's interest.' [The
phrase seems rather unusual,
like ἀφεὶς τὰ συνοίσοντα, 'giving
up what was likely to prove his
interest.' P.]

§§ 15—19. *Again, the witnesses depose to a Challenge as
well as to a Will. Now Challenges are meant to meet the case
of those transactions, which it
is otherwise impossible to bring
before the court. In the present
case, what call was there for
a Challenge? The arbitration
took place in Athens, and they
have deposed that the original
will was produced before the
arbitrator. If this was true,
they ought to have put the
original will into the box and
the producer should have proved
it by evidence. In that case the
jury, after weighing the credi-
bility of the deposition and in-
specting the seals of the will,
would have decided accordingly; and, had I thought myself
wronged by the verdict, I might
have proceeded against the deponent in question. But, as it
is, no single witness has undertaken the whole responsibility;*
*no! they have cleverly divided
it, by one witness (Cephisophon)
deposing to having a document
inscribed 'Pasion's Will'; and
another (Amphias), to having
produced it after being sent to
do so by the former witness; but
whether it was genuine or not,
was 'more than he knew.'—In
fact, Stephanus and his friends
made the Challenge a mere mask
to enable them to depose to a will,
so that the jury were led to believe that the will was my father's,
and I myself was debarred from
being heard on my wrongs, and
so that by these very means my
opponents might ultimately be
convicted of having given false
evidence—a result which they
hardly expected.*

15. μὴ ἐθέλειν] ἐθέλω is the
proper form in Attic prose, θέλω
in Attic verse, but the latter is
occasionally found in Dem. in
such formulae as ἂν θεὸς θέλῃ.
(See Veitch *Gk. Vbs.*) The Paris
MS Σ has θέλειν, which was
adopted in Dindorf's earlier
editions.

πρόκλησεις] Harpocr. s. v.
εἰώθεσαν ὁπότε δικάζοιντό τινες,
ἐξαιτεῖν ἐνίοτε θεραπαίνας ἢ θερά-

μαρτυρεῖν. οἶμαι γὰρ ἅπαντας ὑμᾶς εἰδέναι ὅτι ὅσα μὴ
δυνατὸν πρὸς ὑμᾶς ἀγαγεῖν ἐστι τῶν πεπραγμένων,
τούτων προκλήσεις εὑρέθησαν. οἶον βασανίζειν οὐκ 16
ἔστιν ἐναντίον ὑμῶν· ἀνάγκη τούτου πρόκλησιν εἶναι·
οἶον εἴ τι πέπρακται καὶ γέγονεν ἔξω που τῆς χώρας,
ἀνάγκη καὶ τούτου πρόκλησιν εἶναι πλεῖν ἢ βαδίζειν

ποντας εἰς βάσανον ἢ εἰς μαρτυρίαν
τοῦ πράγματος, καὶ τοῦτο ἐκαλεῖτο
προκαλεῖσθαι, τὸ δὲ γραμματεῖον
τὸ περὶ τούτου γραφόμενον ὠ-
νομάζετο πρόκλησις. παρὰ πολλοῖς δέ ἐστι ῥήτορσι. Δημοσθένης
δ' ἐν τῷ κατὰ Στεφάνου καὶ περὶ
ὧν πρόκλησις γίνεται δηλοῖ. Hermann, *Public Antiquities*, § 141,
20.

16. βασανίζειν οὐκ ἔστιν ἐναντίον
ὑμῶν] In Dobree's *Adversaria*,
we have the suggestive note
'*Qu. interrog. Qu. the fact.*'
As a general rule doubtless this
examination of slaves took place
in private, before a magistrate
or arbitrator or other authorized
person, in the presence of a
number of bystanders either
concerned as witnesses or merely present out of curiosity (Or. 47
§ 12); and the text as it stands
would seem to imply that administration of torture in open
court was not allowed.—We
find Aeschines (Fals. Leg. § 126)
proposing to 'question' certain
slaves in public: ἄγωμεν δὲ καὶ
τοὺς οἰκέτας καὶ παραδιδῶμεν εἰς
βάσανον...παρέσται δὲ ἤδη ὁ δήμιος
καὶ βασανιεῖ ἐναντίον ὑμῶν,
ἂν κελεύητε...κάλει μοι τοὺς οἰκέτας δεῦρο ἐπὶ τὸ βῆμα... At
this point (it is important to
notice) follows a Challenge
which Demosthenes declines.
Thus we have a *proposal* only,
and it may be concluded from
ἂν κελεύητε, that even if the
Challenge had been accepted,

the court would have had to
give a special order for such
departure from ordinary usage.
Again in [Dem.] Or. 47 κατὰ
Εὐέργου ψευδομαρτυριῶν § 17, we
read: ἔδει αὐτόν, εἴπερ ἀληθῆ ἦν
ἅ φασιν αὐτὸν προκαλεῖσθαι, κλη-
ρουμένων τῶν δικαστηρίων κομί-
σαντα τὴν ἄνθρωπον, λαβόντα τὸν
κήρυκα, κελεύειν ἐμέ, εἰ βουλοίμην,
βασανίζειν, καὶ μάρτυρας τοὺς δικαστὰς εἰσιόντας ποιεῖσθαι ὡς
ἕτοιμός ἐστι παραδοῦναι (cf. ib.
§ 6). But it would be idle to
suppose that this passage proves
that the torture might take place
in open court; all that is meant
is that the defendant might
have produced the girl, when
the court was about to sit,
challenged the plaintiff to 'question' her, and called on the
jurors to bear witness that he
was *ready* to hand her over to
be tortured in the usual manner
and *not* in public court.

οἶον—ἔξω τῆς χώρας] As an
illustration of this form of
Challenge, we find in Or. 32 the
plaintiff (Zenothemis) borrowing money in Syracuse (§ 4) and
the defendant challenging him
at Athens to sail to Syracuse
and appear before the authorities there (§ 18). Cf. *ex iure
manum consertum voco* in Cicero
pro Murena § 26 (with Mr
Heitland's note).

πλεῖν ἢ βαδίζειν] Here, as
often, contrasted with one another, as the ordinary words

οὗ τὸ πρᾶγμ' ἐπράχθη· καὶ τῶν ἄλλων τῶν τοιούτων.
ὅπου δ' αὐτὰ τὰ πράγματα ἐφ' αὑτῶν ἔστιν ὑμῖν ἐμφανῆ ποιῆσαι, τί ἦν ἁπλούστερον ἢ ταῦτ' ἄγειν εἰς μέ-
17 σον; Ἀθήνησι μὲν τοίνυν ὁ πατὴρ ἐτελεύτησεν οὑμὸς,
ἐγίγνετο δ' ἡ δίαιτα ἐν τῇ ποικίλῃ στοᾷ, μεμαρτυρήκασι δ' οὗτοι παρέχειν τὸ γραμματεῖον Ἀμφίαν πρὸς
τὸν διαιτητήν. οὐκοῦν εἴπερ ἀληθὲς ἦν, ἐχρῆν αὐτὸ τὸ
γραμματεῖον εἰς τὸν ἐχῖνον ἐμβαλεῖν καὶ τὸν παρέχοντα
μαρτυρεῖν, ἵν' ἐκ τῆς ἀληθείας καὶ τοῦ τὰ σημεῖα ἰδεῖν
οἱ μὲν δικασταὶ τὸ πρᾶγμα ἔγνωσαν, ἐγὼ δὲ, εἴ τις ἠδί-

for 'going by sea or by land,'
Fals. Leg. § 164 οὔτ' ἐπείγεσθαι
βαδίζουσιν οὔτε πλεῖν αὐτοῖς ἐπ-
ήει.

17. ποικίλῃ στοᾷ] 'The painted
portico.' So called from its
pictures, representing the legen-
dary wars of Athens and the
battle of Marathon. See Or. 59
(Neaer.) § 94 and Aeschin.
Ctesiph. § 186. As is well
known, it was this portico which
gave the name of Stoics to the
followers of Zeno of Citium.
Persius III 53, *quaeque docet
sapiens bracatis illita Medis
Porticus.* It is placed east of
the market of the Cerameicus in
Curtius, *Text der sieben Karten*
p. 35.

The *public* arbitrators had
particular buildings assigned
them according to the tribe to
which they belonged : thus in
Or. 47 § 12 the arbitration takes
place in the Heliaea, οἱ γὰρ τὴν
Οἰνηΐδα καὶ τὴν Ἐρεχθηΐδα διαι-
τῶντες ἐνταῦθα κάθηνται.

ἐχρῆν] As usual, without ἄν.
We might have had εἴπερ ἀληθὲς ἦν, ἐνέβαλεν ἂν τὸ γραμματεῖον, implying ἀλλ' οὐκ ἐνέβαλεν,
whereas the sentence as it stands
does not require ἄν because it

implies *not* ἀλλ' οὐκ ἐχρῆν, but
χρὴ μὲν ἐμβαλεῖν ἀλλ' οὐκ
ἐνέβαλεν. So also with ὤφελον,
ἔμελλον, ἔδει, προσῆκεν; '*sed
multo latius patet haec ratio...
Omnino, ubicunque non potest
contrarium opponi, recte abest
particula.*' Hermann *de particula* ἄν § XII. On a similar
principle we have τί ἦν ἁπλούστερον above, which follows the
analogy of δίκαιον ἦν, εἰκὸς ἦν,
&c.

τὰ σημεῖα] Probably the seals
attached to the will (cf. Becker's
Charicles, Sc. IX note 14), and
not those on the deposition-case
or ἐχῖνος (as supposed in Stark's
addenda to Hermann's *Privatalt.*
§ 65, 9). On the ἐχῖνος cf. Or. 39
§ 18, σεσημασμένων τῶν ἐχίνων,
and note on Or. 54 § 27. For
the opening of the seals of a will,
see Ar. Vesp. 584, κλάειν ἡμεῖς
μακρὰ τὴν κεφαλὴν εἰπόντες τῇ
διαθήκῃ, καὶ τῇ κόγχῃ τῇ πάνυ
σεμνῶς τοῖς σημείοισιν ἐπούσῃ.

ᾖα] 'perhaps old Attic, Plat.
Theaet. 180, Rep. 449' Veitch,
Greek Verbs s.v. εἶμι. As *first*
person ᾖειν is rare, but προσῄειν
is not. In § 6 we have had
ἀπῄειν. See Cobet, *Variae Lect.*
p. 307.

κει με, ἐπὶ τοῦτον ᾖα· νῦν δὲ εἰς μὲν οὐδεὶς ὅλον τὸ 18
πρᾶγμα ἀνεδέξατο, οὐδὲ μεμαρτύρηκεν ἁπλῶς, ὡς ἄν
τις τἀληθῆ μαρτυρήσειε, μέρος δ᾽ ἕκαστος, ὡς δὴ σο-
φὸς καὶ διὰ τοῦτο οὐ δώσων δίκην, ὁ μὲν γραμματεῖον
ἔχειν ἐφ᾽ ᾧ γεγράφθαι "διαθήκη Πασίωνος," ὁ δὲ πεμφθεὶς ὑπὸ τούτου παρέχειν τοῦτο, εἰ δ᾽ ἀληθὲς ἢ ψεῦ-
1107 δος, οὐδὲν εἰδέναι.   οἱδὶ δὲ τῇ προκλήσει χρησάμενοι 19
παραπετάσματι διαθήκας ἐμαρτύρησαν, ὡς ἂν μάλισθ᾽
οἱ δικασταὶ ταύτην τὴν διαθήκην ἐπίστευσαν τοῦ πατρὸς εἶναι, ἐγὼ δὲ ἀπεκλείσθην τοῦ λόγου τυχεῖν ὑπὲρ
ὧν ἀδικοῦμαι, οὗτοι δὲ φωραθεῖεν τὰ ψευδῆ μεμαρτυ-

18. εἶς...οὐδεὶς] 'No single witness has accepted the whole responsibility'; cf. § 38 διείλοντο τἀδικήματα. εἶς οὐδεὶς is a much stronger negative than οὐδείς. Or. 21 (Midias) § 12, ἐν γὰρ οὐδέν ἐστιν ἐφ᾽ ᾧ...οὐ δίκαιος ὢν ἀπολωλέναι φανήσεται. Cf. Fals. Leg. § 201, ἐν οὐδ᾽ ὁτιοῦν.

ὁ μὲν...ὁ δὲ] Cephisophon (§§ 21, 22)...Amphias (ὁ Κηφισοφῶντος κηδεστής, § 10).—The subject of ἕκαστος (ὁ μὲν...ὁ δὲ) is μεμαρτύρηκε implied by the former part of the sentence. This is all that is meant by Dobree's punctuation 'Distingue ὁ δὲ, πεμφθεὶς,' to show that πεμφθεὶς is subordinate to παρέχειν and is not to be taken with ὁ δέ. Trans. 'another, that he produced the will on being sent by him (Amphias).'

19. παραπετάσματι] sc. προφάσει (Or. 46 § 9 πρόφασιν...τὴν πρόκλησιν), προσχήματι, as a 'cloak,' or 'pretext,' lit. a 'screen' or 'curtain.' Plat. Protag. 316 E ταῖς τέχναις ταύταις παραπετάσμασιν ἐχρήσαντο, immediately after προσχῆμα ποιεῖσθαι καὶ προκαλύπτεσθαι.

ὡς ἂν μάλισθ᾽ οἱ δικασταί...

ἐπίστευσαν ... ἐγὼ δὲ ἀπεκλείσθην ... οὗτοι δὲ φωραθεῖεν ...] This sentence, as it stands in the MSS, can only mean 'The present witnesses (Stephanus, &c) used the challenge as a pretext for giving evidence of a will, in the very way in which the court *would have* believed that the will was my father's, and I *should have been* debarred from getting a hearing, and in which my opponents *would* now *be* palpably convicted of giving false evidence.' This makes nonsense, as the jury in the former trial *did* believe the witnesses, and Apollodorus *was* debarred from speaking. ἂν is quite out of place with ἐπίστευσαν and ἀπεκλείσθην, but not so with φωραθεῖεν (which cannot here be taken as a simple optative expressing a wish). It thus appears that we should (with G. H. Schaefer) remove ἂν from the aorist indicative and place it with the aor. optative, and read as follows: ὡς (or ὥσθ᾽) οἱ δικασταί...ἐπίστευσαν, ἐγὼ δὲ ἀπεκλείσθην...οὗτοι δ᾽ ἂν μάλιστα φωραθεῖεν. The sense thus gained is fairly satisfactory: 'the

ρηκότες. καίτοι τό γ᾽ ἐναντίον ᾤοντο τούτου. ἵνα δ᾽ εἰδῆτε ταῦτα ὅτι ἀληθῆ λέγω, λαβὲ τὴν τοῦ Κηφισοφῶντος μαρτυρίαν.

witnesses combined the attestation of a challenge with the attestation of a will (made the former a pretext for the latter). The immediate result was that the jury in the previous trial believed the will was really my father's and therefore decided against me without giving me a hearing on my present wrongs. The ultimate result was that by that very means my opponents would be clearly convicted of having given false evidence.'

Hermann attempts to explain the passage by the following translation :

' *Illi vero, provocationis praetextu usi, de testamento testati sunt eo modo, quo facillime judices hoc patris testamentum esse credere, ego autem ab oranda causa mea excludi debebam* [?], *ipsi vero—falsa testati esse deprehenderentur; atqui contrarium sperabant.* Illa enim οὗτοι δέ, (hic voce paullum subsistit orator) φωραθεῖεν τὰ ψευδῆ μεμαρτυρηκότες, ironice dicta esse patet' (*Opuscula* IV 27 de particula ἄν I 7).

Dobree says : ' Sensus est : ita rem administrarunt, ut tunc quidem judices deciperent ; postea autem hoc palam fieret, quamvis id non praeviderent.— Qu. de *modorum* permutatione. Similis locus F. Leg. 424. 16 ' τοσοῦτ᾽ ἀπέχουσι τοῦ τοιοῦτόν τι ποιεῖν, ὥστε θαυμάζουσι καὶ ζηλοῦσι καὶ βούλοιντ᾽ ἂν αὐτὸς ἕκαστος τοιοῦτος εἶναι.

[I suggest ὡς ἂν εἰ μάλιστα, and *perhaps* οὗτοί γε infra (though οὗτοι δέ might mean

'yet these' &c). 'They gave their evidence so, that if the dicasts were ever so much persuaded, and I was stopped from further proceedings then, yet they will be detected in having lied.' ὡς ἂν φωραθεῖεν is a virtual synonym of ὥστε φωραθῆναι. See Aesch. Ag. 357, ὅπως ἂν βέλος ἠλίθιον σκήψειεν.

For the use of δὲ in apodosis, cf. Or. 21 (Mid.) p. 547 § 100, εἰ δέ τις πένης μηδὲν ἠδικηκὼς ταῖς ἐσχάταις συμφοραῖς ἀδίκως ὑπὸ τούτου περιπέπτωκε, τούτῳ δ᾽ οὐδὲ συνοργισθήσεσθε ; and for ὡς ἂν with optative equivalent to ὥστε, see Plat. Phaedr. p. 230 B, καὶ ὡς ἀκμὴν ἔχει τῆς ἄνθης, ὡς ἂν εὐωδέστατον παρέχοι τὸν τόπον, ' see how this willow is in full blossom, so as to fill the place with fragrance !' Symp. p. 187 D, τοῖς μὲν κοσμίοις τῶν ἀνθρώπων, καὶ ὡς ἂν κοσμιώτεροι γίγνοιντο οἱ μήπω ὄντες, δεῖ χαρίζεσθαι. P.]

§§ 19—23. *To prove this, take the evidence of Cephisophon. He deposes to a document having been left him by my father, inscribed ' Pasion's Will'; thinking that to depose to this only was a mere trifle, and that he could not safely go so far as to add (what in itself would have been a simple matter) ' that this was the document produced by the deponent.'—Now, had Phormion's name appeared outside, the deponent might reasonably have kept the document for Phormion; further, had it really been endorsed 'Pasion's Will,' it would have belonged to me by inheritance like the rest of my father's*

ΜΑΡΤΥΡΙΑ.

[n][Κηφισοφῶν Κεφάλωνος 'Αφιδναῖος μαρτυρεῖ καταλειφθῆναι αὐτῷ ὑπὸ τοῦ πατρὸς γραμματεῖον, ἐφ'
ᾧ ἐπιγεγράφθαι διαθήκη Πασίωνος.][n]

Οὐκοῦν ἦν ἁπλοῦν, ὦ ἄνδρες δικασταὶ, τὸν ταῦτα 20
μαρτυροῦντα προσμαρτυρῆσαι " εἶναι δὲ τὸ γραμμα-
" τεῖον, ὃ αὐτὸς παρέχει, τοῦτο," καὶ τὸ γραμματεῖον
ἐμβαλεῖν. ἀλλὰ τοῦτο μὲν, οἶμαι, τὸ ψεῦδος ἡγεῖτο ὀρ-

[n] *testimonium om.* Σ.

---

property, and I should of course have appropriated it, feeling that, with a lawsuit before me, the will, if its terms were those alleged, would be rather detrimental to my interests. The fact that, in spite of the alleged endorsement, it has been produced to Phormion, not to myself, and been let alone by me, proves the forgery of the will and the falsehood of the deposition of Cephisophon. However, I dismiss him for the present, especially as he has given no evidence on the contents of the will, which by the way is a strong proof of the falsehood of the deposition of Stephanus and his friends. Cephisophon, the very person who deposes to having the document, did not dare to depose to its identity with that produced by Phormion; and yet the present witnesses (Stephanus and his friends) have declared that it is a copy of the other, though they cannot claim to have been present when the will was drawn up, never saw it opened before the arbitrator, and indeed have deposed that I refused to open it. If so, have they not clearly charged themselves with having given false evidence?

Μαρτυρία] The wording of this deposition is identical with that of the speech itself (§§ 18 and 20), with the exception of the clause ὑπὸ τοῦ πατρὸς, (naturally suggested by καταλειφθῆναι,) and the description of the witness as Κεφάλωνος 'Αφιδναῖος. Κεφάλων is a parallel form of Κεφαλίων and is found elsewhere (Plut. Arat. 52). One Κηφισοφῶν 'Αφιδναῖος is mentioned in inscriptions as trierarch and commander of the fleet, and it has been proposed to identify him with the witness in this case, though the name of the trierarch's father is not given (Boeckh, *Seewesen* p. 442). The composer of the deposition may have been led to assign Cephisophon to Aphidna by a passage in Or. 59 κατὰ Νεαίρας §§ 9—10, where a person of that name bribes one Stephanus of Erocadae to charge Apollodorus with causing the death of a woman at Aphidna. (A. Westermann *u.s.* pp. 108—9, cf. § 8 *supra.*) The authenticity of the document is, however, confirmed by the fact that an inscription of the year 343 B.C. mentions Κηφισοφῶν Κεφαλίωνος 'Αφιδναῖος (C. I. A. II 1, 114 c. 6 quoted by Kirchner p. 28).

20. ἐμβαλεῖν] sc. εἰς τὸν

γῆς ἄξιον, καὶ δίκην ἂν ὑμᾶς παρ' αὐτοῦ λαβεῖν, γραμματεῖον δ' αὐτῷ καταλειφθῆναι μαρτυρῆσαι φαῦλον
καὶ οὐδέν. ἔστι δὲ τοῦτ' αὐτὸ τὸ δηλοῦν καὶ κατηγο-
21 ροῦν ὅτι πᾶν τὸ πρᾶγμα κατεσκευάκασιν. εἰ μὲν γὰρ
ἐπῆν ἐπὶ τῆς διαθήκης "Πασίωνος καὶ Φορμίωνος" ἢ
"πρὸς Φορμίωνα" ἢ τοιοῦτό τι, εἰκότως ἂν αὐτὴν ἐτήρει τούτῳ· εἰ δ', ὥσπερ μεμαρτύρηκεν, ἐπῆν "διαθήκη
"Πασίωνος," πῶς οὐκ ἂν ἀνῃρήμην αὐτὴν ἐγώ, συνειδὼς μὲν ἐμαυτῷ μέλλοντι δικάζεσθαι, συνειδὼς δ' ὑπε-
ναντίαν οὖσαν, εἴπερ ἦν τοιαύτη, τοῖς ἐμαυτῷ συμ-
φέρουσι, κληρονόμος δὲ ὢν καὶ ταύτης, εἴπερ ἦν τοῦ-
22 μοῦ πατρὸς, καὶ τῶν ἄλλων πατρῴων ὁμοίως; οὐκοῦν

ἐχῖνον, § 17.—ὀργὴ, the indignation of the court.—ἂν λαβεῖν
depends, like the previous
clause, on ἡγεῖτο.

γραμματεῖον δὲ] 'Whereas to
give evidence of a document
having been bequeathed to him,
was a trifle of no importance.'
Kennedy.

'Πασίωνος καὶ Φορμίωνος.'] 'At
ineptus Pasio fuisset, si hoc
inscripsisset ; de utrisque enim,
et Phormione et filiis, in eo
constituerat' (Lortzing Apoll.
p. 78).—ἐτήρει τούτῳ sc. Φορμίωνι.
'If the inscription had been,
This belongs to Pasio, and to
Phormion, or for Phormion, or
anything of that sort, he would
reasonably have kept it for him.'

21. πῶς οὐκ ἂν ἀνῃρήμην...] 'I
should of course have appropriated it.' The plaintiff actually says that if the terms of
the will were such as alleged
and if it had been really inscribed ' Pasion's Will ' (διαθήκη
is emphatic : 'had the endorsement been, not merely, ' This is
Pasion's,' but 'This is Pasion's
will,' &c), then he would certainly have claimed it as heir to his

father's property and, finding it
detrimental to his own interests, would have kept it close.'
The effrontery of this statement
is sufficiently startling.

As regards the phrase διαθήκην
ἀναιρεῖσθαι, it may be noticed that
in Isaeus Or. 6 (Philoct.) §§ 30—
33, we have πείθουσι τὸν Εὐκτή-
μονα τὴν διαθήκην ἀνελεῖν ὡς οὐ
χρησίμην οὖσαν τοῖς παισί· followed by ὁ Εὐκτήμων ἔλεγεν ὅτι
βούλοιτ' ἀνελέσθαι τὴν διαθήκην
and ποιησάμενος πολλοὺς μάρτυρας
ὡς οὐκέτι αὐτῷ κέοιτο ἡ διαθήκη,
ᾤχετο ἀπιών. Cf. also Isaeus
Or. 1 (Cleonym.) § 14, ἀσθενῶν...
ἐβουλήθη ταύτας τὰς διαθήκας
ἀνελεῖν, where Schömann remarks 'ἀναιρεῖν est λύειν tollere,
rescindere: ἀναιρεῖσθαι autem, de
contractuum testamentorum-
que tabulis, proprie est repetere
ab eo, apud quem depositae
fuerunt, quod fit a sublaturo.'
In these passages, however, the
phrase is used of a testator re-
voking his own will; here of an
heir claiming his father's will,
with a view to suppressing it.
Cf. note on Or. 34 § 31.

τῷ παρέχεσθαι μὲν Φορμίωνι, γεγράφθαι δὲ Πασίω-
1108 νος, εἰᾶσθαι δ' ὑφ' ἡμῶν, ἐξελέγχεται κατεσκευασμένη
μὲν ἡ διαθήκη, ψευδὴς δ' ἡ τοῦ Κηφισοφῶντος μαρτυρία. ἀλλ' ἐῶ Κηφισοφῶντα· οὔτε γὰρ νῦν μοι πρὸς
ἐκεῖνόν ἐστιν οὔτ' ἐμαρτύρησεν ἐκεῖνος περὶ τῶν ἐν
ταῖς διαθήκαις ἐνόντων οὐδέν. καίτοι καὶ τοῦτο σκο- 23
πεῖτε, ὅσον ἐστὶ τεκμήριον, ὦ ἄνδρες Ἀθηναῖοι, τοῦ
τούτους τὰ ψευδῆ μεμαρτυρηκέναι. εἰ γὰρ ὁ μὲν αὐτὸς
ἔχειν τὸ γραμματεῖον μαρτυρῶν οὐκ ἐτόλμησεν ἀντίγραφα εἶναι ἃ παρείχετο Φορμίων τῶν παρ' αὐτῷ
μαρτυρῆσαι, οὗτοι δὲ οὔτε ἐξ ἀρχῆς ὡς παρῆσαν ἔχοιεν
ἂν εἰπεῖν οὔτε ἀνοιχθὲν εἶδον πρὸς τῷ διαιτητῇ τὸ
γραμματεῖον, ἀλλὰ καὶ μεμαρτυρήκασιν αὐτοὶ μὴ ἐθέλειν ἐμὲ ἀνοίγειν, ταῦτα ὡς ἀντίγραφά ἐστιν ἐκείνων
μεμαρτυρηκότες, τί ἄλλο ἢ σφῶν αὐτῶν κατήγοροι γεγόνασιν ὅτι ψεύδονται;

Ἔτι τοίνυν, ὦ ἄνδρες Ἀθηναῖοι, ὡς γέγραπταί 24
τις ἂν ἐξετάσας τὴν μαρτυρίαν γνοίη παντελῶς τοῦτο
μεμηχανημένους αὐτούς, ὅπως δικαίως καὶ ἀδίκως δό-

22. τῷ παρέχεσθαι Φορμίωνι]
'By its being produced, not by,
but *to* Phormion.'—εἰᾶσθαι δ'
'and *yet* let alone, (not made
away with,) by myself.' (See last
note.) The pf. pass. εἰᾶσθαι is
apparently never used elsewhere.

23. αὐτὸς ἔχειν] 'That he
had the document in his own
keeping.'

ἐξ ἀρχῆς ὡς παρῆσαν] 'Were
present in the first instance'
as witnesses when Pasion made
his will. But it may be remarked that even supposing
they were so present, it does
not follow that they would know
the *contents* of the document.
(See note on Or. 46 § 2 and

Becker's *Charicles*, Sc. ix note
18.)

§§ 24—26. *Let us now examine
the terms of the deposition and we
shall see that its object is to make
it appear by any means, fair or
foul, that my father made this
will. It speaks of 'the will of
Pasion'; whereas it ought to
have run 'the will which Phormion asserts to have been left by
Pasion'; and you are aware
that there is a vast difference
between a thing being really true
and Phormion's saying so.*

24. ὡς γέγραπται κ.τ.λ.] i.e.
εἴ τις ἐξετάσειεν ὡς γέγραπται ἡ
μαρτυρία, γνοίη κ.τ.λ.

δικαίως καὶ ἀδίκως δόξει] 'That
rightly or wrongly it may ap-

ξει ταῦτα ὁ πατὴρ οὑμὸς διαθέσθαι. λαβὲ δ᾽ αὐτὴν τὴν μαρτυρίαν, καὶ λέγ᾽ ἐπισχὼν οὗ ἄν σε κελεύω, ἵν᾽ ἐξ αὐτῆς δεικνύω.

ΜΑΡΤΥΡΙΑΙ.

[Μαρτυροῦσι παρεῖναι πρὸς τῷ διαιτητῇ Τισίᾳ, ὅτε προὐκαλεῖτο Φορμίων Ἀπολλόδωρον, εἰ μή φησιν ἀντίγραφα εἶναι τῶν διαθηκῶν τῶν Πασίωνος.]

25   Ἐπίσχες.   ἐνθυμεῖσθε ὅτι ʿτῶν διαθηκῶνʾ γέγραπται ʿτῶν Πασίωνοςʾ. καίτοι χρῆν τοὺς βουλομένους τἀληθῆ μαρτυρεῖν, εἰ τὰ μάλιστ᾽ ἐγίγνετο ἡ πρόκλησις, ὡς οὐκ ἐγίγνετο, ἐκείνως μαρτυρεῖν.   λέγε τὴν μαρτυρίαν ἀπ᾽ ἀρχῆς πάλιν.

ΜΑΡΤΥΡΙΑ.   1109

Μαρτυροῦσι παρεῖναι πρὸς τῷ διαιτητῇ Τισίᾳ. Μαρτυροῦμεν· παρῆμεν γὰρ δή.   λέγε. ὅτε προὐκαλεῖτο Φορμίων Ἀπολλόδωρον. Καὶ τοῦτο, εἴπερ προὐκαλεῖτο, ὀρθῶς ἂν ἐμαρτύρουν. εἰ μή φησιν ἀντίγραφα εἶναι τῶν διαθηκῶν τῶν Πασίωνος.

26   Ἔχε αὐτοῦ.   οὐδ᾽ ἂν εἷς ἔτι δήπου τοῦτ᾽ ἐμαρτύρησεν, εἰ μή τις καὶ παρῆν διατιθεμένῳ τῷ πατρὶ τῷ ἐμῷ· ἀλλ᾽ εὐθὺς ἂν εἶπε "τί δ᾽ ἡμεῖς ἴσμεν, εἴ τινές "εἰσι διαθῆκαι Πασίωνος;" καὶ γράφειν ἂν αὐτὸν ἠξίωσεν, ὥσπερ° ἐν ἀρχῇ τῆς προκλήσεως, "εἰ μή "φημ᾽ ἐγὼ ἀντίγραφα εἶναι τῶν διαθηκῶν, ὧν φησι

° *fortasse delendum.*

pear that my father made this will.' A singular expression, the adverbs belonging to δόξει and not to διαθέσθαι.

25. εἰ τὰ μάλιστα] 'If it were *ever so true* that the challenge took place, which I utterly deny.'—ἐκείνως, 'in a form which I am about to show,' viz. in § 26 τῶν διαθηκῶν (*not* τῶν Πασίωνος) but ὧν φησι Φορμίων Πασίωνα καταλιπεῖν.

26. εἴ τινές εἰσι] 'if there *is* any will of Pasion's at all.'

"Φορμίων Πασίωνα καταλιπεῖν," οὐ "τῶν Πασίω-
"νος." τοῦτο μὲν γὰρ ἦν εἶναι διαθήκας μαρτυρεῖν
ὅπερ ἦν τούτοις βούλημα, ἐκεῖνο δὲ φάσκειν Φορ-
μίωνα· πλεῖστον δὲ δήπου κεχώρισται τό τ' εἶναι καὶ
τὸ τοῦτον φάσκειν.

Ἵνα τοίνυν εἰδῆτε ὑπὲρ ἡλίκων καὶ ὅσων ἦν τὸ 27
κατασκεύασμα τὸ τῆς διαθήκης, μικρὰ ἀκούσατέ μου.
ἦν γὰρ, ὦ ἄνδρες Ἀθηναῖοι, τοῦτο πρῶτον μὲν ὑπὲρ
τοῦ μὴ δοῦναι δίκην ὧν διεφθάρκει ἣν ἐμοὶ μὲν οὐ
καλὸν λέγειν, ὑμεῖς δ' ἴστε, κἂν ἐγὼ μὴ λέγω, ἔπειθ'
ὑπὲρ τοῦ κατασχεῖν ὅσα ἦν τῷ ἡμετέρῳ πατρὶ χρήματα
παρὰ τῇ μητρί, πρὸς δὲ τούτοις ὑπὲρ τοῦ καὶ τῶν ἄλλων τῶν ἡμετέρων ἁπάντων κυρίῳ[p] γενέσθαι.   ὅτι δ'

[p] κύριον Lambinus (G. H. Schaefer).

φάσκειν] (sc. εἶναι διαθήκας.)
Here, as often, used with the
collateral notion of saying what
is untrue. Thus both φημί and
φάσκω are used in Soph. El. 319
of promising without perform-
ing: φησίν γε φάσκων δ' οὐδὲν
ὧν λέγει ποιεῖ. [For the whole
sentence, cf. Eur. Alc. 528, χωρὶς
τό τ' εἶναι καὶ τὸ μὴ νομίζεται.]

§§ 27, 28. *An examination
of the terms of the 'Will' proves
that Phormion had important
motives for forging it, viz. (1)
to escape the penalty for se-
ducing one who shall be name-
less, (2) to secure all my father's
money that was in my mother's
hands; and (3) to obtain control over all the rest of the
family property.*

27. κατασκεύασμα] The 'fabrication,' 'forgery,' of the will.
Cf. κατασκευάζειν in §§ 13 and 20.

ὧν διεφθάρκει ἦν ...] 'To
escape the penalty of having
corrupted her whose name I
cannot here mention with-
out impropriety, but whom
you yourselves know without
my naming her.' (For this
delicacy of allusion, cf. note
on § 3.)—ὧν διεφθάρκει ἦν is
equivalent to τῆς διαφθορᾶς τῆς
γυναικὸς ἦν (or τοῦ διεφθαρκέναι
ταύτην ἦν). The substantive is
here 'thrown into' the verb as
in Fals. Leg. § 238 p. 415, ἐν
αὐτοῖς οἷς ἐτιμᾶσθε, 'in the very
honours you enjoyed,' where
Shilleto quotes de Corona § 312
ἐφ' οἷς ἐλυμήνω and a striking
instance from Plato, Phaedo p.
94 c. We may add Midias § 189 p.
576, ἐφ' οἷς ἐλειτούργουν ὑβρίζειν,
and Ar. Ach. 677, οὐ γὰρ ἀξίως
ἐκείνων ὧν ἐναυμαχήσαμεν γηρο-
βοσκούμεσθ' ὑφ' ὑμῶν. Cf. inf.
§ 68 and Or. 55 § 32.

ὑπὲρ τοῦ κατασχεῖν] 'for the
purpose of securing.' So inf. §
47, ὅπως τὴν ἀφορμὴν τῆς τραπέζης κατάσχοι.

κυρίῳ γενέσθαι] The *dative* is
used as though the sentence had
begun with ἡ διαθήκη κατεσκεύ-
αστο Φορμίωνι instead of with
its equivalent in sense ἦν τὸ

οὕτω ταῦτ' ἔχει, τῆς διαθήκης αὐτῆς ἀκούσαντες γνώ-
σεσθε· φανήσεται γὰρ οὐ πατρὸς ὑπὲρ[q] υἱέων γράφον-
τος ἐοικυῖα διαθήκῃ, ἀλλὰ δούλου λελυμασμένου τὰ
28 τῶν δεσποτῶν, ὅπως μὴ δώσει δίκην σκοποῦντος. λέγε 1110
δ' αὐτοῖς τὴν διαθήκην αὐτήν, ἣν οὗτοι μετὰ[r] τῆς προκλήσεως μεμαρτυρήκασιν· ὑμεῖς δ' ἐνθυμεῖσθε ἃ λέγω.

ΔΙΑΘΗΚΗ.

[s][Τάδε διέθετο Πασίων Ἀχαρνεύς· δίδωμι τὴν
ἐμαυτοῦ γυναῖκα Ἀρχίππην Φορμίωνι, καὶ προῖκα
ἐπιδίδωμι Ἀρχίππῃ τάλαντον μὲν τὸ[t] ἐκ Πεπαρήθου,
τάλατον δὲ τὸ[t] αὐτόθεν, συνοικίαν ἑκατὸν μνῶν, θεραπαίνας καὶ τὰ χρυσία καὶ τἆλλ' ὅσα ἐστὶν αὐτῇ ἔνδον.
ἅπαντα ταῦτα Ἀρχίππῃ δίδωμι.][s]

[q] ὥσπερ Z cum libris.   περὶ G. H. Schaefer.   ὑπὲρ Bekk. et
Dindf. cum H. Wolf.   [r] Reiske.   πρὸ libri.

[s—s] om. Σ.   [t] 'Malim τῶν......τῶν.' Dobree.

κατασκεύασμα τὸ τῆς διαθήκης.
The regular construction would
of course require κύριον.

λελυμασμένου] Also a *de-
ponent perfect* in Or. 19 § 105
and Or. 21 § 173 (λελύμαν-
ται). The inf. is found as
pass. in Or. 20 § 142.—The
sense is:—'a slave who is thinking how to escape punishment
for having wronged, *dishonour-
ed*, his master's household,
damaged his master's property.'
τὰ τῶν δεσποτῶν refers to his
master's wife [but is expressed
purposely in a general way.
Aeschylus however uses γυναικὸς λυμαντήριος in this sense,
Ag. 1413 and Cho. 751. P.]

28. διαθήκην μετὰ τῆς προ-
κλήσεως] § 12 προσεμαρτύρουν τῇ
προκλήσει τὴν διαθήκην and § 15
πρόκλησιν ὁμοῦ διαθήκῃ μαρτυρεῖν.
The mss have πρό, which is

altered by Reiske into μετὰ and
by Dobree into διὰ (cf. § 31 τὴν
μίσθωσιν ἣν τὸν αὐτὸν τρόπον διὰ
προκλήσεως ἐνεβάλοντο).

τάδε διέθετο] The usual formula. Thus, Plato's will began:
τάδε κατέλιπε Πλάτων καὶ διέθετο, and Aristotle's: τάδε διέθετο
Ἀριστοτέλης (Diog. Laert. iii 41
and v 11).

τάλαντον κ.τ.λ.] Sums in gross,
charged on land, are meant (as
Pabst and Kennedy understand
it); *not* annual rents (as G. H.
Schaefer supposes).—On συνοικίαν see notes on Or. 36 §§ 6
and 34.

Πεπαρήθου] A small island,
N.W. of Euboea. As it was
an Athenian colony, Athenians
could hold property there (Dareste). Its wine is mentioned
in 35 § 35.

Ἠκούσατε, ὦ ἄνδρες Ἀθηναῖοι, τὸ πλῆθος τῆς προικὸς, τάλαντον ἐκ Πεπαρήθου, τάλαντον αὐτόθεν, συνοικίαν ἑκατὸν μνῶν, θεραπαίνας καὶ χρυσία, καὶ τἄλλα, φησὶν, ὅσα ἐστὶν αὐτῇ, δίδωμι, τούτῳ τῷ γράμματι καὶ τοῦ ζητῆσαί τι τῶν καταλειφθέντων ἀποκλείων ἡμᾶς.

Φέρε δὴ δείξω τὴν μίσθωσιν ὑμῖν καθ᾽ ἣν ἐμεμί- 29 σθωτο τὴν τράπεζαν παρὰ τοῦ πατρὸς οὗτος. καὶ γὰρ ἐκ ταύτης, καίπερ ἐσκευωρημένης, ὄψεσθε ὅτι πλάσμα ὅλον ἐστὶν ἡ διαθήκη. δείξω δ᾽ ἣν οὗτος παρέσχετο μίσθωσιν, οὐκ ἄλλην τινὰ, ἐν ᾗ προσγέγραπται ἕνδεκα τάλαντα ὁ πατὴρ ὀφείλων εἰς τὰς παρακαταθήκας

καὶ τοῦ ζητῆσαι...ἀποκλείων] See on Or. 40 § 15, ἐάν τι οὗτοι τῶν πατρῴων ἐπιζητῶσι.

§§ 29—36. *Again, the 'lease' upon which Phormion took the bank from my father, though itself a fabrication, will prove the 'Will' an absolute forgery.*

It concludes with a clause stating that my father owes eleven talents to the bank. This was added in order that whatever sums were traced to Phormion might be made out to have been 'paid' in discharge of this debt, and not embezzled.—(You imagine perhaps that, as Phormion speaks bad Greek, he is merely a foreigner and a fool. To be sure, he is anything but a good Greek in hating those he ought to honour, but in villany and knavery he is far from a fool.)

The terms of the 'lease' shall now be read and examined.

(1) No one would have paid so large a rent, as that alleged, for the banking business.

(2) No one would have committed the rest of his property to a man under whose management the Bank got into debt.

(3) The stringency of the provision preventing Phormion from doing business as a banker on his own account is inconsistent with the singularly generous terms of the will and proves the latter to be a forgery.

29. τὴν μίσθωσιν κ.τ.λ.] See Or. 36 §§ 4—6.—καὶ γὰρ ἐκ ταύτης, 'for from this *too*,' &c. [The clause καίπερ ἐσκευωρημένης reads unlike the style of Demosthenes. P.]

πλάσμα] Cf. πέπλακε in line 10 of *Argument*, and Or. 36 § 33. Hesychius has πλάσμα· σχηματισμός ('pretence'). ψεῦσμα. ἢ κτίσμα.

ἕνδεκα τάλ.] The origin of this 'debt' is carefully explained in Or. 36 §§ 4—5 (see note on προσώφειλε p. 6), and in the present speech, the plaintiff says nothing that materially shakes that explanation. [The construction is, ὀφείλων τούτῳ εἰς τὰς π., 'owing Phormion eleven talents on the deposits,' or 'for the deposits' which he had put out to interest. Kennedy translates, 'upon the de-

30 τούτῳ. ἔστι δ᾽, οἶμαι, ταῦτα τοιαῦτα. τῶν μὲν οἴκοι
χρημάτων ὡς ἐπὶ τῇ μητρὶ δοθέντων διὰ τῆς διαθήκης αὐτὸν ἐποίησε κύριον, ὥσπερ ἀκηκόατε ἄρτι,
τῶν δ᾽ ἐπὶ τῆς τραπέζης ὄντων, ἃ πάντες ᾔδεσαν καὶ
λαθεῖν οὐκ ἦν, διὰ τοῦ προσοφείλοντα ἀποφῆναι τὸν
πατέρα ἡμῶν, ἵν᾽, ὅσα ἐξελέγχοιτο ἔχων, κεκομίσθαι
φαίη. ὑμεῖς δ᾽ ἴσως αὐτὸν ὑπειλήφατε, ὅτι σολοικίζει
τῇ φωνῇ, βάρβαρον καὶ εὐκαταφρόνητον εἶναι. ἔστι IIII

posits to Phormion.' See § 31
fin. P.]

30. ὡς ἐπὶ τῇ μητρὶ δοθέντων]
'As my mother's dowry.' Or. 40,
περὶ προικὸς, § 6, ἐκδόντος αὐτὴν...
καὶ προῖκα τάλαντον ἐπιδόντος.

πάντες ᾔδεσαν κ.τ.λ.] This
must be taken as a rhetorical
exaggeration. All that the
speaker probably means is that
as Phormion was only the lessee,
not the owner of the bank, he
could be called upon by Apollodorus, the lessor after Pasion's
death, to give an account of all
the moneys held by the bank.
As a contrast we have in § 66
ἐργασίας ἀφανεῖς διὰ τῆς τραπέζης ποιῆται.

κεκομίσθαι] In middle sense.
Or. 41 § 11, οὐκ ἀνενηνόχασι
κεκομισμένοι (τὴν φιάλην). Or.
56 (Dionysod.) § 3, δέον δ᾽ αὐτὸν
ἐν τῇ πέρυσιν ὥρᾳ κεκομίσθαι τὰ
χρήματα. Trans. 'that whatever sums he might be proved
to possess, he might pretend
he had recovered in the way of
debts.'

σολοικίζει τῇ φωνῇ, βάρβαρον]
(See note on Or. 36 § 1, τὴν ἀπειρίαν τοῦ λέγειν.) σόλοικος is a
word of narrower meaning than
βάρβαρος and is applied mainly
to faults of pronunciation or
mistakes in Grammar, especially Syntax, due to foreign

extraction. The word βάρβαρος
originally referred to language
(as an onomatopoetic word connected with the Sanskrit var-
vara, 'a jabberer') and was used
to describe the incoherent jar-
gon (as the Greeks considered
it) of all languages but their
own (Aesch. Ag. 1050). But it
gradually attained a wider sig-
nification and embraced all
that was non-Hellenic in the
customs, the politics, the laws,
and the moral and intellectual
characteristics of foreign na-
tions. (Cf. Isocr. Paneg. § 3 n.)

Hesychius (possibly with the
present passage in view) has
the gloss σολοικίζει· βαρβαρίζει,
and Aristotle (περὶ σοφιστικῶν
ἐλέγχων § 3) explains σολοικίζειν
by τῇ λέξει βαρβαρίζειν and (in
§ 14) illustrates it by instances
from the rules of gender. The
distinction drawn between βαρ-
βαρισμὸς and σολοικισμὸς by
Zeno and the Stoics, and accepted by the writers on Rhetoric,
is perhaps best expressed by
Quintilian: 'vitium quod fit in
singulis verbis, sit barbarismus
...cetera vitia omnia ex pluribus
vocibus sunt, quorum est soloe-
cismus' (1 5, 6 and 34).

βάρβαρον καὶ εὐκαταφρόνητον]
Ar. Nubes 492 ἀμαθὴς...καὶ βάρβαρος.

δὲ βάρβαρος οὗτος τῷ μισεῖν οὓς αὐτῷ προσῆκε
τιμᾶν· τῷ δὲ κακουργῆσαι καὶ διορύξαι πράγματα
οὐδενὸς λείπεται. λαβὲ δὴ τὴν μίσθωσιν, καὶ λέγε, ἣν 31
τὸν αὐτὸν τρόπον διὰ προκλήσεως ἐνεβάλοντο.

ΜΙΣΘΩΣΙΣ ΤΡΑΠΕΖΗΣ[u].

ᵛ[Κατὰ τάδε ἐμίσθωσε Πασίων τὴν τράπεζαν
Φορμίωνι· μίσθωσιν φέρειν Φορμίωνα τῆς τραπέζης
τοῖς παισὶ τοῖς Πασίωνος δύο τάλαντα καὶ τετταράκοντα μνᾶς τοῦ ἐνιαυτοῦ ἑκάστου, χωρὶς τῆς καθ᾽
ἡμέραν διοικήσεως· μὴ ἐξεῖναι δὲ τραπεζιτεῦσαι χωρὶς
Φορμίωνι, ἐὰν μὴ πείσῃ τοὺς παῖδας τοὺς Πασίωνος.
ὀφείλει δὲ Πασίων ἐπὶ τὴν τράπεζαν ἕνδεκα τάλαντα
εἰς τὰς παρακαταθήκας.]ᵛ

Ἃς μὲν τοίνυν παρέσχετο συνθήκας ὡς κατὰ ταύ- 32
τας μισθωσάμενος τὴν τράπεζαν, αὗταί εἰσιν, ὦ ἄνδρες
δικασταί. ἀκούετε δ᾽ ἐν ταύταις ἀναγιγνωσκομέναις
μίσθωσιν μὲν φέρειν τοῦτον, ἄνευ τῆς καθ᾽ ἡμέραν
διοικήσεως, δύο τάλαντα καὶ τετταράκοντα μνᾶς τοῦ
ἐνιαυτοῦ ἑκάστου, μὴ ἐξεῖναι δὲ τραπεζιτεύειν αὐτῷ,

ᵘ μίσθωσις Σ.   ᵛ⁻ᵛ om. Σ.

διορύξαι πράγματα] Lit. 'to
undermine,' 'to ruin' [here,
perhaps, 'to be a rogue in business']. A metaphor from house-
breaking. Or. 9 § 28, κακῶς δια-
κείμεθα καὶ διορωρύγμεθα κατὰ
πόλεις. Or. 35 (Lacr.) § 9, οἷα
ἐτοιχωρύχησαν οὗτοι περὶ τὸ
δάνειον, and Philostratus 552
(quoted by Liddell & Scott), τοιχωρυχεῖν τοὺς λόγους τινός.

31. διὰ προκλήσεως] 'by
means of,' i.e. 'under cover of,'
—'using the Challenge as a
cat's paw.' Cf. Fals. Leg. § 291,
ἔκρινε Φιλόνεικον καὶ δι᾽ ἐκείνου
τῶν σοὶ πεπραγμένων κατηγόρει,
where Shilleto quotes the present passage.

κατὰ τάδε ἐμίσθωσε] Similarly
in an inscription recording a
lease of the year 300 B.C. we
have: κατὰ τάδε ἐμίσθωσαν Ἀντίμαχος Ἀμφιμάχου...τὸ ἐργαστήριον τὸ ἐν Πειραιεῖ...Εὐκράτει
Ἐξηκίου Ἀφιδναίῳ (Revue Ar-
chéol. 1866, xiv 352); and in
an inscription of 345 B.C. κατὰ
τάδε ἐμίσθωσαν Αἰξωνεῖς τὴν Φι-
λαῖδα Αὐτοκλεῖ (C. I. G. 93).
Kirchner p. 39.

32. τῆς καθ᾽ ἡμέραν διοική-
σεως] 'The daily expenditure'
involved in managing the bank,
paying under-clerks, &c.

ἐὰν μὴ ἡμᾶς πείσῃ. προσγέγραπται δὲ τελευταῖον
"ὀφείλει δὲ Πασίων ἔνδεκα τάλαντα εἰς τὰς παρα-
33 "καταθήκας." ἔστιν οὖν ὅστις ἂν τοῦ ξύλου καὶ τοῦ
χωρίου καὶ τῶν γραμματείων τοσαύτην ὑπέμεινε φέρειν μίσθωσιν; ἔστι δ' ὅστις ἂν, δι' ὃν ὠφειλήκει τοσαῦτα χρήματα ἡ τράπεζα, τούτῳ τὰ λοιπὰ ἐπέτρε-
ψεν; εἰ γὰρ ἐνεδέησε τοσούτων χρημάτων, τούτου
διοικοῦντος ἐνεδέησεν. ἴστε γὰρ πάντες, καὶ ὅτ' ἦν
ὁ πατὴρ ἐπὶ τοῦ τραπεζιτεύειν, τοῦτον καθήμενον καὶ
διοικοῦντα ἐπὶ τῇ τραπέζῃ, ὥστε ἐν τῷ μυλῶνι[w] προσ-

----

[w] μυλῶνι Z et Bekker st.   accentum omisit Σ.

----

33. ξύλου…χωρίου…γραμμα-
τείων] The bench (desk or
counter)..the site (in the market-
place)…the banking-books (ledgers, &c).

ὠφειλήκει ἡ τράπεζα] Phormion's account is that Pasion
owed 11 talents to the bank;
whereas Apollodorus unfairly,
as it seems, treating this sum
as a deficit though it stood in
Pasion's hands to the *credit* of
the bank, denounces Phormion
for having caused the bank to
get into *debt*. [Apollodorus
wishes to throw a doubt on
Phormion's ever having had a
lease at all on the terms now
brought forward. He says he
would have been a fool to pay
so much for a business that was
encumbered if not insolvent;
and Pasion would have been
equally foolish if he had let the
bank to one who had managed
it so badly as Phormion. P.]

εἰ γὰρ κ.τ.λ.] A sophistical
argument to bear out the previous clause δι' ὃν ὠφειλήκει ἡ
τράπεζα. It is quite true that
ἡ τράπεζα ἐνεδέησε χρημάτων, but
then the 11 talents in question
were held by Pasion on the

security of land and were part
of the assets of the business.—
On καθήμενον κ.τ.λ. v. Or. 36 § 7, n.

ἐν τῷ μυλῶνι] So far from
being made master of the rest
of the household, Phormion
ought to have been punished, as
a slave, with hard-labour at the
mill, for bad management. For
the mill, as a common part of
slaves' labour, cf. the Phormio
of Terence II 1, 18, *herus si
redierit, Molendum usque in
pistrino, vapulandum, habendae
compedes.* In Lysias Or. 1 § 18
a master threatens his θεράπαινα
with the punishment μαστιγω-
θεῖσαν εἰς μυλῶνα ἐμπεσεῖν, and
Dinarchus, contr. Dem. § 23,
says that Memnon the miller
was condemned to death for
making a freeborn boy work in
his mill. Cf. Eur. Cycl. 240,
εἰς μυλῶνα καταβαλεῖν, and Pollux, ἵνα κολάζονται οἱ δοῦλοι,
μυλῶνες κ.τ.λ. (K. F. Hermann,
Privatalt. § 24, 9, p. 216 Blümner.) The parallel of Samson,
'eyeless in Gaza at the mill
with slaves,' will occur to every
reader (Judges xvi 21, Milton
Samson Agonistes 41, &c).—μύ-
λων is, in respect of accent, a

ἧκεν αὐτὸν εἶναι μᾶλλον ἢ τῶν λοιπῶν κύριον γεν-
1112 έσθαι. ἀλλ' ἐῶ ταῦτα καὶ τἄλλ' ὅσ' ἂν περὶ τῶν 34
ἔνδεκα ταλάντων ἔχοιμι εἰπεῖν, ὡς οὐκ ὤφειλεν ὁ πατὴρ, ἀλλ' οὗτος ὑφῆρηται. ἀλλ' οὗ ἀνέγνων ἕνεκα[x],
τοῦ τὴν διαθήκην ψευδῆ δεῖξαι, τοῦθ' ὑμᾶς ἀναμνήσω.
γέγραπται γὰρ αὐτόθι, μὴ ἐξεῖναι δὲ τραπεζιτεύειν
Φορμίωνι, ἐὰν μὴ ἡμᾶς πείσῃ. τοῦτο τοίνυν τὸ γράμμα
παντελῶς δηλοῖ ψευδῆ τὴν διαθήκην οὖσαν. τίς γὰρ
ἂν[y] ἀνθρώπων, ἃ μὲν ἔμελλε[z] τραπεζιτεύων οὗτος ἐργάζεσθαι[a], ταῦθ' ὅπως ἡμῖν τοῖς αὐτοῦ παισὶν, ἀλλὰ

[x] εἴνεκα Z cum Σ.

[y] ἂν G. H. Schaefer. 'non dubitarem recipere, si modo libri
praeberent...sed necessariam esse voculam ἂν neutiquam mihi
persuadere possum' (Gebauer, *de argumenti ex contrario formis* p.
181). *om. Bekker et Z cum libris.*

[z] ἤμελλε Z cum Σ. (See note on Isocr. Paneg. § 83.)

[a] Bekker. *om.* Z cum Σ. 'quid si [omisso ἐργάζεσθαι] τραπεζιτεύειν scribimus idque praegnanter dictum putamus pro τραπεζιτεύων ἐργάζεσθαι, quem ad modum Horatius carm. iii 16, 26
arandi verbo usus est?' (Gebauer *l. c.*)

false form. (Chandler, *Gk. Acc.*
§ 638.)

34. ἐῶ ταῦτα κ.τ.λ.] The
speaker, it will be observed,
makes no attempt to meet fairly
the statement made on the opposite side, accounting for the
11 talents not being actually
in the bank. (Or. 36 §§ 4—6.)

[ὑφῆρηται. Phormion, he says,
has filched, or secretly with-
drawn, eleven talents from the
bank, which he now pretends
Pasion and Pasion's heirs were
bound to repay. P.]

μὴ τραπεζιτεύειν] The object
of this clause appears to have
been to prevent Phormion's
doing business *on his own account*, apart from the profits
made on the bank. The plaintiff seems rather unfairly to

suggest that Phormion was allowed to make no profit whatever out of the lease.

τίς γὰρ ἂν κ.τ.λ.] 'Is there
any man, I ask, who, after
taking precautions to ensure
his own children receiving the
profits of a lessee's management
of the bank, by preventing him
from doing business on his
own behalf, would have nevertheless actually provided for
that lessee's appropriating the
profits he had himself laid by
in his lifetime and left behind
him on his death?' [The two
things, he says, are inconsistent. If Phormion must bank
only in the interest and for the
benefit of Pasion's family, it was
not likely that he would have
had so much money left him

μὴ τούτῳ γενήσεται προὐνοήθη, καὶ διὰ τοῦτο μὴ
ἐξεῖναι τούτῳ τραπεζιτεύειν ἔγραψεν, ἵνα μὴ ἀφί-
στηται ἀφ᾿ ἡμῶν· ἃ δ᾿ αὐτὸς εἰργασμένος ἔνδον κατ-
35 έλειπε, ταῦθ᾿ ὅπως οὗτος λήψεται παρεσκεύασεν; καὶ
τῆς μὲν ἐργασίας ἐφθόνησεν, ἧς οὐδὲν αἰσχρὸν ἦν
μεταδοῦναι· τὴν δὲ γυναῖκα ἔδωκεν, οὗ μεῖζον οὐδὲν ἂν
κατέλιπεν[b] ὄνειδος,[c] τυχών γε τῆς παρ᾿ ὑμῶν δωρεᾶς,
εἶτα ὥσπερ ἂν δοῦλος δεσπότῃ διδούς, ἀλλ᾿ οὐ τοὐναντίον, εἴπερ ἐδίδου, δεσπότης οἰκέτῃ, προστιθεὶς προῖκα

[b] Bekker.   κατέλειπεν Z cum Σ prima manu.

[c] ὄνειδος; edd.   interrogationis signum ad finem paragraphi
transferendum esse indicavit H. W. Moss.

by Pasion; i.e. he must have
got it unfairly. The sentence
is artificially constructed, and
is one of those sometimes called
'bimembered,' where each clause
is antithetical to the other, as
here προὐνοήθη ὅπως to παρεσκεύασεν ὅπως. P.]

35. καὶ τῆς μὲν ἐργασίας ἐφ-
θόνησεν] The subject is τίς ἀνθρώπων repeated from the previous sentence.

οὗ] sc. ὀνείδους, viz. the disgrace τοῦ γυναῖκα τούτῳ δεδωκέναι.

τυχών γε τῆς παρ᾿ ὑμῶν δω-
ρεᾶς] The fact that Pasion was
made a citizen of Athens in-
creases the disgrace brought on
his family by his providing in his
alleged will that his wife should
marry Phormion.—Or. 59 § 2,
ψηφισαμένου τοῦ δήμου τοῦ ᾿Αθη-
ναίων ᾿Αθηναῖον εἶναι Πασίωνα καὶ
ἐκγόνους τοὺς ἐκείνου διὰ τὰς εὐερ-
γεσίας τὰς εἰς τὴν πόλιν followed
by τῇ τοῦ δήμου δωρεᾷ. Or. 36
§ 47. [τυχών γε seems an imaginary answer in favour of
Phormion; 'very true; but then
it was after he had received the
franchise (that he took the

wife).' 'So then' (the retort
is), 'like a slave who makes a
wife over to his master, rather
than in the converse case, Pasion gave him, it seems, a marriage portion larger than any
citizen ever did!' P.]

ὥσπερ ἂν] sc. διδοίη. Pasion's
gift of his wife with a large
dowry to Phormion, is the kind
of gift a slave might offer his
master in acknowledgment that
all the slave had, belonged by
right to his master, and not
such a gift as might be expected
from a superior to an inferior.
In the latter case a very slight
favour would be enough. At any
rate the inferior would be content with being allowed to have
the honour of being married to
his superior's wife, without any
dowry at all.

εἴπερ ἐδίδου] which Apoll. does
not admit.

προστιθεὶς προῖκα] Or. 40 §
25, προσθέντας (sc. προῖκα) ἐκδοῦναι. Fals. Leg. § 195, προῖκα
προσθεὶς ἐκδώσω καὶ οὐ περι-
όψομαι παθούσας οὐδὲν ἀνάξιον
οὔθ᾿ ἡμῶν οὔτε τοῦ πατρός (cf.
§ 54 infra, προῖκα ἐπιδοὺς ἐκδοῦ-

ὅσην οὐδεὶς τῶν ἐν τῇ πόλει φαίνεται; καίτοι τούτῳ 36
μὲν αὐτὸ τοῦτο ἀγαπητὸν ἦν, τὸ τῆς δεσποίνης ἀξιω-
θῆναι· τῷ πατρὶ δὲ οὐδὲ λαμβάνοντι[d] τοσαῦτα χρήματα, ὅσα φασὶ διδόντα οὗτοι, εὔλογον ἦν πρᾶξαι
ταῦτα. ἀλλ᾽ ὅμως ἃ τοῖς εἰκόσι, τοῖς χρόνοις, τοῖς
πεπραγμένοις ἐξελέγχεται ψευδῆ, ταῦτα μαρτυρεῖν
οὐκ ὤκνησεν οὑτοσὶ Στέφανος.

Εἶτα λέγει περιιὼν ὡς ἐμαρτύρησε μὲν Νικοκλῆς 37

[d] Bekker. λαμβάνοντα Ζ cum Σ.

ναι, n.). Isaeus Or. 3 (Pyrrhus)
§ 51, δοκεῖ δ᾽ ἄν τις ὑμῖν οὕτως
ἀναιδὴς ἢ τολμηρὸς εἰσποίητος γενέσθαι ὥστε μηδὲ τὸ δέκατον μέρος ἐπιδοὺς ἐκδοῦναι τῇ γνησίᾳ
θυγατρὶ τῶν πατρῴων; Eur. Hip-
pol. 628, προσθεὶς…πατὴρ φερνὰς,
ἀπῴκισ᾽…Hyperides, Lycophron
col. 11 line 16 (quoted by Shilleto), εὐθὺς ἐξεδόθη, τάλαντον
ἀργυρίου προσθέντος αὐτῇ Εὐφή-
μου. The commoner term was
ἐπιδοῦναι (cf. §§ 30, 54, &c).

ὅσην οὐδεὶς κ.τ.λ.] The mother
of Demosthenes had a dowry of
only 80ᵐ: the mother of Manti-
theus 60ᵐ; the two daughters of
Polyeuctus 40ᵐ each. (Dareste.)

36. λαμβάνοντι χρήματα] Not
even if he got from Phormion
(viz. as a bribe for leaving him
his wife) the same large amount
which the defendants pretend
that he gave Phormion as a
marriage portion.—φασὶ διδόντα,
supply πρᾶξαι ταῦτα.

τοῖς εἰκόσι…ἐξελέγχεται ψευδῆ]
‘That which the facts, the dates,
the probabilities of the case,
show to be false, Stephanus the
defendant has not scrupled to
bear witness to.’ Kennedy. For
τοῖς εἰκόσι see esp. §§ 9—14. τοῖς
χρόνοις seems inexplicable, except as a rhetorical flourish, for

we have had nothing like an
argument from dates; and Dobree rightly asks Quomodo?.
Even τοῖς πεπραγμένοις is barely
justifiable, unless it is to be
referred to §§ 15—18.

§§ 37—39. *Phormion attempts
to prove the existence of the
‘will,’ by going about saying
that Nicocles gave evidence to
having been guardian, and Pasicles to having been in ward-
ship, under the will. Why then
were not the terms of the will
deposed to by Nicocles and Pasicles, instead of by Stephanus
and his friends? Was it because
the former did not know the
terms? If not, much less could
the latter. How then came the
latter witnesses to depose to one
set of facts, the former to another? It's the old story; they
divided the responsibility of the
wrong; the guardian and ward
deposed to the guardianship as
being under the will, and the
other witnesses, under cloak of a
challenge, deposed to the contents
—the scandalous contents—of
the ‘will.’*

37. Νικοκλῆς] His evidence is
not expressly mentioned in Or.
36; that of Pasicles is referred
to in § 22 of that speech.

ἐπιτροπεῦσαι κατὰ τὴν διαθήκην, ἐμαρτύρησε δὲ Πασικλῆς ἐπιτροπευθῆναι κατὰ τὴν διαθήκην. ἐγὼ δὲ
αὐτὰ ταῦτ' οἶμαι τεκμήρια εἶναι τοῦ μήτ' ἐκείνους τἀληθῆ μήτε τούσδε μεμαρτυρηκέναι. ὁ γὰρ ἐπιτροπεῦ- 1113
σαι κατὰ διαθήκας μαρτυρῶν δῆλον ὅτι καθ' ὁποίας
ἂν εἰδείη, καὶ ὁ ἐπιτροπευθῆναι κατὰ διαθήκας μαρ-
38 τυρῶν δῆλον ὅτι καθ' ὁποίας ἂν εἰδείη. τί οὖν μαθόντες[e] ἐμαρτυρεῖτε ὑμεῖς ἐν προκλήσει διαθήκας, ἀλλ' οὐκ
ἐκείνους εἴᾱτε; εἰ γὰρ αὖ μὴ φήσουσιν εἰδέναι τὰ γεγραμμένα ἐν αὐταῖς, πῶς ὑμᾶς οἷόν τ' εἰδέναι τοὺς μηδαμῇ[f] μηδαμῶς τοῦ πράγματος ἐγγύς; τί ποτ' οὖν οἱ
μὲν ἐκεῖνα, οἱ δὲ ταῦτα ἐμαρτύρησαν; ὅπερ εἴρηκα
39 καὶ πρότερον, διείλοντο τἀδικήματα, καὶ ἐπιτροπεῦσαι
μὲν κατὰ διαθήκην οὐδὲν δεινὸν ἡγεῖτο μαρτυρεῖν ὁ
μαρτυρῶν, οὐδ' ἐπιτροπευθῆναι κατὰ διαθήκην, ἀφαιρῶν ἑκάτερος τὸ μαρτυρεῖν τὰ ἐν ταῖς διαθήκαις ὑπὸ
τούτου γεγραμμένα, οὐδὲ καταλιπεῖν τὸν πατέρα αὐτῷ[g]

---

[e] παθόντες H. Wolf et Dindf. (1867).   μαθόντες Bekker Z et
Dindf. (1846 and 1855) cum libris.

μηδαμῇ Z cum Σ.   [g] αὐτῷ Z.

κατὰ τὴν διαθήκην] Or. 36 § 8,
Φορμίων τὴν μὲν γυναῖκα λαμβάνει κατὰ τὴν διαθήκην, τὸν δὲ
παῖδα ἐπετρόπευεν.

καθ' ὁποίας ἂν εἰδείη] 'would
know the purport of (the terms
of) such will.' [The repetition
of the clause δῆλον—εἰδείη seems
needless, and perhaps is due to
a copyist. P.]

38. τί μαθόντες] Madvig, Gk.
Synt. § 176 (b) R; or Goodwin's
Moods and Tenses § 109 (b).
['What then induced you to
give evidence of a will in con-
nexion with a challenge, instead
of letting them prove it for you?'
P.]

ὑμεῖς] sc. οἱ περὶ Στέφανον.—

ἐκείνους, Nicocles and Pasicles.
οἱ μὲν...οἱ δὲ] Nicocles and
Pasicles...οἱ περὶ Στέφανον.—εἴρηκα καὶ πρότερον refers to § 18.
39. ἀφαιρῶν ἑκάτερος] i.e. both
of them declining to depose to
the terms entered in the will
by Phormion, not by Pasion
himself as is alleged.
καταλιπεῖν] sc. δεινὸν ἡγεῖτο
μαρτυρεῖν. The previous participial sentence is subordinate
only, and does not carry καταλιπεῖν with it. 'There was no
danger in a minor (i.e. Pasicles) deposing, that his father
had left him a document entitled
"a will."' Kennedy. Lit. 'with
the word WILL written upon it';

ἐπιγεγραμμένον γραμματεῖον διαθήκην, οὐδὲ τὰ τοι-
αῦτα· διαθήκας δὲ μαρτυρεῖν, ἐν αἷς χρημάτων τοσούτων κλοπὴ, γυναικὸς διαφθορὰ, γάμοι δεσποίνης,
πράγματα αἰσχύνην καὶ ὕβριν τοσαύτην ἔχοντα, οὐδεὶς ἤθελε πλὴν οὗτοι, πρόκλησιν κατασκευάσαντες,
παρ' ὧν δίκαιον τῆς ὅλης τέχνης καὶ κακουργίας δίκην
λαβεῖν.

Ἵνα τοίνυν, ὦ ἄνδρες Ἀθηναῖοι, μὴ μόνον ἐξ ὧν 40
ἐγὼ κατηγορῶ καὶ ἐλέγχω δῆλος ὑμῖν γένηται τὰ ψευδῆ
μεμαρτυρηκὼς οὑτοσὶ Στέφανος, ἀλλὰ καὶ ἐξ ὧν πεποίηκεν ὁ παρασχόμενος αὐτὸν, τὰ πεπραγμένα ἐκείνῳ
βούλομαι πρὸς ὑμᾶς εἰπεῖν. ὅπερ δ' εἶπον ἀρχόμενος
τοῦ λόγου, δείξω κατηγόρους γιγνομένους αὐτοὺς ἑαυτῶν. τὴν γὰρ δίκην, ἐν ᾗ ταῦτα ἐμαρτυρήθη, παρε-
114 γράψατο Φορμίων πρὸς ἐμὲ μὴ εἰσαγώγιμον εἶναι ὡς
ἀφέντος ἐμοῦ τῶν ἐγκλημάτων αὐτόν. τοῦτο τοίνυν 41
ἐγὼ μὲν οἶδα ψεῦδος ὄν, καὶ ἐλέγξω δὲ, ὅταν εἰσίω

§ 18, ᾧ ἐπιγεγράφθαι διαθήκη
Πασίωνος.

For ἐπιγεγραμμένον διαθήκην
cf. Virg. Ecl. III 196, 'inscripti
nomina regum...flores.'

χρημάτων κλοπὴ] § 34 ὑφῄρηται and § 81 init.—γυναικὸς διαφθορὰ §§ 27 and 3.—On ὕβριν cf.
§ 4, where the γάμος leads to a
γραφὴ ὕβρεως being threatened
by Apollodorus.

§§ 40—42. *In bar of the previous action, Phormion pleaded
a discharge deposed to have
been granted by me, releasing
him from all further claims.
This is false, as I shall prove at
the proper time; but even assuming it to be true, it shows
that Stephanus has given false
evidence and that the will to
which he bears witness is a
forgery. For no one would be*

*so foolish as to take the pre-
caution of having witnesses present when he gave a discharge
to a lessee with a view to getting
rid of any claims against himself on the part of that lessee;
and* yet allow the 'lease' itself and the 'will' to remain
sealed to his detriment. The plea
is therefore inconsistent with the
evidence and the lease is inconsistent with the will; and thus
the whole affair is proved to be
a fabrication and a fraud.

40. παρεγράψατο ... ὡς ἀφέν-
τος] See notes on Or. 36 Argument 1. 23 and *ib.* § 25. The
distinction there drawn between
ἀφιέναι and ἀπαλλάττειν may be
exemplified thus:

ἀφῆκε μὲν Ἀπολλόδωρος ὁ ἀπαλ-
λαγείς, ἀπήλλαξε δὲ Φορμίων ὁ
ἀφεθείς.

πρὸς τοὺς ταῦτα μεμαρτυρηκότας· τούτῳ δὲ οὐχ οἷόν
τε τοῦτ᾽ εἰπεῖν. εἰ τοίνυν ἀληθῆ πιστεύσαιτ᾽ εἶναι τὴν
ἄφεσιν, οὕτω καὶ μάλιστ᾽ ἂν οὗτος φανείη ψευδῆ μεμαρτυρηκὼς καὶ κατεσκευασμένης διαθήκης μάρτυς
γεγονώς. τίς γὰρ οὕτως ἄφρων ὥστε ἄφεσιν μὲν ἐναντίον μαρτύρων ποιήσασθαι, τοῦ βεβαίαν αὐτῷ[h] τὴν
ἀπαλλαγὴν εἶναι, τὰς δὲ συνθήκας καὶ τὰς διαθήκας
καὶ τἄλλα, ὑπὲρ ὧν ἐποιεῖτο τὴν ἄφεσιν, σεσημασμένα
42 ἐᾶσαι καθ᾽ αὑτοῦ κεῖσθαι; οὐκοῦν ἐναντία μὲν ἡ
παραγραφὴ πᾶσι τοῖς μεμαρτυρημένοις, ἐναντία δὲ,
ἣν ἀνέγνων ὑμῖν ἄρτι, μίσθωσις, τῇδε τῇ διαθήκῃ·

[h] αὐτῷ Z.

41. τούτῳ κ.τ.λ.] *Stephanus*,
however, has no right to declare
that the evidence to the release
is false. [The meaning is, that
Stephanus was in league with
Phormion, and therefore was
not in a position to deny, though
he knew it to be untrue, any
plea of Phormion's against
Apollodorus. P.]

τοῦ βεβαίαν αὐτῷ τὴν ἀπαλλαγὴν εἶναι] The plaintiff's object in having witnesses to his
alleged ἄφεσις of Phormion
would be to ensure his own
ἀπαλλαγή, that is, his getting
quit of any counter-claim on
the part of the latter. Or. 33
§ 3, πάντων ἀπαλλαγῆς καὶ ἀφέσεως γενομένης.

If ἀπαλλαγή were synonymous
with ἄφεσις, we should have to
render 'in order to make his
discharge of Phormion's dues
valid.' 'Who would be such a
fool,' he would then ask, ' as to
give an ἄφεσις in presence of witnesses and so lose all right to
further claims?' But the sense
is rather : 'Admit it true that
the plaintiff gave a release to
Phormion in the presence of wit-

nesses with a view to his own
riddance of any counter-claim
on Phormion's part; no one who
had (as alleged) done this, would
be such a fool as to allow the
compacts and agreements, the
will, &c (καὶ τἄλλα sc. περὶ τὴν
μίσθωσιν) to remain in existence
to his own detriment. No! if
he had given a receipt, he would
have opened and suppressed the
documents. But as a fact, he had
not touched them, and his re-
fraining from suppressing them
is thus inconsistent with the
alleged grant of a release to
Phormion. — ποιήσασθαι ἄφεσιν
not 'to get' but 'to give a release,'=ἀφεῖναι, as 'any verb
in Greek may be resolved into
the cognate substantive with
ποιεῖσθαι.' Shilleto on Fals.
Leg. § 103.

42. ἐναντία μίσθωσις...διαθή-
κη] §§ 34—36. For πεπλασμένα cf. Or. 36 § 33.—ἐκ τούτου
τοῦ τρόπου, 'in this manner.'
Kennedy, doubtless following
Bekker's text (ἐκ τοῦ τούτου
τρόπου), translates: 'just what
you might expect from this
man's character.'

οὐδὲν δὲ τῶν πεπραγμένων οὔτ᾽ εὔλογον οὔθ᾽ ἁπλοῦν
οὔθ᾽ ὁμολογούμενον αὐτὸ ἑαυτῷ φαίνεται. ἐκ δὲ τούτου τοῦ τρόπου[1] πάντα πεπλασμένα καὶ κατεσκευα- ◁
σμένα ἐλέγχεται.

῾Ως μὲν τοίνυν ἐστὶν ἀληθῆ τὰ μεμαρτυρημένα, 43
οὔτ᾽ αὐτὸν τοῦτον οὔτ᾽ ἄλλον ὑπὲρ τούτου δεῖξαι δυ-
νήσεσθαι νομίζω. ἀκούω δ᾽ αὐτὸν τοιοῦτόν τι παρεσκευάσθαι λέγειν, ὡς προκλήσεώς ἐστιν ὑπεύθυνος,
οὐχὶ μαρτυρίας, καὶ δυοῖν αὐτῷ[h] προσήκει δοῦναι λόγον, οὐ πάντων τῶν γεγραμμένων, εἴτε προὐκαλεῖτό
με ταῦτα Φορμίων ἢ μὴ, καὶ εἰ μὴ ἐδεχόμην ἐγώ· ταῦτα
μὲν γὰρ ἁπλῶς αὐτὸς μεμαρτυρηκέναι φήσει, τὰ δ᾽
ἄλλα ἐκεῖνον προκαλεῖσθαι, εἰ δ᾽ ἐστὶν ἢ μὴ ταῦτα,
οὐδὲν προσήκειν αὐτῷ[h] σκοπεῖν. πρὸς δὴ τὸν λόγον 44
τοῦτον καὶ τὴν ἀναίδειαν βέλτιόν ἐστι μικρὰ προειπεῖν
1115 ὑμῖν, ἵνα μὴ λάθητε ἐξαπατηθέντες. πρῶτον μὲν, ὅταν
ἐγχειρῇ λέγειν τοῦτο, ὡς ἄρα οὐ πάντων ὑπεύθυνός
ἐστιν, ἐνθυμεῖσθε ὅτι διὰ ταῦτα ὁ νόμος μαρτυρεῖν ἐν
γραμματείῳ κελεύει, ἵνα μήτ᾽ ἀφελεῖν ἐξῇ μήτε προσ-

---

[1] Z et Dind. cum libris.　τοῦ τούτου τρόπου Bekker cum Reiskio.

§§ 43—46. *Stephanus will
urge, that he is not responsible
for a deposition but for a challenge, and for the latter on two
points only,* (1) *the question
whether Phormion made this
challenge or not, and* (2) *whether
I refused it; and that the terms
of the challenge mentioned in the
deposition are Phormion's business, not his. If so, the witness
ought to have had the words
erased when his deposition was
drawn up. It is now too late to
disclaim them, and he is bound
in this trial by the terms of his
own plea that he 'gave true
testimony, in testifying to that*
which is written in the record.'

43. προκλήσεως ὑπεύθυνος] liable
to be prosecuted for giving evidence of a pretended challenge
that never took place. This is
clear from what follows: δεῖ
αὐτὸν δοῦναι λόγον εἴτε προύκα-
λεῖτο Φ. ἢ μή.

44. μαρτυρεῖν ἐν γραμματείῳ]
'All testimonial evidence was
required to be in writing, in
order that there might be no
mistake about the terms and
the witness might leave no sub-
terfuge for himself when convicted of falsehood.' C. R.
Kennedy in Dict. Antiq. s. v.
Martyria.

θεῖναι τοῖς γεγραμμένοις μηδέν. τότ᾽ οὖν αὐτὸν ἔδει
ταῦτ᾽ ἀπαλείφειν κελεύειν, ἃ νῦν οὔ φησι μεμαρτυρη-
45 κέναι, οὐ νῦν ἐνόντων ἀναισχυντεῖν. ἔπειτα καὶ τόδε
σκοπεῖτε, εἰ ἐάσαιτ᾽ ἂν ἐναντίον ὑμῶν ἐμὲ προσγρά-
ψαι τι λαβόντα τὸ γραμματεῖον. οὐ δήπου. οὔκουν
οὐδὲ τοῦτον ἀφαιρεῖν τῶν γεγραμμένων ἐᾶν προσήκει·
τίς γὰρ ἁλώσεται ἔτι ποτὲ[1] ψευδομαρτυριῶν, εἰ μαρ-
τυρήσει τε ἃ βούλεται καὶ λόγον ὧν βούλεται δώσει;
ἀλλ᾽ οὐχ οὕτω ταῦτα οὔθ᾽ ὁ νόμος διεῖλεν οὔθ᾽ ὑμῖν
ἀκούειν προσήκει· ἀλλ᾽ ἐκεῖνο ἁπλοῦν καὶ δίκαιον.
τί γέγραπται; τί μεμαρτύρηκας; ταῦθ᾽ ὡς ἀληθῆ
δείκνυε. καὶ γὰρ ἀντιγέγραψαι ταῦτα " ἀληθῆ μεμαρ-
" τύρηκα, μαρτυρήσας τὰ ἐν τῷ γραμματείῳ γεγραμ-
46 " μένα," οὐ τὸ καὶ τὸ τῶν ἐν τῷ γραμματείῳ. ὅτι δ᾽ οὕτω
ταῦτ᾽ ἔχει, λαβὲ τὴν ἀντιγραφὴν αὐτήν μοι.   λέγε.

[1] ἔτι ποτὲ ('legebatur πώποτε') Dindf.   πώποτε Z cum libris.

ἀπαλείφειν] Used of any ob-
literation or erasure, whether
the document was on a tablet
of wax, or, as in this case, of
some other material, as we
learn from Or. 46 § 11 where
the deposition in question is
described as λελευκωμένον and
not ἐν μάλθῃ γεγραμμένον.

οὐ νῦν, ἐνόντων, ἀναισχυντεῖν]
'The terms being in the deposition, he ought not to have
the impudence to repudiate
them *now*.'

45. εἰ ἐάσαιτ᾽ ἄν] When εἰ
stands for εἴτε or πότερον, to
express an alternative of probabilities, it sometimes takes ἄν,
which would, in the ordinary
sense of εἰ, be inadmissible.

ἁλώσεται.......ψευδομαρτυριῶν]
For the gen. cf. Or. 24 § 103,
ἐάν τις ἁλῷ κλοπῆς καὶ μὴ τι-
μηθῇ θανάτου..., καὶ ἐάν τις ἁλοὺς
τῆς κακώσεως τῶν γονέων..., κἂν

ἀστρατείας τις ὄφλῃ. (Kühner,
Gk. Gr. § 419, 2 p. 331.)—
ὧν βούλεται, supply μόνον.

ἀντιγέγραψαι] 'You have
pleaded' in answer to the indictment or plaint (λῆξις); see
Dict. Antiq. s. v. *Antigraphe.*
'The two pleadings together,
the plaint on the left side, the
plea on the right, form (as we
should say) the issue on the
record. The deposition com-
plained of was annexed' (C. R.
Kennedy). Cf. Meier and Schömann, p. 628.—τὸ καὶ τὸ, 'so
and so'; 'this or that,' cf. τόσα
καὶ τόσα in Or. 34 § 24.

46. τὴν ἀντιγραφὴν] Harpocr.
s.v. τὰ τῶν δικαζομένων γράμματα,
ἃ ἐδίδοσαν περὶ τοῦ πράγματος,
καὶ τὰ τοῦ διώκοντος καὶ τὰ τοῦ
φεύγοντος, ἀντιγραφή, καὶ τὰ
μαρτύρια· Δημ. κατὰ Στεφάνου...
The document that follows, is
the only specimen of an ἀντι-

ΑΝΤΙΓΡΑΦΗ.

k['Απολλόδωρος Πασίωνος 'Αχαρνεὺς Στεφάνῳ Μενεκλέους 'Αχαρνεῖ ψευδομαρτυριῶν, τίμημα τάλαντον. τὰ ψευδῆ μου κατεμαρτύρησε Στέφανος μαρτυρήσας τὰ ἐν τῷ γραμματείῳ γεγραμμένα.

Στέφανος Μενεκλέους 'Αχαρνεὺς[1] τἀληθῆ ἐμαρτύρησα μαρτυρήσας τὰ ἐν τῷ γραμματείῳ γεγραμμένα.]k

1116   Ταῦτα οὗτος αὐτὸς[m] ἀντεγράψατο, ἃ χρὴ μνημονεύειν ὑμᾶς, καὶ μὴ τοὺς ἐπ' ἐξαπάτῃ νῦν λόγους ὑπὸ τούτου ῥηθησομένους πιστοτέρους ποιεῖσθαι τῶν νόμων καὶ τῶν ὑπὸ τούτου γραφέντων εἰς τὴν ἀντιγραφήν.

Πυνθάνομαι τοίνυν αὐτοὺς καὶ περὶ ὧν ἔλαχον 47

k-k om. Σ.

1 Στέφανος Μενεκλέους 'Αχαρνεὺς cum Reiskio Bekker. om. Z cum libris.

m om. Z et Bekker (st. Leipzig ed.) cum Σ.

γραφὴ that has come down to us. Though rejected by Westermann, and bracketed by Dindorf, it is quoted by Pollux 8, 58.

ἐπ' ἐξαπάτῃ] Or. 20 (Lept.) § 98, ἐξαπάτης ἕνεκα.—ῥηθησομένους. This future is used chiefly in the participle and infinitive, while the 'third future' is probably confined to the third person singular εἰρήσεται (Veitch Greek Verbs s. v. *εἴρω). ῥηθήσεται however is found in Thuc. 1 73, Ar. Ethics iv 1, 14, and Rhet. 1 12 and 13.

§§ 47—50. I hear they propose to speak of my original action and to denounce it as fraudulent and vexatious. But I submit that this would be irrelevant to the present issue, and I claim that, instead of their being allowed to go into the proofs of the original claim which they debarred me from adducing, they should be compelled, in the interests of justice and for the convenience of the jury, to keep to the record, and prove that the testimony by which they deprived me of those proofs was true.

47. περὶ ὧν ἔλαχον] The original indictment of Phormion in the δίκη ἀφορμῆς to which Or. 36 is a παραγραφή.—ὅπως κατάσχοι, sup. § 27.—εἶπον καὶ

τὴν ἐξ ἀρχῆς δίκην ἐρεῖν καὶ κατηγορήσειν, ὡς συκο-
φαντήματα ἦν. ἐγὼ δ' ὃν μὲν τρόπον ἐσκευωρήσατο
τὴν μίσθωσιν, ὅπως τὴν ἀφορμὴν τῆς τραπέζης κατάσχοι, εἶπον καὶ διεξῆλθον ὑμῖν, ὑπὲρ δὲ τῶν ἄλλων
οὐκ ἂν οἷός τ' εἴην λέγειν ἅμα καὶ τούτους ἐλέγχειν
περὶ τῆς μαρτυρίας· οὐ γὰρ ἱκανόν μοι τὸ ὕδωρ ἐστίν.

48 ὅτι δ' οὐδ' ὑμεῖς ἐθέλοιτ' ἂν εἰκότως ἀκούειν περὶ τούτων αὐτῶν, ἐκεῖθεν εἴσεσθε, ἂν λογίσησθε πρὸς ὑμᾶς
αὐτοὺς ὅτι οὔτε νῦν ἐστι χαλεπὸν περὶ ὧν μὴ κατηγό-
ρηται λέγειν, οὔτε[n] ψευδεῖς ἀναγνόντα μαρτυρίας
ἀποφεύγειν. ἀλλ' οὐδέτερόν γε δίκαιον τούτων οὐδ'

49 ἂν εἷς φήσειεν εἶναι, ἀλλ' ὃ ἐγὼ προκαλοῦμαι νῦν.
σκοπεῖτε δὲ ἀκούσαντες. ἐγὼ γὰρ ἀξιῶ, οὓς μὲν ἀφεί-
λοντό με ἐλέγχους περὶ τῶν ἐγκλημάτων, οὓς προσῆκον
ἦν ῥηθῆναι, μὴ ζητεῖν αὐτοὺς νῦν, αἷς δὲ ἀφείλοντο
μαρτυρίαις, ὡς εἰσὶν ἀληθεῖς, δεικνύναι. εἰ δ' ὅταν μὲν
τὴν δίκην εἰσίω, τὰς μαρτυρίας με ἐλέγχειν ἀξιώσουσιν, ὅταν δὲ ταύταις ἐπεξίω, περὶ τῶν ἐξ ἀρχῆς ἐγκλημάτων λέγειν με κελεύσουσιν, οὔτε δίκαια οὔτε ὑμῖν

50 συμφέροντα ἐροῦσιν. δικάσειν γὰρ ὀμωμόκατε ὑμεῖς
οὐ περὶ ὧν ἂν ὁ φεύγων ἀξιοῖ, ἀλλ' ὑπὲρ αὐτῶν ὧν ἂν
ἡ δίωξις ᾖ. ταύτην δ' ἀνάγκη τῇ τοῦ διώκοντος λήξει

[n] οὔτε τότε optime Dobree.

διεξῆλθον sc. in §§ 29—36.—On
τὸ ὕδωρ, see note on Or. 54 § 36.
    48. οὔτε νῦν κ.τ.λ.] i. e. 'it
is easy enough for my opponents
to introduce into their reply
matter that is irrelevant to the
case and is no part of my indictment, just as formerly it
was easy enough for them to
get an acquittal by reciting
false depositions.'
    Whether we read οὔτε τότε
ψευδεῖς or not, we must in either
case take the second clause as a
pointed reference to the *former*
trial.
    49. αἷς δὲ ἀφείλοντο μαρτυρίαις]
sc. τοὺς ἐλέγχους.—On τὴν δίκην
εἰσίω, see note on § 7 πρὸς ἐκείνους εἰσίω.
    50. περὶ.. ὑπέρ] § 11 n.
    δίωξις] (Dem.) Or. 47 § 70, οἱ
δὲ νόμοι τούτων κελεύουσι τὴν
δίωξιν εἶναι. The word is also
found in Antiphon Or. 6 § 7,
τὴν δίωξιν εὐσεβείας ἕνεκα ποιεῖσθαι.—On λήξει...εἴληχα cf. Or.
36 § 21 λήξεων.

δηλοῦσθαι, ἣν ἐγὼ τούτῳ ψευδομαρτυριῶν εἴληχα. μὴ
1117 δὴ τοῦτ' ἀφεὶς περὶ ὧν οὐκ ἀγωνίζεται λεγέτω· μηδ'
ὑμεῖς ἐᾶτε, ἂν° ἄρα οὗτος ἀναισχυντῇ.

Οἶμαι[p] τοίνυν αὐτὸν οὐδὲν οὐδαμῇ[q] δίκαιον ἔχοντα 51
λέγειν ἥξειν καὶ ἐπὶ τοῦτο, ὡς ἄτοπον ποιῶ, παραγραφὴν ἡττημένος, τοὺς διαθήκην μαρτυρήσαντας διώκων, καὶ τοὺς δικαστὰς τοὺς τότε φήσειν[r] διὰ τοὺς
ἀφεῖναι μεμαρτυρηκότας ἀποψηφίσασθαι μᾶλλον ἢ
διὰ τοὺς διαθήκην μαρτυρήσαντας. ἐγὼ δ', ὦ ἄνδρες
Ἀθηναῖοι, νομίζω πάντας ὑμᾶς εἰδέναι ὅτι οὐχ ἧττον
τὰ πεπραγμένα εἰώθατε σκοπεῖν ἢ τὰς ὑπὲρ τούτων
παραγραφάς· περὶ δὴ τῶν πραγμάτων αὐτῶν τὰ ψευδῆ καταμαρτυρήσαντες οὗτοί μου ἀσθενεῖς τοὺς περὶ
τῆς παραγραφῆς ἐποίησαν λόγους. χωρὶς δὲ τούτων 52
ἄτοπον, πάντων τὰ ψευδῆ μαρτυρησάντων, τίς μάλιστα ἔβλαψεν ἀποφαίνειν, ἀλλ' οὐχ ὡς αὐτὸς ἕκαστος
ἀληθῆ μεμαρτύρηκε δεικνύναι. οὐ γάρ, ἂν ἕτερον

° ἐὰν Ζ cum Σ.   [p] οἴομαι Ζ cum Σ (cf. Or. 36 § 18).
[q] οὐδαμῇ Ζ cum Σ.

[r] cum Reiskio Bekker.   φήσει Ζ cum libris.

---

§§ 51—52. *The defendant will
urge that the jury in the former
trial were led to dismiss my suit
by reason of the witnesses in support of the discharge on which
Phormion's special plea was
based; and not by reason of those
who (like himself) gave evidence
to the will, as part of the main
issue. But I reply that every one
knows that juries look to the main
issue as well as to the special plea,
and I contend that witnesses to the
main issue (like the defendant)
crippled my case on the special
plea. Where all gave false evidence, it is not enough for any
individual defendant to point
out that some other witness*
*damaged my case more than he
did, but to prove that his own
evidence is true.*

51. ἀφεῖναι] sc. τῶν ἐγκλημάτων Φορμίωνα. Or. 36 §§ 23
—25.

τὰ πεπραγμένα] The facts of
the case on its merits, as opposed to the special plea. See
note on Or. 36 *Argument* 1. 25
ἅπτεται τῆς εὐθείας κ.τ.λ.

ἀσθενεῖς ἐποίησαν κ.τ.λ.]
'Weakened my arguments on
the special plea.' This need
not imply that he actually
spoke; as a matter of fact, we
find the court would not listen
to him (§ 6).

δείξῃ δεινότερα εἰργασμένον, ἀποφεύγειν αὐτῷ προσήκει, ἀλλ' ἂν αὐτὸς ὡς ἀληθῆ μεμαρτύρηκεν ἀποφήνῃ.
53   'Εφ' ᾧ τοίνυν, ὦ ἄνδρες 'Αθηναῖοι, μάλιστ' ἀπολωλέναι δίκαιός ἐστιν οὑτοσὶ Στέφανος, τοῦτ' ἀκούσατέ μου.   δεινὸν μὲν γάρ ἐστιν εἰ καὶ καθ' ὅτου τις
οὖν τὰ ψευδῆ μαρτυρεῖ, πολλῷ δὲ δεινότερον καὶ πλείονος ὀργῆς ἄξιον, εἰ κατὰ τῶν συγγενῶν· οὐ γὰρ τοὺς
γεγραμμένους νόμους ὁ τοιοῦτος ἄνθρωπος μόνον,
ἀλλὰ καὶ τὰ τῆς φύσεως οἰκεῖα[a] ἀναιρεῖ.   τοῦτο τοίνυν

[a] δίκαια Cobet.

§§ 53—56. *By giving false
evidence against* me, *the defendant has done wrong to the unwritten laws of natural affection,
for my wife is his first cousin.
Very different has been the conduct of my wife's father, Deinias,
who holds himself debarred by
the claims of kinship from giving
even true evidence on my behalf
against my opponent Stephanus,
who is his sister's son.*

53.   ἀπολωλέναι] 'To be put
to death' for bearing false witness against his own relations,
Apollodorus having married the
first cousin of Stephanus.

καθ' ὅτου τις οὖν] = καθ'
ὁτουοῦν ὁστισοῦν; like ὁπωστι-
οῦν = ὁτιοῦν καὶ ὁπωσοῦν.

τοὺς γεγραμμένους νόμους...τὰ
τῆς φύσεως οἰκεῖα] Soph. Antig.
454, οὐ γὰρ σθένειν τοσοῦτον ᾠ-
όμην τὰ σὰ κηρύγμαθ' ὥστ' ἄγρα-
πτα κἀσφαλῆ θεῶν νόμιμα δύνασθαι θνητὸν ὄνθ' ὑπερδραμεῖν.
There, as here, the unwritten
law of natural affection is contrasted with human ordinances.

'*Intelligisne* (asks Cobet) *quae
sint* τὰ τῆς φύσεως οἰκεῖα *op-
posita* τοῖς νόμοις τοῖς γεγραμμένοις? *Non opinor.   Sed latet
in* οἰκεῖα *vocabulum quo non est
aliud apud Oratores tritius et
frequentius, nempe* τὰ τῆς φύσεως
δίκαια ἀναιρεῖ, *veluti in Orat.*
xxv 28 προφάσεις πλάττων καὶ
ψευδεῖς αἰτίας συντιθεὶς τὰ κοινὰ
δίκαια ἀνατρέψειν οἴει. *Rectissime
igitur componuntur* τὰ τῆς φύσεως
δίκαια *et* τὰ τῶν νόμων δίκαια,
quae commemorat idem Orator
xxv 3 μεθ' ἑαυτοῦ δεῖξων ἑκάτερος
τὰ τῶν νόμων δίκαια' (*NovaeLec-
tiones* p. 619).—τὰ τῆς φύσεως
οἰκεῖα may however be retained
in spite of the above suggestion,
and we may readily render it
'natural relationship' or better
'the home-ties of nature', 'the
natural ties of home affections.'
In § 65, Stephanus is denounced
as 'the common enemy of all
human nature.'

C. R. Kennedy (Introduction
to κατὰ Στεφ. p. 45) observes,
"To give wilfully false testimony
against the plaintiff was an
aggravation of his offence, ...
for the Athenians excused a man
for being reluctant even to give
true evidence against a relation." [The patriarchal system,
descended from the old Aryan
peoples, made the Greeks view
all family ties as almost invio-
lable. With all their respect for
' written law,' the obligations of
relationship had more of reli-

ἐπιδειχθήσεται πεποιηκὼς οὑτοσί[t]. ἔστι γὰρ ἡ τούτου
μήτηρ καὶ ὁ τῆς ἐμῆς γυναικὸς πατὴρ ἀδελφοί, ὥστε 54
τὴν μὲν γυναῖκα τὴν ἐμὴν ἀνεψιὰν εἶναι τούτῳ, τοὺς
1118 δὲ παῖδας τοὺς ἐκείνου καὶ τοὺς ἐμοὺς ἀνεψιαδοῦς.
ἆρ' οὖν δοκεῖ ποτ' ἂν ὑμῖν οὗτος, εἴ τι δι' ἔνδειαν εἶδε
ποιούσας ὧν οὐ χρὴ τὰς αὑτοῦ συγγενεῖς, ὅπερ ἤδη
πολλοὶ πεποιήκασι, παρ' αὑτοῦ προῖκα ἐπιδοὺς ἐκδοῦναι, ὃς ὑπὲρ τοῦ μηδ' ἃ προσήκει κομίσασθαι
ταύτας τὰ ψευδῆ μαρτυρεῖν ἠθέλησε, καὶ περὶ πλείονος ἐποιήσατο τὸν Φορμίωνος πλοῦτον ἢ τὰ τῆς
συγγενείας ἀναγκαῖα; ἀλλὰ μὴν ὅτι ταῦτ' ἀληθῆ 55
λέγω, λαβέ μοι[u] τὴν μαρτυρίαν τὴν Δεινίου καὶ
ἀναγίγνωσκε, καὶ κάλει Δεινίαν.

ΜΑΡΤΥΡΙΑ.

[v][Δεινίας Θεομνήστου Ἀθμονεὺς μαρτυρεῖ τὴν θυ-

[t] Bekker (Berlin ed.). οὗτος Z et Bekker (st. Leipzig ed.) cum Σ.
[u] Bekker. om. Z cum Σ.   [v-v] om. Σ.

gious sanction. See Cox, *Hist.
of Greece*, ɪ pp. 15—18. P.]

54. ὁ τῆς ἐμῆς γυναικὸς πατήρ]
i. e. Deinias, father of the
Theomnestus who speaks the
first 15 §§ of Or. 59 κατὰ Νεαίρας,
when Apollodorus takes up the
speech. Apollodorus, besides
being brother-in-law to Theomnestus by marrying the sister
of the latter, gave his own
daughter in marriage to him
(Or. 59 § 2).

ἀνεψιαδοῦς] Hesych. ἀνεψια-
δοῦς· ἐκ τοῦ ἀνεψιοῦ γεγονὼς,
ἢ τῆς ἀνεψιᾶς, second cousins.
The form of the word follows
the analogy of λυκιδεὺς, κυνα-
δεὺς, ἀδελφιδοῦς, θυγατριδοῦς,
ἀλωπεκιδεὺς, the terminations
in -ιδεὺς, -ιδέος, -αδεὺς, -αδέος
(οῦς) being a kind of patronymic

form. P.] See Dict. Ant. s. v.
Heres.

πολλοὶ πεποιήκασι κ.τ.λ.] Instances of such generosity are
given in the passages quoted
from Dem. in the note on
§ 35, *supra*, where instead of
ἐπιδοῦναι προῖκα the rather less
common phrase προσθεῖναι προῖκα is used.

τὰ συγγενείας ἀναγκαῖα] 'The
strong ties of kindred.' Cf.
necessitudo. Fals. Leg. § 290,
ὑπὲρ συγγενῶν καὶ ἀναγκαίων. Cf.
Or. 36 § 30, ἀνάγκη...οἰκεῖον.

55. Δεινίας Θεομνήστου Ἀθμο-
νεὺς] The father's name is
very likely to be right, as Deinias had a son named Theomnestus (Or. 59 §§ 2 and 16) and
the grandson very often bore the
same name as the grandfather

γατέρα αὐτοῦ ἐκδοῦναι Ἀπολλοδώρῳ κατὰ τοὺς νόμους
γυναῖκα ἔχειν, καὶ μηδεπώποτε παραγενέσθαι, μηδὲ
αἰσθέσθαι ὅτι Ἀπολλόδωρος ἀφῆκε τῶν ἐγκλημάτων
ἁπάντων Φορμίωνα.]ᵛ

56   Ὅμοιός γε ὁ Δεινίας, ὦ ἄνδρες δικασταὶ, τούτῳ,
ὃς ὑπὲρ τῆς θυγατρὸς καὶ τῶν θυγατριδῶν καὶ ἐμοῦ
τοῦ κηδεστοῦ διὰ τὴν συγγένειαν οὐδὲ τἀληθῆ μαρτυρεῖν ἐθέλει κατὰ τούτου. ἀλλ' οὐχ οὑτοσὶ Στέφανος,
οὐκ ὤκνησε καθ' ἡμῶν τὰ ψευδῆ μαρτυρεῖν, οὐδ', εἰ
μηδένα τῶν ἄλλων, τὴν αὑτοῦ μητέρα ᾐσχύνθη τοῖς
ἀπ' ἐκείνης οἰκείοις τῆς ἐσχάτης ἐνδείας αἴτιος γενόμενος.

(note on Or. 39 § 27). But
of the numerous persons named
Deinias or Theomnestus, not
one is described in any inscription as Ἀθμονεύς, and the
ascription of the witness to the
deme in question is perhaps due
to the invention of the composer of the document.

It is clear that Deinias, on
being called, refused to swear
to the deposition read aloud to
him, οὐδὲ τἀληθῆ μαρτυρεῖν ἐθέλει. The deposition ought therefore to be followed by the word
ἐξωμοσία as in § 60. (A. Westermann, *u. s.* pp. 109—111.)
Cf. Or. 49 § 20.

Apollodorus, be it observed,
assumes that the reason why
Deinias refuses to swear to the
deposition is that it would be
to the detriment of his kinsman
Stephanus; but the disclaimer
may really have been due to
Deinias being aware that the
evidence was false. As the
document before us is untrust-
worthy, we cannot tell what
the proposed evidence really
was,—possibly something re-

ferring to Pasion's will (as suggested by Westermann *u. s.*) or
rather something to the detriment of Stephanus' character,
e.g. his bad behaviour to Apollodorus and his family, or his
receiving bribes from Phormion
to give false evidence against
the plaintiff. (Lortzing, *Apoll.*
p. 80.)

56. ὅμοιός γε] Or. 24 (Timocr.)
§ 106, ὅμοιός γε, οὐ γάρ; Σόλων
νομοθέτης καὶ Τιμοκράτης, ib. 181
and Or. 22 (Androt.) § 73, ὅμοι-
όν γε, οὐ γάρ;

ἀλλ'—οὐκ ὤκνησε] Elsewhere,
we have the ἀλλά repeated, e. g.
Or. 21 (Midias) § 200, ἀλλ' οὐ
Μειδίας, ἀλλ' ἀπὸ τῆς ἡμέρας ταύτης λέγει κ.τ.λ. and Or. 23
(Aristocr.) § 89, ἀλλ' οὐκ Ἀριστοκράτης, ἀλλὰ προπηλακίζει μὲν
κ.τ.λ. Passages like these lead
Dobree to say, ' *malim* ἀλλ' οὐκ
ὤκνησε,' but either construction
is allowable.—οὐδ' εἰ μηδένα τῶν
ἄλλων, sc. ᾐσχύνθη. If he had
no respect for any one else, he
might at least have respected
(had some regard for) his own
mother and her relations.

Ὁ τοίνυν ἔπαθον δεινότατον καὶ ἐφ' ᾧ μάλιστα 57
ἐξεπλάγην, ὅτ' ἠγωνιζόμην, ὦ ἄνδρες δικασταί, τοῦθ'
ὑμῖν εἰπεῖν βούλομαι· τήν τε γὰρ τούτου πονηρίαν
ἔτι μᾶλλον ὑμεῖς ὄψεσθε, καὶ ἐγὼ τῶν γεγενημένων
ἀποδυράμενος τὰ πλεῖστα πρὸς ὑμᾶς ὡσπερεὶ ῥᾴων
1119 ἔσομαι. τὴν γὰρ μαρτυρίαν, ἣν ᾤμην εἶναι καὶ δι' ἧς
ἦν ὁ πλεῖστος ἔλεγχός μοι, ταύτην οὐχ εὗρον ἐνοῦσαν
ἐν τῷ ἐχίνῳ. τότε μὲν δὴ τῷ κακῷ πληγεὶς οὐδὲν ἄλλο 58
εἶχον ποιῆσαι πλὴν ὑπολαμβάνειν τὴν ἀρχὴν ἠδικη-

§§ 57—62. *I must tell the jury, by the way, of an atrocious trick which was played me to my great disadvantage in the former action. At the trial itself, the deposition on which I mainly relied proved to be missing ; and I have since learnt that it was stolen by Stephanus while the suit was still before the arbitrator.*

I call witnesses to prove this : they take an oath of disclaimer. —I thought as much.—Well, to prove they are perjured, I now produce a challenge (duly attested by witnesses) calling on Stephanus to allow his slave to be tortured in the matter of the abstraction of the document; my witnesses depose he refused the challenge.

Now, do the jury suppose that one who thus perpetrated a theft without any personal provocation, would have had the slightest hesitation in giving false evidence in his own interests and at the special instance of another ?

57. ἐξεπλάγην] The form -επλάγην is post-Homeric and is used in compounds with the sense 'strike with terror or amazement' (Veitch Gk. Vbs. s. v. πλήσσω). For the simple verb, ἐπλήγην is used, as in the first line of the very next section, but only in the sense of 'receiving a blow from.' [e.g. Soph. Oed. Col. 605 ὅτι σφ' ἀνάγκη τῇδε πληγῆναι χθονί and Eur. Orest. 497 πληγεὶς θυγατρὸς τῆς ἐμῆς ὑπὲρ (ὑπαὶ) κάρα. πληγεὶς τῷ κακῷ, for ἐκπλαγείς, is remarkable; as if a Roman had said *malo percussus*, for *perculsus*. P.]

ἀποδυράμενος τὰ πλεῖστα πρὸς ὑμᾶς] 'by unburdening to you all that I can of my past sorrows.' Hdt. ii 141 πρὸς τὤγαλμα ἀποδύρεσθαι οἷα κινδυνεύει παθέειν.

ῥᾴων ἔσομαι] 'I shall feel relieved ' or (to translate it still more closely) 'I shall feel *easier*.' For this use of ῥᾴων, cf. Eur. Ion 875 στέρνων ἀπονησαμένη ῥᾴων ἔσομαι. Herc. Fur. 1407, φίλτρον τοῦτ' ἔχων ῥᾴων ἔσει.

58. τὴν ἀρχήν] 'the magistrate,' in whose possession the sealed casket of depositions was kept until the trial. Cf. notes on Or. 53 § 24 τὴν ἀρχήν and on Or. 39 § 9 where ἀρχήν, like *magistratus* in Latin and 'authorities' in English, is used of the holder of the office as well as of the office itself. '*Portentose Reiskius* τὴν Ἀρχίππην,' says Dobree,—Archippe having

κέναι μὲ καὶ τὸν ἐχῖνον κεκινηκέναι. νῦν δὲ ἀφ' ὧν
ὕστερον πέπυσμαι, πρὸς αὐτῷ τῷ διαιτητῇ Στέφανον
τουτονὶ αὐτὴν ὑφῃρημένον εὑρίσκω, πρὸς μαρτυρίαν
τινὰ, ἵν' ἐξορκώσαιμι, ἀναστάντος ἐμοῦ. καὶ ὅτι ταῦτ'
ἀληθῆ λέγω, πρῶτον μὲν ὑμῖν μαρτυρήσουσι τῶν τούτοις παρόντων οἱ ἰδόντες. οὐ γὰρ ἐξομνύναι ἐθελήσειν
59 αὐτοὺς οἶμαι[w]. ἐὰν δ' ἄρα τοῦτο ποιήσωσιν ὑπ' ἀναιδείας, πρόκλησιν ὑμῖν ἀναγνώσεται, ἐξ ἧς τούτους
τ' ἐπιορκοῦντας ἐπ' αὐτοφώρῳ λήψεσθε καὶ τοῦτον
ὁμοίως ὑφῃρημένον τὴν μαρτυρίαν εἴσεσθε. καίτοι
ὅστις, ὦ ἄνδρες Ἀθηναῖοι, κακῶν[x] ἀλλοτρίων κλέπτης

[w] οἴομαι Z cum Σ (cf. § 51).

[x] *fortasse καὶ τῶν vel καὶ ἑκών. eadem quae ipse anno 1875
protuleram, postea eodem Aristophanis loco laudato protulit G.
Gebauer, de argumenti ex contrario formis, 1877, p. 8.*

died eight or ten years before
the suit against Phormion.

τὸν ἐχῖνον κεκινηκέναι] 'had
tampered with the deposition
case.' κινεῖν is similarly used
elsewhere in the sense of 'med-
dling with unlawfully', in Or. 22
Androt. § 71 and Or. 24 Timocr.
§ 179 χρήματα κινῶν ἱερά. Hdt.
vi 134 κινεῖν τὰ ἀκίνητα.

ἵν' ἐξορκώσαιμι] 'that I might
put a witness on his oath,' sc.
τὸν μάρτυρα implied in the preceding μαρτυρίαν. Or. 54 § 26,
τῶν παρόντων ἡμῖν (sc. μαρτύρων) καθ' ἕνα οὑτωσὶ πρὸς τὸν
λίθον ἄγοντες καὶ ἐξορκίζοντες.

ἐξομνύναι] 'to take an oath
of disclaimer.' Cf. Fals. Leg.
§ 176 ἢ μαρτυρεῖν ἢ ἐξόμ-
νυσθαι ἀναγκάσω. ἐὰν δ' ἐξομ-
νύωσιν, ἐπιορκοῦντας ἐξελέγξω
παρ' ὑμῖν φανερῶς. Pollux: ἐξωμοσία δέ, ὅταν τις ἢ πρεσβευτὴς
αἱρεθεὶς ἢ ἐπ' ἄλλην τινὰ δημοσίαν
ὑπηρεσίαν, ἀρρωστεῖν ἢ ἀδυνατεῖν
φάσκων ἐξομνύηται αὐτὸς ἢ δι'
ἑτέρου. ἐξώμνυντο δὲ καὶ οἱ
κληθέντες μάρτυρες, εἰ φάσ-
κοιεν μὴ ἐπίστασθαι ἐφ' ἃ
ἐκαλοῦντο. Isaeus Or. 9 (Astyph.) § 18 κάλει Ἱεροκλέα ἵνα
ἐναντίον τούτων μαρτυρήσῃ ἢ ἐξο-
μόσηται. ΜΑΡΤΥΡΙΑ. ἀκριβῶς
μὲν ᾔδειν· τοῦ γὰρ αὐτοῦ ἀνδρός
ἐστιν, ἃ μὲν οἶδεν, ἐξόμνυσθαι,
τῶν δὲ μὴ γενομένων πίστιν ἐθέλειν ἐπιθεῖναι ἦ μὴν εἰδέναι γενόμενα. Or. 29 § 20; Or. 58 (Theocrines) § 7; Or. 59 § 28.

59. κακῶν ἀλλοτρίων κλέπτης
κ.τ.λ.] 'did not shrink from being
set down as having stolen what
stood in other people's way.'
κακῶν ἀλλοτρίων κλέπτης is a very
singular expression, 'a thief of
other people's ills,' meaning (as
some suppose) one who steals
what is detrimental to other
people's interests, in this case
the μαρτυρία, which is a κακὸν
οἰκεῖον to Phormion and a κακὸν
ἀλλότριον to Stephanus. But
Lambinus justly objects to the
phrase, and Lortzing p. 91
rightly observes, *singulariter*

ὑπέμεινεν ὀνομασθῆναι, τί ἂν ἡγεῖσθε ποιῆσαι τοῦτον ὑπὲρ αὑτοῦ[y]; λέγε τὴν μαρτυρίαν, εἶτα τὴν πρόκλησιν 60 ταύτην.

ΜΑΡΤΥΡΙΑ.

[z][Μαρτυροῦσι φίλοι εἶναι καὶ ἐπιτήδειοι Φορμί-

[y] τοῦτον ἄλλου του Z cum FΣΦ; ὑπὲρ ἄλλου του Voemel. τοῦτον ὑπὲρ αὑτοῦ Bekker cum γρ. FΦ. 'sensui satisfaceret δεομένου vel αἰτοῦντός του. Cf. § 62.' Sauppe.

[z] testimonium om. Σ.

dicta sunt. Reiske says 'Fur alienorum malorum est Graecis ille qui mala, fraudes, scelera, clam, in occulto exsequitur et perficit, non sponte sua, sed iussu alieno'; and similarly C. R. Kennedy (rather vaguely) renders it 'a person who would commit a theft as a tool of another.' G. H. Schaefer, who rightly doubts whether κακὰ ἀλλότρια can mean anything but *mala quae alius patitur*, proposes to read κακιῶν with the sense 'qui quid furatur, ut sceleribus alius accommodet.' Another critic (Beels, *diatribe* p. 100) says: 'κακῶν ἀλλοτρίων κλέπτης lepide vocatur Stephanus, qui in gratiam Phormionis et fortasse eius iussu, testimonium e capsula surripuerat.' In Plato Rep. 346 E we have μηδένα ἐθέλειν ἑκόντα ἄρχειν καὶ τὰ ἀλλότρια κακὰ μεταχειρίζεσθαι ἀνορθοῦντα ('to handle and set right other people's disorders'), but neither this nor any other passage that I can find supports the sense usually assigned to the words before us.

It may therefore be worth while to suggest that κακῶν may be corrupt and should be altered into καὶ τῶν where καὶ emphasizes the *whole* clause τῶν ἀλ-λοτρίων κλέπτης ὑπέμεινεν ὀνομασθῆναι, and not τῶν ἀλλοτρίων only. [The latter construction would inappropriately import into the passage some of the humour of the lines in Aristoph. Ranae 610 εἶτ' οὐχὶ δεινὰ ταῦτα, τύπτειν τουτονὶ κλέπτοντα, πρός τ' ἀλλότρια 'isn't it a shame to beat this poor fellow (Xanthias) for stealing, and that too— another man's goods?' A not uncommon παρὰ προσδοκίαν, as if some other kind of theft were possible. P.] Or again we may alter κακῶν into καὶ ἑκών, comparing § 62 where ὁ τὴν τοῦ κλέπτης φανῆναι (δόξαν) μὴ φυγὼν is parallel to ὃς ἃ μηδεὶς ἐκέλευεν ἐθελοντὴς (=ἑκὼν) πονηρὸς ἦν.

ἀλλοτρίων in any case is intended to point the contrast with ὑπὲρ αὑτοῦ in the second half of the sentence.

[καὶ τῶν ἀλλοτρίων κλέπτης seems a highly probable emendation; nor is there any difficulty in καὶ referring to the general character of a κλέπτης τῶν ἀλλοτρίων. P.] Cf. also Or. 28 § 22 ἀλλὰ καὶ τἀλλότρια ἀποστερῶν ἀποδέδεικται.

60. μαρτυροῦσι κ.τ.λ.] The composer of the present document and the next and of that

ωνι, καὶ παρεῖναι πρὸς τῷ διαιτητῇ Τισίᾳ, ὅτε ἦν
ἀπόφασις τῆς διαίτης Ἀπολλοδώρῳ πρὸς Φορμίωνα,
καὶ εἰδέναι τὴν μαρτυρίαν ὑφῃρημένον Στέφανον, ἣν
αἰτιᾶται αὐτὸν Ἀπολλόδωρος ὑφελέσθαι.]

᾿Η μαρτυρεῖτε, ἢ ἐξομόσασθε.

ΕΞΩΜΟΣΙΑ.

61   Οὐκ ἄδηλον ἦν, ὦ ἄνδρες δικασταί, ὅτι τοῦτο ἔμελλον ποιήσειν, προθύμως ἐξομεῖσθαι. ἵνα τοίνυν παραχρῆμα ἐξελεγχθῶσιν ἐπιωρκηκότες, λαβέ μοι ταύτην
τὴν μαρτυρίαν καὶ τὴν πρόκλησιν. ἀναγίγνωσκε.

ΜΑΡΤΥΡΙΑ.

ᶻ[Μαρτυροῦσι παρεῖναι, ὅτε Ἀπολλόδωρος προὐκαλεῖτο Στέφανον παραδοῦναι τὸν παῖδα τὸν ἀκόλουθον εἰς βάσανον περὶ τῆς ὑφαιρέσεως τοῦ γραμματείου,
καὶ γράμματα ἦν ἕτοιμος γράφειν Ἀπολλόδωρος, καθ᾽
ὅ τι ἔσται ἡ βάσανος. ταῦτα δὲ προκαλουμένου

in Or. 46 § 21, has not taken the trouble to invent any names for the witnesses. He describes them as 'friends of Phormion' to suggest a motive for their disclaiming cognisance of the alleged theft on the part of his witness Stephanus. The writer adds that it was 'on the *declaration* or *award* of the arbitrator between Phormion and Ap.' But so long as there were fresh witnesses being brought forward (as appears from § 58 πρὸς μαρτυρίαν κ.τ.λ.), the case was not ripe for the arbitrator's decision; so we must either suppose that the writer has made a mistake, or that at any rate he uses ἀπόφασις in a vague and general sense for the process of decision and its immediate antecedents. (A. Westermann *u. s.* p. 111—112.)—On

ἀπόφασις, cf. Or. 54 § 27 ad fin. The word in this sense is from ἀποφαίνω, not from ἀπόφημι.

61. μαρτυροῦσι] The fabricator of the document overlooks the fact that the μαρτυρία and the πρόκλησις are two separate documents. It is improbable that he deliberately left out the πρόκλησις, as he has taken the pains to manufacture all the other necessary documents in the case. The two titles μαρτυρία and πρόκλησις are wrongly placed at the head of the document, implying that either the compiler or the transcriber thought that the document included both. Dindorf (ed. 3) has rightly placed the πρόκλησις *after* the document, as in Or. 59 §§ 123, 124.

καθ᾽ ὅ τι ἔσται ἡ βάσανος] 'The terms of the torture.' Cf. Ar.

Ἀπολλοδώρου οὐκ ἐθελῆσαι παραδοῦναι Στέφανον,
ἀλλὰ ἀποκρίνασθαι Ἀπολλοδώρῳ δικάζεσθαι, εἰ βούλοιτο, εἴ τί φησιν ἀδικεῖσθαι ὑφ᾽ ἑαυτοῦ.][z]

ΠΡΟΚΛΗΣΙΣ.

Τίς ἂν οὖν ὑπὲρ τοιαύτης αἰτίας, ὦ ἄνδρες δικα- 62
σταί, εἴπερ ἐπίστευεν αὐτῷ, οὐκ ἐδέξατο τὴν βάσανον;
οὐκοῦν τῷ φεύγειν τὴν βάσανον ὑφῃρημένος ἐξελέγχεται. ἆρ᾽ οὖν ἂν ὑμῖν αἰσχυνθῆναι δοκεῖ τὴν τοῦ
τὰ ψευδῆ μαρτυρεῖν δόξαν ὁ τὴν τοῦ κλέπτης φανῆναι
μὴ φυγών; ἢ δεηθέντος ὀκνῆσαι τὰ ψευδῆ μαρτυρεῖν,
ὃς ἃ μηδεὶς ἐκέλευεν[a] ἐθελοντὴς πονηρὸς ἦν;

Δικαίως τοίνυν, ὦ ἄνδρες Ἀθηναῖοι, τούτων ἀπάν- 63
των δοὺς δίκην, πολὺ μᾶλλον ἂν εἰκότως διὰ τἄλλα
κολασθείη παρ᾽ ὑμῖν. σκοπεῖτε δὲ, τὸν βίον ὃν βεβί-
ωκεν ἐξετάζοντες· οὗτος γὰρ, ἡνίκα μὲν συνέβαινεν εὐ-

---

[a] Bekker.   ἐκέλευσεν Z cum Σ.

Ran. 618—625 (a) καὶ πῶς βασα-
νίσω; (β) πάντα τρόπον κ.τ.λ....
(a) κἂν τι πηρώσω γέ σοι τὸν
παῖδα τύπτων τἀργύριόν σοι κείσε-
ται. Antiphon VI (de Choreuta)
§ 23 ὡμολόγοιν πείσας τὸν δεσπότην παραδώσειν αὐτῷ βασανίζειν
τρόπῳ ὁποίῳ βούλοιτο.

62. τὴν τοῦ κλέπτης φανῆναι
(δόξαν), 'the discredit of being
proved a thief.' ('Who did not
shrink from becoming a thief.'
Kennedy.)

δεηθέντος] sc. τινός. See
Kühner Gk. Gr. § 486 A, 2, p.
641 'on the gen. absol. without
any substantive like ἀνθρώπων,
πραγμάτων being expressed.'

§§ 63—67. Examine the de-
fendant's life and character, and
you will find him cringing to
and flattering the prosperous,
only to desert them when they fall

into destitution. For the present,
he is the creature of Phormion;
and, to compass his own ends,
he is willing to do wrong to his
own relations, regardless of the
ill-repute he thus incurs. He deserves to be abhorred as the common enemy of all humanity.
With all his wealth, he has never
performed a single public service.
Villains who are poor may have
some allowance made them, for
the exigencies of their position;
villains who are rich can claim
no excuse and therefore call for
punishment at your hands.

63. δοὺς...ἂν...κολασθείη = δοίη
ἂν καὶ κολασθείη.

ἡνίκα συνέβαινεν εὐτυχεῖν Ἀρισ-
τολόχῳ] See Or. 36 § 50.—
Note συνέβαινεν followed soon
after by βαίνων.

τυχεῖν Ἀριστολόχῳ τῷ τραπεζίτῃ, ἴσα βαίνων ἐβάδιζεν ὑποπεπτωκὼς ἐκείνῳ, καὶ ταῦτα ἴσασι πολλοὶ τῶν
64 ἐνθάδ' ὄντων ὑμῶν. ἐπειδὴ δ' ἀπώλετ' ἐκεῖνος καὶ
τῶν ὄντων ἐξέστη, οὐχ ἥκιστα ὑπὸ τούτου καὶ τῶν
τοιούτων διαφορηθείς, τῷ μὲν υἱεῖ τῷ τούτου πολλῶν
πραγμάτων ὄντων οὐ παρέστη πώποτε οὐδ' ἐβοήθη-
σεν, ἀλλ' Ἀπόληξις καὶ Σόλων καὶ πάντες ἄνθρωποι
μᾶλλον βοηθοῦσι· Φορμίωνα δὲ πάλιν ἑόρακε[b], καὶ
τούτῳ γέγονεν οἰκεῖος, ἐξ Ἀθηναίων ἁπάντων τοῦτον
ἐκλεξάμενος, καὶ ὑπὲρ τούτου πρεσβευτὴς μὲν ᾤχετο 1121

[b] ἑώρακε Z cum Σ.

ἴσα βαίνων ἐβάδιζεν ὑποπεπτωκὼς ἐκείνῳ] 'Walked in step
with that person and cringed to
him.' 'Cringed to him, as he
walked beside him.' Harpocr.
ἴσα βαίνων Πυθοκλεῖ· Δημοσθένης
ἐν τῷ κατ' Αἰσχίνου (Fals. Leg. §
315) ἀντὶ τοῦ συνὼν ἀεὶ καὶ μηδὲ
βραχὺ ἀφιστάμενος· καὶ ἐν τῷ
κατὰ Στεφάνου α' φησὶν "'Αριστο-
λόχῳ τῷ τραπεζίτῃ ἴσα βαίνων
ἐβάδιζε." Μένανδρος· παρ' αὐτὸν
ἴσα βαίνουσ' ἑταίρα πολυτελής.
(Ἀριστολόχῳ really comes after
συνέβαινεν and is understood
after ἴσα βαίνων.) Shilleto u. s.
explains it here as 'truckling
to, and adapting his pace to his
companion's.' The phrase became common in later Greek,
e. g. Alciphron Ep. III 56 ἑταί-
ρεις σεαυτόν, οὐδὲν δέον, καὶ βαδί-
ζεις ἴσα δὴ [καὶ τύφου πλήρης εἶ]
τοῦτο δὴ τοῦ λόγου, Πυθοκλεῖ.
See note on § 68.

ὑποπεπτωκὼς] inf. 65; Or. 59
(Neaer.) § 43 ὑπέπεσε Καλλιστράτῳ, Isaeus Or. 6 § 29 ὑπο-
πεπτωκότες οἵδε τῇ ἀνθρώπῳ.

64. τῶν ὄντων ἐξέστη] Or.
36 § 50 ἐξέστησαν ἁπάντων τῶν
ὄντων.

διαφορηθείς] In pass. generally of things, here of the person,
plundered. [But it is an uncommon word. Eur. Bacch.
746 θᾶσσον δὲ διεφοροῦντο σαρκὸς
ἔνδυτά, 'the cattle had their
flesh (or hides, perhaps) carried
off in different directions.' Ibid.
739 ἄλλαι δὲ δαμάλας διεφόρουν
σπαράγμασιν. P.]

Ἀπόληξις] Harpocr. εἷς τῶν
ι' συγγραφέων, ὃν Πλάτων κωμῳδεῖ
ἐν Σοφισταῖς. (For ι' the mss
have ν', corrected by Cobet who
explains it of the ten συγγραφεῖς
in Thuc. VIII 67.) Ἀπόληξις
Προσπάλτιος occurs in Or. 43
πρὸς Μακάρτατον, as grandfather
of Macartatus, and there are
others of the same name in
inscriptions. Of this Solon
nothing is known, and Ἀπόληξις
cannot be identified with any
of the above.

ἑόρακε] respexit, 'has had
his eye upon,' i. e. has courted.
A remarkable use. P.]

πρεσβευτής] 'Agent.' Or. 32
Zenoth. § 11 πρεσβευτὴν ἐκ βουλῆς
τινα λαμβάνομεν... One who
negotiates for another is named
after a political custom 'an ambassador.'

εἰς Βυζάντιον πλέων, ἡνίκα ἐκεῖνοι τὰ πλοῖα τὰ τούτου
κατέσχον, τὴν δὲ δίκην ἔλεγε τὴν πρὸς Καλχηδονίους,
τὰ ψευδῆ δ' ἐμοῦ φανερῶς οὕτω καταμεμαρτύρηκεν.
εἶθ' ὃς εὐτυχούντων ἐστὶ κόλαξ, κἂν ἀτυχῶσι, τῶν 65
αὐτῶν τούτων προδότης, καὶ τῶν μὲν ἄλλων πολιτῶν
πολλῶν καὶ καλῶν κἀγαθῶν ὄντων μηδενὶ μηδ' ἐξ
ἴσου χρῆται, τοῖς δὲ τοιούτοις ἐθελοντὴς ὑποπίπτει,
καὶ μήτ' εἴ τινα τῶν οἰκείων ἀδικήσει μήτ' εἰ παρὰ τοῖς
ἄλλοις φαύλην δόξαν ἕξει ταῦτα ποιῶν μήτ' ἄλλο μηδὲν σκοπεῖ, πλὴν ὅπως τι πλέον ἕξει, τοῦτον οὐ μισεῖν
ὡς κοινὸν ἐχθρὸν τῆς φύσεως ὅλης τῆς ἀνθρωπίνης
προσήκει; ἔγωγ' ἂν φαίην. ταῦτα μέντοι τὰ τοσαύτην 66
ἔχοντα αἰσχύνην, ὦ ἄνδρες Ἀθηναῖοι, ἐπὶ τῷ τὴν πόλιν φεύγειν καὶ τὰ ὄντα^c ἀποκρύπτεσθαι προῄρηται
πράττειν, ἵν' ἐργασίας ἀφανεῖς διὰ τῆς τραπέζης ποιῆται καὶ μήτε χορηγῇ μήτε τριηραρχῇ μήτ' ἄλλο μηδὲν
ὧν προσήκει ποιῇ. καὶ κατείργασται τοῦτο. τεκμήριον δέ· ἔχων γὰρ οὐσίαν τοσαύτην ὥστε ἑκατὸν μνᾶς

^c Bekker. χρήματα Z cum Σ.

ἐκεῖνοι] sc. οἱ Βυζάντιοι, implied from Βυζάντιον. See note
on Isocr. Paneg. § 110: φάσκοντες μὲν λακωνίζειν τἀναντία δ'
ἐκείνοις ἐπιτηδεύοντες.

Καλχηδονίους] Phormion, it
seems, must have been implica-
ted in some mercantile suit with
people at Calchedon (opposite
Byzantium). The affair is not
alluded to elsewhere.

65. καλῶν κἀγαθῶν] In good
Greek always *two* words (neither
καλὸς καὶ ἀγαθός nor καλοκἀγαθός)
though the derivative is nevertheless καλοκἀγαθία. Cf. θεοῖς
ἐχθρὸς and θεοισεχθρία. See note
on Isocr. Paneg. § 78.

κοινὸν ἐχθρὸν τῆς φύσεως] § 53
τὰ τῆς φύσεως οἰκεῖα ἀναιρεῖ.

66. ἐπὶ τῷ τὴν πόλιν φεύγειν]
'With a view to escape the
public service.' Kennedy. [An-
other singular expression. Such
citizens were called διαδρασιπο-
λῖται, Ar. Ran. 1014. P.]

ἀποκρύπτεσθαι] 28 § 24 ἀποκρύπτεσθαι μᾶλλον, in contrast
to λειτουργεῖν ἐθελήσειν.

ἐργασίας ἀφανεῖς] 'Sly (un-
returned) profits.' Contrast § 30
ἃ πάντες ᾔδεσαν κ.τ.λ.

χορηγῇ...τριηραρχῇ] See note
on Or. 36 § 39 ἐλειτούργεις.—
κατείργασται τοῦτο (middle) 'he
has accomplished this object.'

τεκμήριον δέ· ἔχων γὰρ] Madvig Gk. Synt. § 196 a, and note
on Isocr. Paneg. § 87.

ἐπιδοῦναι τῇ θυγατρὶ, οὐδ' ἡντινοῦν ἑώραται λειτουργίαν[d] ὑφ' ὑμῶν λειτουργῶν, οὐδὲ τὴν ἐλαχίστην. καίτοι πόσῳ κάλλιον φιλοτιμούμενον ἐξετάζεσθαι καὶ
προθυμούμενον εἰς ἃ δεῖ τῇ πόλει, ἢ κολακεύοντα καὶ
τὰ ψευδῆ μαρτυροῦντα; ἀλλ' ἐπὶ τῷ κερδαίνειν πᾶν
67 ἂν οὗτος ποιήσειεν. καὶ μὴν, ὦ ἄνδρες Ἀθηναῖοι,
μᾶλλον ἄξιον ὀργίλως ἔχειν τοῖς μετ' εὐπορίας πο-
νηροῖς ἢ τοῖς μετ' ἐνδείας. τοῖς μὲν γὰρ ἡ τῆς ἀνάγκης   1122
χρεία φέρει τινὰ συγγνώμην παρὰ τοῖς ἀνθρωπίνως
λογιζομένοις· οἱ δ' ἐκ περιουσίας, ὥσπερ οὗτος, πονηροὶ οὐδεμίαν πρόφασιν δικαίαν ἔχοιεν ἂν εἰπεῖν,
ἀλλ' αἰσχροκερδίᾳ[c] καὶ πλεονεξίᾳ καὶ ὕβρει καὶ τῷ
τὰς αὑτῶν συστάσεις κυριωτέρας τῶν νόμων ἀξιοῦν

[d] Bekker.   λειτουργίαν ἑώραται Z cum F.

[c] -είᾳ Z.   -ίᾳ Σ prima manu.

ἐξετάζεσθαι] 'To be found in
the pursuit of an honourable
ambition for willing service to
the state.' Or, shorter, 'to show
oneself a man of public spirit.'
Harpocr. ἀντὶ τοῦ ὁρᾶσθαι, Δημοσθένης κατὰ Στεφάνου. καὶ ἐν τῷ
κατ' Ἀνδροτίωνος (§ 66) 'ἐξη-
τάσθης' φησὶν ἀντὶ τοῦ ὤφθης,
ἑωράθης.   Cf. de Cor. §§ 115,
173, 197.

ἀλλ' ἐπὶ τῷ κ.τ.λ.] 'Un-
fortunately, the defendant is a
person who will do anything to
get money.'   Kennedy.

67. ἡ τῆς ἀνάγκης χρεία] 'The
force of circumstances ('the pressure of their necessitous lot,'
lit. 'need induced by necessity,')
'leads to some allowance being
made for them in the eyes of
those who view the case with
human fellow-feeling.' Stobaeus
in quoting this passage has the
reading adopted in the text,
instead of the common reading
ἡ τῆς χρείας ἀνάγκη. He also

has οὐδεμίαν δικαίαν πρόφασιν
ἔχουσι, besides, for obvious
reasons, omitting ὥσπερ οὗτος.
(Florilegium 46, 72 p. 316.)
The extract proceeds with the
words πολλὰ δ' οὖν κακὰ πράγματα τοὺς ἐλευθέρους ἡ πενία
βιάζεται ποιεῖν, ἐφ' οἷς ἂν ἐλεοῖντο
δικαιότερον ἢ προσαπολλύοιντο,
which do not appear in the
present passage. They are really taken from Dem. Or. 57
(Eubulides) § 45, as Meineke
might have noted in his edition
of Stobaeus. For the copyist's
patchwork δ' οὖν κακὰ πράγματα
we should therefore restore δου-
λικὰ πράγματα from Demos-
thenes himself, and print the
passage as a separate extract.

συστάσεις] 'plots,' 'conspira-
cies,' parties, political interests,
studia, ἑταιρεῖαι.   Or. 37 § 39
περιστήσας τοὺς μεθ' ἑαυτοῦ, τὸ
ἐργαστήριον τῶν συνεστώτων.
[Eur. Andr. 1088 εἰς δὲ συστάσεις
κύκλους τ' ἐχώρει λαὸς οἰκήτωρ

εἶναι ταῦτα φανήσονται πράττοντες. ὑμῖν δὲ οὐδὲν τούτων συμφέρει, ἀλλὰ τὸν ἀσθενῆ παρὰ τοῦ πλουσίου δίκην, ἂν ἀδικῆται, δύνασθαι λαβεῖν. ἔσται δὲ τοῦτο, ἐὰν κολάζητε τοὺς φανερῶς οὕτως ἐξ εὐπορίας πονηρούς.

Οὐ τοίνυν οὐδ' ἃ πέπλασται καὶ βαδίζει οὗτος 68 παρὰ τοὺς τοίχους ἐσκυθρωπακώς, σωφροσύνης ἄν τις

θεοῦ. Thuc. II 21 κατὰ σvστάσεις γενόμενοι. So also οἱ σvνιστάμενοι in Ar. Lysistr. 577. P.] Cf. Or. 46 § 25.

ἐξ εὐπορίας πονηρούς] 'made bad by their wealth.' Kennedy is hardly correct here in rendering 'men who (for all their riches) are thus flagrantly dishonest.' It is not *in spite of*, but directly *from*, their large means that they become bad citizens. P.]

§§ 68—70. *His affected airs as he sullenly slinks along the sides of the streets, so far from showing a modest reserve, really indicate an unsociable character. All this solemn guise is purposely put on, to veil his real disposition, while it serves to repel the approaches of his fellow-men. He has never contributed to the needs of any one of all the citizens of Athens; but as a usurer, who counts his neighbours' needs his own good fortune, he has ejected relations of his from their homes, and shown himself ruthless in the exaction of interest from his debtors.*

68. ἃ πέπλασται κ.τ.λ.] explained by the contrast immediately after, τοῖς ἁπλῶς ὡς πεφύκασι βαδίζουσι καὶ φαιδροῖς. ἃ πέπλασται καὶ βαδίζει instead of ἣν ἔχει πεπλασμένην ὄψιν καὶ τὸ σεμνὸν βάδισμα, is a fresh instance (like ὧν διεφθάρκει in §

27) of the fondness of the Greeks for throwing into the verb what in other languages would be naturally expressed by a substantive.

ἐσκυθρωπακώς] Or. 54 § 34 μεθ' ἡμέραν μὲν ἐσκυθρωπάκασι καὶ λακωνίζειν φασί... For this and similar words expressing sullen and morose demeanour the student should read the speech of Hercules in Eur. Alc. 773—802.

For a similar passage, showing how keenly the behaviour of persons walking in the streets was criticised at Athens, we may compare Or. 37 (Pant.) § 52 where the defendant anticipates that the plaintiff will bring up against him his fast walking and loud talking, and his constantly carrying a stick. After contrasting their respective characters he adds (§ 55) τοιοῦτος ἐγὼ ὁ ταχὺ βαδίζων καὶ τοιοῦτος σὺ ὁ ἀτρέμας. Again Plato, Charmid. p. 159 B, expressly mentions 'walking quietly in the streets' as a mark of σωφροσύνη. σωφροσύνη τὸ κοσμίως πάντα πράττειν καὶ ἡσυχῇ ἔν τε ταῖς ὁδοῖς βαδίζειν καὶ διαλέγεσθαι. Aristotle ascribes κίνησις βραδεῖα and φωνὴ βαρεῖα to his μεγαλόψυχος (Eth. IV 9 = 3), and Theophrastus characterises the 'Arrogant man' (ὁ ὑπερήφανος) as δεινὸς... ἐν ταῖς ὁδοῖς πορευόμενος μὴ λαλεῖν τοῖς ἐντυγχάνουσι, κάτω

ἡγήσαιτο εἰκότως εἶναι σημεῖα, ἀλλὰ μισανθρωπίας.
ἐγὼ γάρ, ὅστις αὐτῷ μηδενὸς συμβεβηκότος δεινοῦ
μηδὲ τῶν ἀναγκαίων σπανίζων ἐν ταύτῃ τῇ σχέσει
διάγει τὸν βίον, τοῦτον ἡγοῦμαι συνεορακέναι[f] καὶ λε-
λογίσθαι παρ' αὐτῷ ὅτι τοῖς μὲν ἁπλῶς, ὡς πεφύκασι,
βαδίζουσι καὶ φαιδροῖς καὶ προσέλθοι τις ἂν καὶ δεηθείη καὶ ἐπαγγείλειεν οὐδὲν ὀκνῶν, τοῖς δὲ πεπλασμένοις καὶ σκυθρωποῖς ὀκνήσειέ τις ἂν προσελθεῖν
69 πρῶτον.   οὐδὲν οὖν ἄλλο ἢ πρόβλημα τοῦ τρόπου τὸ
σχῆμα τοῦτ' ἔστι, καὶ τὸ τῆς διανοίας ἄγριον καὶ
πικρὸν ἐνταῦθα δηλοῖ.   σημεῖον δέ· τοσούτων γὰρ
ὄντων τὸ πλῆθος Ἀθηναίων, πράττων πολὺ βέλτιον ἢ

[f] -εωρακέναι Z.

κεκυφώς.   Cf. Alexis ap. Athen.
ι p. 21 § 38 ἐν γὰρ νομίζω τοῦτο
τῶν ἀνελευθέρων εἶναι, τὸ βαδίζειν
ἀρρύθμως ἐν ταῖς ὁδοῖς.   Soph.
fragm. 234 b ὡς νῦν τάχος στεί-
χωμεν· οὐ γὰρ ἔσθ' ὅπως σπουδῆς
δικαίας μῶμος ἅψεταί ποτε.   Alciphron ι 34 § 1 ἐξ οὗ φιλοσοφεῖν
ἐπενόησας, σεμνός τις ἐγένου καὶ
τὰς ὀφρῦς ὑπὲρ τοὺς κροτάφους
ἐπῆρας.   εἶτα σχῆμα ἔχων καὶ
βιβλίδιον μετὰ χεῖρας εἰς τὴν Ἀκα-
δημίαν σοβεῖς.   Cf. supr. § 63
ἴσα βαίνων κ.τ.λ. and infr. § 77.

σχέσει] cf. τὸ σχῆμα inf. § 69.
[διάγειν ἐν σχέσει seems unlike
Demosthenes.   The same may
be said of ποιεῖν ἀοίκητον, 'to
deprive of a home,' § 70.   P.]

τοῖς … φαιδροῖς … προσέλθοι τις
ἂν καὶ δεηθείη] The 'Surly man'
(ὁ αὐθάδης) is characterised by
Theophrastus as apt προσαγο-
ρευθεὶς μὴ ἀντιπροσειπεῖν, and the
'Arrogant man' as προσελθεῖν
(to greet) πρότερος οὐδενὶ θελῆσαι.
—φαιδροῖς, 'cheerful,' 'bright'
(as we say).

δεηθείη καὶ ἐπαγγείλειεν] 'prefer a request and make a pro-

mise (or proposal).'   The two
words are correlative to one another like 'asking and granting
a favour.'   ἐπαγγείλειεν is an
emendation for ἀπαγγείλειεν proposed by H. Wolf and accepted
by Reiske and others.   Dobree
unnecessarily suggests 'Quaere
an potest = ἐπαγγέλαιτο, i. e.
opem peteret.'   This would involve a needless repetition of the
idea of δεηθείη.   [Besides, ἐπαγ-
γέλλεσθαι is rather 'to make a
profession of,' 'to propose that
some one should accept your
service' in some matter.   P.]

πεπλασμένοις καὶ σκυθρωποῖς]
'Affected and sullen characters.'

69.   πρόβλημα τοῦ τρόπου]
'A cloak to mask his real character.'   Soph. Phil. 1008 οἵως
μ' ὑπῆλθες, ὥς μ' ἐθηράσω λαβὼν
πρόβλημα σαυτοῦ παῖδα τόνδ'
ἀγνῶτ' ἐμοί.   Cf. παραπέτασμα
supr. § 19, also πρόσχημα in the
sense of 'an excuse.'

ἐνταῦθα δηλοῖ] 'He shows
herein the real rudeness and
malignity of his temper.'

σὲ προσῆκον ἦν, τῷ πώποτε εἰσήνεγκας, ἢ τίνι συμ-
βέβλησαί πω, ἢ τίνα εὖ πεποίηκας[g]; οὐδέν' ἂν εἰπεῖν
ἔχοις· ἀλλὰ τοκίζων καὶ τὰς τῶν ἄλλων συμφορὰς 70
καὶ χρείας εὐτυχήματα σαυτοῦ νομίζων ἐξέβαλες μὲν
1123 τὸν σαυτοῦ θεῖον Νικίαν ἐκ τῆς πατρῴας οἰκίας, ἀφῄ-
ρησαι δὲ τὴν σαυτοῦ πενθερὰν ταῦτα ἀφ' ὧν ἔζη,
ἀοίκητον δὲ τὸν Ἀρχεδήμου παῖδα τὸ σαυτοῦ μέρος
πεποίηκας. οὐδεὶς δὲ πώποτε οὕτω πικρῶς οὐδ' ὑπερήμερον εἰσέπραξεν ὡς σὺ τοὺς ὀφείλοντας τοὺς τόκους.

g Bekker. ἢ τίνα εὖ πεποίηκας om. Z cum Σ.

τῷ πώποτε εἰσήνεγκας] 'to
whose service did you ever con-
tribute?' Cf. Or. 53 § 9 ἔρανον
αὐτῷ...εἰσοίσοιμι.

συμβέβλησαι] 'to whom have
you ever lent any aid?' (Kennedy). συμβάλλεσθαι (with perf.
pass. used as mid.) is here used
in a general sense of helping,
as in Or. 21 (Mid.) § 133 συμ-
βαλουμένους τοῖς συμμάχοις. Cf.
59 § 69 εἰς ἔκδοσιν...τῇ θυγατρὶ
συμβαλέσθαι, followed by εἰσενεγκεῖν εἰς τὴν ἔκδοσιν (§ 70). It
is used of 'contributing' ib.
§ 113 προῖκα...συμβάλλεται, Lys.
4 § 10 τὸ ἥμισυ τοῦ ἀργυρίου
συνεβαλόμην. We have the active use in Or. 34 § 1, συμβόλαια
πολλοῖς συμβάλλοντες.

70. ἐξέβαλες] 'ousted from his
patrimony,' cf. Or. 36 § 49 ἐκβαλεῖν. The debtor in such a case
would be said ἐκπεσεῖν or ἐκστῆναι τῶν ὄντων, ib. § 50. Or. 29
§ 2 λίαν ὠμῶς καὶ πικρῶς ὄντα
συγγενῆ τοῦτον ἐκ τῆς οὐσίας
ἁπάσης ἐκβέβληκα.

θεῖον] his (maternal) uncle,
not patruum. Reiske suggests
that this Nicias may be identified with the person of that
name in Or. 36 § 17 married to
the sister of Apollodorus' wife.
But the relationships that would

thus result are rather complex
(cf. supra §§ 54—56), and it
seems simpler to suppose that
there were two persons of that
name in the same family.

ἀοίκητον] 'a homeless out-
cast.' The word is rare in
this meaning, being generally
used of an uninhabitable country ('ἀοίκητος καὶ ἔρημος Hdt. ii
34, cf. v 10. So in Plat. Legg. 778
B, etc.' L and S). Unless we
accept it in the sense of 'houseless,' it would be necessary
either (as Reiske says) to alter
παῖδα into οἶκον or to read
ἄοικον (as G. H. Schaefer sus-
pects). The latter word is found
in this sense in Plato Symp.
203 D and elsewhere. In Lucian
however (p. 727), the word ἀοίκητος is used as in the present
passage: Gallus § 17 περιέμενον
ἀοίκητος ἐστώς, ἄχρι δὴ ὁ Μνή-
σαρχος ἐξειργάζετό μοι τὸν οἶκον.
(Ἀλεκτρύων loquitur.)

τὸ σαυτοῦ μέρος] 'quod ad te
attinet.' Fals. Leg. § 82 οὕτω
διέθηκας αὐτοὺς τὸ μέρος σύ. So
also τὸ σὸν μέρος Soph. O. C.
1366.

ὑπερήμερον εἰσέπραξεν] 'levied
judgment on a defaulter.' (Kennedy.) Dem. Or. 33 (Apat.) § 6.
Or. 21 (Mid.) §§ 81, 89 συνέβη

εἶτα ὃν ὁρᾶτε ἐπὶ πάντων οὕτως ἄγριον καὶ μιαρὸν,
τοῦτον ὑμεῖς ἠδικηκότα ἐπ' αὐτοφώρῳ λαβόντες οὐ
τιμωρήσεσθε; δεινὰ ἄρα, ὦ ἄνδρες δικασταὶ, ποιήσετε
καὶ οὐχὶ δίκαια.

71   Ἄξιον τοίνυν, ὦ ἄνδρες Ἀθηναῖοι, καὶ Φορμίωνι
τῷ παρασχομένῳ τουτονὶ νεμεσῆσαι τοῖς πεπραγμένοις, τὴν ἀναίδειαν τοῦ τρόπου καὶ τὴν ἀχαριστίαν

δὲ ὑπερημέρῳ γενομένῳ λαθεῖν
αὐτῷ διὰ τὸ ἀδικηθῆναι. In Theophrastus the 'Penurious man' (ὁ
μικρολόγος) is described as δεινὸς
ὑπερημερίαν πρᾶξαι καὶ τόκον τό-
κου ἀπαιτῆσαι. Pollux: (speaking
of debt) ὁ οὐκ ἐκτίσας κατὰ προθεσμίαν ὑπερήμερος.   Harpocr.
ὑπερήμεροι οἱ δίκην ὀφλόντες
ὁποιανοῦν καὶ τὰ ἐπιτίμια τοῖς
ἑλοῦσι μὴ ἀποδιδόντες ἐν ταῖς τακ-
ταῖς προθεσμίαις...

In the whole of this passage
the speaker, dexterously avails
himself of the odium and unpopularity attending the trade
of a money-lender at Athens.
Cf. Or. 37 (Pant.) § 52 μισοῦσιν
Ἀθηναῖοι τοὺς δανείσαντας. Thus,
in the Epistles of Alciphron,
borrowed doubtless in part from
the later Attic Comedy, in a
letter beginning μέγα κακόν εἰσιν
οἱ κατὰ τὴν πόλιν τοκογλύφοι,
the money-lender is described as
πρεσβύτην, ὀφθῆναι ῥικνὸν, συν-
εσπακότα τὰς ὀφρῦς (1 26), cf.
ib. III 3 § 2 ὁ Χρέμης ὁ κατεσκλη-
κώς, ὁ κατεσπακὼς τὰς ὀφρῦς, ὁ
ταυρηδὸν πάντας ὑποβλέπων. In
the same letter we have another
banker, of whom no harm is
said, called by the conventional
name Pasion, doubtless taken
from our Pasion.

εἶτα — ἠδικηκότα λαβόντες]
Compare Midias § 97.

§§ 71—76. At this point the
speaker begins a fierce invective
against Phormion.   Against

Phormion, who produced the defendant as his witness, you have
a right to be indignant for his
effrontery and his ingratitude.
When Phormion was for sale, instead of being bought by a cook,
or what not, and learning his
master's trade, he had the good
fortune to come into the hands of
my father, who taught him the
business of a banker, and conferred on him many other benefits. Yet, with all his wealth,
he is ungrateful enough to allow
the founders of his fortunes to
remain in poverty and distress.
He has not scrupled to marry
her, who was once his own
master's wife, thus securing to
himself a large marriage-portion,
while he suffers my daughters to
languish without a dowry and
become poor old maids in their
father's house. Meanwhile, he
counts and calculates the amount
of my money, and criticises me
as narrowly as a master might
his slave.

71. νεμεσῆσαι] A poetic verb,
rarely found in good Greek
prose. It occurs, however, in
Or. 20 (Lept.) § 161 τοιαῦτα...
οἷς μηδεὶς ἂν νεμεσῆσαι; twice in
Plato, and also in Arist. Rhet.
II 9.   Here, as elsewhere, νεμεσᾶν is used in its regular sense
of 'indignation at undeserved
good fortune' (Arist. Eth. II 7
§ 15 ὁ νεμεσητικὸς λυπεῖται ἐπὶ
τοῖς ἀναξίως εὖ πράττουσι).

ἰδόντας. οἶμαι γὰρ ἅπαντας ὑμᾶς εἰδέναι ὅτι τοῦτον,
ἡνίκ᾽ ὤνιος ἦν, εἰ συνέβη μάγειρον ἤ τινος ἄλλης
τέχνης δημιουργὸν πρίασθαι, τὴν τοῦ δεσπότου τέχνην
ἂν μαθὼν πόρρω τῶν νῦν παρόντων ἦν ἀγαθῶν. ἐπειδὴ 72
δὲ ὁ πατὴρ ὁ ἡμέτερος τραπεζίτης ὢν ἐκτήσατ᾽ αὐτὸν
καὶ γράμματα ἐπαίδευσε καὶ τὴν τέχνην ἐδίδαξε καὶ
χρημάτων ἐποίησε κύριον πολλῶν, εὐδαίμων γέγονε,
τὴν τύχην, ᾗ πρὸς ἡμᾶς ἀφίκετο, ἀρχὴν λαβὼν πάσης
τῆς νῦν παρούσης εὐδαιμονίας. οὐκοῦν δεινόν, ὦ γῆ 73
καὶ θεοὶ, καὶ πέρα δεινοῦ, τοὺς Ἕλληνα μὲν ἀντὶ βαρ-
βάρου ποιήσαντας, γνώριμον δ᾽ ἀντ᾽ ἀνδραπόδου, τοσούτων ἀγαθῶν ἡγεμόνας, τούτους περιορᾶν ἐν ταῖς
ἐσχάταις ἀπορίαις ὄντας ἔχοντα καὶ πλουτοῦντα, καὶ
εἰς τοῦθ᾽ ἥκειν ἀναιδείας ὥστε, ἧς παρ᾽ ἡμῶν τύχης
μετέσχε, ταύτης ἡμῖν μὴ τολμᾶν μεταδοῦναι. ἀλλ᾽ 74
αὐτὸς μὲν οὐκ ὤκνησε τὴν δέσποιναν γῆμαι, καὶ ἣ τὰ
1124 καταχύσματα αὐτοῦ κατέχεε τόθ᾽ ἡνίκα ἐωνήθη, ταύτῃ

ἂν μαθὼν ... ἦν] ἂν belongs
solely to ἦν, the principal verb
of the apodosis, although it is
placed immediately before the
emphatic participle μαθών. See
Goodwin's *Moods and Tenses*
§ 42, 3 note 1.

72. τραπεζίτης ὤν] The participial clause is here, as often,
more emphatic than the principal verb ἐκτήσατο. 'Since my
father, into whose hands he
came, was a *banker*.'

73. γνώριμον] Kennedy renders this : 'a *friend* instead of
a slave.' γνώριμος however is a
weaker word than φίλος, though
it is curiously placed after it by
an anti-climax in Or.18 (de Corona) § 284 ξένος ἢ φίλος ἢ γνώριμος. But in the present passage, the context leads us to
prefer translating it : 'a *man of
note* instead of a mere slave.'

τοσούτων ἀγαθῶν ἡγεμόνας] An
unusual phrase ; 'who had led
him to, showed him the way
to, so many social and political
advantages.' P.]

καὶ πλουτοῦντα is perhaps a
gloss on τὸν ἔχοντα. Cf. Soph.
Aj. 157 πρὸς γὰρ τὸν ἔχονθ᾽ ὁ
φθόνος ἕρπει. P.]

ἀναιδείας] For the gen. cf.
Or. 36 § 48 εἰς τοῦθ᾽ ἥκεις μανίας.

74. καταχύσματα] Harpocr.
Δημοσθένης ἐν τῷ κατὰ Στεφάνου
α΄. ὅτι τῶν νεωνήτων οἱ δεσπόται
τραγήματα κατέχεον Ἀριστοφάνης
Πλούτῳ δηλοῖ (Ar. Plut. 768
φέρε νῦν ἰοῦσ᾽ εἴσω κομίσω καταχύσματα ὥσπερ νεωνήτοισιν ὀφ-
θαλμοῖς ἐγώ). The sweetmeats,
nuts, &c, were scattered over
the newly-purchased slave and
scrambled for by his fellow-
servants. 'This was done, not
on the slave's account, but for

συνοικεῖν, οὐδὲ προῖκα πέντε τάλαντα αὐτῷ γράψαι,
χωρὶς ὧν οὔσης τῆς μητρὸς κυρίας οὗτος ἐγκρατὴς
γέγονε πολλῶν χρημάτων (τί γὰρ αὐτὸν οἴεσθε εἰς
τὰς διαθήκας ἐγγράψαι "καὶ τἄλλα, ὅσα ἐστὶν, Ἀρ-
"χίππῃ δίδωμι" ;) τὰς δ᾽ ἡμετέρας θυγατέρας μελλού-
σας δι᾽ ἔνδειαν ἀνεκδότους ἔνδον γηράσκειν περιορᾷ·
75 καὶ εἰ μὲν πένης οὗτος ἦν, ἡμεῖς δ᾽ εὐποροῦντες ἐτυγ-
χάνομεν, καὶ συνέβη τι παθεῖν, οἷα πολλὰ, ἐμοὶ, οἱ
παῖδες ἂν οἱ τούτου τῶν ἐμῶν θυγατέρων ἐδικάζοντο[h],

h ‘legendum videtur ἐδικάζοντο i.e. ἐπεδικάζοντο cum Wolfio’. Dobree.

the sake of a good omen, as the
Scholiast tells us.’ Becker's
Charicles iii 33 (=p. 368 of
Eng. abridg.). Hermann, *Pri-
vatalt.* § 12, 5, p. 82 Blümner;
St John's *Manners and Customs
of the Greeks* iii 27.

προῖκα πέντε κ.τ.λ.] § 28.

οὔσης κυρίας] He, as the
husband, has got possession of
property, as κύριος (or legal
possessor) of her, as she was of
the said property. P.]

75. εἰ...συνέβη τι παθεῖν κ.τ.λ.]
‘If, in the ordinary course of
nature, anything had happened
to me’; a common euphemism
for death. See note on Or. 54
§ 25.

ἐδικάζοντο] The *regular* word
used of the suitors under such
circumstances was ἐπι-δικάζεσθαι
(Or. 43 Macart. § 55 τῆς ἐπικλήρου
ἐπιδικάζεσθαι and ἐπεδικαζόμην
γένει ὢν ἐγγυτάτω). Hence, ἐπεδικάζοντο has been proposed.
But this suggestion, although
since supported by the discovery of a marginal correction
to that effect in the Paris ms Σ,
is not perhaps absolutely necessary, as the wider general
term includes the narrower
special one. The reference, in
any case, is to the provisions
of the Athenian law, whereby,
when there was no son to
inherit the estate, the heiresses
were bound to be married to
their nearest relatives (not in
the ascending line). The next
of kin brought his claim before
the chief Archon, whose duty
it was ἐπιμελεῖσθαι τῶν ἐπικλήρων
(Or. 43 § 75), public notice was
given of the claim, and if no
one appeared to dispute it, the
Archon adjudged the heiress to
him (ἐπεδίκασεν αὐτῷ τὴν ἐπίκληρον). If another claimant
appeared, a court was held to
decide the suit, according to
the Athenian law of consan-
guinity. Cases even occurred in
which the suitor would get his
wife taken off his hands to
enable him to marry such an
heiress (e.g. Or. 57 § 41). If
the ‘heiress’ was poor, and the
nearest relative did not choose
to marry her, he was bound to
give her a marriage-portion according to his own fortune (C.
R. Kennedy, *Dict. Antiq.* s. v.
Epiclerus). Or. 43 § 54 *lex,*
τῶν ἐπικλήρων ὅσαι θητικὸν τε-
λοῦσιν, ἐὰν μὴ βούληται ἔχειν ὁ
ἐγγυτάτω γένους ἐκδιδότω ἐπιδοὺς

οἱ τοῦ δούλου τῶν τοῦ δεσπότου· θεῖοι γάρ εἰσιν αὐταῖς
διὰ τὸ τὴν μητέρα τὴν ἐμὴν τοῦτον λαβεῖν· ἐπειδὴ
δὲ ἀπόρως ἡμεῖς ἔχομεν, τηνικαῦτα οὐ συνεκδώσει
ταύτας, ἀλλὰ λέγει καὶ λογίζεται τὸ πλῆθος ὧν ἐγὼ
χρημάτων ἔχω. καὶ γὰρ τοῦτο ἀτοπώτατον πάντων. 76
ὧν μὲν ἀπεστέρηκεν ἡμᾶς χρημάτων, οὐδέπω καὶ τήμε-
ρον ἠθέλησεν ὑποσχεῖν τὸν λόγον[1], ἀλλὰ μὴ εἰσαγωγί-
μους εἶναι τὰς δίκας παραγράφεται· ἃ δὲ τῶν πατρῴων
ἐνειμάμην ἐγώ, ταῦτα λογίζεται. καὶ τοὺς μὲν ἄλλους
ἄν τις ἴδοι τοὺς οἰκέτας ὑπὸ τῶν δεσποτῶν ἐξεταζομέ-
νους· οὗτος δ' αὖ τοὐναντίον τὸν δεσπότην ὁ δοῦλος
ἐξετάζει, ὡς δῆτα πονηρὸν καὶ ἄσωτον ἐκ τούτων

<hr>

[1] Bekker. τὸν λόγον om. Z cum Σ.

<hr>

κ.τ.λ. (Cf. K. F. Hermann,
Public Antiq. § 120, notes 6—
12; *Privatalt.* § 64, notes 10
and 11 = *Rechtsalt.* p. 57 Thalheim, with Pollux III 33 ; and
see Aristoph. Vesp. 583—7.)

θεῖοι] Phormion's sons being,
like Apollodorus, sons of Archippe, would be 'uncles' to
the daughters of their half-
brother Apollodorus.—ἡμεῖς is
emphatically contrasted with εἰ
πένης οὗτος ἦν (*supra*), as ὧν
ἐγὼ ἔχω inf. with the implied
ὧν οὗτος (or ὧν αὐτὸς) ἔχει.

76. ἐξεταζομένους] 'scrutinis-
ed', 'narrowly examined', 'called
to account', 'taken to task' (§§
80, 82; 2 § 27 πικρῶς ἐξετάσαι).
Liddell and Scott refer to this
passage, and explain it 'to question by the torture,' comparing
Polybius xv 27 § 7 (φιλοτίμως
ἐξετάσαι πᾶσαν προτιθέντα βάσανον); but in view of the context it
seems better to give it a general
sense, though not to the exclu-
sion of the special meaning
above suggested. Besides, a
reference to the passage in Poly-

bius will show that the verb there
refers not to the torture itself,
but to the close examination *preceding* the torture. The torture
was only to be applied if the
ἐξέτασις failed. [The verb is here
used for ἐλεγχομένους τὴν οὐσίαν,
'having their property inquired
into.' Slaves, in fact, had no
property: but their masters
might inquire if they had, rightly or wrongly, become possessed
of anything, e.g. of means to
purchase their liberty. 'To
make an inventory of property'
is ἐξετάξειν (Ar. Eccl. 729), or ἐξέ-
τασιν ποιεῖσθαι, which is also a
military term. P.]

§§ 77—80. *My aspect of countenance, my quickness of walk
and my loudness of talk may
not, perhaps, be in my favour;
they are not my fault but my
misfortune; they annoy other
people and do me no good; and
yet I can claim that I am moderate in my personal expenditure,
and I thereby show that I lead
a far more orderly life than
Phormion and the like. Towards*

77 ἐπιδείξων. ἐγὼ δ', ὦ ἄνδρες Ἀθηναῖοι, τῆς μὲν ὄψεως
τῇ φύσει καὶ τῷ ταχέως βαδίζειν καὶ λαλεῖν μέγα
οὐ τῶν εὐτυχῶς πεφυκότων ἐμαυτὸν κρίνω· ἐφ' οἷς
γὰρ οὐδὲν ὠφελούμενος λυπῶ τινας, ἔλαττον ἔχω
πολλαχοῦ· τῷ μέντοι μέτριος κατὰ πάσας τὰς εἰς
ἐμαυτὸν δαπάνας εἶναι πολὺ τούτου καὶ τοιούτων 1125
78 ἑτέρων εὐτακτότερον ζῶν ἂν φανείην. τὰ δ' εἰς τὴν
πόλιν καὶ ὅσα εἰς ὑμᾶς, ὡς δύναμαι λαμπρότατα, ὡς
ὑμεῖς σύνιστε, ποιῶ· οὐ γὰρ ἀγνοῶ τοῦθ', ὅτι τοῖς
μὲν γένει πολίταις ὑμῖν ἱκανόν ἐστι λειτουργεῖν ὡς οἱ
νόμοι προστάττουσι, τοὺς δὲ ποιητοὺς ἡμᾶς, ὡς ἀποδι-
δόντας χάριν, οὕτω προσήκει φαίνεσθαι λειτουργοῦν-

the state, I have performed public services in a most liberal manner, passing even beyond the requirements of the law, to express the gratitude due to Athens from one who owes his citizenship to her generous adoption of his father. Don't taunt me then, Phormion, with what is really to my credit, but prove, if you can, that I am guilty of immorality like your own. How dare you *criticise another's life and character?*

77. τῆς ὄψεως τῇ φύσει κ.τ.λ.] These are datives of *respect*,— 'in the matter of appearance,' &c. Kennedy wrongly construes with κρίνω, 'I judge by,' &c. P.]

τῷ ταχέως βαδίζειν καὶ λαλεῖν μέγα κ.τ.λ.] For the general sense, cf. Lysias 16 § 19 οὐκ ἄξιον ἀπ' ὄψεως...οὔτε φιλεῖν οὔτε μισεῖν οὐδένα, ἀλλ' ἐκ τῶν ἔργων σκοπεῖν· πολλοὶ μὲν γὰρ μικρὸν διαλεγόμενοι καὶ κοσμίως ἀμπεχόμενοι μεγάλων κακῶν αἴτιοι γεγόνασιν, ἕτεροι δὲ τῶν τοιούτων ἀμελοῦντες πολλὰ κἀγαθὰ ὑμᾶς εἰσιν εἰργασμένοι. See also note on § 68 and cf. particularly Or.

37 (Pant.) § 52 Νικόβουλος ἐπίφθονός ἐστι καὶ ταχέως βαδίζει καὶ μέγα φθέγγεται καὶ βακτηρίαν φορεῖ, and esp. § 55 where Nicobulus says of himself οὐχὶ λέληθα ἐμαυτόν, οὐδ' ἀγνοῶ οὐ τῶν εὖ πεφυκότων κατὰ ταῦτα ὢν ἀνθρώπων, οὐδὲ τῶν λυσιτελούντων ἑαυτοῖς. εἰ γὰρ ἐν οἷς μηδὲν ὠφελοῦμαι ποιῶν, λυπῶ τινὰς, πῶς οὐκ ἀτυχῶ κατὰ τοῦτο τὸ μέρος; The parallel is so close that it lends some colour to the inference that the two speeches were written by the same orator, and that if Demosthenes wrote either, he probably wrote both. Cf. *Introd.* p. xlvi.

τῷ μέντοι μέτριος — φανείην] This self-complacent assertion may be instructively compared with the passage in Or. 36 §§ 42 and 45, where the present plaintiff is charged with extravagance of expenditure and licentiousness of life.

78. τοὺς ποιητούς] Or. 53 § 18 (of Apollodorus) κατὰ ψήφισμα πολίτης (Hermann, *Political Antiquities* § 117).

τας. μὴ οὖν μοι ταῦτ᾽ ὀνείδιζε ἐφ᾽ οἷς ἐπαίνου τύχοιμ᾽
ἂν δικαίως, ἀλλὰ τίνα, ὦ Φορμίων, τῶν πολιτῶν ἑται- 79
ρεῖν, ὥσπερ σύ, μεμίσθωμαι; δεῖξον. τίνα τῆς πόλεως, ἧς αὐτὸς ἠξιώθην, καὶ τῆς ἐν αὐτῇ παρρησίας
ἀπεστέρηκα, ὥσπερ σὺ τοῦτον ὃν κατῄσχυνας; τίνος
γυναῖκα διέφθαρκα, ὥσπερ σὺ πρὸς πολλαῖς ἄλλαις
ταύτην, ᾗ τὸ μνῆμα ᾠκοδόμησεν ὁ θεοῖς ἐχθρὸς οὗτος
πλησίον τοῦ τῆς δεσποίνης, ἀνηλωκὼς πλέον ἢ τάλαντα δύο; καὶ οὐκ ᾐσθάνετο ὅτι οὐχὶ τοῦ τάφου
μνημεῖον ἔσται τὸ οἰκοδόμημα τοιοῦτον ὄν, ἀλλὰ τῆς
ἀδικίας ἧς τὸν ἄνδρα ἠδίκηκεν ἐκείνη διὰ τοῦτον. εἶτα 80
τοιαῦτα ποιῶν καὶ τηλικαύτας μαρτυρίας ἐξενηνοχὼς
τῆς ὕβρεως τῆς σαυτοῦ σὺ τὸν ἄλλου του βίον ἐξετάζειν τολμᾷς; μεθ᾽ ἡμέραν εἰ σὺ σώφρων, τὴν δὲ νύκτα,

79. ἑταιρεῖν μεμίσθωμαι] Aeschin. Timarch. § 13 τῷ παιδί...
ὅς ἂν ἐκμισθωθῇ ἑταιρεῖν.

τῆς πόλεως ... παρρησίας ἀπε-
στέρηκα] νόμος γὰρ ἦν τὸν ἡται-
ρηκότα μὴ πολιτεύεσθαι *Argument* to Dem. Fals. Leg. p. 338.
Or. 59 § 28. This forms the
main point of the speech κατ᾽
'Ανδροτίωνος. See also Ar. Equit.
877. Aeschin. Timarch. §§ 19
—32 (Hermann, *Privatalt.* § 29,
22 = p. 258 Blümner).

τὸ μνῆμα ᾠκοδόμησεν...ἀνηλω-
κὼς πλέον ἢ τάλαντα δύο] The
tendency to extravagant outlay
on tombs was checked at Athens
by a legal enactment referred to
by Cicero, Legg. ii 64, *post ali-
quanto propter has amplitudines
sepulcrorum...lege sanctum est,
ne quis sepulcrum faceret oper-
osius quam quod decem homines
effecerint triduo*, ib. 66. Cf.
Plato, Legg. p. 959 D ἔστω δὴ
νόμος οὗτος· τῷ μὲν δὴ τοῦ μεγίσ-
του τιμήματος εἰς τὴν πᾶσαν τα-
φὴν ἀναλισκόμενα μὴ πλέον πέντε

μνῶν κ.τ.λ. Plato even suggests
that the tomb or barrow (χῶμα)
should not take more than the
work of five men for five days
and that the inscription on the
stêlô should not be more than
four lines long, ib. p. 958 E.—
Lysias Or. 32 § 31 εἰς τὸ μνῆμα
τοῦ πατρὸς οὐκ ἀναλώσας πέντε
καὶ εἴκοσι μνᾶς ἐκ πεντακισχιλίων
δραχμῶν, τὸ μὲν ἥμισυ αὐτῷ τίθησι
τὸ δὲ τούτοις λελόγισται (cf.
Becker, *Charicles* iii 108 = p.
395 of Engl. Abridg.).

πλησίον τοῦ τῆς δεσποίνης]
Archippe, his former master's
wife. [τῆς ἀδικίας ῆς—ἠδίκηκεν.
The genitive by attraction for
the cognate accusative, ἀδικεῖν
τινα (μεγάλην) ἀδικίαν. P.]

80. σὺ τὸν ἄλλου] strongly
emphatic: 'you (of all men) presume!' &c. On ἐξετάζειν, cf. §
76.

μεθ᾽ ἡμέραν...σώφρων, τὴν δὲ
νύκτα...] Or. 54 § 34 μεθ᾽ ἡμέραν μὲν ἐσκυθρωπάκασι κ.τ.λ.

ἐφ' οἷς θάνατος ἡ ζημία, ταῦτα ποιεῖς. πονηρὸς, ὦ
ἄνδρες Ἀθηναῖοι, πονηρὸς οὗτος ἄνωθεν ἐκ τοῦ ἀνα-
κείου κἄδικος. σημεῖον δέ· εἰ γὰρ ἦν δίκαιος, πένης
ἂν ἦν τὰ τοῦ δεσπότου διοικήσας. νῦν δὲ τοσούτων
χρημάτων τὸ πλῆθος κύριος καταστάς, ὥστε τοσαῦτα
λαθεῖν ἀπ' αὐτῶν κλέψας ὅσα νῦν κέκτηται, οὐκ
81 ὀφείλειν ταῦτα, ἀλλὰ πατρῷα ἔχειν ἡγεῖται. καίτοι
πρὸς θεῶν, εἰ κλέπτην σε ἀπῆγον ὡς ἐπ' αὐτοφώρῳ

ἐφ' οἷς θάνατος ἡ ζημία] e.g.
certain forms of ὕβρις (K. F.
Hermann, *Privatalt.* § 61, 20=
Rechtsalt. p. 37 Thalheim, where
Lysias is quoted, τοὺς ὑβρίζειν
δόξαντας ἔξεστιν ὑμῖν θανάτῳ
ζημιοῦν).

§§ 80—82. *You are a rogue of
old, Phormion, an arrant rogue.
Had you been honest, you would
have remained poor. As it is,
after embezzling the sums under
your control, you choose to regard them as an inherited patrimony! Yet, suppose I could have
clapped your present property on
your shoulders and arrested you
summarily as a thief caught in
the act, then if you denied the
theft, you would have been compelled to confess that you got it
all from my father: you could
not have got it elsewhere, for you
were a barbarian when we bought
you. And yet you ungratefully
resisted a suit for the sums claimed from you on our part; you
abused us, you criticised the
antecedents of our family. Well,
even if I am bound to think less
of myself than of all the rest of
my audience, I am at any rate
bound to think more of myself
than of Phormion; and Phormion, at least, is bound to think
less of himself than of me. You
may make us out what you
please, but you yourself were a*

slave all the same.

πονηρὸς...ἄνωθεν ἐκ τοῦ ἀνα-
κείου] A knave, an arrant knave
and a villain of old since he left
the temple of Castor. ἄνωθεν is
a maioribus, πονηρὸς κἀκ πονηρῶν,
cf. Or. 58 § 17 πονηρὸς ἐκ τρι-
γονίας. Or. 44 (Leochar.) § 5
οὐδὲν ἂν ἔδει ἄνωθεν ἐξετάζειν τὸ
γένος τὸ ἡμέτερον. The ἀνακεῖον
is the temple of the *Dioscuri*
or Ἄνακες, as they were called
(Plut. Thes. 33, Cic. Nat. Deor.
III § 53). It was one of the
places where slaves were sold;
Διοσκούρων ἱερὸν, οὗ νῦν οἱ μισθο-
φοροῦντες δοῦλοι ἑστᾶσιν (Bekker
Anecd. 212). Harpocr. ἀνακεῖον·
ἀνάκτορον· Δημοσθένης ἐν τῷ
κατὰ Στεφάνου. ἱερὸν τῶν Διοσκούρων. Moeris, ἄνακες καὶ ἀνά-
κιον Ἀττικῶς (cf. ἀνακεῖον Thuc.
VIII 93), Διόσκοροι καὶ Διοσκορεῖον
Ἑλληνικῶς. Pollux I 37, ἑορταὶ
δὲ ἔντιμοι...Διοσκοίρων Ἀθήνησιν
Ἀνάκεια. The temple stood S.E.
of the market of the Cerameicus
(E. Curtius, *Text der sieben
Karten* p. 53).

Cf. Seneca de constantia sapi-
entis 13 'non moleste feram, si
mihi non reddiderit nomen ali-
quis, ex his qui ad Castoris
negotiantur, nequam mancipia
ementes vendentesque, quorum
tabernis pessimorum servorum
areae refertae sunt.'

81. κλέπτην σε ἀπῆγον κ.τ.λ.]

1126 εἰληφὼς, τὴν οὐσίαν ἣν ἔχεις, εἴ πως οἷόν τ' ἦν,
ἐπιθείς σοι, εἶτά σε ἠξίουν, εἰ μὴ φῇς ὑφῃρημένος
ταῦτ' ἔχειν, ἀνάγειν ὅθεν εἴληφας, εἰς τίνα ἂν αὐτὰ
ἀνήγαγες; οὔτε γάρ σοι πατὴρ παρέδωκεν, οὔθ' εὗρες,
οὔτε λαβὼν ποθεν ἄλλοθεν ἦλθες ὡς ἡμᾶς· βάρβαρος
γὰρ ἐωνήθης. εἶθ' ᾧ δημοσίᾳ προσῆκεν ἐπὶ τοῖς
εἰργασμένοις τεθνάναι, σύ, τὸ σῶμα σεσωκὼς καὶ
πόλιν ἐκ τῶν ἡμετέρων σαυτῷ κτησάμενος καὶ παῖδας
ἀδελφοὺς τοῖς σεαυτοῦ δεσπόταις ἀξιωθεὶς ποιήσασθαι, παρεγράψω μὴ εἰσαγώγιμον εἶναι τὴν δίκην
τῶν ἐγκαλουμένων χρημάτων ὑφ' ἡμῶν; εἶτα κακῶς
ἡμᾶς ἔλεγες, καὶ τὸν ἡμέτερον πατέρα ἐξήταζες ὅστις
ἦν; ἐφ' οἷς τίς οὐκ ἂν, ὦ ἄνδρες Ἀθηναῖοι, χαλεπῶς 82
ἤνεγκεν; ἐγὼ γάρ, εἰ πάντων τῶν ἄλλων ὑμῶν ἔλαττον
προσήκει μοι φρονεῖν, τούτου γε μεῖζον, οἶμαι, καὶ
τούτῳ γε εἰ μηδενὸς τῶν ἄλλων ἔλαττον, ἐμοῦ γε
ἔλαττον· ὄντων γὰρ ἡμῶν τοιούτων, ὁποίους τινὰς ἂν
καὶ σὺ κατασκευάσῃς τῷ λόγῳ, σὺ δοῦλος ἦσθα.

See Or. 54 § 1 τῇ τῶν λωποδυτῶν ἀπαγωγῇ n.—ἐπ' αὐτοφώρῳ,
flagrante delicto.

ἀνάγειν] ἀναφέρειν, sc. ἐκεῖσε
ὅθεν (or εἰς τοῦτον ἀφ' οὗ) εἴληφας. *Demonstrare unde et qui
facultates illas adeptus sis*
(Reiske). 'Had I then required
you to *name* the person from
whom you got it, to whom
should you have *referred* as the
donor?' Kennedy.

οὔτε πατὴρ παρέδωκεν, οὔθ'
εὗρες] Or. 36 § 43 οὐδὲ γὰρ
Πασίων ὁ σὸς πατὴρ ἐκτήσαθ' εὑρὼν
οὐδὲ τοῦ πατρὸς αὐτῷ παραδόντος.
—πατήρ, here (as often) without
the article.

βάρβαρος ἐωνήθης] Eur. Iph.
Aul. 1400 βαρβάρων Ἕλληνας
ἄρχειν εἰκός, ἀλλ' οὐ βαρβάρους,
μῆτερ, Ἑλλήνων, τὸ μὲν γὰρ

δοῦλον οἱ δ' ἐλεύθεροι, the first
four words of which are quoted
by Arist., Pol. 1 2 § 4, with the
comment ὡς ταὐτὸ φύσει βάρβαρον καὶ δοῦλον ὄν.

ἐπὶ τοῖς εἰργασμένοις] 'for
what you have done,' Aesch.
Suppl. 6 φεύγομεν οὔτιν' ἐφ'
αἵματι δημηλασίαν. Mid. p. 549
φεύγειν ἐφ' αἵματι. P.] Dem. 3
§ 24 τὴν ἐπὶ τοῖς ἔργοις δόξαν.

ἐξήταζες] i.e. in Or. 36 §§ 43
and 48, ἐγένετο Πασίων Ἀρχεστράτου. On ἐξετάζειν, cf.
§ 76.

82. μεῖζον] sc. προσήκει φρονεῖν, which is also understood in
both the next two clauses.

σὺ δοῦλος ἦσθα] Emphatically
placed at the close of the passage.

83   Τάχα τοίνυν ἂν ἴσως καὶ τοῦτό τις αὐτῶν εἴποι,
ὡς ἀδελφὸς ὢν ἐμὸς Πασικλῆς οὐδὲν ἐγκαλεῖ τῶν αὐτῶν τούτῳ πραγμάτων. ἐγὼ δ᾽, ὦ ἄνδρες Ἀθηναῖοι,
καὶ περὶ Πασικλέους, παραιτησάμενος καὶ δεηθεὶς
ὑμῶν συγγνώμην ἔχειν, εἰ προεληλυθὼς εἰς τοῦτο
ὥστε ὑπὸ τῶν ἐμαυτοῦ δούλων ὑβρίσθαι[j] οὐ δύναμαι
κατασχεῖν, ἃ τέως οὐδὲ τῶν ἄλλων λεγόντων ἀκούειν
84 ἐδόκουν, ἐρῶ καὶ οὐ σιωπήσομαι. ἐγὼ γὰρ ὁμομήτριον
μὲν ἀδελφὸν ἐμαυτοῦ Πασικλέα νομίζω, ὁμοπάτριον

[j] Dobree (G. Π. Schaefer, Dindorf).   ὑβρισθεὶς Z cum libris.

§§ 83—84. *Oh, but my brother Pasicles takes no part with
me in these claims against Phormion!*

*As for Pasicles (craving your
forgiveness for being provoked
into uttering what I am about to
say), while I acknowledge him
as my mother's son, yet, judging
from his taking Phormion's side
against me, I have my fears that
his father was another. Say no
more, then, of Pasicles! call him
your son, Phormion, and not
your master; my opponent (as
he is bent upon it)—not my brother.*

83. τούτῳ. Depending on ἐγκαλεῖ, not on τῶν αὐτῶν.

ὑβρίσθαι] The mss have
ὑβρισθεὶς, which makes it necessary to take ὥστε with οὐ δύναμαι
κατασχεῖν and at first sight
leaves εἰ without a verb. To
remove the supposed difficulty,
Dobree reads ὑβρίσθαι, placing
παραιτησάμενος—κατασχεῖν in a
parenthesis. But the emendation is at once unnecessary and
inadequate, and we prefer accepting the arrangement suggested by Shilleto, who was the
first to explain the manuscript
reading correctly. 'Schaefer

ὑβρίσθαι frustra tentat. Inter-
punctionis egebat locus, non con-
iecturae.' The passage should
run as follows: ἐγὼ δ᾽ ὦ ἄνδρες
Ἀθηναῖοι καὶ περὶ Πασικλέους,
(παραιτησάμενος καὶ δεηθεὶς ὑμῶν
συγγνώμην ἔχειν, εἰ, προεληλυθὼς
εἰς τοῦτο ὥστε ὑπὸ τῶν ἐμαυτοῦ
δούλων ὑβρισθεὶς οὐ δύναμαι κατασχεῖν, ἃ τέως οὐδὲ τῶν ἄλλων
λεγόντων ἀκούειν ἐδόκουν ἐρῶ καὶ
οὐ σιωπήσομαι) ἐγὼ γὰρ...νομίζω.
'γὰρ post parenthesin saepe
fraudi fuit criticis' (Fals. Leg.
§ 107 not. crit.).

[The passage is slightly ἀνα-
κόλουθον, but it can hardly be
doubted that we must construe
προεληλυθὼς εἰς τοῦτο ὥστε—
ὑβρισθεὶς οὐ δύναμαι κατασχεῖν,
'having reached such a point
that—I am unable to restrain
(my feelings),' and συγγνώμην
ἔχειν (ἐμοὶ) εἰ——ἐρῶ καὶ οὐ
σιωπήσομαι. The ἐγὼ δ᾽ at the
beginning is resumed at ἐγὼ
γὰρ ὁμομήτριον. There is no
great difficulty in the passage;
certainly it is not made clearer
by any proposed alteration.
He was going to say ἐγὼ καὶ περὶ
Πασικλέους—ἐρῶ, but he lost
himself, as it were, in the maze
of the intervening clauses. P.]

1127 δ᾽ οὐκ οἶδα, δέδοικα μέντοι μὴ τῶν Φορμίωνος ἁμαρτημάτων εἰς ἡμᾶς ἀρχὴ Πασικλῆς ᾖ. ὅταν γὰρ τῷ δού-
λῳ συνδικῇ τὸν ἀδελφὸν ἀτιμῶν, καὶ παραπεπτωκὼς
θαυμάζῃ τούτους ὑφ᾽ ὧν αὐτῷ θαυμάζεσθαι προσῆκε,
τίν᾽ ἔχει δικαίαν ταῦθ᾽ ὑποψίαν; ἄνελε οὖν ἐκ μέσου
μοι Πασικλέα, καὶ σὸς μὲν υἱὸς ἀντὶ δεσπότου καλεί-
σθω, ἐμὸς δὲ ἀντίδικος (βούλεται γάρ) ἀντ᾽ ἀδελφοῦ.

Ἐγὼ δὲ τούτῳ μὲν χαίρειν λέγω, οὓς δ᾽ ὁ πατήρ 85
μοι παρέδωκε βοηθοὺς καὶ φίλους, εἰς τούτους ἥκω,
εἰς ὑμᾶς, ὦ ἄνδρες δικασταί. καὶ δέομαι καὶ ἀντιβολῶ
καὶ ἱκετεύω, μὴ ὑπερίδητέ με καὶ τὰς θυγατέρας δι᾽
ἔνδειαν τοῖς ἐμαυτοῦ δούλοις καὶ τοῖς τούτου κόλαξιν
ἐπίχαρτον γενόμενον. ὁ ἐμὸς ὑμῖν πατὴρ χιλίας ἔδωκεν ἀσπίδας, καὶ πολλὰ χρήσιμον αὐτὸν παρέσχε, καὶ
πέντε τριήρεις ἐθελοντὴς ἐπιδοὺς καὶ παρ᾽ αὐτοῦ πλη-

---

84. παραπεπτωκὼς] 'Court-
ing,' 'flattering.' As this verb
does not seem to occur elsewhere in this sense, H. Wolf
and Dobree would prefer ὑποπεπτωκὼς as in §§ 63, 65; but
the text is supported by the mss
and by Harpocration, who says:
ἀντὶ τοῦ ὑποπεπτωκώς. Δημοσθένης ἐν τῷ κατὰ Στεφάνου.—
παραπεπτωκὼς implies subservi-
ence of a less abject and cringing form than ὑποπεπτωκὼς,
which would be too strong a
word for this context. 'ὑποπίπτειν est ad pedes alicuius,
παραπίπτειν ad latus alicuius
succumbere' (Lortzing, Apoll.
p. 90).
Πασικλέα] The silence of
Pasicles is a point brought
against Apoll. in Or. 36 § 22.
The insinuation in the text
seems quite gratuitous, and its
indelicacy forms a singular contrast to the plaintiff's affectation
of reserve in referring to his

mother in the earlier part of the
speech (§ 3 and § 27).
§ 85. *Farewell, then, to my
so-called brother; while I turn
to my true friends, the jury, and
appeal to them not to allow me
to be laughed to scorn by my own
servants and by those who cringe
to them, like Stephanus.—My
father was a great benefactor to
the state, and it would hardly be
creditable to yourselves that his
son should suffer wrong.*
85. δέομαι...ἀντιβολῶ...ἱκε-
τεύω] Cf. § 1.
τοῖς τούτου κόλαξιν] i.e. Stephanus and his friends (not excluding Pasicles).
ἐπίχαρτον] Thuc. III 67. '*Demosthenes non dixit*' (Lortzing,
Apoll. p. 91). ἐπιχαίρειν occurs
in Dem. 9 § 61 and 21 § 134.
ἀσπίδας] The father, Pasion,
had a shield manufactory, as we
learn from Or. 36 § 4.
ἐπιδοὺς] Used of voluntary
free gifts for state purposes

ρώσας ἐτριηράρχησε τριηραρχίας. καὶ ταῦτα, οὐκ
ὀφείλειν ὑμᾶς νομίζων χάριν ἡμῖν, ὑπομιμνήσκω·
ἡμεῖς γὰρ ὀφείλομεν ὑμῖν· ἀλλ' ἵνα μὴ λάθω τι παθὼν τούτων ἀνάξιον· οὐδὲ γὰρ ὑμῖν ἂν γένοιτο καλόν.

(ἐπιδόσεις) opp. to εἰσφέρειν.
See Wolf's *Leptines* p. 66, ed.
Beatson, notes 109, 110; and
Boeckh, *P. E.* Book ιv, chap. 17,
p. 759 Lamb.

ἐτριηράρχησε τριηραρχίας] At
first sight this is an exception to
the usual idiom, whereby a cognate accusative is not used after
a verb except with an adjective.
Or. 28 § 3 χορηγεῖ καὶ τριηραρχεῖ
καὶ τὰς ἄλλας λειτουργίας λειτουρ-
γεῖ. But the clause πέντε τριη-
ρεῖς ἐθελοντὴς ἐπιδοὺς is virtually
an adjectival phrase descriptive
of the nature of the trierarchies.
Thus, in English we do not say
'he fought a fight' by itself, but
'he has fought a good fight,'
(See Mayor on *dicta dicere* and
servitutem serviunt Cic. Phil. ιι
§ 42 where the absence of the
adj. is explained by the sense
of the acc. being *different* from
that of the governing verb and
therefore cognate in form alone.)
'*Speciose Reiskius* ē ἐτριηράρχησε τριηραρχίας i.e. πέντε' Dobree.   Compare Antiphon 5 § 77
καὶ χορηγίας ἐχορήγει καὶ τέλη
κατετίθει, Andoc. 1 § 73 εὐθύνας
ὦφλον ἄρξαντες ἀρχάς, Dem. 18
§ 114, 24 § 150.   Kühner's *Gk.
Gr.* ιι p. 265 n. 3, Lobeck's *Para-
lipomena* p. 501—538, and Rehdantz, *indices* s.v. *etymologica
figura*, where it is shewn that
this use of the cognate accusative
is specially frequent in legal and
constitutional phrases.   On the
trierarchal services of Apollodorus, see note on Or. 36 § 41.

§§ 86—end. *Time would not
suffice to tell of all the outrages
inflicted on me; but you may
form some notion of their enor-
mity if each one of you would
just think of the slave he left at
home and imagine himself treated
by him as I have been treated by
Phormion. Whatever satisfaction
each of you would claim under
such circumstances, you will allow me to have a right to now,
and I therefore ask you, for the
sake of the laws and of your
solemn oaths, to establish a signal
precedent by the punishment of
the man who by his false evidence
robbed me of that satisfaction.
Remember all that you have
heard on our side and meet my
opponents' suggestions at every
point. If they deny that they
are responsible for all the details
of their deposition, ask them
'What stands in the document?'
'Why did not Stephanus erase
the clause?' If they say that a
will has been deposed to by a
guardian, by a ward, and by
one who has it in his keeping;
then ask these three witnesses
'What will?' 'what are its
terms?' for not one of the three
has gone so far as to attest the
terms of the will, which are
deposed to by the other witnesses
(viz. by Stephanus and his
friends). If they appeal to your
compassion, remember that the
victim of a wrong deserves more
pity than those who are doomed
to be punished; and that if you
inflict that punishment, you will
grant redress to myself, you will
restrain my opponents from their
abject adulation, and you will
be giving a verdict which will be
true to your solemn oath.*

Πολλὰ δ' ἔχων εἰπεῖν περὶ ὧν ὕβρισμαι, οὐχ ἱκα- 86
νὸν ὂν τὸ ὕδωρ ὁρῶ μοι. ὡς οὖν μάλιστ' ἂν ἅπαντας
ὑμᾶς ἡγοῦμαι γνῶναι τὴν ὑπερβολὴν ὧν ἠδικήμεθ'
ἡμεῖς, φράσω· εἰ σκέψαιτο πρὸς ἑαυτὸν ἕκαστος ὑμῶν
τίν' οἴκοι κατέλιπεν οἰκέτην, εἶθ' ὑπὸ τούτου πεπον-
θόθ' ἑαυτὸν θείη ταῦθ' ἅπερ ἡμεῖς ὑπὸ τούτου. μὴ
γὰρ εἰ Σύρος ἢ Μάνης ἢ τίς ἕκαστος ἐκείνων, οὗτος δὲ
Φορμίων· ἀλλὰ τὸ πρᾶγμα τὸ αὐτό· δοῦλοι μὲν ἐκεῖνοι, δοῦλος δ' οὗτος ἦν, δεσπόται δ' ὑμεῖς, δεσπότης
δ' ἦν ἐγώ. ἣν τοίνυν ὑμῶν ἂν ἕκαστος δίκην ἀξιώσειε 87
λαβεῖν, ταύτην νομίζετε κἀμοὶ προσήκειν νῦν· καὶ τὸν
1128 ἀφῃρημένον τῷ μαρτυρῆσαι. τὰ ψευδῆ καὶ ὑπὲρ τῶν
νόμων καὶ ὑπὲρ τῶν ὅρκων, οὓς ὀμωμοκότες δικάζετε,
τιμωρήσασθε καὶ^k παράδειγμα ποιήσατε τοῖς ἄλλοις,
μνημονεύοντες πάντα ὅσα ἀκηκόατε ἡμῶν, καὶ φυλάτ-
τοντες, ἐὰν παράγειν ἐπιχειρῶσιν ὑμᾶς, καὶ πρὸς ἕκαστον ἀπαντῶντες, ἐὰν μὴ φῶσιν ἅπαντα μεμαρτυρηκέναι, "τί οὖν ἐν τῷ γραμματείῳ γέγραπται; τί οὖν
"οὐ τότε ἀπηλείφου; τίς ἡ παρὰ τοῖς ἄρχουσιν ἀντι-
"γραφή;" ἐὰν μεμαρτυρηκέναι τὸν μὲν ἐπιτροπευθῆ- 88
ναι κατὰ διαθήκας, τὸν δ' ἐπιτροπεῦσαι, τὸν δ' ἔχειν,

^k habet Σ a me collatus.   om. Z et Bekker st.

86. οὐχ ἱκανὸν τὸ ὕδωρ] Or. 54
§ 36.

μὴ γὰρ......] sc. σκέψηται, understood from σκέψαιτο in the
previous sentence.

Σύρος ἢ Μάνης] Both com-
mon slave-names. Strabo VII
p. 467 ἐξ ὧν γὰρ ἐκομίζετο ἢ τοῖς
ἔθνεσιν ἐκείνοις ὁμωνύμους ἐκάλουν
τοὺς οἰκέτας ὡς Λυδὸν καὶ Σύρον,
ἢ τοῖς ἐπιπολάζουσιν ἐκεῖ ὀνόμασι
προσηγόρευον, ὡς Μάνην (cf. Or.
53 § 20) ἢ Μίδαν τὸν Φρύγα,
Τίβιον δὲ τὸν Παφλαγόνα (K. F.
Hermann, Privatalt. § 13, 16
p. 92 Blümner). [Ar. Pax 1146,

τόν τε Μανῆν ἡ Σύρα βωστρησάτω
'κ τοῦ χωρίου.   P.]

87. τὸν ἀφῃρημένον] Him (ie.
Stephanus) who by false testimony has robbed me of it (i.e.
of my right to a verdict, τὸ δίκην
λαβεῖν).

μνημονεύοντες...... φυλάττοντες]
Or. 36 § 61.

τί οὖν...γέγραπται] Cf. § 45.
ἀπηλείφου, § 44.   ἡ ἀντιγραφὴ,
§ 46.

88. τὸν μὲν ἐπιτροπευθῆναι
κ.τ.λ.] §§ 37, 38.

τὸν δ' ἔχειν] 'Has the document in his custody,' i.e. the

ποίας ; ἐν αἷς τί γέγραπται ; ταῦτ' ἐρωτᾶτε· ἃ γὰρ
οὗτοι μεμαρτυρήκασιν, οὐδεὶς ἐκείνων προσμεμαρτύ-
ρηκεν. ἐὰν δ' ὀδύρωνται, τὸν πεπονθότα ἐλεεινότερον
τῶν δωσόντων δίκην ἡγεῖσθε. ταῦτα γὰρ ἂν ποιῆτε,
ἐμοί τε βοηθήσετε, καὶ τούτους τῆς[1] ἄγαν κολακείας
ἐπισχήσετε, καὶ αὐτοὶ τὰ εὔορκα ἔσεσθε ἐψηφισμένοι.

[1] Bekker. τὰς Z cum FΣΦ.

γραμματεῖον inscribed διαθήκη
Πασίωνος § 16, ὁ μὲν γραμματεῖον
ἔχειν ἐφ' ᾧ γεγράφθαι διαθήκη
Πασίωνος.

ἃ γὰρ] None of the witnesses
corroborate one another ; one
group depose to one series of
isolated facts ; another to another.—οὗτοι, Stephanus and
his supporters.—ἐκείνων, Pasicles and Nicocles.

ἐὰν ὀδύρωνται] Alluding to
the pathetic appeals of the
peroration. Cf. the *miserabiles
epilogi* of Cicero and the Ἐλέου
εἰσβολὴ of the Greek Rhetoricians (Volkmann's *Rhetorik* §
27).

εὔορκα κ.τ.λ.] So in the
former speech on the other
side ; Or. 36 § 61 αὐτοὶ εὐορκήσετε.

XLVI

ΚΑΤΑ ΣΤΕΦΑΝΟΥ
ΨΕΥΔΟΜΑΡΤΥΡΙΩΝ Β.

ΥΠΟΘΕΣΙΣ.

['Εν τούτῳ τῷ λόγῳ καὶ τῶν φθασάντων τινὰ ἐπι-
κατασκευάζεται, καὶ ἕτερα προσεισάγεται[a], εἰ καὶ[aa]
παράνομοι αἱ διαθῆκαι.]

Argumentum a manu recentiore in Σ supra scriptum.
[a] Wolf. προεισ- *vulgo.*
[aa] '*immo ὡς καὶ vel ὅτι καὶ.*   al Bekkerus addidit' Z.

1. 1. τῶν φθασάντων τινὰ ἐπι-
κατασκευάζεται] 'The speaker
establishes afresh some of the
points of his former speech;
and brings on other new points,
whether the will is not also in
violation of the law.'

φθάνειν in this sense is found
only in late Greek, e.g. Argument
to Or. 4 (Philippic) τῷ φθάσαντι
(λόγῳ), and Aelian Var. Hist.
I 34 τὰ φθάσαντα, 'the matters
before-mentioned.' ἐπικατασκευάζειν (according to Sophocles'
Lex. of late Greek) is found in
Dio Cassius 50, 23, 3 ('to construct on') and Eusebius II 557
A ('to prepare after'). It is here
perhaps middle, and not passive.
—προσεισάγω is found in Diogenes Laertius 9, 88 (quoted by
Liddell and Scott, who take it
as *middle* in the present pas-

sage).

§§ 1—3. *Stephanus has made
a long reply to my former speech,
and, as I suspected, has had a
good deal to say in defence of
his evidence. A cunning rogue
himself, and well primed by
Phormion's numerous advisers,
he has attempted to mislead you
into the notion that he is not
responsible for all the details of
his deposition. He has not
brought a single witness to prove,
either (1) that he was present
when my father made the alleged
will, or (2) that he ever saw it
opened after my father's death;
and yet he has actually deposed
that the copy set forth in his
deposition is a transcript of the
'will.' By so doing he is palpably convicted of having given
false testimony.*

1   "Οτι μὲν οὐκ ἀπορήσειν ἔμελλε Στέφανος οὑτοσὶ 1129
ὅ τι ἀπολογήσεται περὶ τῆς μαρτυρίας, παράγων τῷ
λόγῳ, ὡς οὐ πάντα μεμαρτύρηκε τὰ ἐν τῷ γραμματείῳ
γεγραμμένα, καὶ ἐξαπατῶν ὑμᾶς, καὶ αὐτὸς σχεδόν τι
ὑπενόουν, ὦ ἄνδρες δικασταί. πανοῦργός τε γάρ ἐστι
καὶ οἱ γράφοντες καὶ οἱ συμβουλεύοντες ὑπὲρ Φορμίωνος πολλοί· ἅμα τ' εἰκός ἐστι τοὺς ἐγχειροῦντας τὰ
ψευδῆ μαρτυρεῖν καὶ τὴν ἀπολογίαν εὐθέως ὑπὲρ αὑ-
2 τῶν μελετᾶν. ὅτι δ' ἐν τοσούτῳ λόγῳ οὐδαμοῦ μάρτυρας παρέσχετο ὑμῖν ὡς ἢ διατιθεμένῳ τῷ πατρὶ τῷ
ἐμῷ παρεγένετό που αὐτὸς ταύτην τὴν διαθήκην, ὥστ'
εἰδέναι ταῦτα ὅτι ἀντίγραφά ἐστιν ὧν ὁ πατήρ μου
διέθετο, ἢ ἀνοιχθὲν εἶδε τὸ γραμματεῖον ὅ φασι διαθέμενον ἐκεῖνον καταλιπεῖν, ταῦτα συμμέμνησθέ μοι.

1. παράγων—ὑπενόουν] Apollodorus had already, in his former speech, thrown out his suspicions that Stephanus would have recourse to this line of defence. See Or. 45 §§ 44 and 87.

οἱ γράφοντες...ὑπὲρ Φορμίωνος] e. g. Demosthenes himself.

τὴν ἀπολογίαν...μελετᾶν] 'prepare their defence.' μελετᾶν, like *meditari*, with which it is etymologically connected, is often used of 'rehearsing a part,' 'conning over a task,' 'practising for a performance.'

2. μάρτυρας ... ὡς ... παρεγένετο] The plaintiff objects that Stephanus could not attest to a document being a copy of Pasion's 'will,' as he calls no evidence to prove he was present when the will was made (cf. Or. 45 § 26). But even supposing he had been present, it would not follow that he was familiar with the terms, as even the witnesses to a will would not necessarily know its contents, or be able to attest to

its correspondence with any document purporting to be a copy of the same. Cf. Isaeus Or. 4 (Nicostratus) § 13 τῶν διατιθεμένων οἱ πολλοὶ οὐδὲ λέγουσι τοῖς παραγινομένοις ὅ τι διατίθενται, ἀλλ' αὐτοῦ μόνου, τοῦ καταλιπεῖν διαθήκας, μάρτυρας παρίστανται, τοῦ δὲ συμβαίνοντός ἐστι καὶ γραμματεῖον ἀλλαγῆναι καὶ τἀναντία ταῖς τοῦ τεθνεῶτος διαθήκαις μεταγραφῆναι. οὐδὲν γὰρ μᾶλλον οἱ μάρτυρες εἴσονται εἰ ἐφ' αἷς ἐκλήθησαν διαθήκαις, αὗται ἀποφαίνονται (Becker, *Charicles*, Scene IX note 18).

The inelegance of the triple repetition διατιθεμένῳ..διέθετο.. διαθέμενον is considered open to criticism by A. Schaefer, *Dem. u. s. Zeit*, III 2, 187.

ἐκεῖνον] not αὐτόν, either because it refers to a person deceased, or to distinguish τὸν πατέρα from the subject of the sentence, Στέφανος. P.]

συμμέμνησθε] A verb apparently never used elsewhere, except in late Greek.

ἀλλὰ μὴν ὁπότε μεμαρτύρηκεν ἀντίγραφα εἶναι τῶν 3
διαθηκῶν τῶν Πασίωνος τὰ ἐν τῷ γραμματείῳ γεγραμμένα, τὰς δὲ διαθήκας μὴ ἔχει[b] ἐπιδεῖξαι μήθ᾽ ὡς ὁ
πατὴρ διέθετο ἡμῶν, μήθ᾽ ὡς αὐτὸς εἶδε παραγενόμενος αὐταῖς[c] διατιθεμένου τοῦ πατρὸς, πῶς οὐ περιφανῶς οὗτος ἐξελέγχεται τὰ ψευδῆ μεμαρτυρηκώς;

Εἰ τοίνυν πρόκλησίν φησιν εἶναι καὶ μὴ μαρτυ- 4
ρίαν, οὐκ ἀληθῆ λέγει· ἅπαντα γὰρ ὅσα παρέχονται εἰς
130 τὸ δικαστήριον προκαλούμενοι ἀλλήλους οἱ ἀντίδικοι,
διὰ μαρτυρίας παρέχονται. οὐ γὰρ ἂν εἰδείηθ᾽ ὑμεῖς
εἴτ᾽ ἐστιν ἀληθῆ εἴτε ψευδῆ ἅ φασιν ἑκάτεροι, εἰ μή τις
καὶ τοὺς μάρτυρας παρέχοιτο. ὅταν δὲ παράσχηται,
τούτοις πιστεύοντες ὑποδίκοις οὖσι ψηφίζεσθε ἐκ τῶν
λεγομένων καὶ μαρτυρουμένων ἃ ἂν ὑμῖν δοκῇ δίκαια
εἶναι. βούλομαι τοίνυν καὶ τὴν μαρτυρίαν ἐξελέγξαι, 5
ὅτι οὐ πρόκλησίς ἐστι, καὶ ὡς ἔδει μαρτυρεῖν αὐτοὺς,
εἴπερ ἐγίγνετο ἡ πρόκλησις, ὡς οὐκ ἐγίγνετο. μαρτυροῦσι παρεῖναι πρὸς τῷ διαιτητῇ Τισίᾳ, ὅτε προύκα-
λεῖτο Φορμίων Ἀπολλόδωρον ἀνοίγειν τὸ γραμματεῖον, ὃ παρεῖχεν Ἀμφίας ὁ Κηφισοφῶντος κηδεστὴς,
Ἀπολλόδωρον δ᾽ οὐκ ἐθέλειν ἀνοίγειν. οὕτω μὲν ἂν

[b] *G. II. Schaefer, Z et Bekker* (st. Leipzig ed.).   ἔχειν *Bekker*
1824 *cum libris.*

[c] Bekker *cum libris.*   αὐτὰς Z *cum Baitero.*

3. ὁπότε] See the note on Or.
34 § 33 and cf. inf. § 9 ad fin.

§§ 4—5. *If my opponent
urges that he is responsible for
a Challenge only and not for
a deposition, then he is not
speaking the truth. Every Challenge necessarily involves a deposition, and I shall shew that
he has deposed to something
more than a mere Challenge,
and I shall also criticize the
terms of his deposition.*

4. πρόκλησιν...μὴ μαρτυρίαν]
Or. 45 § 43 προκλήσεώς ἐστιν
ὑπεύθυνος, οὐχὶ μαρτυρίας. Stephanus disclaims responsibility
for the deposition, but the
plaintiff on his part insists that
the deposition is inseparable
from the Challenge, as no Challenge could be put in evidence
at a trial unless attested by the
deposition of a responsible
witness.

μαρτυροῦντες ἐδόκουν ἀληθῆ μαρτυρεῖν· ἀντίγραφα δὲ τῶν διαθηκῶν τῶν Πασίωνος μαρτυρεῖν εἶναι τὰ ἐν τῷ γραμματείῳ ἃ παρείχετο Φορμίων, μήτε παραγενομένους ἐκείνῳ διατιθεμένῳ, μήτ' εἰδότας εἰ διέθετο, πῶς οὐ περιφανῶς ἀναισχυντία[d] δοκεῖ ὑμῖν εἶναι;

6   Ἀλλὰ μὴν εἰ φησὶ Φορμίωνος λέγοντος πιστεύειν ταῦτ' ἀληθῆ εἶναι, τοῦ αὐτοῦ ἀνδρός ἐστι πιστεύειν τε λέγοντι τούτῳ ταῦτα καὶ κελεύοντι μαρτυρεῖν. οἱ δέ γε νόμοι οὐ ταῦτα λέγουσιν, ἀλλ' ἃ ἄν[e] εἰδῇ τις καὶ οἷς ἂν παραγένηται πραττομένοις, ταῦτα μαρτυρεῖν κελεύουσιν ἐν[f] γραμματείῳ γεγραμμένα, ἵνα μήτ' ἀφελεῖν ἐξῇ μηδὲν μήτε προσθεῖναι τοῖς γεγραμμένοις. 7 ἀκοὴν δ' οὐκ ἐῶσι ζῶντος μαρτυρεῖν, ἀλλὰ τεθνεῶτος. τῶν δὲ ἀδυνάτων καὶ ὑπερορίων ἐκμαρτυρίαν γεγραμ-

***

[d] ' Malim περιφανοῦς ἀναισχυντίας.' Dobree.

[e] ἃ ἄν Bekker st. ἂν Z. ἂν Σ prima manu.

[f] ἐν Bekker cum Σ a me collato. ἐν τῷ Z cum Φ.

***

5. περιφανῶς] § 3; the corresponding substantive περιφάνεια has occurred in Or. 45 § 2.

§§ 6—8. *If Phormion's assertion was the defendant's only reason for deposing to the document being a copy of Pasion's will, then he has been guilty of giving hearsay evidence which is false and which he has given in a manner contrary to the law.*

7. ἀκοὴν...μαρτυρεῖν] 'to give hearsay evidence.' Or. 57 (Eubul.) § 4 οὐδὲ μαρτυρεῖν ἀκοὴν ἐῶσιν οἱ νόμοι, 44 (Leoch.) § 55. Isaeus Or. 6 (Philoctemon) § 54 (δίκαιον) οἷς μὴ παρεγένετο, ἀλλ' ἤκουσέ τις, ἀκοὴν μαρτυρεῖν, 8 (Kiron) §§ 6, 14, 29. Examples of this kind of evidence are found in Or. 43 (Macart.) §§ 36, 42, 44—46. Meier and Schömann, *Attische Process* p. 669 fin.

τῶν ἀδυνάτων καὶ ὑπερορίων ἐκμαρτυρίαν] The witness, whether he had been present at the preliminary examination or not, was compelled to attend at the trial itself to confirm his evidence, unless he was either ill or abroad, in which case his evidence might be taken by a commission. Or. 35 (Lacr.) §§ 20, 34. Isaeus Or. 3 (Pyrrhus) §§ 20—27, esp. § 20 παρὰ τῶν ἀσθενούντων ἢ ἀποδημεῖν μελλόντων ὅταν τις ἐκμαρτυρίαν ποιῆται... Harpocration, ἐκμαρτυρία· διαφέρει τῆς μαρτυρίας, ὅτι ἡ μὲν μαρτυρία τῶν παρόντων ἐστίν, ἡ δ' ἐκμαρτυρία τῶν ἀπόντων. σαφέστατα δὲ περὶ τούτων διδάσκουσι Δημοσθένης τε

μένην ἐν τῷ[g] γραμματείῳ· καὶ ἀπὸ τῆς αὐτῆς ἐπισκή-

1131 ψεως τήν τε μαρτυρίαν καὶ ἐκμαρτυρίαν ἀγωνίζεσθαι ἅμα, ἵν' ἐὰν μὲν ἀναδέχηται ὁ ἐκμαρτυρήσας, ἐκεῖνος ὑπόδικος ᾖ τῶν ψευδομαρτυριῶν, ἐὰν δὲ μὴ ἀναδέχηται, οἱ μαρτυρήσαντες[h] τὴν ἐκμαρτυρίαν. Στέφανος 8 τοίνυν οὑτοσὶ, οὔτ' εἰδὼς διαθήκας καταλιπόντα τὸν πατέρα ἡμῶν, οὔτε παραγενόμενος πώποτε διατιθεμένῳ τῷ πατρὶ ἡμῶν, ἀκούσας δὲ Φορμίωνος, μεμαρτύρηκεν ἀκοὴν τὰ ψευδῆ τε καὶ παρὰ τὸν νόμον. καὶ ταῦθ' ὅτι ἀληθῆ λέγω, αὐτὸν ὑμῖν τὸν νόμον ἀναγνώσεται.

ΝΟΜΟΣ.

['Ακοὴν εἶναι μαρτυρεῖν τεθνεῶτος, ἐκμαρτυρίαν δὲ ὑπερορίου καὶ ἀδυνάτου.]

'Ως τοίνυν καὶ παρ' ἕτερον νόμον μεμαρτύρηκεν 9

[g] om. Z cum Reiskio.

[h] Z et Bekker (st. Leipzig ed.) cum Reiskio. ἐκμαρτυρήσαντες Bekker (Berlin ed.) cum libris.

ἐν τῷ κατὰ Στεφάνου καὶ Δείναρχος. Meier and Schömann, p. 670.

ἀπὸ τῆς αὐτῆς ἐπισκήψεως] The laws enact 'that the evidence of the absent witness shall come before the court under the same impeachment as that of the witnesses attesting the same, in order that, if the absent witness acknowledge his evidence, *he* may be liable to a trial for false testimony, and if he disown it, then the attesting witnesses.' For ἐπίσκηψις, the process of bringing an action for false witness, cf. Arist. Pol. ΙΙ 12 § 11 Χαρώνδου ἴδιον οὐδέν ἐστι πλὴν αἱ δίκαι τῶν ψευδομαρτυριῶν, πρῶτος γὰρ ἐποίησε τὴν ἐπίσκηψιν. Or. 47 §§ 1 and 5 Θεόφημος αὐτοῖς ὡς ἀλη-

θῆ μεμαρτυρηκόσιν οὐκ ἐπεσκήψατο οὐδ' ἐπεξέρχεται τῶν ψευδομαρτυριῶν, ib. 51. Or. 29 §§ 7, 41 and Or. 34 § 46 note. Cf. Meier and Schömann, p. 385.

ἐὰν μὴ ἀναδέχηται] 'if he does *not* acknowledge it' e. g. on the ground of its being forged or incorrectly copied. Isaeus Or. 3 §§ 23, 24 tells us 'it was usual to select persons of good character to receive such evidence and to have as many of them as possible' (C. R. Kennedy in Dict. Ant. s. v. ἐκμαρτυρία). Cf. Schol. on Aeschin. Fals. Leg. § 19 εἰ ἐπανελθὼν ἐκεῖνος (sc. ὁ ἐκμαρτυρήσας) εἶπεν, ὅτι οὐδὲν εἶπον, ἐκρίνοντο οὗτοι (sc. οἱ μαρτυρήσαντες) ὡς συκοφάνται.

§§ 9—10. *The defendant has also given evidence contrary to*

ἐπιδεῖξαι ὑμῖν βούλομαι, ἵνα εἰδῆτε ὅτι μεγάλων ἀδικημάτων οὐκ ἔχων καταφυγὴν ὁ Φορμίων, πρόφασιν
λαβὼν λόγῳ τὴν πρόκλησιν, ἔργῳ αὐτὸς αὑτῷ μεμαρτύρηκε προστησάμενος τούτους, δι' ὧν οἱ μὲν δικασταὶ
ἐξηπατήθησαν ὡς ἀληθῆ τούτων μαρτυρούντων, ἐγὼ
δὲ ἀπεστερήθην ¹ὧν ὁ πατήρ μοι κατέλιπε¹ χρημάτων
καὶ τοῦ δίκην λαβεῖν περὶ ὧν ἀδικοῦμαι. μαρτυρεῖν
γὰρ οἱ νόμοι οὐκ ἐῶσιν αὐτὸν αὑτῷ οὔτ' ἐπὶ ταῖς
γραφαῖς οὔτ' ἐπὶ ταῖς δίκαις οὔτ' ἐν ταῖς εὐθύναις. ὁ
τοίνυν Φορμίων αὐτὸς αὑτῷ μεμαρτύρηκεν, ὁπότε
φασὶν οὗτοι ἀκούσαντες ἐκείνου ταῦτα μεμαρτυρη
10 κέναι. ἵνα δὲ εἰδῆτε ἀκριβῶς, αὐτὸν τὸν νόμον μοι
ἀνάγνωθι.

¹⁻¹ ὧν θ' ὁ πατὴρ κατέλιπε (μοι *fortasse per errorem omisso*) Dobree.

*another law. Under cover of
the testimony of the defendant
and his friends, Phormion has
virtually given evidence in his
own cause, which is illegal; and
the law declares that a suit for
false testimony shall be maintainable against a person on the
ground of his having given evidence contrary to the law.*

9. πρόφασιν λαβὼν τὴν πρόκλησιν] In Or. 45 § 19 (which
should be compared with the
whole of the present sentence)
this Challenge is denounced as
a παραπέτασμα. So below, προστησάμενος τούτους 'putting these
men forward as an excuse.' For
the favourite antithesis between
λόγος and ἔργον, cf. Thucydides
passim, and Antiphon, Or. 5 § 5
οὐ γὰρ δίκαιον οὔτε ἔργῳ ἁμαρτόντα διὰ ῥήματα σωθῆναι οὔτε
ἔργῳ ὀρθῶς πράξαντα διὰ ῥήματα
ἀπολέσθαι· τὸ μὲν γὰρ ῥῆμα τῆς
γλώσσης ἁμάρτημά ἐστι τὸ δ'
ἔργον τῆς γνώμης. Cf. *ib.* § 84
and Or. 6 § 47 οἱ μὲν ἄλλοι

ἄνθρωποι τοῖς ἔργοις τοὺς λόγους
ἐλέγχουσιν, οὗτοι δὲ τοῖς λόγοις
τὰ ἔργα ζητοῦσιν ἄπιστα καθιστάναι. See also Blass *Att. Ber.*
1 129, 213.

τούτων is redundant after δι'
ὧν, that is, μαρτυρούντων might
have agreed with ὧν, instead of
a new clause introduced with a
genitive absolute. [The latter
was preferred from its tendency
to combine with ὡς. P.]

γραφαῖς...δίκαις] See note on
Or. 54 § 2.—εὐθύναις, 'audits,'
'examinations on surrendering
office,' as opposed to δοκιμασία,
'the enquiry preliminary to
taking office.'

10. τοῖν ἀντιδίκοιν—μή] 'that
both parties be compelled to
answer one another's questions,
but that neither be allowed to
be a witness in his own cause.'
On ἐρώτησις see Aristot. Rhet.
III 18 and for examples cf.
Lysias Or. 12 §§ 24—26, Or. 22
§ 5; Or. 13 §§ 30—33. Dem.
de Cor. § 52, Plato Apol. p. 25,

ΝΟΜΟΣ.

[Τοῖν ἀντιδίκοιν ἐπάναγκες εἶναι ἀποκρίνασθαι ἀλλήλοις τὸ ἐρωτώμενον, μαρτυρεῖν δὲ μή.]

Σκέψασθε τοίνυν τουτονὶ τὸν νόμον, ὃς κελεύει
1132 ὑποδίκους εἶναι τῶν ψευδομαρτυριῶν καὶ κατ᾽ αὐτὸ τοῦτο, ὅτι μαρτυρεῖ παρὰ τὸν νόμον.

ΝΟΜΟΣ.

[Ἔστω δὲ καὶ ὑπόδικος τῶν ψευδομαρτυριῶν ὁ μαρτυρήσας αὐτοῦ τούτου[j], ὅτι μαρτυρεῖ παρὰ τὸν νόμον· καὶ ὁ προβαλόμενος[k] κατὰ ταὐτά.]

Ἔτι τοίνυν κἂν ἀπὸ τοῦ γραμματείου γνοίη τις, 11 ἐν ᾧ ἡ μαρτυρία γέγραπται, ὅτι τὰ ψευδῆ μεμαρτύρηκεν. λελευκωμένον τε γάρ ἐστι καὶ οἴκοθεν

---

[j] 'immo δι᾽ αὐτοῦ τούτου *vel* αὐτῷ τούτῳ' Z.
[k] Bekker *cum Reiskio.* προβαλλόμενος Z *cum libris.*

Isaeus Or. 11 § 4. 'A favourite instrument of debate with speakers in the public assembly and law courts is the interrogation of the adversary. The object of this is to enforce an argument; or to take the adversary by surprise and extract from him an unguarded admission; or to place him in an awkward dilemma, by shaping your question in such a way, that he must either by avowing it admit something which his antagonist wishes to establish, or by refusing seem to give consent by his silence to that which the questioner wishes to insinuate; or to gain some similar advantage' (Cope's Introduction to Ar. Rhet. p. 362).

αὐτοῦ τούτου]=κατ᾽ αὐτὸ τοῦτο above.

ὁ προβαλόμενος κατὰ ταὐτά] The person who produced the false witness, προὔβάλετο or προὐστήσατο, was liable to what was called a δίκη κακοτεχνιῶν for conspiring to defeat the ends of justice. Or. 47 § 1 τὸν προβαλόμενον ὑπόδικον ἔχῃ τῶν κακοτεχνιῶν.

§ 11. *That the defendant's evidence is false may be concluded from the material on which it is written.*

λελευκωμένον καὶ οἴκοθεν κατεσκευασμένον] The plaintiff curiously argues the falsehood of the defendant's deposition from the nature of the material on which it is inscribed. The document, he points out, is 'whitened, and must have been brought from home purposely prepared.' This would have been proper enough for a deposition attesting to the facts of the past, in which case there is time to draw up an elaborate document. But a deposition purporting to attest a Challenge

κατεσκευασμένον. καίτοι τοὺς μὲν τὰ πεπραγμένα
μαρτυροῦντας προσήκει οἴκοθεν τὰς μαρτυρίας κατεσκευασμένας μαρτυρεῖν, τοὺς δὲ τὰς προκλήσεις
μαρτυροῦντας τοὺς ἀπὸ ταὐτομάτου προστάντας ἐν[1]
μάλθῃ γεγραμμένην τὴν μαρτυρίαν, ἵν᾽, ἄν[m] τι προσ-
γράψαι ἢ ἀπαλεῖψαι βουληθῇ, ῥᾴδιον ᾖ[n].

[1] Z cum Reiskio. καὶ ἐν Bekker cum libris.

[m] εἰ...βουληθῇ Z cum libris. ‘malim ἐβουλήθη vel βουληθείη’ Sauppe.

[n] ᾖ H. Wolf. ἦν Z cum libris.

(evidence to which might be given by any duly qualified person even accidentally present) would naturally be rapidly written on the spot ἐν μάλθῃ, i.e. on a waxen tablet. This would allow of any addition or erasure being made at the request of the witnesses before they attested it. ‘The difference between these methods,’ as C. R. Kennedy remarks, ‘was much the same as between writing with a pen on paper and with a pencil on a slate’ (Dict. Ant. s. v. μαρτυρία). The distinction here drawn is (as Mr Paley observes) between a waxed tablet (δέλτος) scratched with a point like the Roman *stilus*, and a whitened surface on which the letters could be conveniently laid on with black pigment (μέλαν).

For λελευκωμένον cf. Dem. Or. 24 (Timocr.) § 23 *Lex*, ὁ τιθεὶς τὸν καινὸν νόμον, ἀναγράψας εἰς λεύκωμα, ἐκτιθέτω πρόσθε τῶν ἐπωνύμων. Bekker’s Anecd. (λέξεις ῥητορικαί) p. 277 λεύκωμά ἐστι πίναξ γύψῳ ἀληλιμμένος, πρὸς γραφὴν πολιτικῶν γραμμάτων ἐπιτήδειος (we may compare the Roman *album* and contrast the *black boards* of our class-rooms).

For ἐν μάλθῃ ib. p. 278 μάλ- θη· μεμαλαγμένος κηρὸς ἢ ἄλλο τι τοιοῦτον, ᾧ τὰ γραμματεῖα πράττεται. Pollux x 58: ὁ δὲ ἐνὼν τῇ πινακίδι (sc. καλεῖται) κηρὸς ἢ μάλθη ἢ μάλθα. Ἡρόδοτος μὲν γὰρ κηρὸν εἴρηκεν, Κρατῖνος δὲ ἐν τῇ Πυτίνῃ μάλθην ἔφη, Ἀριστοφάνης δὲ ἐν τῷ Γηρυτάδῃ ‘τὴν μάλθαν ἐκ τῶν γραμματείων ἦσθιον.’ Harpocr. μάλθη· ὁ μεμαλαγμένος κηρός· Δημοσθένης ἐν τῷ κατὰ Στεφάνου. Ἱππῶναξ, ἔπειτα μάλθῃ τὴν τρόπιν παραχρί- σας. And similarly Hesychius and Suidas. (Bekker’s *Charicles*, Scene IX notes 12 and 13, and Beels, *diatribe* p. 116—119.)

οἴκοθεν κατεσκευασμένον] a ‘pregnant’ expression, equivalent in sense to οἴκοι κατε- σκευασμένον καὶ οἴκοθεν ἀπηνεγ- μένον. Similarly below, where Reiske unnecessarily proposes οἴκοθεν ἐπιφερομένας τὰς μαρ- τυρίας κατεσκευασμένας μαρτυρεῖν. For the general drift of the argument and its imputation of deliberate design, cf. Cic. Phil. II § 85 *unde diadema? non enim abiectum sustuleras, sed attuleras domo meditatum et cogitatum scelus.*

τοὺς προστάντας] These words are rather obscure. Kennedy

Οὐκοῦν κατὰ μὲν ταῦτα πάντα ἐξελέγχεται τὰ 12
ψευδῆ μεμαρτυρηκὼς καὶ παρὰ τὸν νόμον· βούλομαι
δ' ὑμῖν καὶ αὐτὸ τοῦτο ἐπιδεῖξαι, ὡς οὔτε διέθετο ὁ
πατὴρ ἡμῶν διαθήκην οὐδεμίαν οὔθ' οἱ νόμοι ἐῶσιν.
εἰ γάρ τις ἔροιτο ὑμᾶς καθ' ὁποίους νόμους δεῖ πολιτεύεσθαι ἡμᾶς, δῆλον ὅτι ἀποκρίναισθ' ἂν κατὰ τοὺς
κειμένους. ἀλλὰ μὴν οἵ γε νόμοι ἀπαγορεύουσι μηδὲ
νόμον ἐξεῖναι ἐπ' ἀνδρὶ° θεῖναι, ἂν μὴ τὸν αὐτὸν ἐφ'

° Σ.   ἐπ' ἀνδρὶ ἐξεῖναι Z et Bekker st.

renders προστάντας as equivalent
to παρόντας. Rather, perhaps,
'who stand forward voluntari-
ly.' P.]

ἂν βουληθῇ] The *vulgata
lectio* used to be εἰ, altered by
G. H. Schaefer into ἐὰν to avoid
the anomaly of εἰ with the
subjunctive, a construction described as 'poetical' in Bekker's
Anecdota (p. 144). See, however, the commentators on Thuc.
VI 21 § 1 εἰ ξυστῶσιν, Hermann's
Opuscula I 280 and Kühner's
Gk. Gr. § 398 p. 207. Similarly
in Dem. Or. 24 §§ 79 and 93 we
have the ordinary indicative
followed by the anomalous subjunctive, εἴ τινι...προστετίμηται
...ἢ τὸ λοιπὸν προστιμηθῇ, whereas in § 207 we find the regular
construction εἴ τινι προστετίμη-
ται δεσμοῦ κἂν τὸ λοιπόν τινι
προστιμήσητε (where see Wayte's
notes).

§§ 12—17. *Further, my father
made no will at all, nor do the
laws allow it, laws which bind
every citizen of Athens without
exception. It was not until ten
years after my father's death
that Phormion obtained the citizenship; not foreseeing this, how
could my father have insulted
our family, cast contempt on
your bounty and disregarded the*

*laws, by giving his own wife
in marriage to Phormion, and
that by a will which he was
legally incompetent to make? The
law forbids a man's making a
will if he have male issue lawfully begotten.—Again, the law
only allows those who are not
'adopted' to dispose of their
property by will, and my father
was a citizen by 'adoption' only.
Lastly, it does not permit a
person to make a will if he is of
unsound mind, and the terms of
the alleged 'will' which give
my father's widow to Phormion
are inconsistent with the terms
of the 'lease,' and argue the
absence of sound mind and
therefore my father's incompe-
tence to make any will whatever.*

12. κειμένους...θεῖναι] κεῖμαι
is constantly borrowed as a
perfect passive to τίθημι, while
τέθειμαι is almost invariably
used as a deponent perfect.
Thus the usage of the perfect
in the best writers would be:

ὁ νομοθέτης τέθεικε τὸν νόμον.
ἡ πόλις τέθειται τὸν νόμον.
ὁ νόμος κεῖται.

(See further in notes on Or.
34 § 16, Or. 39 Argument, line
23, and on Isocr. ad Dem. § 36.)
μηδὲ νόμον...ἐπ' ἀνδρὶ θεῖναι]
Just as a *privilegium* was for-

13 ἅπασιν ᾿Αθηναίοις.   οὐκοῦν ὁ μὲν νόμος οὑτοσὶ τοῖς
αὐτοῖς νόμοις πολιτεύεσθαι ἡμᾶς κελεύει καὶ οὐκ ἄλλοις. ὁ δὲ πατὴρ ἐτελεύτησεν ἐπὶ Δυσνικήτου ἄρχοντος, ὁ δὲ Φορμίων ᾿Αθηναῖος ἐγένετο ἐπὶ Νικοφήμου
ἄρχοντος, δεκάτῳ ἔτει ὕστερον ἢ ὁ πατὴρ ἡμῶν ἀπέθανεν. πῶς ἂν οὖν μὴ εἰδὼς ὁ πατὴρ αὐτὸν ᾿Αθηναῖον
ἐσόμενον ἔδωκεν ἂν τὴν ἑαυτοῦ γυναῖκα, καὶ προεπη-
λάκισε μὲν ἂν ἡμᾶς, κατεφρόνησε δ᾽ ἂν τῆς δωρεᾶς I133
ἧς παρ᾽ ὑμῶν ἔλαβε, παρεῖδε δ᾽ ἂν τοὺς νόμους; πότερα δὲ κάλλιον ἦν αὐτῷ ζῶντι πρᾶξαι ταῦτα, εἴπερ
ἐβούλετο, ἢ ἀποθανόντα διαθήκας καταλιπεῖν, ἃς οὐ
κύριος ἦν; ἀλλὰ μὴν αὐτῶν τῶν νόμων ἀκούσαν-
14 τες, γνώσεσθε ὡς οὐ κύριος ἦν διαθέσθαι. λέγε τὸν
νόμον.

ΝΟΜΟΣ.

[῞Οσοι μὴ ἐπεποίηντο, ὥστε μήτε ἀπειπεῖν μήτ᾽

bidden by Roman law, so at
Athens legislation expressly affecting a particular individual,
whether in his interest or to
his detriment, was not allowed,
except in the single instance of
ostracism; cf. the law quoted in
Andocides, de mysteriis § 87
μηδὲ ἐπ᾽ ἀνδρὶ νόμον ἐξεῖναι θεῖναι,
ἐὰν μὴ τὸν αὐτὸν ἐπὶ πᾶσιν ᾿Αθη-
ναίοις, ἐὰν μὴ ἑξακισχιλίοις δόξῃ
κρύβδην ψηφιζομένοις, and see
Dem. Or. 24 (Timocrates) § 59,
and 23 (Aristocr.) § 86.

13. ὁ μὲν νόμος...ὁ δὲ πατὴρ
κ.τ.λ.] The sentence is rather
loosely written, and the sense
might have been brought out
better by some such arrangement as this: ὁ μὲν νόμος...κε-
λεύει, ὁ δὲ πατὴρ Φορμίωνι οὔπω
᾿Αθηναίῳ γενομένῳ ἔδωκε τὴν
ἑαυτοῦ γυναῖκα· ἐτελεύτησε γὰρ
κ.τ.λ. A similar looseness of
structure may be noticed in §§
25 and 15—ἐπὶ Δυσνικήτου B.C.
370. ἐπὶ Νικοφήμου B.C. 360.
τῆς δωρεᾶς] sc. τῆς πολιτείας.
Or. 36 § 30.

14. ὅσοι μὴ ἐπεποίηντο κ.τ.λ.
‘Any citizen (with the exception of such as had been adopted when Solon entered on his archonship, and had thereby become unable either to renounce
or to claim his inheritance), shall
be allowed to dispose of his own
property at his pleasure, provided he have no male issue
lawfully begotten.’ Cf. Isaeus
Or. 6 (Philoctemon) § 28 τοῖς
φύσει υἱέσιν αὐτοῦ οὐδεὶς οὐδενὶ ἐν
διαθήκῃ γράφει δόσιν οὐδεμίαν,
διότι ὁ νόμος αὐτὸς ἀποδίδωσι τῷ
υἱεῖ τὰ τοῦ πατρὸς καὶ οὐδὲ διαθέσθαι ἐᾷ ὅτῳ ἂν ὦσι παῖδες γνήσιοι. K. F. Hermann, *Rechtsalt.*
ed. Thalheim § 10 p. 63.

ἐπιδικάσασθαι, ὅτε Σόλων εἰσῄει τὴν ἀρχὴν, τὰ ἑαυτοῦ διαθέσθαι εἶναι, ὅπως ἂν ἐθέλῃ, ἂν μὴ παῖδες ὦσι
γνήσιοι ἄρρενες, ἂν μὴ μανιῶν ἢ γήρως ἢ φαρμάκων
ἢ νόσου ἕνεκεν, ἢ γυναικὶ πειθόμενος, ὑπὸ τούτων
του παρανοῶν[p], ἢ ὑπ' ἀνάγκης, ἢ ὑπὸ δεσμοῦ κατα-
ληφθείς.]

[p] Z et Dind. cum P. Wesseling. ὑπὸ τούτων τοῦ παρανόμων
libri. ἢ ὑπὸ τῶν του παρανόμων Bekker cum Reiskio.

The law is quoted to prove that Pasion had no right to make a will, (1) because he had male issue lawfully begotten (sc. Apollodorus). But it will be noticed that the law does not forbid such persons from making any will whatsoever. It simply enacts that those who have no male issue may dispose of their property as they please. Pasion was not debarred by this law from making a will, but was not allowed to make any disposition he chose, since (as in our law of entail) the right to the property was secured to the son.

Again (2), Pasion was a citizen by 'adoption', whereas this law implies that no 'adopted' person could dispose of his property as he pleased. But it will be observed on the other side, that the plaintiff has deliberately confounded two different senses of ποιεῖσθαι (1) 'to adopt into a family' and (2) 'to present with the citizenship.' ἐπεποίηντο refers to 'family adoption' (Or. 44 Leoch. ad fin.), and the plaintiff argues as though it meant the same as ἐπεποίητο πολίτης.

ἀπειπεῖν...ἐπιδικάσασθαι] Or. 52 (Callippus) § 19 οὔτε ἀμφισ-βητήσαντα οὔτε ἀπειπόντα περὶ τοῦ ἀργυρίου. ἀπειπεῖν may be paralleled by the phrase in Roman law *eiurare hereditu-tem*. For ἐπιδικάσασθαι cf. note on 45 § 75.

μανιῶν] genitive, like the three subsequent substantives, governed by ἕνεκα at the end of the clause. 'Unless his mind is impaired by lunacy, or dotage, or by drugs or disease.' Kennedy. [The plural μανίαι means, as usual, 'mad fits,' 'delusions.' P.]

ὑπὸ τούτων του παρανοῶν] A certain correction of the old reading ὑπὸ τούτων τοῦ παρανό-μων. Cf. Isaeus Or. 9 ad fin. εἰ τοῦτον ἐποιήσατο υἱὸν οὐ τῷ πατρὶ πολεμιώτατος ἦν, πῶς οὐ δόξει τοῖς ἀκούσασι παρανοεῖν ἢ ὑπὸ φαρμάκων διεφθάρθαι; and ib. Or. 6 (Philoct.) § 9 οὑτοσὶ ὁ νόμος κοινὸς ἅπασι κεῖται, ἐξεῖναι τὰ ἑαυτοῦ διαθέσθαι, ἐὰν μὴ παῖ-δες ὦσι γνήσιοι ἄρρενες, ἐὰν μὴ ἄρα μανεὶς ἢ ὑπὸ γήρως ἢ δι' ἄλλο τι τῶν ἐν τῷ νόμῳ παρανοῶν δια-θῆται, Plut. Sol. 21, [Dem.] 48 § 56.—On φαρμάκων see further in § 16 φαρμακῶντα.—νόσου ἕνε-κεν can only refer to cases where the mind was enfeebled, for bodily infirmity was of course in itself no bar to the validity of a will (Becker, *Charicles*, Scene ix note 19).

15   Τοῦ μὲν νόμου τοίνυν ἀκηκόατε, ὃς οὐκ ἐᾷ διαθήκας διαθέσθαι, ἐὰν παῖδες ὦσι γνήσιοι. οὗτοι δέ
φασι ταῦτα διαθέσθαι τὸν πατέρα, ὡς δὲ παρεγένοντο
οὐκ ἔχουσιν ὑποδεῖξαι[q]. ἄξιον δὲ καὶ τόδε ἐνθυμηθῆ-
ναι, ὅτι ὅσοι μὴ ἐπεποίηντο, ἀλλ᾽ ἦσαν πεφυκότες γνήσιοι, τούτοις ὁ νόμος δίδωσιν, ἐὰν ἄπαιδες ὦσι, διαθέσθαι τὰ ἑαυτῶν. ὁ τοίνυν πατὴρ ἡμῶν ἐπεποίητο
ὑπὸ τοῦ δήμου πολίτης, ὥστε οὐδὲ κατὰ τοῦτο ἐξῆν
αὐτῷ διαθέσθαι διαθήκην, ἄλλως τε καὶ περὶ τῆς
γυναικὸς, ἧς οὐδὲ κύριος ἐκ τῶν νόμων ἦν, παῖδές τε
16   ἦσαν αὐτῷ. σκέψασθε δὲ καὶ διότι οὐδ᾽ ἂν ἄπαις τις
ᾖ, κύριός ἐστι τὰ αὑτοῦ διαθέσθαι, ἐὰν μὴ εὖ φρονῇ·
νοσοῦντα δὲ ἢ φαρμακῶντα ἢ γυναικὶ πειθόμενον ἢ

<hr>

[q] ἐπιδεῖξαι Z.   ὑποδεῖξαι Dind. cum Σ (prima manu).

<hr>

16. διότι] In the same sense
as ὅτι, for which it is not unfrequently used, especially by
Isocrates when a *hiatus* is
thereby avoided, e.g. Isocr.
Lochites § 7 ἐνθυμουμένους ὅτι
followed by καὶ διότι. Isocr.
Paneg. § 48 n.   Here σκέψασθε
δὲ καὶ διότι corresponds in
sense to ἄξιον δὲ καὶ τόδε ἐνθυ-
μηθῆναι, ὅτι in the previous
section.

εὖ φρονῇ] Isaeus Or. 7 § 1
εἴ τις αὐτὸς ζῶν καὶ εὖ φρονῶν
ἐποιήσατο, contrasted with εἴ
τις τελευτήσειν μέλλων διέθετο, εἴ
τι πάθοι, τὴν οὐσίαν ἑτέρῳ. Eur.
Ion 520, εὖ φρονεῖς μέν; i.e. ἆρα
ἔμφρων εἶ;—On νοσοῦντα see
above, § 14 νόσου ἕνεκεν.

φαρμακῶντα] Harpocr. Δη-
μοσθένης ἐν τῷ κατὰ Στεφάνου.
ἔστι δὲ φαρμακῶν ὁ ὑπὸ φαρμακῶν βεβλαμμένος, ὡς καὶ Θεό-
φραστος ἐν ιε΄ Νόμων ὑποσημαίνει.

[φαρμακᾶν is one of a class of
verbs implying mental or bodily
affection, e.g. λημᾶν, 'to have

blear eyes,' ποδαγρᾶν, χαλαζᾶν,
φονᾶν, 'to be blood-thirsty,'
θανατᾶν, 'to have a desire for
death,' Plat. Phaedo p. 64 B,
τομᾶν 'to require the knife' &c.
The verbs themselves are less
commonly used than their participles. P.] Cf. Rutherford's
New Phrynichus p. 153.

εἰ δοκοῦσιν εὖ φρονοῦντος κ.τ.λ.]
It is curious to find the plaintiff
setting up this suggestion of
lunacy when in another speech,
Or. 49 (Timoth.) § 42, delivered
at an earlier date, he describes
his father as not only giving
him a written statement of
debts due, but also, in his last
illness, telling him and his
brother the details of each particular sum, the name of the
debtor, and even the purpose
for which the money was lent.
He might have turned his
argument to more account, if,
instead of insinuating that the
terms of the alleged will suggested that his father was of

ὑπὸ γήρως ἢ ὑπὸ μανιῶν ἢ ὑπὸ ἀνάγκης τινὸς κατα-
ληφθέντα ἄκυρον κελεύουσιν εἶναι οἱ νόμοι. σκοπεῖτε
1134 δή‌ʳ, εἰ δοκοῦσιν ὑμῖν εὖ φρονοῦντος ἀνδρὸς εἶναι αἱ
διαθῆκαι, ἅς φασι διαθέσθαι οὗτοι τὸν πατέρα. μὴ 17
πρὸς ἄλλο δέ τι παράδειγμα σκέψησθε ἢ πρὸς τὴν
μίσθωσιν, εἰ δοκεῖ ὑμῖν ἀκόλουθον εἶναι τῷ τὴν τέχνην
μὴ ἐξουσίαν δόντι ἐν τῷ αὐτῷ ἡμῖν ἐργάζεσθαι, τούτῳ
τὴν γυναῖκα δοῦναι τὴν αὐτοῦ καὶ τῶν παίδων ἐᾶσαι
κοινωνὸν αὐτῷ γενέσθαι. καὶ μὴ θαυμάζετε, εἰ τἄλλα
σκευωρουμένους αὐτοὺς τὰ ἐν τῇ μισθώσει τοῦτο παρ-
έλαθεν. ἴσως μὲν γὰρ οὐδὲ προσεῖχον ἄλλῳ οὐδενὶ ἢ
τῷ τὰ χρήματα ἀποστερῆσαι καὶ τῷ προσοφείλοντα
τὸν πατέρα ἐγγράψαι· εἶτα δὲ οὐδὲ ἐδόκουν ἐμὲ οὕτω
δεινὸν ἔσεσθαι ὥστε ταῦτα ἀκριβῶς ἐξετάσαι.

ʳ Bekker cum correcto Σ. δὲ Z cum Σ (prima manu).

unsound mind, and therefore
legally incompetent to make
any will at all, he had urged
that, his father having been of
sound mind up to the day of
his death, the 'insane' provisions of the will betrayed it to
be a forgery.

17. ἀκόλουθον εἶναι...τῷ δόντι...
τούτῳ δοῦναι] The juxtaposition
of these two datives, referring
to two different persons, is ex-
tremely harsh. The order is:
δοκεῖ ὑμῖν ἀκόλουθον εἶναι (Πασίωνι), τῷ μὴ δόντι ἐξουσίαν ἐργάζεσθαι τὴν τέχνην ἐν τῷ αὐτῷ
ἡμῖν, δοῦναι τούτῳ (sc. Φορμίωνι)
τὴν γυναῖκα τὴν αὐτοῦ; 'Is it
consistent for one who refused
Phormion permission to carry
on business in partnership with
us, actually to give Phormion
his own wife?'

τῶν παίδων κοινωνὸν αὐτῷ]
Kennedy: 'partner with himself in paternity' (by marrying
his widow). For σκευωρουμένους
cf. Or. 45 § 5.

ἐγγράψαι] Specially used of
'registering' a man as debtor.
Cf. Or. 53 § 14.

οὕτω δεινόν] 'They little
dreamt I should be clever
enough to examine all these questions thoroughly.' This passage
has been quoted as an indication
of the plaintiff's consciousness
of his own oratorical skill, and as
a presumption in favour of the
view that Apollodorus is himself the writer of the speeches
delivered by him which have
come down to us among the
orations of Demosthenes (A.
Schaefer, Dem. u. s. Zeit, III 2,
192).

§§ 18—21. The forgery of
the will is also proved by the
law of betrothals, which provides
that a woman may be affianced for
lawful wedlock by her guardians,
i. e. certain near relations, such

18   Σκέψασθε τοίνυν καὶ τοὺς νόμους, παρ' ὧν κελεύουσι τὰς ἐγγύας ποιεῖσθαι, ἵν' εἰδῆτε καὶ ἐκ τούτων
ὡς κατεσκευασμένης διαθήκης ψευδὴς μάρτυς γέγονε
Στέφανος οὑτοσί. λέγε[s].

ΝΟΜΟΣ.

[Ἣν ἂν ἐγγυήσῃ ἐπὶ δικαίοις δάμαρτα εἶναι ἢ
πατὴρ ἢ ἀδελφὸς ὁμοπάτωρ ἢ πάππος ὁ πρὸς πατρός,
ἐκ ταύτης εἶναι παῖδας γνησίους. ἐὰν δὲ μηδεὶς ᾖ
τούτων, ἐὰν μὲν ἐπίκληρός τις ᾖ, τὸν κύριον ἔχειν, ἐὰν
δὲ μὴ ᾖ[t], ὅτῳ ἂν ἐπιτρέψῃ, τοῦτον κύριον εἶναι.]

19   Οὗτος μὲν τοίνυν ὁ νόμος οὓς ἐποίησε κυρίους
εἶναι, ἀκηκόατε· ὅτι δ' οὐδεὶς ἦν τούτων τῇ μητρί, οἱ
ἀντίδικοί μοι αὐτοὶ μεμαρτυρήκασιν. εἰ γὰρ ἦν, παρεί-
χοντ' ἄν. ἢ μάρτυρας μὲν ψευδεῖς οἴεσθ' ἄν[u] παρασχέ-

---

[s] Bekker. *om.* Z *cum* Σ.   [t] Bekker *cum libris.* *om.* Z.

[u] 'cum vocula ἄν…tantummodo ad posterius membrum referri
possit (nam attractione in tali sententiae conformatione non est
locus), pro οἴεσθ' ἄν scribendum duco οἴεσθ' αὐτούς. ellipsin accu-
sativi per se tolerabilem esse putarem, quamquam αὐτόν et αὐτούς,

*as father, brother, or grandfather.
As none of these are in existence,
and you may be sure that the
other side would have produced
them, or pretended to do so, to
suit their purpose, it follows
that my mother was an 'heiress,'
and the law declares that the
son of an heiress, when he comes
of age, shall be his mother's
guardian. Now I was abroad
on public service (and therefore
of full age) when Phormion
married my mother, (and he did
so without obtaining the consent
of myself, her guardian).*

18.   σκέψασθε τοὺς νόμους]
The accusative after the principal verb, where in English
we should prefer making it the
nom. of the subordinate clause.
Cf. Or. 45 § 24. Kennedy partially keeps up the Greek construction by rendering it thus:
'look now at the laws, (to see)
from whom they require betrothals to be obtained.'

ἐγγύας] The betrothal (ἐγ-
γύησιν) was made by the natural or legal guardian of the girl,
in the presence of the relatives
of both parties. 'All children
born from a marriage legally
contracted in this respect were
γνήσιοι, and consequently, if
sons, ἰσόμοιροι, or entitled to
inherit equally.' (Whiston in
Dict. Ant. s. v. *Matrimonium,*
K. F. Hermann, *Privatalt.* § 30,
7 = p. 261 ed. Blümner).

σθαι καὶ διαθήκας οὐκ οὔσας, ἀδελφὸν δὲ ἢ πάππον ἢ
πατέρα οὐκ ἄν, εἴπερ ἦν δυνατὸν ἕνεκα χρημάτων·
ὁπότε τοίνυν μηδεὶς φαίνεται ζῶν τούτων, τότε ἀνάγκη
ἐπίκληρον τὴν μητέρα ἡμῶν εἶναι. τῆς τοίνυν ἐπικλήρου σκοπεῖτε τίνας κελεύουσιν οἱ νόμοι κυρίους εἶναι.
λέγε τὸν νόμον.

20

ΝΟΜΟΣ.

[Καὶ ἐὰν ἐξ ἐπικλήρου τις γένηται, καὶ ἅμα ἡβήσῃ
ἐπὶ δίετες, κρατεῖν τῶν χρημάτων, τὸν δὲ σῖτον μετρεῖν
τῇ μητρί.]

Οὐκοῦν ὁ μὲν νόμος κελεύει τοὺς παῖδας ἡβήσαντας κυρίους τῆς μητρὸς εἶναι, τὸν δὲ σῖτον μετρεῖν τῇ
μητρί. ἐγὼ δὲ φαίνομαι στρατευόμενος καὶ τριηραρχῶν ὑμῖν, ὅτε οὗτος συνῴκησε τῇ μητρί. ἀλλὰ μὴν
ὅτι ἐγὼ μὲν ἀπεδήμουν τριηραρχῶν, ἐτετελευτήκει[v] δ᾽
ὁ πατὴρ πάλαι, ὅτε οὗτος ἔγημε, τὰς δὲ θεραπαίνας

21

nisi generalis est sententia, in contrario non facile omittuntur'
(Gebauer, *de argumenti ex contrario formis* p. 207).

[v] τετελευτήκει Z cum Σ.

20. καὶ ἐὰν—μητρί] 'If a son is born of an heiress, two years after he has attained his puberty he shall enter into possession of the estate, and he shall pay alimony to his mother.' Kennedy. Harpocr. ἐπιδιετὲς ἡβῆσαι· Δημοσθένης ἐν τῷ κατὰ Στεφάνου. At the end of his article he quotes Hyperides (frag. 223) ἐπεὶ δὲ ἐνεγράφην ἐγὼ καὶ ὁ νόμος ἀπέδωκε τὴν κομιδὴν τῶν καταλειφθέντων τῇ μητρί, ὃς κελεύει κυρίους εἶναι τῆς ἐπικλήρου καὶ τῆς οὐσίας ἁπάσης τοὺς παῖδας, ἐπειδὰν ἐπιδιετὲς ἡβῶσιν. Cf. Isaeus frag. 90, id. Or. 10 § 12 and Or. 8 § 31. (See A. Schaefer, Dem. III 2, 19—39, esp. p. 25, *Eintritt der Mündigkeit nach Attischen Rechte*, where

ἐπιδιετὲς ἡβῆσαι is explained to include the 17th and 18th year, and the 'coming of age' is placed at the age of 18. K. F. Hermann, *Privatalt.* § 35, p. 322 Blümner.)

On ἐπίκληρος see note on Or. 45 § 75. (Cf. Lortzing, *Apoll.* p. 85 and A. Schaefer *u. s.* p. 176.)

στρατευόμενος κ.τ.λ.] And therefore of full age; referring back to παῖδας ἡβήσαντας.

21. πάλαι] Pasion died B.C. 370, the trierarchy probably took place in B.C. 368 (Or. 45 § 3), and it was during the plaintiff's absence on this public service that the marriage of Archippe took place. The interval here implied by the vague word πάλαι 'some time before' would seem to be two years. The

αὐτὸν ἐξήτουν καὶ ἠξίουν περὶ αὐτοῦ τούτου βασανίζεσθαι αὐτὰς, εἰ ταῦτ' ἀληθῆ ἐστι, καὶ ὡς προεκαλού-
μην, λαβέ μοι τὴν μαρτυρίαν.

ΜΑΡΤΥΡΙΑ.

[Μαρτυροῦσι παρεῖναι, ὅτε προὐκαλεῖτο Ἀπολλόδωρος Φορμίωνα, ὅτε ἠξίου ἀποδοῦναι Ἀπολλόδωρος
Φορμίωνα τὰς θεραπαίνας εἰς βάσανον, εἰ μή φησι
Φορμίων καὶ πρότερον διεφθαρκέναι τὴν μητέρα τὴν
ἐμὴν, πρὶν οὗ ἀποφαίνει Φορμίων γῆμαι ἐγγυησάμενος αὐτὴν παρὰ Πασίωνος. ταῦτα δὲ προκαλουμένου
Ἀπολλοδώρου οὐκ ἠθέλησε Φορμίων παραδοῦναι τὰς
θεραπαίνας.]

Τὸν τοίνυν νόμον ἐπὶ τούτοις ἀνάγνωθι, ὃς κελεύει
ἐπιδικασίαν εἶναι τῶν ἐπικλήρων ἁπασῶν, καὶ ξένων
καὶ ἀστῶν, καὶ περὶ μὲν τῶν πολιτῶν τὸν ἄρχοντα

plaintiff wishes to insinuate that, though some time elapsed before the marriage proper (ἔγημε), intrigues had been going on at an earlier date, and this is how the writer of the deposition in § 21 seems to have understood it.

τὴν μητέρα τὴν ἐμὴν] These words, which would have been appropriate enough in the mouth of Apollodorus, are absurdly out of place in the deposition, and betray gross carelessness on the part of the fabricator of the document. Even apart from this detail, the general contents of the deposition are different from what we are led to expect by the plaintiff's language in introducing it. (A. Westermann *u. s.* p. 113.)

§§ 22, 23. *The law does not allow any one to marry an* 'heiress,' *without a legal adjudication. Phormion made no legal claim for the hand of my mother, but did exactly as he pleased, in defiance of the law.*

22. τῶν ἐπικλήρων] The plaintiff attempts to prove that his mother was an 'heiress.' If so, her property ought to have passed absolutely into the hands of her eldest son, on his coming of age, whether her husband was alive or not. But there is not a single trace of such a relation between Archippe and Apollodorus in the rest of the speeches of the latter. Archippe was most probably of foreign extraction (cf. Or. 45 § 22) and the plaintiff's argument seems the merest shuffling. (See further, A. Schaefer, *Dem. u. s. Zeit*, III 2, 176.) On ἐπιδικασία τῶν ἐπικλήρων see note on Or. 45 § 75.

εἰσάγειν καὶ ἐπιμελεῖσθαι, περὶ δὲ τῶν μετοίκων τὸν πολέμαρχον, καὶ ἀνεπίδικον μὴ ἐξεῖναι ἔχειν μήτε κλῆρον μήτε ἐπίκληρον.

ΝΟΜΟΣ.

[Κληροῦν δὲ τὸν ἄρχοντα κλήρων καὶ ἐπικλήρων, ὅσοι εἰσὶ μῆνες, πλὴν τοῦ σκιροφοριῶνος. ἀνεπίδικον δὲ κλῆρον μὴ ἔχειν.]

Οὐκοῦν αὐτὸν εἴπερ ἐβούλετο[w] ὀρθῶς διαπράττε- 23 σθαι, λαχεῖν ἔδει τῆς ἐπικλήρου, εἴτε κατὰ δόσιν αὐτῷ[x] προσῆκεν[y] εἴτε κατὰ γένος, εἰ μὲν ὡς ὑπὲρ ἀστῆς, πρὸς τὸν ἄρχοντα, εἰ δὲ ὑπὲρ ξένης, πρὸς τὸν πολέμαρχον, καὶ τότε, εἴπερ τι λέγειν εἶχε δίκαιον, πείσαντα ὑμῶν τοὺς λαχόντας μετὰ τῶν νόμων καὶ

[w] Bekker. ἠβούλετο Z cum Σ.   [x] αὐτῷ Z. αυτω Σ.
[y] G. H. Schaefer. προσήκειν Z cum libris.

κληροῦν κλήρων κ.τ.λ.] i.e. 'assign by lot days for the trial of claims to inheritances or heiresses.' Below, we have the corresponding phrase λαχεῖν τῆς ἐπικλήρου, i.e. 'to have allotted to one a suit for the hand of the heiress.' Compare the common phrases λαγχάνειν and κληροῦν δίκην. So λαγχάνειν τοῦ κλήρου 'to be a suitor for the property,' Isaeus Or. 11 (Hagn.) §§ 22, 40, Or. 3 (Pyrr.) § 74 and Or. 9 (Astyph.) § 4. After κληροῦν Meier and Schömann, *Att. Process* 611, understand δίκας.

τὸν ἄρχοντα] The Archon *Eponymus*, or Chief Archon. See Or. 35 § 48 (where the duties of the Polemarch are also mentioned) and Or. 37 § 33.

πλὴν σκιροφοριῶνος] The last month of the Attic year, nearly corresponding to our June. It is here excepted, apparently

because it was in this month that most of the magistrates vacated office and passed their audit.

ἀνεπίδικον] 'Without legal adjudication.' See K. F. Hermann, *Privatalt.* § 66, notes 1 and 2 = p. 72 Thalheim.

23. εἴπερ...εἴτε...εἴτε...εἰ...εἰ... εἴπερ] εἰ is here repeated in various forms no less than six times in the same sentence; cf. Or. 53 § 23 where εἰ occurs twice. But even the undisputed writings of Demosthenes contain frequent instances of such reiteration, e.g. Or. 54 § 15 (twice); Or. 15 (de Rhod. lib.) § 15 (thrice); Or. 20 (Lept.) § 113 (four times) '*quanquam hic εἰ μὲν et εἰ δὲ inter se opponuntur quae non est vera repetitio.*' (Lortzing, *Apoll.* p. 33.)

ὑμῶν τοὺς λαχόντας] 'Those of your number who were drawn

τῆς ψήφου κύριον εἶναι, καὶ μὴ αὐτὸν αὑτῷ νόμους
ἰδίους θέμενον διαπράξασθαι ἃ ἐβούλετο.

24   Σκέψασθε δὴ καὶ τονδὶ τὸν νόμον, ὃς κελεύει τὴν
διαθήκην, ἣν ἂν παίδων ὄντων γνησίων ὁ πατὴρ δια-
θῆται, ἐὰν ἀποθάνωσιν οἱ παῖδες πρὶν ἡβῆσαι, κυρίαν
εἶναι.

ΝΟΜΟΣ.

[Ὅ τι ἂν γνησίων ὄντων υἱῶν ὁ πατὴρ διαθῆται,
ἐὰν ἀποθάνωσιν οἱ υἱεῖς πρὶν ἐπὶ δίετες ἡβᾶν, τὴν
τοῦ πατρὸς διαθήκην κυρίαν εἶναι.]

25   Οὐκοῦν ὁπότε ζῶσιν, ἄκυρος μὲν ἡ διαθήκη ἐστίν,
ἣν φασιν οὗτοι τὸν πατέρα καταλιπεῖν, παρὰ πάντας
δὲ τοὺς νόμους μεμαρτύρηκε Στέφανος οὑτοσὶ τὰ ψευδῆ, ὡς ἀντίγραφά ἐστι τῆς διαθήκης τῆς Πασίωνος·
πῶς γὰρ σὺ οἶσθα, καὶ ποῦ παραγενόμενος διατιθεμένῳ
τῷ πατρί; κακοτεχνῶν δὲ φαίνει περὶ τὰς διαθήκας,
τὰ ψευδῆ μὲν αὐτὸς μαρτυρῶν ἑτοίμως, κλέπτων δὲ
τὰς ἀληθεῖς μαρτυρίας, ἐξαπατῶν δὲ τοὺς δικαστὰς,
συνιστάμενος δ᾽ ἐπὶ ταῖς δίκαις. οἱ δὲ νόμοι καὶ περὶ
26 τῶν τοιούτων γραφὴν πεποιήκασιν. καί μοι ἀνάγνωθι
τὸν νόμον.

for the jury' ('allotted for the trial of the cause').

§ 24. *Again, there is a law allowing a will made by a father (though he has legitimate sons) to become valid if the sons die before reaching manhood. In the present case, as the sons are alive and grown up the 'will' is invalid.*

ἐὰν ἀποθάνωσιν—πρὶν ἡβῆσαι] 'Every man of full age and sound mind, not under durance or improper influence (cf. § 15), was competent to make a will; but if he had a son he could not disinherit him; al-though his will might take effect on the contingency of the son not completing his seventeenth year' (C. R. Kennedy in Dict. Ant. s. v. *Heres*).

For the latter part of this statement, the present passage is perhaps the only express authority.

§§ 25—26. *Further, the defendant has illegally entered into a conspiracy to defeat the ends of justice.*

κλέπτων…μαρτυρίας] Or. 45 § 58. On συνιστάμενος, see note on συστάσεις Or. 45 § 67.

ΝΟΜΟΣ.

['Εάν τις συνίστηται ἢ συνδεκάζῃ τὴν ἡλιαίαν ἢ
τῶν δικαστηρίων τι τῶν 'Αθήνησιν ἢ τὴν βουλὴν ἐπὶ
δωροδοκίᾳ χρήματα διδοὺς ἢ δεχόμενος, ἢ ἑταιρείαν
συνιστῇ ἐπὶ καταλύσει τοῦ δήμου, ἢ συνήγορος ὢν
λαμβάνῃ χρήματα ἐπὶ ταῖς δίκαις ταῖς ἰδίαις ἢ δη-

26. συνδεκάζῃ] 'Bribe the
Heliœa.' Pollux VIII 42: δώρων
κατὰ τοῦ ἐπὶ δώροις δικάσαντος ἦν
ἡ γραφή, δεκασμοῦ δὲ κατὰ τοῦ
διαφθείραντος· καὶ ὁ μὲν δεκάζε-
σθαι ὁ δὲ δεκάζειν ἐλέγετο (ib. VI
190). Or. 21 (Mid.) § 113 lex, ἐάν
τις...διδῷ ἑτέρῳ ἢ διαφθείρῃ τινὰς
ἐπαγγελλόμενος, ἐπὶ βλάβῃ τοῦ
δήμου...ἄτιμος ἔστω. δεκασμὸς
however (strictly meaning a
systematic bribery by division
into sets of ten) is only a late
word and is not found in the
Attic Orators, though ἀδέκαστος
occurs in Ar. Ethics II 9 § 6, οὐ
γὰρ ἀδέκαστοι κρίνομεν (τὴν ἡδο-
νήν), and Aeschines, Timarch.
§ 86, has συνδεκάζειν τὴν ἐκκλησίαν καὶ τἆλλα δικαστήρια and
ib. § 87 μαρτυρεῖν τὸν μὲν ὡς
ἐδέκαζε τὸν δὲ ὡς ἐδεκάζετο. Cf.
Isocr. Or. 8 § 50 θανάτου τῆς
ζημίας ἐπικειμένης, ἐάν τις ἀλῷ
δεκάζων, and Lysias Or. 29 § 12
δεδεκασμένοι. So in Latin, we
have *decuriare* used of or-
ganised bribery at elections,
Cicero, pro Plancio § 45 *decu-
riatio tribulium* and *decuriasse
Plancium, conscripsisse*. Cf. the
obscure name given to bribed
dicasts at Athens, Λύκου δεκάς
(in wholesale bribery an agent,
it is conjectured, was chosen
from each tribe and the group
of ten thus selected to deal
with their fellow-tribesmen were
comically called Λύκου δεκάς
from the statue of Lycus near

the law-courts. Meier and
Schömann, *Att. Process* p. 150.
Harpocr. s.v. δεκάζων).

The usual phrase for bribery
is χρήμασι φθείρειν (or διαφθεί-
ρειν), though the euphemism
χρήμασι πεῖσαι is still more frequent. It is curious to note
how frequently the word δωροδοκία occurs, and how rarely
δεκασμὸς and its corresponding
verb. Again and again we have
charges of receiving bribes,
seldom of giving them; possibly
because those who gave them
were too powerful to be attacked.
—ἐπὶ δωροδοκίᾳ, 'with a corrupt
motive,' is here a general term,
implying without directly expressing the corresponding term
δεκασμός.

ἑταιρείαν ἐπὶ καταλύσει τοῦ
δήμου] Thuc. VIII 54, ὁ Πείσ-
ανδρος τὰς ξυνωμοσίας...ἁπάσας
ἐπελθὼν καὶ παρακελευσάμενος
ὅπως ... καταλύσουσι τὸν δῆμον
κ.τ.λ. See Grote, H. G. chap. 51
(iv p. 394, ed. 1862).

ἐπὶ ταῖς δίκαις κ.τ.λ.] 'In any
cause either of a public or private nature.' Kennedy. Rather
(as above, § 25), 'with a view
to winning the causes brought
either by private persons or on
public grounds.' It is to a
collusion for such a purpose
between the σύνδικος and the
συνήγορος that Aristophanes al-
ludes in Vesp. 694. P.]

μοσίαις, τούτων εἶναι τὰς γραφὰς πρὸς τοὺς θεσμοθέτας.]

27   Ἡδέως ἂν τοίνυν ὑμᾶς ἐροίμην ἐπὶ τούτοις ἅπασι
κατὰ ποίους νόμους ὀμωμοκότες δικάζετε, πότερα κατὰ
τοὺς τῆς πόλεως ἢ καθ᾽ οὓς Φορμίων αὐτῷ νομοθετεῖ.
ἐγὼ μὲν τοίνυν τούτους παρέχομαι ὑμῖν, καὶ ἐξελέγχω
αὐτοὺς ἀμφοτέρους παραβεβηκότας, Φορμίωνα μὲν ἐξ
ἀρχῆς ἀδικήσαντα ἡμᾶς καὶ ἀποστερήσαντα τὰ χρήματα, ἃ ὁ πατὴρ ἡμῖν κατέλιπε καὶ ἐμίσθωσε τούτῳ
μετὰ τῆς τραπέζης καὶ τοῦ ἐργαστηρίου, Στέφανον
δὲ τουτονὶ τὰ ψευδῆ μεμαρτυρηκότα καὶ παρὰ τὸν
νόμον.

28   Ἄξιον τοίνυν, ὦ ἄνδρες δικασταὶ, καὶ τόδε ἐν-
θυμηθῆναι, ὅτι διαθηκῶν[z] οὐδεὶς πώποτε ἀντίγραφα
ἐποιήσατο, ἀλλὰ συγγραφῶν μὲν, ἵνα εἰδῶσι καὶ μὴ
παραβαίνωσι, διαθηκῶν δὲ οὔ. τούτου γὰρ ἕνεκα καταλείπουσιν[a] οἱ διατιθέμενοι, ἵνα μηδεὶς εἰδῇ ἃ δια-

---

[z] *margo ed. Parisiensis.* διαθήκης Z cum ΣΦ. διαθήκας F.

[a] κατασεσημασμένας καταλείπουσιν (Reiske); κατακλείουσιν (Seager); οὐ καταλείπουσιν, sc. διαθηκῶν ἀντίγραφα (G. H. Schaefer).

θεσμοθέτας] 'The six minor Archons.

§ 27. *The jury has sworn to do justice according to the laws of Athens and not the laws which Phormion chooses to lay down for himself. I produce the laws of Athens and I prove that both of my opponents have broken them, Phormion by defrauding me of the money left me by my father, Stephanus by giving false evidence and that contrary to the law.*

τὰ χρήματα] sc. the Banking-stock, which is the subject of Or. 36. The ἐργαστήριον is the shield-manufactory of Or. 36 § 4.

§ 28. *The jury, by the way, should also notice that no one ever makes a copy of a will. How then came Stephanus and his friends to know that the contents of the document appended to the deposition are a copy of my father's will?*

καταλείπουσιν] is especially used of leaving behind one at death. 'The reason why people leave their wills behind them (instead of publishing them before they die) is to prevent any one knowing their contents.' Kennedy renders it: 'keep wills by them until their death.'

[I incline to think κατακλεί-ουσιν is the true reading. The

τίθενται. πῶς οὖν ὑμεῖς ἴστε ὅτι ἀντίγραφά ἐστι τῶν διαθηκῶν τῶν Πασίωνος τὰ ἐν τῷ γραμματείῳ γεγραμμένα;

Δέομαι δ' ὑμῶν ἁπάντων, ὦ ἄνδρες δικασταὶ, καὶ 29 ἱκετεύω βοηθῆσαι μὲν ἐμοὶ, τιμωρήσασθαι δὲ τοὺς ἑτοίμως οὕτω τὰ ψευδῆ μαρτυροῦντας, ὑπέρ τε ὑμῶν αὐτῶν καὶ ἐμοῦ καὶ τοῦ δικαίου καὶ τῶν νόμων.

reason why people 'leave wills' is to shew how they wish to dispose of their property; the reason why they 'keep them under lock and key' is that no one may have access to them. P.]

For the reiteration διατιθέμενοι...διατίθενται, see §§ 2 and 3.

§ 29. *I implore the jury to grant me redress, that those who are so prompt to give false evidence may be punished on all grounds, particularly for the sake of justice and the laws.*

τῶν νόμων] Placed last for emphasis, since the whole speech has dealt with quotations of laws and not with εἰκότα, or 'presumptive proofs,' as in the former oration.

LIII.

ΠΡΟΣ ΝΙΚΟΣΤΡΑΤΟΝ
ΠΕΡΙ ΑΝΔΡΑΠΟΔΩΝ ΑΠΟΓΡΑΦΗΣ
ΑΡΕΘΟΥΣΙΟΥ[a].

ΥΠΟΘΕΣΙΣ.

Ἀπολλόδωρος γραψάμενος ψευδοκλητείας Ἀρεθούσιον εἷλεν. ὀφείλοντος δὲ τοῦ Ἀρεθουσίου τάλαντον τῇ πόλει καὶ ἀποδοῦναι μὴ δυνηθέντος, καὶ διὰ
τοῦτο εἰς τὰ δημόσια ἀπογραφομένης αὐτοῦ τῆς οὐ-
5 σίας, ἀπογράφει ὁ Ἀπολλόδωρος οἰκέτας ὡς ὄντας
Ἀρεθουσίου, ὁ δὲ Νικόστρατος[b] μεταποιεῖται ὡς ἰδίων
καὶ ἐκείνῳ προσηκόντων οὐδέν. ἐπεὶ δὲ τὸ πρᾶγμα
μοχθηρόν ἐστι[c], διὰ τοῦτο ὁ ῥήτωρ διηγεῖται πηλίκα

[a] πρὸς Νικόστρατον περὶ τῶν Ἀρεθουσίου ἀνδραπόδων Ζ.
[b] [ο δὲ Νικόστρατος] Ζ. ‘addidit Bekker cum II. Wolf.’
[c] om. Ζ. addidit Dindf. ex Σ.

1. ψευδοκλητείας] § 15 note.
8. μοχθηρὸν] ‘vexatious,’ sc.
συκοφαντικόν.
§§ 1—4. (Arethusius has incurred a debt to the public treasury and has neglected to discharge it.) I have accordingly
laid an information against him
and drawn up a specification of
his property. I have done so,
not in the spirit of an informer,
but in the simple desire to exact
vengeance for having been out-
rageously wronged by Arethusius
and his brother Nicostratus.
The purity of my motives will
be proved, (1) by the small a-
mount at which the two slaves
are valued (two-and-a-half
minae), so that the pecuniary
gain to which I am legally entitled for bringing this information is small, while the loss
which I should incur, if I fail,
is 1000 drachmae, (or four times
the value of the slaves). (2)
The fact that I have laid the
information in my own name,
proves that I am prompted by
the personal motive of revenge
alone. Content with that revenge, I am willing to waive all

πέπονθεν Ἀπολλόδωρος ὑπ᾽ Ἀρεθουσίου, ἵνα δοκῇ μὴ
246 φύσει πονηρὸς ὢν ταῦτα πράττειν, ἀλλὰ ἀμυνόμενος
τὸν ἀδικοῦντα.

Ὅτι μὲν οὐ συκοφαντῶν, ἀλλ᾽ ἀδικούμενος καὶ ὑβρι- 1
ζόμενος ὑπὸ τούτων καὶ οἰόμενος δεῖν τιμωρεῖσθαι τὴν
ἀπογραφὴν ἐποιησάμην, μέγιστον ὑμῖν ἔστω τεκμήριον, ὦ ἄνδρες δικασταὶ, τό τε μέγεθος τῆς ἀπογραφῆς,
καὶ ὅτι αὐτὸς ἐγὼ ἀπέγραψα. οὐ γὰρ δήπου συκοφαν-

claim to the reward which the
law in such cases allows the
bringer of the information (viz.
three-fourths of the valuation).

The court will now permit me
to justify myself by shewing how
ungratefully I have been dealt
with by my opponents and by relating, so far as time permits,
the most atrocious and flagrant
of all the wrongs which they
have inflicted upon me.

οἰόμενος δεῖν τιμωρεῖσθαι] 'To
avoid the fatal charge of *syco-
phantia*, any one prosecuting a
fellow-citizen for some public
offence endeavoured to shew
that he had private and personal grounds of enmity against
the accused; and if he succeeded in proving this, it was
considered the most natural
and reasonable thing in the
world that he should endeavour
to satisfy his hatred by becoming public prosecutor.' Wilkins'
Light of the World p. 30 (where
a reference is made to Lewes'
History of Philosophy i 108).
For illustrations of the Greek
view of the reasonableness of
revenge, see note on Isocr. ad
Dem. § 26.

τὸ μέγεθος] 'the size', 'the
amount', a neutral word, here
meaning probably 'the *small*

amount', 'the *paltriness* of the
specification.' Herod. ii 74,
μεγάθεϊ μικρός. The sum of two
and a half minae seems to refer
to the value of the two slaves
taken together (Boeckh, *Publ.
Econ.* i chap. xiii p. 96 Lamb).
Reiske, however, explains τὸ
μέγεθος τῆς ἀπογραφῆς: *magni-
tudo mulctae mihi luendae, si
causa cadam.*

τῆς ἀπογραφῆς] 'the specification', or 'inventory', of property, used especially of information as to State property
alleged to be unlawfully held
by a private person. Harpocration, ἀπογραφή· ὅταν τις
λέγῃ τινὰ ἔχειν τι τῶν τῆς πόλεως, ἀπογραφὴν ποιεῖται ὁ ἐνα-
γόμενος, δηλῶν πόθεν ἔχει τὰ
χρήματα καὶ πόσα ταῦτα εἴη...τί
δὲ ἦν τὸ κινδύνευμα τῷ τὴν ἀπογραφὴν ποιουμένῳ, ἐν τῷ Δημοσθένους πρὸς Νικόστρατον περὶ
τῶν Ἀρεθουσίου ἀνδραπόδων, εἰ
γνήσιος, δῆλον γίγνεται. Hesychius, ἀπογραφή· ἀρίθμησις· ἢ
ἡ γινομένη μήνυσις. Cf. Or. 22
(Androt.) § 51, τὸ τὰ χωρία δη-
μεύειν καὶ τὰς οἰκίας, καὶ ταῦτ᾽
ἀπογράφειν, 37 § 7, 40 § 22.
Meier and Schömann, pp. 253—
260.

οὐ δήπου..ἀπέγραψα ἄν..ἀνδρά-
ποδα] 'I should not have sche-

τεῖν γε βουλόμενος ἀπέγραψα ἂν[d] πένθ᾽ ἡμιμναίων
ἄξια ἀνδράποδα, ὡς αὐτὸς ὁ ἀμφισβητῶν τετίμηται
αὐτά, ἐκινδύνευον δ᾽ ἂν περί τε χιλίων δραχμῶν καὶ
τοῦ μηδέποτε μηδένα αὖθις ὑπὲρ ἐμαυτοῦ γράψασθαι·
οὐδ᾽ αὖ οὕτως ἄπορος ἦν οὐδ᾽ ἄφιλος[e] ὥστ᾽ οὐκ ἂν
2 ἐξευρεῖν τὸν ἀπογράψοντα· ἀλλὰ τῶν ἐν ἀνθρώποις
ἁπάντων ἡγησάμενος δεινότατον εἶναι ἀδικεῖσθαι μὲν
αὐτός, ἕτερον δ᾽ ὑπὲρ ἐμοῦ τοῦ ἀδικουμένου τοὔνομα
παρέχειν, καὶ εἶναι ἄν τι τούτοις τοῦτο τεκμήριον,
ὁπότε ἐγὼ λέγοιμι τὴν ἔχθραν πρὸς ὑμᾶς, ὡς ψεύδομαι

[d] ἀπέγραψα μὲν ἄν.... Dobree.
[e] οὐδ᾽ ἄφιλος Bekker.   om. Z cum Σ.

duled slaves worth two minas
and a half.' Kennedy.

χιλίων δραχμῶν] The fine
inflicted on a prosecutor who
in a public accusation failed to
obtain a fifth part of the votes.
This fine was attended by complete or partial disfranchisement. Hyper. Eux. 44, 5 τὸν
ἐγχειρήσαντα συκοφαντεῖν αὐτοὺς
(in an ἀπογραφή) εὐθὺς ἠτίμωσαν
τὸ πεμπτὸν μέρος τῶν ψήφων οὐ
μεταδόντες, Lysias 18 § 14 χιλί-
αις δραχμαῖς ἐζημίωσατε τὸν βουλόμενον τὴν ἡμετέραν γῆν δημοσίαν ποιῆσαι. Or. 58 (Theocrin.)
§ 6 ἐὰν ἐπεξιών τις μὴ μεταλάβῃ
τὸ πεμπτὸν μέρος τῶν ψήψων,
χιλίας ἀποτίνειν, κἂν μὴ ἐπεξίῃ,
χιλίας ἑτέρας, ἵνα μὴ συκοφαντῇ
μηδεὶς μήτ᾽ ἄδειαν ἔχων ἐργολαβῇ
καὶ καθυφιῇ τὰ τῆς πόλεως.

μηδέποτε—γράψασθαι] Lipsius
(in note 320 to p. 260 of Meier
and Schömann) regards this as
an exaggeration. Cf. Hager in
Journ. of Philology VI 15.

ὥστ᾽ οὐκ ἂν ἐξευρεῖν] A mixed
phrase between ὥστ᾽ οὐκ ἂν
ἐξεύροιμι and ὥστε μὴ ἐξευρεῖν.
The use of ἄν with ὥστε and the

infinitive is rare, but it occurs
when a mere contingent result
is described. P.]

2. αὐτός is kept in the nom.,
referring back to ἡγησάμενος, in
spite of the interposition of
δεινότατον εἶναι which leads us
to expect an acc. with the infinitive ἀδικεῖσθαι (Shilleto on Fals.
Leg. § 337).

τοὔνομα παρέχειν] 'to lend
his name,' i.e. allow himself
to be used as a cat's paw. [Eu-
ripides has παρασχεῖν ὄνομα in
Helena 1100 and 1653, where
Helen is said to have 'lent her
name' for the fraud put upon
Paris in marrying a mere εἴδω-
λον. In both passages however
the genuineness of the verse
may be doubted. P.]

τεκμήριον—ὡς ψεύδομαι] My
opponents might have said, 'If
you *really* had a quarrel against
us, why did you not file the
action against us in your own
name?' Perhaps we should
read: οὐ γὰρ ἂν ἐὰν ποτε ἕτερον
ἀπογράψαι, 'for I never should
have allowed another, &c.' P.]

(οὐ γὰρ ἄν ποτε ἕτερον ἀπογράψαι, εἴπερ ἐγὼ αὐτὸς ἠδικούμην), διὰ μὲν ταῦτ᾽ ἀπέγραψα. ἀπογράψας δὲ ἐὰν ἀποδείξω τἀνδράποδα ᾿Αρεθουσίου ὄντα, οὗπερ ἐγέγραπτο εἶναι, τὰ μὲν τρία μέρη, ἃ ἐκ τῶν νόμων τῷ ἰδιώτῃ τῷ ἀπογράψαντι γίγνεται, τῇ πόλει ἀφίημι, αὐτῷ δ᾽ ἐμοὶ τετιμωρῆσθαι ἀρκεῖ μόνον. εἰ μὲν οὖν 3 μοι ἦν ἱκανὸν τὸ ὕδωρ διηγήσασθαι πρὸς ὑμᾶς τὰ ἐξ ἀρχῆς, ὅσ᾽ ἀγαθὰ πεπονθότες ὑπ᾽ ἐμοῦ οἷά με εἰργασμένοι εἰσὶν, εὖ οἶδ᾽ ὅτι ὑμεῖς τ᾽ ἄν μοι ἔτι μᾶλλον συγγνώμην εἴχετε τοῦ ὀργίζεσθαι αὐτοῖς, τούτους τ᾽ ἀνοσιωτάτους ἀνθρώπων ἡγήσασθε εἶναι· νῦν δ᾽ οὐδὲ διπλάσιόν μοι τούτου ὕδωρ ἱκανὸν ἂν γένοιτο. τὰ μὲν οὖν μέγιστα καὶ περιφανῆ τῶν ἀδικημάτων, καὶ ὁπόθεν ἡ ἀπογραφὴ αὕτη γέγονεν, ἐρῶ πρὸς ὑμᾶς, τὰ δὲ πολλὰ ἐάσω.

τὰ τρία μέρη] Three-fourths of the valuation was allowed by law to be paid to the individual who brought the action. Boeckh, *Sec-urkunden* p. 535 ἀφεῖκε Πολύευκτος ὁ ἀπογράψας τὰ ἐκ τῶν νόμων καὶ τῆς ἀπογραφῆς Σωπόλιδι τὰ γιγνόμενα εἰς τὴν ἐπιτιμίαν (penalty). It has been inferred from the inscription just quoted that this regulation was not confined (as Boeckh supposed) to concealed property, which was discovered by the informer. (*Publ. Econ.* iii chap. xiv p. 395 Lewis², p. 512 Lamb). Cf. Meier and Schömann p. 260, note 321 Lipsius, and Hermann, *Public Antiquities* § 136, 14.—τῷ ἰδιώτῃ τῷ ἀπογράψαντι, 'to the individual informer' Kennedy. ὁ ἰδιώτης is here contrasted with ἡ πόλις.

ἀφίημι] *remitto atque condono*, Reiske.

3. εἰ ἦν ἱκανὸν...ὑμεῖς ἄν συγγνώμην εἴχετε...νῦν δὲ οὐδὲ διπλάσιον...ἱκανὸν ἂν γένοιτο] The student will be careful to distinguish between the two forms of conditional sentences here combined. 'If the time allowed *had been* sufficient, you *would have* made allowance for me ..., but, as the case is, even twice as much time *would* not suffice.' (Goodwin, *Greek Moods* § 49, 2 and § 50, 2.)—On τὸ ὕδωρ cf. Or. 54 § 36.

ὅσα...οἷα] 'What benefits they have received from me and what a requital they have paid me for them,' or, better, 'the return they have given me for all the benefits I have conferred upon them.' For this idiomatic use of the double relative, cf. Soph. El. 751, οἷ᾽ ἔργα δράσας οἷα λαγχάνει κακά, also Ovid, Fasti v 460, *cernite sim qualis qui modo qualis eram;* and Cornelius Nepos, *Atticus*, 18, 3, *notans quis a quo ortus quos honores quibusque temporibus cepisset.*

4   Νικόστρατος γὰρ οὑτοσὶ[f], ὦ ἄνδρες δικασταὶ, γείτων μοι ὢν ἐν ἀγρῷ καὶ ἡλικιώτης γνωρίμως μέν μοι
εἶχε καὶ πάλαι, ἐπειδὴ δ' ἐτελεύτησεν ὁ πατὴρ καὶ ἐγὼ
ἐν ἀγρῷ κατῴκουν, οὗπερ καὶ νῦν οἰκῶ, καὶ μᾶλλον
ἀλλήλοις ἤδη ἐχρώμεθα διὰ τὸ γείτονές τε εἶναι καὶ

[f] Bekker.   om. Z cum Σ.   (οὗτος A[1]r.)

§§ 4—9. *My opponent's brother Nicostratus, was my neighbour in the country, and, being
about the same age, we were
thrown much together and became more and more intimate
with one another. I granted him
whatever he asked of me, and he
on his part was of some service
to me in taking charge of my
property whenever I was abroad
on public or private business.*

*On one of these occasions,
when I had left him in charge,
three of his servants ran away
from him. While pursuing them,
he was taken prisoner by a
privateer, and sold as a slave.
On my return, I was told of his
unhappy plight by one of his
brothers, Deinon, and I supplied
the latter with travelling expenses and thus enabled him to
go to the rescue of Nicostratus.
The latter, on his return, informed me that he had been
ransomed for a considerable sum.
He appealed to me with tears in
his eyes and pointed to the marks
left by the galling fetters (though
he is now ashamed enough of
those scars that are the memorials
of his slavery). He thus succeeded in inducing me to for-
give him the three minae, which
I had advanced for his brother's
travelling expenses, and to con-
tribute, as a free gift towards the
twenty-six minae required for
the ransom, the sum of ten minae
which I raised on the security
of some of my property.*

4. Νικόστρατος γὰρ] γὰρ is
almost invariably used at the
beginning of narratives like the
present; the English idiom generally requires us to omit it
in translation, though we may
sometimes render it, 'Well, then,'
'to proceed, then.' Cf. Or. 55
§ 10 τοῦ γὰρ χωρίου κ.τ.λ., 27
§ 4.

γνωρίμως εἶχε] γνώριμος is a
much weaker word than φίλος,
as has already been noticed, on
Or. 45 § 73. The gradually in-
creasing intimacy between Apollodorus and Nicostratus is well
expressed by the successive
phrases (1) γνωρίμως εἶχε, (2)
μᾶλλον ἀλλήλοις ἐχρώμεθα, (3)
πάνυ οἰκείως διεκείμεθα of the
present section, and (4) φίλος
ἀληθινὸς of § 12. Cf. 33 § 5
γνωρίμως ἔχω...πάνυ οἰκείως χρῶ-
μαι.

ἐτελεύτησεν ὁ πατήρ] The
death of Pasion took place B.C.
370 (Or. 46 § 13).

κατῴκουν...οἰκῶ] If any distinction is to be drawn, the
compound verb should be rendered 'I settled' and the simple 'I live'; but it is more likely
that οἰκῶ is intended as a virtual
repetition of the preceding κατῴκουν. In such cases it is unnecessary to repeat the preposition, e.g. Eur. Bacc. 1065 κατ-
ῆγεν ἦγεν ἦγεν εἰς μέλαν πέδον
and Orest. 181, διοιχόμεσθ', οἰχό-
μεθα, where Porson remarks that,
when a verb is repeated, it is
generally used first in its com-

ἡλικιῶται. χρόνου δὲ προβαίνοντος καὶ πάνυ οἰκείως
διεκείμεθα, καὶ ἐγώ θ᾽ οὕτως οἰκείως διεκείμην πρὸς
τοῦτον ὥστ᾽ οὐδενὸς πώποτε ὧν ἐδεήθη οὗτος ἐμοῦ
ἀπέτυχεν, οὗτός τ᾽ αὖ ἐμοὶ οὐκ ἄχρηστος ἦν πρὸς τὸ
ἐπιμεληθῆναι καὶ διοικῆσαι, καὶ ὁπότε ἐγὼ ἀποδημοίην
ἢ δημοσίᾳ τριηραρχῶν ἢ ἰδίᾳ κατ᾽ ἄλλο τι, κύριον τῶν
ἐν ἀγρῷ τοῦτον ἁπάντων κατέλειπον. συμβαίνει δή 5
μοι τριηραρχία περὶ Πελοπόννησον, ἐκεῖθεν δ᾽ εἰς
Σικελίαν ἔδει τοὺς πρέσβεις ἄγειν, οὓς ὁ δῆμος ἐχει-
ροτόνησεν. ἡ οὖν ἀναγωγὴ διὰ ταχέων ἐγίγνετό μοι.
ἐπιστέλλω δὴ αὐτῷ ὅτι αὐτὸς μὲν ἀνῆγμαι καὶ οὐχ

pound, then in its simple form.
Or. 36 § 4 προσώφειλε...ὤφειλε,
33 § 18 ἐξοίσειν...ἐνήνοχεν.

μᾶλλον...ἡλικιῶται] 'We grew
more and more familiar with
one another from being not
only neighbours but also of the
same age.' Or. 55 § 23 ad fin.
and Or. 35 § 6 ἐπιτήδειοί μοι εἰσι
καὶ χρώμεθ᾽ ἀλλήλοις ὡς οἷόν τε
μάλιστα.

χρόνου προβαίνοντος] Soph.
Phil. 285, ὁ μὲν χρόνος δὴ διὰ
χρόνου προὔβαινέ μοι.

δημοσίᾳ τριηραρχῶν] This reference to the speaker's public
services is dexterously inserted
to ingratiate him with his audience, as well as to lead up to the
subsequent narrative συμβαίνει
δή μοι τριηραρχία.—On some of
the later trierarchal services of
Apollodorus cf. note on Or. 36
§ 41.

5. τριηραρχία περὶ Πελοπόννησον κ.τ.λ.] The date of this event,
if it could be determined with cer-
tainty would assist materially
in determining the date of the
delivery of the speech. It seems
very probable that this trierarchy should be identified with
that referred to in Or. 45 § 3,

which, as we have already seen,
may be placed in the year 368
B.C. See *Introd.* p. lvii.

διὰ ταχέων] Thuc. I 80, διὰ
ταχέων ἐλθεῖν, Isocr. 14 § 3 διὰ
βραχέων ἂν ἐποιησάμεθα τοὺς
λόγους followed by ἀναγκαῖον διὰ
μακροτέρων δηλῶσαι (Kühner
Greek Grammar II § 434, 1, d).
Or. 50 (Polycl.) § 12 ἀναγόμενος
διὰ τάχους, 47 (Euerg.) § 49.

ἀνῆγμαι] ἀνάγεσθαι is constantly contrasted with κατά-
γεσθαι; the latter word occurs
in § 6 κατήχθη εἰς Αἴγιναν. The
verb, with its corresponding
substantive ἀναγωγὴ, implies a
notion that ships in the open
sea or, as we say, on the '*high
seas*', are at a greater elevation
than vessels in harbour. So in
Thuc. I 48 and VIII 10 μετέωρος
is an epithet of ships at sea.
Similar references to this familiar optical illusion may be
noted in Milton's *Paradise Lost*
II 636, *Far off at sea a fleet
descried Hangs in the clouds*,
and in Ruskin's *thymy slopes
of down overlooked by the blue
line of lifted sea* (Modern
Painters III iv 14 § 51).

ἐπιστέλλω ... ὅτι ἀνῆγμαι καὶ

οἷός τ᾽ εἴην[g] οἴκαδε ἀφικέσθαι, ἵνα μὴ κατακωλύοιμι 1248
τοὺς πρέσβεις· τούτῳ δὲ προσέταξα ἐπιμελεῖσθαί τε
τῶν οἴκοι καὶ διοικεῖν, ὥσπερ καὶ ἐν τῷ ἔμπροσθεν
6 χρόνῳ. ἐν δὲ τῇ ἐμῇ ἀποδημίᾳ ἀποδιδράσκουσιν αὐτὸν
οἰκέται τρεῖς ἐξ ἀγροῦ παρὰ τούτου, οἱ μὲν δύο ὧν ἐγὼ
ἔδωκα αὐτῷ, ὁ δὲ εἷς ὧν αὐτὸς ἐκτήσατο. διώκων οὖν
ἁλίσκεται ὑπὸ τριήρους καὶ κατήχθη εἰς Αἴγιναν, καὶ
ἐκεῖ ἐπράθη. ἐπειδὴ δὲ κατέπλευσα ἐγὼ τριηραρχῶν,
προσέρχεταί μοι Δείνων ὁ ἀδελφὸς ὁ τούτου λέγων
τήν τε τούτου συμφορὰν, αὐτός τε ὅτι δι᾽ ἀπορίαν
ἐφοδίων οὐ πεπορευμένος εἴη ἐπὶ τοῦτον πέμποντος
τούτου αὐτῷ[h] ἐπιστολὰς, καὶ ἅμα λέγων πρὸς ἐμὲ ὡς
7 ἀκούοι αὐτὸν δεινῶς διακεῖσθαι. ἀκούσας δ᾽ ἐγὼ ταῦτα
καὶ συναχθεσθεὶς ἐπὶ τῇ ἀτυχίᾳ τῇ τούτου πέμπω
τὸν Δείνωνα τὸν ἀδελφὸν αὐτοῦ[i] εὐθὺς ἐπὶ τοῦτον,

[g] Bekker.   ἦν Z cum ΣrA[1] et Φ (prima manu).

[h] αὐτῷ Z.

οὐχ οἷός τ᾽ εἴην] The historic
present ἐπιστέλλω being virtually a secondary tense has the
optative εἴην in the dependent
clause.   For the combination
of the indicative ἀνῆγμαι with
the optative εἴην, we may compare Or. 59 (Neaer.) § 81 λέγων
ὅτι οὐκ ἤδει…ἀλλ᾽ ἐξαπατηθείη,
47 (Euerg.) § 50 λέγων ὅτι…δεῖ
…καὶ κελεύοι, ib. 68 ὡς εἶχον…
καὶ…τελευτήσειεν, and esp. 27
(Aphob. A) § 19 ἐτόλμα…λέγειν
ὡς χρέα τε παμπολλὰ ἐκτέτικεν…
καὶ ὡς πολλὰ τῶν ἐμῶν λάβοιεν.
The optative of the perfect and
future was less familiar than
the optative of the other tenses.
It is apparently for this reason
that the indicative of the perfect
or the future was often retained
after secondary tenses, even
when the present or the aorist

was changed from the indicative to the optative (Goodwin,
Moods and Tenses § 70, 2, R 2).
The mss appear to have been
misled by the indicative ἀνῆγμαι
into writing ἦν instead of εἴην.

κατακωλύοιμι] Or. 33 § 13 τοῦ
εἰς Σικελίαν πλοῦ διὰ τοῦτον κα-
τεκωλύθη.

6.   παρὰ τούτου] ‘From the
defendant’s house.’ — ὧν ἐγὼ
κ.τ.λ. i.e. ‘of the number of
those whom I had given him.’

κατέπλευσα τριηραρχῶν] ‘When
my voyage as trierarch came to
an end.’ Or. 50 § 12 κατέπλευσα
τοὺς πρέσβεις ἄγων. For the preposition in κατέπλευσα cf. κατήχθη infra, and see note on
ἀνῆγμαι supra § 5.

ἐπὶ τοῦτον] ‘In quest of him,’
‘to fetch him back.’

δοὺς ἐφόδιον αὐτῷ τριακοσίας δραχμάς. ἀφικόμενος
δ' οὗτος καὶ ἐλθὼν ὡς ἐμὲ πρῶτον μὲν ἠσπάζετο, καὶ
ἐπήνει ὅτι παρέσχον τὰ ἐφόδια τῷ ἀδελφῷ αὐτοῦ, καὶ
ὠδύρετο τὴν αὐτοῦ συμφορὰν, καὶ κατηγορῶν ἅμα
τῶν ἑαυτοῦ οἰκείων ἐδεῖτό μου βοηθῆσαι αὐτῷ, ὥσπερ
καὶ ἐν τῷ ἐμπροσθεν χρόνῳ ἦν περὶ αὐτὸν ἀληθινὸς
φίλος· καὶ κλάων[j] ἅμα, καὶ λέγων ὅτι ἓξ καὶ εἴκοσι
μνῶν λελυμένος εἴη, εἰσενεγκεῖν αὐτῷ τι ἐκέλευέ με 8
εἰς τὰ λύτρα. ταῦτα δ' ἐγὼ ἀκούων καὶ ἐλεήσας
τοῦτον, καὶ ἅμα ὁρῶν κακῶς διακείμενον καὶ δεικνύ-
οντα ἕλκη ἐν ταῖς κνήμαις ὑπὸ δεσμῶν, ὧν ἔτι τὰς

[i] τούτου Z cum Σ. αὐτοῦ A¹r. 'Fortasse verba τὸν ἀδελφὸν
τούτου delenda sunt' Sauppe.

[j] Bekk. cum A¹r. κλαίων Z cum Σ.

7. ἐπήνει] Not 'praised,'
but, rather, 'thanked.' Cf. § 13,
ἐπαινέσας με ἐκέλευσε κ.τ.λ. So
also in Ar. Ranae 508, κάλλιστ',
ἐπαινῶ, 'thank you!' where
however the notion of declining
the offer is also involved.

ἀληθινὸς φίλος] ἀληθινὸς is
the Latin verus; ἀληθὴς verax.
'We may affirm of the ἀληθὴς
that he fulfils the promise of
his lips, but the ἀληθινὸς the
wider promise of his name'
(Trench, Synonyms of the New
Testament § VIII). See also
Donaldson, New Cratylus § 258
and Kühner Greek Gr. I § 334.
7. [ἀληθινὸς is 'genuine,' as
χρυσὸς, ἀρετὴ, &c.; ἀληθὴς is
more directly contrasted with
ψευδὴς, as ἀληθὴς λόγος. But the
distinction is not always observed. Euripides has ἀληθὴς
φίλος Suppl. 867, and σαφὴς
φίλος is not unusual in the same
sense. P.] Cf. note on Or. 40
§ 20.

κλάων] 'In Tragedy κλαίω

and κλάω; in Aristophanes κλάω
prevails, in Attic prose κλαίω
and κλάω, the latter gaining
ground.' Veitch, Greek Verbs.

εἴκοσι μνῶν] Aristotle, Eth.
v 10 § 9, gives as an example
of νομικὸν δίκαιον, conventional
right, τὸ μνᾶς λυτροῦσθαι, the
right of every man to claim his
freedom on payment of one
mina,—perhaps referring only
to slaves. P.]

λελυμένος] Isaeus Or. 5 § 44
οὐδ' ἐκ τῶν πολεμίων ἐλύσω οὐδένα, Lysias Or. 19 § 59, Dem.
Fals. Leg. § 169.

ἐκέλευε] 'urged me,' 'asked
me,'—less strong than the aorist
ἐκέλευσε (inf. § 9). The impf.
of this verb is often found in
passages where we should expect the aorist, especially in
Herodotus and Thucydides. It
may be regarded as used in a
tentative sense, in so far as the
result of the request is uncer-
tain.

8. ἕλκη ἐν ταῖς κνήμαις] Ar.

οὐλὰς ἔχει, καὶ ἐὰν κελεύσητε αὐτὸν δεῖξαι, οἳ μὴ
ἐθελήσει[k], ἀπεκρινάμην αὐτῷ ὅτι καὶ ἐν τῷ ἔμ-   1249
προσθεν χρόνῳ εἴην αὐτῷ φίλος ἀληθινὸς, καὶ νῦν ἐν
τῇ συμφορᾷ βοηθήσοιμι[l] αὐτῷ, καὶ τάς τε τριακοσίας,
ας τῷ ἀδελφῷ αὐτοῦ ἔδωκα ἐφόδιον ὅτε ἐπορεύετο
ἐπὶ τοῦτον, ἀφείην αὐτῷ, χιλίας τε δραχμὰς ἔρανον

[k] ἐθελήσει Dobree.   οὐ μὴ 'θελήσῃ Z.   θελήσῃι Σ.   ἐθελήσῃ Bekker.
[l] G. II. Schaefer.   βοηθήσαιμι libri.

Eq. 907, τὰν τοῖσιν ἀντικνημίοις
ἑλκύδρια περιαλείφειν.

οὐ μὴ ἐθελήσει] 'There is
little chance of his consenting.'

Nicostratus would naturally
refuse to display the scars left
by the galling fetters : to do so
would be to confess that he had
incurred the disgrace of having
been sold as a slave.

The future indicative with οὐ
μὴ has here, as elsewhere, the
force of an emphatic future with
οὐ. The subjunctive, especially
in the aorist tense, is still more
common in this sense, and is
indeed the reading of the mss
in the present passage, the indicative being an apparently
unnecessary emendation due to
Dobree. [The Greeks said οὐ
μὴ φύγῃ, οὐ μὴ ἔλθῃ, and οὐ μὴ
ληφθῶ, but seem to have preferred οὐ μὴ πράξει to οὐ μὴ
πράξῃ. But here too mss generally vary. P.] This construction
must be distinguished from the
special use of οὐ μὴ with the
second person of the fut. indic.,
to express a strong prohibition
(Goodwin, Moods and Tenses
§ 89, 1 and 2).

ἀπεκρινάμην] The Attic form
corresponding to ὑπεκρινάμην in
Herodotus and ἀπεκρίθην in late
Greek, e.g. in the New Testa-
ment (Winer's Gr. p. 327, ed.
Moulton). Cf. Rutherford's New

Phrynichus p. 186.

ὅτι ἐν τῷ ἔμπροσθεν χρόνῳ
εἴην φίλος, καὶ νῦν βοηθήσοιμι]
'That I had been his true friend
formerly, and would assist him
now.' The opt. εἴην represents
not the present or future but
the imperfect of direct discourse; while the future optative
βοηθήσοιμι corresponds to the
future ind. of oratio recta. 'The
fut. opt. in Classic Greek is
used only in indirect discourse
after secondary tenses to represent a fut. indic. of the
direct discourse' (Goodwin,
Moods and Tenses § 26). βοηθήσαιμι is wrong, because it
would represent ἐβοήθησα of the
oratio recta and would therefore be inconsistent with νῦν.—
Similarly below, εἰσοίσοιμι (contrasted with ἀφείην) represents
the fut. indic. of direct discourse. Cf. 36 § 6 ἔσοιτο, and
Rehdantz, index I, s.v. opta-
tivus.

ἀφείην] inf. § 13.   Fals. Leg.
p. 394 § 171 ὅσα...ἀφῆκα χρήματα καὶ δωρεὰν ἔδωκα.

ἔρανον κ.τ.λ.] 'I would con-
tribute 1000 drachmae towards
his ransom,' i.e. 10 minae out
of the total amount of 26 minae
mentioned in § 7 ad fin. On
ἔρανος cf. Hermann, Privatalt.
§ 65, 13, esp. p. 65 of Rechtsalt.
ed. Thalheim. 'L'éranos, dit

αὐτῷ εἰς τὰ λύτρα εἰσοίσοιμι. καὶ τοῦτο οὐ λόγῳ 9
μὲν ὑπεσχόμην, ἔργῳ δ' οὐκ ἐποίησα, ἀλλ' ἐπειδὴ
οὐκ ηὐπόρουν[m] ἀργυρίου διὰ τὸ διαφόρως ἔχειν τῷ
Φορμίωνι καὶ ἀποστερεῖσθαι ὑπ' αὐτοῦ τὴν οὐσίαν ἥν
μοι ὁ πατὴρ κατέλιπε, κομίσας ὡς Θεοκλέα τὸν τότε
τραπεζιτεύοντα ἐκπώματα καὶ στέφανον χρυσοῦν,
ἅπερ[n] ἐμοὶ ἐκ τῶν πατρῴων ὄντα ἐτύγχανεν, ἐκέλευσα
δοῦναι τούτῳ χιλίας δραχμάς, καὶ τοῦτο ἔδωκα δωρεὰν
αὐτῷ τὸ ἀργύριον, καὶ ὁμολογῶ δεδωκέναι. ἡμέραις 10
δ' οὐ πολλαῖς ὕστερον προσελθών μοι κλάων[o] ἔλεγεν

[m] εὐπόρουν Ζ.

[n] A¹r. ἃ παρ' Ζ et Bekker st. cum ΣΦΒ.

[o] Bekk. cum rA¹. κλαίων Ζ.

très - exactement M. Foucart (*des associations religieuses chez les Grecs*, Paris, 1873, p. 143), n'était ni un don, ni un secours, mais un prêt qu'il fallait rembourser' (Dareste).

9. οὐ λόγῳ μὲν ὑπεσχόμην, ἔργῳ δ' οὐκ ἐποίησα] Cf. de Corona § 179 οὐκ εἶπον μὲν ταῦτα οὐκ ἔγραψα δέ, οὐδ' ἔγραψα μὲν οὐκ ἐπρέσβευσα δέ, οὐδ' ἐπρέσβευσα μὲν οὐκ ἔπεισα δὲ τοὺς Θηβαίους. Kennedy neatly translates: 'nor did I content myself with mere words; but what I promised I performed.'

διαφόρως—τῷ Φορμίωνι] The context shews that the reference is to the estrangement between Apollodorus and Phormion shortly after the death of Pasion in 370 B.C.—τὴν οὐσίαν refers mainly to the banking-stock which forms the subject of Or. 36, the claim to which was not brought forward until some twenty years later.

δωρεὰν] not as a loan, but as a free gift.

§§ 10—13. *Not many days afterwards, he came once more and told me with tears in his eyes that the persons who had advanced the ransom were demanding payment of the remaining sixteen minae, and that the agreement required him to refund the money within thirty days, or, failing payment, to be liable for twice the amount. He could raise no money, he said, on the farm in my neighbourhood, as that property was already encumbered by a claim upon it on the part of his brother Arethusius; and he asked me to advance the remainder, as otherwise my former gifts would be thrown away, and himself carried off to prison as the lawful property of the ransomer. He further promised to collect the whole amount and to repay me. Accordingly, I raised the remaining sixteen minae on the security of my lodging-house, and lent him this sum for a year without interest.*

ὅτι οἱ ξένοι ἀπαιτοῖεν αὐτὸν[P], οἱ δανείσαντες τὰ λύτρα,
τὸ λοιπὸν ἀργύριον, καὶ ἐν ταῖς συγγαφαῖς εἴη τριά-
κονθ᾽ ἡμερῶν αὐτὸν ἀποδοῦναι ἢ διπλάσιον ὀφείλειν,
καὶ ὅτι τὸ χωρίον τὸ ἐν γειτόνων μοι τοῦτο οὐδεὶς
ἐθέλοι οὔτε πρίασθαι οὔτε τίθεσθαι· ὁ γὰρ ἀδελφὸς ὁ

[P] αὐτὸν Z.

10. ἀπαιτοῖεν] ἀπαιτεῖν (cf.
ἀπολαμβάνειν) is 'to ask for
one's due,' 'to request repayment of what is one's own.'
Andocides II § 22, ἀ...ἀφείλεσθε,
ταῦθ᾽ ὑμᾶς, εἰ μὲν βούλεσθε, αἰτῶ,
εἰ δὲ [μὴ] βούλεσθε, ἀπαιτῶ.
Or. 33 § 6 οἱ χρῆσται κατήπειγον
αὐτὸν ἀπαιτοῦντες, and Or. 49
§ 2.

So ἀποδοῦναι 'to pay what is
due,' 'to make full payment of
the sum borrowed.' Or. 49 § 2
οὐ μόνον οὐκ ἀπέδωκε χάριν ἀλλὰ
καὶ τὸ δοθὲν ἀποστερεῖ με. In
Arist. Rhet. II 7 § 5, among the
reasons which indicate the absence of real gratitude, we have
ὅτι ἀπέδωκαν ἀλλ᾽ οὐκ ἔδωκαν
('they merely returned the favour,' simply repaid a debt, and
nothing more). Cf. St Luke
vi 34, 35, ἁμαρτωλοὶ ἁμαρτω-
λοῖς δανείζουσιν, ἵνα ἀπολάβωσι
τὰ ἴσα.

διπλάσιον ὀφείλειν] Or. 56 §
20. Cf. Revue archéologique,
1866 no. 11 (quoted by Dareste),
ἐὰν δὲ μὴ ἀποδιδῷ τὴν μίσθωσιν
κατὰ τὰ γεγραμμένα ἢ μὴ ἐπισκευ-
άζῃ, ὀφείλειν αὐτὸν τὸ διπλάσιον,
and the stipulatio duplae of Roman law.

τὸ χωρίον τὸ ἐν γειτόνων μοι]
'the property (or farm) in my
immediate neighbourhood.' ἐν
γειτόνων seems to be an elliptical phrase equivalent to ἐν τοῖς
τῶν γειτόνων 'in my neighbours'
lands,' 'in my own neighbourhood.' In early Greek there is
probably no other instance of

this phrase, and as ἐκ γειτόνων
is not without example in the
Attic Orators, it appears preferable to the reading in the text,
which is obtained by Reiske
from τὸ ἐγγειτόνων, found in
three good mss (ΣΑ¹Β). Inepte
Reiskius, says Dobree, who
refers to Ar. Plut. 435, ἡ καπη-
λὶς ἧκ τῶν γειτόνων. For ἐκ γειτόνων cf. Lycurgus, (Leocrates)
§ 21 οὐδὲ τὰ ὅρια τῆς χώρας αἰσχυ-
νόμενος ἀλλ᾽ ἐκ γειτόνων τῆς ἐκ-
θρεψάσης αὐτὸν πατρίδος μετοικῶν
(cf. e vicinia and exadversum in
the sense of prope). For ἐν γειτόνων we find no parallel earlier
than Lucian, φιλοψευδής § 25 ἐν
γειτόνων δὲ ἡμῖν ᾤκει and con-
vivium § 22; also Icaromenippus
§ 8, ἐν γειτόνων ἐστὶ τὰ δόγματα
καὶ μὴ πολὺ διεστηκότα ('their
doctrines are next door to one
another and differ but slightly').

πρίασθαι ...... ὠνεῖσθαι] The
former is used as the aorist of
the latter; ὠνησάμην (though
common in Lucian and Plu-
tarch) being never found in
early Greek Prose, and perhaps
once only in Greek comedy (in
a doubtful fragment of Eupolis).
The correct aorist and present
are found side by side in § 21,
πρίαιντο followed by ὁ ὠνούμενος;
similarly in Lysias, Or. 7 § 4,
πριάμενος occurs with ὠνούμην
in the very next sentence. Cf.
Rutherford's New Phrynichus
p. 210.

τίθεσθαι] lit. 'to get security
given you,' hence 'to lend

'Αρεθούσιος, οὗ τἀνδράποδ' ἐστὶ ταῦτα ἃ νῦν ἀπογέγραπται, οὐδένα ἐῴη οὔτε ὠνεῖσθαι οὔτε τίθεσθαι ὡς ἐνοφειλομένου αὐτῷ ἀργυρίου. σὺ οὖν μοι, ἔφη, πό- 11 ρισον τὸ ἐλλεῖπον τοῦ ἀργυρίου, πρὶν τὰς τριάκονθ' ἡμέρας παρελθεῖν, ἵνα μὴ ὅ τε ἀποδέδωκα, ἔφη, τὰς χιλίας δραχμὰς, ἀπόλωνται, καὶ αὐτὸς ἀγώγιμος γένωμαι. συλλέξας δ', ἔφη, τὸν ἔρανον, ἐπειδὰν τοὺς ξένους ἀπαλλάξω, σοὶ ἀποδώσω ὃ ἄν μοι χρήσῃς. οἶσθα 1250 δ', ἔφη, ὅτι καὶ οἱ νόμοι κελεύουσι τοῦ λυσαμένου ἐκ τῶν πολεμίων εἶναι τὸν λυθέντα, ἐὰν μὴ ἀποδιδῷ τὰ

money on security' of land, &c; 'to lend on mortgage,' as opposed to τίθεναι, lit. 'to give security,' 'to put in pledge,' 'to mortgage,' 'to borrow on security.' — Hermann, *Privatalt.* § 68, 15 = p. 90 Thalheim, quotes Dionys. de Isaeo 13 (Is. frag. 29), which illustrates the general sense of the present passage; δανειζομένῳ οὐδεὶς ἂν ἔδωκεν ἐπ' αὐτοῖς ἔτι πλέον οὐδὲν ἀποδεδωκότι τὰς μισθώσεις.

ἃ νῦν ἀπογέγραπται] 'which have been scheduled in the present snit (entered in the ἀπογραφὴ, or specification).'

ὡς ἐνοφειλομένου — ἀργυρίου] 'on the ground that money was due to himself thereon.' The property was already saddled with a debt due to Arethusius, to whom it was (in part at least) mortgaged. Arethusius, in other words, had a *lien* of money upon the property. In another speech delivered by Apollodorus, Or. 49 (Timoth.) § 45, we have the words ἐνεπισκήψασθαι ἐν τῇ οὐσίᾳ τῇ ἐκείνου ἐνοφειλόμενον αὐτῷ τοῦτο τὸ ἀργύριον.

To contract a fresh loan on the security of property already mortgaged was of course fraudulent and was very properly forbidden. Cf. Bekker's *Anecdota* p. 259 μὴ ἐπιδανείσασθαι ἐπὶ τοῖς αὐτοῖς ἐνεχύροις. Or. 35 (Lacrit.) § 21 ἔστιν ἐν τῇ συγγραφῇ ὅτι ὑποτιθέασι ταῦτ' ἐλεύθερα (unencumbered) καὶ οὐδενὶ οὐδὲν ὀφείλοντες, καὶ ὅτι οὐδ' ἐπιδανείσονται ἐπὶ τούτοις παρ' οὐδένος. See also Or. 34 §§ 6, 50.

11. ἵνα μὴ ὅ τε ἀποδέδωκα, τὰς χιλίας δραχμὰς, ἀπόλωνται] i.e. ἵνα μὴ αἵ τε χίλιαι δραχμαὶ, ἃς ἀποδέδωκα, ἀπόλωνται. τὰς δραχμὰς is here attracted into the same case as the relative ὅ, the object of ἀποδέδωκα. Or. 20 (Lept.) § 18, οὐδείς ἐστ' ἀτελὴς, οὐδ' οὓς αὐτὸς ἔγραψε, τοὺς ἀφ' Ἁρμοδίου καὶ Ἀριστογείτονος. See Kühner, *Gk. Gr.* II § 556, 4.

ἀγώγιμος] 'liable to seizure.' Or. 23 (Aristocr.) § 11 ἄν τις αὐτὸν ἀποκτείνῃ, ἀγώγιμον εἶναι.

ἀπαλλάξω] Or. 34 § 22 τοὺς δανείσαντας ἀπήλλαξεν. See note on Or. 36 § 25.

τοῦ λυσαμένου...εἶναι τὸν λυθέντα] 'the laws enact that a person ransomed from the enemy shall be the property of the ransomer, if the former fail to pay the redemption money.' Hermann, *Rechtsalt.* ed. Thalheim p. 18 note 6.

12 λύτρα. ἀκούων δ' αὐτοῦ ταῦτα καὶ δοκῶν οὐ ψεύδεσθαι ἀπεκρινάμην αὐτῷ ἅπερ ἂν νέος τε ἄνθρωπος καὶ οἰκείως χρώμενος, οὐκ ἂν νομίσας ἀδικηθῆναι, ὅτι, ὦ Νικόστρατε, καὶ ἐν τῷ πρὸ τοῦ[q] σοι χρόνῳ φίλος ἦν ἀληθινὸς, καὶ νῦν ἐν ταῖς συμφοραῖς σου, καθ' ὅσον ἐγὼ ἐδυνάμην, βεβοήθηκα. ἐπειδὴ δ' ἐν τῷ παρόντι οὐ δύνασαι πορίσαι ἅπαντα τὰ χρήματα, ἀργύριον μὲν ἐμοὶ οὐ πάρεστιν, οὐδ' ἔχω οὐδ' αὐτὸς, τῶν δὲ κτημάτων σοι τῶν ἐμῶν κίχρημι ὅ τι βούλει, θέντα τοῦ

[q] Bekker. πρὸ τούτου Z *cum* FΣΦ.

12. ἅπερ ἂν] sc. ἀποκρίναιτο.

οὐκ ἂν νομίσας ἀδικηθῆναι] i.e. οὐ νομίσας ἀδικηθῆναι ἄν. ἂν is often separated from its verb by such words as οἶμαι, δοκῶ, οἶδα, νομίζω. Xen. Cyrop. VIII 7 § 25 ἡδέως ἄν μοι δοκῶ κοινωνῆσαι (Goodwin, *Moods and Tenses*, § 42, 2, p. 62). This is most frequently the case when ἂν is closely attracted to an emphatic negative, e.g. Or. 36 § 49, οὐ γὰρ ἄλλο γ' ἔχοις οὐδὲν ἂν ποιῆσαι.

ὅτι, ὦ Νικόστρατε, κ.τ.λ.] ὅτι, which usually introduces an indirect construction, is here followed by *oratio recta*, and need not be translated. Xen. Cyrop. VII 3 § 3 ἀπεκρίνατο ὅτι, ὦ δέσποτα, οὐ ζῇ (Goodwin, *Moods and Tenses*, § 79).

ἐπειδὴ...οὐ δύνασαι κ.τ.λ.] G. H. Schaefer suggests ἐπειδὴ δ' οὐ δύναμαι (for δύνασαι) πορίσαι...ἀργύριον γὰρ (for μὲν) ἐμοὶ οὐ πάρεστιν...τῶν (*om.* δὲ) κτημάτων...κίχρημι ὅ τι βούλει. He holds that this reply suits the request of Nicostratus in § 11, πόρισον τὸ ἐλλεῖπον τοῦ ἀργυρίου, better than the manuscript reading. The proposed alteration does not, however, commend itself as conclusive; indeed, the emphatic pronoun ἐμοί, and the words οὐδ' ἔχω οὐδ' αὐτὸς, are more appropriate as a contrast to the *second* person δύνασαι than to the proposed substitution δύναμαι. The sense of the text is simply this: 'inasmuch as you are at present unable to pay the whole of the debt, although I have no money by me, nor indeed have I any at all (e.g. at my banker's) any more than yourself, I freely grant you the loan of any part of my property; you may mortgage it for the remainder of your debt and have the use of the money for a year without interest.'

κίχρημι] here, as elsewhere, of a friendly loan, *commodare*, as contrasted with δανείζω, which is generally used of a money-lender's loan on interest, *mutuo dare*. Or. 49 (Timoth.) § 23, στρώματα καὶ ἱμάτια καὶ φιάλας ἀργυρᾶς δύο ... ἔχρησε, καὶ τὴν μνᾶν τοῦ ἀργυρίου. ἣν ἐδανείζετο, ἐδάνεισεν, where, in the very next section, ἐδανείσατο is applied to the furniture as well as to the money; τὰς φιάλας... ἃς ἠτήσατο ὅτεπερ καὶ τὰ στρώματα καὶ τὴν μνᾶν τοῦ ἀργυρίου ἣν ἐδανείσατο. Fals. Leg. p. 394 ἔχρησα τἀργύριον.

ἐπιλοίπου ἀργυρίου ὅσον ἐνδεῖ σοι, ἐνιαυτὸν ἀτόκῳ χρῆσθαι τῷ ἀργυρίῳ καὶ ἀποδοῦναι τοῖς ξένοις. συλλέξας
δ' ἔρανον, ὥσπερ αὐτὸς φῇς, λῦσαί μοι. ἀκούσας δ' 13
οὗτος ταῦτα καὶ ἐπαινέσας με ἐκέλευσε τὴν ταχίστην
πρᾶξαι, πρὶν ἐξήκειν τὰς ἡμέρας ἐν αἷς ἔφη δεῖν τὰ
λύτρα καταθεῖναι. τίθημι οὖν τὴν συνοικίαν ἐκκαίδεκα
μνῶν Ἀρκέσαντι Παμβωτάδῃ, ὃν αὐτὸς οὗτος προὐ-
ξένησεν^r, ἐπὶ ὀκτὼ ὀβολοῖς τὴν μνᾶν δανείσαντι τοῦ

^r Bekker. προεξένησεν Σ cum A¹r (προεξένισεν F, προσεξένησεν
Σ 'litera σ in προσ a manu recentiore deleta' Dind.).

θέντα κ.τ.λ.] sc. θεῖναί τι (τῶν κτημάτων) τοῦ ἀργυρίου καὶ χρῆσθαι κ.τ.λ. For the genitive (of price) cf. infra § 13, τίθημι τὴν συνοικίαν ἐκκαίδεκα μνῶν. (For numerous instances of gen. after words like ὠνεῖσθαι, πωλεῖν, περιδίδοσθαι, see Kühner, II § 418, 6 a).—ὅσον ἐνδεῖ sc. 16 minae, Apollodorus having already (§ 8 fin.) provided 10 out of the 26 minae (§ 7 fin.).

συλλέξας ἔρανον] Mid. § 184, ἐγὼ νομίζω πάντας ἀνθρώπους ἐράνους φέρειν παρὰ τὸν βίον αὐτοῖς, οὐχὶ τούσδε μόνους οὓς συλλέγουσί τινες κ.τ.λ. Cf. Antiphon, p. 117, 19. P.]

λῦσαί μοι] sc. τὸ κτῆμα. 'Release my property from the mortgage,' or (with Kennedy), 'pay off my mortgage as you promise.' So, in another speech delivered by Apollodorus, Or. 50 (Polycles) § 28 ἵνα λύσωνταί μοι τὸ χωρίον, ἀποδόντες...τριάκοντα μνᾶς.

13. τὴν συνοικίαν] not 'the 'lodging-house' mentioned in Or. 45 § 28, for that belonged to his mother who did not die until 360 b.c; but another, possibly of equal value (100 minae). Such a security would amply suffice for a loan of 16 minae,

and the rate of 16 per cent. below mentioned would, if paid on the value of the house, exactly produce the 16 minae required. In consideration of lending this sum on the security in question, Arcesas would further receive interest (from Apollodorus) at the rate of 16 per cent. on the 16 minae. Cf. Or. 36 § 6, ἐπὶ συνοικίαις δεδανεικὼς ἦν (with note). Aeschin. Timarch. § 124 ὅπου πολλοὶ μισθωσάμενοι μίαν οἴκησιν διελόμενοι ἔχουσι, συνοικίαν καλοῦμεν, ὅπου δὲ εἷς ἐνοικεῖ, οἰκίαν.

Παμβωτάδῃ] Harpocration, Δημοσθένης ἐν τῷ πρὸς Νικόστρατον. Παμβωτάδαι τῆς Ἐρεχθηΐδος δῆμος. Suidas gives the name of the deme as Παμβῶται. On προὐξένησεν, 'introduced,'cf. Or. 37 (Pant.) § 11.

ἐπὶ ὀκτὼ ὀβολοῖς τὴν μνᾶν τοῦ μηνὸς ἑκάστου] 'Who lent me the money at an interest of 8 obols per mina per month,' i.e. 12×8 obols per 600 obols (or '16 per cent.'), per annum. When the interest is quoted at so many obols per mina per month, we have simply to double the number of obols to find the rate per cent. per annum. Thus ἐπὶ πέντε ὀβολοῖς is 10 per

μηνὸς ἑκάστου. λαβὼν δὲ τὸ ἀργύριον οὐχ ὅπως χάριν
τινά μοι ἀποδίδωσιν ὧν εὖ ἔπαθεν, ἀλλ᾽ εὐθέως ἐπε-
βούλευσέ μοι, ἵν᾽ ἀποστερήσειε τἀργύριον καὶ εἰς ἔχθραν κατασταίη, καὶ ἀπορούμενος ἐγὼ τοῖς πράγμασι
νέος ὢν ὅ τι χρησαίμην, καὶ ἄπειρος πραγμάτων, ὅπως
μὴ εἰσπράττοιμι αὐτὸν τἀργύριον οὗ ἡ συνοικία ἐτέθη,
14 ἀλλ᾽ ἀφείην αὐτῷ.   πρῶτον μὲν οὖν ἐπιβουλεύει μοι
μετὰ τῶν ἀντιδίκων, καὶ πίστιν αὐτοῖς δίδωσιν· ἔπειτ᾽ 1251

cent.: again ἐπὶ δραχμῇ (i.e. ἐφ᾽
ἐξ ὀβολοῖς) is 12 per cent. and ἐπὶ
τρίτῳ ἡμιωβελίῳ (i.e. 2½ obols
per mina per month) is 5 per
cent. per annum. From 12 to 18
per cent. appear to have been the
commonest rates of interest at
Athens. (For this, and another
Athenian method of reckoning
rates of interest, see Donaldson's *Greek Grammar* ad fin., or
Dict. Antiq. s. v. *Fenus*.)

§§ 13 *cont.*—15. *As soon as
he had got the sixteen minae, so
far from being grateful, he actually laid a plot to rob me of them,
calculating on my being driven
by my youthful inexperience into
foregoing the attempt to recover
the money which he owed me.
First, as I was then engaged in
lawsuits against my relations,
he made overtures to them and
pledged himself to make common
cause with them. Next, as he
was acquainted with my proposed
pleadings, he disclosed them to
my opponents, and further got
me condemned to pay a fine in a
case for which I had never really
received a summons, though he
fraudulently entered the name
of his brother Arethusius as one
of the witnesses to the summons
alleged. Moreover, in the event
of my bringing to a preliminary
hearing the lawsuits which I
had obtained leave to institute*

*against my relations, they were
preparing to inform against me
as a debtor to the treasury and
to get me thrown into prison.
Lastly, Arethusius actually got
me condemned as a debtor to the
treasury, made a forcible entry
into my house, and carried off
all my furniture, though it was
worth far more than the ‘debt’
in question.*

οὐχ ὅπως] *non modo non.*
Lit. I do not say that he did,
(because he did not do it).
Trans. ‘so far from making any
grateful return, &c.’

ὅ τι χρησαίμην] ‘What to do
with (how to treat) the matter.’
Or. 40 § 18 and Lysias 9 § 5
ἀπορούμενος δὲ καὶ συμβουλευό-
μενός τινι τῶν πολιτῶν τί χρήσω-
μαι τῷ πράγματι.

ἵν᾽ ἀποστερήσειε...καὶ ἀπορούμενος ἐγὼ κ.τ.λ., ὅπως μὴ εἰσπράτ-
τοιμι] ὅπως μὴ is somewhat
out of place, indeed ὅπως is
really superfluous, as the whole
sentence depends on the parti-
cle of purpose ἵνα.—ἀφείην, § 8.

14. τῶν ἀντιδίκων] Referring
principally to his opponent
Phormion (cf. § 9, διαφόρως ἔχειν
τῷ Φορμίωνι, and § 14 ad fin. τῶν
οἰκείων τῶν ἀδικούντων με). But
a litigious person like Apollodorus doubtless had many such
opponents, even apart from those
whose lawsuits are expressly

ἀγώνων μοι συνεστηκότων πρὸς αὐτοὺς τούς τε
λόγους ἐκφέρει μου εἰδὼς, καὶ ἐγγράφει[s] τῷ δημοσίῳ

[s] καὶ ἐκγράφει ΓΦ.   om. Σ.

recorded in the orations that have come down to us (see Or. 36 § 53).

τοὺς λόγους ἐκφέρει μου εἰδώς] 'Divulges my arguments, with which he was acquainted.'

ἐγγράφει τῷ δημοσίῳ ἀπρόσκλητον κ.τ.λ.] Lit. 'registers (against me) for the state-treasury an unsummoned fine of 610 drachmae arising from production of property in court,' i.e. 'enters me as a state-debtor to the amount of 610 drachmae, demanded from me without formal citation, as a fine for non-production of property in court'; or, as Prof. Kennedy renders it, 'registers (against me) a fine to the treasury... upon a writ of *exhibit* of which I had no notice by legal summons.'

The note on this sentence in Jerome Wolf's edition of Demosthenes (A.D. 1547) deserves to be quoted not only for its modesty and candour, but also as an illustration of the difficulties which embarrassed a commentator in the sixteenth century, owing to the inadequacy of the books of reference then accessible. '*Sententia quae sit, Oedipus divinet. Me et Budaeus* (sc. Budaei commentarii linguae Graecae) *et lexica Graeca Latinaque omnia destituunt. Quaesivi* ἀπόκληρος (sic), *quaesivi* ἐμφανής, *quaesivi* κατάστασις, *quaesivi ἐξ ἐμφανῶν καταστάσεως. Sed aut muta aut ἀπροσδιόνυσα omnia. Doctiores, si boni viri sunt, explicanto potius, quam me sugillanto.*'

Before entering on the details,

it may be well to explain the general drift of the passage. Apollodorus is engaged in a variety of lawsuits, in one of which we must suppose that he was alleged to be in possession of certain articles, probably documents, either actually belonging to one of his opponents or such that the latter had a legal right to demand production of them. The proper course on the part of Nicostratus, who had made common cause with one of these opponents, would have been to serve Apollodorus with a summons, duly attested by witnesses, requiring him to produce the articles in question. If Apollodorus had, without assigning a legally valid reason, refused to do so, Nicostratus would have been entitled to have a fine levied on Apollodorus and to get him entered as a debtor to the state for the amount of that fine. Instead of this, it appears that Nicostratus served no summons on Apollodorus (the ἐπιβολή was ἀπρόσκλητος), thus giving the latter no opportunity for shewing cause against the production of the articles demanded; he then proceeded to obtain a verdict against his opponent *in contumaciam*, and to have him registered as owing 610 drachmae to the public treasury. Cf. Meier and Schömann, *Att. Process*, p. 758.

ἐγγράφει] 'registers (against me),'—a common term for a formal entry or registration, especially of a debt or fine. Or. 43 § 71 *lex*, ἐγγραφόντων οἱ ἄρ-

ἀπρόσκλητον ἐξ ἐμφανῶν καταστάσεως ἐπιβολὴν[t] ἑξ-
ακοσίας καὶ δέκα δραχμὰς, διὰ Λυκίδου τοῦ μυλωθροῦ
ποιησάμενος τὴν δίκην. κλητῆρα δὲ κατ' ἐμοῦ τόν τε[u]

[t] Valesius ad Harpocrationem p. 52.   ἐπιβουλὴν libri.

[u] Bekker.   om. Ζ cum Σ (prima manu).   'τε in margine a
manu prima Σ' Dind.

χοντες...τοῖς πράκτορσιν (the col-
lectors) ὃ τῷ δημοσίῳ γίγνεται.
Or. 27 § 38 προσοφείλοντας ἡμᾶς
ἐνέγραψεν.   Or. 25 (Aristog. a)
§ 4, ὀφείλοντα τῷ δημοσίῳ καὶ
ἐγγεγραμμένον ἐν ἀκροπόλει (cf.
ib. § 70, ἐγγράφονται πάντες οἱ
ὀφλισκάνοντες, ὅρος δ' ἡ σανὶς ἡ
παρὰ τῇ θεῷ κειμένη).   Or. 40
§ 23.

τῷ δημοσίῳ]   For τὸ δημόσιον
in the sense of τὸ κοινὸν 'the
treasury,' cf. Isaeus, Or. 10 § 20
ἐμοί τι ἀτύχημα πρὸς τὸ δημόσιον
συνέβη.   Mid. § 182 and Deinarchus, Or. 2 § 2, ὀφείλων τῷ
δημοσίῳ. See Or. 39 (Boeot.) § 14.

ἀπρόσκλητον]   This is the
reading of the codex Augustanus
primus (A¹), first accepted by
Reiske for the vulgata lectio
ἀπόκληρον which is unintel-
ligible.   ἀπρόσκλητος ἐπιβολὴ
'a fine without a citation,' here
means 'a fine inflicted in a case
for which no citation has been
issued.'   Similarly infra § 15
ἀπρόσκλητον δίκην and Mid. §
92 τὴν κατὰ τοῦ διαιτητοῦ γνῶσιν,
ἣν ἀπρόσκλητον κατεσκεύασεν, αὐτὸς κυρίαν ἑαυτῷ πεποίηται.

ἐξ ἐμφανῶν καταστάσεως κ.τ.λ.]
'a fine upon a writ of exhibit,'
lit. 'arising out of an ἐμφανῶν
κατάστασις, i. e. a case of formal
production of property in court.'
Isaeus, Or. 6 § 31, ἀπῄτει τὸν
Πυθόδωρον τὸ γραμματεῖον καὶ
προσεκαλέσατο εἰς ἐμφανῶν κα-
τάστασιν. καταστάντος δὲ ἐκείνου
πρὸς τὸν ἄρχοντα, ἔλεγεν ὅτι βούλοιτ' ἀνελέσθαι τὴν διαθήκην.

Dem. Or. 56 § 3 τὸ ἐνέχυρον κα-
θίστησιν εἰς τὸ ἐμφανές.   ib. § 38,
ἐὰν μὴ παρασχῇς τὰ ὑποκείμενα
ἐμφανῆ.   Or. 52 § 10 μάρτυρας
ἔχων ἠξίουν ἐμφανῆ καταστῆσαι τὰ
χρήματα.   Cf. the Roman exhibitio (Ulpian, Digest, 29, 3, 2,
exhibitio tabularum testamenti);
and actio ad exhibendum (Ulpian, Digest, 43, 29, 1, exhi-
bere est in publicum producere).
Hence comes our common legal
term, an exhibit or writ of production.   With ἐμφανῆ καταστῆσαι, we may further compare
our ordinary phrase sub paena
duces tecum, used when a soli-
citor (for instance) holds a document which the court can require to be put in, for the fur-
therance of the ends of justice.
Cf. Meier and Schömann, p. 374.

ἐπιβολήν]   Harpocr. ἐπιβολή·
ἡ ζημία.   Lysias, Or. 20 § 14
ἠνάγκαζον, ἐπιβολὰς ἐπιβάλλοντες
καὶ ζημιοῦντες, and ib. Or. 30 § 3.
ἐπιβολὴν is a certain correction
for ἐπιβουλὴν, a mistake possibly due to τὴν ἐπιβουλὴν in the
middle of the next section.
Another instance of the same
confusion may be noticed in
Isocr. Paneg. § 148 διαμαρτὼν
τῆς ἐπιβουλῆς where the best ms
wrongly has ἐπιβολῆς.

διὰ Λυκίδου...ποιησάμενος τὴν
δίκην]   'having got the case
brought on by means of Lycidas', who as the tool of Nicostratus was either a merely nominal prosecutor or possibly a
venal arbitrator.   For this use

ἀδελφὸν τὸν αὑτοῦ[v] Ἀρεθούσιον τοῦτον ἐπιγράφεται,
οὗπέρ ἐστι τἀνδράποδα ταῦτα, καὶ ἄλλον τινά· καὶ
παρεσκευάζοντο, εἰ ἀνακρινοίμην κατὰ τῶν οἰκείων
τῶν ἀδικούντων με τὰς δίκας ἃς εἰλήχειν αὐτοῖς, ἐνδεικνύναι με[w] καὶ ἐμβάλλειν εἰς τὸ δεσμωτήριον. ἔτι 15
δὲ πρὸς τούτοις ὁ Ἀρεθούσιος[x] ἀπρόσκλητόν μου ἑξακοσίων[y] καὶ[y] δέκα δραχμῶν δίκην καταδικασάμενος ὡς
ὀφείλοντος[z] τῷ δημοσίῳ[a], κλητῆρας ἐπιγραψάμενος καὶ

[v] Bekker *cum* A[1]r.   +τὸν Z *cum* FΣΦ.

[w] ἐνδεικνύναι με [ὡς ὀφείλοντα τῷ δημοσίῳ] Z (Sauppe).   ἐνδεικνύναι με Bekker. 'cf. § 15 l. 4. *fortasse verba* ὡς—δημοσίῳ *etiam*
hoc loco a grammatico addita sunt' Z.

[x] Bekker *cum libris*.   ὁ Ἀρεθούσιος *om.* Z (Sauppe).

[y] *om.* Bekker *cum libris*.   *addidit Ullrichius, quaest. Aristoph.*
i p. 40.   [ἑξακοσίων καὶ] δέκα Z.

[z] Reiske.   ὀφείλοντα *libri*.

[a] ὡς ὀφείλοντος τῷ δημοσίῳ *om.* Z (Sauppe), *seclusit Bekker st.*

of διὰ referring to a mere 'cat's-
paw' see note on Or. 45 § 31.

κλητῆρα ... ἐπιγράφεται] 'enters as witness to the citation.'
Mid. § 87 κλητῆρα οὐδ' ὁντινοῦν
ἐπιγραψάμενος, and Or. 54 § 31
ἐπιγράφεται μάρτυρας, i.e. 'en-
dorses on the deposition the
names of certain persons as
witnesses.'

ἀνακρινοίμην ... τὰς δίκας] 'in
the event of my bringing to a
preliminary hearing the suits
which I had instituted against
my relatives (Phormion, &c) who
were doing me wrong.' Harpocr.
ἀνάκρισίς ἐστιν ἐξέτασις ὑφ' ἑκασ-
της ἀρχῆς γινομένη πρὸ τῶν δικῶν
περὶ τῶν συντεινόντων εἰς τὸν
ἀγῶνα· ἐξετάζουσι δὲ καὶ εἰ ὅλως
εἰσάγειν χρή. Cf. Meier and
Schömann, p. 622.

ἐνδεικνύναι με] 'to lay an information (ἔνδειξις) against me'
for undertaking a prosecution,
while still a debtor to the trea-

sury. Or. 58 (Theocrin.) § 14
κελεύει (ὁ νόμος) κατά τε τῶν
ὀφειλόντων τῷ δημοσίῳ τὰς ἐν-
δείξεις τὸν βουλόμενον ποιεῖσθαι
τῶν πολιτῶν... By ἔνδειξις is
meant a criminal information
against a person acting when
under legal disability. It was
brought in writing before the
Archon and was a very summary process. Hermann, *Public
Antiquities*, § 137, 11. (Cf.
Or. 39 § 14 and Pollux there
quoted.)

15. ἀπρόσκλητος δίκη] Hesychius, ἡ μὴ τυχοῦσα τῶν κα-
λουμένων κλητόρων κατὰ τὸν νό-
μον· καὶ διὰ τοῦτο οὐκ ἦν εἰσαγώγιμος.

κλητῆρας ἐπιγραψάμενος] i. e.
'having endorsed it with the
names of witnesses to a citation.' As the δίκη was ἀπρόσκλητος, i.e. as there were no
κλητῆρες, this endorsement was
virtually a forgery.

εἰσελθὼν εἰς τὴν οἰκίαν βίᾳ τὰ σκεύη πάντα ἐξεφό-
ρησε, πλέον ἢ εἴκοσι μνῶν ἄξια, καὶ οὐδ' ὁτιοῦν κατέλιπεν. ὅτε δὲ τιμωρεῖσθαι ᾤμην δεῖν καὶ[b] ἐκτίσας[b] τῷ
δημοσίῳ τὸ ὄφλημα, ἐπειδὴ ἐπυθόμην τὴν ἐπιβουλὴν,
ἐβάδιζον[b] ἐπὶ τὸν κλητῆρα τὸν ὁμολογοῦντα κεκλητευκέναι τὸν Ἀρεθούσιον[c] τῆς ψευδοκλητείας κατὰ τὸν

[b] Σ. ἐκτίσας...καὶ ἐβάδιξον Bekker.
[c] Bekker. κεκλητευκέναι, τόνδ' Ἀρεθούσιον, Z cum ΣΦ.

τὰ σκεύη πάντα ἐξεφόρησε]
'carried out all my furniture'
(i.e. distrained upon me for
my alleged debt). Or. 22 (Androt.) § 57, βαδίζειν ἐπ' οἰκίας
καὶ σκεύη φέρειν μηδὲν ὀφειλόντων
ἀνθρώπων. Arethusius seized
property worth more than 20
minae, although the 'debt'
amounted to little more than
six. (610 dr. = 6 m. 10 dr.)

§§ 15—18. *On my proceeding
against Arethusius for fraudulent citation, he came into my
property at night and laid waste
my orchard with all its fine
fruit-grafts, its vines and its
olive-trees. Further they put up
a boy of free birth to go in broad
daylight and pluck the flowers
of my rose-bed, hoping I would
mistake him for a slave and strike
him, and thus make myself liable to an indictment for assault.
In this they were disappoint-
ed. Thereupon, as soon as I had
brought to the preliminary stage
before the magistrate my indictment of Arethusius for fraudulent citation, and was on the
point of taking it before the jury,
he lay in wait for me when I was
coming up from the Peiraeus late
at night and violently assaulted
me, and was only prevented from
dashing me into the quarries by
some people hearing my cries and
rushing to the rescue.*

*Not many days after, I
brought my case before the jury
and with the greatest ease got
Arethusius convicted. Though
the jury proposed to condemn
him to death, I begged them to
acquiesce in the penalty proposed by my opponents themselves, a fine of one talent.*

ὅτε δὲ—ἐβάδιζον] lit. 'When
I thought it my duty to avenge
myself, and on hearing of the
plot, was proceeding, after payment of the debt, to take mea-
sures against Arethusius, &c.' In
translating the whole sentence
it is convenient to omit ὅτε, to
render ᾤμην and ἐβάδιζον as principal verbs, and to begin a new
English sentence with the first
words of the apodosis, ἐλθὼν
εἰς τὸ χωρίον κ.τ.λ.

τὸν Ἀρεθούσιον] to be taken
in apposition with τὸν κλητῆρα,
unless indeed the words are
only an interpolated explanation of τὸν κλητῆρα (cf. § 10).

τῆς ψευδοκλητείας] Harpocr.
ψευδοκλητεία ὄνομα δίκης ἐστιν,
ἣν εἰσίασιν ἐγγεγραμμένοι ὀφείλειν τῷ δημοσίῳ, ἐπειδὰν αἰτιῶν-
ται τινας ψευδῶς κατεσκευάσθαι
κλητῆρας καθ' ἑαυτῶν πρὸς τὴν
δίκην ἀφ' ἧς ὦφλον. Meier and
Schömann, p. 319.
The genitive is here used
after βαδίζειν ἐπί τινα on the
analogy of the construction

*νόμον, ἐλθὼν εἰς τὸ χωρίον τῆς νυκτός, ὅσα ἐνῆν φυτὰ
ἀκροδρύων γενναῖα ἐμβεβλημένα, καὶ τὰς ἀναδενδρά-*

commonly found after διώκειν,
εἰσάγειν and ἐπεξέρχεσθαι (in
the legal sense). Plato, Leg.
886 B, ἐπεξίτω φόνου τῷ κτείναντι.
Or. 49 (Apollodorus v. Timotheus) § 56 μὴ...ἐπὶ τόνδε κακοτεχνιῶν ἔλθοιμι. The phrase βαδίζειν ἐπί τινα is found in a similar
sense in Or. 52 (Apollod. v.
Callippus) § 32 ἐπὶ τὸν Κηφισιάδην βαδίζειν. Cf. 56 §§ 15, 18,
and 42 § 12 εἰς τὸ δικαστήριον
βαδίζειν.

ὅσα ἐνῆν φυτὰ—διαθεῖεν] 'he
cut off all the choice fruit-grafts
that were there, and the trained
vines besides ; he also broke
down the nursery-beds of olive-
trees set in rows around my
plantations, making worse havoc
than would ever be made, even
by enemies in war.'

ἀκροδρύων] The primary sense
of the word is 'fruit,' the secondary 'fruit-trees.' Though used
in early writers of any edible
fruit, later authorities restrict
it to the hard-shelled varieties
alone. Cramer's *Anecdota Ox-
oniensia* III 357 Ὀρφεὺς ἀκρόδρυα
πᾶσαν ὀπώραν καλεῖ· Γάληνος δὲ
καὶ οἱ τὰ φυτουργικὰ συνταξάμενοι
ἀκρόδρυά φασι τὰ σκέπην ἔχοντα,
οἷον ῥοίας, κάρυα, ἀμυγδάλας καὶ
εἴ τι ὅμοιον (pomegranates, nuts,
almonds and the like), ὀπώρας
δὲ τὰ ἀσκεπῆ ὡς μῆλα, ἀπίους καὶ
τὰ ὅμοια (apples, pears, &c).
Similarly Democritus, Geoponica x 74, ἀκρόδρυα καλεῖται ὅσα
ἔξωθεν κέλυφος ἔχει. In Xenophon, Oeconom. 19 § 12 we
have τἄλλα ἀκρόδρυα πάντα after
mention of vines and fig-trees,
and in Plato, Critias, 115 B, τὸν
ἥμερον καρπόν, τόν τε ξηρὸν (different kinds of grain)...καὶ τὸν
ὅσος ξύλινος (fruits of hard rind).

παιδιᾶς τε ὃς ἕνεκα ἡδονῆς τε γέγονε δυσθησαύριστος ἀκροδρύων
καρπός, ὅσα τε παραμύθια πλησ-
μονῆς μεταδόρπια ἀγαπητὰ κάμ-
νοντι τίθεμεν. Aristot. Hist. An.
VIII 28, 4 οὔτ' ἀκρόδρυα οὔτ'
ὀπώρα χρόνιος. Athenaeus, II
§ 38 p. 52, οἱ Ἀττικοὶ καὶ ἄλλοι
συγγραφεῖς κοινῶς πάντα τὰ ἀκρόδρυα χάρυα λέγουσιν, ib. III § 20
p. 81, Γλαυκίδης δέ φησιν ἄριστα
τῶν ἀκροδρύων εἶναι μῆλα κυδώνια
(quinces), φαύλια, στρουθία (two
other kinds of quince).

The etymological formation
of the word, referring as it does
originally to what we may call
the 'tree-tips,' or the fresh
growth at the furthest extremi-
ties of the branches, may be
illustrated by the passage in Hesiod's *Works and Days* 231, οὔ-
ρεσι δὲ δρῦς ἄκρη μέν τε φέρει
βαλάνους, μέσση δὲ μελίσσας, and
Theocritus, XV 112, πὰρ δέ οἱ
ὥρια κεῖται, ὅσα δρυὸς ἄκρα φέ-
ροντι.

[It seems to me that ἀκρόδρυα
meant trees which produced
fruit chiefly on the upper boughs,
as distinguished from vines,
from which the grapes hang in
clusters nearer to the ground.
The edible acorn, βάλανος, may
have been specially so described,
if we limit δρῦς to the sense of
'oak-tree.' P.]

γενναῖα] 'of a choice kind,'
'of a good stock.' Plato, Leg.
844 E, τὴν γενναίαν νῦν λεγομένην
σταφυλὴν ἢ τὰ γενναῖα σῦκα ἐπ-
ονομαζόμενα ὀπωρίζειν. (Cf. nobilis in Martial III 47, 7 *frutice
nobili caules* and as an epithet
of *uva* ib. IV 44, 2 and *olivae*
v 78, 19.) Athenaeus, XIV § 68
p. 653, γενναῖα λέγει ὁ φιλό-
σοφος (sc. Plato u. s.), ὡς καὶ

δας ἐξέκοψε, καὶ φυτευτήρια ἐλαῶν[d] περιστοίχων κατ-
έκλασεν, οὕτω δεινῶς ὡς οὐδ' ἂν οἱ πολέμιοι διαθεῖεν.
16 πρὸς δὲ τούτοις μεθ' ἡμέραν παιδάριον ἀστὸν εἰσπέμ-

[d] Bekker cum ΓΑ¹.   ἐλαιῶν Z cum FΣΦ.

'Αρχίλοχος· πάρελθε, γενναῖος γὰρ εἷς. ἢ τὰ ἐπιγεγεννημένα, οἷον τὰ ἐπεμβεβλημένα· ὁ γὰρ 'Αριστοτέλης καὶ ἐπεμβολάδας ἀπίους ὀνομάζει τὰς ἐγκεκεντρισμένας. (The second explanation is clearly wrong. I only cite it to illustrate the next note.)

ἐμβεβλημένα] 'grafted.' Harpocration s. v. ἀντὶ τοῦ ἐγκεκεντρισμένα Δημοσθένης ἐν τῷ πρὸς Νικόστρατον, καὶ 'Αριστοτέλης δ' ἐμβολάδας ἀπίους λέγει τὰς τοιαύτας.

ἀναδενδράδας] 'trained vines' growing on trees, 'tree-vines.' The climbing vine is contrasted with the ground-vine of Lesbos in the *Pastor* of Longus, II 1 πᾶσα κατὰ τὴν Λέσβον ἄμπελος ταπεινὴ, οὐ μετέωρος οὐδὲ ἀναδενδρὰς, ἀλλὰ κάτω τὰ κλήματα ἀποτείνουσα καὶ ὥσπερ κιττὸς νεμομένη. Cf. Polyb. xxxiv 11 § 1, ἀναδενδρίτης οἶνος and Geoponica v 61, ἀναδενδρῖτις, also Strabo v p. 231, τὸ δὲ Καίκουβον (*Caecubum*) ἑλῶδες ὂν εὐοινοτάτην ἄμπελον τρέφει τὴν δενδρῖτιν. Columella iv 1, 8, *vitis arbustiva*, and Pliny N. H. xvii 23 § 199 sqq. *nobilia vina non nisi in arbustis gigni.* The best trees for the purpose were, according to Pliny, the elm (*amicta vitibus ulmo* of Hor. Ep. i 16, 3) and the poplar; next to these the ash, the fig-tree and the olive. (See further St John's *Manners and Customs of Ancient Greece*, ii 344—8.)

φυτευτήρια] nursery-beds of young olive-trees.

ἐλαῶν περιστοίχων] i.e. 'olives planted round the beds of the garden.' Harpocr. περίστοιχοι· Δημοσθένης ἐν τῷ πρὸς Νικόστρατον περὶ τῶν 'Αρεθουσίου ἀνδραπόδων. Δίδυμος δέ τι γένος ἐλαιῶν περιστοίχους καλεῖ ἃς Φιλόχορος στοιχάδας προσηγόρευσε. μήποτε (' perhaps ') δὲ περιστοίχους κέκληκεν ὁ ῥήτωρ τὰς κύκλῳ περὶ τὸ χωρίον ἐν στοίχῳ πεφυκυίας (cf. Ar. Ach. 997, περὶ τὸ χωρίον ἅπαν ἐλᾴδας ἐν κύκλῳ). Pollux v 36, Σόλων δὲ καὶ στοιχάδας τινὰς ἐλάας ἐκάλεσε ταῖς μορίαις ἀντιτιθείς, ἴσως τὰς κατὰ στοῖχον πεφυτευμένας [Lucr. v 1373, *utque olearum caerula distinguens inter plaga currere posset.* P.] On the laws protecting the cultivation of the olive in Attica and providing for the preservation of the sacred olives (or μορίαι) and even of the hollow trunk of an olive tree, see the interesting speech of Lysias, Or. 7, περὶ τοῦ σηκοῦ, esp. § 2, ἀπεγράφην τὸ μὲν πρῶτον ἐλαίαν ἐκ τῆς γῆς ἀφανίζειν, καὶ πρὸς τοὺς ἐωνημένους τοὺς καρποὺς τῶν μοριῶν πυνθανόμενοι προσῇσαν ... νυνί με σηκόν φασιν ἀφανίζειν. See also Dem. Or. 43 (Macart.) §§ 69—71.

16. παιδάριον ἀστὸν] i.e. a little boy, who was free born. It was expected that Apollodorus would have mistaken the boy for a slave and either bound or beaten him, thereby rendering himself liable to an indictment for assault (ὕβρις).

Aeschines (Timarch. § 16) quotes a 'law of Solon': ἄν τις 'Αθηναίων ἐλεύθερον παῖδα ὑβρίσῃ,

ψαντες διὰ τὸ γείτονες εἶναι καὶ ὅμορον τὸ χωρίον,
ἐκέλευον τὴν ῥοδωνιὰν βλαστάνουσαν ἐκτίλλειν, ἵν᾽, εἰ

γραφέσθω ὁ κύριος τοῦ παιδὸς πρὸς τοὺς θεσμοθέτας...ἔνοχοι δὲ ἔστωσαν ταῖσδε ταῖς αἰτίας καὶ οἱ εἰς τὰ οἰκετικὰ σώματα ἐξαμαρτάνοντες, and similarly Dem. Mid. §§ 47—48. According to these two passages, it was permissible to institute a γραφὴ ὕβρεως even for outrage done to a slave, and though the text appears at first sight to imply that in such a case an indictment could not be brought, yet all that is necessarily meant is that if the lad maltreated were free born, the indictment (however unjustifiable in the present instance) would have been easier to bring forward than in the case of a slave. (Becker's *Charicles* III p. 31—32 = p. 367 of English Abridgement. Hermann, *Privatalt.* § 60.)

ἐκέλευον—ἐκτίλλειν] 'prompted him to pluck off the flowers of my rose-bed.' ἐκέλευον, 'put him up to...,' 'persuaded him.' [ἐκτίλλειν is perhaps ' to pick off the young shoots as they were growing.' P.].

The rhetorician Hermogenes quotes the phrase τὴν ῥοδωνιὰν ἐκτίλλειν as an instance of ἀφέλεια (Spengel, *Rhetores Graeci* II 353). Harpocration has the following article, ῥοδωνιά· Δημοσθένης ἐν τῷ περὶ τῶν Ἀρεθουσίου ἀνδραπόδων. ῥοδωνιά ἐστιν ἡ τῶν ῥόδων φυτεία ὥσπερ ἰωνιὰ ἡ τῶν ἴων, ὡς Ἑκαταῖος ἐν αʹ περιηγήσεως δηλοῖ. Similarly Pollux I 229, who gives ἰωνιὰ as the only parallel he can remember to the formation of the word ῥοδωνιά (cf. *rosaria, violaria*).

To a modern reader, the mention of a rose-bed is immediately suggestive of a pleasure garden; but whether we look to the character of its owner who seems to have been a dry man of business and little more, or to the context with its fruit-trees, its vines and its olives, we are driven to the conclusion that his roses were mere articles of trade, grown to be sold in town for crowns and garlands. Just so, among the blessings of Peace, in the *Pax* of Aristophanes, 577, we find 'the violet-bed beside the well' mentioned in the very same breath as ' cakes and figs and myrtle - berries, sweet new wine and olive-trees.'

In Or. 50 § 61, Apollodorus says of his garden, τὸ ὕδωρ...ἐκ τῶν φρεάτων ἀπέλιπεν, ὥστε μηδὲ λάχανον γενέσθαι ἐν τῷ κήπῳ. The Greek appreciation of the rose seems to have been mainly utilitarian. Thus it is under the head of στεφανώματα that Theophrastus dilates on the many beauties of the rose and on its numerous varieties (πλήθει τε φύλλων καὶ ὀλιγότητι καὶ τραχύτητι καὶ λειότητι καὶ χροιᾷ καὶ εὐοσμίᾳ, *Hist. Plant.* VI 6). To the Greek, says Ruskin, ' a rose was good for scent, and a stream for sound and coolness; for the rest one was no more than leaves, the other no more than water ' (*Modern Painters* III 4 13 § 13). ' A Greek despises flowers,' says Mr Bent, unless ' they are sweet-smelling or useful for something ' (*Cyclades*, p. 276). It is indeed a noteworthy fact, attributable partly to the insignificance of the Attic flora, and still more to the defective development of Greek taste in this particular, that in what is known as the

καταλαβὼν αὐτὸν ἐγὼ δήσαιμι ἢ πατάξαιμι ὡς δοῦλον
ὄντα, γραφήν με γράψαιντο ὕβρεως. ὡς δὲ τούτου 1252
διήμαρτον, κἀγὼ μάρτυρας μὲν ὧν ἔπασχον ἐποιούμην,
αὐτὸς δ' οὐδὲν ἐξημάρτανον εἰς αὐτούς, ἐνταῦθα ἤδη
17 μοι ἐπιβουλεύουσι τὴν μεγίστην ἐπιβουλήν· ἀνακεκρι-
μένου γὰρ ἤδη μου κατ' αὐτοῦ τὴν τῆς ψευδοκλητείας
γραφὴν καὶ μέλλοντος εἰσιέναι εἰς τὸ δικαστήριον,
τηρήσας με ἀνιόντα ἐκ Πειραιῶς ὀψὲ περὶ τὰς λιθοτομίας παίει τε πὺξ καὶ ἁρπάζει μέσον, κἂν ἐώθει° με εἰς

° ἁρπάζει με (sic Σ) μέσον καὶ ὠθεῖ Ζ. 'Malim ἐώθει' Bekker.
κἂν pro καὶ G. H. Schaefer.

best period of Greek literature
there is scarcely a single instance of a refined appreciation
of the attractions of a flower-
garden. One of the rare exceptions is the mention of κήπους
εὐώδεις in Ar. Aves 1067. The
passage in Eur. El. 777, κυρεῖ δὲ
κήποις ἐν καταρρίτοις βεβώς, δρέ-
πων τερείνης μυρσίνης κάρᾳ πλό-
κους, is hardly an exception, as
the epithet 'well-watered' is
somewhat prosy, and the context shows that the only reason
why Aegisthus is in his garden
is for the purely practical object
of making himself a myrtle-
wreath for his sacrifice to the
mountain-nymphs. (Cf. Becker's *Charicles* p. 203—4, esp. i
p. 349 sqq., of the 2nd German
ed. with the excellent addenda
of K. F. Hermann; also the
latter's *Privatalt.* § 15 note 20
p. 106 ed. Blümner; St John's
*Manners and Customs of Ancient
Greece*, i 301—334, esp. p. 304,
305: Büchsenschütz, *Besitz u.
Erwerb* p. 72, and Schleiden,
die Rose.)

17. ἀνακεκριμένου] passive form
in middle sense (§ 14 ἀνακρινοίμην τὰς δίκας): 'when I had
brought to the preliminary ex-

amination my indictment for
false citation, &c.'

τηρήσας—ἐβοήθησαν] The attack reminds us partly of the
murder mentioned by Cicero,
pro Cluentio § 37, *in arenarias
quasdam extra portam Esquili-
nam perductus occiditur.*

The quarries referred to in
the text were possibly near the
Museum hill where the Long
Walls leading to the Peiraeus
strike the wall enclosing Athens
itself, or still more probably
at a point immediately outside
the ἄστυ, south of the Peiraic
gate of Athens. In the excellent *Atlas von Athen* by Dr E.
Curtius, the third map indicates
'recent quarries' at this point,
just north of the ancient βά-
ραθρον. In Murray's *Greece*,
1884, i 341, the incident described in the text is oddly supposed to have happened to Demosthenes.

πύξ] Or. 47 § 38 παίει πὺξ
τὸ στόμα.

κἂν ἐώθει] The MSS have καὶ
ὤθει, 'struck me with his fist
and gripped me round the waist
and was pushing me into the
quarries, had not some people,
hearing my cries, come up and

τὰς λιθοτομίας, εἰ μή τινες προσιόντες, βοῶντός μου
ἀκούσαντες, παρεγένοντο καὶ ἐβοήθησαν. ἡμέραις δ᾽
οὐ πολλαῖς ὕστερον εἰσελθὼν εἰς τὸ δικαστήριον πρὸς
ἡμέραν διαμεμετρημένην, καὶ ἐξελέγξας αὐτὸν τὰ
ψευδῆ κεκλητευκότα καὶ τὰ ἄλλα ὅσα εἴρηκα ἠδικηκότα, εἷλον. καὶ ἐν τῇ τιμήσει βουλομένων τῶν δικα-   18
στῶν θανάτου τιμῆσαι αὐτῷ, ἐδεήθην᾽ ἐγὼ τῶν δικα-

᾽ ἐδεήθην Bekker cum A¹r.   + μὲν Z cum BF et editione Aldina
(ἐδεήθημεν ΣΦ).

rescued me.' This is more graphic than the sense given by Schaefer's emendation κἂν ὤθει.

εἰσελθών...πρὸς ἡμέραν διαμεμετρημένην] 'having entered into court upon a day divided out among several causes, i.e. the day on which I came into court was allotted to several law-suits, and the number of motions was so great that the time at my disposal was therefore very limited. Apollodorus wishes to indicate the ease with which after a necessarily short speech he had got a conviction against Arethusius. Cf. Aeschines, Fals. Leg. § 126, ἐνδέχεται δὲ τὸ λοιπὸν μέρος τῆς ἡμέρας ταῦτα πρᾶξαι (i.e. βασανίσαι)· πρὸς ἔνδεκα γὰρ ἀμφορέας ἐν διαμεμετρημένῃ τῇ ἡμέρᾳ κρίνομαι. Dem. Fals. Leg. § 120, ὃς γὰρ ἀγῶνας καινοὺς ὥσπερ δράματα, καὶ τούτους ἀμαρτύρους πρὸς διαμεμετρημένην τὴν ἡμέραν αἱρεῖς διώκων, δῆλον ὅτι πάνδεινος εἶ τις. Harpocr. s. v. μέρος τι ὕδατός ἐστι πρὸς μεμετρημένον ἡμέρας μέρος ῥέον· διεμετρεῖτο δὲ τῷ Ποσειδεῶνι...i.e. the standard length of time for calculating the measurement of the *Clepsydra* was taken from a day near the end of our December. The length of the twelfth part of the day would

vary with the time of the year, and the running out of the water would indicate the lapse of a particular portion of the whole day. Thus the water-clock might indicate a time equivalent to (say) the fourth part of the shortest day (Dec. 21) and this length of time might be taken as a unit of the measurement during the rest of the year (Heslop's note on Fals. Leg. *l.c.*; see however Meier and Schömann p. 716).

τὰ ψευδῆ κεκλητευκότα] § 15.

18. ἐν τῇ τιμήσει] In an ἀγὼν τιμητὸς, the declaration of the *first* verdict, that of condemnation, was followed by the τίμησις or fixing of the penalty, with the ἀντίτιμησις, in which latter the defendant on *his* part submitted to the court an alleviation of the penalty claimed by the plaintiff. (Plato Apol. p. 36 A.)

τιμῆσαι......ἐτιμῶντο] The active is used of the court, the middle of the parties to the suit (αὐτοί sc. the defendant Arethusius and his friends). Plato Apol. p. 38 A εἰ μὲν γὰρ ἦν χρήματα, says Socrates, ἐτιμησάμην ἂν χρημάτων ὅσα ἔμελλον ἐκτίσειν· νῦν δὲ οὐ γὰρ ἔστιν, εἰ μὴ ἄρα ὅσον ἂν ἐγὼ δυναίμην ἐκτῖσαι τοσούτου βούλεσθέ μοι τιμῆσαι (of the Jury).

στῶν μηδὲν δι' ἐμοῦ τοιοῦτον πρᾶξαι, ἀλλὰ συγχωρῆσαι ὅσουπερ αὐτοὶ ἐτιμῶντο, ταλάντου, οὐχ ἵνα μὴ
ἀποθάνῃ ὁ 'Αρεθούσιος (ἄξια γὰρ αὐτῷ θανάτου εἴργαστο εἰς ἐμέ), ἀλλ' ἵν' ἐγὼ Πασίωνος ὢν καὶ κατὰ
ψήφισμα πολίτης μηδένα 'Αθηναίων ἀπεκτονὼς εἴην.
ὡς δ' ἀληθῆ εἴρηκα πρὸς ὑμᾶς, τούτων ὑμῖν μάρτυρας
πάντων παρέξομαι.

ΜΑΡΤΥΡΕΣ.

19   ῍Α μὲν τοίνυν ἀδικούμενος, ὦ ἄνδρες δικασταὶ, ὑπ'
αὐτῶν τὴν ἀπογραφὴν ἐποιησάμην δεδήλωκα ὑμῖν· ὡς
δ' ἔστιν 'Αρεθουσίου τἀνδράποδα ταῦτα καὶ ὄντα ἐν
τῇ οὐσίᾳ τῇ ἐκείνου ἀπέγραψα ἐπιδείξω ὑμῖν. τὸν μὲν
γὰρ Κέρδωνα ἐκ μικροῦ παιδαρίου ἐξεθρέψατο· καὶ ὡς

δι' ἐμοῦ] 'through my agency,'
'on a prosecution of mine.'
Reiske conjectures δι' ἐμὲ, 'on
my account,' which would also
make good sense, though dis-
approved by Dobree, who refers
in support of δι' ἐμοῦ to Or. 51
§ 17 ὥσπερ...χάριν τιθεμένων διὰ
τῶν τοιούτων τοῖς ἀμελοῦσιν ὑμῶν,
ἀλλ' οὐ διὰ τῶν βελτιόνων τοῖς
ὑπηρετοῦσιν ἃ δεῖ χαρίζεσθαι
προσῆκον.

Πασίωνος ὢν] i.e. the son of
one who, originally a banker's
slave, had received the citizenship by adoption. Neither the
father nor the son was a citizen
by birth, and it would have been
peculiarly invidious had the
latter compassed the death of
one who was by birth a citizen
of Athens.

§§ 19—21. *Having now re-
counted some of the wrongs done
me by Arethusius and his brother
Nicostratus, I will call evidence
in detail to prove that the two
slaves entered by me in the specification do not belong to Nicos-*

*tratus who is now attempting to
claim them, but are really part
of the property of Arethusius
and are thus liable to be confiscated to the state, as a partial payment of his debt to the treasury.*

§ 19. At this point the
speaker, after having shewn
the reasons which justified him
in regarding Arethusius as his
enemy and exacting vengeance
from him, reaches the real
point at issue, viz. the proof
that the slaves specified in the
schedule belong to Arethusius,
and not, as is alleged, to his
brother Nicostratus.

τὸν μὲν γὰρ Κέρδωνα] con-
trasted with τὸν δὲ Μάνην in
§ 20. Κέρδων is a slave-name
expressive of knavish cunning
(cf. ἡ κερδώ, 'the wily one,' i.e.
'the fox'). Digest xxxviii 1,
42 *Cerdonem servum meum ma-
numitti volo* (quoted by Mayor
on Juv. iv 153 *tollat sua mu-
nera Cerdo*).

ἐκ μικροῦ παιδαρίου] Plat.
Symp. 207 D ἐκ παιδαρίου, Or.

ἦν Ἀρεθουσίου, τούτων ὑμῖν τοὺς εἰδότας μάρτυρας
παρέξομαι.

ΜΑΡΤΥΡΕΣ.

1253   Παρ' οἶς τοίνυν εἰργάσατο πώποτε, ὡς τοὺς μι- 20
σθοὺς Ἀρεθούσιος ἐκομίζετο ὑπὲρ αὐτοῦ, καὶ δίκας
ἐλάμβανε καὶ ἐδίδου, ὁπότε κακόν τι ἐργάσαιτο, ὡς
δεσπότης ὤν, τούτων ὑμῖν τοὺς εἰδότας μάρτυρας
παρέξομαι.

ΜΑΡΤΥΡΕΣ.

Τὸν δὲ Μάνην, δανείσας ἀργύριον Ἀρχεπόλιδι τῷ

59 (Apoll. κατὰ Νεαίρας) § 18, ταύτας παιδίσκας ἐκ μικρῶν παιδίων ἐκτήσατο, and similarly the far more frequent phrases ἐκ παιδός (Or. 27 § 4), ἐκ νέου, ἐκ μειρακίου.

20. παρ' οἶς τοίνυν—δεσπότης ὤν] sc. ὡς Ἀρεθούσιος ἐκομίζετο τοὺς μισθοὺς παρ' ἐκείνων παρ' οἶς εἰργάσατο πώποτε ὁ Κέρδων κ.τ.λ. 'I shall shew also that Arethusius got the wages on his account from all the persons with whom he ever worked ; and that he used to receive compensation or to pay it when Cerdon did any mischief, as a master would be bound to do.' Kennedy.—[πώποτε in the earlier Attic is never used without the negative, but often in Plato and Demosthenes. P.]

Slaves were sometimes let out by their owners either for work in the mines or for any kind of labour; or again (as here) to work as hired servants for wages (ἀποφορά) which went to their masters. Aeschin. Timarch. § 97 οἰκέτας δημιουργοὺς τῆς σκυτοτομικῆς τέχνης ἐννέα ἢ δέκα ὧν ἕκαστος τούτῳ δυ' ὀβο-λοὺς ἀποφορὰν ἔφερε τῆς ἡμέρας. Isaeus Or. 8 (Ciron) § 35 ἀνδρά-ποδα μισθοφοροῦντα (Hermann, Privatalt. § 13, 10 and § 49 ad fin. pp. 91, 463 ed. Blümner).

δίκας ἐλάμβανε] A slave was incapacitated from conducting a law-suit either on his own account or on behalf of another. Plato Gorg. 483 B, ἀνδραπόδου, ὅστις ἀδικούμενος καὶ προπηλακι-ζόμενος μὴ οἶός τ' ἐστὶν αὐτὸς αὑτῷ βοηθεῖν μηδ' ἄλλῳ οὗ ἂν κήδηται. Or. 37 (Pant.) § 51 ἔδει...λαχόντα ἐκείνῳ (sc. τῷ δού-λῳ) τὴν δίκην τὸν κύριον διώκειν ἐμέ. (Hermann, Privatalt. § 59, 1 = Rechtsalt. p. 19 Thalheim.)

δίκας...ἐδίδου, ὁπότε κακόν τι ἐργάσαιτο] The law by which the master had to make good any damage done by his slave is quoted as a law of Solon by Lysias, Or. 10 (Theomnest. A) § 19, οἰκῆος καὶ δούλης τὴν βλάβην ὀφείλειν.—The clause containing ἐργάσαιτο refers of course to δίκας ἐδίδου alone; otherwise we should have had some such phrase as ὁπότε κακόν τι πάθοι ἢ ἐργάσαιτο.

τὸν δὲ Μάνην] governed by ἐναπετίμησεν but placed early

Πειραιεῖ, ἐπειδὴ οὐχ οἷός τ᾽ ἦν αὐτῷ ἀποδοῦναι ὁ
Ἀρχέπολις οὔτε τὸν τόκον οὔτε τὸ ἀρχαῖον ἅπαν, ἐναπετίμησεν αὐτῷ[g]. καὶ ὅτι ἀληθῆ λέγω, τούτων ὑμῖν
τοὺς μάρτυρας παρέξομαι.

ΜΑΡΤΥΡΕΣ.

21   Ἔτι τοίνυν καὶ ἐκ τῶνδε γνώσεσθε, ὦ ἄνδρες δικασταὶ, ὅτι εἰσὶν Ἀρεθουσίου οἱ ἄνθρωποι· ὁπότε γὰρ
οἱ ἄνθρωποι οὗτοι ἢ ὀπώραν πρίαιντο ἢ θέρος μισθοῖν-

[g] οὔτε τὸ ἀρχαῖον, ἅπαν ἐναπετίμησεν αὐτῷ Reiske, G. H. Schaefer, Z, Dind. (Oxon. 1846), et Bekker st.

for emphatic contrast with τὸν
μὲν Κέρδωνα in § 19. It may
almost be regarded as an accusative absolute.

Μάνης was one of the commonest slave-names. Theophrastus
in his will, which is preserved
by Diogenes Laertius, v 55,
mentions among his slaves Cal-
lias and Manes, and the latter
name occurs in Ar. Ran. 965,
Lys. 908, 1213, and Pax 1146,
while in the Aves, 523, it is
used in the plural as a synonym
for 'slaves,' νῦν δ᾽ ἀνδράποδ᾽ ἠλι-
θίους Μανᾶς. See further on Or.
45 § 86.

ἐναπετίμησεν]   Archepolis
handed over Manes to Are-
thusius as an equivalent for
part of the debt due to the
latter. The nominative to this
verb is not Arethusius, the subject of the participle δανείσας,
but Archepolis, the subject of
the subordinate clause ἐπειδὴ
οὐχ οἷός τ᾽ ἦν. It will further
be noticed that, while the verb
ἀποτιμάω is generally used in
the active of *borrowing* and in
the middle of *lending* money on
security, the compound ἐναπο-
τιμάω is in the present passage
applied to the debtor's transfer-

ence of a part of his property
on valuation in lieu of direct
payment of his debt. The same
compound occurs in the passive
form in Dio Cassius XII 37 τὰ
ἐνέχυρα πρὸς τὴν ἀξίαν ἐναποτι-
μηθῆναι ἐκέλευσε (i.e. Caesar
ordained that the securities on
which money had been borrowed should be valued and transferred to the creditors in place
of a money payment).

The editors who place a
comma after τὸ ἀρχαῖον, construe ἅπαν with ἐναπετίμησεν αὐτῷ, 'handed him over in full
payment,' 'paid off the whole
sum in the person of Manes.'

21. ὀπώραν πρίαιντο κ.τ.λ] de
Cor. § 51 τοὺς θεριστὰς ἢ τοὺς
ἄλλο τι μισθοῦ πράττοντας and
ib. § 262 σῦκα καὶ βότρυς καὶ
ἐλάας συλλέγων ὥσπερ ὀπωρώ-
νης ἐκ τῶν ἀλλοτρίων χωρίων.
'Whenever they bought up the
produce of an orchard or hired
themselves out to reap a har-
vest, it was Arethusius who
made the bargain on their behalf for the purchase or for the
wages respectively.' μισθούμενος refers back to θέρος μισθοῖντο
ἐκθερίσαι, just as ὠνούμενος corresponds to πρίαιντο. The latter

το ἐκθερίσαι ἢ ἄλλο τι τῶν περὶ γεωργίαν ἔργων ἀναιροῖντο, Ἀρεθούσιος ἦν ὁ ὠνούμενος καὶ μισθούμενος ὑπὲρ αὐτῶν. ὡς δ᾽ ἀληθῆ λέγω, καὶ τούτων ὑμῖν τοὺς μάρτυρας παρέξομαι.

ΜΑΡΤΥΡΕΣ.

Ὅσας μὲν τοίνυν μαρτυρίας παρασχέσθαι εἶχον 22 ὑμῖν, ὡς ἔστιν Ἀρεθουσίου τἀνδράποδα, δεδήλωκα ὑμῖν. βούλομαι δὲ καὶ περὶ τῆς προκλήσεως εἰπεῖν, ἣν οὗτοί με προὐκαλέσαντο καὶ ἐγὼ τούτους. οὗτοι μὲν γάρ με προὐκαλέσαντο, ὅτε ἡ πρώτη ἀνάκρισις ἦν, φάσκοντες ἕτοιμοι εἶναι παραδιδόναι ἐμοὶ αὐτῷ τἀνδράποδα

verb having no present participle of its own, ὠνούμενος commonly takes its place and is so used in the present passage. Cf. note on § 10, where πρίασθαι is followed by ὠνεῖσθαι.

§§ 22—25. *I now propose to deal with the Challenge which my opponents proposed to me, and also with that which I myself proposed to them.*

At the preliminary hearing of my case against Arethusius, they put in a Challenge, and offered therein to deliver up the slaves, to be tortured by myself, their object being to claim the Challenge as a piece of evidence in their own favour in the event of my refusing to accept it.

I replied to the Challenge by stating in the presence of witnesses, that since this was not a private but a public cause and since the slaves, as I contended, were the property of the state, it was not for myself to torture them, as I was only a private person. On the contrary, it was a question for the board of police or for certain persons chosen by the Council of the state. *On these conditions I was willing to accept their Challenge, and I challenged them to accept my own proposal. They declined my offer.*

22. προκλήσεως] On the subject of Challenges, see Or. 45 § 15.

ἣν ... με προὐκαλέσαντο] For the double acc. cf. Or. 56 § 17 προκαλεῖσθαί τινα πρόκλησιν.

ἡ πρώτη ἀνάκρισις] 'the first preliminary investigation,' see note on ἀνακρινοίμην § 14 *supra*.

παραδιδόναι ... τἀνδράποδα βασανίσαι] The principle of extracting evidence by the torture of slaves, was one of the weakest points in the judicial system of Athens (some interesting criticisms on it may be found in Forsyth's *Hortensius* p. 40, and in Mahaffy's *Social Life in Greece* p. 226—8).—ἐμοὶ αὐτῷ is emphatic, just as, six lines further, εἰ ἐμοὶ ἐξεδίδοσαν contrasted with δημοσίᾳ. The speaker holds that the slaves belong to the state and should have been handed over to the public official and not to a private individual like himself.

βασανίσαι, βουλόμενοι μαρτυρίαν τινὰ αὐτοῖς ταύτην
23 γενέσθαι. ἐγὼ δ' ἀπεκρινάμην αὐτοῖς ἐναντίον μαρτύρων ὅτι ἕτοιμός εἰμι ἰέναι εἰς τὴν βουλὴν μετ' αὐτῶν
καὶ παραλαμβάνειν μετ' ἐκείνης ἢ μετὰ τῶν ἔνδεκα, 1254
λέγων ὅτι, εἰ μὲν ἰδίαν δίκην ἐδικαζόμην αὐτοῖς, εἰ
ἐμοὶ ἐξεδίδοσαν, παρελάμβανον ἄν, νῦν δὲ τῆς πόλεως
εἴη τἀνδράποδα καὶ ἡ ἀπογραφή· δεῖν οὖν δημοσίᾳ
24 βασανίζεσθαι. ἡγούμην γὰρ οὐ προσήκειν ἐμοὶ ἰδιώτῃ
ὄντι τοὺς δημοσίους βασανίζειν· οὔτε γὰρ τῆς βασάνου
κύριος ἐγιγνόμην οὔτε καλῶς ἔχειν τὰ λεγόμενα ὑπὸ
τῶν ἀνθρώπων ἐμὲ κρίνειν.[h] ἡγούμην τε δεῖν τὴν
ἀρχὴν ἢ τοὺς ᾑρημένους ὑπὸ τῆς βουλῆς γράφεσθαι,

[h] κρίνειν, Z.

ταύτην] Not the evidence given by the slaves, but the mere offer to allow them to be tortured, 'wishing this (offer) to be a kind of evidence on their own side.' ταύτην is attracted into the same gender as μαρτυρίαν; τοῦτο would have made the same sense, but would have been less idiomatic.

23. εἰ... εἰ] Two or even three protases, not co-ordinate, may belong to one apodosis, e.g. Plat. Men. 74 B, εἴ τίς σε ἀνέροιτο τοῦτο, τί ἐστι σχῆμα; εἰ αὐτῷ εἶπες ὅτι στρογγυλότης, εἴ σοι εἶπεν ἅπερ ἐγώ, εἶπες δήπου ἂν ὅτι σχῆμά τι (Goodwin, *Moods and Tenses* § 55. 1).

The reiteration of εἰ in the present passage has been considered open to objection; it occurs however in Or. 54 § 15, in an undoubtedly genuine speech of Demosthenes (A. Schaefer, *Dem. u. s. Zeit* III 2, 188 and Lortzing, *Apoll.* 33).

δημοσίᾳ βασανίζεσθαι] 'to be questioned publicly,' i.e. 'to be tortured by a state-officer.'

24. οὔτε τῆς βασάνου κύριος ἐγιγνόμην] i.e. I did not acquire control of the 'question,'—authority over the examination.

οὔτε καλῶς ἔχειν] sc. ἡγούμην, 'it was unsuitable, I thought, for *myself* to decide as to the answers of the slaves.'

τὴν ἀρχήν] sc. τοὺς ἔνδεκα, as appears by comparing § 23, μετὰ (τῆς βουλῆς) ἢ μετὰ τῶν ἔνδεκα. Reiske wrongly renders : '*illum Archontem ad cuius tribunal haec causa pertineret, aut delectos a senatu.*' Frequently it is the context alone that decides whether ἡ ἀρχή or even οἱ ἄρχοντες refers to the Archons or to some other public functionaries. Thus in Or. 22 (Androt.) § 26, τοῖς ἄρχουσιν ἐφήγου refers to the Eleven, and in Lysias, Or. κατὰ τῶν σιτοπώλων §§ 5—10, οἱ ἄρχοντες is several times used of the five σιτοφύλακες in the Peiraeus. On τὴν ἀρχὴν for 'the authorities,' *abstract* for *concrete*, see note on Or. 45 § 58.

γράφεσθαι] 'to have the answers written down,' or 'to

καὶ κατασημηναμένους τὰς βασάνους, ὅ τι εἴποιεν[1]
οἱ ἄνθρωποι, παρέχειν εἰς τὸ δικαστήριον, ἵν᾽ ἀκούσαντες ἐκ τούτων ἐψηφίσασθε ὁποῖόν τι ὑμῖν ἐδόκει.
ἰδίᾳ μὲν γὰρ βασανιζομένων τῶν ἀνθρώπων ὑπ᾽ ἐμοῦ 25
ἀντελέγετ᾽ ἂν ἅπαντα ὑπὸ τούτων, εἰ δὲ δημοσίᾳ,
ἡμεῖς μὲν ἂν ἐσιωπῶμεν, οἱ δ᾽ ἄρχοντες ἢ οἱ ᾑρημένοι
ὑπὸ τῆς βουλῆς ἐβασάνιζον ἂν μέχρι οὗ αὐτοῖς ἐδόκει. ταῦτα δ᾽ ἐμοῦ ἐθέλοντος οὐκ ἂν ἔφασαν τῇ
ἀρχῇ παραδοῦναι, οὐδ᾽ εἰς τὴν βουλὴν ἤθελον ἀκο-
λουθεῖν. ὡς οὖν ἀληθῆ λέγω, κάλει μοι τοὺς τούτων
μάρτυρας.

[1] εἴπαιεν Z cum BF.   εἴποιεν Ar.   ειπεν Σ.

take down the answers.' Plato
Theaet. 143 A, ἐγραψάμην ὑπομνήματα, 'I wrote me down some
memoranda.' This sense of
the middle must not be confounded with the technical
meaning 'to indict.'

κατασημηναμένους] 'having
sealed up the testimony extorted.' The documents were
put into an ἐχῖνος or 'casket,'
which was sealed up and afterwards produced in court and
there opened. Or. 54 § 17 ση-
μανθῆναι τοὺς ἐχίνους.

βασάνους, as is proved by the
subsequent clause, 'whatever
the slaves said,' is here used,
not of the torture itself, but of
the extorted evidence. Harpocr. βάσανος· Ἀντιφῶν· λίθος
οὕτω καλεῖται, ᾗ τὸ χρυσίον παρα-
τριβόμενον δοκιμάζεται. Ὑπερεί-
δης δ᾽ ἐν τῷ κατ᾽ Ἀντίου τὰ ἐν
τοῖς βασάνοις εἰρημένα ὑπὸ
τῶν βασανιζομένων καὶ ἀναγρα-
φέντα βασάνους ὠνόμασε. (Anaxi-
menes) rhet. XVI 1, βάσανός ἐστι
μὲν ὁμολογία παρὰ συνειδότος,
ἄκοντος δέ.

παρέχειν κ.τ.λ.] 'to produce

in court' the evidence obtained
by torture. The torture itself,
it appears, did not take place
in court (see note on Or. 45 § 16).

ἵνα—ἐψηφίσασθε] For ἵνα 'in
which case,' cf. Or. 36 § 47.
ἐκ τούτων should be taken with
ἐψηφίσασθε and not with ἀκούσαντες, cf. Or. 45 § 2 ἐξ ὧν (ἀκούσαντες)…γνώσεσθε.

25. ἰδίᾳ βασανιζομένων τῶν
ἀνθρώπων] equivalent to εἰ ἰδίᾳ
ἐβασανίζοντο. Hence in the corresponding clause, instead of
δημοσίᾳ δέ, which would have
been equally good Greek, we have
εἰ δὲ δημοσίᾳ sc. ἐβασανίζοντο
(Goodwin, *Moods and Tenses*
§ 109, 6).

[The drift of the argument is:
'I objected to a *private* examination, because my opponents
would have said that my report
of their statements was untrue;
whereas if the examination
were *public*, the responsibility
would have rested wholly on
the authorities.' P.]

οἱ ἄρχοντες] 'The Eleven.'
See note on τὴν ἀρχὴν in §
24.

ΜΑΡΤΥΡΕΣ.

26   Κατὰ πολλὰ μὲν οὖν ἔμοιγε δοκοῦσιν εἶναι ἀναί-
σχυντοι ἀμφισβητοῦντες τῶν ὑμετέρων, οὐχ ἥκιστα
δὲ ὑμῖν αὐτοὺς ἐπιδείξω ἐκ τῶν νόμων τῶν ὑμετέρων.
οὗτοι γάρ, ὅτε οἱ δικασταὶ ἐβούλοντο θανάτου τιμῆσαι
τῷ Ἀρεθουσίῳ, ἐδέοντο τῶν δικαστῶν χρημάτων τιμῆσαι καὶ ἐμοῦ συγχωρῆσαι, καὶ ὡμολόγησαν αὐτοὶ
27 συνεκτίσειν.   τοσούτου δὴ δέουσιν ἐκτίνειν καθ᾽ ἃ
ἠγγυήσαντο ὥστε καὶ τῶν ὑμετέρων ἀμφισβητοῦσιν.
καίτοι οἵ γε νόμοι κελεύουσι τὴν οὐσίαν εἶναι δημο-   1255
σίαν, ὃς ἂν ἐγγυησάμενός τι τῶν τῆς πόλεως μὴ ἀπο-

---

§§ 26—29. *My opponents are really claiming what is public property, that is, your own property, men of the jury, and I shall prove this by your own laws. When the jury were proposing to condemn Arethusius to death, my opponents proposed a pecuniary penalty and promised jointly to pay it. So far from fulfilling their guarantee, they are actually claiming your own property; and the laws declare that the property of persons who guarantee the payment of a sum to the state and fail to do so shall be confiscated; so that even on this ground alone, the laws would require the slaves in question to be state property.*

As soon as Arethusius becomes indebted to the treasury, instead of being, as was admitted in former days, the wealthiest of the brothers, he is now made out to be ever so poor, and part of his property is claimed by his mother, part by his brothers, as in the present instance by Nicostratus.

I must ask you in conclusion to consider that there will never be any lack of claimants to contest your property, and to defraud the state of her dues, by making pitiful appeals to your compassion. If you disregard all such pleas in the present case, you will do wisely in finding a verdict against Nicostratus.

26. τιμῆσαι] See § 18.

ἐμοῦ συγχωρῆσαι] sc. ἐδέοντο, implored me to acquiesce in my opponents having a pecuniary penalty imposed on them.—ὡμο-λόγησαν αὐτοὶ συνεκτίσειν, ' they agreed that they would be jointly responsible for the payment.' Kennedy.

27. τῶν ὑμετέρων] The slaves claimed by the state, for non-payment of the fine due from Arethusius, are here dexterously represented as the property of the jury.

ὃς ἂν ἐγγυησάμενος κ.τ.λ.] Andoc. de Myst. § 73 οἱ μὲν ἀργύριον ὀφείλοντες τῷ δημοσίῳ, ὁπόσοι εὐθύνας ὦφλον ἄρξαντες ἀρ-χάς...ἢ ἐγγύας ἠγγυήσαντο πρὸς τὸ δημόσιον, τούτοις ἡ μὲν ἔκτισις ἦν ἐπὶ τῆς ἐνάτης πρυτανείας, εἰ δὲ μὴ διπλάσιον ὀφείλειν καὶ τὰ κτή-ματα αὐτῶν πεπρᾶσθαι. Her-mann, *Public Antiquities*, § 124, 17.

διδῷ τὴν ἐγγύην· ὥστε καὶ εἰ τούτων ἦν τἀνδράποδα,
προσῆκεν αὐτὰ δημόσια εἶναι, εἴπερ τι τῶν νόμων
ὄφελος. καὶ πρὶν μὲν ὀφείλειν τῷ δημοσίῳ ὁ Ἀρε- 28
θούσιος ὡμολογεῖτο τῶν ἀδελφῶν εὐπορώτατος εἶναι·
ἐπειδὴ δ' οἱ νόμοι κελεύουσι τἀκείνου ὑμέτερα εἶναι,
τηνικαῦτα πένης ὢν φαίνεται ὁ Ἀρεθούσιος, καὶ τῶν
μὲν ἡ μήτηρ ἀμφισβητεῖ, τῶν δ' οἱ ἀδελφοί. χρῆν δ'
αὐτούς, εἴπερ ἐβούλοντο δικαίως προσφέρεσθαι πρὸς
ὑμᾶς, ἀποδείξαντας ἅπασαν τὴν οὐσίαν τὴν ἐκείνου,
τὰ τούτων αὐτῶν εἴ τις ἀπέγραφεν, ἀμφισβητεῖν. ἐὰν 29
οὖν ἐνθυμηθῆτε ὅτι οὐδέποτ' ἔσται ἀπορία τῶν ἀμ-
φισβητησόντων ὑμῖν περὶ τῶν ὑμετέρων,—ἢ γὰρ
ὀρφανοὺς ἢ ἐπικλήρους κατασκευάσαντες ἀξιώσουσιν
ἐλεεῖσθαι ὑφ' ὑμῶν, ἢ γῆρας καὶ ἀπορίας καὶ τροφὰς
μητρὶ λέγοντες, καὶ ὀδυρόμενοι δι' ὧν μάλιστ' ἐλ-
πίζουσιν ἐξαπατήσειν ὑμᾶς, πειράσονται ἀποστερῆσαι
τὴν πόλιν τοῦ ὀφλήματος. ἐὰν οὖν ταῦτα παριδόντες
πάντα καταψηφίσησθε, ὀρθῶς βουλεύσεσθε.

28. πένης ὢν φαίνεται] 'is made out to be a poor man.'

προσφέρεσθαι] 'to behave,' Or. 40 § 40.

ἀποδείξαντας] 'having disclosed' (delivered a formal specification of) 'the estate of Arethusius'—τούτων αὐτῶν i.e. Nicostratus and Deinon.

29. ἐὰν οὖν—ἐὰν οὖν ταῦτα] The sentence is suspended by a parenthesis of several lines from ἢ γὰρ ὀρφανοὺς to ὀφλή-ματος, and it is then resumed by the repetition of ἐὰν οὖν.

ὀρφανοὺς ἢ ἐπικλήρους] 'orphan-sons or heiresses,' meaning by the latter 'orphan-daughters,' 'portionable-sisters'; 'an 'heiress' under the Athenian law was by no means necessarily in good circumstances. (See note on Or. 45 § 75.)

ἀπορίας] 'embarrassments,' 'distresses.' For the plural cf. Fals. Leg. § 146, εὐπορίας κτή-ματα πλοῦτον ἀντὶ τῶν ἐσχάτων ἀποριῶν.—τροφὰς μητρί, 'a mother's maintenance.'

ὀδυρόμενοι κ.τ.λ.] 'Appeals ad misericordiam formed the staple conclusion of every speech, and it was not held undignified for the greatest aristocrats, or grotesque for the most notorious scamps, to burst out crying in court, and to bring up their children to excite the compassion of the jury by their tears.' Mahaffy, *Social Life in Greece* p. 369. Cf. Or. 45 § 88 and Or. 54 § 38.

καταψηφίσησθε] sc. Νικοστρά-του.

LIV.

ΚΑΤΑ ΚΟΝΩΝΟΣ ΑΙΚΙΑΣ.

ΥΠΟΘΕΣΙΣ.

Ἀρίστων Ἀθηναῖος δικάζεται Κόνωνι αἰκίας, λέγων ὑπ' αὐτοῦ καὶ τοῦ παιδὸς αὐτοῦ τετυπτῆσθαι, καὶ
μάρτυρας τούτου παρεχόμενος. ὁ δὲ Κόνων ἀρνεῖται
τὸ πρᾶγμα καὶ μάρτυρας ἀντιπαρέχεται, οὓς ὁ Δημοσθένης οὔ φησι πιστούς· βεβιωκέναι γὰρ φαύλως 1256
καὶ εὐχερῶς ἔχειν πρὸς τὸ ψεύδεσθαι.

---

1. 2. τετυπτῆσθαι] In Classical Greek, we should have had
the phrase πληγὰς εἰληφέναι.
The tenses from * τυπτέω, with
the exception of the future τυπτήσω (used in Attic Prose and
Comedy), are characteristic of
late Greek. Thus, in the first
Argument to the *Midias*, we
have τετύπτηκεν and τετυπτημένος. Again, in Lucian (Demo-
nax § 16) we read ἐπεὶ δέ τις
ἀθλητὴς…ἐπάταξεν αὐτὸν εἰς
τὴν κεφαλὴν λίθῳ καὶ αἷμα ἐρρύη,
οἱ μὲν παρόντες ἠγανάκτουν ὡς
αὐτὸς ἕκαστος τετυπτημένος,
where ἐπάταξεν is correctly used
(as in Classical Greek Prose) instead of the aorist active of
τύπτω, while τετυπτημένος is
only a late form, for which
writers of the best age would
have written either πεπληγμένος
or πληγὴν εἰληφώς.
The κατὰ Κόνωνος affords an
instructive study on this point
of Greek usage, as will further
appear in *Excursus (A)* at the
end of the speech (p. 221).

6. εὐχερῶς ἔχειν κ.τ.λ.] 'make
no difficulty about lying.' Or. 21
(Mid.) § 103, τὸν μιαρὸν καὶ
λίαν εὐχερῆ, τὸν κονιορτὸν Εὐκτή-
μονα. So ῥᾳδίως ὀμνύναι *infra*
§ 39. P.]

§§ 1, 2. *I was grossly assaulted
by the defendant Conon, and, for
a very long time, indeed, my life
was despaired of. When I was
restored to health and strength,
instead of going beyond my
years by bringing against him
a public indictment for brutal
outrage, I followed the advice
of my friends and took the
easier course of instituting a
private suit for a common
assault. I ask for your indul-
gent hearing, while I briefly
relate to you my wrongs, and
I trust that, if I prove my case,
you will help me to my rights.*

Ὑβρισθεὶς, ὦ ἄνδρες δικασταὶ, καὶ παθὼν ὑπὸ 1
Κόνωνος τουτουὶ τοιαῦτα ὥστε πολὺν χρόνον πάνυ
μήτε τοὺς οἰκείους μήτε τῶν ἰατρῶν μηδένα προσδοκᾶν
περιφεύξεσθαί με, ὑγιάνας καὶ σωθεὶς ἀπροσδοκήτως
ἔλαχον αὐτῷ τὴν δίκην τῆς αἰκίας ταυτηνί. πάντων

1. ὑβρισθεὶς—ταυτηνί] The
opening sentence is best rendered by treating ὑβρισθεὶς and
παθὼν as principal verbs, and
beginning a fresh sentence with
the word ὑγιάνας, e.g. 'I was
the victim of wanton outrage,
and I suffered such maltreatment at the hands of Conon
the defendant, that, for a very
long time indeed, neither my
friends nor any of my medical
attendants expected my recovery. Contrary to expectation,
I was restored to health and
strength; and I thereupon
brought against him the present action for the assault in
question.'

This exordium is quoted by
the rhetorician Hermogenes as
an example of perspicuity and
directness of expression (καθαρότης, Spengel, *Rhetores Graeci*
II 276). Here, as in Or. 45,
the keynote of the whole speech
is struck by the opening word,
ὑβρισθεὶς. Cf. also Or. 21 (Mid.)
§ 1 τὴν μὲν ἀσέλγειαν, ὦ ἄνδρες
δικασταί, καὶ τὴν ὕβριν κ.τλ.

πολὺν χρόνον πάνυ] For this
position of πάνυ, placed *after*
πολὺν, and even separated from
it, cf. Plato, Hipp. Maj. 282 E
ἐν ὀλίγῳ χρόνῳ πάνυ, Or. 30 § 2
ὑβριστικῶς ὑπ' αὐτοῦ πάνυ ἐξε-
βλήθην, and (Dem.) Prooem. 18
βραχύ τί μοι πεισθῆτε πάνυ.

ἔλαχον...δίκην] lit. 'obtained
this suit by lot,' 'had it allotted
to me,' i.e. 'obtained leave
(from the Archon) to bring this
action.' Where several lawsuits

were instituted at the same
time, the Archon decided by
lot the order in which they
were to be heard (κληροῦν τὰς
δίκας); hence the applicant for
leave to bring an action is commonly said λαγχάνειν δίκην. See
Meier and Schömann, p. 595—8.

τῆς αἰκίας] 'the assault in
question.' Ariston, as he further
explains in the next sentence,
is bringing against Conon a
private suit for assault (αἰκίας
δίκη), instead of a public indictment for wanton outrage
(ὕβρεως γραφή). The penalty
in the former was light, namely,
a pecuniary fine paid to the
plaintiff; in the latter, it was
either a fine paid to the state,
or, in extreme cases, death.
The former implied that the
complainant had been simply
assaulted and struck, the latter
that he had been subjected to
malicious and brutal indigni-
ties.

Harpocration s.v. αἰκίας· εἶδος δίκης ἰδιωτικῆς ἐπὶ πληγαῖς
λαγχανομένης, ἧς...ὁ μὲν κατή-
γορος τίμημα ἐπιγράφεται, ὁπόσου
δοκεῖ ἄξιον εἶναι τὸ ἀδίκημα, οἱ δὲ
δικασταὶ ἐπικρίνουσι (Isocr. 20
Loch. § 16). See Meier and
Schömann p. 547 ff.=p. 646
ed. Lipsius.

Lexica Segueriana p. 355, αἰκία διαφέρει ὕβρεως, ὅτι αἰκία
μὲν ἡ διὰ πληγῶν, ὕβρις δὲ καὶ
ἄνευ πληγῶν μετὰ προπηλακισμοῦ
καὶ ἐπιβουλῆς· διὸ καὶ εὐθῦναι
ἐλάττονες τῆς αἰκίας. See also Or.
37 § 33.

δὲ τῶν φίλων καὶ τῶν οἰκείων, οἷς συνεβουλευόμην,
ἔνοχον μὲν φασκόντων αὐτὸν ἐκ τῶν πεπραγμένων
εἶναι καὶ τῇ τῶν λωποδυτῶν ἀπαγωγῇ καὶ ταῖς τῆς
ὕβρεως γραφαῖς, συμβουλευόντων δέ μοι καὶ παραι-
νούντων μὴ μείζω πράγματα ἢ δυνήσομαι φέρειν
ἐπάγεσθαι, μηδ᾽ ὑπὲρ τὴν ἡλικίαν ὧν[a] ἐπεπόνθειν ἐγκαλοῦντα φαίνεσθαι, οὕτως ἐποίησα καὶ δι᾽ ἐκείνους

[a] περὶ ὧν Rauchenstein, *Philologus* ix 739.

συνεβουλευόμην … συμβουλευόντων] 'consulted'…'counselled.' The active and middle senses of this verb are also found side by side in Xen. Anab. II 1 § 17, ξυμβουλευομένοις ξυνεβούλευσε τάδε.

τῇ τῶν λωποδυτῶν ἀπαγωγῇ] 'the summary process directed against footpads,' i.e. 'summary arrest and imprisonment for highway robbery.' The plaintiff's friends meant that Conon might have been captured *flagrante delicto*, and carried off to prison as a λωποδύτης (lit. 'a clothes-stealer'). According to the plaintiff's subsequent statement, this would be actually true, as Conon and his friends had stripped him of his cloak and carried it off (§ 8 ἐξέδυσαν, and § 10 ἀπεκομίσθην γυμνός, οὗτοι δὲ ᾤχοντο θοἰμάτιον λαβόντες μου). Cf. Isocr. antid. § 90, τοῦτον ἀπαγαγὼν ἀνδραποδιστὴν καὶ κλέπτην καὶ λωποδύτην, Dem. Or. 22 § 26, Aeschin. Timarch. § 91, Lysias Or. 10 § 10, and 13 § 68 ἐνθάδε λωποδύτην ἀπήγαγε, καὶ ὑμεῖς κρίναντες αὐτὸν ἐν τῷ δικαστηρίῳ καὶ καταγνόντες αὐτοῦ θάνατον ἀποτυμπανίσαι παρέδοτε. Hermann, *Rechtsalt.* p. 41 Thalheim; Meier and Schömann p. 229 (n. 208 Lipsius).

ὕβρεως γραφαῖς] here contrasted with αἰκίας δίκη.—Harpocr. γραφή· δημοσίου τινὸς ἐγκλήματος ὄνομα. δίκη· ἰδίως λέγεται ἐπὶ ἰδιωτικῶν ἐγκλημάτων, ὡς σαφὲς ποιεῖ Δημοσθένης ἐν τῷ κατὰ Κόνωνος.
[The plural γραφαὶ shows that more than one public indictment could have been framed. See also Or. 21 (Mid.) § 28, καὶ δίκας ἰδίας δίδωσιν ὁ νόμος μοι καὶ γραφὴν ὕβρεως. P.]
ἐπάγεσθαι] 'to take upon my shoulders a greater burden than I should be able to bear.' —πράγματα, in taking legal action. P.]
ὑπὲρ τὴν ἡλικίαν — φαίνεσθαι] 'to incur the imputation of going beyond my years in undertaking to prosecute for the maltreatment I had received.' Or. 58 § 1 (of a youthful citizen appearing as a prosecutor) μήθ᾽ ἡλικίαν μήτ᾽ ἄλλο μηδὲν ὑπολογισάμενος, 29 § 1. The task of instituting and carrying to its issue a γραφὴ ὕβρεως would be more laborious and would require greater skill and experience than was involved in a δίκη αἰκίας. A young man like Ariston would find himself in an awkward and invidious position, as prosecutor in so ambitious a case as a γραφὴ ὕβρεως,

ἰδίαν ἔλαχον δίκην, ἥδιστ' ἂν, ὦ ἄνδρες Ἀθηναῖοι,
θανάτου κρίνας τουτονί. καὶ τούτου συγγνώμην ἕξετε, 2
εὖ οἶδ' ὅτι, πάντες, ἐπειδὰν ἃ πέπονθ' ἀκούσητε· δεινῆς γὰρ οὔσης τῆς τότε συμβάσης ὕβρεως οὐκ ἐλάτ-
257 των ἡ μετὰ ταῦτ' ἀσέλγειά ἐστι τουτουί. ἀξιῶ δὴ
καὶ δέομαι πάντων ὁμοίως ὑμῶν πρῶτον μὲν εὐνοϊκῶς
ἀκοῦσαί μου περὶ ὧν πέπονθα λέγοντος, εἶτ', ἐὰν ἠδι-

not to mention his being une-
qually matched against an unscrupulous opponent who was
older than himself and had
numerous connexions to support him. He would also be
deterred (though he does not
here confess it) by the rule requiring the prosecutor to pay a
fine of a thousand drachmae
in the event of his not obtaining at least one-fifth part of the
votes (Or. 21 § 47).

The construction is, ἐγκαλοῦντα τούτων ἃ ἐπεπόνθειν. For
the gen. cf. Or. 36 § 9 πῶς ἔνεστ'
ἐγκαλεῖν αὐτῷ μισθώσεως.

[ὑπὲρ τὴν ἡλικίαν may mean,
'beyond the resentment suited
to my years,' implying that a
young man ought to put up
with a little affront, and not
make a serious matter of it. P.]

ἰδίαν] ἀντὶ τοῦ ἰδιωτικὴν Δημοσθένης ἐν τῷ κατὰ Κόνωνος.
ἐλέγετο δὲ τὸ ἴδιον καὶ ἰδιωτικὸν
ὡς ὁ αὐτὸς ῥήτωρ ἐν τῷ κατὰ
Ζηνόθεμιν (§ 32 πρᾶγμα ἴδιον),
Harpocration.

[ἥδιστ' ἂν κρίνας, for καίτοι
ἥδιστ' ἂν ἔκρινα, well illustrates
the fondness of the Greeks for
participial construction. The
sense is, 'though I would most
gladly have brought him to
trial on the capital charge.' P.]

Cf. Or. 53 § 18 οὐχ ἵνα μὴ ἀποθάνῃ κ.τλ.

'Ce cri de haine a quelque
chose de naïf et de sauvage; le
plaignant semble le laisser é-
chapper malgré lui, sous l'impression trop vive encore des
injures, qu'il a reçues. Cet
involontaire et rapide oubli de
la modération qu'il s'est com-
mandée donne à son langage un
accent de sincérité plus marqué;
il lui sert aussi pour amener la
récit des faits de la cause' (Perrot, *Revue des deux mondes*,
1873, 3, p. 946).

θανάτου] The penalty of
death was inflicted in cases of
λωποδυτῶν ἀπαγωγή, and even
in special cases of ὕβρεως γρα-
φή· For the former, cf. Xen.
Mem. 1 2 § 62, ἐάν τις φανερὸς
γένηται λωποδυτῶν ἢ βαλαν-
τιοτομῶν ἢ τοιχωρυχῶν, τούτοις
θάνατός ἐστιν ἡ ζημία. For
the latter, cf. Lysias, fragm. 44,
καίτοι τις οὐκ οἶδεν ὑμῶν ὅτι τὴν
μὲν αἰκίαν χρημάτων ἔστι μόνον
τιμῆσαι, τοὺς δὲ ὑβρίζειν δόξαντας ἔξεστιν ὑμῖν θανάτῳ ζημιοῦν, Dem. Or. 21 § 49, inf. § 23.
—'θάνατος articulo carere solet,
si supplicium significat et cum
vocabulo iudicali coniungitur'
Zink (quoting Procksch in *Philologus* xxxvii 306).

2. δεινῆς—τουτουί] 'The original outrage, atrocious as it was,
does not surpass the subsequent brutality of the defendant.' See § 26. The first clause
may perhaps be taken as a genitive absolute.

κῆσθαι καὶ παρανενομῆσθαι δοκῶ, βοηθῆσαί μοι τὰ
δίκαια. ἐξ ἀρχῆς δ᾽ ὡς ἕκαστα πέπρακται, διηγήσομαι
πρὸς ὑμᾶς, ὡς ἂν οἷός τε ὦ διὰ βραχυτάτων.

παρανενομῆσθαι] The passive is formed just as if the verb were directly transitive in the active, i.e. as if the active construction were παρανομεῖν τινα, and not εἴς τινα. So also the active παροινεῖν εἴς τινα has παροινεῖσθαι for its corresponding passive (see below § 4 *init.* and § 5 *fin.*).

βοηθῆσαί μοι τὰ δίκαια] 'assist me to my rights.' For the phrase and the context, cf. Or. 27 § 3 δέομαι ὑμῶν...μετ᾽ εὐνοίας τ᾽ ἐμοῦ ἀκοῦσαι κἂν ἠδικῆσθαι δοκῶ, βοηθῆσαί μοι τὰ δίκαια, ποιήσομαι δ᾽ ὡς ἂν δύνωμαι διὰ βραχυτάτων τοὺς λόγους, ib. § 68, Or. 35 § 5; 38 § 2; 40 § 61. A fuller phrase may be noticed in § 42 of this speech, βοηθεῖν καὶ τὰ δίκαια ἀποδιδόναι. Kühner, *Gk. Gr.* 264 § 410 c, quotes Xen. Mem. II 6 § 25 ὅπως αὐτός τε μὴ ἀδικῆται καὶ τοῖς φίλοις τὰ δίκαια βοηθεῖν δύνηται, —*zum Rechte verhelfen.* It is an extension of the cogn. acc. βοηθεῖν βοήθειαν.

The exordium has several points of coincidence with that of Or. 45. See p. 56.

In the next four sections the plaintiff states the origin of the bad blood between the defendant's family and himself. The narrative, though part of the διήγησις which naturally follows immediately after the προοίμιον of a forensic speech, is only preliminary to the recital of the facts on which the suit is really founded. It is to this portion of the statement of the case that Rhetoricians like Theodorus of

Byzantium would have given the name of προδιήγησις (Arist. Rhet. III 13).

§§ 3—6. *Two years ago, we were ordered out to Panactum on garrison duty, and, as ill luck would have it, the sons of Conon pitched their tents close to our own. They picked quarrels with our servants and were persistently guilty of drunken and indecent conduct at the expense of our attendants and ourselves. My messmates and myself represented the case to the general, and he reprimanded them severely for their treatment of ourselves and for their misbehaviour in the camp. Notwithstanding, they burst in upon us on that very evening and violently assaulted us; indeed, serious consequences might have ensued, but for the arrival of the officers on the scene of disorder. On our return to Athens, there was naturally some ill blood between Conon's sons and myself, but I simply made up my mind to have nothing more to do with them. However, as the result proved, my collision with the sons in the camp led to my being grossly maltreated by their father the defendant, who instead of rebuking his sons for the original outrage, has himself been guilty of a much more shameful aggression.*

'Par sa vive et familière simplicité, ce récit dut plaire aux juges, viellards auxquels il rappelait les compagnes de leur jeunesse, les nuits passées sous la tente, les repas au grand air, dans ces beaux sites où se dres-

Ἐξήλθομεν, ἔτος τουτὶ τρίτον, εἰς Πάνακτον φρου- 3
ρᾶς ἡμῖν προγραφείσης. ἐσκήνωσαν οὖν οἱ υἱεῖς οἱ
Κόνωνος τουτουὶ ἐγγὺς ἡμῶν, ὡς οὐκ ἂν ἐβουλόμην·
ἡ γὰρ ἐξ ἀρχῆς ἔχθρα καὶ τὰ προσκρούσματ᾽ ἐκεῖθεν
ἡμῖν συνέβη, ἐξ ὧν δ᾽, ἀκούσεσθε. ἔπινον ἑκάστοτε
οὗτοι τὴν ἡμέραν, ἐπειδὴ τάχιστα ἀριστήσαιεν, ὅλην,
καὶ τοῦθ᾽ ἕως περ ἦμεν ἐπὶ τῇ φρουρᾷ, διετέλουν ποιοῦντες. ἡμεῖς δ᾽ ὥσπερ ἐνθάδ᾽ εἰώθαμεν, οὕτω διή-
γομεν καὶ ἔξω. ἦν οὖν δειπνοποιεῖσθαι τοῖς ἄλλοις 4
ὥραν συμβαίνοι, ταύτην ἂν ἤδη ἐπαρῴνουν οὗτοι, τὰ

saient, au milieu des montagnes, les forteresses destinées à protéger les frontières de l'Attique' (Perrot *u. s.* p. 947).

3. ἐξήλθομεν] not as youthful περίπολοι, but as part of the regular troops. This may be inferred from § 5, where the στρατοπέδον, στρατηγός and ταξίαρχοι are mentioned, and where there is apparently an absence of the strict discipline which was usual in the case of ἔφηβοι (Zink p. 19).

ἔτος τουτὶ τρίτον] 'two years ago' (sc. ἐστί). Dem. Ol. 3 § 4 ἀπηγγέλθη...τρίτον ἢ τέταρτον ἔτος τουτί, Ἡραῖον τεῖχος πολιορκῶν.

The present passage places the date of the speech in the 'third year after,' or, as we should say, 'two years after,' an expedition to Panactum. See *Introd.* p. lxiii.

On Panactum, or Panactus, a fort on the borders of Attica and Boeotia (Leake's *Demi* p. 128), Harpocration has this article; Πάνακτος· Δημοσθένης κατὰ Κόνωνος· πόλις ἐστὶ μεταξὺ τῆς Ἀττικῆς καὶ τῆς Βοιωτίας. He further notes that Thucydides (v 42) makes the word neuter, and Menander masculine.

φρουρᾶς..προγραφείσης] 'being ordered out on garrison duty.' For προγράφειν, in the sense of 'putting up a public notice' at head-quarters, compare Arist. Aves 448, ἀκούετε λεῴ· τοὺς ὁπλίτας νυνμενὶ | ἀνελομένους θὤπλ᾽ ἀπιέναι πάλιν οἴκαδε, | σκοπεῖν δ᾽ ὅ τι ἂν προγράφωμεν ἐν τοῖς πινακίοις, and Aristotle ἐν Ἀθηναίων πολιτείᾳ (quoted by Harpocration s. v. στρατεία), ὅταν ἡλικίαν ἐκπέμπωσι, προγράφουσιν ἀπὸ τίνος ἄρχοντος ἐπωνύμου μέχρι τίνος δεῖ στρατεύεσθαι.

ὡς οὐκ ἂν ἐβουλόμην] sc. σκηνῶσαι αὐτούς, 'and would to heaven they had not!'

προσκρούσματα] 'collisions.' Or. 39 § 18, πολλοῖς προσκρούει and Or. 37 § 15, ᾧ φίλος ἦν... τούτῳ προσκεκρουκότα, 33 § 7.

ἐξ ὧν δ᾽, ἀκούσεσθε] Or. 14 § 17 δι᾽ ὅ δ᾽, εἴσεσθε.

ἀριστήσαιεν.....δειπνοποιεῖσθαι] On ἄριστον and δεῖπνον, see Becker's *Charicles* p. 313, ed. 3. —The optative ἀριστήσαιεν denotes frequent and repeated action, which is also clearly brought out by ἑκάστοτε and διετέλουν ποιοῦντες.

4. ὥραν] Not to be translated 'hour,' but 'time,' as

μὲν πολλὰ εἰς τοὺς παῖδας ἡμῶν τοὺς ἀκολούθους, τελευτῶντες δὲ καὶ εἰς ἡμᾶς αὐτούς· φήσαντες γὰρ καπ-
νίζειν αὐτούς[b] ὀψοποιουμένους τοὺς παῖδας ἢ κακῶς
λέγειν, ὅ τι τύχοιεν, ἔτυπτον καὶ τὰς ἀμίδας[c] κατεσκε-
δάννυον[d] καὶ προσεούρουν καὶ ἀσελγείας καὶ ὕβρεως
οὐδ' ὁτιοῦν ἀπέλειπον[e]. ὁρῶντες δ' ἡμεῖς ταῦτα καὶ
λυπούμενοι τὸ μὲν πρῶτον ἀπεπεμψάμεθα, ὡς δ'

[b] αὐτοὺς Z.   [c] *Bekker.* ἀμίδας Z cum r ; αμιδας Σ.
[d] *Bekker st.* κατεσκεδάννυσαν.
[e] *Bekker.* ἀπέλιπον Z cum ΦΣΦρ.

ὥρα in the former sense is
found in late Greek only, and
was probably first so used by
Hipparchus the Alexandrine
astronomer in the second century B.C. In phrases like ἔθυον
ὥραν οὐδένος κοινὴν θεῶν (Eumen.
109) and τὴν τεταγμένην ὥραν
(Bacch. 724), the rendering
'hour' should be avoided as
open to misconstruction.

ταύτην....ἐπαρῴνουν....εἰς τοὺς
παῖδας] Liddell and Scott (ed. 6)
inadvertently quote this passage
as an instance of παροινεῖν being
used transitively 'like ὑβρίζειν,'
whereas ταύτην is obviously the
accusative of time (sc. τὴν ὥραν)
and the object of παροινεῖν is
expressed by εἰς τοὺς παῖδας
(this has been corrected in ed.
7). For the corresponding passive to this intransitive active,
see § 5 *fin.* παροινουμένους. [πάρ-
οινος and παροινεῖν mean, not
'to be intoxicated,' but 'to be
abusive over one's cups.' P.]

ὅ τι τύχοιεν] This clause is to
be taken ἀσυνδέτως. 'Pretend-
ing, in short, anything they
pleased.' The full construction
would be: φήσαντες ὅ τι τύχοιεν
φήσαντες.

ἔτυπτον] See *Excursus* (A) on
p. 221.

τὰς ἀμίδας κ.τ.λ.] 'They emp-
tied the chamber-pots on them.'
Kennedy. Hermogenes, who
selects the present narrative as
an instance of ἁπλῆ διήγησις,
draws attention to the orator's
plain-speaking in the clauses
before us, and quotes them from
memory with this comment: οὐ
γὰρ εἶχε μᾶλλον δεινῶσαι τῷ
λόγῳ ἢ τὰ πράγματα λέγων αὐτὰ
ὁ ῥήτωρ ψιλά, ἃ ἔπραττον ἐκεῖνοι·
γυμνὰ γάρ τοι λεγόμενα πλείονα
ἰσχὺν ἔλαβεν ἢ εἴ τις αὐτὰ ἐκόσ-
μει λόγοις (Spengel, *Rhet. Gr.*
II 199.)

ἀπεπεμψάμεθα] Either 'we
drove them away,' 'told them
to be off' (Westermann), a sense
which is supported by Hdt. I 120
τὸν παῖδα τοῦτον ἐξ ὀφθαλμῶν
ἀπόπεμψαι and VI 63; or (more
probably) 'we took no notice,'
literally, 'we put the matter
(ταῦτα) aside from ourselves,'
'dismissed it from our thoughts.'
*primum quidem satis habuimus
talia aversari, detestari* (G. H.
Schaefer); 'at first only expressed our disgust' (Kennedy and
Dareste). [Cf. Eur. Hec. 72,
ἀποπέμπομαι ἔννυχον ὄψιν. In
the present passage it is a remarkable use. P.]

ἐχλεύαζον ἡμᾶς καὶ οὐκ ἐπαύοντο, τῷ στρατηγῷ τὸ
πρᾶγμα εἴπομεν κοινῇ πάντες οἱ σύσσιτοι προσελθόν-
τες, οὐκ ἐγὼ τῶν ἄλλων ἔξω. λοιδορηθέντος δ' αὐτοῖς 5
ἐκείνου καὶ κακίσαντος αὐτοὺς οὐ μόνον περὶ ὧν εἰς
ἡμᾶς ἠσέλγαινον, ἀλλὰ καὶ περὶ ὧν ὅλως ἐποίουν ἐν
τῷ στρατοπέδῳ, τοσούτου ἐδέησαν παύσασθαι ἢ αἰσχυνθῆναι ὥστ', ἐπειδὴ θᾶττον συνεσκότασεν, εὐθὺς
258 ὡς ἡμᾶς εἰσεπήδησαν ταύτῃ τῇ ἑσπέρᾳ, καὶ τὸ μὲν
πρῶτον κακῶς ἔλεγον, τελευτῶντες δὲ καὶ πληγὰς ἐνέτειναν ἐμοί, καὶ τοσαύτην κραυγὴν καὶ θόρυβον περὶ
τὴν σκηνὴν ἐποίησαν ὥστε καὶ τὸν στρατηγὸν καὶ
τοὺς ταξιάρχους ἐλθεῖν καὶ τῶν ἄλλων στρατιωτῶν
τινάς, οἵπερ ἐκώλυσαν μηδὲν ἡμᾶς ἀνήκεστον παθεῖν
μηδ' αὐτοὺς ποιῆσαι παροινουμένους ὑπὸ τουτωνί[f].
τοῦ δὲ πράγματος εἰς τοῦτο προελθόντος, ὡς δεῦρ' 6
ἐπανήλθομεν, ἦν ἡμῖν, οἷον εἰκός, ἐκ τούτων ὀργὴ καὶ

[f] Σ. τούτων Z.

πάντες οἱ σύσσιτοι] 'not I alone, but all the messmates in a body.' Kennedy. Cf. Lysias Or. 13 § 79 οὔτε συσσιτήσας τούτῳ οὐδεὶς φανήσεται οὔτε σύσκηνος γενόμενος.

ἔξω] placed last for emphasis and also to avoid *hiatus* (Rehdantz on Phil. 1 § 34).

5. λοιδορηθέντος κ.τ.λ.] 'He censured and rebuked them severely, not only for their brutal treatment of ourselves, but also for their general behaviour in the camp.' For λοιδορηθεὶς used in the sense of the aorist *middle*, cf. διαλεχθεὶς in § 7.— On κακίσαντος, cf. note on Or. 34 § 2.

ἐπειδὴ θᾶττον συνεσκότασεν] 'As soon as ever it grew dark,' 'no sooner was it dusk than...' For ἐπειδὴ θᾶττον (which is less common than ἐπειδὴ τάχιστα, § 3), cf. Or. 37 § 41 ἐπειδὴ θᾶττον ἀνείλετο, Plato Protag. 425 c, ἐπειδὰν θᾶττον συνίῃ τις, Xen. Cyrop. III 3—20 ἦν θᾶττον.

εἰσεπήδησαν] Aeschin. 1 § 59 εἰσπηδήσαντες νύκτωρ εἰς τὴν οἰκίαν.

ποιῆσαι] sc. μηδὲν ἀνήκεστον. The plaintiff candidly admits that the arrival of the authorities prevented himself and his friends doing violence to Conon's sons in self-defence, provoked and exasperated as they were by the brutal assaults of their opponents.

παροινουμένους] Fals. leg. § 198 ἀπώλετ' ἂν παροινουμένη. The active construction is παροινεῖν εἴς τινα, cf. § 4 and see note on Isocr. ad Dem. § 30, πιστευθέντες.

ἔχθρα πρὸς ἀλλήλους. [g]οὐ μὴν ἔγωγε ᾤμην δεῖν οὔτε δίκην λαχεῖν αὐτοῖς οὔτε λόγον ποιεῖσθαι τῶν συμβάντων οὐδένα, ἀλλ' ἐκεῖνο ἁπλῶς ἐγνώκειν τὸ λοιπὸν εὐλαβεῖσθαι καὶ φυλάττεσθαι μὴ πλησιάζειν τοῖς τοιούτοις. πρῶτον μὲν οὖν τούτων ὧν εἴρηκα βούλομαι τὰς μαρτυρίας παρασχόμενος, μετὰ ταῦτα οἷα ὑπ' αὐτοῦ τούτου πέπονθα ἐπιδεῖξαι, ἵνα εἰδῆτε ὅτι ᾧ προσῆκε τοῖς τὸ πρῶτον ἁμαρτηθεῖσιν ἐπιτιμᾶν, οὗτος αὐτὸς πρότερος πολλῷ δεινότερ' εἴργασται.

ΜΑΡΤΥΡΙΑΙ.

7   Ὧν μὲν τοίνυν οὐδένα ᾤμην δεῖν λόγον ποιεῖσθαι,

[g] μὰ τοὺς θεούς, οὐ μὴν ἔγωγε Z cum libris Demosthenis; οὐ μὴν ἔγωγε μὰ τοὺς θεοὺς Bekker cum Dionysio.

6. μετὰ ταῦτα οἷα—προσῆκε] These few words as printed in Dindorf's ed. include no less than seven instances of *hiatus*, five of which can however be readily removed by elision. Benseler, who has exhaustively treated this subject in his volume *de hiatu in oratoribus Graecis*, says of the speeches of Dem. against Conon and Callicles: *orator solet verba ita coniungere et collocare, ut plerumque vocalium concursus evitetur.* p. 152.

τοῖς...ἁμαρτηθεῖσιν] Neuter, sc. ὑπὸ τῶν υἱέων τῶν Κόνωνος.

πρότερος] as a ringleader in acts of aggression.

Here follows the narrative proper.

§§ 7—9. *Not long after our return from the camp, I was taking my usual evening walk in the market-place with a friend of mine, when a son of the defendant, Ctesias by name, who was intoxicated at the time, caught sight of us, and after raising a yell and muttering something indistinctly to himself, went off to a part of the town where a large party, including his father, had met for a carouse; summoned them to his standard, and made them march with him down to the market-place. On closing with us, one of them fell upon my friend and pinned him, while Conon and his son and another attacked myself, stripped me of my cloak, dashed me into the mud, jumped upon me, and otherwise grossly maltreated me. The language I heard them use, as I lay helpless on the ground, was simply awful, and would hardly bear repeating. Conon himself meanwhile set up a crowing like a victorious game-cock. When they had left me, some people, who happened to come up, carried me home, and afterwards took me to a public bath, where they washed me all over, and brought the surgeons to see me. I will now call evidence, to attest to these facts.*

ταῦτ' ἔστιν. χρόνῳ δ' ὕστερον οὐ πολλῷ περιπατοῦντος, ὥσπερ εἰώθειν, ἑσπέρας ἐν ἀγορᾷ μου μετὰ
Φανοστράτου τοῦ Κηφισιέως, τῶν ἡλικιωτῶν τινός,
παρέρχεται Κτησίας ὁ υἱὸς ὁ τούτου, μεθύων, κατὰ
τὸ Λεωκόριον, ἐγγὺς τῶν Πυθοδώρου. κατιδὼν δ' ἡμᾶς
καὶ κραυγάσας, καὶ διαλεχθείς τι πρὸς αὐτὸν οὕτως ὡς
ἂν μεθύων, ὥστε μὴ μαθεῖν ὅ τι λέγοι, παρῆλθε πρὸς

7. περιπατοῦντος κ.τ.λ.] Hor.
Sat. 1 6, 113 vespertinumque
pererro Saepe forum.

ἑσπέρας.] Cf. νυκτὸς in § 28;
Madvig's *Gk. Syntax* § 66 a,
Farrar's *Gk. Syntax* § 46 n. and
Abbott's *Shaksp. Gr.* § 176.

ἐν ἀγορᾷ] The article is omitted, as in ἄστυ and πόλις (when
used of Athens); below we have
εἰς τὴν ἀγοράν. Similarly εἰς
βαλανεῖον in § 9, followed by εἰς
τὸ βαλανεῖον in § 10.

The *agora* probably extended
at this time over the inner Cerameicus, the district to the N.W.
of the Acropolis.

τοῦ Κηφισιέως] The deme
Κηφισία belonged to the tribe
Erechtheis, and lay 12 miles
N.E. of Athens at the foot of
Pentelicus. It still retains its
ancient name.

κατά] 'opposite to,' as Aesch.
Theb. 528, τύμβον κατ' αὐτὸν
διογενοῦς 'Αμφίονος, and so frequently in Thucyd. in the sense
of 'off a coast, or river.' P.]

Λεωκόριον] The monument
of the daughters of Leos
(Praxithea, Theope, Eubule),
who, at the command of an
oracle, sacrificed themselves for
their country. Or. 60 (Epitaph.)
§ 29 (αἱ Λεὼ κόραι) ἑαυτὰς ἔδοσαν
σφάγιον τοῖς πολίταις ὑπὲρ τῆς
χώρας. Cicero de Nat. Deor. III
§ 50. Harpocration states that
it was ἐν μέσῳ τῷ Κεραμεικῷ,
i.e. in the midst of the *inner*

Cerameicus, the N.W. district
of Athens, lying within the walls,
as opposed to the *outer* Cerameicus, the κάλλιστον προάσ-
τειον where the Athenian war-
riors were buried (Thuc. 11 34,
Arist. Aves 395). It was close
to the *Leocorium* that Hipparchus was slain by Har-
modius and Aristogeiton (Thuc.
VI 57).

τῶν Πυθοδώρου] 'The premises
(or shop) of Pythodorus,' either
understanding οἰκιῶν, or more
probably δωμάτων, like the expression which occurs twice in
Or. 43 Macart. § 62 (νόμος) εἰς
τὰ τοῦ ἀποθανόντος εἰσιέναι.
Theocr. 11 76 μέσαν κατ' ἀμαξι-
τόν, ᾆ τὰ Λύκωνος. [Ar. Vesp.
1440, οὕτω δὲ καὶ σὺ παράτρεχ'
ἐς τὰ Πιττάλου. P.]

Pythodorus is possibly the
friend of Pasion mentioned in
Isocr. Trapez. § 33 Πυθόδωρον
τὸν σκηνίτην καλούμενον, quoted
by Harpocr. s.v. σκηνίτης: ἔοικεν
ἐπώνυμον εἶναι. μήποτε (perhaps)
δὲ ὡς ἀγοραῖον καλούμενον,
ἐπειδὴ ἐν σκηναῖς ἐπιπράσκετο
πολλὰ τῶν ὠνίων.

διαλεχθείς] Cf. § 5 λοιδορηθείς.
—ὡς ἂν μεθύων, sc. διαλεχθείη.
See on Or. 34 § 32.—μαθεῖν, sc.
ἡμᾶς.

πρὸς Μελίτην ἄνω] A hilly
district within the walls, comprising part of the western half
of Athens, and including the
hill of the 'Pnyx' and that of

Μελίτην ἄνω· ἔπινον γὰρ ἐνταῦθα (ταῦτα γὰρ ὕστερον ἐπυθόμεθα) παρὰ Παμφίλῳ τῷ κναφεῖ Κόνων 1259
οὑτοσὶ, Θεότιμός τις, Ἀρχεβιάδης, Σπίνθαρος ὁ Εὐβούλου, Θεογένης ὁ Ἀνδρομένους, πολλοί τινες, οὓς
8 ἐξαναστήσας ὁ Κτησίας ἐπορεύετο εἰς τὴν ἀγοράν. καὶ
ἡμῖν συμβαίνει ἀναστρέφουσιν ἀπὸ τοῦ Φερρεφαττίου

the Nymphs. Schol. on Ar. Aves
997 τὸ χωρίον...ᾧ περιλαμβάνεται
καὶ ἡ Πνύξ...Μελίτη γὰρ ἅπαν
ἐκεῖνο, ὡς ἐν τοῖς ὁρισμοῖς γέγραπται τῆς πόλεως. That it was
near the *agora* is implied by
the present passage, as well as
by Plato Parm. 126 c, where Ce-
phalus meets Adeimantus and
Glaucon in the *agora*, and they
conduct him to Antiphon, οἰκεῖ
δὲ ἐγγὺς ἐν Μελίτῃ. It was so
called from the nymph Melite,
wife of Hercules (Leake's *Athens*
1 441, 485; Dyer's *Athens* 97).

ἔπινον κ. τ. λ.] Either Pam-
philus had invited Conon and
his set to a friendly symposium,
or, which is more probable, his
shop was their place of lounge.
Lysias 24 § 20 ἕκαστος ὑμῶν
εἴθισται προσφοιτᾶν ὁ μὲν πρὸς
μυροπωλεῖον, ὁ δὲ πρὸς κουρεῖον
ὁ δὲ πρὸς σκυτοτομεῖον, ὁ δ' ὅποι
ἂν τύχῃ, καὶ πλεῖστοι μὲν ὡς τοὺς
ἐγγυτάτω τῆς ἀγορᾶς κατεσκευ-
ασμένους, ἐλάχιστοι δὲ ὡς τοὺς
πλεῖστον ἀπέχοντας αὐτῆς. (See
Becker's *Charicles* p. 279.)

τῷ κναφεῖ] 'the fuller.' As
woollen cloaks would be spoiled
by ordinary washing, they were
regularly sent to the fuller to
be scoured. The process con-
sisted in rubbing in a kind of
alkaline marl (fullers' earth),
Κιμωλία γῆ, Ran. 713, and card-
ing (κνάπτειν) to raise the nap
(Jebb's *Theophrastus* xxv 13, and
St John's *Manners and Customs
of Ancient Greece* iii 232).

Ἀρχεβιάδης] § 34 note.

Σπίνθαρος ὁ Εὐβούλου] This
Eubulus was probably the
orator and statesman, one of
Demosthenes' most formidable
opponents. This supposition
is strongly confirmed by the
fact that the orator in question
is known as Εὔβουλος Σπινθάρου
Προβαλίσιος. The person mentioned in the text would, according to the common custom,
be called Spintharus, after his
grandfather. Cf. note on Or.
39 § 27. (A. Schäfer's *Dem.
u. s. Zeit,* 1 190 n.)

ἐξαναστήσας] The word is
sometimes used as a military
term of starting soldiers from
ambush, as in Thuc. 11 68, 111 7
and 108 § 3 ἐξανάσταντες, and
Xen. Hell. IV 8 § 37; cf. Iliad
1 191. The orator makes his
client, a young soldier, charac-
teristically describe the scuffle
in the language of military life.
Similarly, a few lines below,
ἀνεμίχθημεν, 'when we closed
with one another.'

8. συμβαίνει...καὶ περιτυγχάνο-
μεν] A simple and somewhat
archaic form of phrase instead
of ὅτε περιτυγχάνομεν. Thuc.
1 50, ἤδη ἦν ὀψὲ καὶ οἱ Κορίνθιοι
ἐξαπίνης πρύμναν ἐκρούοντο. Soph.
Phil. 354 (Kühner § 518, 8).

Φερρεφαττίου] The site of the
temple of Persephone is un-
certain; it is supposed to have
been south of the Leocorium,
and close to the statue of

καὶ περιπατοῦσι πάλιν κατ' αὐτό πως τὸ Λεωκόριον
εἶναι, καὶ τούτοις περιτυγχάνομεν. ὡς δ' ἀνεμίχθημεν, εἷς μὲν αὐτῶν, ἀγνώς τις, [h]Φανοστράτῳ προσπίπτει καὶ κατεῖχεν ἐκεῖνον, Κόνων δ' οὑτοσὶ καὶ ὁ υἱὸς
αὐτοῦ καὶ ὁ Ἀνδρομένους υἱὸς ἐμοὶ περιπεσόντες τὸ
μὲν πρῶτον ἐξέδυσαν, εἶθ' ὑποσκελίσαντες καὶ ῥάξαν-
τες εἰς τὸν βόρβορον οὕτω διέθηκαν ἐναλλόμενοι καὶ
ὑβρίζοντες ὥστε τὸ μὲν χεῖλος διακόψαι, τοὺς δ'
ὀφθαλμοὺς συγκλεῖσαι· οὕτω δὲ κακῶς ἔχοντα κατέ-
λιπον[i] ὥστε μήτε ἀναστῆναι μήτε φθέγξασθαι δύνασθαι. κείμενος δ' αὐτῶν ἤκουον πολλὰ καὶ δεινὰ λεγόντων. καὶ τὰ μὲν ἄλλα καὶ βλασφημίαν ἔχει τινά, 9
καὶ ὀνομάζειν ὀκνήσαιμ' ἂν ἐν ὑμῖν ἔνια, ὃ δὲ τῆς

[h] Σ. +τῷ Bekker et Z.

[i] Bekker cum Dionysio. καταλιπεῖν Z cum ΦΣΦ. καταλείπειν kr.

Triptolemus, but we have no
data worth mentioning besides
the vague indications of the
present passage (Leake's *Athens*
I 488, and Wordsworth's *Athens
and Attica*, p. 150).

εἷς μὲν—ἐκεῖνον] 'One of
them, whom I failed to identify,
suddenly fell on Phanostratus,
and pinned *him*.' The present
προσπίπτει gives a vivid effect
to the description, and the imperfect κατεῖχεν must also be
noticed as implying that the
plaintiff's friend was held fast
during the whole of the ensuing
scuffle, and therefore could offer
no assistance.—ὁ υἱὸς αὐτοῦ,
Ctesias.— ἐξέδυσαν, 'stripped
me' of my cloak; § 9, ᾤχοντο
θοἰμάτιον λαβόντες μου.

εἶθ'—συγκλεῖσαι] 'next, they
tripped me up, and made me
fall heavily into the mud, and
by leaping upon me, and mal-
treating me, they put me in

such a condition that they cut
my lip right through, and
bunged up my eyes.'

9. τὰ μὲν ἄλλα—ἐν ὑμῖν ἔνια]
i. e. 'much of what they said
was most abusive, and some of
it I should be sorry to repeat in
your presence.' Cf. Or. 18 §
103, ὅσ' ὀκνήσαιμ' ἂν πρὸς ὑμᾶς
εἰπεῖν, 21 § 79, οὐ γὰρ ἔγωγε
προαχθείην ἂν εἰπεῖν πρὸς ὑμᾶς
τῶν τότε ῥηθέντων οὐδέν, 2 § 19,
and esp. Aeschin. 1 § 55, τοιαῦτα
ἁμαρτήματα καὶ τοιαύτας ὕβρεις...
οἵας ἐγὼ μὰ τὸν Δία τὸν Ὀλύμπιον
οὐκ ἂν τολμήσαιμι πρὸς ὑμᾶς
εἰπεῖν· ἃ γὰρ οὗτος ἔργῳ πράττων
οὐκ ᾐσχύνετο, ταῦτ' ἐγὼ λόγῳ
σαφῶς ἐν ὑμῖν εἰπὼν οὐκ ἂν
ἐδεξάμην ζῆν. Cic. Ver. II 1
§ 32.

This rhetorical device of pro-
fessing to have compunctions at
repeating the bad language of
one's opponent is sufficiently obvious. The effect is threefold.

ὕβρεώς ἐστι τῆς τούτου σημεῖον καὶ τεκμήριον τοῦ πᾶν
τὸ πρᾶγμα ὑπὸ τούτου γεγενῆσθαι, τοῦθ᾽ ὑμῖν ἐρῶ·
ᾖδε γὰρ τοὺς ἀλεκτρυόνας μιμούμενος τοὺς νενικηκό-
τας, οἱ δὲ κροτεῖν τοῖς ἀγκῶσιν αὐτὸν ἠξίουν ἀντὶ
πτερύγων τὰς πλευράς. καὶ μετὰ ταῦτα ἐγὼ μὲν ἀπεκομίσθην ὑπὸ τῶν παρατυχόντων γυμνός, οὗτοι δ᾽
ᾤχοντο θοἰμάτιον λαβόντες μου. ὡς δ᾽ ἐπὶ τὴν θύ-
ραν ἦλθον, κραυγὴ καὶ βοὴ τῆς μητρὸς καὶ τῶν θερα-

(1) The court is left to imagine that the terms of abuse were singularly offensive. (2) The plaintiff is accredited with being a man of high principle for hesitating to repeat the abominable language of his opponent, —for what Aristotle would call his δυσχέρεια τῶν αἰσχρῶν. (3) The court is flattered by the compliment implied in the assurance that the language was too indecent to be repeated in their hearing. Cf. Arist. Rhet. iii 7, παθητικὴ δέ, ἐὰν μὲν ᾖ ὕβρις, ὀργιζομένου λέξις, ἐὰν δὲ ἀσεβῆ καὶ αἰσχρά, δυσχεραίνοντος καὶ εὐλα- βουμένου καὶ λέγειν.

σημεῖον] To be taken with ὕβρεως; τεκμήριον with τοῦ γε- γενῆσθαι. The former is 'an indication,' 'a sign'; the latter 'a conclusive proof' (note on Isocr. ad Dem. § 2). Or. 36 § 12.

ᾖδε—πλευράς] 'he began to crow, mimicking the fighting- cocks that have won a victory, while the rest bade him flap his elbows against his sides, like (lit. in lieu of) wings.'

We find representations of cock-fighting on ancient gems and vase-paintings; and, if the authority of Aelian (var. hist. ii 28) may be trusted, it was a political institution at Athens, and took place in the public theatre once a year. (See esp. Becker's *Charicles* p. 77 n., also pp. 80—81, where the whole scene described in the text is admirably woven in with the adventures of Charicles.)

[Plato, Theaet. p. 164, φαινό- μεθά μοι ἀλεκτρύονος ἀγεννοῦς δίκην, πρὶν νενικηκέναι, ἀπο- πηδήσαντες ἀπὸ τοῦ λόγου ᾄδειν. Ar. Vesp. 705, κᾆθ᾽ ὅταν οὗτός γ᾽ ἐπισίξῃ ἐπὶ τῶν ἐχθρῶν τιν᾽ ἐπιρρύξας, ἀγρίως αὐτοῖς ἐπιπηδᾷς. The fighting-cock springs upon its adversary, and uses its spur to strike the head. P.]

γυμνός] sc. ἄνευ τοῦ ἱματίου, stripped of his cloak, as is clearly shown by the following clause. Or. 21 § 216 γυμνὸς ἐν τῷ χιτωνίσκῳ. Aeschin. 1 § 26 ῥίψας θοἰμάτιον γυμνὸς ἐπαγκρα- τίαζεν. Ar. Lys. 150 ἐν τοῖς χιτωνίοισι…γυμναί. Nub. 497, κατάθου θοἰμάτιον…γυμνοὺς εἰσιέ- ναι νομίζεται. Hermann *Pri- vatalt.* § 21 p. 175 Blümner.— ᾤχοντο, in its usual pluperfect sense, 'after stripping me of my cloak, they had taken to their heels.'—ἦλθον, possibly first person singular, but more probably third person plural, referring to οἱ παρατυχόντες. But cf. § 20, ὑγιὴς ἐξελθὼν φορά- δην ἦλθον οἰκάδε.

παινίδων ἦν, καὶ μόλις[j] ποτὲ εἰς βαλανεῖον ἐνεγκόν-
τες με καὶ περιπλύναντες ἔδειξαν τοῖς ἰατροῖς. ὡς
οὖν ταῦτ' ἀληθῆ λέγω, τούτων ὑμῖν τοὺς μάρτυρας
παρέξομαι.

1260 ΜΑΡΤΥΡΕΣ.

Συνέβη τοίνυν, ὦ ἄνδρες δικασταί, καὶ Εὐξίθεον 10
τουτονὶ τὸν Χολλείδην, ὄνθ' ἡμῖν συγγενῆ, καὶ Μειδίαν μετὰ τούτου ἀπὸ δείπνου ποθὲν ἀπιόντας περιτυ-
χεῖν πλησίον ὄντι μοι τῆς οἰκίας ἤδη, καὶ εἰς τὸ βαλανεῖον φερομένῳ παρακολουθῆσαι, καὶ ἰατρὸν ἄγουσι
παραγενέσθαι. οὕτω δ' εἶχον ἀσθενῶς ὥσθ', ἵνα μὴ
μακρὰν φεροίμην οἴκαδε ἐκ τοῦ βαλανείου, ἐδόκει τοῖς
παροῦσιν ὡς τὸν Μειδίαν ἐκείνην τὴν ἑσπέραν κομίσαι
με[k] καὶ ἐποίησαν οὕτως· λαβὲ οὖν καὶ τὰς τούτων
μαρτυρίας, [l]ἵν' εἰδῆθ' ὅτι πολλοὶ συνίσασιν ὡς ὑπὸ
τούτων ὑβρίσθην[l].

[j] μόγις Z et Bekker st. cum Σ.

[k] Bekker. om Z cum Σ.   [l-l] ἵν'—ὑβρίσθην om. r.

εἰς βαλανεῖον] a *public* bath, as
is shown by § 10, ἵνα μὴ μακρὰν
φεροίμην οἴκαδε ἐκ τοῦ βαλανείου.
See Becker's *Charicles* p. 147—
152.—For the context, cf.
Lysias, fragm. 75 (of a boy who
had been severely thrashed)
οὐ δυναμένου δὲ βαδίζειν ἐκόμισαν
αὐτὸν εἰς τὸ δεῖγμα ἐν κλίνῃ, καὶ
ἐπέδειξαν πολλοῖς Ἀθηναίων.

§ 10. *I was followed to the
bath by Midias and by a
relative of mine who was returning with him from dinner; and
as I was too weak to be carried
home again that evening, I was
taken to the house of Midias
for the night, as will be proved
by evidence.*

10. Χολλείδην] 'Οἱ Χολλεῖδαι,'
(Or. 35 § 20), a *deme* of the
tribe Leontis, probably situated

south of Hymettus and west
of *Mons Anhydrus*, or Hymettus minor (Leake's *Athens*, 11
57 and Wordsworth's *Athens
and Attica*, chap. xxv).—τού-
τονὶ implies that Euxitheus was
present in court; the other,
Midias (probably the same as
the subject of the well-known
oration of Dem.), was absent.—
τῆς οἰκίας, Ariston's home.

τὸ βαλανεῖον] *with* the article,
in reference to βαλανεῖον already
mentioned *without* the article.
So in § 7, ἐν ἀγορᾷ...εἰς τὴν
ἀγοράν.

ἄγουσι] The construction is
καὶ παραγενέσθαι αὐτοῖς ἄγουσιν
ἰατρόν.

ὡς τὸν Μειδίαν] 'to Midias'
house.' For ὡς introducing an
accusative of motion towards a

ΜΑΡΤΥΡΙΑΙ.

Λαβὲ δὴ καὶ τὴν τοῦ ἰατροῦ μαρτυρίαν.

ΜΑΡΤΥΡΙΑ.

11   Τότε μὲν τοίνυν παραχρῆμα ὑπὸ τῶν πληγῶν ὧν[m] ἔλαβον καὶ τῆς ὕβρεως οὕτω διετέθην, ὡς ἀκούετε καὶ μεμαρτύρηται παρὰ πάντων ὑμῖν τῶν εὐθὺς ἰδόντων. μετὰ δὲ ταῦτα τῶν μὲν οἰδημάτων τῶν ἐν τῷ προσώπῳ καὶ τῶν ἑλκῶν οὐδὲν ἔφη φοβεῖσθαι λίαν ὁ ἰατρός, πυρετοὶ δὲ παρηκολούθουν μοι συνεχεῖς καὶ ἀλγήματα ὅλου μὲν τοῦ σώματος πάνυ σφοδρὰ καὶ δεινά, μάλιστα δὲ τῶν πλευρῶν καὶ τοῦ ἤτρου, καὶ τῶν σιτίων 12 ἀπεκεκλείμην[n]. καὶ ὡς μὲν ὁ ἰατρὸς ἔφη, εἰ μὴ κάθαρσις αἵματος αὐτομάτη μοι πάνυ πολλὴ συνέβη περιωδύνῳ ὄντι καὶ ἀπορουμένῳ ἤδη, κἂν ἔμπυος γενόμενος

[m] *Bekker.* ἇς Z cum ΣΦΑ¹rk.
[n] *Bekker* cum Α¹. ἀπεκεκλείσμην Z cum FΦr. απεκλεισμην Σ.

person, cf. Thuc. iv 79, ἀφίκετο ὡς Περδίκκαν καὶ ἐς τὴν Χαλκιδικήν.

§§ 11, 12. *The surgeon and others have deposed to the immediate consequences of the assault; afterwards, though he expressed no great fears about my external bruises, unintermittent attacks of fever ensued, attended by extreme internal pain. I was quite unable to eat; and, but for a violent discharge of blood at a critical time, death would have resulted, as will be proved by medical evidence.*

11. τῶν σιτίων ἀπεκεκλείμην] 'I was cut off from, debarred from, my food,' 'too ill to eat anything.' Hesychius explains ἀποκεκλῆσθαι σιτίων· ἀνορέκτως ἔχειν τροφῆς.—Strict Atticists prefer ἀπεκεκλήμην (from old Attic κλήω) to ἀπεκεκλείμην

and ἀπεκεκλείσμην (Veitch *Gk. Verbs*).—ἤτρου, 'the pit of the stomach.'

12. εἰ μὴ—διεφάρην] 'If a copious discharge of blood had not spontaneously occurred, while I was in extreme agony and at the very crisis of the malady, I should have died of internal suppuration.' [An injury caused by the stamping upon him when down, was relieved at last by passing blood from some internal hemorrhage. P.] περιωδύνῳ is possibly a technical term; at any rate it is used by Hippocrates, 'the Father of Medicine,' and he also has περιωδυνεῖν, περιωδυνία and περιωδυνᾶσθαι [μοῖρα μὴ περιώδυνος μηδὲ δεμνιοτήρης occurs in Aesch. *Ag.* 1423. P.].—ἀπορουμένῳ is either *passive,* 'despaired of,' or more probably *middle,* 'doubtful of my recovery', οὐκ εἰδὼς εἰ πε-

διεφθάρην· νῦν δὲ τοῦτ᾽ ἔσωσε τὸ αἷμα ἀποχωρῆσαν.
ὡς οὖν καὶ ταῦτ᾽ ἀληθῆ λέγω, καὶ παρηκολούθησέ μοι
1261 τοιαύτη νόσος ἐξ ἧς εἰς τοὔσχατον ἦλθον, ἐξ ὧν ὑπὸ
τούτων ἔλαβον πληγῶν, λέγε τὴν τοῦ ἰατροῦ μαρτυρίαν καὶ τὴν τῶν ἐπισκοπούντων.

ΜΑΡΤΥΡΙΑΙ.

῞Οτι μὲν τοίνυν οὐ μετρίας τινὰς καὶ φαύλας λα- 13
βὼν πληγάς, ἀλλ᾽ εἰς πᾶν ἐλθὼν διὰ τὴν ὕβριν καὶ τὴν
ἀσέλγειαν τὴν τούτων πολὺ τῆς προσηκούσης ἐλάττω

ριφεύξομαι § 28.—On the quantity of ἔμπνος, see *Excursus* (B), p. 236.

τοῦτ᾽ ἔσωσε] The construction is τοῦτο τὸ αἷμα, ἀποχωρῆσαν, ἔσωσέ με, 'the passing of this blood saved my life.'

παρηκολούθησε—πληγῶν] Constr. τοιαύτη νόσος, ἐξ ἧς εἰς τοὔσχατον ἦλθον, παρηκολούθησέ μοι ἐκ τῶν πληγῶν, ἃς ὑπὸ τούτων (sc. Conon, Ctesias and Theogenes) ἔλαβον.

τῶν ἐπισκοπούντων] 'those who came to see me,' 'visited me in illness.' Xen. Cyrop. VIII 2 § 25, ὁπότε τις ἀσθενήσειε τῶν θεραπεύεσθαι ἐπικαιρίων, ἐπεσκόπει καὶ παρεῖχε πάντα ὅτου ἔδει; also in *middle*, Xen. Mem. III 11 § 10, ἀρρωστήσαντος φίλου φροντιστικῶς ἐπισκέψασθαι. Or. 59 § 56, τὰ πρόσφορα τῇ νόσῳ φέρουσαι καὶ ἐπισκοπούμεναι.

§§ 13—15. *Let me now tell you beforehand of the course which Conon will take in his reply. He will divert your attention from the facts and try to throw ridicule on the whole affair. He will tell you it was only the playful pleasantry that is common among young men about town. He will misrepresent us as just like his sons in character, and only*

different in being hard on other people. But the jury will be inflicting what I may call a fresh outrage upon me, if they are going to believe the defendant's bare assertion about our respective characters and to allow no weight to the evidence of our life and conduct.

13. εἰς πᾶν ἐλθών] While πᾶν ποιεῖν and πάντα ποιεῖν are invariably used in the active sense of 'straining every nerve,' 'leaving no stone unturned,' εἰς πᾶν ἐλθεῖν and similar phrases have often (like εἰς τοὔσχατον ἐλθεῖν of the last section) the passive notion of being reduced to the utmost extremity, as in the present passage.

Thus (i) in *active* sense we have Xen. Cyr. V 4 § 26 πάντα ἐποίουν πείθοντες τὸν βασιλέα, Anab. III 1 § 18 ἐπὶ πᾶν ἔλθοι, ὡς ἡμᾶς τὰ ἔσχατα αἰκισάμενος πᾶσιν ἀνθρώποις φόβον παράσχοι, Soph. O. T. 265 κἀπὶ πάντ᾽ ἀφίξομαι ζητῶν τὸν αὐτόχειρα.

(ii) in *passive*; Xen. Hell. VI 1 § 12 οἶδα δέ, ὑφ᾽ οἵας δυνάμεως...εἰς πᾶν ἀφίκετο βασιλεύς, and V 4 § 29. Plato Symp. 194A, μάλ᾽ ἂν φοβοῖο καὶ ἐν παντὶ εἴης.

τῆς προσηκούσης ἐλάττω δίκην] 'I have entered on an action much below the merits

δίκην εἴληχα, πολλαχόθεν νομίζω δῆλον ὑμῖν γεγενῆσθαι. οἶμαι° δ᾽ ὑμῶν ἐνίους θαυμάζειν τίνα[p] ποτ᾽
ἐστὶν ἃ πρὸς ταῦτα τολμήσει Κόνων λέγειν. βούλομαι
δὴ προειπεῖν ὑμῖν ἃ ἐγὼ πέπυσμαι λέγειν αὐτὸν παρεσκευάσθαι, ἀπὸ τῆς ὕβρεως καὶ τῶν πεπραγμένων
τὸ πρᾶγμ᾽ ἄγοντα εἰς γέλωτα καὶ σκώμματα ἐμβαλεῖν
14 πειράσεσθαι, καὶ ἐρεῖν ὡς εἰσὶν ἐν τῇ πόλει πολλοί,
καλῶν κἀγαθῶν ἀνδρῶν υἱεῖς, οἳ παίζοντες οἷα ἄνθρωποι νέοι σφίσιν αὐτοῖς ἐπωνυμίας πεποίηνται, καὶ κα-
λοῦσι τοὺς μὲν ἰθυφάλλους, τοὺς δὲ αὐτοληκύθους,

° οἴομαι Z cum Σ.   [p] A¹kr.   τί Z cum Σ.

of the case.' Cf. latter half of § 1.

τίνα ποτ᾽ ἐστὶν ἅ] The Zürich editors and Westermann prefer *τί ποτ᾽ ἐστὶν ἅ*, 'what is the import (*sing.*) of the points (*plur.*) that Conon will urge in his defence.' *τί...ἅ* is more idiomatic than *τίνα...ἅ*, and is found in Or. 4 § 10; 19 § 288; 21 § 154; 36 § 28; 37 § 36.

ἀπὸ τῆς ὕβρεως—ἐρεῖν] In apposition to λέγειν παρεσκευάσθαι, and loosely dependent on πέ-πυσμαι. A simpler construction might have been brought about by closing the sentence with παρεσκευάσθαι and then begin-ning afresh with some such sentence as the following; ἀπὸ γὰρ τῆς ὕβρεως καὶ τῶν πεπραγ-μένων τὸ πρᾶγμ᾽ ἀπαγαγών, εἰς γέλωτα καὶ σκώμματ᾽ ἐμβαλεῖν πειράσεται, καὶ ἐρεῖ κ.τ.λ., and in English translation this would give a clearer sense than any slavishly literal rendering of the more complex construc-tion in the text. 'He will di-vert your attention from the wanton outrage and the actual facts of the case; and will endeavour to turn the whole

affair into mere jest and ridi-cule.' That εἰς γέλωτα καὶ σκώμματ᾽ ἐμβαλεῖν is the con-struction (and not καὶ σκώμματ᾽ ἐμβαλεῖν πειράσεσθαι, καὶ ἐρεῖν,) appears from (Dem.) Phil. 4 § 75, τὸ πρᾶγμα εἰς γέλωτα καὶ λοιδορίαν ἐμβαλόντες, cf. Aeschin. 1 § 135 τὸ πρᾶγμα εἰς ὄνειδος καὶ κινδύνους καθιστάς and εἰς γέλωτα καὶ λῆρόν τινα προτρεπό-μενος ὑμᾶς, Lysias frag. 75, 1 εἰς σκώμματά τε αὐτοῖς καὶ ἀν-τιλογίαν καὶ ἔχθρον καὶ λοιδορίαν κατέστησαν.—Hesychius, refer-ring perhaps to the present pas-sage, has σκώμματα· λοιδορήματα γέλωτος χάριν.

14. *ὡς εἰσὶν*] followed in the latter half of the sentence by acc. c. inf.

καλῶν κἀγαθῶν] See note on Or. 4, 5 § 65. Trans. 'sons of respectable people, who in their youthful frolics have given them-selves nicknames.' σφίσιν αὐτοῖς is not necessarily limited to the reflexive sense, but is sometimes almost equivalent to the *re-ciprocal* pronoun ἀλλήλοις (see Isocr. Paneg. § 34).

ἰθυφάλλους ...... αὐτοληκύθους] 'Priapi and Sileni.' Kennedy

ἐρῶσι δ' ἐκ τούτων ἑταιρῶν τινές, καὶ δὴ καὶ τὸν υἱὸν
τὸν ἑαυτοῦ εἶναι τούτων ἕνα, καὶ πολλάκις περὶ[q] ἑται-
ρας καὶ εἰληφέναι καὶ δεδωκέναι πληγάς, καὶ ταῦτ'
εἶναι νέων ἀνθρώπων. ἡμᾶς δὲ πάντας τοὺς ἀδελφοὺς
παροίνους μέν τινας καὶ ὑβριστὰς κατασκευάσει[r], ἀγνώμονας δὲ καὶ πικρούς. ἐγὼ δ', ὦ ἄνδρες δικασταὶ, 15
χαλεπῶς ἐφ' οἷς πέπονθα ἐνηνοχὼς, οὐχ ἧττον τοῦτ'
ἀγανακτήσαιμ' ἂν καὶ ὑβρισθῆναι νομίσαιμι, εἰ οἷόν τ'

[q] *Bekker.* καὶ περὶ Z cum Σ.

[r] *Bekker.* παρασκευάσειν Z cum Σ, κατεσκευάκασι ΓΦ, κατασκευάσει A[1]kr.

(following the French translation of Auger). For an account
of the word αὐτολήκυθος, see *Excursus (C),* p. 227.

ἐρῶσι κ.τ.λ.] The construction
is τινὲς ἐκ τούτων ἐρῶσιν ἑταιρῶν.
—καὶ δὴ καὶ, used in descending
to particulars after a general
statement. Or. 55 § 10. The
construction here changes from
ὡς εἰσὶν to the acc. with infin.—
περὶ ἑταίρας gen. sing., not acc.
pl. [See Or. 21 § 36 p. 525 and
Ar. Vesp. 1345. P.]

εἰληφέναι καὶ δεδωκέναι πλη-
γὰς] These phrases are used
to supply the lack of a perf.
passive and active of τύπτω, as
the Attic prose writers know
nothing of the forms τετύφθαι
and τετυφέναι. See *Excursus
(A)* on τύπτω, p. 221.

παροίνους...ὑβριστὰς...ἀγνώμο-
νας... πικρούς] 'drunken' and
'insolent'; 'unforgiving' and
'ill-tempered.' The four epi-
thets, separated into pairs by
μὲν and δὲ, refer, in the case of
the first couple, to the actual
'assault and battery'; in the
case of the second, to the lawsuit that had since resulted.
Conon will in his artful way represent us as really wild sparks

like himself, who are yet inconsistent enough to be churlish
and ill-tempered, instead of
genial and good-humoured as
πάροινοι and ὑβρισταί ought
to be.

κατασκευάσει] in bad sense,
'to misrepresent,' 'trump up
a story,' 'make out falsely.'
Cf. Or. 45 § 82. παρασκευάσειν,
the reading of the Paris ms
Σ, depends, like the previous in-
finitives, on the remote verb
πέπυσμαι.

15. χαλεπῶς — ἐνηνοχὼς]
'deeply indignant as I am at the
wrongs I have suffered.' Or. 21
§ 108 ἐγὼ γὰρ ἐνηνοχὼς χαλεπῶς
ἐφ' οἷς περὶ τὴν λειτουργίαν ὑβρίσθην, ἔτι πολλῷ χαλεπώτερον...
τούτοις τοῖς μετὰ ταῦτα ἐνήνοχα
καὶ μᾶλλον ἠγανάκτησα, 58 § 55
πράως ἐπὶ τοῖς γιγομένοις φέρειν.

τοῦτ' ἀγανακτήσαιμ' ἂν] Or.
8 § 55, ἀγανακτῶ αὐτὸ τοῦτο, εἰ
τὰ μὲν χρήματα λυπεῖ τινας ὑμῶν
εἰ διαρπασθήσεται. ἀγανακτεῖν
and similar verbs implying
mental emotion, though occasionally followed by a dative
with or without ἐπί, may have
an accusative neuter pronoun
(Kühner, *Gk. Gr.* § 410 c 5).
τοῦτο is explained by εἰ ἀληθη

εἰπεῖν, εἰ ταῦτ᾽ ἀληθῆ δόξει Κόνων οὑτοσὶ λέγειν περὶ
ἡμῶν, καὶ τοσαύτη τις ἄγνοια παρ᾽ ὑμῖν ἐστιν ὥσθ᾽
ὁποῖος ἄν τις ἕκαστος εἶναι φῇ ἢ ὁ πλησίον αὐτὸν αἰ- 12
τιάσηται, τοιοῦτος νομισθήσεται, τοῦ δὲ καθ᾽ ἡμέραν
βίου καὶ τῶν ἐπιτηδευμάτων μηδ᾽ ὁτιοῦν ἔσται τοῖς
16 μετρίοις ὄφελος. ἡμεῖς γὰρ οὔτε παροινοῦντες οὐδ᾽[s]
ὑβρίζοντες ὑπ᾽ οὐδενὸς ἀνθρώπων ἑωράμεθα, οὔτ᾽ ἄγνω-

[s] Baiter (Dind. et Westermann): οὔθ᾽ retinet Bekker st. qui
in versu proximo οὐδὲ scribit.

δόξει οὑτοσὶ λέγειν, 'deeply indignant as I am at the wrongs
I have suffered, I should (if
you will pardon the expression)
feel no less resentment at this,
and should deem myself the
victim of a fresh outrage at
your hands, if Conon shall be
held by you to be speaking the
truth about us...' εἰ οἷόν τ᾽
εἰπεῖν must be understood as a
parenthetical apology for using
the strong word ὑβρισθῆναι to
express the outrage that will be
done to the feelings of honest
men like the plaintiff, if the
defendant's bare assertion is
believed outright, and if no
weight is given to the unimpeachable testimony presented
on the other hand by the exemplary lives of himself and
his brothers. Cf. esp. § 43 εἰ
προσυβρισθεὶς ἄπειμι καὶ δίκης
μὴ τυχών.

αὐτὸν αἰτιάσηται] sc. εἶναι,
'that, whatever sort of person
each one shall assert that he is,
or his neighbour shall accuse
him of being, such he shall be
considered to be, and respectable
citizens shall have no advantage
at all from their daily life or
conduct.' Aeschin. 1 § 153 and
2 § 5.

§§ 16—17. *As to our own*
character, no one has ever seen
us playing drunken pranks on
other people, and we cannot see
how our opponents can call us
' hard ' on others, if we claim
redress. Conon's sons are welcome to belong to their disorderly
clubs, but I shall be surprised
if this or any similar plea will
enable them to escape with impunity.

16. οὔτε παροινοῦντες οὐδ᾽
ὑβρίζοντες...οὔτ᾽ ἄγνωμον κ.τ.λ.]
This refers to § 14, παροίνους...
καὶ ὑβριστὰς...ἀγνώμονας δὲ καὶ
πικρούς. The Mss have οὔθ᾽
ὑβρίζοντες, which Baiter alters
into οὐδ᾽ ὑβρίζοντες. It would
be better perhaps (with Bekker)
to leave οὔθ᾽ ὑβρίζοντες, and to
alter οὔτ᾽ into οὐδ᾽ before ἄγνωμον. The break between the
second clause and the first is
clearly greater than between
the two parts of the first (viz.
παροινοῦντες and ὑβρίζοντες).

ἑωράμεθα] This form of the
perf. of ὁρᾶν (for the older
Attic ὦμμαι, the 2nd and 3rd
sing. of which occur in Dem.)
is also found in Isocr. antid.
§ 110, μηδ᾽ ὑφ᾽ ἑνὸς ἑωρᾶσθαι,
possibly the earliest extant instance (the *antidosis* belongs to
B.C. 355; the present speech to
B.C. 355 or 341).

μον οὐδὲν ἡγούμεθα ποιεῖν, εἰ περὶ ὧν ἠδικήμεθ' ἀξιοῦ-
μεν κατὰ τοὺς νόμους δίκην λαβεῖν. ἰθυφάλλοις δὲ
καὶ αὐτοληκύθοις συγχωροῦμεν εἶναι τοῖς υἱέσι τοῖς
τούτου, καὶ ἔγωγ' εὔχομαι τοῖς θεοῖς εἰς Κόνωνα καὶ
τοὺς υἱεῖς τοὺς τούτου καὶ ταῦτα καὶ τὰ τοιαῦτα ἅπαντα
τρέπεσθαι. οὗτοι γάρ εἰσιν οἱ τελοῦντες ἀλλήλους τῷ 17
ἰθυφάλλῳ, καὶ τοιαῦτα‹ ποιοῦντες ἃ πολλὴν αἰσχύνην
ἔχει καὶ λέγειν, μὴ ὅτι γε δὴ ποιεῖν ἀνθρώπους μετρίους. ἀλλὰ τί ταῦτ' ἐμοί; θαυμάζω γὰρ ἔγωγε, εἴ τίς
ἐστι πρόφασις παρ' ὑμῖν ἢ σκῆψις εὑρημένη δι' ἣν, ἂν
ὑβρίζων τις ἐξελέγχηται καὶ τύπτων, δίκην οὐ δώσει.
οἱ μὲν γὰρ νόμοι πολὺ τἀναντία καὶ τὰς ἀναγκαίας

‹ *Bekker.*   τὰ τοιαῦτα Z cum Σ.

συγχωροῦμεν κ.τ.λ.] They are
welcome, so far as we are concerned, to the attributes of
Priapi and Sileni. For the
dat. cf. § 44, πονηροτέροις ἡμῖν
εἶναι συνέβαινεν.

εἰς Κόνωνα...τρέπεσθαι] Passive; 'recoil upon the head of
Conon.' Ar. Ach. 833, πολυπραγμοσύνη νῦν εἰς κεφαλὴν τρέ-
ποιτ' ἐμοί. (Dem.) Epist. 4 §
10, οἱ θεοί...τὴν ἄδικον βλασφημίαν εἰς κεφαλὴν τῷ λέγοντι τρέ-
πουσι.

οἱ τελοῦντες κ.τ.λ.] 'who ini-
tiate one another with Priapic
rites.'— πολλὴν αἰσχύνην ἔχει,
'involve deep disgrace even to
speak of.'—μὴ ὅτι γε, *nedum.*
Cf. Plato, Phaedr. 240 D, Crat.
427 E, and see note on Or. 34
§ 14.

§§ 17 *cont.*—20. *Compare the
spirit of our laws with the course
which Conon proposes to take.
The laws, I understand, affix a
penalty even to minor offences,
to preclude the perpetration of
graver crimes, to prevent men
(for instance) being gradually led*

*from wrangling to blows, from
blows to wounding, from wounding to murder. Conon, on the
contrary, will make light of the
whole affair and will raise a
laugh to get himself acquitted.
Why! none of you would have
laughed had you seen me when
I was being brutally maltreated,
and when I was carried helpless
to my home.*

17. θαυμάζω γάρ] The Eng-
lish idiom requires us to leave
γάρ untranslated, or else to render it by the exclamation 'why!'
—'What has all this to do with
me? Why! for my part, I am
surprised if in *your* court they
have discovered any plea or pretext, thanks to which a man,
if convicted of outrage and
assault, shall escape punishment.'

οἱ μὲν γὰρ νόμοι κ.τ.λ.] The
influence of μέν extends over the
whole of the two following sections, it is then caught up and
reiterated in the clause εἶτ' ἐν
μὲν τοῖς νόμοις οὕτως. Thus the
first μέν has no δέ corresponding

προφάσεις, ὅπως μὴ μείζους γίγνωνται, προείδοντο,
οἷον (ἀνάγκη γάρ μοι ταῦτα καὶ ζητεῖν καὶ πυνθάνε-
18 σθαι διὰ τοῦτον γέγονεν) εἰσὶ κακηγορίας δίκαι· φασὶ
τοίνυν ταύτας διὰ τοῦτο γίγνεσθαι, ἵνα μὴ λοιδορού-

to it, until we reach the words ἂν δ' εἴπῃ Κόνων. 'The laws say so and so...' 'Not so Conon.'

τὰς ἀναγκαίας προφάσεις κ.τ.λ.] i.e. προείδοντο ὅπως μηδ' αἱ ἀναγκαίαι προφάσεις μείζους γίγνωνται. Thus, to use the illustration supplied below by Demosthenes himself, abusive language is a πρόφασις for dealing blows; blows again are a πρόφασις for inflicting wounds; lastly wounding, for homicide. The laws, by ordaining a legal remedy at each stage, (1) defamation, (2) assault, (3) unlawful wounding, interpose to prevent defamation, which is a pretext for assault, growing into actual assault; similarly assault developing into unlawful wounding, and ultimately into homicide. 'The laws on *their* part have, on the very contrary, made provision, even in the case of pleas of necessity, against the development of those pleas into greater proportions.'

[The meaning is, that the law, by providing an action for every kind of insult, has made it unnecessary for the aggrieved to resort to extremes in avenging himself. By ἀναγκαία πρόφασις he means, for instance, the plea, that a man was insulted and he was *obliged* to resent it. The law says, 'that obligation must not be pressed too far, so as to justify you in taking very violent revenge.' P.]

ἀνάγκη γάρ...γέγονεν] The plaintiff, a quiet, common-place soldier, is here on the verge of

displaying a familiarity with legal technicalities which would be not only out of keeping with his ordinary character, but would be resented by those of the jury who happened to be less versed in legal learning. The court would be apt to ascribe his acquaintance with the details of the law of defamation, assault, and homicide to that over-litigiousness of character which was as unpopular, as it was common, at Athens; or, at the very least, they would put him down as a pedant. Hence Demosthenes introduces a passing apology, explaining that the plaintiff, honest man, owes all his legal lore to the enquiries rendered imperative by the maltreatment he had received from the defendant. Hence, too, the skilful disclaimer of superior knowledge involved in the subsequent phrases; φασὶ... γίγνεσθαι and ἀκούω...εἶναι. Cf. Lysias Or. 19 §§ 5, 53.

κακηγορίας δίκαι] Isocr. κατὰ Λοχίτου (an αἰκίας δίκη like the present case), § 3 (οἱ θέντες ἡμῖν τοὺς νόμους) οὕτω...ἡγήσαντο δεινὸν εἶναι τὸ τύπτειν ἀλλήλους, ὥστε καὶ περὶ κακηγορίας νόμον ἔθεσαν, ὃς κελεύει τοὺς λέγοντάς τι τῶν ἀπορρήτων πεντακοσίας δραχμὰς ὀφείλειν. Cf. Lysias, Or. 10 §§ 6—12, Dem. Or. 23 § 50, Or. 21 § 32.

18. λοιδορούμενοι] 'reviling *one another*.' For the reciprocal sense, cf. Or. 54 § 40, ἐχθροὺς ἀλλήλοις ... λοιδορουμένους καὶ πλύνοντας αὐτοὺς τἀπόρρητα, and

μενοι τύπτειν ἀλλήλους προάγωνται. πάλιν αἰκίας
εἰσίν· καὶ ταύτας ἀκούω διὰ τοῦτ' εἶναι τὰς δίκας, ἵνα
μηδεὶς, ὅταν ἥττων ᾖ, λίθῳ μηδὲ τῶν τοιούτων ἀμύνη-
ται μηδενὶ, ἀλλὰ τὴν ἐκ τοῦ νόμου δίκην ἀναμένῃ.
τραύματος πάλιν εἰσὶ γραφαὶ τοῦ μὴ τιτρωσκομένων
τινῶν φόνους γίγνεσθαι. τὸ φαυλότατον, οἶμαι, τὸ 19
τῆς λοιδορίας, πρὸ τοῦ τελευταίου καὶ δεινοτάτου προ-

Ar. Ranae 857, πραόνως ἔλεγχ'
ἐλέγχου, λοιδορεῖσθαι δ' οὐ θέμις
ἄνδρας ποιητὰς ὥσπερ ἀρτοπω-
λίδας.

As λοιδορεῖσθαι is used in the
sense of κακῶς ἀγορεύειν ἀλλήλους, so also λοιδορία sometimes occurs as an equivalent
for the precise technical term
κακηγορία. Hence we have in
Ar. Vesp. 1207 εἶλον διώκων λοιδορίας (sc. κακηγορίας), and Athenaeus (XII 525 B) quotes from
Antiphon ἐν τῷ κατ' Ἀλκιβιάδου
λοιδορίας, possibly meaning a
speech in a δίκη κακηγορίας.

αἰκίας] sc. δίκαι, of which the
present case is an instance.

For the general sense of the
following sentences, cf. Isocr.
κατὰ Λοχίτου Or. 20 § 8 πολλάκις
ἤδη μικραὶ προφάσεις μεγάλων
κακῶν αἴτιαι γεγόνασι, καὶ...διὰ
τοὺς τύπτειν τολμῶντας εἰς τοῦτ'
ἤδη τινὲς ὀργῆς προήχθησαν ὥστ'
εἰς τραύματα καὶ θανάτους
καὶ φυγὰς καὶ τὰς μεγίστας
συμφορὰς ἐλθεῖν.

ἵνα μηδεὶς—μηδενί] 'to prevent anyone, when he is the
weaker party, defending himself
with a stone or any similar
missile,' e. g. an ὄστρακον, Lysias Or. 4 § 6. See Mahaffy's
Social Greece pp. 358—360.

τραύματος...γραφαί] (Lysias)
Or. 6 κατ' Ἀνδοκίδου § 15 ἄν τις
ἀνδρὸς σῶμα τρώσῃ, κεφαλὴν ἢ
πρόσωπον ἢ χεῖρας ἢ πόδας, αὐτὸς
κατὰ τοὺς νόμους τοὺς ἐξ Ἀρείου

πάγου φεύξεται τὴν ἀδικηθέντος
πόλιν, καὶ ἐὰν κατίῃ, ἐνδειχθεὶς
θανάτῳ ζημιωθήσεται.

The fourth oration of Lysias
is a very brief defence in a case
of 'malicious wounding,' περὶ
τραύματος ἐκ προνοίας. The defendant endeavours to prove the
absence of πρόνοια (malice pre-
pense), and implores the βουλή
(ἡ ἐξ Ἀρείου πάγου) to rescue
him from banishment (§§ 6, 12,
20). In Aeschin. Ctesiph. § 51
a τραύματος γραφή instituted by
Demosthenes is mentioned; and
Demosthenes himself (Aristocr.
§ 24) quotes the law τὴν βουλὴν
δικάζειν φόνου καὶ τραύματος ἐκ
προνοίας κ.τ.λ.

τοῦ μὴ...φόνους γίγνεσθαι] The
genitive of a clause containing
an accusative of the subject
and an infinitive is often used
(especially with μὴ) to denote
the object or motive; the dative,
the means and instrument or
cause (Madvig's Greek Syntax,
§ 170, and the commentators
on Thuc. II 102; VI 33; VIII 87
§ 3.)

19. τὸ τῆς λοιδορίας κ.τ.λ.]
'the least of these evils, namely,
abusive language, has been
provided for by the laws, for the
avoidance of (πρὸ) &c.'—προεώραται, which may have either a
middle or a passive sense, has
here almost certainly the latter,
especially as we have just had
ἑωράμεθα as a passive in § 16.

εώραται, τοῦ μὴ φόνον γίγνεσθαι μηδὲ κατὰ μικρὸν
ὑπάγεσθαι ἐκ μὲν λοιδορίας εἰς πληγάς, ἐκ δὲ πληγῶν 1263
εἰς τραύματα, ἐκ δὲ τραυμάτων εἰς θάνατον, ἀλλ᾽ ἐν
τοῖς νόμοις εἶναι τούτων ἑκάστου τὴν δίκην, μὴ τῇ τοῦ
προστυχόντος ὀργῇ μηδὲ βουλήσει ταῦτα κρίνεσθαι.
20 εἶτ᾽ ἐν μὲν τοῖς νόμοις οὕτως· ἂν δ᾽ εἴπῃ Κόνων "ἰθύ-
"φαλλοί τινές ἐσμεν ἡμεῖς συνειλεγμένοι, καὶ ἐρῶντες
"οὓς ἂν ἡμῖν δόξῃ παίομεν καὶ ἄγχομεν," εἶτα γελάσαντες ὑμεῖς ἀφήσετε; οὐκ οἶμαί[u] γε. οὐ γὰρ ἂν
γέλως ὑμῶν ἔλαβεν οὐδένα, εἰ παρὼν ἐτύγχανεν, ἡνίκα
εἱλκόμην καὶ ἐξεδυόμην καὶ ὑβριζόμην, καὶ ὑγιὴς ἐξελθὼν φοράδην ἦλθον οἴκαδε, ἐξεπεπηδήκει δὲ μετὰ
ταῦθ᾽ ἡ μήτηρ, καὶ κραυγὴ καὶ βοὴ τῶν γυναικῶν
τοσαύτη παρ᾽ ἡμῖν ἦν ὡσπερανεὶ τεθνεῶτός τινος,

.[u] οἶμαι Ζ cum Σ.

προεώραμαι occurs as passive in Arist. Met. ΙΙ 1, and προεωρᾶσθαι as middle in Diod. Sic. xx 102. Westermann here supplies ὁ νόμος, and thus takes it as a middle ; but Dem. in the present passage and its context appears to prefer the plural οἱ νόμοι, though ἐκ τοῦ νόμου occurs four lines back.

ἐκ λοιδορίας εἰς πληγάς] 40 § 32 ἐξ ἀντιλογίας καὶ λοιδορίας πληγὰς συναψάμενος.

20. ἐν μὲν τοῖς νόμοις] re-iterates οἱ μὲν γὰρ νόμοι in § 17.

ἰθύφαλλοι—ἄγχομεν] 'we belong to the Priapus-club (§ 34, ἐπειδὰν συλλεγῶσι) and in our love-affairs (§ 14) strike and throttle whom we choose.'

εἶτα] an indignant exclamation. — γελάσαντες ... ἀφήσετε. Cf. Or. 23 § 206, ἂν ἐν ᾖ δύ᾽ ἀστεῖα εἴπωσι...ἀφίετε. Horace, Sat. ΙΙ 1, 86, solventur risu tabulae ; tu missus abibis.

εἱλκόμην—οἴκαδε] The rhe-torician Aristides (Spengel, Rhet. Graeci ΙΙ 495) quotes this sentence to exemplify σφοδρότης, or vehemence of style. On ἐξεπεπηδήκει he remarks, οὐκ εἶπεν ἐξεληλύθει, ἀλλὰ ἐμφαντι-κώτερον τῇ ὀνομασίᾳ, ἐξεπεπη-δήκει ἡ μήτηρ· ἐν γὰρ τῷ ὀνόματι ἡ ἔμφασις.

φοράδην] Hesychius, ὁ φερό-μενος βασταγμῷ [by the hands of men (not in a wheeled car) P.].

τεθνεῶτος] The compound tenses ἀποθνήσκω, ἀποθανοῦμαι, ἀπέθανον (which are frequent in Attic prose and comedy, but are not used in tragedy) have no corresponding perfect, but take instead the *simple* forms τέθνηκα, τεθνάναι, τεθνεώς. ἀποτεθνεὼς and the like are never found in Attic verse or prose (Cobet, nov. lect. 29 and Veitch, *Greek verbs*). Cf. Plato, Phaedo 64 A, ἀποθνήσκειν τε καὶ τεθνάναι, and 71 c, ἐκ τῶν τεθνεώτων, followed

ὥστε τῶν γειτόνων τινας πέμψαι πρὸς ἡμᾶς ἐρησομέ-
νους ὅ τι ἐστὶ τὸ συμβεβηκός. ὅλως δ', ὦ ἄνδρες 21
δικασταί, δίκαιον μὲν οὐδενὶ δήπου σκῆψιν οὐδεμίαν
τοιαύτην οὐδὲ ἄδειαν ὑπάρχειν παρ' ὑμῶν᾽ δι' ἣν
ὑβρίζειν ἐξέσται· εἰ δ' ἄρ' ἐστί τῳ, τοῖς δι' ἡλικίαν
τούτων τι πράττουσι, τούτοις ἀποκεῖσθαι προσήκει
τὰς τοιαύτας καταφυγάς, κἀκείνοις᾽ οὐκ εἰς τὸ μὴ
δοῦναι δίκην, ἀλλ' εἰς τὸ τῆς προσηκούσης ἐλάττω. 22
ὅστις δ' ἐτῶν μέν ἐστι πλειόνων ἢ πεντήκοντα, παρὼν
δὲ νεωτέροις ἀνθρώποις καὶ τούτοις υἱέσιν, οὐκ ὅπως
ἀπέτρεψεν ἢ διεκώλυσεν, ἀλλ' αὐτὸς ἡγεμὼν καὶ πρῶτος καὶ πάντων βδελυρώτατος γεγένηται, τίν' ἂν
οὗτος ἀξίαν τῶν πεπραγμένων ὑπόσχοι δίκην; ἐγὼ
μὲν γὰρ οὐδ' ἀποθανόντα οἶμαι. καὶ γὰρ εἰ μηδὲν

ᵛ Bekker st. cum ΣΛ¹k : legebatur ὑμῖν.

ʷ Α¹kr. καὶ ἐκείνοις Ζ cum Σ.

in the very next line by ἐκ τῶν
ἀποθανόντων.

§§ 21—23. *It is only those
who are misled by their youth into
acts of outrage that deserve any
indulgence, and even in their
case, such indulgence ought not
to get them off altogether, but
should extend simply to mitigation of their penalty. But Conon
is more than fifty years of age,
and therefore inexcusable; and
yet, instead of stopping younger
men, and those his sons, from
doing wrong, he was the ringleader of them all.*

*Even the penalty of death
would be too small for his crimes,
for the conduct of his sons in
their father's presence proves that
he himself had no reverence for
his own father.*

21. δίκαιον μὲν] The rule
of strict justice, stated broadly
(ὅλως, 'speaking generally'), as
contrasted with the concessions
granted in special cases on the
principles of equity (or ἐπιείκεια)
implied in the next sentence.

τούτοις] repeats the previous
dative τοῖς...πράττουσι ('to these,
I say'), and is itself emphatically
reiterated in the subsequent
κἀκείνοις, referring pointedly to
the plaintiff's opponents.

εἰς] 'to the extent of.' For
this sense, see my note on Eur.
El. 1072. P.]

22. παρὼν δὲ—γεγένηται] Cf.
§ 6 ad fin.

τίν' ἂν—δίκην ;] i.e. 'Is there
any punishment to which he
could submit, that would be
adequate to his crimes?'—On
ἀποθανόντα, cf. note on § 20,
τεθνεῶτος.—With οἶμαι we understand ἀξίαν ἂν τῶν πεπραγμένων
ὑποσχεῖν δίκην.—ἅπερ νυνί, sc.
πεποιηκὼς φαίνεται.

αὐτὸς εἴργαστο τῶν πεπραγμένων, ἀλλ᾽ εἰ παρεστη- 1264
κότος τούτου Κτησίας ὁ υἱὸς ὁ τούτου ταῦθ᾽ ἅπερ[x]
νυνὶ πεποιηκὼς ἐφαίνετο, τοῦτον ἐμισεῖτ᾽ ἂν δικαίως.
23 εἰ γὰρ οὕτω τοὺς ἑαυτοῦ προῆκται παῖδας ὥστ᾽ ἐνάν-
τίον ἐξαμαρτάνοντας ἑαυτοῦ, καὶ ταῦτα ἐφ᾽ ὧν ἐνίοις
θάνατος ἡ ζημία κεῖται, μήτε φοβεῖσθαι μήτ᾽ αἰσχύνεσθαι, τί τοῦτον οὐκ ἂν εἰκότως παθεῖν οἴεσθε; ἐγὼ
μὲν γὰρ ἡγοῦμαι ταῦτ᾽ εἶναι σημεῖα τοῦ μηδὲ τοῦτον
τὸν ἑαυτοῦ πατέρα αἰσχύνεσθαι· εἰ γὰρ ἐκεῖνον αὐτὸς
ἐτίμα καὶ ἐδεδίει, κἂν τούτους αὐτὸν ἠξίου.
24   Λαβὲ δή μοι καὶ τοὺς νόμους, τόν τε[y] τῆς ὕβρεως

---

[x] *Bekker st. cum* Σ.   +οὗτος A¹kr.
[y] τόν τε *addidit* Dind.   τοὺς A¹kr.   *om.* Z *et Bekker st. cum* ΣΦ.

τοῦτον ἐμισεῖτ᾽ ἂν δικαίως]
'even then you would have
abhorred the defendant, and
rightly too!' or (with Kennedy)
'even then he would have deserved your execration.'

23. προῆκται] Perfect passive
with *middle* sense 'has had
them brought up' (Liddell and
Scott), or simply 'has trained
them,' (*gezogen hat*). This explanation is due to Reiske, and
is probably right. But the
general sense of προάγω, 'to
lead on by little and little'
(§ 18, προάγωνται), may perhaps
warrant our understanding it of
Conon's permitting his sons to
be constantly taking liberties,
and going step by step from bad
to worse. προῆκται may in the
latter case be rendered 'has
spoilt' (*verzogen hat*, Westermann and G. H. Schaefer), but
the two meanings are almost
identical, and the general sense
the same.

καὶ ταῦτα ἐφ᾽ ὧν—κεῖται] 'and
that too in the case of acts, for

some of which the penalty ordained is death' (referring to
laws against ὕβρις and περὶ τῶν
λωποδυτῶν, cf. § 1 *ad fin.*). ἐφ᾽
ὧν ἐνίοις stands for ἐπὶ τούτων
ὧν ἐνίοις [or, perhaps, καὶ ταῦτα
(ἐξαμαρτάνοντας) ἐφ᾽ ὧν ἐνίοις. P.]

τοῦτον] Conon; ἐκεῖνον, his
father (who was probably dead,
as we may take αἰσχύνεσθαι as
an *imperfect* imperative); τούτους, his sons.—The construction of the last clause is ἠξίου
ἂν καὶ τούτους (τιμᾶν καὶ δεδιέναι)
αὐτόν.

§§ 24, 25.   *Take and read the
statutes on brutal outrage and
on highway robbery, to both of
which the defendant is amenable,
though I have declined to claim
redress under these statutes.
Further, had death ensued, he
would have been chargeable with
murder.*

24.   τόν τε τῆς ὕβρεως] In Or.
21 (Mid.) § 46, a document is
given, purporting to be the law
in question.

καὶ τὸν περὶ τῶν λωποδυτῶν· καὶ γὰρ τούτοις ἀμφοτέροις ἐνόχους τούτους ὄψεσθε. λέγε.

ΝΟΜΟΙ.

Τούτοις τοῖς νόμοις ἀμφοτέροις ἐκ τῶν πεπραγμένων ἔνοχος Κόνων ἐστὶν οὑτοσί· καὶ γὰρ ὕβριζε
καὶ ἐλωποδύτει. εἰ δὲ μὴ κατὰ τούτους προειλόμεθ'
ἡμεῖς δίκην λαμβάνειν, ἡμεῖς μὲν ἀπράγμονες καὶ μέτριοι φαινοίμεθ' ἂν εἰκότως, οὗτος δ' ὁμοίως πονηρός.
καὶ μὴν εἰ παθεῖν τί μοι συνέβη, φόνου καὶ τῶν δεινο- 25
τάτων ἂν ἦν ὑπόδικος. τὸν γοῦν τῆς Βραυρωνόθεν
ἱερείας πατέρα ὁμολογουμένως οὐχ ἁψάμενον τοῦ τε-

τὸν περὶ τῶν λωποδυτῶν] The
periphrasis is due to the fact
that the crime has no name
specially appropriated to it in
Attic Greek of the best age
(λωποδυσία is found only in a
glossary, and λωποδυσίου δίκη in
the rhetorician Hermogenes,
fl. A.D. 170). Cf. § 1, where
λωποδυτῶν ἀπαγωγὴ is parallel
to ὕβρεως γραφαί.—See Mayor's
note on Cicero, Phil. II § 8.—
Xen. Mem. I 2 § 62 κατὰ τοὺς
νόμους, ἐάν τις φανερὸς γένηται
κλέπτων ἢ λωποδυτῶν ἢ βα-
λαντιοτομῶν ἢ τοιχωρυχῶν ...
τούτοις θάνατός ἐστιν ἡ ζημία.

ἀπράγμονες καὶ μέτριοι] 'Quiet
and inoffensive,' Or. 42 § 12
μετρίου καὶ ἀπράγμονος πολίτου
μὴ εὐθὺς ἐπὶ κεφαλὴν εἰς τὸ
δικαστήριον βαδίζειν. Cf. Or.
36 § 53.

25. εἰ παθεῖν τί μοι συνέβη] a
common euphemism for death.
Or. 23 (Aristocr.) § 59 ἂν ἄρα
συμβῇ τι παθεῖν ἐκείνῳ. A frequent formula at the beginning
of a Greek will was : ἔσται μὲν
εὖ, ἐὰν δέ τι συμβαίνῃ, τάδε διατί-
θεμαι (Diog. Laert. v 11 § 51).
Cf. Cicero, Phil. 1 § 10, si quid

mihi humanitus accideret, and
Sheridan's Rivals, v 3 (just before a duel), 'But tell me now,
Mr Acres, in case of an ac-
cident, is there any little will or
commission I could execute for
you?'

γοῦν] 'for instance,' or, ' at
any rate,' one person was condemned for such an offence.
Tr. ' the father of the priestess
at Brauron, though he confess-
edly had not laid a finger on the
deceased, and merely because
he encouraged the assailant to
hit him again, was outlawed by
the court of the Areopagus.' P.]

τῆς Βραυρωνόθεν ἱερείας] Priestess of Artemis, who was specially
worshipped at Brauron, the
ancient deme near the western
coast of Attica, where Orestes
and Iphigenia are said to have
landed with the statue of the
Taurian goddess. Wordsworth's
Athens and Attica c. xxviii :
'The daughter of Agamemnon
was brought here, as the legend
related [Iph. T. 1461], from the
gloomy regions of the Tauric
Chersonesus, and placed as a
priestess of Diana's temple in

λευτήσαντος, ὅτι τῷ πατάξαντι τύπτειν παρεκελεύ-
σατο, ἐξέβαλεν ἡ βουλὴ ἡ ἐξ Ἀρείου πάγου. δικαίως·
εἰ γὰρ οἱ παρόντες, ἀντὶ τοῦ κωλύειν τοὺς ἢ δι᾽ οἶνον
ἢ δι᾽ ὀργὴν ἤ τιν᾽ ἄλλην αἰτίαν ἐξαμαρτάνειν ἐπι-
χειροῦντας, αὐτοὶ παροξυνοῦσιν, οὐδεμί᾽ ἐστὶν ἐλπὶς
σωτηρίας τῷ περιπίπτοντι τοῖς ἀσελγαίνουσιν, ἀλλ᾽
ἕως ἂν ἀπείπωσιν, ὑβρίζεσθαι ὑπάρξει· ὅπερ ἐμοὶ
συνέβη.

this cheerful valley, where she was said to have lived and died; and where her supposed tomb was shown in after ages.' The principal ceremony in the Brauronia, held every five years, was the rite performed by the young girls of Attica, dressed in saffron-coloured attire, who played as bears in honour of the goddess. Ar. Lys. 645 κᾆτ᾽ ἔχουσα τὸν κροκωτὸν ἄρκτος ἦ Βραυρωνίοις. Leake's *Athens* II 72, and Dict. Ant. s. v. *Brauronia*.

πατάξαντι τύπτειν] See *Excursus* (*A*) p. 221.

ἐξέβαλεν] not 'expelled' from its own body, but 'banished' from the country. A. Schaefer, *Dem. u. s. Zeit* III 2, 114 n.

The charge in this case would be what is technically called βούλευσις, which is best defined as 'id crimen, quo quis, quacunque sit ratione, ipse tamen a necando manus abstinens hominem morti studeat dare' (Forchhammer, *de Areopago*, p. 30). Harpocration s. v. says that the term is used ὅταν ἐξ ἐπιβουλῆς τίς τινι κατασκευάσῃ θάνατον, ἐάν τι ἀποθάνῃ ὁ ἐπιβουλευθεὶς ἐάν τε μή. He adds that, according to Isaeus and Aristotle, such charges came before the court ἐπὶ Παλλαδίῳ; but, according to Deinarchus, before the

Areopagus,—as in the present instance. The apparent discrepancy as to the tribunal for hearing such cases, may be reconciled by the fact that the court at the Palladium was reserved for charges of φόνος ἀκούσιος (Aristocr. § 72), whereas that of the Areopagus had cognisance of φόνος ἐκ προνοίας (Sauppe, *Or. Att.* II. 235; see also Meier and Schömann, p. 312, note 532 Lipsius; and the discussion in Zink's *Dissertatio* pp. 3—10).

Ἀρείου πάγου] The form Ἀρειόπαγος is apparently only found in late inscriptions. (See note on Isocr. Paneg. § 78 καλοῖς κἀγαθοῖς.)

ἕως ἂν ἀπείπωσιν] 'till they are tired,' sc. οἱ ἀσελγαίνοντες. Cf. § 27, ἐπειδὴ δ᾽ οὖν ποτ᾽ ἀπεῖπον. Reiske (*index Graec.*) is clearly wrong in his rendering *deliquerint animis sub verberibus:* had the clause referred to the victim, the singular would have been used, to correspond to τῷ περιπίπτοντι.

§§ 26—29. *At the arbitration my opponents, by wasting time and introducing irrelevant matters, protracted the proceedings beyond midnight, to the disgust of all the bystanders, and at last even of themselves. They then, with an evasive object, put in a challenge, offer-*

1265   Ἃ τοίνυν, ὅθ' ἡ δίαιτα ἐγίγνετο, ἐποίουν, βούλο- 26
μαι πρὸς ὑμᾶς εἰπεῖν· καὶ γὰρ ἐκ τούτων τὴν ἀσέλγειαν θεάσεσθε αὐτῶν. ἐποίησαν μὲν γὰρ ἔξω μέσων
νυκτῶν τὴν ὥραν, οὔτε τὰς μαρτυρίας ἀναγιγνώσκειν
ἐθέλοντες οὔτε ἀντίγραφα διδόναι, τῶν τε παρόντων
ἡμῖν καθ' ἕνα οὑτωσὶ πρὸς τὸν λίθον[z] ἄγοντες καὶ ἐξ-

[z] Dind. et Westermann. βωμὸν Z et Bekker st. cum libris.

*ing to surrender certain slaves
to be examined by torture as to
the assault, and they will make
much of this challenge. But
had it been a bona fide offer, it
would have been made not at the
last moment, but long before.*

26. ἡ δίαιτα] Civil actions at
Athens, before being brought
into court, were almost invariably referred to arbitration.
The Arbitrators (διαιτηταί) were
either public and appointed by
lot (κληρωτοί) or private and
chosen (αἱρετοί) by the parties to
the impending suit. In cases
brought before a public arbitrator the parties might appeal to
a higher Court; whereas the decision of a private arbitrator
was final. See esp. Or. 21
(Mid.) § 94 τὸν τῶν διαιτῶν νόμον.
The δίαιτα here described was
of the former kind. (See further
Dict. Antiq. s. v. δίαιτα and
Excursus to Kennedy's Demosth.
Leptines &c pp. 395—403, or
Hermann's *Public Antiquities*,
§ 145, 10 &c. Cf. Wayte on
Androt. § 27.)

ἐποίησαν—ὥραν] 'They prolonged the time beyond midnight.' For the plural νύκτες
in the sense *nocturna tempora*
cf. Plato Phileb. 50 D νῦν οὖν
λέγε πότερα ἀφίης με ἢ μέσας
ποιήσεις νύκτας, Protag. 310 c,
and Symp. 217 D πόρρω τῶν νυκτῶν. Ar. Nub. 1, τὸ χρῆμα τῶν
νυκτῶν ὅσον.

οὔτε—διδόναι] 'by refusing to
read aloud the depositions or to
put in copies of the same.' The
depositions were indispensable,
and the defendants' refusal
would obviously protract the
proceedings, and lead to lengthy
debates between the Arbitrator
and the parties to the suit.—
τῶν παρόντων sc. μαρτύρων.—
καθ' ἕνα = ἕκαστον, 'one by
one,' *singillatim.* Or. 9 § 22,
καθ' ἕν' οὑτωσὶ περικόπτειν καὶ
λωποδυτεῖν τῶν Ἑλλήνων (index
to Buttmann's *Midias* s. v.
κατά).

οὑτωσὶ] 'merely,' *sic temere*,
Homer's αὔτως, or μάψ οὔτως,
'just bringing our witnesses up
to the altar and putting them
on their oath and *nothing
more*,' without allowing them
to proceed with their depositions.

λίθον] The MSS have βωμόν,
which is retained by the Zürich
editors but altered into λίθον by
others on the authority of Harpocration : λίθος· Δημοσθένης ἐν
τῷ κατὰ Κόνωνος 'τῶν τε παρόντων
καθ' ἕνα ἡμῖν οὑτωσὶ καὶ πρὸς
τὸν λίθον ἄγοντες καὶ ἐξορκοῦντες
(sic).' ἐοίκασι δ' Ἀθηναῖοι πρός
τινι λίθῳ τοὺς ὅρκους ποιεῖσθαι ὡς
Ἀριστοτέλης ἐν τῇ Ἀθηναίων πο-
λιτείᾳ καὶ Φιλόχορος ἐν τῷ γ
ὑποσημαίνουσι. So Hesychius,
λίθος· βῶλος, βωμὸς καὶ βάσις.
τὸ ἐν τῇ Ἀθηναίων ἐκκλησίᾳ βῆμα. Plutarch, Solon 25, ὤμνυεν

ορκίζοντες, καὶ γράφοντες μαρτυρίας οὐδὲν πρὸς τὸ πρᾶγμα, ἀλλ' ἐξ ἑταίρας εἶναι παιδίον αὐτῷ τοῦτο καὶ πεπονθέναι τὰ καὶ τὰ, ἃ μὰ τοὺς θεούς, ὦ ἄνδρες δικασταὶ, οὐδεὶς ὅστις οὐκ ἐπετίμα τῶν παρόντων καὶ ἐμί-

27 σει, τελευτῶντες δὲ καὶ αὐτοὶ οὗτοι ἑαυτούς. ἐπειδὴ δ' οὖν ποτ' ἀπεῖπον καὶ ἐνεπλήσθησαν ταῦτα ποιοῦντες, προκαλοῦνται ἐπὶ διακρούσει καὶ τῷ μὴ σημαν-

ὅρκον ἕκαστος τῶν θεσμοθετῶν ἐν ἀγορᾷ πρὸς τῷ λίθῳ. Similarly what Theophrastus (ap. Zenob. proverb. iv 36) calls the ὕβρεως καὶ ἀναιδείας βωμούς on the Areopagus, Pausanias describes as λίθους (ι 28 § 5).

The word βωμόν was perhaps originally an interlinear or marginal explanation of λίθον, and subsequently thrust the right word from the text.

The διαιτηταὶ might hold their arbitration in any temples, halls or courts available, e. g. in the temple of Hephaestus as in Isocr. Trapez. § 15, ἑλόμενοι δὲ βασανιστὰς ἀπηντήσαμεν εἰς τὸ Ἡφαιστεῖον (Dem. 33 § 18). So in Or. 36 § 16 we have seen the temple of Athene on the Acropolis mentioned as the scene of an arbitration. In any case an altar for the administration of oaths would be readily at hand, and it is unnecessary to suppose that in the present passage any special public altar is intended. Indeed, βωμός, with its synonym λίθος, does not always mean an altar, as it may also be used of a small platform or step of stone. Cf. Favorinus (quoted by Hager in *Journ. of Philol.* vi 21) βωμός· οὐ μόνον ἐφ' ὧν ἔθυον ἀλλὰ καὶ κτίσμα τι ἁπλῶς καὶ ἀνάστημα, ἐφ' οὗ ἐστι βῆναί τι καὶ τεθῆναι. βωμοῖς· βαθμοῖς.

ἐξορκίζοντες] Also used in Aeschin. fals. leg. § 85, ἐξώρκιζον τοὺς συμμάχους, in the same sense as the more common ἐξορκοῦν (for which see Or. 45 § 58).

οὐδὲν πρὸς τὸ πρᾶγμα] sc. οὔσας, 'utterly irrelevant.'—τοῦτο, sc. Ctesias. They brought all sorts of irrelevant depositions, one of which was that Conon's son was illegitimate [and therefore Conon was not legally responsible for his actions; further that he, Ctesias, has undergone certain ill treatment which justified the outrage he committed on Ariston. P.]

ἅ] The antecedent is not τὰ καὶ τὰ, but the general sense of the whole of the preceding clauses; 'a course of conduct which, &c.'

τελευτῶντες—ἑαυτούς] sc. ἐπετίμων καὶ ἐμίσουν, 'at last they were indignant at and disgusted with themselves.' The speaker feeling that, by implying that his opponents had had the sense to desist, he has made too much of a concession to them, hurries over his admission, and in the next sentence cuts the matter short by the opening words ἐπειδὴ δ' οὖν, i.e. 'whether this was the real reason or no, at any rate when at last they *did* desist, &c.'

27. προκαλοῦνται——γράψαντες] 'with a view to gaining

θῆναι τοὺς ἐχίνους ἐθέλειν ἐκδοῦναι περὶ τῶν πληγῶν
παῖδας, ὀνόματα γράψαντες. καὶ νῦν οἶμαι[a] περὶ τοῦτ'
ἔσεσθαι τοὺς πολλοὺς τῶν λόγων αὐτοῖς. ἐγὼ δ' οἶμαι[b]
δεῖν πάντας ὑμᾶς ἐκεῖνο σκοπεῖν, ὅτι οὗτοι, εἰ τοῦ
γενέσθαι τὴν βάσανον ἕνεκα προὐκαλοῦντο, καὶ ἐπί-
στευον τῷ δικαίῳ τούτῳ, οὐκ ἂν ἤδη τῆς διαίτης ἀπο-
φαινομένης, νυκτός, οὐδεμιᾶς ὑπολοίπου σκήψεως 28
οὔσης, προὐκαλοῦντο, ἀλλὰ πρῶτον μὲν πρὸ τοῦ τὴν

[a] οἴομαι Ζ cum Σ. [b] Σ. οἴομαι Ζ.

time, and preventing the cases
for the documents from being
sealed up, they put in a challenge, tendering certain slaves,
whose names they wrote down,
to be examined as to the assault.'

The προκλησις, or challenge,
demanding or offering an inquiry into a special 'issue'
before an Arbitrator very frequently related to the testimony
of slaves presumably cognisant
of the matter in dispute. In
many cases the challenge would
take the form of demanding
that the opponent's slaves
should be given up to torture,
(to elicit facts which that
opponent was alleged to have
concealed or misrepresented
(Dict. Antiq. p. 398 a). Harpocr. quoted on Or. 45 § 15.
(See Or. 45 § 59—62, and Or.
59 § 124—5.)

In the present instance Conon
offers to allow certain slaves to
be examined. The plaintiff
evidently refuses, and this refusal, he says, is sure to be
made a strong point against
him. He therefore insists that
the προκλησις in question was a
mere ruse to protract the proceedings before the Arbitrator,
and that had it been a *bona
jide* offer it would have been

made at an earlier date, and
with all the proper formalities
(§ 27—29).

τοὺς ἐχίνους] All the legal
documents (μαρτυρίαι, προκλήσεις &c.) produced during an
arbitration or, indeed, any
preliminary examination, e.g.
an ἀνάκρισις, were enclosed in
one or more caskets, or ἐχῖνοι
(possibly of a cylindrical shape),
which were sealed up and carefully preserved, to be ready in
the event of an appeal. See
Or. 45 §§ 17 and 57, Or. 39
§ 17, Or. 47 § 16, and cf. Or. 48
(Olymp). § 48, τὰς συνθήκας πάλιν
σημήνασθαι, τὰ δ' ἀντίγραφα ἐμ-
βαλέσθαι εἰς τὸν ἐχῖνον.

τῷ δικαίῳ τούτῳ] 'this plea.'

ἤδη διαίτης ἀποφαινομένης]
'when the award was just
being announced.' ἀποφαινεσ-
θαι, (1) in *middle* of the διαι-
τητής Or. 33 (Apat.) § 19, εἷς
ὢν (sc. ἄνευ τῶν συνδιαιτητῶν
ἀποφανεῖσθαι ἔφη τὴν δίαιταν,
§ 20 ἐρήμην κατ' αὐτοῦ ἀπε-
φήνατο τὴν δίαιταν (cf. § 21
τὴν ἀπόφασιν ἐποιήσατο: (2)
in *passive* (as here) of the award
itself. Reiske's Index (to which
these references are due) is
wrong in rendering it as a
past sense, *sententia iam pro-
nuntiata*.

δίκην ληχθῆναι, ἡνίκ' ἀσθενῶν ἐγὼ κατεκείμην καὶ,
οὐκ εἰδὼς εἰ περιφεύξομαι, πρὸς ἅπαντας τοὺς εἰσιόντας τοῦτον ἀπέφαινον τὸν πρῶτον πατάξαντα καὶ τὰ
πλεῖσθ' ὧν ὑβρίσμην διαπεπραγμένον, τότ' ἂν εὐθέως
ἧκεν ἔχων μάρτυρας πολλοὺς ἐπὶ τὴν οἰκίαν, τότ' ἂν
τοὺς οἰκέτας παρεδίδου καὶ τῶν ἐξ Ἀρείου πάγου τινὰς
παρεκάλει· εἰ γὰρ ἀπέθανον, παρ' ἐκείνοις ἂν ἦν ἡ 1266
29 δίκη.   εἰ δ' ἄρ' ἠγνόησε ταῦτα καὶ τοῦτο τὸ δίκαιον
ἔχων, ὡς νῦν φήσει, οὐ παρεσκευάσατο ὑπὲρ τηλικούτου κινδύνου, ἐπειδή γ' ἀνεστηκὼς ἤδη προσεκαλεσάμην[c] αὐτὸν, ἐν τῇ πρώτῃ συνόδῳ πρὸς τῷ
διαιτητῇ παραδιδοὺς ἐφαίνετ' ἄν· ὧν οὐδὲν πέπρακται
τούτῳ.   ὅτι δ' ἀληθῆ λέγω καὶ διακρούσεως ἕνεκα ἡ
πρόκλησις ἦν, λέγε ταύτην τὴν μαρτυρίαν· ἔσται γὰρ
ἐκ ταύτης φανερόν.

[c] προεκαλεσάμην A¹kr.

28. τὸν πρῶτον πατάξαντα] 'I
was pointing out the defendant,
to all who came to see me. as
the man who struck the first
blow.' In a case of assault, the
question who struck the first
blow would be, of course, important.   Or. 47 § 40 βούλομαι
τοὺς μάρτυρας παρασχέσθαι οἳ
εἰδόν με πρότερον πληγέντα.
ἡ δ' αἰκία τοῦτ' ἐστιν, ὃς ἂν ἄρξῃ
χειρῶν ἀδίκων πρότερος. Cf.
Or. 23 § 50, Isocr. Or. 20 § 1,
Lysias, Or. 4 § 11.

ἔχων μάρτυρας πολλούς] To
give full and legal attestation
to the πρόκλησις. So also in
Or. 45 § 61, and elsewhere, a
πρόκλησις is attested by a μαρτυρία.

ἐξ Ἀρείου πάγου τινάς] as
special witnesses. § 25 εἰ παθεῖν
τί μοι συνέβη, φόνου...ἂν ἦν ὑπόδικος. The speaker implies that
had death ensued, Conon would
have been liable to a charge

of φόνος ἐκ προνοίας. On the
jurisdiction of the Areopagus in
cases of homicide, see especially
§§ 65—70 of the speech against
Aristocrates, Or. 23.

τοῦτο τὸ δίκαιον sc. τὴν πρόκλησιν.

29. εἰ...οὐ] Cf. § 33 ad fin.
προσεκαλεσάμην] 'I cited,
summoned him,' served him
with a πρόσκλησις, not to be
confounded with προὐκαλεσάμην,
'I challenged him, put in a
πρόκλησις.' Several mss actually
have προεκαλεσάμην,—a mani-
fest blunder.—'If he did not
know this serious responsibility,
and if having (as he will now tell
you) this plea on his side (i.e.
the offer of the slave), he took
no precautions against so serious
a peril (i.e. the charge of murder), yet at least, when on my
recovery I issued a summons
against him, in our *first* meeting before the Arbitrator he

ΜΑΡΤΥΡΙΑ.

Περὶ μὲν τοίνυν τῆς βασάνου ταῦτα μέμνησθε, 30
τὴν ὥραν ἡνίκα προὐκαλεῖτο, ὧν ἕνεκ' ἐκκρούων ταῦτ'
ἐποίει, τοὺς χρόνους τοὺς πρώτους, ἐν οἷς οὐδαμοῦ
τοῦτο βουληθεὶς τὸ δίκαιον αὑτῷ γενέσθαι φαίνεται,
οὐδὲ προκαλεσάμενος, οὐδ' ἀξιώσας. ἐπειδὴ τοίνυν
ταῦτα πάντα ἠλέγχετο, ἅπερ παρ' ὑμῖν, πρὸς τῷ διαιτητῇ, καὶ φανερῶς ἐδείκνυτο πᾶσιν ὧν ἔνοχος τοῖς
ἐγκεκλημένοις, ἐμβάλλεται μαρτυρίαν ψευδῆ, καὶ 31
ἐπιγράφεται μάρτυρας ἀνθρώπους οὓς οὐδ' ὑμᾶς

would have shown himself willing to give up the slaves.'

§§ 30—33. *He thereupon put
in false evidence, alleging that
certain witnesses, boon companions of his own, deposed that
they found the defendant's son
and myself fighting in the market-place and that the defendant
did not strike me. On my own
part, I produce the evidence of
strangers who came up by ac-
cident, attesting that they saw
me struck by the defendant.
What motive could these strangers have had for giving 'false
evidence' on my side ?*

30. ὧν ἕνεκ' ἐκκρούων ταῦτ'
ἐποίει] As delay and evasion
were the object (ὧν ἕνεκα) of the
defendant's conduct (§ 27 ἐπὶ
διακρούσει and § 29 διακρούσεως
ἕνεκα), we may at first sight suspect (with Westermann) that
ἐκκρούων is an interpolation;
it may, however, be defended
on the ground that it enables
the speaker to reiterate emphatically the real motive of
his opponent,—'his purpose,
his *evasive* purpose, in so
doing.' In this view, we may,
if we please, punctuate the
passage thus: ὧν ἕνεκα, ἐκκρούων,
ταῦτ' ἐποίει. Cf. Fals. leg. § 144,

ἐκκρούσας εἰς τὴν ὑστεραίαν, and
see Or. 36 § 2; 45 § 4; 40 §§ 44,
45.

ἀξιώσας] sc. τὸ δίκαιον γενέσθαι, 'to have claimed to have
this plea allowed him,' i.e. the
plea founded on his appeal to
the evidence of his slaves.

ἠλέγχετο] The construction
is, οὗτος ἠλέγχετο ταῦτα πάντα
πρὸς τῷ διαιτητῇ ἅπερ (accusative) νῦν παρ' ὑμῖν ἐλέγχεται.
Thus the nominative to ἠλέγχετο is the same as that of ἐδείκνυτο in the next clause, and no
change of construction is re-
quisite.

πᾶσι] not masc., but to be
taken with τοῖς ἐγκεκλημένοις.

31. ἐμβάλλεται] Or. 40 § 21
μαρτυρίαν οὐδεμίαν ἐμβεβλημένος,
ib. §§ 28, 58; cf. 27 §§ 51, 54;
28 § 1; sc. εἰς τὸν ἐχῖνον (§ 27),
Or. 49 § 65, ἐμβαλομένου ἐμοῦ
ὅρκον εἰς τὸν ἐχῖνον, and 45 § 6.
Trans. 'puts in a false deposition endorsed with names which,
I take it, *you* will recognise,
when you hear them.'

ἐπιγράφεται] Or. 53 § 14, κλητῆρα ἐπιγράφεται. The phrase
hardly means 'to give in one's
list of witnesses' (L and S), but
rather 'to have their names
inscribed as witnesses.' ἐπι-

ἀγνοήσειν οἶμαι[d], ἐὰν ἀκούσητε, "Διότιμος Διοτίμου
"Ἰκαριεὺς, Ἀρχεβιάδης Δημοτέλους Ἁλαιεὺς, Χαι-
"ρέτιμος[e] Χαριμένους[f] Πιτθεὺς[g] μαρτυροῦσιν ἀπιέναι
"ἀπὸ δείπνου μετὰ Κόνωνος, καὶ προσελθεῖν ἐν ἀγορᾷ
"μαχομένοις Ἀρίστωνι καὶ τῷ υἱεῖ τῷ Κόνωνος, καὶ
32 "μὴ πατάξαι Κόνωνα Ἀρίστωνα," ὡς ὑμᾶς εὐθέως
πιστεύσοντας, τὸ δ' ἀληθὲς οὐ λογιουμένους, ὅτι πρῶτον μὲν οὐδέποτ' ἂν οὔθ' ὁ Λυσίστρατος οὔθ' ὁ Πα-
σέας οὔθ' ὁ Νικήρατος οὔθ' ὁ Διόδωρος, οἳ διαρρήδην

[d] οἴομαι Z cum Σ.
[e] *Bekk.* cum r. Χαιρήτιος Z cum FΣ ; χαιρίτιος Φ.
[f] *Bekk.* Χαιριμένους Z cum ΣrA[1].
[g] Πιθεὺς Σ (Dind. ed. Oxon. 1846).

γράφεται, it will be noticed, is previous in order of time to ἐμβάλλεται. This ὕστερον πρότερον enables the speaker to lead up more easily to the mention of the names of the witnesses.

The following μαρτυρία is indisputably authentic, and therefore serving as a standard by which others purporting to be original depositions may be tested. See notes on Or. 35 (Iacr.) § 10 and Or. 45 § 8.

Ἰκαριεὺς ...Ἁλαιεὺς ...Πιτθεὺς] The names of the corresponding *demes* are (1) Ἰκαρία, belonging to the tribe *Aegeis*, and placed by Leake p. 103 'in the southern part of Diacria, not far from the Marathonian district.' (Bursian, however, identifies the Ἰκάριον ὄρος with the southern spur of Cithaeron towards Megara, *Geogr.* I 251.)

(2) Ἁλαί, a name common to two sea-coast *demes*, the first Ἁλαί Αἰξωνίδες of the tribe *Cecropis* S.W. of Athens and N.W. of Cape Zoster; the second Ἁλαί Ἀραφηνίδες of the tribe *Aegeis* on the east coast of Attica near Brauron.

(3) Πίθος, of the tribe *Cecropis*, placed by Bursian N.E. of Athens, near the southern spurs of Pentelicus (*Geogr.* I. 345). The spelling Πιθεὺς is found in the Paris MS Σ, instead of Πιτθεύς of other MSS. The latter is recognised by Harpocr. s. v. Πιτθεύς· δῆμος τῆς Κεκροπίδος ἡ Πιτθός (*sic*).—For Ἀρχεβιάδης see note on § 34.

μὴ πατάξαι Κόνωνα Ἀρίστωνα] The sense shows that Conon is the subject, Ariston the object. The order of the words is, in itself, inconclusive.

ὡς—λογιουμένους] The accusative absolute of the participle is here used with ὡς, as often with ὥσπερ (*quasi vero*): 'imagining that you will at once give credence, instead of drawing the true inference.'

32. ἂν] is constructed with ἠθέλησαν, five lines distant.

Νικήρατος] possibly the Niceratos to whom Demosthenes pathetically refers in Or. 21 (Mid) § 165 Νικήρατος ὁ τοῦ Νικίου ἀγαπητὸς παῖς, ὁ παντά-

μεμαρτυρήκασιν ὁρᾶν ὑπὸ Κόνωνος τυπτόμενον ἐμὲ
καὶ θοἰμάτιον ἐκδυόμενον καὶ τἄλλα ὅσα ἔπασχον
ὑβριζόμενον, ἀγνῶτες ὄντες καὶ ἀπὸ ταὐτομάτου παρα-
267 γενόμενοι τῷ πράγματι τὰ ψευδῆ μαρτυρεῖν ἠθέλησαν, εἰ μὴ ταῦθ' ἑώρων πεπονθότα· ἔπειτ' αὐτὸς ἐγὼ
οὐδέποτ' ἂν, μὴ παθὼν ὑπὸ τούτου ταῦτ', ἀφεὶς τοὺς
καὶ παρ' αὐτῶν τούτων ὁμολογουμένους τύπτειν ἐμὲ,
πρὸς τὸν οὐδ' ἁψάμενον πρῶτον εἰσιέναι προειλόμην.
τί γὰρ ἄν; ἀλλ' ὑφ' οὗ γε πρώτου ἐπλήγην καὶ μάλισθ' 33
ὑβρίσθην, τούτῳ καὶ δικάζομαι καὶ μισῶ καὶ ἐπεξέρχομαι. καὶ τὰ μὲν παρ' ἐμοῦ πάνθ' οὕτως ἐστὶν ἀληθῆ
καὶ φαίνεται· τούτῳ δὲ μὴ παρασχομένῳ τούτους 'μάρ-

πασιν ἀσθενῆς τῷ σώματι. If so,
he would be a great-grandson
of the Nicias, who commanded
in the Sicilian expedition.

θοἰμάτιον ἐκδούμενον] § 35.
Lysias Or. 10 § 40 (with reference to the term λωποδύτης) εἰ
τις ἀπάγοι τινὰ φάσκων θοἰμάτιον
ἀποδεδύσθαι ἢ τὸν χιτωνίσκον
ἐκδεδύσθαι, where θοἰμάτιον (as
here) and χιτωνίσκον are the
object and not the subject.

τὰ ψευδῆ] Cf. Or. 45 § 2
'if they had not actually seen
the assault, they would never
have consented to give false
evidence,' i.e. evidence which,
on that supposition, would have
been false, τὰ ψευδῆ ἂν ὄντα εἰ
μὴ ταῦθ' ἑώρων.

ἔπειτ' αὐτὸς ἐγὼ] refers to ὅτι
πρῶτον μὲν (οἱ μάρτυρες) and still
subordinate to the distant ὅτι.

πρῶτον] adverb, to be taken
with εἰσιέναι, contrasted with
ὑφ' οὗ πρώτου ἐπλήγην. 'I prosecute *first* the man who struck
me first of all the assailants.'
This seems better than to take
it with ἁψάμενον, 'him who did
not even touch me first.'

εἰσιέναι] εἰς τὸ δικαστήριον.
Reiske's index shows that this
verb is used in Dem. of either
litigant or both, or again of the
cause itself, or even with δίκην
or γραφὴν as accusative after it.
See note on Or. 45 § 7.

33. τί γὰρ ἄν] 'Why should I?'
The mss have the interpolation,
ἢ διὰ τί; probably a mere explanation of τί; as equivalent
to διὰ τί;

δικάζομαι ... μισῶ ... ἐπεξέρχο-
μαι] 'Sue ... abhor ... prosecute
(visit with vengeance),' 'he it
is whom I sue and prosecute
as my enemy.' The collocation
of μισῶ, expressive of inward
feeling, between δικάζομαι and
ἐπεξέρχομαι, indicating outward
acts, is curious. The latter
word is probably immediately
suggested by μισῶ, 'not only do I
hate him in my heart, but I carry
out that hatred to its practical
issue by prosecuting him.'

φαίνεται] sc. ἀληθῆ ὄντα, not
'appears,' but 'is proved to
be,' 'is clearly true':—μὴ παρασχόμενος = εἰ μὴ παρέσχετο.

τυρας ἦν δήπου λόγος οὐδεὶς, ἀλλ' ἡλωκέναι παραχρῆμα ὑπῆρχε σιωπῇ. συμπόται δ' ὄντες τούτου καὶ
πολλῶν τοιούτων ἔργων κοινωνοὶ, εἰκότως τὰ ψευδῆ
μεμαρτυρήκασιν. εἰ δ' ἔσται τὸ πρᾶγμα τοιοῦτον, [h]ἐὰν
ἅπαξ ἀπαναισχυντήσωσί τινες καὶ τὰ ψευδῆ φανερῶς
τολμήσωσι μαρτυρεῖν, οὐδὲν δὲ [h]τῆς ἀληθείας ὄφελος,
34 πάνδεινον ἔσται πρᾶγμα. ἀλλὰ νὴ Δία οὐκ εἰσὶ τοιοῦ-

[h] 'Reiskius, (ὥστ') ἐὰν ἅπαξ—οὐδὲν εἶναι τῆς ἀληθ. *Hoc quidem speciose, sed illud non puto necesse.*' Dobree.

εἰκότως] to be taken with τα ψευδῆ μεμαρτύρηκασι, not with κοινωνοί.

εἰ δ' ἔσται κ.τ.λ.] 'If it comes to such a pass, if once certain persons are lost to all sense of shame and openly dare to give false evidence, and (consequently) truth has no advantage, it will be an atrocious state of things.' The simple construction would have been as follows: ἐὰν δὲ ἅπαξ ἀπαναι-σχυντήσωσί τινες καὶ τὰ ψευδῆ φανερῶς τολμήσωσι μαρτυρεῖν, οὐδὲν ἔσται τῆς ἀληθείας ὄφελος· εἰ δὲ ἔσται τὸ πρᾶγμα τοιοῦτον, πάνδεινον ἔσται.

As it is, Demosthenes, by writing τοιοῦτον in the early part of the sentence, leads us to expect ὥστε, which however never comes; we have, instead, the clause ἐὰν, κ.τ.λ., exegetical of τοιοῦτον. Again οὐδὲν τῆς ἀληθείας ὄφελος is *in sense* the apodosis of ἐὰν...τὰ ψευδῆ τολ-μήσωσι μαρτυρεῖν, but in con-struction is made part of the protasis, πάνδεινον ἔσται πρᾶγμα being left to do duty as an apo-dosis, and πρᾶγμα necessarily repeated owing to the long interval that separates the apodosis from τὸ πρᾶγμα in the protasis.

For εἰ—οὐδὲν, see note on

Or. 34 § 48.

ἀπαναισχιντήσωσι] used of unblushing effrontery. Cf. ἀπ-ανθαδίζεσθαι. Or. 29 § 20, τὸ μὲν πρῶτον ἀπηναισχύντει, τοῦ δὲ διαιτητοῦ κελεύοντος μαρτυρεῖν ἢ ἐξομνύειν, ἐμαρτύρησε πάνυ μόλις.

34. ἀλλὰ νὴ Δία] used, as often, like *at enim*, to introduce emphatically an anticipated re-joinder on the part of the op-ponents. 'Oh but, good hea-vens! they are not such cha-racters as I make them out.' The phrase may be seen in its fullest form in Or. 20 § 3 ἀλλὰ νὴ Δί' ἐκεῖνο ἂν ἴσως εἴποι πρὸς ταῦτα.

§§ 34—37. *Many of you know the characters of the wit-nesses for the defence,—men who, in the daytime, affect an aus-terity which is very inconsistent with their conduct when they meet together. They will un-scrupulously contradict the evi-dence on our side; but you will remember that I rely on medical witnesses, whereas my oppo-nents have no independent tes-timony, and, but for themselves, could get no evidence at all a-gainst me. People who break into houses, and assault persons in the streets, would surely have no scruple about putting down false evidence on a paltry piece of paper.*

τοι. ἀλλ᾽ ἴσασιν ὑμῶν, ὡς ἐγὼ νομίζω, πολλοὶ καὶ τὸν
Διότιμον καὶ τὸν Ἀρχεβιάδην καὶ τὸν Χαιρέτιμον¹ τὸν
ἐπιπόλιον τουτονί, οἳ μεθ᾽ ἡμέραν μὲν ἐσκυθρωπάκασι
καὶ λακωνίζειν φασὶ καὶ τρίβωνας ἔχουσι καὶ ἁπλᾶς

¹ Bekk. Χαιρήτιον Z cum ΦΣΦ. Cf. § 31.

31. Ἀρχεβιάδην] This worthy, who has already been mentioned among the witnesses in §§ 7 and 31, and must not be confounded with the still less known Ἀρχεβιάδης ὁ Λαμπτρεύς (Or. 52 § 3), was evidently quite a 'character,' judging from Plutarch's description of him as 'a man of sour countenance who always wore a coarse cloak and had grown a prodigious beard.' Phocion x *init.* ἦν δέ τις Ἀρχεβιάδης ἐπικαλουμένος Λακωνιστής, πώγωνά τε καθειμένος ὑπερφυῆ μεγέθει καὶ τρίβωνα φορῶν ἀεὶ καὶ σκυθρωπάζων· τοῦτον ἐν βουλῇ θορυβούμενος ὁ Φωκίων ἐπεκαλεῖτο τῷ λόγῳ μάρτυν ἅμα καὶ βοηθόν. ὡς δὲ ἀναστὰς ἐκεῖνος ἃ πρὸς χάριν ἦν τοῖς Ἀθηναίοις συνεβούλευεν, ἁψάμενος αὐτοῦ τῶν γενείων "ὦ Ἀρχεβιάδη" εἶπε "τί οὖν οὐκ ἀπεκείρω;" It will be observed that Plutarch's anecdote contains several points of coincidence with the passage before us.

τὸν ἐπιπόλιον] 'the grey-headed man yonder' (present in court). Aristot. de gen. anim. v 5 § 3 ἐπιπολιοῦνται αἱ τρίχες 'the hair grows *grizzled.*' [ἐπιπόλιος is perhaps much the same as the Homeric μεσαιπόλιος, *Il.* xiii 361, whether the sense is 'grey on the top,' or 'half grey,' 'grizzled.' P.]

μεθ᾽ ἡμέραν κ.τ.λ.] Or. 45 § 80.

ἐσκυθρωπάκασι] i. e. 'assume a sour expression and a frown-

ing brow.' Cf. Or. 45 § 68.

λακωνίζειν φασί] i. e. 'pretend to imitate the Laconians.' Plato Protag. 342 B, οἱ μὲν (sc. ἐν ταῖς πόλεσι λακωνίζοντες) ὦτά τε κατάγνυνται (i.e. get their ears battered in boxing) μιμούμενοι αὐτούς, καὶ ἱμάντας περιειλίττονται καὶ φιλογυμναστοῦσι καὶ βραχείας ἀναβολὰς φοροῦσιν, ὡς δὴ τούτοις κρατοῦντας τῶν Ἑλλήνων τοὺς Λακεδαιμονίους. Ar. Aves 1281 ἐλακωνομάνουν ἅπαντες ἄνθρωποι τότε | ἐκόμων, ἐπείνων, ἐρρύπων, ἐσωκράτουν, | ἐσκυταλιοφόρουν (v. Becker's *Charicles* p. 63 with n. 8).

τρίβωνας] Sometimes mentioned as characteristic of Laconians. Plutarch Nicias 19: τοὺς Σικελιώτας...σκώπτοντας εἰς τὸν τρίβωνα καὶ τὴν κόμην (of Gylippus the Spartan general)...ἐν τῇ βακτηρίᾳ καὶ τῷ τρίβωνι τὸ σύμβολον καὶ τὸ ἀξίωμα τῆς Σπάρτης καθορῶντες... Athenaeus xii 50, p. 535 (quoting the historian Douris) Παυσανίας ὁ τῶν Σπαρτιατῶν βασιλεύς, καταθέμενος τὸν πάτριον τρίβωνα, τὴν Περσικὴν ἐνεδύετο στολήν. [At the same time, the regular dress of the old Athenian dicast or ecclesiast was the τρίβων and the βακτηρία, both often mentioned in Aristoph. e.g. Vesp. 33. P.]

ἁπλᾶς ὑποδέδενται] 'wear single-soled shoes,' sc. ἐμβάδας. Harpocration ἁπλᾶς· Δημ. κατά Κόνωνος. Καλλίστρατός φησι τὰ μονόπελμα τῶν ὑποδημάτων οὕτω καλεῖσθαι. Στράττις Λημνομέδᾳ 'ὑποδήματα σαυτῷ πρίασθαι τῶν

ὑποδέδενται, ἐπειδὰν δὲ συλλεγῶσι καὶ μετ' ἀλλήλων
35 γένωνται, κακῶν καὶ αἰσχρῶν οὐδὲν ἐλλείπουσι· καὶ
ταῦτα τὰ λαμπρὰ καὶ νεανικά ἐστιν αὐτῶν· "οὐ γὰρ
"ἡμεῖς μαρτυρήσομεν ἀλλήλοις; οὐ γὰρ ταῦθ' ἑταίρων
"ἐστὶ καὶ φίλων; τί δὲ καὶ δεινόν ἐστιν ὧν παρέξεται
"κατὰ σοῦ; τυπτόμενόν φασί τινες ὁρᾶν; ἡμεῖς δὲ
"μηδ' ἧφθαι τὸ παράπαν μαρτυρήσομεν. ἐκδεδύσθαι 1268
"θοἰμάτιον; τοῦτ' ἐκείνους πρότερον πεποιηκέναι ἡμεῖς
"μαρτυρήσομεν. τὸ χεῖλος ἐρράφθαι; τὴν κεφαλὴν δέ
36 "γ' ἡμεῖς ἢ ἕτερόν τι κατεαγέναι φήσομεν." ἀλλὰ καὶ
μάρτυρας ἰατροὺς παρέχομαι. τοῦτ' οὐκ ἔστιν, ὦ ἄνδρες δικασταί, παρὰ τούτοις· ὅσα γὰρ μὴ δι' αὐτῶν,
οὐδενὸς μάρτυρος καθ' ἡμῶν εὐπορήσουσιν. ἡ δ' ἀπ'
αὐτῶν ἑτοιμότης οὐδ' ἂν εἰπεῖν μὰ τοὺς θεοὺς δυ-

ἁπλῶν.' Bekker, *Anecd.* 205
ἁπλαῖ· ὑποδήματος εἶδος Λακωνι-
κοῦ κ.τ.λ. They had only one
thickness of sole and were apparently more like slippers than
shoes. (Becker, *Charicles*, p.
449.) There was also a more
elaborate kind of shoes known as
Λακωνικαί (Ar. Vesp. 1158). For
the general drift of the sentence
cf. Isaeus Or. 5 § 11 ὀνειδίζει καὶ
ἐγκαλεῖ αὐτῷ ὅτι ἐμβάδας καὶ
τριβώνια φορεῖ ὥσπερ ἀδικούμενός
τι εἰ ἐμβάδας Κηφισόδοτος φορεῖ,
ἀλλ' οὐκ ἀδικῶν ὅτι ἀφελόμενος
αὐτὸν τὰ ὄντα πένητα πεποίηκεν.

συλλεγῶσι] sc. νυκτός, contrasted with μεθ' ἡμέραν μέν.

κακῶν καὶ αἰσχρῶν] 'wicked-
ness and indecency.'

35. τὰ λαμπρὰ καὶ νεανικά]
'their splendid and spirited
pleas.'

οὐ γὰρ κ.τ.λ.] 'What! sha'n't
we, &c.' *quidni igitur?*

ὧν παρέξεται] constr. τί δὲ καὶ
δεινόν ἐστιν ἐκ τούτων ἃ παρέξεται
ὁ 'Αρίστων κατὰ σοῦ; 'is there
any serious harm, anything
really worth fearing?'

ἧφθαι] passive, referring to
Ariston, like τυπτόμενον just be-
fore. ' ἧμμαι is pf. mid. in Soph.
Tr. 1009 (ἧπται) and Pl. Phaedr.
260 (ἧφθαι)' (we may add Dem.
Or. 51 § 5, ἧφθαι τῆς τριήρους
τούτους); 'pf. passive in Eur.
Hel. 107, Ar. Pl. 301 and Thuc.
IV 100.' Veitch, *Greek Verbs.*

ἐρράφθαι] § 41, τὸ χεῖλος διακοπεὶς οὕτως ὥστε ῥαφῆναι.
This was doubtless part of the
surgeon's evidence in § 10.

κατεαγέναι] second perfect in
passive sense. For other constructions, cf. Plato Gorg. 469 D,
τῆς κεφαλῆς κατεαγέναι and Lys.
Or. 3 § 40 καταγεὶς τὴν κεφαλὴν
ὑπ' αὐτοῦ.

36. ὅσα μὴ] 'except what is (deposed) by means of themselves';
'*nam nisi quod sibi ipsi testa-
buntur nullum adversus nos tes-
tem habebunt.* Plutarch *Timol.*
3, πρᾶος διαφερόντως ὅσα μὴ μι-
σοτύραννος εἶναι καὶ μισοπόνηρος.'
G. H. Schaefer.

ἡ—ἑτοιμότης] On this circum-

ναίμην ὅση καὶ οἷα πρὸς τὸ ποιεῖν ὁτιοῦν ὑπάρχει. ἵνα δ' εἰδῆτε οἷα καὶ διαπραττόμενοι περιέρχονται, λέγε αὐτοῖς ταυτασὶ τὰς μαρτυρίας, σὺ δ' ἐπίλαβε τὸ ὕδωρ.

ΜΑΡΤΥΡΙΑΙ.

Τοίχους τοίνυν διορύττοντες καὶ παίοντες τοὺς 37 ἀπαντῶντας, ἆρ' ἂν ὑμῖν ὀκνῆσαι δοκοῦσιν ἐν γραμματειδίῳ τὰ ψευδῆ μαρτυρεῖν ἀλλήλοις[j] οἱ κεκοινωνη-

j *Bekk.* om. Σ *prima manu.*

locution, see Kühner, *Gk. Gr.* II p. 288.

ὅση καὶ οἷα] *quanta et qualis.* 'In heaven's name, I could not tell you the *extent* and the *character* of the readiness existing on their part to perpetrate anything in the world.' Cf. the common collocation τοσοῦτος καὶ τοιοῦτος (e. g. § 37), which may often be conveniently paraphrased as above.

ἵνα εἰδῆτε] The speaker uses the plural in addressing the δικασταί, and passes off to the singular λέγε, on turning to the clerk of the court.

ἐπίλαβε τὸ ὕδωρ] Or. 45 § 8; 57 § 21; Lysias Or. 23 §§ 4, 8, 11, 13, 15; Isaeus Or. 2 § 34; 3 § 12. The κλεψύδρα (Becker's *Charicles,* p. 212 n.) was always stopped by the functionary in charge of it (ὁ ἐφ' ὕδωρ) during the recitation of documents: it was only the duration of the speech proper that was reckoned in the allowance of time measured by the κλεψύδρα. Or. 36 ends with the words ἔξερα τὸ ὕδωρ 'pour out the water,' implying that the orator had found it unnecessary to avail himself of the full allowance of time. The Orators frequently used ὕδωρ in the sense of 'time

allotted' for a speech, e. g. ἐν τῷ ἐμῷ ὕδατι· ἐν μικρῷ μέρει τοῦ παντὸς ὕδατος. So Or. 41 fin. πρὸς ὀλίγον ὕδωρ ἀναγκαζόμενος λέγειν, infra § 44; 40 § 38; 44 § 45; 53 § 3; 59 § 20; Deinarchus Or. 1 § 114; 2 § 6. Aeschin. Fals. leg. § 126 πρὸς ἔνδεκα ἀμφορέας ... κρίνομαι, Dem. Or. 43 § 8. Cf. Pliny, Ep. II 11 § 14 *dixi horis paene quinque; nam duodecim* clepsydris *quas spatiosissimas acceperam sunt additae quattuor.*

When Goethe visited Venice, in Oct. 1786, and went to see a trial in the Ducal Palace, he found a custom in force singularly similar to that implied in the text. Whenever the advocate spoke, the time that elapsed was measured with an hourglass, which was laid on its side while the depositions were read: 'so lange nämlich der Schreiber liest, so lange läuft die Zeit nicht' etc. (*Italiänische Reise* p. 68 Düntzer).

37. τοίχους διορύττοντες] The documents just read have deposed to the defendant's witnesses being guilty *inter alia* of housebreaking (τοιχωρυχία). Hermann, *Rechtsalt.* ed. Thalheim p. 40 f.

γραμματειδίῳ] 'a mere bit of

κότες τοσαύτης καὶ τοιαύτης φιλαπεχθημοσύνης καὶ
πονηρίας καὶ ἀναιδείας καὶ ὕβρεως ; πάντα γὰρ ταῦτ᾽
ἔμοιγ᾽ ἐν τοῖς ὑπὸ τούτων πραττομένοις ἐνεῖναι δοκεῖ.
καίτοι καὶ τούτων ἕτερ᾽ ἐστὶ πεπραγμένα τούτοις δεινότερα, ἀλλ᾽ ἡμεῖς οὐχ οἷοί τε γενοίμεθ᾽ ἂν πάντας
ἐξευρεῖν τοὺς ἠδικημένους.

38 ῾Ο τοίνυν πάντων ἀναιδέστατον μέλλειν αὐτὸν
ἀκούω ποιεῖν, βέλτιον νομίζω προειπεῖν ὑμῖν εἶναι.
φασὶ γὰρ παραστησάμενον τοὺς παῖδας αὐτὸν κατὰ
τούτων ὀμεῖσθαι, καὶ ἀράς τινας δεινὰς καὶ χαλεπὰς

paper,' 'a paltry document.'
Or. 56 § 1 ἐν γραμματειδίῳ δυοῖν
χαλκοῖν ἐωνημένῳ καὶ βιβλιδίῳ
μικρῷ πάνυ. Isocr. Trapez. § 34.
The diminutive is thrown into
effective contrast by the subsequent τοσαύτης καὶ τοιαύτης.

φιλαπεχθημοσύνης] 'malignity,'
'quarrelsomeness,' used also by
Isocr. antid. § 315, ὠμότητα καὶ
μισανθρωπίαν καὶ φιλαπεχθημο-
σύνην. Dem. Or. 24 § 6 πονηρῷ
καὶ φιλαπεχθήμονι καὶ θεοῖς ἐχ-
θρῷ.

καίτοι—τούτοις] a fortuitous
hexameter.

§§ 38—41. *I must warn you
that Conon will try to impose
upon you by swearing by the
lives of his own sons and by
other strange imprecations. His
recklessness about oaths is proved
by what I have heard of the
profanity of his youthful days;
and surely Conon, who would
think nothing of perjury, is not
to be credited in comparison with
myself, who, so far from swearing
by the lives of my children, would
not swear at all, except under
compulsion, and even then, only
in a lawful manner. Such an
oath I was willing to take for
the truth's sake; and, in self-
defence against the perjury of*

*my opponent, I challenged him
to accept my offer to take the
oath, and I now solemnly swear
that Conon whom I now prosecute really assaulted and brutally maltreated me.*

38. παραστησάμενον τοὺς παῖ-
δας] The practice of exciting
the compassion of the jury by
bringing the children into court
is often referred to, e.g. Or. 21
§ 99, παιδία γὰρ παραστήσεται
καὶ κλαήσει καὶ τούτοις αὐτὸν ἐξ-
αιτήσεται, and Hyperides, Euxe-
nipp. ad fin. ἐγὼ μὲν οὖν σοὶ
Εὐξένιππε βεβοήθηκα ὅσα εἶχον.
λοιπὸν δ᾽ ἐστὶ δεῖσθαι τῶν δικαστῶν καὶ τοὺς φίλους παρακα-
λεῖν καὶ τὰ παιδία ἀναβιβάζεσθαι,
(see especially Aristophanes'
ridicule of the custom in *Vespae*
568—74 and 976—8). But in
the present case a still more
sensational effect is to be produced by Conon's laying his
hands upon his children's heads
and praying that the direst
curses may come down upon
them, if his statements are
false.

κατὰ τούτων ὀμεῖσθαι] 'to
swear by them,—by their lives.'
κατὰ implies the basis on which
the oath rests [or, perhaps, hos-
tile action directed against the

ἐπαράσεσθαι[k] καὶ τοιαύτας, οἵας ἀκηκοώς γέ τις θαυμάσας ἀπήγγειλεν[l] ἡμῖν. ἔστι δὲ, ὦ ἄνδρες δικασταὶ, ἀνυπόστατα μὲν τὰ τοιαῦτα τολμήματα· οἱ γὰρ οἶμαι βέλτιστοι καὶ ἥκιστ᾽ ἂν αὐτοί τι ψευσάμενοι μάλισθ᾽ ὑπὸ τῶν τοιούτων ἐξαπατῶνται· οὐ μὴν ἀλλὰ δεῖ πρὸς τὸν βίον καὶ τὸν τρόπον ἀποβλέποντας πιστεύειν. τὴν δὲ τούτου πρὸς τὰ τοιαῦτ᾽ ὀλιγωρίαν ἐγὼ πρὸς ὑμᾶς ἐρῶ· πέπυσμαι γὰρ ἐξ ἀνάγκης. ἀκούω γὰρ, ὦ ἄνδρες δικασταὶ, Βάκχιόν τέ τινα, ὃς παρ᾽ ὑμῖν ἀπέθανε, καὶ

1269

39

---

[k] 'Bekk. cum H. Wolfio et corr. Σ.' -σασθαι Z cum k.
[l] ἀπήγγελλεν Z et Bekker st. cum ΣΦ.

---

object sworn by. So in Ar. Equit. 660, κατὰ χιλίων παρῇνεσα εὐχὴν ποιήσασθαι χιμάρων, the vow is, as it were, aimed at the lives of the creatures to be sacrificed. P.]. Thuc. v 47, ὀμνύντων τὸν ὅρκον κατὰ ἱερῶν τελείων, Isaeus Or. 7 § 16, ὀμνύναι καθ᾽ ἱερῶν, Lys. Or. 32 § 13, ἐπιορκήσασα κατὰ τῶν παίδων τῶν ἐμαυτῆς, Dem. 29 § 26 ἡ μήτηρ κατ᾽ ἐμοῦ καὶ τῆς ἀδελφῆς πίστιν ἠθέλησεν ἐπιθεῖναι, 19 § 292; 21 § 119. (Kühner's Greek Grammar, § 433 fin.)

We find a curious parallel in a charge made as follows against Demosthenes himself by Deinarchus, Or. 1 § 71, ποῦ τοῦτ᾽ ἐστὶ δίκαιον...τοὺς μὲν νόμους προλέγειν...παιδοποιεῖσθαι κατὰ τοὺς νόμους...σὲ δὲ τοὺς οὐ γεγενημένους υἱεῖς σαυτῷ προσποιεῖσθαι παρὰ τοὺς νόμους τῶν ἐν ταῖς κρίσεσιν ἕνεκα γιγνομένων ὅρκων.

ἀκηκοώς—ἀπήγγειλεν] i.e. 'our informant listened to them in amazement.'

ἀνυπόστατα] not exactly 'intolerable' but 'irresistible,' 'impossible to withstand.' The most upright of men and those who are least likely to tell a

falsehood themselves (the jury for instance) are most likely to be deceived by such asseverations (ὑπὸ τῶν τοιούτων sc. τολμημάτων).

οἱ οἶμαι βέλτιστοι] For the position of οἶμαι, cf. Plato Gorg. 483 c, ἡ δέ γε οἶμαι φύσις, and Rep. 504 A, ἐξ οἶμαι τῆς ἀκροτάτης ἐλευθερίας.

οὐ μὴν ἀλλὰ]= 'not but that.' The phrase is always elliptical: here we may supply οὐ μὴν (ὑπὸ τῶν τοιούτων δεῖ ἐξαπατᾶσθαι) ἀλλὰ...

πρὸς τὸν βίον—πιστεύειν] 'You must turn your eyes (away from ἀπὸ... his solemn assurances in court) to his life and character, and *then* believe him (if you can).'

39. πρὸς τὰ τοιαῦτα] sc. ὅρκους.

πέπυσμαι—ἀνάγκης] i.e. the defendant has forced the enquiry upon me (cf. § 17 fin. ἀνάγκη...)

παρ᾽ ὑμῖν ἀπέθανε] 'was condemned to death in your court, —by your verdict.'

Ἀριστοκράτην] Probably identical with the person mentioned in Or. 38 § 27 τῶν αἰσχρῶν ἐστὶ

Ἀριστοκράτην τὸν τοὺς ὀφθαλμοὺς διεφθαρμένον καὶ
τοιούτους ἑτέρους καὶ Κόνωνα τουτονὶ ἑταίρους εἶναι
μειράκια ὄντας καὶ Τριβαλλοὺς ἐπωνυμίαν ἔχειν· τούτους τά τε Ἑκαταῖα κατεσθίειν[m], καὶ τοὺς ὄρχεις τοὺς

[m] *Bekk.* cum Aᵇkr et Maximo Sophista in Fabricii Bibl. Gr. ix
584. κατακαίειν ΓΣΦ. *om.* Z et Westermann.

..τὰ μὲν ὄντα κατεσθίοντας καὶ παροινοῦντας μετὰ Ἀριστοκράτους καὶ Διογνήτου καὶ τοιούτων ἑτέρων αἰσχρῶς καὶ κακῶς ἀνηλωκέναι.

τὸν τοὺς ὀφθ. διεφθαρμένον] 'the man with the bad eyes' (perhaps blind from ophthalmia, *luscus*). For pass. of διαφθείρω used of impaired sight or hearing, and similar physical defects, cf. Aeschin. 1 § 102 πρεσβύτης διεφθαρμένος τοὺς ὀφθαλμούς, Hdt. 1 34 ἦσαν τῷ Κροίσῳ δύο παῖδες, τῶν οὕτερος μὲν διέφθαρτο, ἦν γὰρ δὴ κωφός, and *ib.* 38 διεφθαρμένος τὴν ἀκοήν. Dem. Or. 13 § 13 δεῖ τὰ ὦτα πρῶτον ὑμῶν ἰάσασθαι, διέφθαρται γάρ.

Τριβαλλοὺς] See *Excursus* (D) p. 228.

τὰ Ἑκαταῖα] Once every month, at the time of the new moon, dishes of food were set out for Hecate in the evening at the places where three roads met; and the food thus offered was not unfrequently eaten by poor people. Cf. Arist. Plutus, 594—7, παρὰ τῆς Ἑκάτης ἔξεστιν τοῦτο πυθέσθαι | εἴτε τὸ πλουτεῖν εἴτε τὸ πεινῆν βέλτιον. φησὶ γὰρ αὕτη | τοὺς μὲν ἔχοντας καὶ πλουτοῦντας δεῖπνον κατὰ μῆν' ἀποπέμπειν, τοὺς δὲ πένητας τῶν ἀνθρώπων ἁρπάζειν πρὶν καταθεῖναι (with the *Scholia*). [Juvenal v 85, '*exigua feralis cena patella,*' Psalm cvi 28, 'they ate the offerings of the dead.' This act, and the eating of the καθάρματα, which had a mysti-

cal import, are cited as instances of impious bravado in things sacred, which augured ill for Conon's paying any regard to the obligations of a solemn oath. P.] In Lucian's dialogues of the dead (1 § 1 = p. 331 R) Diogenes asks Pollux to invite from the upper world Menippus the Cynic, who is sure to bring his wallet well stocked with broken victuals, λέγε αὐτῷ..., ἐμπλησάμενον τὴν πήραν ἥκειν θέρμων τε πολλῶν καὶ εἴ που εὕροι ἐν τῇ τριόδῳ Ἑκάτης δεῖπνον κείμενον ἢ ᾠὸν ἐκ καθαρσίου ἤ τι τοιοῦτον.

Hemsterhuis in an exhaustive note on the above passage (Vol. 11 p. 397—400 ed. Bipont.) also quotes Plutarch 11 p. 290 D, (the dog) χθονίᾳ δεῖπνον Ἑκάτῃ πεμπόμενος εἰς τριόδους ἀποτροπαίων καὶ καθαρσίων ἐπέχει μοῖραν, Quaest. Rom. p. 280 B, Symp. vii p. 708 F. We may add Charicleides cited by Athenaeus vii 325, δέσποιν' Ἑκάτη, τριοδῖτι, τρίμορφε, τριπρόσωπε, τρίγλαις (mullet) κηλευμένα.

After the word Ἑκαταῖα some of the mss (including Σ) have κατακαίειν, 'to burn up,' which is not likely to be the right reading; others have κατεσθίειν, which makes good sense and is commonly accepted. Of Reiske's conjectures (κατ' ἀγυιὰς and καταπίνειν) neither can be considered probable. Baiter leaves out the verb, thus making συλλέγοντας

ἐκ τῶν χοίρων¹¹, οἷς καθαίρουσιν ὅταν εἰσιέναι μέλλωσι,
συλλέγοντας ἑκάστοτε συνδειπνεῖν ἀλλήλοις, καὶ ῥᾷον
ὀμνύναι καὶ ἐπιορκεῖν ἢ ὁτιοῦν. οὐ δὴ Κόνων ὁ τοιοῦτος 40

¹¹ τὰς ὄρνεις (ὄρνις kB) τὰς ἐκ τῶν χωρῶν (χορῶν krA¹) αἷς libri.

govern Ἑκαταῖα as well as ὄρχεις.
Westermann suggests κλέπτειν
but follows Baiter. κατακαίειν
may perhaps be accounted for
by supposing that Ἑκαταῖα or
καταῖα was erroneously written
twice by an early copyist; a
subsequent copyist might alter
this into the nearest verb he
could think of, κατακαίειν; this
would be seen to be wrong by a
still later writer, who would
substitute the intelligible word
κατεσθίειν.

τοὺς ὄρχεις τοὺς ἐκ τῶν χοί-
ρων] The мss have τὰς ὄρνεις
(or ὄρνις) τὰς ἐκ τῶν χωρῶν (or
χορῶν) αἷς. But birds are out of
place in an expiatory sacrifice
prior to a public assembly, and
the use of young pigs for this
purpose is distinctly attested by
ancient authorities (e.g. Schol.
on Ar. Ach. 44). We must
therefore accept the certain
emendations given in the text,
and originally proposed by Hemsterhuis (in his note on Lucian
above referred to).

Harpocr. (and Photius) κα-
θάρσιον· Αἰσχίνης κατὰ Τιμάρχου
(§ 23, speaking of the ἐκκλησία,
ἐπειδὰν τὸ καθάρσιον περιενεχθῇ),
ἔθος ἦν Ἀθήνησι καθαίρειν τὴν
ἐκκλησίαν καὶ τὰ θέατρα καὶ ὅλως
τὰς τοῦ δήμου συνόδους μικροῖς
πάνυ χοιριδίοις ἅπερ ὠνόμαζον
καθάρσια· τοῦτο δ'ἐποίουν οἱ λεγό-
μενοι περιστίαρχοι, οἵπερ ὠνομάσ-
θησαν οὕτως ἤτοι ἀπὸ τοῦ περι-
στείχειν ἢ ἀπὸ τῆς ἑστίας. (Ar.
Eccl. 128, ὁ περιστίαρχος περι-
φέρειν χρὴ τὴν...γαλῆν, Ach. 44
ὡς ἂν ἐντὸς ἦτε τοῦ καθάρματος.)

καθαίρουσιν] A plural indefinite, with the subject omitted;
cf. the frequent use of φασί,
λέγουσι, ὀνομάζουσι.

εἰσιέναι] sc. εἰς τὴν ἐκκλησίαν, etc. Hence εἰσιτήρια (Fals.
leg. § 210 with Shilleto's note).

ἢ ὁτιοῦν] 'They think less of
swearing and perjuring themselves than anything else whatsoever,' 'than anything else in
the world.' Or. 56 § 15 οὐδέν γε
μᾶλλον ἢ ὁτιοῦν.

40. οὐ δὴ...οὐδὲ πολλοῦ δεῖ]
Here, as usual in this phrase,
οὐδὲ reiterates the preceding negation (οὐ δὴ), but does not negative πολλοῦ δεῖ although closely
pronounced with it. (Cf. Fals.
leg. § 33 οὐ γάρ...τὰ πράγματ'
ἐστὶ φαῦλα...οὐδὲ πολλοῦ δεῖ,
with Shilleto's note.) We have
an apparent exception to this
rule in Or. 18 § 20 φανήσεται
γὰρ οὐδὲ πολλοῦ δεῖ τῆς γενησομένης ἄξιον αἰσχύνης, where
there is no preceding negative
expressed. The exception may
however be explained on the
supposition that φανήσεται is
ironical and therefore implies
a negative: οὐ γὰρ φανήσεται τῆς
γενησομένης ἄξιον αἰσχύνης, οὐδὲ
πολλοῦ δεῖ.

οὐ δὴ κ.τ.λ. A very elegant
and idiomatic passage: 'Conon
then, as a character such as
I have described, is not to be
trusted on oath; far from it,
indeed. No! the man who
would not take even an oath
that he intends to observe by
any object you do not recognise
(i.e. such as Conon swears by),

πιστός ἐστιν ὀμνύων· οὐδὲ πολλοῦ δεῖ· ἀλλ᾽ ὁ μηδ᾽ εὔορκον μηδὲν ἂν ὀμόσας[o] ὧν μὴ νομίζετε[p], κατὰ δὲ δὴ
παίδων μηδ᾽ ἂν[q] μελλήσας, ἀλλὰ κἂν[r] ὁτιοῦν παθὼν

[o] ἂν ὀμόσας μηδὲν r.

[p] Σ. νομίζεται A¹kr. ὀμόσας, κατὰ δὲ δὴ παιδων ὧν μὴ νομίζετε
Bekker cum libris, quod ad verborum ordinem attinet, 'sententia
perversa iam a Wolfio notata.'—'Lege ὧν μὴ νομίζεται μηδὲν μηδ᾽
ἂν μελλήσας, qui ne in animum quidem induxerit ut novo et inusitato
more per liberorum capita iuret…Imo transpone, ὀμόσας ὧν μὴ νομίζεται, κατὰ δὲ δὴ τῶν παίδων μηδ᾽ ἂν μελλήσας.' Dobree. ὀμ. ὧν μὴ
νομίζετε, κατὰ δὲ δὴ παίδων μηδ᾽ ἂν μελλήσας Sauppe.

[q] μηδὲν ΣΓΦ.   [r] καὶ A¹kr.

and would not for a moment think of doing so on the lives of his children, but would rather suffer anything than that,—and who, even when constrained, will take none but a customary oath,—I say, such a man is more to be trusted than one who swears by his sons and offers to undergo the fiery ordeal.' P.]

ὁ μηδ᾽—μελλήσας] The mss have ὧν μὴ νομίζετε (or νομίζεται) after κατὰ δὲ δὴ παίδων. There are two objections to this: (i) the plaintiff describes himself as one who is 'reluctant to swear even to the truth' (μηδ᾽ εὔορκον μηδὲν ἂν ὀμόσας), whereas in § 41 he publicly swears to having been assaulted by the defendant: (ii) an oath by the lives of one's children is described as 'contrary to usage' (ὧν μὴ νομίζετε), whereas this very oath is elsewhere attributed to the mother of Demosthenes. Or. 29 §§ 26, 33, 54, 56 ἡ μήτηρ κατ᾽ ἐμοῦ καὶ τῆς ἀδελφῆς…πίστιν ἠθέλησεν ἐπιθεῖναι…ἣν μηδεὶς ὑμῶν νομιζέτω καθ᾽ ἡμῶν ποτ᾽ ἂν ὀμνύναι ταῦτ᾽ ἂν ἐθέλειν, εἰ μὴ σαφῶς ᾔδει τὰ εὔορκα ὀμουμένη. Or. 19 § 292.

These objections are removed by the transposition adopted in the text.

If an easier alteration is preferred, we may retain the order as it stands in the mss, simply inserting μηδὲν after ὧν μὴ νομίζετε, and accounting for its loss by its similarity to the subsequent μηδ᾽ ἄν. The mss vary between μηδ᾽ ἄν and μηδέν, and this proposal combines the two alternative readings. The sentence would then run thus: ὁ μηδ᾽ εὔορκον μηδὲν ἂν ὀμόσας, κατὰ δὲ δὴ παίδων, ὧν μὴ νομίζετε μηδὲν μηδ᾽ ἂν μελλήσας. Thus ὧν μὴ νομίζετε depends on μηδὲν and does not refer to παίδων, the sense of the second clause being that Ariston would never dream of taking any such oath, by his children's lives, as would be contrary to general usage. Below, he describes himself as ὀμνύων ὡς νόμιμον. See Dobree quoted in critical notes.

μηδ᾽ εὔορκον] Isocr. ad Dem. § 23 ἕνεκα δὲ χρημάτων μηδένα θεῶν ὀμόσῃς, μηδ᾽ ἂν εὐορκεῖν μέλλῃς.

κἂν ὁτιοῦν παθὼν πρότερον] 'Would submit to anything sooner than that,' i.e. rather than swear by an oath contrary

πρότερον, εἰ δ᾿ᵇ ἀναγκαῖον, ὀμνύων ὡς νόμιμον, ἀξιο-
πιστότερος τοῦ κατὰ τῶν παίδων ὀμνύοντοςᵗ καὶ διὰ
τοῦ πυρός. ἐγὼ τοίνυν ὁ δικαιότερόν σου πιστευθεὶς
ἂν κατὰ πάντα, ὦ Κόνων, ἠθέλησα ὀμόσαι ταυτί, οὐχ

ᵇ δ᾿ ἄρ᾿ *Bekker cum* A¹kr. ᵗ ὀμνύοντος *Bekk. cum* A¹kr.

to the country's use, or by the lives of his children.

The whole sentence is intended to be descriptive of the *character* of a man who has a solemn regard for the obligations of an oath; hence the use of μή. A person of such a character, says the plaintiff, is more trustworthy than one who is ready to take any oath you please. The characters contrasted are of course those of the plaintiff and defendant respectively, but this is only *implied* until we reach the next sentence, ἐγώ...ὁ δικαιότερόν σου πιστευθεὶς ἄν, when the contrast is brought home to the case at issue.

καὶ διὰ τοῦ πυρός] It is doubtful whether we can explain this of any ordeal by fire like that referred to in Soph. Antig. 264 (ἦμεν δ᾿ ἕτοιμοι καὶ μύδρους αἴρειν χεροῖν, καὶ πῦρ διέρπειν καὶ θεοὺς ὀρκωμοτεῖν), and possibly implied in Ar. Lysistr. 133, ἀλλ᾿ ἀλλ᾿ ὅ τι βούλει, κἄν με χρὴ, διὰ τοῦ πυρὸς ἐθέλω βαδίζειν, which however may be only a strong metaphor expressive of readiness to endure any amount of torture. Sometimes διὰ πυρὸς is used of 'braving the extremest perils,' 'going through fire and water' as in Xen. Symp. iv 16, ἔγωγ᾿ οὖν μετὰ Κλεινίου κἂν διὰ πυρὸς ἰοίην, and Oec. xxi 7, ἀκολουθητέον...καὶ διὰ πυρὸς καὶ διὰ παντὸς κινδύνου (L and S s. v. πῦρ).

In the present passage διὰ τοῦ πυρός possibly contains an allusion to some strange form of self-devotion, one of the ἀραὶ δειναὶ καὶ χαλεπαὶ obscurely hinted at in § 38. G. H. Schaefer simply says: 'vertam, *vel dum ara ardet*,' i.e. 'one who swears by his children even while the flame is burning on the altar,' and C. R. Kennedy renders the words: 'and before the burning altar.' (Cf. Or. 43 § 14 λαβόντες τὴν ψῆφον καομένων τῶν ἱερείων.)

This is hardly satisfactory, and it is not improbable that the text is corrupt and that we should read καὶ διὰ τοῦ πυρὸς ἰόντος, where the participle would easily have been lost by *homoeoteleuton* with ὀμνύοντος.

πιστευθεὶς ἄν] See on § 1 *ad fin*. For the passive, formed just as if the active were directly transitive, and took the accusative, cf. § 5 παροινουμένους and § 2 παρανενομῆσθαι.

ἠθέλησα ὀμόσαι ταυτί] The general drift of this oath must have been given by the πρόκλησις which was read to the jury; it is also indicated in the asseverations of § 41.

It is clear that this Challenge was refused by the defendant. The plaintiff would therefore be able to point to this refusal as a fact in his own favour, just as the defendant would in the case of the πρόκλησις tendered by him and rejected by the plaintiff (§ 27).—In the next line καὶ emphasizes ὁτιοῦν.

ὑπὲρ τοῦ μὴ δοῦναι δίκην ὧν ἠδίκηκα, καὶ ὁτιοῦν
ποιῶν, ὥσπερ σύ, ἀλλ' ὑπὲρ τῆς ἀληθείας καὶ ὑπὲρ
τοῦ μη προσυβρισθῆναι, ὡς οὐ κατεπιορκηθησόμενος[u]
τὸ πρᾶγμα. λέγε τὴν πρόκλησιν.

ΠΡΟΚΛΗΣΙΣ.

41   Ταῦτ' ἐγὼ καὶ τότ' ἠθέλησα ὀμόσαι, καὶ νῦν ὀμνύω
τοὺς θεοὺς καὶ τὰς θεὰς ἅπαντας καὶ ἁπάσας[v] ὑμῶν
ἕνεκα, ὦ ἄνδρες δικασταὶ, καὶ τῶν περιεστηκότων, ἦ
μὴν παθὼν ὑπὸ Κόνωνος ταῦτα ὧν δικάζομαι, καὶ λα- 1270
βὼν πληγὰς, καὶ τὸ χεῖλος διακοπεὶς οὕτως ὥστε καὶ
ῥαφῆναι, καὶ ὑβρισθεὶς τὴν δίκην διώκειν. καὶ εἰ μὲν
εὐορκῶ, πολλά μοι ἀγαθὰ γένοιτο καὶ μηδέποτ' αὖθις
τοιοῦτο μηδὲν πάθοιμι, εἰ δ' ἐπιορκῶ, ἐξώλης ἀπολοίμην

[u] Dobree.   κατεπιορκησόμενος Z et Bekker st. cum libris.
[v] πάσας Z cum Σ.

κατεπιορκηθησόμενος] An e-
mendation for κατεπιορκησόμενος, the future middle, which
if retained, must be taken as
passive in sense, 'inasmuch as
I am determined not to lose the
case by your perjury.' [Or, 'as
one who had no idea of having
the case decided against him by
perjury.' P.] For the use of
κατα- cf. καταρρᾳθυμεῖν ('to
lose by negligence') in Or. 4 § 7,
τὰ κατερρᾳθυμημένα πάλιν ἀναλ-
ήψεσθε, and κατεπάδειν, 'to
subdue by charming' (Pl. Gorg.
483 E).

41. τῶν περιεστηκότων] Aeschin. Ctesiph. § 56 ἀποκρίνομαι
ἐναντίον σοι τῶν δικαστῶν καὶ τῶν
ἄλλων πολιτῶν ὅσοι δὴ ἔξωθεν πε-
ριεστᾶσι, and Dem. de Cor.
§ 196.

What applies above to private
orations of great public importance, applies *mutatis mutandis*
to the present speech, which
was probably listened to by a
considerable body of citizens,
besides the forty δικασταί before
whom this case was apparently
tried (see *Introduction* p. lxi).

καὶ εἰ μὲν εὐορκῶ—ἔσεσθαι]
Quoted by Aristeides (ii 487
Rhet. Graeci, Spengel), together
with the famous adjurations of
the speech *de Corona* (§§ 1 and
141), to exemplify ἀξιοπιστία
brought about by ὅρκοι and ἀρά.

ἐξώλης] Or. 49 § 66; Fals.
leg. § 172, ἐξώλης ἀπολοίμην καὶ
προώλης εἰ..., and in § 70 (after
quoting the solemn form of
imprecation used before the
meetings of the βουλή and
ἐκκλησία) the orator adds: εὔ-
χεσθ' ἐξώλη ποιεῖν αὐτὸν καὶ γένος
καὶ οἰκίαν.

Ariston is here taking an oath
almost as strong as that which
he finds fault with in Conon;
but he would probably plead
that he was only swearing 'in
the customary manner,' ὡς νόμιμον (§ 40).

αὐτός τε καὶ εἴ τί μοι ἔστιν ἢ μέλλει ἔσεσθαι. ἀλλ'
οὐκ ἐπιορκῶ, οὐδ' ἂν Κόνων διαρραγῇ. ἀξιῶ τοίνυν 42
ὑμᾶς, ὦ ἄνδρες δικασταί, πάνθ' ὅσα ἐστὶ δίκαια ἐπι-
δείξαντος ἐμοῦ καὶ πίστιν προσθέντος ὑμῖν, ὥσπερ ἂν
αὐτὸς ἕκαστος παθὼν τὸν πεποιηκότα ἐμίσει, οὕτως
ὑπὲρ ἐμοῦ πρὸς Κόνωνα τουτονὶ τὴν ὀργὴν ἔχειν, καὶ
μὴ νομίζειν ἴδιον τῶν τοιούτων μηδὲν ὃ κἂν ἄλλῳ τυχὸν συμβαίη, ἀλλ' ἐφ' ὅτου ποτ' ἂν συμβῇ, βοηθεῖν
καὶ τὰ δίκαια ἀποδιδόναι, καὶ μισεῖν τοὺς πρὸ μὲν τῶν
ἁμαρτημάτων θρασεῖς καὶ προπετεῖς, ἐν δὲ τῷ δίκην
ὑπέχειν ἀναισχύντους καὶ πονηροὺς καὶ μήτε δόξης
μήτε ἔθους μήτ' ἄλλου μηδενὸς φροντίζοντας πρὸς
τὸ μὴ δοῦναι δίκην. ἀλλὰ δεήσεται Κόνων καὶ κλαή- 43

διαρραγῇ] sc. λέγων ὡς ἐπιορκῶ,
'not even if Conon burst with
saying that I forswear myself'—
or (as we should put it)—'say
so *till he bursts.*' De Cor. § 21
ὁ σὸς κοινωνὸς, οὐχ ὁ ἐμὸς, οὐδ'
ἂν σὺ διαρραγῇς ψευδόμενος.
πίστιν]=ὅρκον, Or. 49 § 42
πίστιν ἠθέλησα ἐπιθεῖναι.

§§ 42—43. *This is no private
interest of myself alone; Conon
will appeal to the compassion of
the jury, though the victim of
such an outrage deserves their
pity, rather than its perpetrators.
I therefore claim from the jury
the same feeling of resentment
against Conon, as each one of
them would have felt in his own
case.*

42. πάνθ'—δίκαια] perhaps =
πάντα δίκαια ὅσα ἐστι (not πάντα
ὅσα δίκαιά ἐστι). If so, we should
read ἐστι for ἐστι.—πίστιν προσθέντος § 41, alluding to νῦν ὀμνύω
κ.τ.λ.—παθὼν = εἰ ἔπαθεν.

τὴν ὀργὴν ἔχειν] Or. 21 (Mid.)
§ 70, εἰ τοίνυν τις ὑμῶν ἄλλως
πως ἔχει τὴν ὀργὴν ἐπὶ Μειδίαν ἢ
ὡς δέον αὐτὸν τεθνάναι, οὐκ ὀρθῶς

ἔχει. P.]

δ—συμβαίη]=ὃ καὶ ἄλλῳ (τυχὸν) συμβαίη ἄν, 'which might,
perchance, happen to another.'
For acc. abs. τυχὸν (like παρα-
σχόν, ἐξόν, μετόν, Kühner § 487, 3)
cf. Isocr. Paneg. § 171 τυχὸν ἄν
τι συνεπέραναν and Dem. de Cor.
§ 221 ἐπεπείσμην δ' ὑπὲρ ἐμαυτοῦ,
τυχὸν μὲν ἀναισθητῶν, ὅμως δ'
ἐπεπείσμην.

τὰ δίκαια ἀποδιδόναι] 'To
grant him the claims which are
his due'; ἀπο-, as in ἀπολαμβάνειν, 'to receive one's due,'
'to accept full payment.' See
note on Or. 53 § 10.

πρὸ] Not 'previous to,' but
'in the presence of,' 'at.' [Cf.
however Or. 21 (Mid.) § 30 νόμους
ἔθεσθε πρὸ τῶν ἀδικημάτων ἐπ'
ἀδήλοις τοῖς ἀδικήσουσιν. P.]

μήτε ἔθους...φροντίζοντας] Cf.
§ 10 ὧν μὴ νομίζετε.

43. δεήσεται...καὶ κλαήσει] Or.
30 § 32 ἀναβὰς ἐπὶ τὸ δικαστήριον
ἐδεῖτο, ἱκετεύων ὑπὲρ αὐτοῦ καὶ
ἀντιβολῶν καὶ δάκρυσι κλαίων.
Cf. Or. 53 § 29.—προσυβρισθεὶς
is further explained by δίκης

σει[w]· σκοπεῖτε δὴ πότερός ἐστιν ἐλεεινότερος, ὁ πεπον-
θὼς οἷα ἐγὼ πέπονθα ὑπὸ τούτου, εἰ προσυβρισθεὶς
ἄπειμι καὶ δίκης μὴ τυχών, ἢ Κόνων, εἰ δώσει
δίκην; πότερον δ' ὑμῶν ἑκάστῳ συμφέρει ἐξεῖναι τύπτειν καὶ ὑβρίζειν ἢ μή; ἐγὼ μὲν οἶμαι[x] μή. οὐκοῦν,
ἂν μὲν ἀφιῆτε, ἔσονται πολλοί, ἐὰν δὲ κολάζητε,
ἐλάττους.

44 Πόλλ' ἂν εἰπεῖν ἔχοιμι, ὦ ἄνδρες δικασταί, καὶ
ὡς ἡμεῖς χρήσιμοι, καὶ αὐτοὶ[y] καὶ ὁ πατήρ, ἕως ἔζη,
καὶ τριηραρχοῦντες καὶ στρατευόμενοι καὶ τὸ προσ-
ταττόμενον ποιοῦντες, καὶ ὡς οὐδὲν οὔθ' οὗτος οὔτε
τῶν τούτου οὐδείς· ἀλλ' οὔτε τὸ ὕδωρ ἱκανὸν οὔτε 1271
νῦν περὶ τούτων ὁ λόγος ἐστίν. εἰ γὰρ δὴ ὁμολογουμένως ἔτι τούτων καὶ ἀχρηστοτέροις καὶ πονηροτέροις
ἡμῖν εἶναι συνέβαινεν, οὐ τυπτητέοι οὐδὲ ὑβριστέοι
δήπου ἐσμέν.

[w] κλαιήσει Ζ cum Σ.   [x] οἴομαι Ζ cum Σ.
[y] καὶ αὐτοὶ A[1]kr.   om. Ζ cum ΦΣΦ.

μὴ τυχών. See note on § 15, ὑβρισθῆναι.

ἢ μή] sc. ἐξεῖναι, not συμφέρει. The latter would require οὔ.

ἂν μὲν ἀφιῆτε κ.τ.λ.] Isocr. κατὰ Λοχίτου (αἰκίας) § 18, τοὺς ἄλλους πολίτας κοσμιωτέρους ποιήσετε καὶ τὸν βίον τὸν ὑμέτερον αὐτῶν ἀσφαλέστερον καταστήσετε.

§ 44. *I might say much of the public services of my family, and show that my opponents have done you no such service. But time would not suffice, nor is this the point at issue. For even supposing we were ever so inferior to our opponents, that is no reason why we should be beaten and insulted.*

44. χρήσιμοι] χρήσιμος is almost invariably used with εἴς τι, πρός τι, ἐπί τι or the simple dat.,

but is here placed absolutely.

τριηραρχοῦντες] See Or. 36 § 41.

ὡς οὐδέν] = ὡς κατ' οὐδὲν γέγονε χρήσιμος (understood from χρήσιμοι above).—On τὸ ὕδωρ, see § 36.

τούτων...ἀχρηστοτέροις] More unserviceable, more useless, to the state than our opponents. For the dat. συνέβαινεν ἡμῖν εἶναι ἀχρηστοτέροις cf. § 16 αὐτοληκύθοις συγχωροῦμεν εἶναι τοῖς υἱέσι.

ἄχρηστος is here contrasted with χρήσιμος and, as often in the Orators, is used in the same sense as ἀχρεῖος in earlier Greek writers.

τυπτητέοι] formed like τυπτήσω as if from *τυπτέω, cf. τετυ-πτῆσθαι in *Argument* 1. 2. See Excursus (A), *infra*.

Οὐκ οἶδ’ ὅ τι δεῖ πλείω λέγειν· οἶμαι[x] γὰρ ὑμᾶς οὐδὲν ἀγνοεῖν τῶν εἰρημένων.

[x] οἴομαι Z cum Σ.

οὐκ οἶδ’—εἰρημένων] The very same sentence (with the addition of the phrase ἐξέρα τὸ ὕδωρ) occurs at the close of Or. 36. On ὅ τι δεῖ, see note on 36 § 62.

A longer speech might appropriately have closed with a recapitulation and a formal peroration; but in the present instance neither is necessary. Arist. Rhet. iii 13 ὁ ἐπίλογός ἐστιν οὐδὲ δικανικοῦ (λόγου) παντός, οἷον ἐὰν μικρὸς ὁ λόγος καὶ τὸ πρᾶγμα εὐμνημόνευτον.

EXCURSUS (A).

On the defective verb τύπτω (§§ 4, 25, 32, 35, &c.).

The verb τύπτω forms a familiar paradigm in almost all the elementary Greek Grammars in ordinary use, where, as every schoolboy knows, it is conjugated at full length with its three perfect tenses, its five futures, and its six aorists; and it must be admitted that, for the purposes of a paradigm, the verb in question is in several respects admirably adapted. Had the selection fallen on a verb ending in -ω with a *vowel* for the last letter of its stem, e.g. λύ-ω, or τιμά-ω, our model verb would have had one aorist only in each voice, ἔλυσα, ἐλυσάμην, ἐλύθην; ἐτίμησα, ἐτιμησάμην, ἐτιμήθην. Had a *verbum purum* ending in -μι been taken, e.g. φη-μί, δίδω-μι, ἵστη-μι, the beginner would have had to face a very complex conjugation at the very outset of his task. τύπτω is unencumbered with the special irregularities of verbs ending in -μι, and has the advantage of two *theoretically possible* aorists in each voice; indeed, as Veitch has pointed out, it is 'one of the very few verbs that have the second aorist active and passive in actual use' (though the former is very rare, while in *Attic prose* neither is ever found). Again, as compared with some other *verba impura*, with a *consonant* for their characteristic letter, it has this advantage; that the stem-vowel remains unchanged throughout, and is thus identical in (for instance) the aorist and present participle alike (τυπ-είς and τύπ-τ-ων), whereas in λείπω, φαίνω, τήκω as compared with ἔ-λιπ-ον, ἐ-φάν-ην, ἐ-τάκ-ην, the stem-vowels which appear in the aorist have suffered modification in the present; also the consonantal relations between the different tenses are simpler than in the case of some other verbs; thus, while β in ἐ-βλάβ-ην becomes π in βλάπ-τ-ω, no such alteration is necessary in passing from the -τυπ- of the second aorist to the strengthened form τυπτ- of the present.

The verb is not without an interest of its own in the history of grammar; and though it may be rash to conjecture whether it owed its first selection to the grim humour of some *plagosus Orbilius* of old times, intent on bringing each tense's meaning home to his pupils' memories by the help of his ferule, it may be interesting to note that this particular paradigm is found in the early Greek Grammars which appeared in Italy at the revival of learning, as for instance in the *Erotemata* of Chrysoloras, a distinguished scholar, who (in the dedication of a copy in my possession, printed at Venice at the Aldine press in 1517) is described as *Manuel Chrysoloras, qui primus Iuniorum reportauit in Italiā literas graecas**. The paradigm may also be traced still further

---

* On Chrysoloras, see Hody, *de viris illustribus* cap. ii, and Voigt's *Humanismus* 1² 225, 234; and cf. Hallam's *Literature of Europe* 1 99 ed. 1854, where the *Erotemata* is described as 'the first, and long the only, channel to a knowledge of Greek, save oral instruction,' and Mullinger's *History of the University of Cambridge*, 1 pp. 391—396, where it is called 'the Greek Grammar

back to the Canons of Theodosius, an Alexandrine grammarian of the age of Constantine the Great, who expounds
all the parts, regardless of usage, and at considerable length
(viz. on pp. 1008—1044 of Θεοδοσίου γραμματικοῦ εἰσαγωγικοὶ κανόνες περὶ κλίσεως ῥημάτων in Bekker's *Anecdota
Græca*, vol. III). The Grammar of Theodosius is in its
turn founded on that of a more celebrated Greek scholar,
Dionysius the Thracian, who taught at Rome in B.C. 80.
The τέχνη γραμματική of the latter is a short work, occupying only pp. 629—643 in Bekker's *Anecdota Græca*,
vol. II; it was a standard text-book for many centuries
and is the original basis of all subsequent grammars. I
quote a few words from chap. xv, which bear on our
present subject: διαθέσεις δέ εἰσι τρεῖς, ἐνέργεια, πάθος,
μεσότης· ἐνέργεια μὲν οἷον τύπτω, πάθος δὲ οἷον τύπτομαι,
μεσότης δὲ ἡ ποτὲ μὲν ἐνέργειαν, ποτὲ δὲ πάθος παριστῶσα,
οἷον πέποιθα, διέφθορα, ἐποιησάμην, ἐγραψάμην*. Shortly
after, he proceeds: ἀριθμοὶ δὲ τρεῖς, ἑνικός, δυϊκὸς καὶ πληθυντικός· ἑνικὸς μὲν οἷον τύπτω, δυϊκὸς δὲ οἷον τύπτετον,
πληθυντικὸς δὲ οἷον τύπτομεν· πρόσωπα δὲ τρία, πρῶτον,
δεύτερον, τρίτον· πρῶτον μὲν οἷον τύπτω, δεύτερον οἷον
τύπτεις, τρίτον οἷον τύπτει.

of the first century of the Renaissance.' 'It served Reuchlin for a
model at Orleans, was used by Linacre at Oxford and Erasmus
at Cambridge, and long continued to hold its ground against
formidable rivals,' p. 395. The date of his arrival in Italy was
about 1396.—The Aldine edition above referred to is of course
a reprint. It was first printed in 1484. Hallam I p. 180 ascribes
to about the year 1480 a small quarto tract of great rarity, entitled
*coniugationes verborum Graecae, Daventria noviter extremo labore
collectae et impressae*, containing nothing but τύπτω in all its
voices and tenses, with Latin explanations.

* It is quoted ἐτυψάμην in Graefenhan, *Geschichte der Classischen Philologie*, II p. 481, q.v.; but Dionysius appears in the rest
of the chapter to confine himself to *tenses in actual use* and is
therefore likely to have avoided ἐτυψάμην.

But, however well this verb may be adapted as a typical form for the beginner, and however interesting it may be as a tradition of the earlier grammarians, it cannot be too clearly understood that very few of the tenses are really used by the best Greek authors. The tenses given in the paradigm are all formed regularly on the principles of *analogy* alone, regardless of the opposite principles of *anomaly* which prevail in the usage of the Greek writers themselves. In *Attic Prose* none of the tenses given in the grammars are found except the present and imperfect, active and passive, τύπτω and ἔτυπτον, τύπτομαι and ἐτυπτόμην. The future active is not τύψω but τυπτήσω, and the aorists in use are borrowed from other verbs, and are really ἐπάταξα and ἐπλήγην. ἔτυψα is never found in Attic Prose, and the reference to Lysias, *fragment* 10, 2, given in Veitch's *Greek Verbs*, and repeated, apparently without verification, in Liddell and Scott's Lexicon, supplies us with no real exception. The passage, when examined, proves to be part of an exposition of a possibly genuine speech of Lysias, written by the anonymous author of the προλεγόμενα τῶν στάσεων (*Rhetores Graeci* VII p. 15 Walz, cf. Spengel's *Artium Scriptores* p. 137). The words used by this late writer are: ἐγκύμονά τις ἔτυψε κατὰ γαστρὸς καὶ κρίνεται φόνου, where Lysias himself would undoubtedly have written ἐπάταξεν, as is proved by a passage in Or. 13 § 71, ὁ Θρασύβουλος τύπτει τὸν Φρύνιχον καὶ καταβάλλει πατάξας. The following passages will further illustrate the prose usage of this defective verb, Lysias, Or. 4 § 15, πότερον ἐπλήγην ἢ ἐπάταξα; id. Or. 1 §§ 25—27, where πατάξας καταβάλλω is followed by the corresponding passive forms πληγεὶς κατέπεσεν, Dem. Or. 4 § 40, ὁ πληγεὶς κἂν ἑτέρωσε πατάξῃς, Thuc. VIII 92, ὁ Φρύνιχος πληγεὶς followed by ὁ πατάξας διέφυγεν. Again in Plato's *Laws*, p. 879 D—2, we have τύπτοντα and τύπτειν followed by πατάξαι, and soon after, τύπτει τῇ μάστιγι followed by ὅσας ἂν αὐτὸς πατάξῃ: so in p. 880 B, ἐάν τις τύπτῃ τὸν πρεσβύτερον...τῇ τοῦ πληγέντος ἡλικίᾳ, and in p. 882 the last two forms occur twice over. Cf. Aristot. *Eth.* v 5 § 4, ὅταν ὁ μὲν πληγῇ ὁ δὲ πατάξῃ, *Rhet.* I 15 § 29, ὁμοῖα καὶ εἰ ἰσχυρὸς ἀσθενῆ πατάξαι ἢ πληγῆναι προκαλέσαιτο, *Eth.* v 5 § 4, εἰ ἀρχὴν ἔχων ἐπάταξεν, οὐ δεῖ ἀντι-πληγῆναι, καὶ εἰ ἄρχοντα ἐπάταξεν, οὐ πληγῆναι μόνον δεῖ ἀλλὰ καὶ κολασθῆναι. *Rhet.* I 15 § 29, πατάξαι ἢ πληγῆναι, *de anima* B, 8, p. 419 b 15, τὸ τύπτον καὶ τὸ τυπτόμενον...ἂν πληγῇ, p. 420 a 24, οὐ δὴ πᾶν ψοφεῖ τυπτόμενον καὶ τύπτον, οἷον ἐὰν πατάξῃ βελόνη βελόνην, p. 423 b 16, πληγεῖσα ἐπάταξεν, *Soph. Elench.* p. 168 a 6, ἄν τις τύπτῃ τοῦτον καὶ τοῦτον, ἄνθρωπον ἀλλ᾽ οὐκ ἀνθρώπους τυπτήσει, and *Meteorologica*, p. 368 a 18, τύπτων...τύπτον...τύπτεται, p. 371 b 10, ᾗ μέλλει πατάξειν κινεῖται πρὶν πληγῆναι, while three lines below we find ὃ ἐὰν πατάξῃ.—Among other parts similarly borrowed we have πέπληγα, πέπληγμαι, πεπλήξομαι and πληγήσομαι.— So in Latin, *ferio*, *percussi*, etc.

But one of the best studies on this point of usage is the Speech of Demosthenes κατὰ Κόνωνος, where we find the following forms; in § 81 τύπτειν, in § 17 τύπτων, in § 4 ἔτυπτον, in §§ 32 and 35 τυπτόμενον, with the verbal τυπτητέος in § 44. Again in § 31 we have πατάξαι (*not* τύψαι or πλῆξαι), and in § 33 ἐπλήγην (not ἐπατάχθην, or ἐτύπην, much less ἐτύφθην). Further in § 25 πατάξαντι stands side by side with τύπτειν; and lastly we have the phrases πληγὰς ἐνέτειναν (§ 5) and εἰληφέναι καὶ δεδωκέναι πληγὰς (§ 14), which assist in making up for the defective tenses. It is reserved for the late writer who composed the *Argument* to use the unclassical form τετυπτῆσθαι.

For the usage of this verb in Attic *Verse*, see Veitch's excellent book on *Greek Verbs*, where it will be noticed that almost the only part used besides those found in Prose is τυπείς; the student should also read the interesting criticisms of Cobet in pp. 330—343 of his *Variae lectiones*, and the corresponding passage in Rutherford's *New Phrynichus*, p. 257 ff.

[The above Excursus, in the form in which it appeared in 1875, has been translated into German by Dr L. Schmidt in the *Paedogogisches Archiv*, xxv(I) 1883, p. 62—5.]

·EXCURSUS (B).

On the quantity of ἔμπυος (*Or.* 54 § 12).

In Soph. *Phil.* 1378, the phrase ἔμπυος βάσις is used with reference to the festering foot of Philoctetes, but the position of the words, at the end of an iambic line, leaves the quantity undetermined. This may however be ascertained (1) by the accent of the word from which it is derived, viz. πύον, which according to the express statement of the grammarian Arcadius should never be written πῦον; (ii) by the fact that Empedocles makes the first syllable of πύον short. We may further notice that the adjective and its derivatives occur (as might be expected) not unfrequently in Hippocrates and the medical writers; and that one of these, Galen (lib. xiii p. 876), quotes in full an Elegiac poem in which Andromachus the elder, in describing the virtues of his potent antidote, or θηριακὴ δι' ἐχιδνῶν, has the following couplet, which determines the quantity of the word:

καὶ μογερῶν στέρνων ἀπολύσεται ἔμπυον ἰλύν
πινομένη πολλοὺς μέχρις ἐπ' ἠελίους.

Hence we conclude that the lexicons of Liddell and Scott (ed. 6 *) and of Pape are unwarranted in marking

* In ed. 7 (1883) the quantity is not marked.

the penultimate as long;—an oversight which does not occur in the fourth edition of the former lexicon, and is doubtless due to a confusion between the quantities of τὸ πῦον, the Latin *pus*, and ὁ πυός, the Lat. *colostra* (or beestings).

EXCURSUS (C).

On the meaning of αὐτολήκυθος (*Or.* 54 § 14).

The exact meaning of this word is difficult to determine, and the Grammarians content themselves with giving us a wide choice of conflicting explanations. Harpocration, for instance, has the following article.

Αὐτολήκυθοι: Δημοσθένης κατὰ Κόνωνος, (1) ἤτοι ἀντὶ τοῦ εὐζώνους τινὰς καὶ ἑτοίμους πᾶν ὁτιοῦν ποιεῖν καὶ ὑπομένειν, (2) ἢ ἀντὶ τοῦ πένητας καὶ μηδὲν ἄλλο κεκτημένους ἢ ληκύθους, (3) ἢ αὐτουργούς, (4) ἢ ἀντὶ τοῦ εἰς πληγὰς ἑτοίμους καὶ οἷον τύπτοντας καὶ μαστιγοῦντας καὶ ὑβρίζοντας, (5) ἢ λέγοι ἂν τοὺς ἐκ προχείρου διδόντας ἀργύριον....

He further states that Menander used the word in two of his comedies, and attempts to support the last of the above interpretations by showing from Diphilus, that money was occasionally carried about in the λήκυθος: and the last but one by appealing to Menander for the fact that the thong or strap (ἱμάς), by which the λήκυθος was suspended about the person, might be detached from the flask and used as a whip. None of these five explanations is convincing and the last two are almost certainly wrong. An indication of the true meaning may however be gathered from the second. Any respectable Athenian in going to the public baths would be naturally attended by his slave carrying the master's λήκυθος or oil-flask, &c. Compare, for the Roman custom, Varro *R. R.* 1 55 § 4 (*olea*) *dominum in balnea sequitur*. The fraternity of young men alluded to in the text, may have gone on the principle of discarding the attendance of their slaves and carrying their own λήκυθοι, either to be free from the slight restraint which the company of their servants might put upon their practical jokes and wild escapades, or by way of assuming a lower grade of respectability than their birth would warrant, and availing themselves of that disguise either as a mere freak of youthful pleasantry or as a cloak for acts of outrage and disorder. If this view is tenable, the general sense of the title may be kept up by some such rendering as 'gentleman beggars,' 'amateur tramps.'

This explanation is in part confirmed by one of the guesses recorded in Bekker's *Anecdota Graeca* 465, 17 where αὐτολήκυθος is explained ὁ πένης ἀπὸ τοῦ ἑαυτῷ τὰς ληκύθους εἰς τὰ βαλανεῖα εἰσφέρειν. Again, Hesychius has αὐτολήκυθοι· οἱ πένητες, οἱ μόνην λήκυθον ἔχοντες· ἢ δι' ἑαυτῶν βαστάζοντες τὴν λήκυθον, οὐ δι' οἰκετῶν. Pollux x 62, refers to the passage in Demosthenes, and quotes a parallel from the comic poet Antiphanes, Meineke *Com. Graec. fragm.* III 7, καὶ αὐτοληκύθους δέ τινας Δημοσθένης ἐν τῷ κατὰ Κόνωνος ὀνομάζει οὓς σαφέστερον ἄν τις ἐν τῷ Ἀντιφάνους Ἀθάμαντι κεκλῆσθαι λέγοι·

χλαμύδα καὶ λόγχην ἔχων
ἀξυνακόλουθος ξηρὸς αὐτολήκυθος.

As another nickname attaching to one of these Clubs we have Τριβαλλοὶ in § 39 ; and in Athenaeus a coterie of Athenian wits is mentioned in the time of Philip of Macedon and therefore nearly coincident in date with the Clubs in the text; these wits or γελωτοποιοί went by the name of 'the sixty' (Athen. xiv 614). Cf. also Lysias, *fragm.* 53, κατὰ Κινησίου: οὐ μετὰ τούτου ποτὲ Ἀπολλοφάνης καὶ Μυσταλίδης καὶ Λυσίθεος συνειστιῶντο, μίαν ἡμέραν ταξάμενοι τῶν ἀποφράδων, ἀντὶ νουμηνιαστῶν κακοδαιμονιστὰς σφίσιν αὐτοῖς τοὔνομα θέμενοι;

EXCURSUS (D).

On the Τριβαλλοὶ of Or. 54 § 39.

The Triballi were a wild Thracian people occupying the region north of the range of Haemus and south of the Danube, now known as Servia. Their character is often described in unfavourable terms : thus Isocrates (*de pace* § 50) speaks of their δυσγένεια as opposed to the εὐγένεια of Athens, and (*Panath.* § 227) denounces them as leagued against all their neighbours : ἅπαντές φασιν ὁμονοεῖν μὲν (τοὺς Τριβαλλοὺς) ὡς οὐδένας ἄλλους ἀνθρώπους, ἀπολλύναι δ᾽ οὐ μόνον τοὺς ὁμόρους καὶ τοὺς πλησίον οἰκοῦντας ἀλλὰ καὶ τοὺς ἄλλους ὅσων ἂν ἐφικέσθαι δυνηθῶσιν. Lastly the comic poet Alexis (who flourished in B.C. 356, a date but slightly anterior to the present speech), attacking, apparently, some rude and uncivilised custom, describes it as too barbarous even for the Triballi, οὐδ᾽ ἐν Τριβαλλοῖς ταῦτά γ᾽ ἐστὶν ἔννομα | οὗ φασὶ τὸν θύοντα τοῖς κεκλημένοις | δείξαντ᾽ ἰδεῖν τὸ δεῖπνον, εἰς τὴν αὔριον | πωλεῖν ἀδείπνοις ἅπερ ἔθηκ᾽ αὐτοῖς ἰδεῖν (ap. Athen. xv p. 671). Cf. Ar. *Aves* 1530.

According to the speaker, Conon and his two companions were, as mere striplings (μειράκια), known by a name borrowed from these lawless Triballi. Now if the speech was (as is very probable) delivered in B.C. 341 (see p. lxiii) when Conon was rather more than 50 years of age (§ 22), he would be a μειράκιον, or about 15 years of age, 35 years previous, viz. B.C. 376. By a coincidence which has apparently remained unnoticed, this brings us to the very year in which the wild Triballi crossed the Haemus with a strong force, ravaged the southern coast of Thrace near Abdera and were forced to retreat by the Athenian commander Chabrias (Diodor. xv 36). The name of the barbarous tribe would therefore be on the lips of all Athens during the youth of Conon and his friends, and would readily find currency as a slang term of the day.

We may compare with the Τριβαλλοὶ, the disorderly Clubs to which Conon's son belonged, the ἰθύφαλλοι and αὐτολήκυθοι of § 14 ; and we may suggest in passing that the special form of the appellation, apart from its general applicability, probably turned on a play of words (e.g. τρι-βειν τοὺς ἄλλους or others more or less obvious). Cf. Photius s.v. (quoting this passage) οἱ ἐν τοῖς βαλανείοις ἀνα-γώγως διατριβόμενοι·...οἱ δὲ τοὺς εἰκαίους καὶ τοὺς βίους κατατρίβοντας. Hesychius (*inter alia*) οἱ ἐπὶ τὰ δεῖπνα ἑαυτοὺς καλοῦντες. The *Scholia* on Aeschines i § 52 (τούσδε τοὺς ἀγρίους ἄνδρας) couple together Τριβαλλοὶ (cf. Plin. *N. H.* vii 2) and Κένταυροι as infamous appellatives, and lastly the comic poet Eubulus (fl. B.C. 375) has the line Τριβαλλοποπανόθρεπτα μειρακύλλια.

As an exact parallel to the Triballi in the text and the other clubs already mentioned, we have in English literature the 'nocturnal fraternity of the Mohock-club,— a name borrowed from a sort of cannibals in India' (i.e. North America). The practical jokes of that 'worthy society of brutes,' and 'well-disposed savages,' will be familiar to the readers of the Spectator (Nos. 324, 332 and 347 ; *anno* 1712). Cf. also Gay's *Trivia* iii 325— 328 :

> Who has not heard the *Scowrer's* midnight fame?
> Who has not trembled at the *Mohock's* name?
> Was there a watchman took his hourly rounds,
> Safe from their blows, or new-invented wounds?

As German parallels we have the names *Polacken, Tartaren, Husaren,* and *Kroaten* (quoted by Reiske); similarly in French, *Cosaques* and *Pandours* (mentioned by M. Dareste).

LV.

ΠΡΟΣ ΚΑΛΛΙΚΛΕΑ ΠΕΡΙ ΧΩΡΙΟΥ.

ΥΠΟΘΕΣΙΣ.

Καλλικλῆς, πρὸς ὃν ὁ λόγος, καὶ ὁ τὴν δίκην ὑπ᾽ ἐκείνου φεύγων[a] γείτονες ἦσαν ἐν χωρίῳ, ὁδῷ μέσῃ διειργόμενοι. δυσομβρίας[b] δὲ συμβάσης, εἰς τὸ Καλλικλέους χωρίον ὕδωρ ἐμπεσὸν ἐκ τῆς ὁδοῦ κατελυμή- νατο. ἐπὶ τούτῳ διώκει βλάβης τὸν γείτονα· εἶναι 5 γάρ φησιν ἐν τῷ Τισίου χωρίῳ χαράδραν εἰς ὑπο- δοχὴν τοῦ ὕδατος τοῦ ἐκ τῆς ὁδοῦ ποιηθεῖσαν, ἣν ἀποι- κοδομήσαντα[c] νῦν αἰτίαν ἑαυτῷ βλάβης γενέσθαι. ὁ δὲ τοῦ Τισίου παῖς πρῶτον μὲν παλαιὸν καὶ οὐ δι᾽ ἑαυτοῦ τὸ ἔργον δείκνυσι· ζῶντος γὰρ ἔτι καὶ τοῦ 10 Καλλικλέους πατρὸς ἀποικοδομηθῆναι τὴν χαράδραν φησὶν ὑπὸ τοῦ Τισίου· ἔπειτα συνίστησιν ὡς οὐδὲ χαράδρα τις τὸ χωρίον ἐστί[d]. διασύρει δὲ καὶ τὴν

* Bekker st. cum H. Wolfio. διώκων libri. διωκόμενος Z, coniecit Sauppe.

b δηωβίας Φ. δη βίας B. δύο βίας Σ. margo editionis Parisi- ensis (1570) habet et δυσομβρίας quod nusquam alias legitur, et ἐπομβρίας (Z et Bekker st.) quod occurrit infra § 11 γενομένης ἐπομβρίας.

c ἀποικοδομήσαντα Sauppe, coll. § 12. ἀπωκοδομήσας ΒΦΣ. ἀποικοδομηθεῖσαι Reiske (Bekker st.).

d οὐδὲ χαράδρα τις ἀλλὰ χωρίον ἐστί ed. Parisiensis in margine (cf. § 12 ἀποδείξω χωρίον ὂν τοῦτ᾽ ἀλλ᾽ οὐ χαράδραν).

12. συνίστησιν] The word is used in late Greek in the sense 'to give proof of,' e. g. Polyb. III 108 § 4 ἐπειρᾶτο συνιστάνειν ὅτι... We may therefore per-haps render it 'he attempts to prove.' [Perhaps ἐνίστησιν, 'he objects.' P.]

13. διασύρει] makes light of the damage done. See §§ 23—

σvμβᾶσαν τῷ Καλλικλεῖ βλάβην ὡς μικρὰν καὶ
15 οὐκ ἀξίαν τηλικαύτης δίκης, καὶ τὸ ὅλον ἠδικῆσθαι
μὲν οὐδέν φησι τὸν Καλλικλέα, ἐπιθυμεῖν δὲ τῶν
χωρίων τῶν ἑαυτοῦ καὶ διὰ τοῦτο συκοφαντίας μηχα-
νᾶσθαι πάσας.

---

1   Οὐκ ἦν ἄρ', ὦ ἄνδρες 'Αθηναῖοι, χαλεπώτερον οὐδὲν ἢ γείτονος πονηροῦ καὶ πλεονέκτου τυχεῖν, ὅπερ
ἐμοὶ νυνὶ συμβέβηκεν. ἐπιθυμήσας γὰρ τῶν χωρίων
μου Καλλικλῆς οὕτω διατέθεικέ με συκοφαντῶν ὥστε
πρῶτον μὲν τὸν ἀνεψιὸν τὸν ἑαυτοῦ κατεσκεύασεν
2 ἀμφισβητεῖν μοι τῶν χωρίων, ἐξελεγχθεὶς δὲ φανερῶς
καὶ περιγενομένου μου τῆς τούτων σκευωρίας, πάλιν
δύο δίκας ἐρήμους μου κατεδιῃτήσατο, τὴν μὲν αὐτὸς

---

26. Dem. Or. 13 § 12 διέσυρε
('depreciated') τὰ παρόντα καὶ
τοὺς προγόνους ἐπήνεσε.

§§ 1, 2. *There is really no
greater nuisance, gentlemen,
than a greedy neighbour, as I
have found to my cost in the
case of the plaintiff Callicles.
He has set his heart upon my
property, and has therefore by
every legal means, direct or indirect, made me the victim of a
vexatious persecution.*

*Though I am no speaker my-
self, yet, if the court will give
me their attention, the facts
themselves will prove the base-
lessness of the present action.*

1. οὐκ ἦν ἄρ'—τυχεῖν] For
οὐκ ἦν ἄρα, 'there is not really
after all,' cf. Soph. O. C. 1697
πόθος καὶ κακῶν ἄρ' ἦν τις, and for
this use of ἦν, especially with
ἄρα, to express a fact which is
and always has been the same,
see the examples given in Liddell and Scott, s.v. εἰμί, F.
For the general sense, cf.

Hesiod's *Works and Days* 345
πῆμα κακὸς γείτων, and esp.
Aristot. Rhet. II 21 § 15 εἴ τις
γείτοσι τύχοι κεχρημένος... φαύ-
λοις, ἀποδέξαιτ' ἂν τοῦ εἰπόντος
ὅτι οὐδὲν γειτονίας χαλεπώτερον.

συκοφαντῶν] 'by his vexa-
tious litigation, his petty persecution.' The word is always
difficult to render, and we have
generally to be guided by the
context for the exact equivalent
in English.

κατεσκεύασεν] 'suborned his
cousin to claim it from me.'
The verb, here followed by the
infinitive, most commonly takes
an accusative, e.g. § 34 τὸν
ἀνεψιὸν κατεσκεύασε, Or. 54 § 14.

2. σκευωρίας] 'intrigue, job-
bery.' Or. 36 § 33 πλάσμα καὶ
σκευώρημα.

δίκας ἐρήμους—κατεδιῃτήσατο]
'got two awards (in arbitration)
decided against me by default
(for non-appearance).' Or. 21
(Mid.) §§ 84, 85 (Στράτων ὁ

χιλίων δραχμῶν, τὴν δὲ τὸν ἀδελφὸν τουτονὶ πείσας
Καλλικράτην[e]. δέομαι δὴ πάντων ὑμῶν ἀκοῦσαί μου
καὶ προσέχειν τὸν νοῦν, οὐχ ὡς αὐτὸς δυνησόμενος εἰπεῖν, ἀλλ' ἵν' ὑμεῖς ἐξ αὐτῶν τῶν πραγμάτων καταμά-
θητε ὅτι φανερῶς συκοφαντοῦμαι.

Ἓν μὲν οὖν, ὦ ἄνδρες Ἀθηναῖοι, πρὸς ἅπαντας 3
τοὺς τούτων λόγους παρέχομαι δίκαιον. τὸ γὰρ χωρίον τοῦτο περιῳκοδόμησεν ὁ πατὴρ μικροῦ δεῖν πρὶν
ἐμὲ γενέσθαι, ζῶντος μὲν ἔτι Καλλιππίδου τοῦ τούτων[f]

[e] Καλλικρατίδην Z et Bekker st.   καλλικρατίτην ΣΒ et γρ. ΓΦ.
[f] Bekk. cum r.   του του τοῦ Σ.   τοῦ τούτου Z.

διαιτητὴς) ὡς οὔτ' ἐγὼ συνεχώρουν
οὔθ' οὗτος (Midias) ἀπήντα, τῆς
δ' ὥρας ἐγίγνετο ὀψέ, κατεδιή-
τησεν. ἤδη δ' ἑσπέρας οὔσης
καὶ σκότους ἔρχεται Μειδίας...
καὶ καταλαμβάνει τὸν Στράτωνα
ἀπιόντ' ἤδη, τὴν ἔρημον δεδωκότα.
τὸ μὲν οὖν πρῶτον οἷός τ' ἦν
πείθειν αὐτόν, ἣν καταδεδιῃτή-
κει, ταύτην ἀποδεδιῃτημένην ἀπο-
φέρειν.

ἔρημος in Attic has usually
two terminations only: hence
ἐρήμους δίκας, which was perhaps preferred to ἐρήμας δίκας
on grounds of euphony. In § 6
however we find ἐρήμην κατεδιῃτήσασθε, possibly to avoid
the ambiguity arising from the
ellipse of δίκην, and in § 31 we
have ἐρήμην μου καταδεδιῄτηται
τοιαύτην ἑτέραν δίκην.

τὴν μὲν χιλίων] The same
suit is described in § 31 (quoted
in last note) as similar to the
suit in which this speech is
spoken. The damages in the
latter are also fixed at 1000
drachmae, § 25.

πείσας] sc. καταδιαιτήσασθαι.

Καλλικράτην] On the part
taken in these lawsuits by Callicrates, the brother of the

plaintiff Callicles, see A. Schaefer, Dem. und seine Zeit iii 2,
p. 254 note.

§§ 3—7. (My opponents bring
an action for damages on the
ground that the building of a
wall enclosing my property has
stopped a water-course, and thus
diverted the drainage of the
surrounding hills on to the property of the plaintiff on the opposite side of the road.)

In answer to all their arguments, I have simply to plead
that my father built that wall
fifteen years before his death,
without any objection, formal or
informal, on the part of the
plaintiff's family, who are now
attempting to take advantage of
my youth and inexperience.

I also challenge them to prove
the existence of the alleged water-
course (§ 6).

3. δίκαιον] 'a fair and legal
plea.' Or. 54 §§ 27, 29, 42.

γὰρ] See note on Or. 53 § 4.
—ὁ πατήρ, sc. Tisias § 5.—μικροῦ δεῖν πρὶν, 'almost before' '
(i.e. 'a very short time after')
I was born; not 'within a little
before,' 'just before.'

Καλλιππίδου τοῦ τούτων πατρὸς]

πατρὸς καὶ γειτνιῶντος, ὃς ἀκριβέστερον ᾔδει δήπου
τούτων, ὄντος δὲ Καλλικλέους ἀνδρὸς ἤδη καὶ ἐπιδη-
4 μοῦντος Ἀθήνησιν· ἐν δὲ τούτοις τοῖς ἔτεσιν ἅπασιν
οὔτ' ἐγκαλῶν οὐδεὶς πώποτ' ἦλθεν οὔτε μεμφόμενος
(καίτοι δῆλον ὅτι καὶ τόθ' ὕδατα πολλάκις ἐγένετο[g]),
οὔτ' ἐκώλυσεν ἐξ ἀρχῆς, εἴπερ ἠδίκει τινὰ περιοικοδο-   1273
μῶν ὁ πατὴρ τὸ ἡμέτερον χωρίον, ἀλλ' οὐδ' ἀπηγόρευσεν οὐδὲ διεμαρτύρατο, πλέον μὲν ἢ πεντεκαίδεκ' ἔτη

[g] Z et Bekk. st. cum ΣΒΓΦ.   ἐγίγνετο Bekk. 1824 cum A[1]r.

The two sons Καλλικλῆς and
Καλλικράτης bear names similar
to their father's, Καλλιπίδης,
all three being compounds of
κάλλος. 'Thus we have Ναυ-
σίφιλος Ναυσινίκου, and Καλ-
λίστρατος Καλλικράτους. So also brothers' names sometimes
varied but slightly, as Diodotus
and Diogeiton' (Becker's *Charicles* p. 220 Eng. ed.). Cf. part
i p. 136.

ἀνδρὸς ἤδη] Having attained
to man's estate and being resident at Athens, Callicles might
have brought an action long ago,
if he felt himself aggrieved. P.]

4. καίτοι — ὕδατα πολλάκις
ἐγένετο] 'and yet of course it
often rained then, just as it
does now,'—a touch of quiet
humour characteristic of this
speech. (ὕδωρ γενέσθαι literally
refers to *rain*, though floods are
implied as a necessary consequence. Ar. Vesp. 265 δεῖται
......ὕδωρ γενέσθαι κἀπιπνεῦσαι
βόρειον αὐτοῖς.)

εἴπερ ἠδίκει] (As he would
have done) if my father was
wronging any one... (But he did
not prevent him; and not only
so,) but &c. P.]

ἀπηγόρευσε] 'forbade.' In
Classical Greek, ἀγορεύω and
its compounds are seldom found
except in the present and imperfect tenses; the remaining
tenses and the verbal derivatives being generally borrowed
from ἐρῶ, εἶπον, εἴρηκα, εἴρημαι,
ἐρρήθην, ῥηθήσομαι, with ῥῆσις,
ῥητός, ῥητέον. Thus ἀναγορεύω
(to proclaim) has for its imperfect ἀνηγόρευον, while the
correct forms for the other
parts are, ἀνερῶ, ἀνείρηκα, ἀνεῖ-
πον, ἀνερρήθην and ἀνάρρησις
&c, instead of ἀναγορεύσω...
ἀναγόρευσις &c. The strict rule,
however, as to this verb and
its compounds, has its exceptions, in the case of προσαγορεύω
(e.g. προσαγορευθῇ 40 § 1), and
partially also in ἀπαγορεύω.
Thus,instead of the more usual
ἀπεῖπε, we here find ἀπηγόρευσε,
which also occurs in Dem. Or.
40 § 44 ἀπηγόρευσεν αὐτῷ μὴ
διαιτᾶν and Arist. Oecon. ii 24;
Plat. Theaet. p. 200 ἀπαγο-
ρεύσῃς. In Ar. Pax 107 we have
καταγορεύσῃ. (See Cobet's variae lectiones p. 35-39 and novae
lectiones p. 778; Mnemosyne n.s.
ii p. 127; also Veitch, *Greek
Verbs* p. 10, ed. 1871; Shilleto
on *Fals. Leg.* p. 397, and Rutherford's *New Phrynichus*, p. 326.)

διεμαρτύρατο] 'formally pro-
tested.' Or. 33 § 20 διαμαρτυ-
ραμένου τοῦ ἀνθρώπου ἐναντίον

τοῦ πατρὸς ἐπιβιοῦντος, οὐκ ἐλάττω δὲ τοῦ τούτων
πατρὸς Καλλιππίδου. καίτοι, ὦ Καλλίκλεις, ἐξῆν δή- 5
που τόθ᾽ ὑμῖν, ὁρῶσιν ἀποικοδομουμένην τὴν χαράδραν, ἐλθοῦσιν εὐθὺς ἀγανακτεῖν καὶ λέγειν πρὸς τὸν

μαρτύρων, de Cor. § 28 μὴ σιγῆ-
σαι…ἀλλὰ βοᾶν καὶ διαμαρτύρεσ-
θαι (ib. 143); Or. 42 § 28. It
must not be confounded with
διεμαρτύρησε, ‘put in a διαμαρ-
τυρία’ (see Meier and Schömann,
p. 639).

ἐπιβιοῦντος] Sense and usage
alike show that this, though at
first sight an ambiguous form,
is certainly aorist, and not present. Cf. § 32 ἐπεβίω, which
also occurs in Thuc. ii 65 (of
Pericles) ἐπεβίω δύο ἔτη καὶ
μῆνας ἓξ καὶ ἐπειδὴ ἀπέθανεν
κ.τ.λ. So also Or. 41 §§ 19 and
18 ἐπιβιοῦντος μετὰ ταῦτα πλεῖον
ἢ πένθ᾽ ἡμέρας. The *first* person
ἐπεβίων is naturally rare, as the
aorist of this verb is mainly ap-
plicable to those who are no
longer living; but Thuc. v 26
has, ἐπεβίων διὰ παντὸς (τοῦ πολέμου). In Attic Greek ἐβίων,
like βιώσομαι, βεβίωκα and βε-
βιωμένος, is used to supplement
the defects of ζῆν, which is itself
hardly used except in the present and imperfect active. ζήσω
is very rare. (See Cobet, *variae
lect.* p. 610.)

5. ἐξῆν] As usual, without
ἄν. See note on ἐχρῆν Or. 45
§ 17, followed, as here, by ἵνα
with the indicative.

ὑμῖν] ‘You and yours,’ i.e.
your father, your brother and
(when at home, and not at
Athens § 3) yourself. ὑμεῖς
never stands for σύ, and it has
been shown elsewhere that the
passages quoted from Isocrates
to prove the contrary will not
bear examination (Isocr. ad

Dem. § 2). So also, in Eur.
Bacch. 252 ἀναίνομαι πάτερ | τὸ
γῆρας ὑμῶν εἰσορῶν νοῦν οὐκ ἔχον,
the plural ὑμῶν refers to Cad-
mus and Teiresias, not to the
former only. Again in Homer,
Odyss. xii 81, we have ᾗπερ ἂν
ὑμεῖς νῆα παρὰ γλαφυρὴν ἰθύνετε,
φαίδιμ᾽ Ὀδυσσεῦ, where ὑμεῖς
refers to Odysseus and his com-
rades.

In Latin however the rule is
perhaps less strictly kept, and
vester appears to be used for
tuus in Catullus 71, 3 *Aemulus
iste tuus qui vestrum exercet
amorem*, probably the only instance of this exceptional use
of plural for singular. The rule
is only apparently broken in
Virg. Aen. ix 525 *Vos, o Calliope, precor, aspirate canenti*.
Here *vos* refers to all the Muses,
though Calliope alone is mentioned. (Cf. Aen. i 140 *ves-
tras, Eure, domos*.) So too
Cicero pro Deiot. § 29 *vos vestra
secunda fortuna, Castor, non
potestis sine propinquorum ca-
lamitate esse contenti?* (The
plural *vos* is at once explained
by *felix ista domus* in the previous sentence.)

τὴν χαράδραν] The word is
not only used of the torrent
itself, but also of the channel
cut by the torrent’s course (der.
χαράσσω). Hesychius χαράδρα·
χείμαρρος ποταμός. κατάγει δὲ
οὗτος παντοῖα ἐν τῷ ῥεύματι καὶ
κατασύρει. χαράδραι· αἱ χα-
ράξεις τοῦ ἐδάφους. καὶ οἱ κοῖλοι
τόποι ἀπὸ τῶν καταφερομένων
ὀμβρίων ὑδάτων. The rendering

πατέρα, "Τισία, τί ταῦτα ποιεῖς ; ἀποικοδομεῖς τὴν χα-
"ράδραν ; εἶτ᾽ ἐμπεσεῖται τὸ ὕδωρ εἰς τὸ χωρίον τὸ
"ἡμέτερον"· ἵν᾽ εἰ μὲν ἐβούλετο παύσασθαι, μηδὲν
ὑμῖν[h] ἦν δυσχερὲς πρὸς ἀλλήλους[h], εἰ δ᾽ ὠλιγώρησε
καὶ συνέβη τι τοιοῦτον, μάρτυσιν εἶχες τοῖς τότε
6 παραγενομένοις χρῆσθαι.   καὶ νὴ Δί᾽ ἐπιδεῖξαί σε[l]
ἔδει πᾶσιν ἀνθρώποις χαράδραν οὖσαν, ἵνα μὴ λόγῳ

[h] ἡμῖν ἦν δυσχερὲς πρὸς ἀλλήλους Bekk. st. ὑμῖν δυσχερὲς πρὸς
ἀλλήλους ἦν Bekk. 1824. ὑμῖν Σ a me collatus ; ἡμῖν manu prima in
ὑμῖν mutatum r. ὑμῖν ἦν (η Σ, ᾖ ΦΦ) δυσχερὲς πρὸς ἀλλήλους Ζ ; δυσχερὲς πρὸς ἀλλήλους ᾖ r (ᾖ A¹).

[l] 'ἐπιδεῖξαί σέ γε, Reiskius e mss, sed vel lege γέ σε, vel potius
dele σε.' Dobree.

'water-course' will suit all the passages in which it occurs in the present speech.

τί ταῦτα ποιεῖς ;] 'What are you about?' lit. 'why are you doing this?' 'Are you cutting off the water-course?'

ἀποικοδομεῖς] *ἀντὶ τοῦ ἀπο-φράττεις ἀπολαβών τινα (?) οἰκο-δομήματι· Δημοσθένης ἐν τῷ πρὸς Καλλικλέα.* The above explanation from Harpocration, with the awkward *τινὰ*, does not entirely suit this passage, though he specially refers to this speech. But in Thuc. i 134, we read of Pausanias, *ἔνδον ὄντα τηρήσαντες αὐτὸν καὶ ἀπολαβόντες εἴσω ἀπῳκοδόμησαν*, and it seems likely that the lexicographer, or his transcribers, either had that passage itself in view, or carelessly incorporated into an explanation of Demosthenes the note of some previous expositor of Thucydides.

ἵνα...ἦν] Goodwin's *Moods and Tenses* § 44, 3, and Or. 36 § 47. As an exact parallel to the whole of this sentence, we have Or. 28 § 5 *ἐχρῆν* (like *ἐξῆν, supra*)...*εἰσκαλέσαντας μάρτυρας* πολλοὺς παρασημήνασθαι κελεῦ-σαι τὰς διαθήκας, *ἵν᾽, εἴ τι ἐγίγ-νετο ἀμφισβητήσιμον, ἦν εἰς τὰ γράμματα ταῦτ᾽ ἐπανελθεῖν.*

ὑμῖν] (which is really the reading of the Paris ms Σ, although the contrary would be inferred from the *apparatus criticus* of Dindorf and the Zürich editors), must refer to the defendant's father Tisias and the family of Callicles the plaintiff. With *ἡμῖν* which is found in the *codex Augustanus primus* and approved by G. H. Schaefer, the sense is: 'in which case you and I would have been having no disputes with one another (as we now have).'

εἰ...συνέβη τι τοιοῦτον] i.e. *εἰ ἐνέπεσεν τὸ ὕδωρ εἰς τὸ χωρίον τὸ ὑμέτερον.—μάρτυσι*, referring to *διεμαρτύρατο* in § 4.

εἶχες] without *ἂν*, being dependent on *ἵνα*, like the preceding *ἦν*. '*intelligendum de Callicle, qui si tale quid olim factum esset, testibus nunc uti posset.*' G. H. Schaefer.

6. *ἐπιδεῖξαι ... χαράδραν οὖ-σαν*] § 12 *ἐγὼ ἀποδείξω χωρίον ὃν τοῦτ᾽ ἀλλ᾽ οὐ χαράδραν.*

μόνον, ὥσπερ νῦν, ἀλλ' ἔργῳ τὸν πατέρ' ἀδικοῦντ'
ἀπέφαινες. τούτων τοίνυν οὐδὲν πώποτ' οὐδεὶς ποιεῖν
ἠξίωσεν. οὐ γὰρ ἂν οὔτ' ἐρήμην, ὥσπερ ἐμοῦ νῦν,
κατεδιῃτήσασθε, οὔτε πλέον ἂν ἦν ὑμῖν συκοφαντοῦσιν
οὐδὲν, ἀλλ' ʲεἰ ἠνέγκατε τότε μάρτυρα καὶ ἐπεμαρτύ- 7
ρασθε, νῦνʲ ἀπέφαινεν ἂν ἐκεῖνος εἰδὼς ἀκριβῶς ὅπως
εἶχεν ἕκαστα τούτων, καὶ τοὶς ῥᾳδίως τούτουςᵏ μαρτυροῦντας ἐξήλεγχεν. ἀνθρώπου δ', οἶμαι, τηλικούτου
καὶ ἀπείρου τῶν πραγμάτων ἅπαντες καταπεφρονή-

ʲ⁻ʲ Bekk. 1824, et G. H. Schaefer. εἰ ἠνέγκατε—νῦν om. Z et
Bekk. st. cum ΣrAˡ.

ᵏ Bekk. 1824 cum A¹A⁵. τούτοις Z et Bekk. st. cum ΓΣΦΒ.

ἵνα—ἀπέφαινες] Constr. ἵνα
μὴ λόγῳ μόνον ἀπέφαινες τὸν
πατέρα ἀδικοῦντα, ὥσπερ νῦν
(ἀποφαίνεις), ἀλλ' ἔργῳ (ἀπέφαινες ἀδικοῦντα). λόγῳ and
ἔργῳ (on which see Or. 46 § 9)
are not to be taken with ἀδικοῦντα.—In the next sentence
οὐδεὶς means οὐδεὶς ὑμῶν.

ἐρήμην...κατεδιῃτήσασθε] See
§ 2.

εἰ ἠνέγκατε — ἐπεμαρτύρασθε,
νῦν] If we retain these words,
ἐκεῖνος will refer to ὁ μάρτυς. If
(with the best mss) we omit them,
it can only refer to ὁ πατήρ
(Tisias, who was no longer
alive). The latter makes quite
as good sense as the former;
if we lose the antithesis between ὁ μάρτυς and τοὺς ῥᾳδίως
μαρτυροῦντας, we gain the contrast between the father who
would certainly have held his
own, and the son whose youth
and inexperience are held fair
game by the plaintiff's party
(τηλικούτου—καταπεφρονήκατε).

7. ῥᾳδίως] 'only too readily,' 'recklessly,' 'at random.'
Plat. Apol. p. 24 c ῥᾳδίως εἰς
ἀγῶνας καθιστὰς ἀνθρώπους, Leg.

917 β θεῶν ὀνόματα μὴ χραίνειν
ῥᾳδίως, Meno 94 ε ῥᾳδίως κακῶς λέγειν ἀνθρώπους.

τούτους] The reading τού-
τοις is open to the objection
that between κατεδιῃτήσασθε in
the previous and καταπεφρονήκατε in the subsequent context,
we expect, not the third person
τούτοις, but the second person
ὑμῖν, just as above we have
οὐδὲν πλέον ἂν ἦν ὑμῖν.
If we retain the doubtful
words at the beginning of § 7,
the argument in favour of τούτους is yet stronger, and τούτοις
is then still less defensible.
('melior vulgata lectio, τούτους,
μάρτυρας scilicet,' Seager, Classical Journal, 1825, no. 61 p.
63.)

τηλικούτου] more commonly
of great age (tantae aetatis),
but here of extreme youth
(tantulae aetatis). Soph. El.
614 ἥτις τοιαῦτα τὴν τεκοῦσαν
ὕβρισεν, καὶ ταῦτα τηλικοῦτος (sc.
οὖσα). Antig. 726. Plat. Apol.
25 D τοσοῦτον σὺ ἐμοῦ σοφώτερος
εἶ τηλικούτου ὄντος (so old, of
Socrates) τηλικόσδε ὤν (so young,
of Meletus).

κατέ μου.   ἀλλ᾽ ἐγὼ πρὸς ἅπαντας τούτους, ὦ ἄνδρες
Ἀθηναῖοι, τὰς αὐτῶν¹ πράξεις ἰσχυροτάτας μαρτυρίας
παρέχομαι.   διὰ τί γὰρ οὐδεὶς οὔτ᾽ ἐπεμαρτύρατο οὔτ᾽
ἐνεκάλεσεν, ἀλλ᾽ οὐδ᾽ ἐμέμψατο πώποτε, ἀλλ᾽ ἐξήρκει
ταῦτ᾽ αὐτοῖς ἠδικημένοις περιορᾶν;

8   Ἐγὼ τοίνυν ἱκανὰ μὲν ἡγοῦμαι καὶ ταῦτ᾽ εἶναι 1274
πρὸς τὴν τούτων κατηγορίαν.   ἵνα δ᾽ εἰδῆτε, ὦ ἄνδρες
Ἀθηναῖοι, καὶ περὶ τῶν ἄλλων, ὡς οὔθ᾽ ὁ πατὴρ οὐδὲν
ἠδίκει περιοικοδομῶν τὸ χωρίον, οὗτοί τε κατεψευσμέ-
νοι πάντ᾽ εἰσὶν ἡμῶν, ἔτι σαφέστερον ὑμᾶς πειράσομαι διδάσκειν.   τὸ μὲν γὰρ χωρίον ὁμολογεῖται καὶ
9 παρ᾽ αὐτῶν τούτων ἡμέτερον ἴδιον εἶναι· τούτου δ᾽

¹ Bekk.   αὐτῶν Z (αιτῶν Σ).

ἐξήρκει—περιορᾶν] 'they were content to submit to these wrongs.' The dative ἠδικημένοις, subordinate to περιορᾶν, follows the case of αὐτοῖς, which again depends on ἐξήρκει. Cf. Or. 54 §§ 16 and 44.   Or. 3 § 23 εὐδαίμοσιν ὑμῖν ἔξεστι γίγνεσθαι. Madvig *Gk. Synt.* § 158 2) 3).— ταῦτ᾽, acc. after ἠδικημένοις.— περιορᾶν, a verb characteristic of Greek prose and comedy (Porson on Eur. Med. 284 and Cobet *var. lect.* p. 338).

§§ 8, 9.   *I contend that my father had a perfect right to build the enclosure, as even the plaintiff himself admits that the land is our own property. This being admitted, a personal in-spection would in itself have sufficed to show the jury how groundless the present action is. And this was why I wanted (and my opponents refused) to submit the matter to the arbitration of impartial persons who knew the neighbourhood. Failing this, I must ask the jury for their closest attention while I describe* the position of the properties in question.

8.   οὔθ᾽...τε]   Or. 54 § 26, Madv. *Gk. Synt.* § 208.

ἡμέτερον ἴδιον]   'our own pri-vate property,' stronger than ἡμέτερον.   So in § 13. — The grammarian Priscian, who cu-riously regards ἴδιος as an exact equivalent to the Latin *suus*, has the following remark: *quod mi-rum est, hoc ipsum* [id est τὸ ἴδιον] *etiam primae et secundae adiun-gitur personae apud illos ut* Ἰσαῖος ἐν τῷ πρὸς Εὐκλείδην: οὐκ ἂν τὰ ἴδια τὰ ἐμαυτοῦ (fragm. 60). *Demosthenes* ἐν τῷ πρὸς Πολυ-κλέα: οὐ περὶ τῶν ἐμῶν ἰδίων μᾶλ-λον τιμωρήσεσθε Πολυκλέα ἢ οὐχ ὑπὲρ ὑμῶν αὐτῶν καὶ ἐν τῷ αὐτῷ οὐ περὶ πλείονος ἐποιησάμην τὰ ἐμαυτοῦ ἴδια ἢ τὰ ὑμέτερα (Dem. Or. 50 §§ 66, 63).   ἐν δὲ τῷ πρὸς Καλλικλέα περὶ χωρίου βλάβης· τὸ μὲν γὰρ χωρίον— ἡμέτερον ἴδιον εἶναι.   *Phroe-nichus* ποαστρίαις: ὥσπερ ἐμοῦ αὐτῆς ἴδιον, *pro quo nos dicimus* 'meum proprium,' *et* 'tuum proprium.' *dicitur tamen etiam*

ὑπάρχοντος, ὦ ἄνδρες Ἀθηναῖοι, μάλιστα μὲν ᾔδειτε
ἂν ἰδόντες τὸ χωρίον ὅτι συκοφαντοῦμαι. διὸ καὶ τοῖς
εἰδόσιν ἐπιτρέπειν ἐβουλόμην ἐγώ, τοῖς ἴσοις. ἀλλ᾽
οὐχ οὗτοι, καθάπερ νυνὶ λέγειν ἐπιχειροῦσι· δῆλον δ᾽
ὑμῖν καὶ τοῦτ᾽ αὐτίκ᾽ ἔσται πᾶσιν. ἀλλὰ προσέχετε,
ὦ ἄνδρες Ἀθηναῖοι, πρὸς Διὸς καὶ θεῶν τὸν νοῦν.   τοῦ 10

'suum proprium illius,' *ut non
putetur abundare* 'suum,' *sed
indubitabilem discretionem sig-
nificare.* Priscian, *Instit.* p. 1089
—90.

9. τούτου δ᾽ ὑπάρχοντος] 'this
being admitted,' 'with this fact
to begin upon.' Plat. Tim.
p. 29 A τούτων ὑπαρχόντων = τούτων ὑποκειμένων, *his positis.*

ἰδόντες] = εἰ εἴδετε, Goodwin's
Moods and Tenses § 52, 1.

τοῖς εἰδόσι...τοῖς ἴσοις] § 35
ἑτοῖμοι ἦμεν ἐπιτρέπειν τοῖς εἰδόσιν, ἴσοις καὶ κοινοῖς. Or. 40
§ 39 ἐπιτρέπειν...διαιτητῇ ἴσῳ.
On 'private arbitrators' see note
on Or. 54 § 26 ἡ δίαιτα.

In the present instance, the
consent of the speaker's opponents was essential, and he insists (for all they urge to the
contrary) that it was to their
refusal that the failure of his
attempt to secure an amicable
settlement must be ascribed.

οὐχ οὗτοι] ἐπιτρέπειν ἐβούλοντο.—In the next sentence
ὑμῖν and πᾶσι go together, καὶ
emphasizing τοῦτο.

προσέχετε—τὸν νοῦν] 'I implore the jury, in the name of
all that's sacred, to give me
their best attention.' The ear-
nestness of this appeal (πρὸς
Διὸς καὶ τῶν θεῶν) is explained
by the fact that unless the
jury clearly understood the to-
pographical details which here
follow, the remainder of the
speech would be almost unin-

telligible, and what applies to
the original hearers holds
equally good for the modern
reader. The defendant has
just informed the court that an
actual inspection of the premises would have been decisive
in his favour. He therefore
naturally endeavours to com-
pensate for that disadvantage
by giving his audience a distinct description of the relative
situation of the properties of the
contending parties. [In modern
courts a map or plan made by
a surveyor would be produced.
P.]

§§ 10, 11. *The estate of my
opponents is separated from my
own by a public road, and both
are surrounded by a tract of
mountainous country. Thus, the
drainage from the hills flows
partly into our properties, partly
on to the road, and in the latter
case, it is either carried down
the road itself, or, if anything
stops its course, it inundates the
properties. On one occasion, the
water made an inroad into what
was subsequently my father's
property, and, owing to neglect,
made further inroad. Accordingly my father, on coming into
possession, built this wall to
protect his lands from the encroachments of his neighbours as
well as from the inroad of the
water.*

10. τοῦ γὰρ—ὁδός ἐστι] lit.
'for the space between their

γὰρ χωρίου τοῦ τ' ἐμοῦ καὶ τοῦ τούτων τὸ μέσον[m] ὁδός
ἐστιν, ὅρους δὲ περιέχοντος κύκλῳ τοῖς χωρίοις τὸ
καταρρέον ὕδωρ τῇ μὲν εἰς τὴν ὁδὸν, τῇ δ' εἰς τὰ χωρία
συμβαίνει φέρεσθαι. καὶ δὴ καὶ τοῦτ' εἰσπῖπτον εἰς[n]
τὴν ὁδὸν, ᾗ μὲν ἂν εὐοδῇ, φέρεται κάτω κατὰ τὴν ὁδὸν,
ᾗ δ' ἂν ἐνστῇ τι, τηνικαῦτα τοῦτ' εἰς τὰ χωρία ὑπεραί-

[m] μέσον Z et Bekk st.   τὸ manu antiqua insertum habet Σ.

[n] εἰς FΣΦ.   legebatur ἐνίοτε εἰς.

property and mine is a road,'
i.e. 'there is a road between
their property and my own.'
τὸ μέσον, however, seems a
less satisfactory reading than
μέσον.

ὅρους περιέχοντος κύκλῳ] Xen.
Hellen. iv 6 § 8 διὰ τὰ κύκλῳ
περιέχοντα ὄρη. Plat. Critias
Λ τὸ περὶ τὴν πόλιν πᾶν πεδίον
ἐκείνην μὲν περιέχον αὐτὸ δὲ
κύκλῳ περιεχόμενον ὄρεσι.

τοῖς χωρίοις] This can hardly
be taken with περιέχοντος κύκλῳ,
which would require an accusative, nor again with καταρρέον,
as we should then expect τὸ
τοῖς χωρίοις καταρρέον ὕδωρ,
which indeed is actually printed
in Reiske's *Index Graecitatis*
(with the explanation '*id est
εἰς τὰ χωρία*'). Reiske's erroneous quotation may account
for this passage being cited in
Liddell and Scott as an instance
of καταρρεῖν 'c. dat. *to rush
down to a place*' (corrected in
ed. 7, 1883).

A better explanation is either
to construct it with συμβαίνει
(which however is objectionable
on account of the repetition of
τὰ χωρία in the same sentence),
or, better still, to understand
it as a kind of *dativus incommodi*. In the latter case we
might render as follows: 'between their property and mine

there is a road; a hilly district
encircles both; and *unfortu-
nately for the properties* the
water that flows down runs (it
so happens) partly into the
road, partly into the properties.'

[I should regard χωρίοις as
the dative in relation to position; 'as these farms have
mountains enclosing them on
every side.' P.]

καὶ δὴ καί] 'and in particular.'
After making a general reference to τὸ καταρρέον ὕδωρ, the
speaker narrows his description
to the water which runs down
the road. In the next section,
again, καὶ δή limits the subject
still further to the water which
on a special occasion made inroad into his own property.

ᾗ ἂν εὐοδῇ] 'wherever it has
a free course.' Arist. gen. anim.
i 18 ῥεῖ ὅπου ἂν εὐοδήσῃ τοῦ
σώματος, and (as a passive in
intransitive sense) ib. ii 4 εὐ-
οδεῖται μᾶλλον. Cf. *infra* § 11 τὸ
ὕδωρ...μᾶλλον ὡδοποίει.

ᾗ ἂν ἐνστῇ τι] 'wherever anything stands in the way', 'any
obstacle intervenes.' Plat.
Phaedo, 77 B ἔτι ἐνέστηκεν (in-
stat, obstat) τὸ τῶν πολλῶν (of an
objection in argument, ἔνστασις).

τηνικαῦτα κ.τ.λ.] 'why! thereupon it must of course over-
flow the properties.' τηνικαῦτα,

ρεῖν ἀναγκαῖον ἤδη. καὶ δὴ κατὰ τοῦτο τὸ χωρίον, 11
ὦ ἄνδρες δικασταί, γενομένης ἐπομβρίας συνέβη τὸ
ὕδωρ ἐμβαλεῖν· ἀμεληθὲν δέ, οὔπω τοῦ πατρὸς ἔχοντος
αὐτό, ἀλλ' ἀνθρώπου δυσχεραίνοντος ὅλως τοῖς τόποις
καὶ μᾶλλον ἀστικοῦ, δὶς καὶ τρὶς ἐμβαλὸν τὸ ὕδωρ τά
τε χωρία ἐλυμήνατο καὶ μᾶλλον ὡδοποίει. διὸ δὴ
ταῦθ' ὁ πατὴρ ὁρῶν, ὡς ἐγὼ τῶν εἰδότων ἀκούω,
καὶ τῶν γειτόνων ἐπινεμόντων ἅμα καὶ βαδιζόντων

though almost always used of
time, occasionally (as here after
ᾗ, which indicates *place*) bears
a more general meaning, 'in
that case,' 'under these circumstances.'

11. ἀμεληθὲν] It seems best
to regard this as an accusative
neuter *absolute* ('neglect having
ensued'), and not to take it
with τὸ ὕδωρ, much less with
αὐτό, i.e. τὸ χωρίον. So in
Plat. Phaedr. 265 D ὁρισθὲν
'it having been defined.' Or.
50 (Polycl.) § 12 προσταχθέν.
(Kühner § 487, 3, and Goodwin's *Moods and Tenses* §
110. 2.)

In translating, we can best
bring out the sense by reserv-
ing ἀμεληθὲν to a later point
in the English sentence, and
rendering the clause οὔπω...
ἔχοντος as though it contained
the principal verb. Thus:
'now my father was not yet
in possession of the property,
but a man who disliked the
neighbourhood and preferred
town life; accordingly neglect
ensued, and the water overflowed
several times, damaged the land,
and was making further inroad.'—For ὡδοποίει, cf. *supra*
§ 10, εὐοδῇ.

[By μᾶλλον ὡδοποίει, the speaker wishes to show how the rain
had made a way for itself al-

most amounting to a χαράδρα,
though he denies the existence
of any recognised χαράδρα by
the road-side in § 16. P.]

ὁρῶν...ἐπινεμόντων] For the
nominative participle combined
with the genitive absolute, cf.
Thuc. VIII 45 Ἀλκιβιάδης τοῖς
Πελοποννησίοις ὕποπτος ὢν καὶ
ἀπ' αὐτῶν ἀφικομένης ἐπιστολῆς
...ὑποχωρεῖ (Goodwin's *Moods
and Tenses* § 111).

τῶν γειτόνων—χωρίου] 'as the
neighbours *also* (ἅμα) encroached and trespassed on the property.' ἐπινέμειν and ἐπινομία
are specially used of turning
cattle on to a neighbour's land
for pasture. Hence the meta-
phorical use of the word in
Aesch. Ag. 485 πιθανὸς ἄγαν
ὁ θῆλυς ὅρος ἐπινέμεται ταχύπορος.
Among other words compounded
with ἐπί and used of encroachments on the debateable border-
land of two countries, or on the
boundaries of adjacent properties, we have ἐπεργάζεσθαι and
ἐπεργασία.

In Plato's Laws (pp. 843—4)
there is a long and interesting
passage, in which the annoy-
ances caused by neighbours are
dwelt upon, and suggestions
made for legal remedies. We
transcribe those portions only
which illustrate the clause before us, and indeed the speech

διὰ τοῦ χωρίου, τὴν αἱμασιὰν περιῳκοδόμησε ταύτην.
12 καὶ ὡς ταῦτ' ἀληθῆ λέγω, παρέξομαι μὲν καὶ μάρτυρας
ὑμῖν τοὺς εἰδότας, πολὺ δὲ, ὦ ἄνδρες Ἀθηναῖοι, τῶν
μαρτύρων ἰσχυρότερα τεκμήρια. Καλλικλῆς μὲν γάρ

in general. p. 843 B βλάβαι
πολλαὶ καὶ σμικραὶ γειτόνων
γιγνόμεναι, διὰ τὸ θαμίζειν ἔχθρας
ὄγκον μέγαν ἐντίκτουσαι, χαλεπὴν
καὶ σφόδρα πικρὰν γειτονίαν
ἀπεργάζονται. διὸ χρὴ πάντως
εὐλαβεῖσθαι γείτονα γείτονι μηδὲν
ποιεῖν διάφορον, τῶν τε ἄλλων
πέρι καὶ δὴ καὶ ἐπεργασίας ξυμ-
πάσης σφόδρα διευλαβούμενον...
ὃς δ' ἂν ἐπεργάζηται τὰ τοῦ
γείτονος ὑπερβαίνων τοὺς ὅρους,
τὸ μὲν βλάβος ἀποτινέτω, τῆς δὲ
ἀναιδείας ἅμα καὶ ἀνελευθερίας
ἕνεκα ἰατρευόμενος διπλάσιον τοῦ
βλάβους ἄλλο ἐκτισάτω τῷ βλαφθέντι...καὶ ἐάν τις βοσκήματα
ἐπινέμῃ, τὰς βλάβας (ἀγρο-
νόμοι) ὁρῶντες κρινόντων καὶ
τιμώντων.

See esp. Donaldson's *New
Cratylus* § 174, where this class
of words is discussed. He apparently understands ἐπινέμειν
in this passage to refer to a
'common trespass'; but this is
sufficiently expressed by βαδιζόντων διὰ τοῦ χωρίου, and it is
therefore better to give ἐπινεμόντων that special application
to the 'encroachment of cattle'
which it constantly bears.

αἱμασιὰν] Never used in the
sense of a 'hedge', but always
of a 'wall of dry stones.' In
Odyss. XVIII 359 and XXIV
224—230 αἱμασίας λέγειν is
explained in a *scholium*, οἰκο-
δομῶν ἐκ συλλεκτῶν λίθων, and
Hesychius paraphrases the word
τὸ ἐκ πολλῶν λίθων λογάδων ἄ-
θροισμα. Thus in Theocr. I 45,
a boy watching a vineyard is described as sitting ἐφ' αἱμασιαῖσι,
and in V 93 we have roses

growing in beds beside the
garden-wall, ῥόδα τῶν ἄνδηρα
παρ' αἱμασιαῖσι πεφύκει. Cf.
Plat. legg. 881 A περιβόλους αἱμα-
σιώδεις τινάς, τειχῶν ἐρύματα.

In Bekker's *Anecdota Graeca*
p. 356, we have the definition,
τὸ ἐκ χαλίκων ᾠκοδομημένον
τειχίον, where the next few
words, κυρίως δὲ τοῖς ἠκανθωμένοις
λέγεται φραγμοῖς, show that such
walls were sometimes topped
with thorns (Odyss. XIV 10
αὐλήν...δείματο...ῥυτοῖσιν λάεσ-
σιν καὶ ἐθρίγκωσεν ἀχέρδῳ, cf.
XXIV 230), just as in England
rough stone-walls are frequently
finished off with furze and other
prickly shrubs. The Greek
peasants still give the name
αἱμασιὰς to the walls built to
support the artificial terraces of
earth on the hillsides of the
Morea (Ross, *Archaeologische
Aufsaetze* II 500).

§§ 12—15. *The plaintiff contends I have damaged his estate
by obstructing 'the water-course.'
In reply, I shall prove that what
he calls a water-course is no such
thing, but really part of our own
ground, for it has fruit-trees
growing in it, which were planted
before my father built the enclosure, and it contains a burial-
place, made before we acquired
the property.*

*All this is in evidence, gentle-
men, as also the fact that the
wall was built while the plaintiff's father was still alive, and
without any protest on the part
of my opponents or the rest of
my neighbours.*

φησι τὴν χαράδραν ἀποικοδομήσαντα βλάπτειν ἐμὲ
αὐτόν°· ἐγὼ δ' ἀποδείξω χωρίον ὂν τοῦτ' ἀλλ' οὐ
χαράδραν. εἰ μὲν οὖν μὴ συνεχωρεῖτο ἡμέτερον ἴδιον 13
εἶναι, τάχ' ἂν τοῦτο ἠδικούμεν, εἴ τι τῶν δημοσίων
ᾠκοδομοῦμεν· νυνὶ δ' οὔτε τοῦτο ἀμφισβητοῦσιν, ἔστι
τ' ἐν τῷ χωρίῳ δένδρα πεφυτευμένα, ἄμπελοι καὶ
συκαῖ. καίτοι τίς ἐν χαράδρᾳ ταῦτ' ἂν φυτεύειν
ἀξιώσειεν; οὐδείς γε. τίς δὲ πάλιν τοὺς αὑτοῦ
προγόνους θάπτειν; οὐδὲ τοῦτ' οἶμαι. ταῦτα τοίνυν 14
ἀμφότερ', ὦ ἄνδρες δικασταί, συμβέβηκεν· καὶ γὰρ

° αὐτὸν Z.

12. τὴν χαράδραν] emphatic,
as is shown by its prominent
position and by the next sentence.

βλάπτειν ἐμὲ αὐτὸν] The
order of words, (1) the infinitive, (2) the subject, (3) the object, is exactly parallel to that
in Or. 54 § 31 μὴ πατάξαι Κόνωνα Ἀρίστωνα.

χωρίον......ἀλλ' οὐ χαράδραν]
'private ground and no water-
course.' Isocr. ad Dem. § 2
τῶν σπουδαίων ἀλλὰ μὴ τῶν
φαύλων εἶναι μιμητάς.

13. εἰ μὴ συνεχωρεῖτο ἴδιον
εἶναι, τάχ' ἂν ἠδικοῦμεν, εἴ τι τῶν
δημοσίων ᾠκοδομοῦμεν] In this
conditional sentence, we have
one apodosis ἠδικοῦμεν ἄν, corresponding to a double protasis.
The second protasis εἰ...ᾠκοδο-
μοῦμεν reiterates the first with
a slight change of idea. The
supposition stated at the beginning of the sentence is thus
re-stated with some slight redundancy at the end, and
reaches the hearer in two parts,
which enter his mind separately
and there unite. So in Plat.
Phaedo 67 E εἰ φοβοῖντο καὶ
ἀγανακτοῖεν, οὐ πολλὴ ἂν ἀλογία

εἴη,...εἰ μὴ ἄσμενοι ἐκεῖσε ἴοιεν.
The idiom may be illustrated
by the effect upon the brain of
the double images of external
objects entering the eyes separately and subsequently uniting.
Numerous varieties of construction, of which the present is a
single instance, are grouped
under the general heading of
'Binary Structure' in Riddell's
Digest of Platonic idioms, § 204.

ἡμέτερον ἴδιον] See note on
§ 8, ad fin.

πεφυτευμένα] 'planted' and
not growing wild, like the ἐρι-
νεὸς or συκῆ ἀγρία.

τίς ... θάπτειν;] The telling
question, 'who would think of
burying his ancestors in a
water-course?' (a question seriously put, unless perhaps we
ought to take it as one of
the touches of humour characteristic of this speech), is of
course not meant to apply to all
the tombs subsequently mentioned (§ 14). Some of them were
there even before the land came
into the speaker's possession.

14. καὶ γὰρ...καὶ] 'for not only
...but.' A frequent idiom, though
one but little observed. P.]

16—2

τὰ δένδρα πεφύτευται πρότερον ἢ τὸν πατέρα περιοι-
κοδομῆσαι τὴν αἱμασιὰν, καὶ τὰ μνήματα παλαιὰ καὶ
πρὶν ἡμᾶς κτήσασθαι τὸ χωρίον γεγενημένα ἐστίν.
καίτοι τούτων ὑπαρχόντων τίς ἂν ἔτι λόγος ἰσχυρότε-
ρος, ὦ ἄνδρες Ἀθηναῖοι, γένοιτο; τὰ γὰρ ἔργα φανερῶς
ἐξελέγχει. καί μοι λαβὲ πάσας νυνὶ τὰς μαρτυρίας,
καὶ λέγε.

ΜΑΡΤΥΡΙΑΙ.

15 Ἀκούετε, ὦ ἄνδρες Ἀθηναῖοι, τῶν μαρτυριῶν.
ἆρ᾽ ὑμῖν δοκοῦσι διαρρήδην μαρτυρεῖν καὶ τὸ[p] χωρίον
εἶναι δένδρων μεστὸν καὶ μνήματ᾽ ἔχειν τινὰ καὶ τἆλλ᾽
ἅπερ καὶ τοῖς ἄλλοις χωρίοις συμβέβηκεν ; καὶ πάλιν
ὅτι περιῳκοδομήθη τὸ χωρίον ζῶντος μὲν ἔτι τοῦ τούτων[q] πατρὸς, οὐκ ἀμφισβητούντων δ᾽ οὔτε τούτων οὔτ᾽
ἄλλου τῶν γειτόνων οὐδενός ;

[p] om. Z et Bekker st. cum FΣΦB.

[q] Bekk. τοῦ τούτου Z cum FΦB. τῶν τούτου Σ.

τούτων ὑπαρχόντων] Cf. § 9
init.

15. ἆρ᾽] We should expect
ἆρ᾽ οὐχ, which, like *nonne*, distinctly implies an affirmative
answer. But ἆρα is not unfrequently used alone, to denote a
simple interrogation, the context showing whether a negative or, as here, an affirmative
reply is expected. Xen. Cyr.
IV 6 § 4 ἆρα βέβληκα δὶς ἐφεξῆς ;
(L and S).

μνήματα...τινὰ] Not μνήματα
παλαιὰ as before. The de-
scription is made as general as
possible to show that the piece
of ground in question had all
the essential characteristics of
private property.—τἆλλ᾽ ἅπερ]
The speaker does not specify
what is included in this *et
cetera*, but the depositions probably went into further detail.

§§ 16—18. The plaintiff
speaks of the stoppage of a water-
course. Now, firstly, I don't
suppose that in the whole of
Attica there is such a thing as
a water-course by the side of a
public road. The water would
naturally flow down the road
and a water-course would be
quite unnecessary. Next, no one
surely would think of allowing
water passing down the highway
to flow into his own land ; on
the contrary, he would of course
dam it off, if it ever made inroad.

Now the plaintiff wants me to
let the water flow into my own
land, and to turn it off into the
road again after it has passed
his property. Why then, the
owner next below my neighbour
opposite will complain. In short,
if I take the water from off the

"Αξιον δ', ὦ ἄνδρες δικασταὶ, καὶ περὶ τῶν ἄλλων 16
1276 ὧν εἴρηκε Καλλικλῆς ἀκοῦσαι. καὶ σκέψασθε᾽ πρῶτον
μὲν εἴ τις ὑμῶν ἑόρακεν᾽ ἢ ἀκήκοε πώποτε παρ᾽ ὁδὸν
χαράδραν οὖσαν. οἶμαι γὰρ ἐν πάσῃ τῇ χώρᾳ μηδεμίαν εἶναι. τοῦ γὰρ ἕνεκα, ὃ διὰ τῆς ὁδοῦ τῆς δημοσίας

^r Bekk. σκέψασθαι Ζ cum ΣΦ.   ^s ἑώρακεν Ζ.

road, I cannot let it out again either into the road or into my neighbours' properties. And no other course is open to me; for I presume the plaintiff won't compel me to drink it up.

16. σκέψασθε] The other reading σκέψασθαι (closely connected by καί with ἀκοῦσαι) is perhaps less preferable.

οἶμαι — ἐποίησέ τις;] The speaker, after asking whether any of his audience has ever seen or even heard of a water-course running by the side of a public way, takes upon himself to declare that he does not believe there is anything of the kind in the whole of Attica. The startling character of this assertion, which could hardly have been untrue, is only equalled by the delightful frankness with which he assigns the reason. 'What could induce any one,' he asks, 'to make a channel through his private grounds for water, which, if let alone, would be sure to flow down along the public road?' The passage is singularly suggestive on the state of the mountain roads of Attica. The public road, so called, would in numbers of cases be little better than the path of a mountain-torrent, which might be used in dry weather for purposes of transit, but in very wet seasons would revert to the possession of the waters. In the days of Demosthenes many of the mountain roads were, we presume, not much better than those of modern Attica, as described with perfect accuracy in Edmond About's lively book on Greek brigandage, *Le Roi des Montagnes:*

"I crossed at a leap the Eleusinian Cephisus ... One hundred paces further on, the road was lost in a wide and deep ravine, hollowed by the rains of two or three thousand winters. I supposed with some show of justice that the ravine must be the road, for I had noticed in my previous excursions that the Greeks dispense with making a road wherever the water has been kind enough to take that duty on itself. In this country, where man but slightly thwarts the laws of nature, the torrents are royal roads, the rivers turnpike-roads; the rivulets cross-country roads. Storms do the office of highway engineers and the rain is an inspector who keeps up without any control the means of communication, great and small" (p. 45 = p. 42 *Eng. transl.* 1862).

[We must remember that road-making, as we have it, is a modern art, and that the want of roads is still the cause of backward civilisation and commerce in many countries. The hollow or sunken lanes, common

ἔμελλε βαδιεῖσθαι φερόμενον, τούτῳ διὰ τῶν ἰδίων
17 χωρίων χαράδραν[1] ἐποίησέ τις ; ἔπειτα τίς ἂν ὑμῶν
εἴτ' ἐν ἀγρῷ νὴ Δί' εἴτ' ἐν ἄστει τὸ διὰ τῆς ὁδοῦ ῥέον
ὕδωρ εἰς τὸ χωρίον ἢ τὴν οἰκίαν δέξαιτ' ἂν αὑτοῦ ;
ἀλλ' οὐκ αὐτὸ τοὐναντίον, κἂν βιάσηταί ποτε, ἀποφράττειν ἅπαντες καὶ παροικοδομεῖν εἰώθαμεν ; οὗτος τοίνυν ἀξιοῖ με ἐκ τῆς ὁδοῦ τὸ ὕδωρ εἰσδεξάμενον
εἰς τὸ ἐμαυτοῦ χωρίον, ὅταν τὸ τούτου παραλλάξῃ
χωρίον, πάλιν εἰς τὴν ὁδὸν ἐξαγαγεῖν. οὐκοῦν πάλιν
ὁ μετὰ τοῦτόν μοι γεωργῶν τῶν γειτόνων ἐγκαλεῖ·

[1] ἄν, vocabuli antecedentis in syllaba ultima absorptum, restitu-
endum esse indicavit H. W. Moss.

in many parts of England, are
caused by the excavating power
of water running along tracks.
The Romans *raised* their roads
(*viam munire*) apparently to
avoid this. As an illustrative
passage, we may quote Iliad
XXIII 420 ῥωχμὸς ἔην γαίης, ᾗ
χειμέριον ἀλὲν ὕδωρ ἐξέρρηξεν
ὁδοῖο, βάθυνε δὲ χῶρον ἅπαντα. P.]

βαδιεῖσθαι] The *Classic* future of βαδίζω (retained even
by Plutarch and Lucian); the
other forms, βαδίσω and βαδιῶ,
are characteristic of the worst
Greek, *extrema barbaries* (Cobet, *var. lect.* 329).

17. αὐτὸ τοὐναντίον] 'on the
very contrary,' so also in Or. 22
(Androt.) § 6.—ἂν τοὐναντίον was
the common text until corrected
by Reiske, on the authority of
two mss and the margin of Σ;
but the correction is so certain
that authority is hardly wanted.

ἀποφράττειν καὶ παροικοδομεῖν]
'dam and wall it off.' The
former implies an abrupt cutting off of the water by a trans-
verse dam athwart the stream;
the latter probably expresses a
wall built parallel to the stream

to narrow its course.

οὗτος τοίνυν — ἐγκαλεῖ] 'This
man, Callicles, expects me to
take the water from the road
(where it has no χαράδρα) into
my farm, and, when it has passed his, again to carry it out of
my farm into the road. But,
in that case, the farmer who
occupies next to *him* would
complain'; i.e. he would say
that I ought to carry it beyond
his farm also, lest it should
come in from the road. It is
clear that the defendant's farm,
on one side of the road (§ 10),
extended considerably beyond
that of the plaintiff Callicles on
the other. For he says that, if
bound to carry it beyond one
farm, he was bound to carry it
beyond a second or a third, before he allowed it to re-enter
the public road. P.]

ἐξαγαγεῖν] 'draw off,' 'let
out,' *derivare*, Xen. Oec. 20
§ 12 τὸ ὕδωρ ἐξάγεται τάφροις.

ἐγκαλεῖ] Not present, but
future. The context is decisive
and the margin of the Paris ms
has ἐγκαλέσει, pointing to the
same conclusion, though the

τὸ γὰρ ὑπὲρ τούτου δίκαιον δῆλον ὅτι κἀκείνοις ὑπάρ-
ξει πᾶσι λέγειν. ἀλλὰ μὴν εἴ γε εἰς τὴν ὁδὸν ὀκνήσω 18
τὸ ὕδωρ ἐξάγειν, ἢ που σφόδρα θαρρῶν εἰς τὸ τοῦ
πλησίον χωρίον ἀφείην ἄν. ὅπου γὰρ δίκας ἀτιμήτους φεύγω διότι τὸ ἐκ τῆς ὁδοῦ ῥέον ὕδωρ εἰς τὸ
τούτου χωρίον διέπεσε, τί πείσομαι πρὸς Διὸς ὑπὸ
τῶν ἐκ τοῦ χωρίου τοῦ ἐμοῦ τοῦ ὕδατος εἰσπεσόντος
βλαπτομένων; ὅπου δὲ μήτ᾽ εἰς τὴν ὁδὸν μήτ᾽ εἰς τὰ

note seems due to a copyist who did not recognise in ἐγκαλεῖ the regular Attic future. In Or. 23 (Aristocr.) § 123, we have ἐγκαλέσουσιν; so also in Or. 19 § 133. The *simple* verb καλῶ hardly ever (Cobet says, *never*) has any other future than καλῶ (*var. lect.* 28, 29).

18. ἢ που] 'Surely, I should scarcely be rash enough to turn it on to my neighbour's land';—'I should be a very rash man indeed to do so.' For this slightly ironical use of ἢ που, 'to be sure,' cf. Lycurgus § 71 ἢ που τάχεως ἂν ἠνέσχετό τις ἐκείνων τῶν ἀνδρῶν τοιοῦτον ἔρ-γον. Soph. Aj. 1008 ἢ πού με Τελαμών...δέξαιτ᾽ ἂν εὐπρόσωπος ἵλεώς τ᾽ ἴσως χωροῦντ᾽ ἄνευ σοῦ.

ὅπου] 'whereas,' 'in a case where' (without any direct notion of *place*). Isocr. ad Dem. § 49.

δίκας ἀτιμήτους φεύγω] 'am sued for a fixed penalty,' 'am put on my trial in law-suits where the damages are already assessed by law.' The plural refers to the fact that the speaker has been sued by Callicrates as well as by Callicles (§ 2).

δίκη τιμητὸς means 'a suit to be assessed,' i.e. 'a suit in which the penalty or damages have *not* been determined by law.' δίκη ἀτίμητος means the opposite; 'a suit not to be assessed,' i.e. a suit in which the penalty has *already* been fixed by law.

So Harpocration : ἀτίμητος ἀγὼν καὶ τιμητός. ὁ μὲν τιμητὸς ἐφ᾽ ᾧ τίμημα ὡρισμένον ἐκ τῶν νόμων οὐ κεῖται, ἀλλὰ τοὺς δικασ-τὰς ἔδει τιμᾶσθαι ὅ τι χρὴ παθεῖν ἢ ἀποτῖσαι· ὁ δὲ ἀτίμητος τοὐ-ναντίον ᾧ πρόσεστιν ἐκ τῶν νόμων ὡρισμένον τίμημα, ὡς μηδὲν δεῖν τοὺς δικαστὰς διατιμῆσαι. Αἰσ-χίνης κατὰ Κτησιφῶντος (§ 210), Δημοσθένης κατὰ Μειδίου (§ 90). Cf. Or. 37 § 40.

Again Pollux (VIII 63) has: ἀτίμητος δὲ δίκη, ἣν οὐκ ἔστιν ὑποτιμήσασθαι ἀλλὰ τοσούτου τε-τίμηται ὅσον ἐπιγέγραπται.

The above explanation is wrongly reversed by Suidas (quoted in Telfy's *Corpus iuris Attici* 747 note), by the *Lexica Segueriana* (on p. 202 and 469 of Bekker's *Anecdota Graeca*), and even in a scholium on § 25 *infra*, χιλίων δραχμῶν δίκην ἀτίμητον φεύγω, a passage which is decisive in favour of Harpo-cration's distinction.

ὅπου δὲ μήτε] There would seem to have been a law prohibiting the draining of farms on to a public way. Hence he says εἰ εἰς τὴν ὁδὸν ὀκνήσω τὸ ὕδωρ ἐξάγειν. It was equally illegal, of course,

χωρία ἀφεῖναί[u] μοι τὸ ὕδωρ ἐξέσται[u] δεξαμένῳ, τί λοιπόν, ὦ ἄνδρες δικασταί, πρὸς θεῶν; οὐ γὰρ ἐκπιεῖν
19 γε δήπου με Καλλικλῆς αὐτὸ προσαναγκάσει. ταῦτα
τοίνυν ἐγὼ πάσχων ὑπὸ τούτων καὶ πολλὰ ἕτερα καὶ
δεινά, μὴ ὅτι δίκην λαβεῖν, ἀλλὰ μὴ προσοφλεῖν ἀγα-
πήσαιμ᾽ ἄν. εἰ μὲν γὰρ ἦν, ὦ ἄνδρες δικασταί, χαρά-   1277
δρα πάλιν ὑποδεχομένη, τάχ᾽ ἂν ἠδίκουν ἐγὼ μὴ δεχό-

[u] ἀφιέναι Z et Bekker st. cum ΓΦΒ (ἀφειεναι Σ). ἔξεστι Z cum ΓΣΦ.

to drain on to another's land.
Hence he asks what he was to
do with the water, if once he
admitted it on his farm? And
the inference is, that he was
right in not admitting it, but
in damming it back as far as
he could, and letting it run as
it might along the road. P.]

οὐ γὰρ ἐκπιεῖν—αὐτὸ προσ-
αναγκάσει] This passage is
quoted by Aristides (II 470 in
Spengel's *Rhet. Graeci*), ὅταν
εἰς ἄτοπον ἀπάγῃς τὸν λόγον,
βαρύτητα εἴργασαι, ὡς ἐν τῷ πρὸς
Καλλικλέα, οὐ γὰρ δὴ ἐκπιεῖν με
αὐτὸ Καλλικλῆς ἀναγκάσει. The
rhetorician recognises the force
and effectiveness of the sentence, but fails to draw attention to its humour.

§ 19. *Now had there been a
water-course below my property,
to take off the drainage, I might
have been doing wrong in refusing to let the water into my
land; but, as it is, the water-
course alleged is neither passed
down to me by any neighbour
immediately above me, nor is it
passed down by myself to any
one else below.*

19. μὴ ὅτι—ἀλλὰ μή...ἀγαπή-
σαιμ᾽ ἄν] 'I must be content, I
do not say, with obtaining a verdict, but with escaping conviction.' The sense is: 'victimised
as I have been, instead of gain-

ing legal satisfaction from my
opponents, I must think myself
fortunate if I am not convicted
to pay them an additional
penalty.'

εἰ μὲν γὰρ—παραλαμβάνουσιν
ὡσαύτως] In Plato's Laws provisions are suggested to prevent
damage being incurred in times
of heavy rain, either owing to
neglect on the part of neighbours in providing an outlet
for streams that pass down to
them from the higher ground
immediately adjacent, or again
owing to careless transmission
of the streams on the part of
the neighbours higher up the
hill:—

ἐὰν δὲ ἐκ Διὸς ὕδατα γιγνόμενα,
τὸν ἐπάνω γεωργοῦντα ἢ καὶ
ὁμότοιχον οἰκοῦντα τῶν ὑποκάτω
βλάπτῃ τις μὴ διδοὺς ἐκροήν, ἢ
τοὐναντίον ὁ ἐπάνω μεθιεὶς εἰκῇ
τὰ ῥεύματα βλάπτῃ τὸν κάτω,
καὶ περὶ ταῦτα μὴ ἐθέλωσι διὰ
ταῦτα κοινωνεῖν ἀλλήλοις, ἐν ἄστει
μὲν ἀστυνόμον, ἐν ἀγρῷ δὲ ἀγρονό-
μον ἐπάγων ὁ βουλόμενος ταξάσθω
τί χρὴ ποιεῖν ἑκάτερον· ὁ δὲ μὴ
ἐμμένων ἐν τῇ τάξει φθόνου θ᾽ ἅμα
καὶ δυσκόλου ψυχῆς ὑπεχέτω
δίκην, καὶ ὄφλων διπλάσιον τὸ
βλάβος ἀποτινέτω τῷ βλαφθέντι,
μὴ ἐθελήσας τοῖς ἄρχουσι πείθεσ-
θαι. Leg. VIII 844 c.

ἠδίκουν...μὴ δεχόμενος] Thus
in the fens near Cambridge, an

μενος, ὥσπερ ἀνὰ χἄτερ[v] ἄττα[w] τῶν χωρίων εἰσὶν
ὁμολογούμεναι χαράδραι· καὶ ταύτας δέχονται μὲν
οἱ πρῶτοι, καθάπερ τοὺς ἐκ τῶν οἰκιῶν χειμάρρους,
παρὰ τούτων δ' ἕτεροι παραλαμβάνουσιν ὡσαύτως·
ταύτην δ' οὔτε παραδίδωσιν οὐδεὶς οὔτε παρ' ἐμοῦ
παραλαμβάνει. πῶς ἂν οὖν εἴη τοῦτο χαράδρα; τὸ δ' 20
εἰσπεσὸν ὕδωρ ἔβλαψε μὲν[x], οἶμαι, πολλάκις ἤδη πολλοὺς μὴ φυλαξαμένους, ἔβλαψε δὲ νῦν καὶ τουτονί.
.ὃ καὶ πάντων ἐστὶ δεινότατον, εἰ Καλλικλῆς μὲν εἰς
τὸ χωρίον εἰσπεσόντος τοῦ ὕδατος ἁμαξιαίους λίθους

[v] ἀν' ἕτερ' Z cum H. Wolfio. ἂν θάτερ' ΓΣΦ. ἀνὰ θάτερ' Bekk.
'ἀνὰ χἄτερ' ἄττα lege; partim e mss' (Dobree).
[w] om. A¹r.   [x] Bekk. ἔβλαψεν Z cum ΓΣΦΒ.

obligation lies on each tenant
to clear out the ditch or dyke
bounding his land on one side,
and so to give free passage to
the water from his neighbour's
land. P.] Cf. the *ius aquae
ducendae* which was one of the
servitutes (or limiting obligations), under which property
was held in Roman law.

ὁμολογούμεναι χαράδραι] 'recognised, acknowledged, undisputed water-courses.' A curious
expression. The nearest ap-
proach to it that I can find is
(Andoc.) Or. 4 § 17 οὐδὲν ἧττον
τῶν ὁμολογουμένων δούλων.

τοὺς χειμάρρους] here 'water-
drains,' 'gutters,' like ὑδρορρόα
Ar. Ach. 922. The word has
lost all trace of its primary
meaning 'a winter torrent.'

§ 20. *The fact is, that simply owing to the plaintiff's own
carelessness, he has suffered from
a flood, as others have before
him; and the strangest incon-
sistency of all is, that the plaintiff, while he himself brings to the
spot large stones to dam off the
water when it makes inroad, has
actually brought against me a
suit for damages, just because
my father built a wall round his
property with the very same object.*

20. μὴ φυλαξαμένους] 'for
not being on their guard,' 'owing to their neglect.' μὴ here
implies the *reason*, as distinguished from οὐ which would
only denote the fact.

ὃ καὶ...δεινότατον, εἰ] Isocr.
Archidamus § 56 ὃ δὲ πάντων
σχετλιώτατον, εἰ φιλοπονώτατοι
δοκοῦντες εἶναι...ῥᾳθυμότερον βου-
λευσόμεθα. Paneg. § 128 ὃ δὲ
πάντων δεινότατον, ὅταν...(Dem.)
Aristog. (25) § 31 ὃ καὶ θαυμασ-
τόν ἐστιν, εἰ κ.τ.λ. In such sentences ὃ δὲ implies a less close
connexion with the previous
context than ὃ καὶ, and ἐστὶ is
frequently omitted (Kühner §
406, 9. Madvig *Gr. Synt.* § 197).

ἁμαξιαίους λίθους] Xen. Anab.
IV 2 § 3 ἐκυλίνδουν ὀλοιτρόχους
ἁμαξιαίους (huge boulders) and
Hell. II 4 § 27, Eur. Phoen. 1157
λᾶαν ἐμβαλὼν κάρᾳ ἁμαξοπληθῆ.

προσκομίσας ἀποικοδομεῖ, τοῦ δὲ πατρὸς, ὅτι τούτο
παθόντος τοῦ χωρίου περιῳκοδόμησεν, ὡς ἀδικοῦντος,
ἐμοὶ βλάβης εἴληχε δίκην. καίτοι εἰ ὅσοι κακῶς πεπόνθασιν ὑπὸ τῶν ὑδάτων τῶν ταύτῃ ῥεόντων ἐμοὶ
λήξονται δίκας, οὐδὲ πολλαπλάσια γενόμενα τὰ ὄντα
21 ἐξαρκέσειεν ἄν μοι. τοσοῦτον τοίνυν διαφέρουσιν
οὗτοι τῶν ἄλλων ὥστε πεπονθότες μὲν οὐδὲν, ὡς αὐτίκα ὑμῖν ἐγὼ σαφῶς ἐπιδείξω, πολλῶν δὲ πολλὰ καὶ
μεγάλα βεβλαμμένων μόνοι δικάζεσθαι τετολμήκασιν
οὗτοί μοι. καίτοι πᾶσι μᾶλλον ἐνεχώρει τοῦτο πράττειν. οὗτοι μὲν γάρ, εἰ καί τι πεπόνθασιν, αὐτοὶ δι'
αὑτοὺς βεβλαμμένοι συκοφαντοῦσιν· ἐκεῖνοι δὲ, εἰ καὶ
μηδὲν ἄλλο, τοιαύτην γ' οὐδεμίαν αἰτίαν ἔχουσιν. ἀλλ'

ἐμοὶ βλάβης εἴληχε δίκην] Or.
29 § 30 ἐγὼ τὴν δίκην ἔλαχον
τούτῳ τῆς ἐπιτροπῆς. Kühner
§ 419, 12.

οὐδὲ πολλαπλάσια] So in § 35
the defendant speaks of his
μικρὰ οὐσία.

§ 21. *If all my neighbours
were to treat me as the plaintiff
has done, I should soon be a ruined man. But while the rest, who
have had great losses, are content
to bear their misfortune, my present opponents alone, who have
lost nothing to speak of, are
bringing against me a groundless
action for damage entirely due
to their own neglect.*

21. πεπονθότες...βεβλαμμένων]
cf. § 11 ὁρῶν...ἐπινεμόντων n.

τετολμήκασιν] τολμᾶν and its
tenses are regularly used in
Greek prose, while τλῆναι is
almost entirely confined to
Greek verse (note on Isocr.
Paneg. § 96 ἔτλησαν).—τοῦτο
πράττειν = δικάζεσθαι.—πᾶσι sc.
τοῖς ἄλλοις.

εἰ καί] *Notwithstanding —
even if*—they have had some

trifling losses. εἰ καί, without
disputing the condition (here
εἰ πεπόνθασι), represents it as of
little consequence. καὶ εἰ or κεἰ
'*even supposing*' introduces a
condition which is utterly improbable. Kühner § 378.

αὐτοὶ — βεβλαμμένοι] 'they
have incurred damage owing to
their own fault alone (by not
damming off the water as I
did), though they vexatiously
throw the blame upon me.' The
participle here is quite as emphatic as a principal verb.

ἐκεῖνοι αἰτίαν ἔχουσιν] 'whereas the rest of my neighbours,
not to mention any other point,
at any rate are open to no such
imputation as this.' With μηδὲν
ἄλλο I understand διαφέρουσι,
and I refer αἰτίαν ἔχουσι to
αὐτοὶ δι' αὑτοὺς βεβλαμμένοι συ-
κοφαντοῦσι. The imputation is
συκοφαντία, bringing a vexatious
charge when they are themselves to blame for want of pre-
caution. Cf. next § τούτους μὲν
μηδὲν ἐγκαλεῖν...τουτονὶ δὲ συκοφαντεῖν.

ἵνα μὴ πάντα ἅμα συνταράξας λέγω, λαβέ μοι τὰς τῶν γειτόνων μαρτυρίας.

ΜΑΡΤΥΡΙΑΙ.

Οὐκοῦν δεινόν, ὦ ἄνδρες δικασταὶ, τούτους μὲν 22 1278 μηδὲν ἐγκαλεῖν μοι τοσαῦτα βεβλαμμένους, μηδ' ἄλλον μηδένα τῶν ἠτυχηκότων, ἀλλὰ τὴν τύχην στέργειν, τουτονὶ δὲ συκοφαντεῖν; ὃν ὅτι μὲν αὐτὸς ἐξημάρτηκε

['while the rest, however negligent they may have been, are at all events chargeable with nothing of this kind,' Kennedy. This seems to give the sense; but the precise ellipse with εἰ καὶ μηδὲν ἄλλο is obscure. P.]

G. II. Schaefer explains τοιαύτην αἰτίαν by the words τοῦ αὐτοὺς (*qu.* αὐτοί) δι' αὐτοὺς βεβλάφθαι, and with εἰ καὶ μηδὲν ἄλλο he understands πεποιήκασι τοῦ φυλάττεσθαι τὴν ἐκ τοῦ ὕδατος ἐσομένην βλάβην.

αἰτίαν ἔχειν (except in Pl. Phaedo 101 c, where it means 'have you, i.e. do you know, any cause?')' is nearly equivalent to δόξαν ἔχειν, 'to have the reputation (i.e. either the credit or the imputation) of...' It occurs in the better sense, 'to have the credit of', in Isocr. de pace § 138 τούτων τῶν ἀγαθῶν τὴν αἰτίαν ἕξομεν. The worse sense, 'to be open to an imputation' (as here), is far more common (e.g. Lysias Or. 22 § 18, 10 § 28, 13 § 62). Both meanings are combined in Thuc. I 83 § 3 τῶν ἀποβαινόντων τὸ πλέον ἐπ' ἀμφότερα αἰτίας ἕξομεν (note on Isocr. Paneg. § 109). αἰτίαν ἔχειν is 'the usual passive of αἰτιᾶσθαι' (Wayte on Timocr. § 187).

§ 22. *The plaintiff has himself done wrong by advancing his wall and thus narrowing the road, and by shooting his rubbish on to the road and thus raising its level.*

22. δεινόν, τούτους μὲν μηδὲν ἐγκαλεῖν... τουτονὶ δὲ συκοφαντεῖν] The clause containing μὲν is coordinate with that containing δὲ, but in English must be subordinate to it. 'Is it not atrocious, that, *while* my neighbours make no complaint..., the plaintiff brings a vexatious action against me?' The influence of δεινὸν affects the second clause in its contrast with the first. Dem. Lept. § 9 πῶς γὰρ οὐκ αἰσχρὸν κατὰ μὲν τὴν ἀγορὰν ἀψευδεῖν νόμον γεγράφθαι...ἐν δὲ τῷ κοινῷ μὴ χρῆσθαι τῷ νόμῳ τούτῳ (Isocr. ad Dem. § 11 n. Madvig *Gr. Synt.* § 189 n, Cicero II Phil. § 110 l. 6 ed. Mayor, n.).

τὴν τύχην στέργειν] στέργειν, in the sense of contented submission, usually has the dative with or without ἐπί, e.g. Isocr. de pace § 6 στέργειν τοῖς παροῦσι. The acc. however occurs again in § 30 *infra*, also in Hdt. IX 117 ἔστερξαν τὰ παρεόντα, Eur. Phoen. 1685 τἄμ' ἐγὼ στέρξω κακά, Soph. Ant. 292, and Isocr. ad Dem. § 29 στέργε μὲν τὰ παρόντα ζήτει δὲ τὰ βέλτιστα.

ὅν] ὃν εἴσεσθε σαφέστερον...ὅτι αὐτὸς ἐξημάρτηκε. The subject of the subordinate here becomes the accusative of the principal sentence, and all the

πρῶτον μὲν τὴν ὁδὸν στενοτέραν[y] ποιήσας, ἐξαγαγὼν
ἔξω τὴν αἱμασιὰν, ἵνα τὰ δένδρα τῆς ὁδοῦ ποιήσειεν
εἴσω[z], ἔπειτα δὲ τὸν χλῆδον ἐκβαλὼν[a] εἰς τὴν ὁδὸν, ἐξ
ὧν ὑψηλοτέραν τὴν ὁδὸν καὶ στενοτέραν[y] πεποιῆσθαι

[y] Σ.   στενωτέραν Z cum A¹.
[z] (1) *Lego* τὰ δένδρα τὰ τῆς ὁδοῦ ποιήσειεν εἴσω, *scil.* τῆς αἱμασιᾶς.
—(2) *Imo deleta glossa lege* τὰ δένδρα ποιήσειεν εἴσω (Dobree).
[a] *Bekker st. cum* γρ. ΓΦ *et Harpocrat. s.v.* χλῆδος, cf. § 27.
ἐμβαλὼν Z et Bekk. 1824.   ἐμβάλλων ΓΣΦ.

words down to συμβέβηκεν inclusive form an object-sentence to the principal verb εἴσεσθε. Lysias, Or. 20 § 34 οὓς οὔπω ἴστε εἴτε ἀγαθοὶ εἴτε κακοί...γενήσονται (Madvig, *Gr. Synt.* § 191. Kühner § 600 p. 1083).

στενοτέραν] The old Greek grammarians (e. g. Choeroboscus) state that στενός (*Ionic* στεινός) and κενός have o, not ω, in the comparative and superlative (cf. *Ionic* στεινότερος). But the forms in ω have better authority than those grammarians supposed (Kühner ι § 154 note 2).

ἐξαγαγὼν...] 'by advancing—carrying-out—his wall beyond the boundary.' Thuc. ι 93 μείζων ὁ περίβολος πανταχῆ ἐξήχθη τῆς πόλεως. § 27 *infra* αἱμασιὰν προαγαγόντες κ.τ.λ.

ἵν'—εἴσω] Not 'to get his trees within the road' (Kennedy), but 'to take in, enclose, the trees of the road.' A thrust at the πλεονεξία of the plaintiff.

χλῆδον] 'rubbish'; the word is only found in § 27 and in a fragment of Aeschylus quoted below. Harpocration s.v. χλῆδος· Δημοσθένης ἐν τῷ πρὸς Καλλικλέα περὶ χωρίου βλάβης· ἔπειτα δὲ τὸν χλῆδον ἐκβαλὼν ἐξ ὧν ὑψηλοτέραν καὶ στενωτέραν τὴν αὐτὴν

ὁδὸν πεποιῆσθαι συμβέβηκεν. πᾶν πλῆθος χλῆδος λέγεται καὶ ἐστὶν οἷον σωρός τις, μάλιστα δὲ τῶν ἀποκαθαρμάτων τε καὶ ἀποψημάτων, καὶ ἡ τῶν ποταμῶν πρόσχωσις, καὶ πολὺ μᾶλλον τῶν χειμάρρων ὃ καὶ χέραδος καλεῖται (Iliad xxi 319). νῦν δὲ ἔοικεν ὁ ῥήτωρ λέγειν ὅτι χοῦν καὶ φρυγανώδη τινα ἐκ τοῦ χωρίου σωρὸν ὁ Καλλικλῆς εἰς τὴν ὁδὸν ἐμβέβληκεν, ὡς καὶ αὐτὸς ἐξῆς ὑποσημαίνει. κέχρηνται δὲ τῷ ὀνόματι πολλοί. Αἰσχύλος Ἀρχείοις "καὶ παλτὰ κἀγκυλητὰ καὶ χλῆδον βαλών" (fr. 14). Bekker's *Anecd. Gr.* 315 ὁ κλῆρος τῶν ἀποκαθαρμάτων, ὁ ἔχων ἰλύν τινα καὶ βοτανώδη καὶ φρυγανώδη. Hesychius χλῆδος· ὁ σωρὸς τῶν λίθων. [The article shows that χλῆδον does not here mean rubbish generally, but the soil or gravel thrown up from altering the fences. P.]

ἐξ ὧν] The pl. refers to ἐξαγαγὼν ...αἱμασιὰν and χλῆδον ἐκβαλών. The first adjective ὑψηλοτέραν is explained by the latter, the second στενωτέραν by the former:—one of the many forms of χιασμὸς or 'introverted parallelism.' This enables the speaker to put his main point in the most emphatic positions (first and last) and the subordinate point between them (note

συμβέβηκεν, ἐκ τῶν μαρτυριῶν αὐτίκ' εἴσεσθε σαφέστερον, ὅτι δ' οὐδὲν ἀπολωλεκὼς οὐδὲ καταβε- 23
βλαμμένος ἄξιον λόγου τηλικαύτην μοι δίκην εἴληχε,
τοῦθ' ὑμᾶς ἤδη πειράσομαι διδάσκειν. τῆς γὰρ μητρὸς τῆς ἐμῆς χρωμένης τῇ τούτων μητρὶ πρὶν τούτους ἐπιχειρῆσαί με συκοφαντεῖν, καὶ πρὸς ἀλλήλας
ἀφικνουμένων, οἷον εἰκὸς ἅμα μὲν ἀμφοτέρων οἰκου-
σῶν ἐν ἀγρῷ καὶ γειτνιωσῶν, ἅμα δὲ τῶν ἀνδρῶν
χρωμένων ἀλλήλοις ἕως ἔζων, ἐλθούσης δὲ τῆς ἐμῆς 24
μητρὸς ὡς τὴν τούτων καὶ ἀποδυραμένης ἐκείνης τὰ
συμβάντα καὶ δεικνυούσης, οὕτως ἐπυθόμεθα πάντα
ἡμεῖς, ὦ ἄνδρες δικασταί· καὶ λέγω μὲν ἅπερ ἤκουσα
τῆς μητρός, οὕτω μοι[b] πολλὰ ἀγαθὰ γένοιτο, εἰ δὲ
ψεύδομαι, τἀναντία τούτων· ἦ μὴν ὁρᾶν καὶ τῆς τούτων μητρὸς ἀκούειν ἔφη κριθῶν μὲν βρεχθῆναι, καὶ
ξηραινομένους ἰδεῖν αὐτὴν[c], μηδὲ τρεῖς μεδίμνους,
ἀλεύρων δ' ὡς ἡμιμέδιμνον· ἐλαίου δ' ἀποκλιθῆναι
μὲν κεράμιον φάσκειν, οὐ μέντοι παθεῖν γε[d] οὐδέν.

[b] Bekk.   οὕτως ἐμοὶ Z cum FΣΦΒ.

[c] Bekk.   αὐτὴν Z cum G. H. Schaefer.

[d] Bekk.   μέντοι γε Z cum Σ.

on Isocr. ad Dem. § 7, Paneg.
§ 54).—αὐτίκα, sc. at the end of
§ 27.—τηλικαύτην δίκην. Cf. §
25 χιλίων δραχμῶν δίκην.

§§ 23—25. *The actual loss
sustained was very trifling, as
I know on good authority; and as
for the old wall which he makes
out he was compelled to repair,
that must not be put to my account, as the wall neither fell
down nor incurred any damage.*

23. χρωμένης ... μητρὶ] 'intimate with.' Dem. Or. 29 § 15
Ἀφόβῳ χρώμενον, Or. 33 (Apatur.) § 7, Or. 35 (Lacrit.) § 6
ἐπιτήδειοί μοί εἰσι καὶ χρώμεθ'
ἀλλήλοις.—τῶν ἀνδρῶν, 'their
husbands.'

24. ἐκείνης] sc. τῆς τούτων
μητρός.

οὕτω—γένοιτο] Or. 54 § 41.
Ter. Eun. IV 1, 1 *ita medii bene
ament.* Prop. I 7, 3 *ita sim
felix.* Cic. ad Att. V 15 *ita
vivam.*

τἀναντία] a kind of euphemism for πολλὰ κακά. So also
Soph. Phil. 503 παθεῖν μὲν εὖ
παθεῖν δὲ θάτερα.

κριθῶν—παθεῖν γε οὐδέν] Quoted by Aristeides (II 544 Spengel
Rhet. Gr.) ἐνίοτε δὲ ἡ μὲν ἔννοια
ἀφελής ἐστιν, ἡ δὲ ἀπαγγελία
πολιτική, ὡς καὶ ἐν τῷ πρὸς
Καλλικλέα ὁ Δημοσθένης, κριθῶν

25 τοσαῦτα, ὦ ἄνδρες δικασταὶ, τὰ συμβάντ' ἦν τούτοις,
ἀνθ' ὧν ἐγὼ χιλίων δραχμῶν δίκην ἀτίμητον φεύγω.
οὐ γὰρ δὴ, τειχίον γ' εἰ* παλαιὸν ἐπῳκοδόμησεν, ἐμοὶ
καὶ τοῦτο λογιστέον ἐστὶν, ὃ μήτ' ἔπεσε μήτ' ἄλλο
δεινὸν μηδὲν ἔπαθεν. ὥστ' εἰ συνεχώρουν αὐτοῖς ἁπάν- 1279
των αἴτιος εἶναι τῶν συμβεβηκότων, τά γε βρεχθέντα
26 ταῦτ' ἦν. ὁπότε δὲ μήτε ἐξ ἀρχῆς ὁ πατὴρ ἠδίκει τὸ
χωρίον περιοικοδομῶν, μήθ' οὗτοι πώποτε ἐνεκάλεσαν
τοσούτου χρόνου διελθόντος, οἵ τ' ἄλλοι πολλὰ καὶ
δεινὰ πεπονθότες μηδὲν μᾶλλον ἐγκαλοῦσιν ἐμοὶ, πάντες τε ὑμεῖς τὸ ἐκ τῶν οἰκιῶν καὶ τὸ ἐκ τῶν χωρίων
ὕδωρ εἰς τὴν ὁδὸν ἐξάγειν εἰώθατε, ἀλλ' οὐ μὰ Δί'
εἴσω τὸ ἐκ τῆς ὁδοῦ δέχεσθαι, τί δεῖ πλείω λέγειν; οὐδὲ
γὰρ ἐκ τούτων ἄδηλον ὅτι φανερῶς συκοφαντοῦμαι,
27 οὔτ' ἀδικῶν οὐδὲν οὔτε βεβλαμμένων ἅ φασιν. ἵνα

---

* Bekk. et corr. Σ. εἰ τειχίον Σ (εἰ in margine manu eadem
addito). τειχίον γε Γ. τειχίον εἰ FB.

μὲν—παθεῖν γε οὐδέν. καὶ
τοῦτο δὲ μετὰ σεμνότητος, ὅπου
γε αὐτὸ τὸ κύριον λεχθὲν κινδυνεύει εὐτέλειαν ποιῆσαι, ὥσπερ
εἰ ἔλεγες, οὐ μέντοι ἐκχυθῆναί
γε. ἐνταῦθα ὁ δὲ ἀντὶ τοῦ κυρίου
καὶ τοῦ κατ' εἶδος, ἐν γένει με-
ταβαλὼν εἶπεν, οὐ μέντοι παθεῖν
γε οὐδέν.

πάσχειν is seldom applied to
an inanimate subject; cf. Or. 56
§ 23 τοῦτο συνέβη παθεῖν τῇ νηί.

κριθῶν—μεδίμνους] 'not even
three *medimni* (or four and a
half bushels) of barley.' The
μεδίμνος = six ἑκτεῖς = six *modii* =
about 12 gallons, or a bushel
and a half.—κεράμιον used like
the Roman *amphora* as a liquid
measure = about six gallons or
two-thirds of the Greek ἀμφορεύς
(μετρητής).

25.   χιλίων δραχμῶν δίκην
ἀτίμητον] See note on § 18.
ἐπῳκοδόμησεν] (cf. ἐπισκευά-
ζειν) refers to repairing the old
wall.
ὃ μήτ' ἔπεσε] 'if the wall
neither fell nor incurred any
damage whatsoever.' ὃ μήτε...
would in Latin be represented
by *quod nec cecidisset nec....*
§§ 26, 27. *Summary of previous arguments, and calling of
witnesses.*
26. οἵ τ' ἄλλοι—ἐμοί] Cf. § 21
πολλῶν πολλὰ ... βεβλαμμένων—
πάντες—εἰώθατε. See § 17 *init.*
οὔτε βεβλαμμένων ἅ φασι] βεβλαμμένων, not neuter, but
masc. 'they have not incurred
the damage they allege.' § 21
πολλῶν πολλὰ καὶ μεγάλα βεβλαμμένων.

δ' εἰδῆτε ὅτι καὶ τὸν χλῆδον εἰς τὴν ὁδὸν ἐκβεβλήκασι[f]
καὶ τὴν αἱμασιὰν προαγαγόντες στενοτέραν[g] τὴν ὑδὸν
πεποιήκασιν, ἔτι δ' ὡς ὅρκον ἐδίδουν ἐγὼ τῇ τούτων
μητρὶ καὶ τὴν ἐμαυτοῦ τὸν αὐτὸν ὀμόσαι προυκαλού-
μην, λαβέ μοι τάς τε μαρτυρίας καὶ τὴν πρόκλησιν.

ΜΑΡΤΥΡΙΑΙ. ΠΡΟΚΛΗΣΙΣ.

Εἶτα τούτων ἀναισχυντότεροι γένοιντ' ἂν ἄνθρω- 28
ποι ἢ περιφανέστερον συκοφαντοῦντες, οἵτινες αὐτοὶ
τὴν αἱμασιὰν προαγαγόντες καὶ τὴν ὁδὸν ἀνακεχωκότες ἑτέροις βλάβης δικάζονται, καὶ ταῦτα χιλίων δραχμῶν ἀτίμητον, οἵ γ' οὐδὲ πεντήκοντα δραχμῶν τὸ
παράπαν ἅπαντα ἀπολωλέκασι; καίτοι σκοπεῖτ', ὦ
ἄνδρες δικασταί, πόσους ὑπὸ τῶν ὑδάτων ἐν τοῖς
ἀγροῖς βεβλάφθαι συμβέβηκε, τὰ μὲν Ἐλευσῖνι, τὰ δ'

[f] Z et Bekk. st. ἐκβεβλήκασιν ΓΣΦ. ἐμβεβλήκασι Bekk. 1824.
[g] στενωτ- Ζ.

27. χλῆδον] See note on § 22.
ὅρκον ἐδίδουν] 'offered an oath'
in the sense of 'proposed to
administer an oath.' On ὅρκον
διδόναι καὶ λαμβάνειν, see esp.
Arist. Rhet. ι 15 §§ 27—33.
§§ 28—30. *My opponents, after
having themselves advanced their
wall and raised the road's level,
are most shamelessly suing the
very victims of their own wrong,
for a penalty of a thousand
drachmae, while their own loss
is less than fifty.*
*If the plaintiff may enclose
his land, we may enclose ours.
If my father wronged you, by
enclosing, you are just as much
wronging me, for if you dam off
the water, it will be swept back
on my own property and will
throw down my wall. But I am
not going to complain; I shall
simply do my best to protect my*

*land. The plaintiff shows his
prudence in protecting his own
property; but in prosecuting me,
he only shows his villany and
his infatuation.*
28. ἀνακεχωκότες] Cf. § 22
ὑψηλοτέραν τὴν ὁδὸν...πεποιῆσθαι
συμβέβηκεν.
Ἐλευσῖνι] Commonly with-
out ἐν. So also Μαραθῶνι and
other locatives of Attic demes.
Cobet var. lect. p. 69, 201 and
nov. lect. p. 95, 96.
'Eleusis was subject to...oc-
casional encroachments from
the river Cephissus, which—although for the greater part of
the year quite dry, or finding
its way to the sea in three or
four slender rills, almost lost in
a gravelly bed—sometimes de-
scends from the mountains with
such impetuosity as to spread
itself over a wide extent of the

ἐν τοῖς ἄλλοις τόποις. ἀλλ' οὐ δήπου τούτων, ὦ γῆ
καὶ θεοὶ, παρὰ τῶν γειτόνων ἕκαστος ἀξιώσει τὰς
29 βλάβας κομίζεσθαι, καὶ ἐγὼ μὲν, ὃν προσῆκεν ἀγανακτεῖν τῆς ὁδοῦ στενοτέρας[h] καὶ μετεωροτέρας γεγενημένης[h], ἡσυχίαν ἔχω· τούτοις δὲ τοσοῦτον περίεστιν,
ὡς ἔοικεν, ὥστε τοὺς ἠδικημένους πρὸς συκοφαντοῦσιν[i]. 1280
καίτοι, ὦ Καλλίκλεις, εἰ καὶ ὑμῖν περιοικοδομεῖν
ἔξεστι τὸ ὑμέτερον αὐτῶν χωρίον, καὶ ἡμῖν δήπου τὸ
ἡμέτερον ἐξῆν. εἰ δ' ὁ πατὴρ ὁ ἐμὸς ἠδίκει περιοικοδομῶν ὑμᾶς, καὶ νῦν ὑμεῖς ἐμὲ ἀδικεῖτε περιοικοδομοῦν-
30 τες οὕτως· δῆλον γὰρ ὅτι, μεγάλοις λίθοις ἀποικο-
δομηθέντος, πάλιν τὸ ὕδωρ εἰς τὸ ἐμὸν ἥξει χωρίον, εἶθ'
ὅταν τύχῃ καταβαλεῖ τὴν αἱμασιὰν ἀπροσδοκήτως.
ἀλλ' οὐδὲν μᾶλλον ἐγκαλῶ τούτοις ἐγὼ διὰ τοῦτο,
ἀλλὰ στέργω τὴν τύχην καὶ τἀμαυτοῦ φυλάττειν
πειράσομαι. καὶ γὰρ τοῦτον φράττοντα μὲν τὰ
ἑαυτοῦ σωφρονεῖν ἡγοῦμαι, δικαζόμενον δέ μοι

h Σ. γεγενημένης καὶ μετεωροτέρας Ζ.

i προσσυκοφαντοῦσιν Ζ.

plain, damaging the lands and buildings.' Leake's *Demi* of Attica, p. 154.

τὰς βλάβας κομίζεσθαι] 'to recover the damages.'—μετεω-ροτέρας = ὑψηλοτέρας, cf. § 22.

29. περίεστιν] More com-monly with a genitive: but cf. Mid. § 17 οὐδ' ἐνταῦθ' ἔστη τῆς ὕβρεως, ἀλλὰ τοσοῦτον αὐτῷ πε-ριῆν ὥστε τὸν...ἄρχοντα διέφθειρε.

[τοσοῦτον, i.e. ἀναισχιντίας (or συκοφαντίας), to be supplied from ἀναισχυντότεροι (ἢ περιφα-νέστερον συκοφαντοῦντες) above, in § 28.—περίεστιν, i.e. ἐκ περι-ουσίας ἔχουσιν. P.] L and S less well explain it; 'So far are matters come with them that....'

πρὸς συκοφαντοῦσιν] Cf. An-drot. § 75 τοσοῦτ' ἀπέχει τοῦ τιμῆς τινὸς...τυχεῖν ὥστ' ἀπειλό-καλος πρὸς ἔδοξεν εἶναι. See note on Or. 37 § 49 πρὸς ἀτιμῶσαι, and 39 § 23 πρὸς μισεῖν.

καὶ ὑμῖν...καὶ ἡμῖν] This idiomatic repetition of καὶ can-not be literally rendered in English.

περιοικοδομῶν ...... -δομοῦντες] Rosses παροικοδ. bis: sed care facias. construe ἠδίκει ὑμᾶς περι-οικοδομῶν 'by hedging in' etc. Dobree.

30. ἀποικοδομηθέντος] Geni-tive neuter absolute. We can-not understand either τοῦ ὕδατος or τοῦ χωρίου. Malim ἀποικοδο-μηθὲν, says Dobree.—στέργω, see § 22.

πονηρότατόν τ᾽ εἶναι καὶ διεφθαρμένον ὑπὸ νόσου νομίζω.

Μὴ θαυμάζετε δ᾽, ὦ ἄνδρες δικασταὶ, τὴν τούτου 31 προθυμίαν, μηδ᾽ εἰ τὰ ψευδῆ κατηγορεῖν νῦν ʲ τετόλμηκεν. καὶ γὰρ τὸ πρότερον πείσας τὸν ἀνεψιὸν ἀμφισβητεῖν μοι τοῦ χωρίου συνθήκας οὐ γενομένας ἀπήνεγκε, καὶ νῦν αὐτὸς ἐρήμην μου καταδεδιήτηται τοιαύτην ἑτέραν δίκην, Κάλλαρον ἐπιγραψάμενος τῶν ἐμῶν δούλων. πρὸς γὰρ τοῖς ἄλλοις κακοῖς καὶ τοῦτο εὕρηνται σόφισμα· Καλλάρῳ τὴν αὐτὴν δίκην δικάζονται. καίτοι τίς ἂν οἰκέτης τὸ τοῦ δεσπότου 32 χωρίον περιοικοδομήσειε μὴ προστάξαντος τοῦ δεσπότου; Καλλάρῳ δ᾽ ἕτερον ἐγκαλεῖν οὐδὲν ἔχοντες, ὑπὲρ ὧν ὁ πατὴρ πλέον ἢ πεντεκαίδεκα ἔτη φράξας ἐπεβίω

ʲ κατηγορεῖν Z et Bekker st. μαρτυρεῖν FΣΦΒ.

διεφθαρμένον ὑπὸ νόσου] 'Blindly infatuated,' 'having his judgment (or reason) impaired by some malady,' contrasted with σωφρονεῖν in the previous clause.

§§ 31, 32. *The plaintiff's assurance in bringing false charges against me is only of a piece with his producing a forged document on a former occasion, when he prompted his cousin to claim my land. Apart from this, simply to spite me (§ 34), he has brought the same charge against my servant, Callarus, as against myself, though the servant could not have enclosed the land on his own responsibility.*

Their interested motive is proved by the fact that, if I let them have my property, by purchase or exchange, then Callarus is at once held to be doing them no wrong; if I refuse, they make themselves out to be grievously wronged by him, and try to get an award or a compromise which will secure them my estate.

31. μὴθαυμάζετε...εἰ] Goodwin's *Moods and Tenses*, § 56.

συνθήκας οὐ γενομένας ἀπήνεγκε] 'put in (or, 'made a return of') false documents, forged contracts that had never been really made.' This is the σκευωρία alluded to in § 2.

ἐρήμην...καταδεδιήτηται] See § 2.

ἐπιγραψάμενος] Having entered on the indictment the name of Callarus, one of my slaves; [for the same action could not be brought twice in the same name. P.]

For another use of ἐπιγράφεσθαι, cf. Or. 54 § 31.

32. ὑπὲρ ὧν κ.τ.λ.] = δικάζονται ὑπὲρ τούτων ἃ ἔφραξεν ὁ πατὴρ καὶ πλέον ἢ πεντεκαίδεκα ἔτη ἐπεβίω. See esp. notes on Or. 45 § 27 ὧν διεφθάρκει and § 68 ἃ πέπλασται.

δικάζονται. κᾶν μὲν ἐγὼ τῶν χωρίων ἀποστῶ τούτοις
ἀποδόμενος ἢ πρὸς ἕτερα χωρία ἀλλαξάμενος, οὐδὲν
ἀδικεῖ Κάλλαρος· ἂν δ' ἐγὼ μὴ βούλωμαι τἀμαυτοῦ 1281
τούτοις προέσθαι, πάντα τὰ δεινότατα ὑπὸ Καλλάρου
πάσχουσιν οὗτοι, καὶ ζητοῦσι καὶ διαιτητὴν ὅστις
αὐτοῖς τὰ χωρία προσκαταγνώσεται, καὶ διαλύσεις
33 τοιαύτας ἐξ ὧν τὰ χωρία ἕξουσιν. εἰ μὲν οὖν, ὦ ἄνδρες δικασταὶ, τοὺς ἐπιβουλεύοντας καὶ συκοφαντοῦν-
τας δεῖ πλέον ἔχειν, οὐδὲν ἂν ὄφελος εἴη τῶν εἰρημένων·
εἰ δ' ὑμεῖς τοὺς μὲν τοιούτους μισεῖτε, τὰ δὲ δίκαια
ψηφίζεσθε, μήτ' ἀπολωλεκότος Καλλικλέους μηδὲν,
μήτ' ἠδικημένου μήθ' ὑπὸ Καλλάρου μήθ' ὑπὸ τοῦ
34 πατρὸς, οὐκ οἶδ' ὅ τι δεῖ πλείω λέγειν. ἵνα δ' εἰδῆτε
ὅτι καὶ πρότερον ἐπιβουλεύων μου τοῖς χωρίοις τὸν
ἀνεψιὸν κατεσκεύασε, καὶ νῦν τὴν ἑτέραν αὐτὸς κατεδιῃτήσατο Καλλάρου ταύτην τὴν δίκην, ἐπηρεάζων
ἐμοὶ διότι τὸν ἄνθρωπον περὶ πολλοῦ ποιοῦμαι, καὶ
Καλλάρῳ πάλιν εἴληχεν ἑτέραν, ἁπάντων ὑμῖν
ἀναγνώσεται τὰς μαρτυρίας.

ΜΑΡΤΥΡΙΑΙ.

35   Μὴ οὖν πρὸς Διὸς καὶ θεῶν, ὦ ἄνδρες δικασταὶ,
προῆσθέ με τούτοις μηδὲν ἀδικοῦντα. οὐ γὰρ τῆς ζη-

διαιτητὴν ὅστις ... προσκατα-
γνώσεται] an arbitrator who shall
actually (go so far as to) ad-
judge their property to them ;
give a verdict of condemnation
adjudging the property to them.

διαλύσεις] 'compromises,'
'settlements.'

§§ 33, 34. *Now if conspiracy
and paltry persecution are to
win the day, my words are merely
wasted. But if you detest such
conduct and intend to give a just
verdict on the ground that neither my father nor my servant*

*has done any damage or wrong
to the plaintiff, then I have already said enough.*

§ 35. *Lastly, I entreat the
jury not to sacrifice me to my opponents, when I have done them
no wrong. It is not so much the
penalty that I care for, hard
though that is for a poor man to
pay; but they want to turn me
out of the parish by their petty
persecution. To prove we were
in the right, we were ready to
submit to a fair arbitration, and
to swear the customary oath; for*

μίας τοσοῦτόν τί μοι μέλει, χαλεπὸν ὂν πᾶσι τοῖς
μικρὰν οὐσίαν ἔχουσιν· ἀλλ' ἐκβάλλουσιν ὅλως ἐκ
τοῦ δήμου με ἐλαύνοντες καὶ συκοφαντοῦντες. ὅτι δ'
οὐκ ἀδικοῦμεν οὐδέν, ἕτοιμοι μὲν ἦμεν ἐπιτρέπειν τοῖς
εἰδόσιν, ἴσοις καὶ κοινοῖς, ἕτοιμοι δ' ὀμνύναι τὸν
νόμιμον ὅρκον· ταῦτα γὰρ ᾠόμεθα ἰσχυρότατα παρασχέσθαι[k] τοῖς αὐτοῖς ὑμῖν ὀμωμοκόσιν. καί μοι λαβὲ
τήν τε πρόκλησιν καὶ τὰς ὑπολοίπους ἔτι μαρτυρίας.

ΠΡΟΚΛΗΣΙΣ. ΜΑΡΤΥΡΙΑΙ.

[k] *Malim* παρέξεσθαι, *vel, quandoquidem* παρασχέσθαι *dat* Ms, *possis*
ἰσχυρότατ' ἂν παρασχέσθαι.   Dobree.

*we felt that that would be the
strongest argument with you,
gentlemen, who are yourselves
upon your solemn oath.*

35. χαλεπὸν ὂν] sc. τὸ
ζημιοῦσθαι. Hard though it
falls on those whose property
is but small.

ἐλαυνόντες καὶ συκοφαντοῦντες]
by their persecution and petty
litigation.

ἕτοιμοι μὲν...ἕτοιμοι δὲ] § 20
ἔβλαψε μὲν...ἔβλαψε δέ.

τοῖς εἰδόσιν, ἴσοις καὶ κοινοῖς]
'impartial, fair and unbiassed
persons, acquainted with the
facts.' § 9 τοῖς εἰδόσι...τοῖς ἴσοις.

τὸν νόμιμον ὅρκον] The defendant appears to have offered
to take an oath in the ἀντωμοσία
at the ἀνάκρισις, or preliminary
examination. Such an oath
might be taken by either of the
parties, with a view to decide
the cause, or some particular
point in dispute. But it was
only taken by the consent of
the adversary, upon a challenge
given and accepted (C. R. Kennedy in *Dict. Antiq.*).   Cf. Or.
54 § 40, ἠθέλησα ὀμόσαι ταυτί.
Aristot. Rhet. i. 15 §§ 27—33.

τοῖς αὐτοῖς ὑμῖν ὀμωμοκόσι] 'to
you who are yourselves on oath';
'*vobis iudicibus qui et ipsi
iurastis.*' Seager *Classical Journal* 1825, no. 61 p. 63.

GREEK INDEX.

*The first figure refers to the number of the Speech, the second
to the Section.*

A.

ἀγανακτεῖν, c. acc. neut. pron.,
  54. 15
ἀγνωμοσύνη 36. 46
ἀγνώμων 54. 14, 16
ἀγορὰ, without article, 54. 7
ἀγορεύω (usage of) 55. 4 n.
ἀγώγιμος 53. 11
ἀδυνάτως ἔχει 36. 1
αἰκία 54. 1, 28
αἱμασιὰ 55. 11
αἰτίαν ἔχειν 55. 21
αἰτιᾶσθαι 36. 40; 54. 15
ἀκοὴν μαρτυρεῖν 46. 7
ἀκόλουθοι 36. 45
ἀκρόδρυα 53. 15
'Αλαιεὺς 54. 31
ἀληθινὸς (ἀληθής) 53. 7
ἀλίσκεσθαι, c. gen., 45. 45
ἀλλὰ 45. 56; 55. 12
ἀλλὰ νὴ Δία 54. 34; 36. 39
ἄλλος, c. gen., 45. 13
ἀμαξιαῖος 55. 20
ἀμεληθὲν 55. 11
ἀμὶς 54. 4
ἄν, attracted to negative, 36.
  49; 45. 7; 53. 12; *consopitum*,
  45. 12; separated from verb,
  53. 12; 54. 32: see also notes
  on 45. 17, 18, 35, 71; 53. 17
ἀνάγειν 45. 81; -άγεσθαι 53. 5
ἀναγκαία πρόφασις 54. 17
ἀνάγκη, 'a family tie,' 36. 30;
  cf. 45. 54
ἀνάγκης χρεία 45. 67
ἀναδενδράδες 53. 15

ἀναδέχεσθαι 46. 7
ἀναίνεσθαι 36. 31
ἀναιρεῖσθαι διαθήκην 45. 21
ἀνακεῖον 45. 80
ἀνακεχωκότες 55. 28
ἀνακρίνεσθαι δίκην 53. 14, 17
ἀνάκρισις 53. 22
ἀνασκευάζεσθαι, 'become bankrupt,' 36. 50 n.
ἀνατρέπειν τράπεζαν 36. 58 n.
ἀνεκδότους ἔνδον γηράσκειν p. xlvii
ἀνεπίδικος 46. 22
ἀνεψιαδοῦς 45. 54
ἀνὴρ γεγονὼς 36. 20
ἄνωθεν πονηρὸς 45. 80
ἀντιγράφεσθαι 45. 45
ἀντιμοιρεῖ 36. 8
ἀνυπόστατος 54. 38
ἀξιοπιστία (rhet.) 54. 41 n.
ἀοίκητος, 'houseless,' 45. 70
ἀπάγειν κλέπτην 45. 81
ἀπαγωγὴ 54. 1
ἀπαιτεῖν 53. 10; 36. 10
ἀπαλείφειν 45. 44
ἀπαλλαγὴ 45. 41; 36. 2
ἀπαλλάττειν 36. 25; ἀπηλλάττετο τῆς μισθώσεως 36. 10
ἀπαναισχυντεῖν 54. 33
ἀπειπεῖν 46. 14; 54. 25
ἀπειρία 36. 1
ἀπεκεκλείμην, τῶν σιτίων, 54. 11
ἀπεκρινάμην 53. 8
ἀπεπεμψάμεθα 54. 4
ἀπήγγειλεν 54. 38
ἀπηγόρευσε 55. 4
ἁπλᾶς ὑποδέδενται 54. 34

ἀποβλέπειν 54. 38
ἀπογραφή 53. 1; p. li sq.
ἀποδεικνύναι, 53. 28
ἀποδιδόναι 36. 9; 53. 10 n.
ἀποδιδόναι τὰ δίκαια 54. 42
ἀποδύρεσθαι 45. 57
ἀποθνήσκειν (usage of), 54. 20, 22, 39
ἀποικοδομεῖν 55. 5
ἀπορίαι, 53. 29
ἀπορούμενος 54. 12
ἀποφαίνειν δίαιταν 54. 27
ἀπόφασις 45. 60
ἀποφράττειν 55. 17
ἀπράγμων 36. 53; 54. 24
ἀπρόσκλητος 53. 14, 15
ἆρα 55. 15
ἀραί, imprecations in wills, 36. 52
Ἄρειος πάγος 54. 25, 28
ἀριστήσαιεν 54. 3
Ἀριστοκράτης 54. 39
Ἀριστόλοχος 36. 49; 45. 63
Ἀρχεβιάδης, Plutarch's description of, 54. 34
ἄρχειν χειρῶν ἀδίκων 54. 28 n.
Ἀρχέστρατος 36. 43
ἀρχή, 'magistrate,' 45. 58; 53. 24
ἄρχοντες, the 'Eleven,' 53. 24
ἄρχων, eponymus, 46. 22
ἀσπιδοπηγεῖον 36. 11
ἀτίμητος δίκη 55. 18, 25
αὐτὸ τοὐναντίον 55. 17
αὐτολήκυθοι 54. 14; p. 227
ἐπ' αὐτοφώρῳ 45. 81
ἀφανεῖς ἐργασίαι 45. 66
ἀφεὶς καὶ ἀπαλλάξας, ἀφῆκε καὶ ἀπήλλαξεν, 36. 25; ἀφήκατε, ἀφῆκαν, 36. 10, 12; ἀφεθείς 36. 3
ἄφεσις 45. 41
ἀφιέναι 36. 25, 32; 45. 40, 51
ἀφορμή 36. 12, 11, 44: ἀφορμῆς δίκη 36. Arg. 22; p. xxiv
ἄχρηστος (ἀχρεῖος) 54. 44

B.

βαδιεῖσθαι 55. 16
βαδίζειν ἐπί τινα 53. 15; p. li
βαδίζειν παρὰ τοὺς τοίχους 45. 68

βαδίζειν ταχέως 45. 77
βαλανεῖον 54. 9
βάρβαρος 45. 30, 81
βασανίζειν 45. 16; βάσανος, terms of, 45. 61; 'evidence extorted,' 53. 24
βλάβης δίκη 55. 20
βοηθεῖν…τὰ δίκαια 54. 2, 42
βουλεύσεως γραφή note ou 54. 25
Βραυρωνόθεν 54. 25

Γ.

γάρ, idiomatic uses of, 45. 83; 53. 4; 54. 17; 55. 3
ἐν γειτόνων, ἐκ γειτόνων, 53. 10
γελάσαντες…ἀφήσετε 54. 20
γενναῖος 53. 15
γνώριμος 45. 73; 53. 4
γνῶσις, 'award,' 36. 16; ἔγνω 36. 60
γοῦν, 36. 52; 54. 25
τὰ γράμματα (τὰ τραπεζιτικὰ) 36. 18, 21, 36; 45. 33
γραμματείδιον 54. 37
γραφαί…δίκαι 54. 2; 46. 9
γράφεσθαι 53. 24
γυμνὸς 54. 9

Δ.

δανείζειν ἐπὶ γῇ 36. 6
δεινὸς 46. 17
δεῖται καὶ ἱκετεύει 36. 5, 7; 45. 1
δεκασμὸς 46. 26 n.
δημοσίᾳ ἀποδημεῖν 45. 3
——— βασανίζεσθαι 53. 23
τὸ δημόσιον 53. 14
διὰ 45. 31; 53. 14, 18
διὰ ταχέων 53. 5
διὰ τοῦ πυρὸς 54. 40
δίαιτα 54. 26; 36. 16
διαλεχθεὶς 54. 7
διαλογισμὸς 36. 23
διαλύειν 36. 3, 50
διαλύσεις 55. 32
διαμεμετρημένη ἡμέρα 53. 17
διαρραγῇ 54. 41
διασύρειν 55. Arg. 13
διαφορηθείς, of *person* plundered, 45. 64
διεμαρτύρατο 55. 4

διεφθαρμένος τοὺς ὀφθαλμοὺς 54. 39

———————— ὑπὸ νόσου 55. 33

διήγησις ἀπλῆ (rhet.) 59. 4 n.

δικάζεσθαι, ἐπιδικάζεσθαι, 45. 75

δίκαιον, 'a plea,' 54. 27, 42; 55. 3

δίκαιον (and ἐπιεικὲς) 54. 21

δίκαιος 36. 43

δίκη ἰδία, opp. to γραφὴ ὕβρεως, 45. 4

διορύττειν τοίχους 54. 37

———————— πράγματα 45. 30

διότι, for ὅτι, 46. 16

δίωξις 45. 50

δοκιμασθεὶς 36. 10

δόξαι…εἶναι 36. 44

δ' οὖν 54. 27

δωροδοκία 46. 26

E.

ἔγγειος οὐσία 36. 5

ἐγγράφειν 53. 14

ἐγγύη 46. 18

ἐγκαλεῖ, future, 55. 17

ἐγκαλεῖν c. gen. 36. 9; 54. 2; c. acc. 36. 12

ἐθέλειν (θέλειν) 45. 15

εἰ 54. 44; repeated, 46. 23; c. subj. 46. 11 n.

εἰᾶσθαι 45. 22

εἰ καί 55. 21

εἰπεῖν…λέγειν 36. 33

εἰς, ' to the extent of,' 54. 21

εἰς γέλωτα…ἐμβαλεῖν 54. 13

εἰς οὐδεὶς 45. 18

εἰς πᾶν ἐλθών 54. 13

εἰσαγώγιμος 36. 3, 23

εἰσιέναι δίκην 45. 49; (εἰς δικαστήριον) 45. 7; 54. 32; (εἰς τὴν ἐκκλησίαν) 54. 39

εἰσφέρειν 45. 69

εἶτα 54. 20

ἐκ μικροῦ παιδαρίου 53. 19

Ἑκαταῖα 54. 39

ἐκβαλεῖν, 'eject,' 36. 49; 45. 70; 'banish,' 54. 25

ἐκδιδόναι, 'give in marriage,' 36. 45

ἐκδύεσθαι 54. 32

ἐκκρούειν 36. 2; 54. 30

ἐκμαρτυρία 46. 7

ἐκστῆναι τῶν ὄντων, of bankrupts, 36. 50 (passive to ἐκβαλεῖν); 45. 64

ἐκτίλλειν 53. 16

ἐκφέρειν λόγους 53. 14

ἐλᾶαι περίστοιχοι 53. 15

ἐλαύνεις, συκοφαντεῖς, διώκεις, 36. 52

ἐλέγχεσθαι 54. 30

ἐλευθέρους ἀφεῖσαν 36. 14

Ἐλευσῖνι 55. 28

ἕλκη…ὑπὸ δεσμῶν 53. 8

ἐμβαλεῖν (εἰς τὸν ἐχῖνον) 45. 20

ἐμβάλλεται (εἰς τὸν ἐχῖνον) 54. 31

ἐμβεβλημένα 53. 15

ἐμποιεῖν χρόνους 36. 2

ἔμπνος 54. 12; p. 226

ἐμφανῶν κατάστασις 53. 14

ἐναποτιμᾶν 53. 20

ἐνδεικνύναι 53. 14

ἐνεργὸς 36. 5

ἐνθήκη (late Greek) 36. Arg. 23

ἐνοφειλομένου…ἀργυρίου 53. 10

ἐνστῆναι 55. 10

ἐξ εὐπορίας πονηροὶ 45. 67

ἐξαγαγὼν αἱμασιὰν 55. 22; ὕδωρ 55. 17

ἐξαναστήσας 54. 7

ἐξαπάτη 45. 46

ἐξεπλάγην 45. 57

ἐξέρα τὸ ὕδωρ 36. 62

ἐξετάζειν 45. 66, 76, 80, 82; cf. 34. 8

ἐξῆν without ἂν 55. 5

ἐξομνύναι 45. 58, 60

ἐξορκίζειν 54. 26

ἐξορκοῦν 45. 58

ἐξώλης 54. 41

ἑόρακε, respexit, 45. 64

ἐπαγγέλλειν 45. 68

ἐπάγεσθαι 54. 1

ἐπαινεῖν 53. 6

ἐπεβίω 55. 32

ἐπειδὴ θᾶττον 54. 5

ἐπὶ 45. 30

ἐπὶ δίετες ἡβῆσαι 46. 20

ἐπὶ δύο παισὶν 36. Arg. 1

ἐπὶ προικὶ 36. Arg. 6

ἐπὶ τοῖς εἰργασμένοις 45. 81

ἐπιβιοῦντος 55. 5

ἐπιβολὴ…ἐπιβουλὴ 53. 14, 15

ἐπιγεγραμμένος followed by acc. 45. 39

ἐπιγράφεσθαι 53. 14, 15; 54. 31; 55. 31

ἐπιδιδόναι 45. 85; προῖκα 45. 35, 54

ἐπιδικασία 46. 22

ἐπικαθῆσθαι ἐπὶ τραπέζης 36. 7

ἐπικατασκευάζειν (late Greek) 46. Arg. 1

ἐπίκληρος 45. 75; 46. 20, 22; 53. 29

ἐπιμονή (rhet.) 36. 52 n.

ἐπινέμειν 55. 11

ἐπιπόλιος 54. 34

ἐπίσκηψις 46. 7

ἐπισκοπεῖν 54. 12

ἐπιτρέπειν, ἀνατρέπειν, 36. 58

ἐπιτρέπειν (δίαιταν) 36. 15

ἐπιτροπὴ 36. 20

ἐπίτροπος 36. 22

ἐπίχαρτος 45. 85

ἐποικοδομεῖν 55. 25

ἐπωβελία 45. 6

ἔρανος 53. 8, 12

ἐργάζεσθαι χρήμασι 36. 44

ἐρήμην sc. δίκην 55. 6

ἐρήμους δίκας 55. 2

ἐρράφθαι 54. 35

ἐρώτησις (rhet.) 46. 10 n.

ἑσπέρας 54. 7

ἑταιρεία 46. 26

ἑταιρεῖν 45. 79

ἔτεσι καὶ χρόνοις ὕστερον 36. 53

ἔτος τουτὶ τρίτον 54. 3

εὐθεῖα (δίκη) 36. Arg. 25

εὐθυδικία 45. 6

εὔθυναι 46. 9

εὐμενῶς and εὐνοϊκῶς 45. 1

εὐοδεῖν 55. 10

εὔορκος 45. 88; 54. 40

εὐπορεῖν χρήματα 36. 57 n.

εὑρεῖν, 'to get by good luck,' 36. 43; 45. 81

εὖ φρονεῖν 46. 16

Εὔφραιος 36. 37

εὐχερῶς ἔχειν 54. Arg. 6

ἐχῖνος 54. 27; 45. 8, 17, 58; 53. 24

ἐχρῆν without ἂν 45. 17

ἑωράμεθα 54. 16

Z.

ζῆν (usage of) 54. 4 n.

H.

ἦ που, ironical, 55. 18

ἦα 45. 17

ἡγεμών...ἀγαθῶν 45. 73

ἡλικία 54. 1

ἧφθαι 54. 35

Θ.

θεῖος 45. 70, 75

θεσμοθέται 46. 26

I.

ἰδίαν δίκην 54. 1

ἴδιος 55. 8

ἰδιώτης 53. 2

ἰθύφαλλος 54. 14, 16, 20

Ἰκαριεὺς 54. 31

ἵνα...ὅπως 53. 13

ἵνα c. indic. 36. 47; 45. 13; 53. 24; 55. 5, 6

ἴσα βαίνειν, 45. 63

ἴσοι 55. 9, 35

K.

καθαρότης (rhet.) 54. 1 n.

καθ' ἑαυτὸν 36. 4

καθ' ἕνα 54. 26

καί, for ὅτε, 54. 8

καὶ γάρ...καὶ 55. 13

καὶ δὴ καὶ 54. 14; 55. 10

καί...καὶ 55. 29

καὶ ταῦτα 36. 45

κακηγορίας δίκαι 54. 17, 18

κακοτεχνιῶν δίκη 46. 10 n.; p. xxxii

κακῶν ἀλλοτρίων κλέπτης 45. 59

Κάλλιππος 36. 53; p. xxix

καλῶν κἀγαθῶν 45. 65; 54. 14

κἂν εἰ 45. 12

κατὰ in composition 36. 39; 54. 40 ad fin.

κατὰ παίδων ὀμνύναι 54. 38, 40

καταλείπειν 46. 28

καταλειτουργεῖν 36. 39

κατασκευάζειν 46. 11; 54. 14; 55. 1

κατασκεύασμα 45. 27, cf. § 42

καταχύσματα 45. 73

καταψευδομαρτυρηθεὶς 45. 1

κατεαγέναι 54. 35

κατεδιῃτήσατο 55. 2, 6

κατείργασται, middle, 45. 66
κατεπιορκηθησόμενος 54. 40 ad fin.
κατῴκουν...οἰκῶ 53. 4
κεῖμαι and τίθημι 46. 12
κεκομίσθαι, deponent, 45. 30
κεράμιον 55. 24
Κέρδων 53. 19
κηδεστής 36. 31
Κηφισιεὺς 54. 7
κινεῖν 45. 58
κίχρημι (and δανείζω) 53. 12
κλάω, κλαίω, 53. 7
κληρόνομος 36. 32
κληροῦν κλήρων 46. 22
κναφεὺς 54. 7
κοινὸς ἐχθρὸς τῆς φύσεως 45. 53
κομίζεσθαι τὰς βλάβας 55. 29
κοσμεῖν καὶ περιστέλλειν 36. 47
κτῆμα...ἐργασία 36. 11
κύριος 45. 74

Λ.

λαγχάνειν δίκην 54. 1
λακωνίζειν 54. 34
λαλεῖν μέγα 45. 77
λαχεῖν τῆς ἐπικλήρου 46. 23
λαχεῖν, of jury, 46. 23; δίκην
    54. 1
λέγειν καὶ διδάσκειν 36. 1
λειτουργεῖν 36. 39
λελευκωμένον γραμματεῖον 46. 11
λελυμασμένος, deponent, 45. 27
λέλυσαι 36. 45
Λεωκόριον 54. 7
λῆξις 36. 21; 45. 50
λίθος (βωμὸς) 54. 26
λιθοτομίαι 53. 17
λόγος, 'mere talk,' 36. 60
λόγῳ...ἔργῳ 46. 9; 55. 6
λοιδορεῖσθαι 54. 18; λοιδορηθεὶς
    54. 5
λοιδορία 54. 19
λωποδυτής 54. 1, 24, 32

M.

μάλθη 46. 11
μάλιστα 45. 25
Μάνης 45. 86; 53. 20
μανιῶν ἕνεκα 46. 14
μαρτυρεῖν ἐν γραμματείῳ 45. 44
μέγεθος, neutral word, 53. 1

μέδιμνος 55. 24
Μειδίας 54. 10
μελετᾶν, *meditari,* 46. 1
Μελίτη 54. 7
μὲν...δὲ 53. 9; 54. 14, 17;
    55. 22, 35
μέρος, 'in part alone,' 36. 54;
    τὸ σαυτοῦ μέρος 45. 70
μέσον, τὸ μέσον, 55. 10
μετεωρότερος 55. 29
μέτοικος 36. 6
μέτριοι λόγοι 45. 4
μὴ 54. 40
μὴ ὅτι 36. 39; 54. 16; 55. 19
μικροῦ δεῖν πρὶν 55. 3
μισθοῦν 36. 12, 13
μίσθωσις, 'rent,' 36. 33, 36
μοχθηρὸς 53. Arg. 8
μυλὼν 45. 33

N.

νεανικὰ 54. 35
νέμειν, νέμεσθαι, 36. 8
νεμεσᾶν, rare in prose, 45. 71
Νικήρατος 54. 32
νόμοι γεγραμμένοι 45. 53
νόμον ἐπὶ ἀνδρὶ θεῖναι 46. 12
νύκτες 54. 26

Ξ.

ξύλον, 'bench,' 45. 33

O.

ὃ καὶ δεινότατον εἰ 55. 20
ὃ μὴ 55. 25
ὅ τι τύχοιεν 54. 4
ὁδοποιεῖν 55. 11; p. lxxi
ὀδύρεσθαι 45. 88
οἶμαι (parenthetical) 36. 44;
    54. 38
ὅμοιός γε 45. 56
ὁμολογουμέναι (curious use of)
    55. 19
ὄνομα παρέχειν 53. 2
ὄντι καὶ ζῶντι 36. 29
ὅπου, 'whereas,' 55. 18
ὀπώραν πρίασθαι 53. 21
ὁρᾶν, to observe, 36. 1
τὴν ὀργὴν ἔχειν 54. 42
ὅρκον διδόναι 55. 27

ὅρκος νόμιμος 55. 35
ὅρχεις (χοίρων) 54. 39
ὅσα μὴ 54. 36
ὅση καὶ οἷα 54. 36;   ὅσα...οἷα 53. 3
ὅτι, superfluous, 53. 12
ὅ τι δεῖ 36. 62;   54. 44
ὅ τι τύχοιεν 54. 4
ὁτιοῦν 54. 39
ὅτου τις οὖν 45. 53
οὐ and μὴ 36. 6;   54. 43;   55. 20
οὐ μὴ ἐθελήσει 53. 8
οὐ μὴν ἀλλά 45. 9;   54. 38
οὐδὲ πολλοῦ δεῖ 54. 40
οὐδὲν πρὸς τὸ πρᾶγμα 54. 26
οὐκ ἦν ἄρα 55. 1
οὔτε,   οὐδὲ,   54. 16;   οὔτε...τε 55. 8
οὗτος, ambiguous uses of, 36. 12, 20, 22, 42, 83
οὗτος...ἐκεῖνος 54. 21, 23
οὕτω...γένοιτο 55. 24
οὑτωσὶ 54. 26
οὐχ ὅπως 53. 13

П.

παθεῖν τι, euphemism, 54. 25; of inanimate things, 55. 24
πάλαι, vaguely used, 46. 21
Πάνακτον 54. 3; p. lxiii
πάνυ, separated from its adj., 54. 1
παραγραφή 36. Arg. 23; 45. 5, 6, 51
παρακαταθήκη 36. 5
παρανενομῆσθαι 54. 2
παρανοεῖν 46. 14
παραπεπτωκὼς 45. 84
παραπέτασμα, 'pretext,' 45. 19
παραστήσασθαι παῖδας 54. 38
παρέχεσθαι 36. Arg. 23
παροικοδομεῖν 55. 17
παροινεῖν 54. 4, 16
παροξυσμὸς 45. 14
παρρησίας ἀποστερεῖν 45. 79
πατάξαι and πληγῆναι p. 224
Πεπάρηθος 45. 28
περὶ...ὑπὲρ 45. 11, 50
περιάγειν, περιάγεσθαι, 36. 45
περιεστηκότες 54. 41
περίεστιν, absolute, 55. 29

περιέχειν κύκλῳ 55. 10
περιορᾶν 55. 7
περιφάνεια 45. 2
περιφανῶς 46. 5
περιώδυνος 54. 12
πικρὸς 54. 14
πιστευθεὶς 54. 40
πίστις, 'credit,' 36. 44, 57
Πιτθεὺς 54. 31
πλάσμα 36. 33;   45. 29
πλάσσειν 45 Arg. 12;   45. 42, 68
πλεῖν...βαδίζειν 45. 16
πληγὰς εἰληφέναι 54. 14
πληγεὶς τῷ κακῷ 45. 57
ποιεῖσθαι ἄφεσιν 45. 41
ποιεῖσθαι, double sense, 46. 14
ποιητὸς (πολίτης) 45. 78
ποικίλη στοά 45. 17
ποτέ, first word in sentence, 36. 50
πράγματα 36. 53;   54. 1
πρεσβεῖα 36. 34
πρεσβευτὴς, 'agent,' 45. 64
πρίασθαι...ὠνεῖσθαι 53. 10, 21
πρὸ 54. 42
πρὸ τοῦ 36. 33
προβαίνειν 53. 4
πρόβλημα 45. 69
προδιήγησις (rhet.) 54. 2
προειμένος 36. 6
προεισάγειν (late Gk.) 46 Arg. 1
προέσθαι 36. 58
προεώραται 54. 19
προῆκται 54. 23
προθεσμία 36. 26—27
προκαλεῖσθαι 54. 27
πρόκλησις 36. 7;   45. 15, 16
πρὸς, adverbial, 55. 29
πρὸς μέρος 36. 32
προσεκαλεσάμην 54. 29
προσηυπορηκὼς χρήματα 36. 57
προσκρούσματα 54. 3
προσοφείλειν 36. 4, 7, 10
πρόστανταs 46. 11
προστιθέναι προῖκα 45. 35
προσυβρισθεὶς 54. 43
προσφέρεσθαι 53. 28
πρόφασις 46. 9
πρῶτον, ambiguous use of, 54. 32
πώποτε, without negative, 53. 20

P.

ῥᾳδίως 55. 7
ῥᾴων ἔσομαι 45. 57
ῥηθησόμενος 45. 46
ῥοδωνιά 53. 16

Σ.

σημεῖα, 'seals,' 45. 17
σημεῖον...τεκμήριον 54. 9
σκεύη ἐκφορεῖν 53. 14
σκευώρημα 36. 33;   45. Arg. 12
σκευωρία 55. 2
σκευωρουμένους 46. 17; ἐσκευωρήσατο 45. 47
σκιροφοριῶν 46. 22
σκυθρωπάζειν 45. 68;   54. 34
σολοικίζειν, 45. 30
Σόλων 36. 27
Σπίνθαρος ὁ Εὐβούλου 54. 7
στενότερος 55. 22
στέργειν τὴν τύχην 55. 22
Στέφανος Ἀχαρνεὺς 45. 8
συγγενείας ἀναγκαῖα 45. 54
συκοφαντεῖν 55. 1, 35;   36. 3, 12
συκοφαντία disclaimed, 53. 1
συμβάλλεσθαι 45. 69
συμβουλεύειν 54. 1
συμμέμνησθε 46. 1
συμπλάσας 36. 16
συνδεκάζειν 46. 26
συνεσκότασεν 54. 5
συνιστάμενος 46. 25
συνίστησιν (in late Gk.) 55 Arg.
   12
συνοικία 36. 6, 34;   53. 13
Σύρος 45. 86
σύσσιτοι 54. 4
συστάσεις 45. 67
σφίσιν αὐτοῖς and ἀλλήλοις 54. 14
σφοδρότης (rhet.) 54. 20 n.
σχέσις 45. 68

T.

τεθνεὼς 54. 20
τεκμήριον δὲ...γὰρ 45. 66
τετυπτῆσθαι (late Gk.) 54. Arg. 2
τηλικοῦτος, 'so young,' 55. 7
τηνικαῦτα, 'in that case,' 55. 10
τί...ᾷ, 54. 13
τί γὰρ ἄν; 54. 33
τί μαθόντες 45. 37

τίθεσθαι...τιθέναι 53. 10, 12
τίθημι and κεῖμαι 46. 12
τιμᾶν...τιμᾶσθαι 53. 18, 26
τίμησις 53. 18
τιμητὸς δίκη 55. 18 n.
Τιμόμαχος 36. 53
τιμωρεῖσθαι δεῖν 53. 1
τίς, ὅς, 36. 59 n.
τίς οὔ; 36. 53
τὸ καὶ τὸ 45. 45
τοιοῦτος 54. 6, 33
τοσαῦτα, tantilla, 36. 41
τοῦ μὴ...γίγνεσθαι 54. 18
τράπεζα 36. 11
τρέπεσθαι 54. 16
Τριβαλλοί 54. 39 and p. 214—6
τρίβων 54. 34
τριηραρχίας τριηραρχεῖν 45. 85
τοίχους διορύττειν 54. 37
τοιχωρυχεῖν (metaph.) 45. 30 n.
τολμᾶν (τλῆναι), 55. 21
τραύματος γραφαὶ 54. 18
τυπτήσω p. 211
τυπτητέοι 54. 44
τύπτω (prose usage of), p. 221
τυχὸν, acc. abs., 54. 42
τριηραρχία 36. 14
τῶν Πυθοδώρου 54. 7

Υ.

ὑβρίζων αὐτὸν 36. 30
ὕβρις 45. 4; 53. 16; 54. 1; penalty in certain cases death,
   45. 79;   54. 23
ὑβρισθῆναι 54. 15
ὕδωρ γενέσθαι 55. 4
ὕδωρ (κλεψύδρα) 54. 36, 44;
   53. 17;   36. 62;   45. 86
ὑμεῖς, 'you and yours,' 55. 5;
   36. 30
ὑπάρχειν 55. 8, 14
ὑπερήμερος 45. 70
ὑπεύθυνος 45. 53
ὑπόλογος 36. 48
ὑποπεπτωκὼς 45. 63, cf. § 84

Φ.

φαιδροὶ 45. 68
φαίνεται 54. 33; φ. ὤν 53. 28
φαρμακᾶν 46. 16
φάσκειν 45. 26

φέρειν, tolerate, 36. 3
φέρειν χαλεπῶς 54. 15
Φερρεφάττιον 54. 8
φεύγειν τὴν πόλιν 45. 66
φθάνειν (late Gk.) 46. Arg. 1
φιλάνθρωπος 45. 4
φιλαπεχθημοσύνη 54. 37
φοράδην 54. 20
φρουρᾶς προγραφείσης 54. 3
φυλάττειν 36. 61;   45. 87
φύσεως οἰκεῖα 45. 53

X.

χαράδρα 55. 5, 12, 19
χειμάρρους 55. 19
χιασμὸς (rhet.) 55. 22 n.
χιλίων δραχμᾶν, fine, 53. 1
χλανὶς 36. 45
χλῆδος 55. 22, 27

Χολλείδης 54. 10
χρήσιμος, used absolutely, 54. 44
χρήστης 36. 6
χρόνους ἐμποιεῖν 36. 2
χρώμενος, 'intimate with,' 55. 23
χωρίον 55. 12

Ψ.

τὰ ψευδῆ 54. 32; μαρτυρεῖν, 45. 2
ψευδοκλητεία 53. 17 n.; p. liii
ψευδομαρτυριῶν δίκη, pp. xxxii,
   liii

Ω.

ὥρα, not 'hour,' 54. 4
ὡς (with acc. absolute) 54. 31
ὡς, 'to the house of,' 54. 10
ᾤχοντο 54. 9

ENGLISH INDEX.

*The first figure refers to the number of the Speech, the second
to the Section.*

A.

About, quoted, 55. 16
accusative, 46. 18
— absolute, 54. 31;   55. 11
— cognate, 45. 85
— double, 53. 22
— duration of time, 36. 35
adverbs in -εί, 36. 8
Aeschines, p. xl
Alciphron, quoted, 45. 68, 70
anacoluthon, 36. 2;   45. 83
Andocides, 36. 58
Antiphon, 46. 9;   54. 18
antithesis, 53. 9
aorist, 53. 9
Apollodorus, πρὸς Τιμόθεον, 36.
   20, 53;   46. 16
— πρὸς Πολυκλέα, 36. 41, 45, 53
— trierarchies, 36. 41;   45. 3;
   53. 5; p. lvii

apology to audience, 45. 83;
   54. 15, 17, 39
appeals *ad misericordiam*, 45. 88;
   53. 29;   54. 43
apposition, 53. 15;   54. 13, 15
arbitration, 45. 17;   54. 26;   55.
   2, 32
Areopagus, 54. 25, 28
Aristides (rhetorician), 54. 20, 41;
   55. 18, 24
Aristotle, Politics, 46. 7
— Rhetoric, 46. 10;   53. 10;   54.
   2, 9, 44
article, 54. 7, 10
Athenian audience, sensitiveness
   of, 36. 1
Athenian clubs, pp. 227—230
Athenian places of lounge, 54. 7
Athens, demeanour in the streets
   of, 45. 68;   p. 227, p. lxvi

Attica, country-roads in, 55. 16
attraction, 45. 79; 53. 22; 54. 12
attraction of antecedent into case of relative, 53. 11
audience, compliments to, 36. 30; 54. 9

B.

bankruptcy, 36. 49, 50, 58
'bimembered' construction, 45. 34
'binary structure,' 55. 13
Blass, F., p. xli, xlix, &c.
bribery, 46. 26
Butcher, S. H., quoted, p. l, lxvi
bystanders in court, 54. 41

C.

Catullus, use of *vester*, 55. 5
Cerdo, 53. 19
change of subject, 36. 3
Chysoloras (Gk. Grammar), p. 222
Cicero. *Phil. II.* 54. 24; 45. 85
— *pro Murena*, 45. 16
citizens by adoption, 36. 30
citizens, rights of, 36. 4 and 6
Cobet, quoted, 36. 45; 45. 7, 11; 53, 64; 54. 20; p. 226; 55. 4, 17
cock-fighting, 54. 9 ·
compound verb followed by simple, 36. 4; 53. 4
conditional sentences, 53. 3, 23; 55. 13
construction changed, 54. 36
— suspended, 53. 29
copyists' errors, 54. 39
court, sensational scenes in, 54. 38
curious collocation, 54. 33

D.

dative, double, 54. 16, 44; 55. 8
— of respect, 42. 77
dativus incommodi, 55. 10
decuriare 46. 26
Deinarchus, charges against Demosthenes, 54. 38; p. xxvii; p. xli; p. lxiv

demonstrative pronoun, redundant, 46. 9
Demosthenes Or. 37 (Pant.), 45. 77; p. xlvi, p. l
— (Or. 57) quoted by Stobaeus, 45. 67
— alleged duplicity of, p. xli, xlviii
depositions forged by copyists, 45. 8, 19, 55, 60, 61; 46. 21; 54. 31
Dion of Syracuse, 36. 53
Dionysius I and Athens, 45. 3
Dionysius Halic., lxiv
Dionysius Thrax, p. 209
Dobree's *Adversaria*, quoted, 36. 53; 45. 7, 13, 16, 18, 28, 48, 56, 58, 68, 83, 84; 46. 5, 9; 53. 1, 8; 54. 33, 40 *bis*; 55. 6, 22, 29, 30, 35

E.

Eleusis, floods at, 55. 28
Eusebius, p. lix
ellipse, 36. 7; 54. 26; 55. 21
emendations discussed, 53. 12; 54. 39
emendations proposed, 36. 5, 53; 45. 18, 19, 37, 59, 73; 53. 2; 54. 16, 40; p. 217 col. 2; 55. 16
emphasis, 54. 30
epilogue, same in several speeches, 36. 50; 54. 44
euphemism, 45. 3, 27, 75; 54. 25; 55. 24
evidence, hearsay, 46. 7
exhibitio (an 'exhibit'), 53. 14
exordium similar in several speeches, 45. 1; 54. 2
expiatory sacrifices, 54. 39

F.

farms in Attica, 55. 10—11
flower-gardens, little appreciated by the Greeks, 53. 16
forged documents, 55. 31; (see 'depositions')
future optative, 53. 8

G.

Gay, quoted, p. 230
Gebauer, G., 45. 34, 59;　46. 19
genitive absolute, 45. 62;　55. 26, 30
— exceptional use of, 45. 13
— with nom. 55. 11, 21
genitives, accumulation of, 36. 23, 41
— εἰς τοῦθ᾽ ἥκειν, 36. 48;　45. 73
— of charge, 53. 15
— of price, 53. 12
— of time, 54. 7, 28
Goethe, quoted, 54. 36
Goodwin, W. W., 45. 6; p. xviii, &c.
Greek Testament, 45. 14;　53. 8; 53. 10
Gregorius Nazianzen, p. lxvii

H.

Harpocration, corrected, 55. 5
Harpocration, quoted, 36. 25, 26, 31;　45. 1, 15, 63, 64, 66, 70, 74, 80, 84;　46. 7, 11, 20; 53. 1, 13, 14, 15, 16, 18, 24; 54. 1, 3, 26, 27, 34, 39;　p. 213;　55. 5, 22;　p. l, liii
harsh construction, 46. 17
Hermann, quoted, 45. 18
Hermogenes, 53. 16;　54. 1, 4
Hesychius, quoted, 36. 33;　45. 29, 30;　53. 15;　54. 11, 13, 20, 26, 34;　p. 228;　p. 230;　55. 5, 22
hiatus, 46. 16;　54. 6;　p. xliii
honesty the best policy, 36. 52
humour, 55. 4, 13, 18;　p. lxx
Hyperides, p. xlvi, lxx

I.

imperfect combined with present, 54. 8
— tentative, 53. 7, 16
indicative with optative, 53. 5
infinitive in relative clause, 36. 25;　45. 10
— with two accusatives, 54. 31; 55. 12
innuendo, 36. 42;　45. 84
interest, 53. 13
interpolation, 54. 33

Isocrates, 55. 5; p. 228
— κατὰ Λοχίτου, 54. 17, 18, 43
— *Trapeziticus*, 36. 3, 5, 43; 54. 26;　p. xix
ita sim felix, 55. 24

J.

Jebb, R. C., quoted, p. xxx
Juvenal, 54. 39

K.

Kennedy, C. R., criticised, 36. 35, 38, 57;　45. 59, 62, 67, 73, 74; 46. 26;　54. 40;　55. 22

L.

lawcourts closed, 45. 4
Liddell and Scott, criticised, 36. 2, 58;　45. 76;　54. 4;　p. 224; p. 226;　55. 10
— supplemented, 36. 43;　45. 84
loose construction, 46. 13;　53. 20;　54. 33
loudness of talk, 45. 77;　p. xlv
Lucian, 45. 70;　54. Arg. 2;　54. 39
lunacy, 46. 14, 16
Lysias, p. xxx, lxiv;　54. 9, 18; p. 224, p. 228
Lysias *de olea sacra*, 53. 15

M.

Mahaffy, J. P., quoted, 53. 29, p. xxi
Milton, quoted, 45. 33;　53. 5
mixed construction, 53. 1
Mohocks, p. lxvi; p. 230
money-lenders, unpopularity of, 45. 70
mortgage, 53. 10
Moss, H. W., 45. 35;　55. 16

N.

name, emphatic, 36. 53
names, similar in the same family, 55. 3
negative, double, (1) 36. 22, 46; (2) 45. 14
— repeated, 54. 40

Nicias, 54. 32
nobilis, 53. 15

O.

oaths, 54. 40;　55. 35
oaths taken by jurors, 36. 26;
　55. 35
object-sentence, 55. 22
olive-trees, varieties of, 53. 15
orchard, 53. 15
ordeal by fire, 54. 40 n.

P.

participial clause, emphatic, 45.
　72
participial construction, 54. 1
participle, emphatic, 55. 21
— followed by subordinate par-
　ticiples, 36. 25;　45. 3
— used for hypothetical clause,
　36. 28;　45. 13, 24;　53. 25;
　55. 8
Pasicles, 36. 8, 22;　45. 84;　p.
　xlvi
Pasion, 36. 3, 7, 43;　45. 35;　p.
　xix
passive of intransitive verbs, 54.
　2, 5, 40
periphrasis, 54. 24
Perrot, G., quoted, 54. 2, 3
Phormion, character of, 36. 57—
　59;　45. 71—82;　p. xxi
Plato's Laws, 45. 79;　55. 11, 19;
　p. lxxii
plural, indefinite, 54. 39
Plutarch, p. xli, lvi
Pollux, quoted, 45. 58;　46. 26;
　53. 15, 16;　p. 228;　55. 18
Polybius, passage explained, 45.
　76
predicative article, 36. 8
'pregnant' expression, 46. 11
present, historic, 53. 5
Priscian, 55. 8
pronoun, emphatic, 36. 31;　45.
　80;　53. 22

Q.

questions, direct and indirect,
　36. 81

R.

Reiske corrected, 54. 25, 27;　55.
　10
relationship, obligations of, 45.
　53
relative, double, 53. 3
— with sentence for antecedent,
　54. 26;　55. 22
repetitions of same word at short
　intervals, 45. 4;　46. 2, 23, 28;
　53. 23
revenge, 53. 1
rhetorical artifices, 36. 2;　45. 5;
　53. 4, 27;　54. 9
— evasions, 45. 34, 36
— exaggeration, 45. 30
rights of water, p. lxxi, 55. 19
road-making, 55. 16
Ruskin, quoted, 53. 5, 16

S.

Sauppe, 54. 40
Schaefer, Arnold, quoted, p. xlv;
　36. 53;　46. 17, 20;　54. 3 etc.
Seager, quoted, 36. 53;　53. 28;
　55. 7, 35
seals on wills, 45. 17
sense-construction, 45. 27, 64
sentences recast for clearness of
　translation, 53. 15;　54. 13;
　55. 11, 12
servitus, 55. 19
Sheridan, quoted, 54. 25
Shilleto, quoted, 36. 33, 53;　45.
　4, 7, 27, 41, 63, 83;　54. 39,
　40
slaves, 45. 74, 80, 81
— names of, 45. 86;　and 53.
　19, 20
statute of limitations, 56. 26
Stobaeus, corrected, 45. 67
subject of subordinate made ob-
　ject of principal sentence, 55.
　22
substantive thrown into verb,
　45. 27, 68;　55. 32
Suidas, mistake of, 55. 18
synonymous verbs combined,
　45. 1

T.

Theodosius (grammarian), p.209
Theophrastus, quoted, 45.68, 70
theoric fund, p. xlviii
Thucydides, 55.5
Tiberius (rhetorician), 36.52
Timotheus (general), 36.20, 53
tombs, 55.13, 15
— extravagant outlay on, 45.79
torture, 53.22;   54.27
— not applied in court, 45.16
trespass, 55.11

V.

various readings discussed, 54.
  39;   55.6, 7
Veitch's *Greek Verbs*, corrected,
  p. 224
verses in prose, 36.44;   54.37
vester and *tuus*, 55.5
vine trained, 53.15

W.

walking, Athenian notions on,
  45.68, 69;   63.67
water, rights of, p. lxxi, 55.19
Weil, H., quoted, pp. xlii, xlix
Westermann quoted, 54.19, 26,
  30, 31; see also 'depositions
  forged by copyists'
widows, marriage to guardians,
  36.8
wills, 36.7;   46.14, 24, 28
— phraseology of, 54.25
— seals attached to, 45.17
witnesses to wills ignorant of
  their contents, 45.23;   46.2
Wolf, Jerome, quoted, 53.14
writing-materials, 46.11

Z.

Zosimus, p. xliii

PUBLICATIONS OF

The Cambridge University Press.

THE HOLY SCRIPTURES, &c.

The Cambridge Paragraph Bible of the Authorized English Version, with the Text revised by a Collation of its Early and other Principal Editions, the Use of the Italic Type made uniform, the Marginal References remodelled, and a Critical Introduction, by F. H. A. Scrivener, M.A., LL.D. Crown 4to., cloth gilt, 21*s*.

The Student's Edition of the above, on *good writing paper*, with one column of print and wide margin to each page for MS. notes. Two Vols. Crown 4to., cloth, gilt, 31*s*. 6*d*.

The Lectionary Bible, with Apocrypha, divided into Sections adapted to the Calendar and Tables of Lessons of 1871. Cr. 8vo. 3*s*. 6*d*.

The Old Testament in Greek according to the Septuagint. Edited by the Rev. Professor H. B. Swete, D.D. Vol. I. Genesis—IV Kings. Crown 8vo. 7*s*. 6*d*. Vol. II. I Chronicles—Tobit. [*Nearly ready.*

The Book of Psalms in Greek according to the Septuagint. Being a portion of Vol. II. of above. Crown 8vo. 2*s*. 6*d*.

The Book of Ecclesiastes. Large Paper Edition. By the Very Rev. E. H. Plumptre, Dean of Wells. Demy 8vo. 7*s*. 6*d*.

Breviarium ad usum insignis Ecclesiae Sarum. Juxta Editionem maximam pro Claudio Chevallon et Francisco Regnault a.d. MDXXXI. in Alma Parisiorum Academia impressam : labore ac studio Francisci Procter, A.M., et Christophori Wordsworth, A.M.

Fasciculus I. In quo continentur Kalendarium, et Ordo Temporalis sive Proprium de Tempore totius anni, una cum ordinali suo quod usitato vocabulo dicitur Pica sive Directorium Sacerdotum. Demy 8vo. 18*s*.

Fasciculus II. In quo continentur Psalterium, cum ordinario Officii totius hebdomadae juxta Horas Canonicas, et proprio Completorii, Litania, Commune Sanctorum, Ordinarium Missae cum Canone et xiii Missis, &c. &c. Demy 8vo. 12*s*.

Fasciculus III. In quo continetur Proprium Sanctorum quod et Sanctorale dicitur, una cum Accentuario. Demy 8vo. 15*s*.

Fasciculi I. II. III. complete £2. 2*s*.

Breviarium Romanum a Francisco Cardinali Quignonio editum et recognitum iuxta editionem Venetiis a.d. 1535 impressam curante Johanne Wickham Legg. Demy 8vo. 12*s*.

The Pointed Prayer Book, being the Book of Common Prayer with the Psalter or Psalms of David, pointed as they are to be sung or said in Churches. Royal 24mo. cloth, 1*s*. 6*d*.

The same in square 32mo. cloth, 6*d*.

The Cambridge Psalter, for the use of Choirs and Organists. Specially adapted for Congregations in which the "Cambridge Pointed Prayer Book" is used. Demy 8vo. cloth, 3*s*. 6*d*. Cloth limp cut flush, 2*s*. 6*d*.

London: Cambridge Warehouse, Ave Maria Lane.

The Paragraph Psalter, arranged for the use of Choirs by the Right Rev. B. F. WESTCOTT, D.D., Lord Bp. of Durham. Fcp. 4to. 5*s.*
The same in royal 32mo. Cloth, 1*s.* Leather, 1*s. 6d.*

Psalms of the Pharisees, commonly known as the Psalms of Solomon, by H. E. RYLE, M.A. and M. R. JAMES, M.A. Demy 8vo. 15*s.*

The Authorised Edition of the English Bible (1611), its Subsequent Reprints and Modern Representatives. By F. H. A. SCRIVENER, M.A., D.C.L., LL.D. Crown 8vo. 7*s. 6d.*

The New Testament in the Original Greek, according to the Text followed in the Authorised Version, together with the Variations adopted in the Revised Version. Edited by F. H. A. SCRIVENER, M.A., D.C.L., LL.D. Small Crown 8vo. 6*s.*

The Parallel New Testament Greek and English. The New Testament, being the Authorised Version set forth in 1611 Arranged in Parallel Columns with the Revised Version of 1881, and with the original Greek, as edited by F. H. A. SCRIVENER, M.A., D.C.L., LL.D. Crown 8vo. 12*s. 6d.* (*The Revised Version is the joint Property of the Universities of Cambridge and Oxford.*)

Greek and English Testament, in parallel columns on the same page. Edited by J. SCHOLEFIELD, M.A. *New Edition, with the marginal references as arranged and revised by* DR SCRIVENER. 7*s. 6d.*

Greek and English Testament. THE STUDENT'S EDITION of the above on *large writing paper.* 4to. 12*s.*

Greek Testament, ex editione Stephani tertia, 1550. Sm. 8vo. 3*s. 6d.*

The Four Gospels in Anglo-Saxon and Northumbrian Versions. By Rev. Prof. SKEAT, Litt.D. One Volume. Demy Quarto. 30*s.* Each Gospel separately. 10*s.*

The Missing Fragment of the Latin Translation of the Fourth Book of Ezra, discovered and edited with Introduction, Notes, and facsimile of the MS., by Prof. BENSLY, M.A. Demy 4to. 10*s.*

The Harklean Version of the Epistle to the Hebrews, Chap. XI. 28—XIII. 25. Now edited for the first time with Introduction and Notes on this version of the Epistle. By ROBERT L. BENSLY. Demy 8vo. 5*s.*

Codex S. Ceaddae Latinus. Evangelia SSS. Matthaci, Marci, Lucae ad cap. III. 9 complectens, circa septimum vel octavum saeculum scriptvs, in Ecclesia Cathedrali Lichfieldiensi servatus. Cum codice versionis Vulgatae Amiatino contulit, prolegomena conscripsit, F. H. A. SCRIVENER, A.M., LL.D. Imp. 4to. £1. 1*s.*

The Origin of the Leicester Codex of the New Testament. By J. R. HARRIS, M.A. With 3 plates. Demy 4to. 10*s. 6d.*

Notitia Codicis Quattuor Evangeliorum Græci membranacei viris doctis hucusque incogniti quem in museo suo asservat Eduardus Reuss Argentoratensis. 2*s.*

London: Cambridge Warehouse, Ave Maria Lane.

THEOLOGY—(ANCIENT).

Theodore of Mopsuestia's Commentary on the Minor Epistles of
S. Paul. The Latin Version with the Greek Fragments, edited from the
MSS. with Notes and an Introduction, by H. B. SWETE, D.D. Vol. I.,
containing the Introduction, and the Commentary upon Galatians—Colos·
sians. Demy Octavo. 12*s*.

Volume II., containing the Commentary on 1 Thessalonians—Philemon,
Appendices and Indices. 12*s*.

Chagigah from the Babylonian Talmud. A Translation of the
Treatise with Notes, etc. by A. W. STREANE, M.A. Demy 8vo. 10*s*.

The Greek Liturgies. Chiefly from original Authorities. By C. A.
SWAINSON, D.D., late Master of Christ's College. Cr. 4to. 15*s*.

Sayings of the Jewish Fathers, comprising Pirqe Aboth and
Pereq R. Meir in Hebrew and English, with Critical Notes. By C.
TAYLOR, D.D., Master of St John's College. 10*s*.

Sancti Irenæi Episcopi Lugdunensis libros quinque adversus
Hæreses, edidit W. WIGAN HARVEY, S.T.B. Collegii Regalis olim
Socius. 2 Vols. Demy Octavo. 18*s*.

The Palestinian Mishna. By W. H. LOWE, M.A. Royal 8vo. 21*s*.

M. Minucii Felicis Octavius. The text newly revised from the
original MS. with an English Commentary, Analysis, Introduction, and
Copious Indices. By H. A. HOLDEN, LL.D. Cr. 8vo. 7*s*. 6*d*.

Theophili Episcopi Antiochensis Libri Tres ad Autolycum. Edidit
Prolegomenis Versione Notulis Indicibus instruxit GULIELMUS GILSON
HUMPHRY, S.T.B. Post Octavo. 5*s*.

Theophylacti in Evangelium S. Matthæi Commentarius Edited
by W. G. HUMPHRY, B.D. Demy Octavo. 7*s*. 6*d*.

Tertullianus de Corona Militis, de Spectaculis, de Idololatria
with Analysis and English Notes, by G. CURREY, D.D. Crown 8vo. 5*s*.

Fragments of Philo and Josephus. Newly edited by J. RENDEL
HARRIS, M.A. With two Facsimiles. Demy 4to. 12*s*. 6*d*.

The Teaching of the Apostles. Newly edited, with Facsimile Text
and Commentary, by J. R. HARRIS, M.A. Demy 4to. 21*s*.

The Rest of the Words of Baruch: A Christian Apocalypse of
the year 136 A.D. The Text revised with an Introduction by J. RENDEL
HARRIS, M.A. Royal 8vo. 5*s*.

The Acts of the Martyrdom of Perpetua and Felicitas; the ori-
ginal Greek Text now first edited from a MS. in the Library of the
Convent of the Holy Sepulchre at Jerusalem, by J. RENDEL HARRIS and
SETH K. GIFFORD. Royal 8vo. 5*s*.

Biblical Fragments from Mount Sinai, edited by J. RENDEL
HARRIS, M.A. Demy 4to. 10*s*. 6*d*.

The Diatessaron of Tatian. By J. RENDEL HARRIS, M.A. Royal
8vo. 5*s*.

THEOLOGY—(ENGLISH).

Works of Isaac Barrow, compared with the original MSS. A new Edition, by A. NAPIER, M.A. 9 Vols. Demy 8vo. £3. 3*s.*

Treatise of the Pope's Supremacy, and a Discourse concerning the Unity of the Church, by I. BARROW. Demy 8vo. 7*s.* 6*d.*

Pearson's Exposition of the Creed, edited by TEMPLE CHEVALLIER, B.D. 3rd Edition revised by R. SINKER, D.D. Demy 8vo. 12*s.*

An Analysis of the Exposition of the Creed, written by the Right Rev. Father in God, JOHN PEARSON, D.D. Compiled by W. H. MILL, D.D. Demy Octavo. 5*s.*

Wheatly on the Common Prayer, edited by G. E. CORRIE, D.D. late Master of Jesus College. Demy Octavo. 7*s.* 6*d.*

The Homilies, with Various Readings, and the Quotations from the Fathers given at length in the Original Languages. Edited by G. E. CORRIE, D.D. late Master of Jesus College. Demy 8vo. 7*s.* 6*d.*

Two Forms of Prayer of the time of Queen Elizabeth. Now First Reprinted. Demy Octavo. 6*d.*

Select Discourses, by JOHN SMITH, late Fellow of Queens' College, Cambridge. Edited by H. G. WILLIAMS, B.D. late Professor of Arabic. Royal Octavo. 7*s.* 6*d.*

De Obligatione Conscientiæ Prælectiones decem Oxonii in Schola Theologica habitæ a ROBERTO SANDERSON, SS. Theologiæ ibidem Professore Regio. With English Notes, including an abridged Translation, by W. WHEWELL, D.D. Demy 8vo. 7*s.* 6*d.*

Cæsar Morgan's Investigation of the Trinity of Plato, and of Philo Judæus. 2nd Ed., revised by H. A. HOLDEN, LL.D. Cr. 8vo. 4*s.*

Archbishop Usher's Answer to a Jesuit, with other Tracts on Popery. Edited by J. SCHOLEFIELD, M.A. Demy 8vo. 7*s.* 6*d.*

Wilson's Illustration of the Method of explaining the New Testament, by the early opinions of Jews and Christians concerning Christ. Edited by T. TURTON, D.D. Demy 8vo. 5*s.*

Lectures on Divinity delivered in the University of Cambridge. By JOHN HEY, D.D. Third Edition, by T. TURTON, D.D. late Lord Bishop of Ely. 2 vols. Demy Octavo. 15*s.*

S. Austin and his place in the History of Christian Thought. Being the Hulsean Lectures for 1885. By W. CUNNINGHAM, D.D. Demy 8vo. Buckram, 12*s.* 6*d.*

Christ the Life of Men. Being the Hulsean Lectures for 1888. By Rev. H. M. STEPHENSON, M.A. Crown 8vo. 2*s.* 6*d.*

The Gospel History of our Lord Jesus Christ in the Language of the Revised Version, arranged in a Connected Narrative, especially for the use of Teachers and Preachers. By Rev. C. C. JAMES, M.A. Crown 8vo. 3*s.* 6*d.*

GREEK AND LATIN CLASSICS, &c.

(*See also* pp. 16, 17.)

Sophocles: the Plays and Fragments. With Critical Notes, Commentary, and Translation in English Prose, by R. C. JEBB, Litt.D., LL.D., Regius Professor of Greek in the University of Cambridge.

Part I. Oedipus Tyrannus. Demy 8vo. *Second Edit.* 12s. 6d.

Part II. Oedipus Coloneus. Demy 8vo. *Second Edit.* 12s. 6d.

Part III. Antigone. Demy 8vo. *Second Edit.* 12s. 6d.

Part IV. Philoctetes. Demy 8vo. 12s. 6d.

Select Private Orations of Demosthenes with Introductions and English Notes, by F. A. PALEY, M.A., & J. E. SANDYS, Litt.D.

Part I. Contra Phormionem, Lacritum, Pantaenetum, Boeotum de Nomine, de Dote, Dionysodorum. Cr. 8vo. *New Edition.* 6s.

Part II. Pro Phormione, Contra Stephanum I. II.; Nicostratum, Cononem, Calliclem. Crown 8vo. *New Edition.* 7s. 6d.

Demosthenes, Speech of, against the Law of Leptines. With Introduction and Critical and Explanatory Notes, by J. E. SANDYS, Litt.D. Demy 8vo. 9s.

Demosthenes against Androtion and against Timocrates, with Introductions and English Commentary by WILLIAM WAYTE, M.A. Crown 8vo. 7s. 6d.

Euripides. Bacchae, with Introduction, Critical Notes, and Archæological Illustrations, by J. E. SANDYS, Litt.D. New Edition, with additional Illustrations. Crown 8vo. 12s. 6d.

Euripides. Ion. The Greek Text with a Translation into English Verse, Introduction and Notes by A. W. VERRALL, Litt.D. Demy 8vo. 7s. 6d.

An Introduction to Greek Epigraphy. Part I. The Archaic Inscriptions and the Greek Alphabet. By E. S. ROBERTS, M.A., Fellow and Tutor of Gonville and Caius College. Demy 8vo. 18s.

Aeschyli Fabulae.—ΙΚΕΤΙΔΕΣ ΧΟΗΦΟΡΟΙ in libro Mediceo mendose scriptae ex vv. dd. coniecturis emendatius editae cum Scholiis Graecis et brevi adnotatione critica, curante F. A. PALEY, M.A., LL.D. Demy 8vo. 7s. 6d.

The Agamemnon of Aeschylus. With a translation in English Rhythm, and Notes Critical and Explanatory. **New Edition, Revised.** By the late B. H. KENNEDY, D.D. Crown 8vo. 6s.

The Theætetus of Plato, with a Translation and Notes by the same Editor. Crown 8vo. 7s. 6d.

P. Vergili Maronis Opera, cum Prolegomenis et Commentario Critico pro Syndicis Preli Academici edidit BENJAMIN HALL KENNEDY, S.T.P. Extra fcp. 8vo. 3s. 6d.

Essays on the Art of Pheidias. By C. WALDSTEIN, Litt.D., Phil.D. Royal 8vo. With Illustrations. Buckram, 30s.

M. Tulli Ciceronis ad M. Brutum Orator. A Revised Text. Edited with Introductory Essays and Critical and Explanatory Notes, by J. E. SANDYS, Litt.D. Demy 8vo. 16s.

M. Tulli Ciceronis pro C. Rabirio [Perduellionis Reo] Oratio ad
Quirites. With Notes, Introduction and Appendices. By W. E. HEIT-
LAND, M.A. Demy 8vo. 7s. 6d.

M. T. Ciceronis de Natura Deorum Libri Tres, with Introduction
and Commentary by JOSEPH B. MAYOR, M.A. Demy 8vo. Vol. I. 10s. 6d.
Vol. II. 12s. 6d. Vol. III. 10s.

M. T. Ciceronis de Officiis Libri Tres with Marginal Analysis, an
English Commentary, and Indices. New Edition, revised, by H. A.
HOLDEN, LL.D. Crown 8vo. 9s.

M. T. Ciceronis de Officiis Libri Tertius, with Introduction,
Analysis and Commentary by H. A. HOLDEN, LL.D. Cr. 8vo. 2s.

M. T. Ciceronis de Finibus Bonorum libri Quinque. The Text
revised and explained by J. S. REID, Litt.D. *[In the Press.*
Vol. III., containing the Translation. Demy 8vo. 8s.

Plato's Phædo, literally translated, by the late E. M. COPE, Fellow
of Trinity College, Cambridge. Demy Octavo. 5s.

Aristotle. The Rhetoric. With a Commentary by the late
E. M. COPE, Fellow of Trinity College, Cambridge, revised and
edited by J. E. SANDYS, Litt.D. 3 Vols. Demy 8vo. 21s.

Aristotle.—ΠΕΡΙ ΨΥΧΗΣ. Aristotle's Psychology, in Greek and
English, with Introduction and Notes, by E. WALLACE, M.A. Demy 8vo. 18s.

ΠΕΡΙ ΔΙΚΑΙΟΣΥΝΗΣ. The Fifth Book of the Nicomachean
Ethics of Aristotle. Edited by H. JACKSON, Litt.D. Demy 8vo. 6s.

Pronunciation of Ancient Greek translated from the Third German
edition of Dr BLASS by W. J. PURTON, B.A. Demy 8vo. 6s.

Pindar. Olympian and Pythian Odes. With Notes Explanatory
and Critical, Introductions and Introductory Essays. Edited by C. A. M.
FENNELL, Litt.D. Crown 8vo. 9s.

— **The Isthmian and Nemean Odes** by the same Editor. 9s.

The Types of Greek Coins. By PERCY GARDNER, Litt.D., F.S.A.
With 16 plates. Impl. 4to. Cloth £1. 11s. 6d. Roxburgh (Morocco
back) £2. 2s.

<hr>

SANSKRIT, ARABIC AND SYRIAC.

Lectures on the Comparative Grammar of the Semitic Languages
from the Papers of the late WILLIAM WRIGHT, LL.D. Demy 8vo. 14s.

The Divyâvadâna, a Collection of Early Buddhist Legends, now
first edited from the Nepalese Sanskrit MSS. in Cambridge and Paris.
By E. B. COWELL, M.A. and R. A. NEIL, M.A. Demy 8vo. 18s.

Nalopakhyânam, or, The Tale of Nala; containing the Sanskrit
Text in Roman Characters, with Vocabulary. By the late Rev. T.
JARRETT, M.A. Demy 8vo. 10s.

Notes on the Tale of Nala, for the use of Classical Students, by
J. PEILE, Litt.D., Master of Christ's College. Demy 8vo. 12s.

<hr>

London: Cambridge Warehouse, Ave Maria Lane.

The History of Alexander the Great, being the Syriac version of the Pseudo-Callisthenes. Edited from Five Manuscripts, with an English Translation and Notes, by E. A. BUDGE, M.A. Demy 8vo. 25*s*.

The Poems of Beha ed dín Zoheir of Egypt. With a Metrical Translation, Notes and Introduction, by the late E. H. PALMER, M.A. 2 vols. Crown Quarto.
    Vol. I. The ARABIC TEXT. Paper covers. 10*s*. 6*d*.
    Vol. II. ENGLISH TRANSLATION. Paper covers. 10*s*. 6*d*.

The Chronicle of Joshua the Stylite edited in Syriac, with an English translation and notes, by W. WRIGHT, LL.D. Demy 8vo. 10*s*. 6*d*.

Kalīlah and Dimnah, or, the Fables of Bidpai; with an English Translation of the later Syriac version, with Notes, by the late I. G. N. KEITH-FALCONER, M.A. Demy 8vo. 7*s*. 6*d*.

Maķála-i-Shakhsí Sayyáḥ ki dar Ķaẓiyya-i-Báb Navishta-Ast (a Traveller's Narrative written to illustrate the Episode of the Báb). Persian text, edited, translated and annotated, in two volumes, by E. G. BROWNE, M.A., M.B. [*Nearly ready.*

MATHEMATICS, PHYSICAL SCIENCE, &c.

Mathematical and Physical Papers. By Sir G. G. STOKES, Sc.D., LL.D. Reprinted from the Original Journals and Transactions, with additional Notes by the Author. Vol. I. Demy 8vo. 15*s*. Vol. II. 15*s*.
    [Vol. III. *In the Press.*

Mathematical and Physical Papers. By Sir W. THOMSON, LL.D., F.R.S. Collected from different Scientific Periodicals from May, 1841, to the present time. Vol. I. Demy 8vo. 18*s*. Vol. II. 15*s*. Vol. III. 18*s*.

The Collected Mathematical Papers of ARTHUR CAYLEY, Sc.D., F.R.S. Demy 4to. 10 vols.
    Vols. I., II. and III. 25*s*. each. [Vol. IV. *In the Press.*

A History of the Study of Mathematics at Cambridge. By W. W. ROUSE BALL, M.A. Crown 8vo. 6*s*.

A History of the Theory of Elasticity and of the Strength of Materials, from Galilei to the present time. Vol. I. GALILEI TO SAINT-VENANT, 1639–1850. By the late I. TODHUNTER, Sc.D., edited and completed by Prof. KARL PEARSON, M.A. Demy 8vo. 25*s*.
    Vol. II. By the same Editor. [*In the Press.*

The Elastical Researches of Barre de Saint-Venant (extract from Vol. II. of TODHUNTER'S History of the Theory of Elasticity), edited by Professor KARL PEARSON, M.A. Demy 8vo. 9*s*.

Theory of Differential Equations. Part I. Exact Equations and Pfaff's Problem. By A. R. FORSYTH, Sc.D., F.R.S. Demy 8vo. 12*s*.

A Treatise on the General Principles of Chemistry, by M. M. PATTISON MUIR, M.A. **Second Edition.** Demy 8vo. 15*s*.

Elementary Chemistry. By M. M. PATTISON MUIR, M.A., and CHARLES SLATER, M.A., M.B. Crown 8vo. 4*s*. 6*d*.

Practical Chemistry. A Course of Laboratory Work. By M. M. PATTISON MUIR, M.A., and D. J. CARNEGIE, M.A. Cr. 8vo. 3*s*.

A Treatise on Geometrical Optics. By R. S. HEATH, M.A. Demy 8vo. 12s. 6d.

An Elementary Treatise on Geometrical Optics. By R. S. HEATH, M.A. Crown 8vo. 5s.

A Treatise on Dynamics. By S. L. LONEY, M.A. Cr. 8vo. 7s. 6d.

A Treatise on Analytical Statics. By E. J. ROUTH, Sc.D., F.R.S. [*Nearly ready.*

A Treatise on Plane Trigonometry. By E. W. HOBSON, M.A. Demy 8vo. [*Nearly ready.*

Lectures on the Physiology of Plants, by S. H. VINES, Sc.D., Professor of Botany in the University of Oxford. Demy 8vo. 21s.

A Short History of Greek Mathematics. By J. GOW, Litt. D., Fellow of Trinity College. Demy 8vo. 10s. 6d.

Notes on Qualitative Analysis. Concise and Explanatory. By H. J. H. FENTON, M.A., F.C.S. New Edit. Crown 4to. 6s.

Diophantos of Alexandria; a Study in the History of Greek Algebra. By T. L. HEATH, M.A. Demy 8vo. 7s. 6d.

A Catalogue of the Portsmouth Collection of Books and Papers written by or belonging to SIR ISAAC NEWTON. Demy 8vo. 5s.

A Treatise on Natural Philosophy. By Prof. Sir W. THOMSON, LL.D., and P. G. TAIT, M.A. Part I. Demy 8vo. 16s. Part II. 18s.

Elements of Natural Philosophy. By Professors Sir W. THOMSON, and P. G. TAIT. *Second Edition.* Demy 8vo. 9s.

An Elementary Treatise on Quaternions. By P. G. TAIT, M.A. *Second Edition.* Demy 8vo. 14s.

A Treatise on the Theory of Determinants and their Applications in Analysis and Geometry. By R. F. SCOTT, M.A. Demy 8vo. 12s.

Counterpoint. A practical course of study. By the late Prof. Sir G. A. MACFARREN, Mus. D. 5th Edition, revised. Cr. 4to. 7s. 6d.

The Analytical Theory of Heat. By JOSEPH FOURIER. Translated with Notes, by A. FREEMAN, M.A. Demy 8vo. 12s.

The Scientific Papers of the late Prof. J. Clerk Maxwell. Edited by W. D. NIVEN, M.A. 2 vols. Royal 4to. £3. 3s. (net.)

The Electrical Researches of the Honourable Henry Cavendish, F.R.S. Written between 1771 and 1781. Edited by J. CLERK MAXWELL, F.R.S. Demy 8vo. 18s.

Practical Work at the Cavendish Laboratory. Heat. Edited by W. N. SHAW, M.A. Demy 8vo. 3s.

Hydrodynamics, a Treatise on the Mathematical Theory of Fluid Motion, by HORACE LAMB, M.A. Demy 8vo. 12s.

The Mathematical Works of Isaac Barrow, D.D. Edited by W. WHEWELL, D.D. Demy Octavo. 7s. 6d.

Illustrations of Comparative Anatomy, Vertebrate and Invertebrate. Second Edition. Demy 8vo. 2s. 6d.

London: Cambridge Warehouse, Ave Maria Lane.

A Catalogue of Australian Fossils. By R. ETHERIDGE, Jun., F.G.S. Demy 8vo. 10*s.* 6*d.*

The Fossils and Palæontological Affinities of the Neocomian Deposits of Upware and Brickhill, being the Sedgwick Prize Essay for 1879. By W. KEEPING, M.A. Demy 8vo. 10*s.* 6*d.*

The Bala Volcanic Series of Caernarvonshire and Associated Rocks, being the Sedgwick Prize Essay for 1888, by A. HARKER, M.A., F.R.S. Demy 8vo. 7*s.* 6*d.*

A Catalogue of Books and Papers on Protozoa, Coelenterates, Worms, etc. published during the years 1861–1883, by D'ARCY W. THOMPSON, M.A. Demy 8vo. 12*s.* 6*d.*

A Revised Account of the Experiments made with the Bashforth Chronograph, to find the resistance of the air to the motion of projectiles. By FRANCIS BASHFORTH, B.D. Demy 8vo. 12*s.*

An attempt to test the Theories of Capillary Action, by F. BASHFORTH, B.D., and J. C. ADAMS, M.A. Demy 4to. £1. 1*s.*

A Catalogue of the Collection of Cambrian and Silurian Fossils contained in the Geological Museum of the University of Cambridge, by J. W. SALTER, F.G.S. Royal Quarto. 7*s.* 6*d.*

Catalogue of Osteological Specimens contained in the Anatomical Museum of the University of Cambridge. Demy 8vo. 2*s.* 6*d.*

Astronomical Observations made at the Observatory of Cambridge from 1846 to 1860, by the late Rev. J. CHALLIS, M.A.

Astronomical Observations from 1861 to 1865. Vol. XXI. Royal 4to., 15*s.* From 1866 to 1869. Vol. XXII. 15*s.*

LAW.

Elements of the Law of Torts. A Text-book for Students. By MELVILLE M. BIGELOW, Ph.D. Crown 8vo. 10*s.* 6*d.*

A Selection of Cases on the English Law of Contract. By GERARD BROWN FINCH, M.A. Royal 8vo. 28*s.*

Bracton's Note Book. A Collection of Cases decided in the King's Courts during the Reign of Henry the Third, annotated by a Lawyer of that time, seemingly by Henry of Bratton. Edited by F. W. MAITLAND. 3 vols. Demy 8vo. £3. 3*s.* (net.)

Tables shewing the Differences between English and Indian Law. By Sir ROLAND KNYVET WILSON, Bart., M.A., LL.M. Demy 4to. 1*s.*

The Influence of the Roman Law on the Law of England. Being the Yorke Prize Essay for the year 1884. By T. E. SCRUTTON, M.A. Demy 8vo. 10*s.* 6*d.*

Land in Fetters. Being the Yorke Prize Essay for 1885. By T. E. SCRUTTON, M.A. Demy 8vo. 7*s.* 6*d.*

Commons and Common Fields, or the History and Policy of the Laws of Commons and Enclosures in England. Being the Yorke Prize Essay for 1886. By T. E. SCRUTTON, M.A. Demy 8vo. 10*s.* 6*d.*

History of the Law of Tithes in England. Being the Yorke Prize Essay for 1887. By W. EASTERBY, B.A., LL.B. Demy 8vo. 7*s.* 6*d.*

History of Land Tenure in Ireland. Being the Yorke Prize Essay
for 1888. By W. E. MONTGOMERY, M.A., LL.M. Demy 8vo. 10s. 6d.

History of Equity as administered in the Court of Chancery. Being
the Yorke Prize Essay for 1889. By D. M^cKENZIE KERLY, M.A., St John's
College. Demy 8vo. 12s. 6d.

An Introduction to the Study of Justinian's Digest. By HENRY
JOHN ROBY. Demy 8vo. 9s.

Justinian's Digest. Lib. VII., Tit. I. De Usufructu, with a Legal
and Philological Commentary by H. J. ROBY. Demy 8vo. 9s.
The Two Parts complete in One Volume. Demy 8vo. 18s.

A Selection of the State Trials. By J. W. WILLIS-BUND, M.A.,
LL.B. Crown 8vo. Vols. I. and II. In 3 parts. 30s.

The Institutes of Justinian, translated with Notes by J. T. ABDY,
LL.D., and BRYAN WALKER, M.A., LL.D. Cr. 8vo. 16s.

Practical Jurisprudence. A comment on AUSTIN. By E. C.
CLARK, LL.D., Regius Professor of Civil Law. Crown 8vo. 9s.

An Analysis of Criminal Liability. By the same. Cr. 8vo. 7s. 6d.

The Fragments of the Perpetual Edict of Salvius Julianus, Arranged, and Annotated by the late BRYAN WALKER, LL.D. Cr. 8vo. 6s.

The Commentaries of Gaius and Rules of Ulpian. Translated
and Annotated, by J. T. ABDY, LL.D., and BRYAN WALKER, M.A.,
LL.D. New Edition by Bryan Walker. Crown 8vo. 16s.

Grotius de Jure Belli et Pacis, with the Notes of Barbeyrac and
others; an abridged Translation of the Text, by W. WHEWELL, D.D.
Demy 8vo. 12s. The translation separate, 6s.

Selected Titles from the Digest, by BRYAN WALKER, M.A., LL.D.
Part I. Mandati vel Contra. Digest XVII. I. Cr. 8vo. 5s.

Part II. De Adquirendo rerum dominio, and De Adquirenda vel
amittenda Possessione, Digest XLI. 1 and 2. Crown 8vo. 6s.

Part III. De Condictionibus, Digest XII. 1 and 4—7 and Digest
XIII. 1—3. Crown 8vo. 6s.

HISTORICAL WORKS.

The Life and Letters of the Reverend Adam Sedgwick, LL.D.,
F.R.S. (Dedicated, by special permission, to Her Majesty the Queen.) By
JOHN WILLIS CLARK, M.A., F.S.A., and THOMAS M^cKENNY HUGHES,
M.A. 2 vols. Demy 8vo. 36s.

The Growth of English Industry and Commerce during the Early
and Middle Ages. By W. CUNNINGHAM, D.D. Demy 8vo. 16s.

The Architectural History of the University of Cambridge and
of the Colleges of Cambridge and Eton. by the late Professor WILLIS,
M.A., F.R.S. Edited with large Additions and a Continuation to the
present time by J. W. CLARK, M.A. 4 Vols. Super Royal 8vo. £6. 6s.
Also a limited Edition of the same, consisting of 120 numbered Copies
only, large paper Quarto; the woodcuts and steel engravings mounted
on India paper; of which 100 copies are now offered for sale, at Twenty-
five Guineas **net** each set.

London: Cambridge Warehouse, Ave Maria Lane.

The University of Cambridge from the Earliest Times to the
Royal Injunctions of 1535. By J. B. MULLINGER, M.A. Demy 8vo. 12s.
—— Part II. From the Royal Injunctions of 1535 to the Accession of Charles
the First. Demy 8vo. 18s.

History of the College of St John the Evangelist, by THOMAS
BAKER, B.D., Ejected Fellow. Edited by JOHN E. B. MAYOR, M.A.,
Fellow of St John's. Two Vols. Demy 8vo. 24s.

Scholae Academicae: some Account of the Studies at the English
Universities in the Eighteenth Century. By CHRISTOPHER WORDS-
WORTH, M.A. Demy 8vo. 10s. 6d.

Life and Times of Stein, or Germany and Prussia in the Napoleonic
Age, by J. R. SEELEY, M.A. Portraits and Maps. 3 vols. Demy 8vo. 30s.

The Constitution of Canada. By J. E. C. MUNRO, LL.M.
Demy 8vo. 10s.

Studies in the Literary Relations of England with Germany in
the Sixteenth Century. By C. H. HERFORD, M.A. Crown 8vo. 9s.

Chronological Tables of Greek History. By CARL PETER. Translated from the German by G. CHAWNER, M.A. Demy 4to. 10s.

Travels in Arabia Deserta in 1876 and 1877. By CHARLES
M. DOUGHTY. With Illustrations. Demy 8vo. 2 vols. £3. 3s.

History of Nepāl, edited with an introductory sketch of the Country
and People by Dr D. WRIGHT. Super-royal 8vo. 10s. 6d.

A Journey of Literary and Archæological Research in Nepal and
Northern India, 1884—5. By C. BENDALL, M.A. Demy 8vo. 10s.

Cambridge Historical Essays.

Political Parties in Athens during the Peloponnesian War, by
L. WHIBLEY, M.A. (Prince Consort Dissertation, 1888.) Second Edition. Crown 8vo. 2s. 6d.

Pope Gregory the Great and his relations with Gaul, by F. W.
KELLETT, M.A. (Prince Consort Dissertation, 1888.) Crown 8vo. 2s. 6d.

The Constitutional Experiments of the Commonwealth, being the
Thirlwall Prize Essay for 1889, by E. JENKS, B.A., LL.B. Cr. 8vo. 2s. 6d.

On Election by Lot at Athens, by J. W. HEADLAM, B.A. (Prince
Consort Dissertation, 1890.) Crown 8vo. [*In the Press.*

The Destruction of the Somerset Religious Houses and its Effects.
By W. A. J. ARCHBOLD, B.A., LL.B. (Prince Consort Dissertation,
1890.) Crown 8vo. [*In the Press.*

MISCELLANEOUS.

The Engraved Gems of Classical Times with a Catalogue of the
Gems in the Fitzwilliam Museum by J. H. MIDDLETON, M.A. Royal 8vo.
12s. 6d.

Erasmus. The Rede Lecture, delivered in the Senate-House, Cambridge, June 11, 1890, by R. C. JEBB, Litt.D. Cloth, 2s. Paper Covers, 1s.

The Literary remains of Albrecht Dürer, by W. M. CONWAY. With
Transcripts from the British Museum Manuscripts, and Notes upon them
by LINA ECKENSTEIN. Royal 8vo. 21s.

The Collected Papers of Henry Bradshaw, including his Memoranda
and Communications read before the Cambridge Antiquarian Society.
With 13 facsimiles. Edited by F. J. H. JENKINSON, M.A. Demy 8vo. 16s.

London: Cambridge Warehouse, Ave Maria Lane.

Memorials of the Life of George Elwes Corrie, D.D. formerly Master of Jesus College. By M. HOLROYD. Demy 8vo. 12s.

The Latin Heptateuch. Published piecemeal by the French printer WILLIAM MOREL (1560) and the French Benedictines E. MARTÈNE (1733) and J. B. PITRA (1852—88). Critically reviewed by JOHN E. B. MAYOR, M.A. Demy 8vo. 10s. 6d.

Kinship and Marriage in early Arabia, by W. ROBERTSON SMITH, M.A., LL.D. Crown 8vo. 7s. 6d.

Chapters on English Metre. By Rev. JOSEPH B. MAYOR, M.A. Demy 8vo. 7s. 6d.

A Catalogue of Ancient Marbles in Great Britain, by Prof. ADOLF MICHAELIS. Translated by C. A. M. FENNELL, Litt.D. Royal 8vo. Roxburgh (Morocco back). £2. 2s.

From Shakespeare to Pope. An Inquiry into the causes and phenomena of the Rise of Classical Poetry in England. By E. GOSSE, M.A. Crown 8vo. 6s.

The Literature of the French Renaissance. An Introductory Essay. By A. A. TILLEY, M.A. Crown 8vo. 6s.

A Latin-English Dictionary. Printed from the (Incomplete) MS. of the late T. H. KEY, M.A., F.R.S. Demy 4to. £1. 11s. 6d.

Ecclesiae Londino-Batavae archivum. TOMVS PRIMVS. ABRAHAMI ORTELII et virorum eruditorum ad eundem et ad JACOBVM COLIVM ORTELIANVM Epistulae, (1524—1628). TOMVS SECVNDVS. EPISTVLAE ET TRACTATVS cum Reformationis tum Ecclesiae Londino-Batavae Historiam Illustrantes 1544—1622. Ex autographis mandante Ecclesia Londino-Batava edidit JOANNES HENRICVS HESSELS. Demy 4to. Each vol., separately, £3. 10s. Taken together £5. 5s. Net.

An Eighth Century Latin-Anglo-Saxon Glossary preserved in the Library of Corpus Christi College, Cambridge, edited by J. H. HESSELS. Demy 8vo. 10s.

Contributions to the Textual Criticism of the Divina Commedia. Including the complete collation throughout the *Inferno* of all the MSS. at Oxford and Cambridge. By the Rev. E. MOORE, D.D. Demy 8vo. 21s.

The Despatches of Earl Gower, English Ambassador at the court of Versailles, June 1790 to August 1792, and the Despatches of Mr Lindsay and Mr Monro. By O. BROWNING, M.A. Demy 8vo. 15s.

Rhodes in Ancient Times. By CECIL TORR, M.A. With six plates. 10s. 6d.

Rhodes in Modern Times. By the same Author. With three plates. Demy 8vo. 8s.

The Woodcutters of the Netherlands during the last quarter of the Fifteenth Century. By W. M. CONWAY. Demy 8vo. 10s. 6d.

Lectures on the Growth and Training of the Mental Faculty. delivered in the University of Cambridge. By FRANCIS WARNER, M.D., F.R.C.P. Crown 8vo. 4s. 6d.

Lectures on Teaching, delivered in the University of Cambridge. By J. G. FITCH, M.A., LL.D. Cr. 8vo. 5s.

Lectures on Language and Linguistic Method in the School. By S. S. LAURIE, M.A., LL.D. Crown 8vo. 4s.

Occasional Addresses on Educational Subjects. By S. S. LAURIE, M.A., F.R.S.E. Crown 8vo. 5s.

London: Cambridge Warehouse, Ave Maria Lane.

A Manual of Cursive Shorthand, by H. L. CALLENDAR, M.A. Extra Fcap. 8vo. 2s.

A System of Phonetic Spelling, adapted to English by H. L. CALLENDAR, M.A. Extra Fcap. 8vo. 6d.

A Primer of Cursive Shorthand. By H. L. CALLENDAR, M.A. 6d.

Reading Practice in Cursive Shorthand. Easy extracts for Beginners. St Mark, Pt. I. Vicar of Wakefield, Chaps. I.—IV. Alice in Wonderland, Chap. VII. Price 3d. each.

Essays from the Spectator in Cursive Shorthand, by H. L. CALLENDAR, M.A. 6d.

Gray and his Friends. Letters and Relics in great part hitherto unpublished. Edited by the Rev. D. C. TOVEY, M.A. Crown 8vo. 6s.

A Grammar of the Irish Language. By Prof. WINDISCH. Translated by Dr NORMAN MOORE. Crown 8vo. 7s. 6d.

A Catalogue of the Collection of Birds formed by the late Hugh EDWIN STRICKLAND, now in the possession of the University of Cambridge. By O. SALVIN, M.A., F.R.S. £1. 1s.

Admissions to Gonville and Caius College in the University of Cambridge March 1558—9 to Jan. 1678—9. Edited by J. VENN, Sc.D., and S. C. VENN. Demy 8vo. 10s.

A Catalogue of the Hebrew Manuscripts preserved in the University Library, Cambridge. By the late Dr SCHILLER-SZINESSY. 9s.

Catalogue of the Buddhist Sanskrit Manuscripts in the University Library, Cambridge. Edited by C. BENDALL, M.A. 12s.

A Catalogue of the Manuscripts preserved in the Library of the University of Cambridge. Demy 8vo. 5 Vols. 10s. each.

    Index to the Catalogue. Demy 8vo. 10s.

A Catalogue of Adversaria and printed books containing MS. notes, in the Library of the University of Cambridge. 3s. 6d.

The Illuminated Manuscripts in the Library of the Fitzwilliam Museum, Cambridge, by W. G. SEARLE, M.A. 7s. 6d.

A Chronological List of the Graces, etc. in the University Registry which concern the University Library. 2s. 6d.

Catalogus Bibliothecæ Burckhardtianæ. Demy Quarto. 5s.

Graduati Cantabrigienses: sive catalogus exhibens nomina eorum quos gradu quocunque ornavit Academia Cantabrigiensis (1800—1884). Cura H. R. LUARD, S.T.P. Demy 8vo. 12s. 6d.

Statutes for the University of Cambridge and for the Colleges therein, made, published and approved (1878—1882) under the Universities of Oxford and Cambridge Act, 1877. Demy 8vo. 16s.

Statutes of the University of Cambridge. 3s. 6d.

Ordinances of the University of Cambridge. 7s. 6d. Supplement to ditto. 1s.

Trusts, Statutes and Directions affecting (1) The Professorships of the University. (2) The Scholarships and Prizes. (3) Other Gifts and Endowments. Demy 8vo. 5s.

A Compendium of University Regulations. Demy 8vo. 6d.

Books of Ezra and Nehemiah. By Rev. Prof. RYLE, M.A.
Book of Psalms. Part I. By Rev. Prof. KIRKPATRICK, B.D.
Book of Isaiah. By Prof. W. ROBERTSON SMITH, M.A.
Book of Ezekiel. By Rev. A. B. DAVIDSON, D.D.
Epistles to Colossians & Philemon. By Rev. H. C. G. MOULE, M.A.
Epistles to Timothy and Titus. By Rev. A. E. HUMPHREYS, M.A.

𝕿𝖍𝖊 𝕾𝖒𝖆𝖑𝖑𝖊𝖗 𝕮𝖆𝖒𝖇𝖗𝖎𝖉𝖌𝖊 𝕭𝖎𝖇𝖑𝖊 𝖋𝖔𝖗 𝕾𝖈𝖍𝖔𝖔𝖑𝖘.

The Smaller Cambridge Bible for Schools *will form an entirely new series of commentaries on some selected books of the Bible. It is expected that they will be prepared for the most part by the Editors of the larger series (the Cambridge Bible for Schools and Colleges). The volumes will be issued at a low price, and will be suitable to the requirements of preparatory and elementary schools.*

Now ready. Price 1s. *each.*

First and Second Books of Samuel. By Prof. KIRKPATRICK, B.D.
First and Second Books of Kings. By Rev. Prof. LUMBY, D.D.
Gospel according to St Matthew. By Rev. A. CARR, M.A.
Gospel according to St Mark. By Rev. G. F. MACLEAR, D.D.
Gospel according to St Luke. By Archdeacon FARRAR, D.D.
Gospel according to St John. By Rev. A. PLUMMER, D.D.
Acts of the Apostles. By Professor LUMBY, D.D.

THE CAMBRIDGE GREEK TESTAMENT
FOR SCHOOLS AND COLLEGES

with a Revised Text, based on the most recent critical authorities, and English Notes, prepared under the direction of the General Editor,

J. J. S. PEROWNE, D.D., BISHOP OF WORCESTER.

Gospel according to St Matthew. By Rev. A. CARR, M.A. 4s. 6d.
Gospel according to St Mark. By Rev. G. F. MACLEAR, D.D. 4s. 6d.
Gospel according to St Luke. By Archdeacon FARRAR. 6s.
Gospel according to St John. By Rev. A. PLUMMER, D.D. 6s.
Acts of the Apostles. By Prof. LUMBY, D.D. 4 Maps. 6s.
First Epistle to the Corinthians. By Rev. J. J. LIAS, M.A. 3s.
Second Epistle to the Corinthians. By Rev. J. J. LIAS, M.A.
[Preparing.
Epistle to the Hebrews. By Archdeacon FARRAR, D.D. 3s. 6d.
Epistles of St John. By Rev. A. PLUMMER, M.A., D.D. 4s.

London: Cambridge Warehouse, Ave Maria Lane.

THE PITT PRESS SERIES.

*** *Copies of the Pitt Press Series may generally be obtained in two volumes,
Text and Notes separately.*

1. GREEK.

Aristophanes. Aves—Plutus—Ranae. By W. C. GREEN, M.A.,
late Assistant Master at Rugby School. 3*s.* 6*d.* each.

Euripides. Heracleidæ. By E. A. BECK, M.A. 3*s.* 6*d.*

Euripides. Hercules Furens. By A. GRAY, M.A., and J. T.
HUTCHINSON, M.A. 2*s.*

Euripides. Hippolytus. By W. S. HADLEY, M.A. 2*s.*

Euripides. Iphigeneia in Aulis. By C. E. S. HEADLAM, B.A. 2*s.* 6*d.*

Herodotus. Book V. By E. S. SHUCKBURGH, M.A. 3*s.*

Herodotus. Book VI. By the same Editor. 4*s.*

Herodotus. Books VIII., IX. By the same Editor. 4*s.* each.

Herodotus. Book VIII., Ch. 1—90. Book IX., Ch. 1—89. By the
same Editor. 3*s.* 6*d.* each.

Homer. Odyssey, Book IX. Book X. By G. M. EDWARDS, M.A.
2*s.* 6*d.* each.

Homer. Odyssey, Book XXI. By the same Editor. 2*s.*

Homer. Iliad. Book XXII. By the same Editor. 2*s.*

Homer. Iliad. Book XXIII. By the same Editor. [*Nearly ready.*

Luciani Somnium Charon Piscator et De Luctu. By W. E.
HEITLAND, M.A., Fellow of St John's College, Cambridge. 3*s.* 6*d.*

Lucian. Menippus and Timon. By E. C. MACKIE, M.A.
[*Nearly ready.*

Platonis Apologia Socratis. By J. ADAM, M.A. 3*s.* 6*d.*

—— **Crito.** By the same Editor. 2*s.* 6*d.*

—— **Euthyphro.** By the same Editor. 2*s.* 6*d.*

Plutarch's Lives of the Gracchi.—Sulla—Timoleon. By H. A.
HOLDEN, M.A., LL.D. 6*s.* each.

Plutarch's Life of Nicias. By the same Editor. 5*s.*

Sophocles.—Oedipus Tyrannus. School Edition. By R. C. JEBB,
Litt.D., LL.D. 4*s.* 6*d.*

Thucydides. Book VII. By Rev. H. A. HOLDEN, M.A., LL.D.
[*Nearly ready.*

Xenophon—Agesilaus. By H. HAILSTONE, M.A. 2*s.* 6*d.*

Xenophon—Anabasis. By A. PRETOR, M.A. Two vols. 7*s.* 6*d.*

—— —— **Books I. III. IV. and V.** By the same Editor.
Price 2*s.* each. **Books II. VI. and VII.** 2*s.* 6*d.* each.

Xenophon—Cyropaedeia. Books I. II. By Rev. H. A. HOLDEN,
M.A., LL.D. 2 vols. 6*s.*

—— —— **Books III. IV. and V.** By the same Editor. 5*s.*

—— —— **Books VI. VII. and VIII.** By the same Editor. 5*s.*

II. LATIN.

Beda's Ecclesiastical History, Books III., IV. Edited by J. E. B. MAYOR, M.A., and J. R. LUMBY, D.D. Revised Edit. 7s. 6d.

Caesar. De Bello Gallico Comment. I. By A. G. PESKETT, M.A. 1s. 6d. **Com. II. III.** 2s.

—— **Comment. I. II. III.** 3s. **Com. IV. V.** 1s. 6d. **Com. VI.** and **Com. VIII.** 1s. 6d. each. **Com. VII.** 2s.

—— **De Bello Civili. Comment. I.** By the same Editor. 3s.

M. T. Ciceronis de Amicitia.—de Senectute.—pro Sulla Oratio. By J. S. REID, Litt.D., Fellow of Gonville and Caius College. 3s. 6d. each.

M. T. Ciceronis Oratio pro Archia Poeta. By the same. 2s.

M. T. Ciceronis pro Balbo Oratio. By the same. 1s. 6d.

M. T. Ciceronis in Gaium Verrem Actio Prima. By H. COWIE, M.A., Fellow of St John's Coll. 1s. 6d.

M. T. Ciceronis in Q. Caecilium Divinatio et in C. Verrem Actio. By W. E. HEITLAND, M.A., and H. COWIE, M.A. 3s.

M. T. Ciceronis Oratio pro Tito Annio Milone. By JOHN SMYTH PURTON, B.D. 2s. 6d.

M. T. Ciceronis Oratio pro L. Murena. By W. E. HEITLAND, M.A. 3s.

M. T. Ciceronis pro Cn. Plancio Oratio, by H. A. HOLDEN, LL.D. Second Edition. 4s. 6d.

M. Tulli Ciceronis Oratio Philippica Secunda. By A. G. PESKETT, M.A. 3s. 6d.

M. T. Ciceronis Somnium Scipionis. By W. D. PEARMAN, M.A. 2s.

Horace. Epistles, Book I. By E. S. SHUCKBURGH, M.A. 2s. 6d.

Livy. Books IV., XXVII. By H. M. STEPHENSON, M.A. 2s. 6d. each.

—— **Book V.** By L. WHIBLEY, M.A. 2s. 6d.

—— **Book XXI. Book XXII.** By M. S. DIMSDALE, M.A. 2s. 6d. each.

M. Annaei Lucani Pharsaliae Liber Primus. By W. E. HEITLAND, M.A., and C. E. HASKINS, M.A. 1s. 6d.

Lucretius, Book V. By J. D. DUFF, M.A., Fellow of Trinity College. *Price* 2s.

P. Ovidii Nasonis Fastorum Liber VI. By A. SIDGWICK, M.A. 1s. 6d.

Quintus Curtius. A Portion of the History (Alexander in India). By W. E. HEITLAND, M.A. and T. E. RAVEN, B.A. 3s. 6d.

P. Vergili Maronis Aeneidos Libri I.—XII. By A. SIDGWICK, M.A. 1s. 6d. each.

P. Vergili Maronis Bucolica. By the same Editor. 1s. 6d.

P. Vergili Maronis Georgicon Libri I. II. By the same Editor. 2s. **Libri III. IV.** By the same Editor. 2s.

Vergil. The Complete Works. By the same Editor. Two Vols. Vol. I. Introduction and Text. 3s. 6d. Vol. II. Notes. 4s. 6d.

III. FRENCH.

Bataille de Dames. By SCRIBE and LEGOUVÉ. By Rev. H. A. BULL, M.A. 2s.

Dix Années d'Exil. Livre II. Chapitres 1—8. Par MADAME LA BARONNE DE STAËL-HOLSTEIN. By the late G. MASSON, B.A. and G. W. PROTHERO, M.A. New Edition, enlarged. 2s.

London: Cambridge Warehouse, Ave Maria Lane.

Histoire du Siècle de Louis XIV. par Voltaire. Chaps. I.—XIII. By GUSTAVE MASSON, B.A. and G. W. PROTHERO, M.A. 2s. 6d. Chaps. XIV.—XXIV. 2s. 6d. Chap. XXV. to end. 2s. 6d.

Fredégonde et Brunehaut. A Tragedy in Five Acts, by N. LE-MERCIER. By GUSTAVE MASSON, B.A. 2s.

Jeanne D'Arc. By A. DE LAMARTINE. By Rev. A. C. CLAPIN, M.A. Revised Edition by A. R. ROPES, M.A. 1s. 6d.

La Canne de Jonc. By A. DE VIGNY. By Rev. H. A. BULL, M.A. 2s.

La Jeune Sibérienne. Le Lépreux de la Cité D'Aoste. Tales by COUNT XAVIER DE MAISTRE. By GUSTAVE MASSON, B.A. 1s. 6d.

La Picciola. By X. B. SAINTINE. By Rev. A. C. CLAPIN, M.A. 2s.

La Guerre. By MM. ERCKMANN-CHATRIAN. By the same Editor. 3s.

La Métromanie. A Comedy, by PIRON. By G. MASSON, B.A. 2s.

Lascaris ou Les Grecs du XVᴱ Siècle, Nouvelle Historique, par A. F. VILLEMAIN. By the same. 2s.

La Suite du Menteur. A Comedy by P. CORNEILLE. By the same. 2s.

Lazare Hoche—Par EMILE DE BONNECHOSE. With Four Maps. By C. COLBECK, M.A. 2s.

Le Bourgeois Gentilhomme, Comédie-Ballet en Cinq Actes. Par J.-B. Poquelin de Molière (1670). By Rev. A. C. CLAPIN, M.A. 1s. 6d.

Le Directoire. (Considérations sur la Révolution Française. Troisième et quatrième parties.) Revised and enlarged. By G. MASSON, B.A. and G. W. PROTHERO, M.A. 2s.

Les Plaideurs. RACINE. By E. G. W. BRAUNHOLTZ, M.A., Ph.D. 2s.

—— —— (Abridged Edition.) 1s.

Les Précieuses Ridicules. MOLIÈRE. By E. G. W. BRAUNHOLTZ, M.A., Ph.D. 2s.

—— —— (Abridged Edition.) 1s.

L'École des Femmes. MOLIÈRE. By GEORGE SAINTSBURY, M.A. 2s. 6d.

Le Philosophe sans le savoir. Sedaine. By Rev. H. A. BULL, late Master at Wellington College. 2s.

Lettres sur l'histoire de France (XIII—XXIV). Par AUGUSTIN THIERRY. By G. MASSON, B.A. and G. W. PROTHERO. 2s. 6d.

Le Verre D'Eau. A Comedy, by SCRIBE. Edited by C. COLBECK, M.A. 2s.

Le Vieux Célibataire. A Comedy, by COLLIN D'HARLEVILLE. With Notes, by G. MASSON, B.A. 2s.

M. Daru, par M. C. A. SAINTE-BEUVE (Causeries du Lundi, Vol. IX.). By G. MASSON, B.A. Univ. Gallic. 2s.

Recits des Temps Merovingiens I—III. THIERRY. By the late G. MASSON, B.A. and A. R. ROPES, M.A. Map. 3s.

London: Cambridge Warehouse, Ave Maria Lane.

IV. GERMAN.

A Book of Ballads on German History. By WILHELM WAGNER, PH.D. 2s.

A Book of German Dactylic Poetry. By WILHELM WAGNER, Ph.D. 3s.

Benedix. Doctor Wespe. Lustspiel in fünf Aufzügen. By KARL HERMANN BREUL, M.A., Ph.D. 3s.

Culturgeschichtliche Novellen, von W. H. RIEHL. By H. J. WOLSTENHOLME, B.A. (Lond.). 3s. 6d.

Das Jahr 1813 (THE YEAR 1813), by F. KOHLRAUSCH. By WILHELM WAGNER, Ph.D. 2s.

Der erste Kreuzzug (1095—1099) nach FRIEDRICH VON RAUMER. THE FIRST CRUSADE. By W. WAGNER, Ph. D. 2s.

Der Oberhof. A Tale of Westphalian Life, by KARL IMMERMANN. By WILHELM WAGNER, Ph.D. 3s.

Der Staat Friedrichs des Grossen. By G. FREYTAG. By WILHELM WAGNER, PH. D. 2s.

Die Karavane, von WILHELM HAUFF. By A. SCHLOTTMANN, Ph.D. 3s. 6d.

Goethe's Hermann and Dorothea. By W. WAGNER, Ph. D. Revised edition by J. W. CARTMELL. 3s. 6d.

Goethe's Knabenjahre. (1749—1761.) Goethe's Boyhood. By W. WAGNER, Ph.D. Revised edition by J. W. CARTMELL, M.A. 2s.

Hauff, Das Bild des Kaisers. By KARL HERMANN BREUL, M.A., Ph.D. 3s.

Hauff, Das Wirthshaus im Spessart. By A. SCHLOTTMANN, Ph.D., late Assistant Master at Uppingham School. 3s. 6d.

Mendelssohn's Letters. Selections from. By JAMES SIME, M.A. 3s.

Schiller. Wilhelm Tell. By KARL HERMANN BREUL, M.A., Ph.D. 2s. 6d.

—— —— (Abridged Edition.) 1s. 6d.

Selected Fables. Lessing and Gellert. By KARL HERMANN BREUL, M.A., Ph.D. 3s.

Uhland. Ernst, Herzog von Schwaben. By H. J. WOLSTENHOLME, B.A. (Lond.). 3s. 6d.

Zopf und Schwert. Lustspiel in fünf Aufzügen von KARL GUTZKOW. By H. J. WOLSTENHOLME, B.A. (Lond.). 3s. 6d.

V. ENGLISH.

An Apologie for Poetrie by Sir PHILIP SIDNEY. By E. S. SHUCKBURGH, M.A. The text is a revision of that of the first edition of 1595. 3s.

An Elementary Commercial Geography. A Sketch of the Commodities and Countries of the World. By H. R. MILL, Sc. D., F.R.S.E. 1s.

An Atlas of Commercial Geography. (Companion to the above.) By J. G. BARTHOLOMEW, F.R.G.S. With an Introduction by Dr H. R. MILL. 3s.

London: Cambridge Warehouse, Ave Maria Lane.

Ancient Philosophy from Thales to Cicero, A Sketch of,
JOSEPH B. MAYOR, M.A. 3s. 6d.

Bacon's History of the Reign of King Henry VII. By the Re
Professor LUMBY, D.D. 3s.

British India, a Short History of. By Rev. E. S. CARLOS, M.A.

Cowley's Essays. By Prof. LUMBY, D.D. 4s.

General Aims of the Teacher, and Form Management. Two Le
tures by F. W. FARRAR, D.D. and R. B. POOLE, B.D. 1s. 6d.

John Amos Comenius, Bishop of the Moravians. His Life ai
Educational Works, by S. S. LAURIE, A.M., F.R.S.E. 3s. 6d.

Locke on Education. By the Rev. R. H. QUICK, M.A. 3s. 6(

Milton's Arcades and Comus. By A. W. VERITY, M.A. 3s.

Milton's Tractate on Education. A facsimile reprint from t
Edition of 1673. Edited by O. BROWNING, M.A. 2s.

More's History of King Richard III. By J. RAWSON LUMBY, D.
3s. 6d.

On Stimulus. A Lecture delivered for the Teachers' Traini
Syndicate at Cambridge, May 1882, by A. SIDGWICK, M.A. New Ed.

Outlines of the Philosophy of Aristotle. Compiled by EDW
WALLACE, M.A., LL.D. Third Edition, Enlarged. 4s. 6d.

Sir Thomas More's Utopia By Prof. LUMBY, D.D. 3s. 6d.

Theory and Practice of Teaching. By E. THRING, M.A. 4s. 6d

The Teaching of Modern Languages in Theory and Practi
By C. COLBECK, M.A. 2s.

The Two Noble Kinsmen. By Professor SKEAT, Litt.D. 3s. 6d.

Three Lectures on the Practice of Education. I. On Marki
by H. W. EVE, M.A. II. On Stimulus, by A. SIDGWICK, M.A. III. (
the Teaching of Latin Verse Composition, by E. A. ABBOTT, D.D. 2s

VI. MATHEMATICS.

Euclid's Elements of Geometry, Books I. and II. By H.]
TAYLOR, M.A. 1s. 6d. **Books III. and IV.** By the same Editor. 1s. (
———— ———— Books I.—IV. in one volume. 3s.

Elementary Algebra (with Answers to the Examples). By W. 1
ROUSE BALL, M.A. 4s. 6d.

Elements of Statics and Dynamics. By S. L. LONEY, M.A. Part
Elements of Statics. 4s. 6d. Part II. Elements of Dynamics.
[Nearly rea

𝕷𝖔𝖓𝖉𝖔𝖓: C. J. CLAY AND SONS,
CAMBRIDGE WAREHOUSE, AVE MARIA LANE.

𝕲𝖑𝖆𝖘𝖌𝖔𝖜: 263, ARGYLE STREET.

𝕮𝖆𝖒𝖇𝖗𝖎𝖉𝖌𝖊: DEIGHTON, BELL AND CO. 𝕷𝖊𝖎𝖕𝖟𝖎𝖌: F. A. BROCKHAUS.

𝕹𝖊𝖜 𝖄𝖔𝖗𝖐: MACMILLAN AND CO.

CAMBRIDGE: PRINTED BY C. J. CLAY, M.A. & SONS, AT THE UNIVERSITY PRESS.